Tales of the Circle

Book one: Welcome to the Circle

By

L.L. Craft

PUBLISHED BY:
L.L. Craft Publications

ISBN: 0615678866
ISBN 13: 9780615678863

Acknowledgments:

The Circle couldn't have happened without a lot of help and support, so some thanks are in order. First, the fine folks behind erotic story site Literotica. There, through the feedback readers and advice from fellow authors, I gained the confidence to begin publishing. There are too many authors to name so one big thank you to the knowledgeable crazies of the Authors hangout. To Vivian Vincent for her editing assistance and lit editor "La Cuchilla", who was always supportive with comments like "Keep making the same mistakes and I'm done with you!" Most importantly, is my wife Gina. Gina is my best friend, my light and my inspiration, truly my twin flame. Without her support and encouragement, I would have never begun writing. This one's for you my love.

Tales of the Circle
Book one: Welcome to the Circle

Part One

Chapter One

"There is an expression all men are created equal.
This statement is a lie, no doubt created to help those who
wallow in mediocrity feel better about themselves."
The Lady Persephone, High Mistress of the Circle.

Sitting at the head of the conference table, Justine Bates struggled to pay attention. The fact Bill Reynolds, was saying the same thing the speaker before him had, wasn't helping. No, that wasn't the problem. Most meetings were like this and normally she had no trouble focusing. The problem was this was the first of three meetings today, and the other two promised to be far more entertaining.

Justine wiped her forehead and looked at the sweat on her hand. Adding to the distractions of the morning was the air conditioning was on the fritz. It was over eighty degrees and felt even warmer inside. The thermostat was off to her left, but she refused to look over. Knowing what it said would just make things worse.

"So what are your thoughts, Justine?"

Coming out of her fog, she looked over at Bill. Only in his late thirties, he was already balding with at least fifty extra pounds on him, most of it hanging over his belt. How he looked would be of no concern of hers, except she had overheard him many times judge the appearance of his female coworkers and women in general. Locking her cold blue gaze onto his watery brown eyes, she spoke. "My first thought is I don't remember saying this was an informal meeting. I think you should rephrase the question."

Bill hesitated, trying to decide if she were kidding. He started to grin, but stopped as Justine widened her eyes, as if saying 'oh really?' Swallowing nervously, he answered, "My apologies, Miss Bates. I was wondering what your thoughts were on my strategy for the upcoming quarter."

"Well, *Bill,"* Justine began, "Your strategy seems to be that of Paul's, which pretty much echoed what Roger said." She paused, and without looking away from him addressed the table. "Please remove the smirks from your faces gentlemen, this isn't high school." She sighed for effect. "If it was, I might be getting some original ideas."

Justine took a moment to let her comment sink in. She normally wasn't insulting during meetings, but had never had work on the one day a month she wanted off. One thing was for certain, she knew without looking around there would be no one smiling now.

"Now," she continued having left the room in awkward silence long enough. "I'll make this easy, and try to get us out of here early. Does anyone have anything to say that hasn't already been said?"

She glanced around the table where no one would meet her gaze. "Very well," She nodded. "I'm sure Mr. Williams will be thrilled there's nothing new to report except stagnant sales and stale ideas."

Justine paused to let that sink in, before sighing dramatically, "My meeting with Mr. Williams is on Friday. Therefore each of you is to have a fresh, and I stress *fresh* proposal, on my desk by Wednesday." She tapped the table with a long red fingernail. "Understood?" There were a few murmurs and she raised her voice. "I'll not allow my district to fall behind the others. If it does, heads will roll. Am I clear?"

This time there were several solid affirmatives and she nodded. Looking towards the end of the table, she pointed to her director of sales. "Paul, if you'd please go over the numbers for the last quarter so everyone here can see why they may not be getting the pay increase they expect every year."

Paul opened his laptop and when everyone turned in their seats to watch the presentation appear on the far wall, Justine slumped back in her seat. She'd been over these numbers a dozen times in the last week, and they weren't bad, in fact they were decent. Decent however, wasn't good enough. Knowing that listening to the numbers again wouldn't change them, Justine allowed her mind the rare treat of wandering.

Wiping again at her face, she thought of how the day should have gone. During the course of the week it wasn't unusual for her to put in sixty hours. That was usually followed up by at least a half a day on Saturday, and more often than not a couple of hours on Sunday from home. But not the first weekend of the month, that was her time. She generally started by sleeping in until ten o'clock. Justine then replaced her morning workout with a trip to the spa. Manicure, pedicure, and full body massage.

From the spa it was back home for the rare indulgence of a good long nap. That nap would always start off with a nice slow masturbation session. Justine would use her silver bullet vibrator, teasing herself with the speeds while she envisioned the evening to come. Depending on who was entertaining, it could determine how powerful her orgasm was. Some members were just more suited to her taste than others. Tonight was The Lady Felicia's turn and she never failed to deliver.

After the nap, and a long hot shower, which occasionally involved more self pleasuring, Justine would dress to kill, have dinner with a group of amazing men and women, and then attend a very different meeting than this one. Justine smiled at the thought of what after the meeting would bring. A night of hardcore fucking with a man a dozen years younger than her, a night that always led into an amazing Sunday morning and...

Justine was beginning to get warm for reasons other than the failed air conditioning. While Paul droned on, she looked about the room, shaking her head again at Bill and a couple of the other men who seemed as if they were cast in the same mold. There was only one other woman in the room, a sales rep named Evelyn. Evelyn was four years younger than Justine, but seemed much older. A decent looking woman who dressed and acted as if she were afraid to let people think she'd ever had any fun in her life.

As for the men, they were mostly early forties, all married, and like Evelyn just seemed as if fun was no longer a word they knew the meaning of. Focused on jobs, kids, bills, they all on the surface seemed to have the lives people wanted, but no one here ever seemed overly happy. Not for the first time Justine wondered why people had the urge to settle down, to spend the rest of their lives with one person, falling into the rut of the same everything, every day. Feeling eyes on her, Justine looked over at Bill and saw him quickly look away. He was always staring at her. She had once overheard him tell someone she was damn hot for her age, but probably wouldn't know what to do with it if it hit her in the face.

Justine had no doubt that's what they all thought. Strong professional women like her didn't know what sex was like. Frigid, prude, those were the words used. Still, Justine had no doubt every man at the table had jerked off thinking of her. Masturbating to the thought of 'giving her what she needed'. Picturing her demure and desiring them, getting to her knees to go down on them.

If they only knew how wrong they were. Few were the men Justine had gone to her knees for. Even then it was as a reward to those who had not only pleased her, but fully appreciated the gift she was bestowing upon them. Not that the men around the table thinking of her in that light bothered her. It's not like any of them; even the single ones, would have the nerve to approach her, and she found it flattering at her age to still be so desired.

At forty-eight Justine could easily pass for a dozen years younger. Her deep blue eyes were set in a face with a fair complexion still unmarred by lines or wrinkles, and she had been asked many times if her full lips were the product of injections. With the exception of plucking a few grays here and there, nothing about Justine, from her smooth features and auburn red hair, to her long tapered nails and still very firm breasts gave away her age. A strict diet, daily workouts and those monthly trips to the spa had kept her looking and feeling young.

Justine would be the first to admit she was narcissistic, but if you had it, why not flaunt it? She was a beautiful sensual woman, and proud of it. Not that she flaunted it around the office. As the VP of sales of Speakeasy wireless, currently number two to only Verizon in sales throughout the US, she certainly couldn't dress like a teenager.

Justine's eyes wandered to her left, where they landed on Mark Phillips. Mark was her district's corporate attorney, and generally didn't attend the board meetings. Since however, he would be involved in the next two meetings of the day, she figured she may as well have him sit in. Mark was staring intently at the graphs on the monitor, but Justine knew him well enough to know that didn't necessarily mean he was paying attention, but it did give her an opportunity to observe him.

When looking at him, one word always came to Justine's mind: perfection. Without a doubt Mark was the most beautiful man she knew. Currently Mark was playing the part of the professional. His thick black hair was gelled back and he was clean shaven, as opposed to the perpetual five o'clock shadow he sported when he was not attending court. Although Mark's bad boy look never failed to make her sweat in a more pleasant way then she was now, there was something to be said for this look as well.

Mark's features were smooth and flawless, with a pair of high cheekbones that had him bordering on being pretty. His beauty didn't stop at his face. Like the other men in the room, Mark had removed his suit jacket, and unbuttoned the first two buttons of his shirt. Aside from that, there was nothing the rest of them had in common with him. His light blue Armani shirt was stretched across a pair of broad shoulders, and large biceps that were the product of an intense two hour a day workout. His sleeves were currently rolled up to expose a pair of well tanned, muscular forearms.

Sitting next to someone like Bill, his beauty stood out even more. Mark was also a practicing Satanist, who followed the teachings of Anton Levay and spoke of 'herds and lemmings'. How some were born to simply be better than others. Justine herself didn't believe she was better than, but felt for him it added to his all around mystique, and the fact that he really didn't care if anyone liked him. Good thing, because very few did, and those were only the few who had truly gotten to know him.

Sensing her staring at him, Mark turned his head to face her, giving Justine a look at his most startling feature, his eyes. They were not one color, but several. The most prominent color was a light shade of golden brown, but blended in was a deep green, along with small flecks of blue. Mark's eyes also changed color. When angry, they darkened to the point they appeared black.

Mark was from Rhode Island where he worked for the largest firm in the state. At thirty-five he had made senior partner and had a reputation as one of the most cut throat attorneys to ever enter a court house. Mark had also been dubbed by the press as The Bad Boy Attorney. This nickname had been earned as much from his questionable tactics as his legendary nightlife, and checkered past. Mark, who she was sure was drunk at the time, had once been quoted in the papers as saying that every woman wanted him and every man wanted to be him. Sitting here staring at him, it was hard to argue with either.

Justine looked at her watch and shook her head. Mark nodded and shrugged. He then let his eyes leave her face, and trail down towards her chest. Justine was wearing a blazer, which she'd unbuttoned due to the heat. Underneath she was wearing a tight black sleeveless shirt, cut low enough to show off the swells of her breasts, which is where his gaze was focused. When he looked up, Justine raised her eyebrows at him and made to close the blazer.

Mark lowered his eyes and mouthed the word 'please'. Justine smiled delightedly, even playing around, he knew his place. It was the fact he did that gave him his place in her bed on these normally glorious Saturdays. Then again, Mark should know his place, seeing it was Justine herself who had broken him years ago. Mark was still watching her, and after glancing around the room, Justine leaned forward and pressed her arms together, pushing her tits further up through the top of the shirt.

Mark smiled in appreciation. Like the rest of him, his teeth were perfect, and the smile itself one that had gotten him his way with women of all ages. Mark looked towards the end of the table where Paul was wrapping up his presentation, then back to her. Reaching up to his shirt, he made a gesture as if removing it and winked at her. She shook her head. Whether she wanted to be here or not, work was work. Mark shrugged, and with an audible sigh of disappointment that was his way of mocking her, sat back in his chair.

Justine stared at him, noticing that as she did, he was trying hard not to smile. No, she wouldn't be goaded. In this setting she was Justine Bates, a respected business woman, not The Lady Scarlett, who was not only respected, but feared as well. As Paul finished speaking he sat down and everyone once again faced her her.

"Now that Paul has shown where we stand in sales, I'd like Robert to speak on what's been going on in R&D, tell you about the new products you'll be presenting to our customers."

"Thank you, Miss Bates." Robert said softly.

Opening a folder, Robert handed a stack of papers to Paul to pass around the table. As with Paul's presentation, Justine already knew about the new phone they were hoping to launch for the holiday season, and had no desire to hear Robert explain it. No, Justine's attention was focused on other desires. As Robert began speaking, heads turned towards him. Justine smiled, knowing damn well Mark was still watching her.

There was a game brewing, and she wanted to give in and play. Glancing around the room she saw everyone was sweating, especially some of the heavier men. Looking over at Mark, she took in the sheen of sweat that covered his forearms. Justine was feeling mischievous; after all, this was supposed to be her day. Turning to look at Mark, Justine mimicked his gesture with the shirt and mouthed, "You first."

Mark hesitated, and with a shrug Justine closed her blazer. Rolling his eyes, he pushed his chair back, and began unbuttoning his shirt. Justine could see he was wearing a white shirt underneath and after waiting until he had gotten to the last button, said, "Excuse me, Mr. Phillips, what are you doing?"

Mark paused as all eyes in the room focused on him. With his hands still on his shirt he answered, "I'm sorry, Miss Bates, but it has to be ninety in here."

"So you should undress as if this were a locker room?"

"My apologies," Mark said softly. "I'm not sure what I was thinking."

"You weren't, obviously." She told him coolly. To say Mark was not well liked in the room would be like saying the sun was warm, and Justine could see the smirks starting. "But it is ridiculous in here," she went on. "I'll tell you what, gentlemen, if you'd like to remove your shirts you can, providing you have something on underneath."

"Thank you, Miss Bates," Mark replied, keeping a straight face. "I know you're big on professionalism, so this is greatly appreciated."

Justine noticed three or four of the others beginning to unbutton their shirts. She saw Mark had also noticed and had slowed up, letting them get close to removing their shirts. Standing up, he un-tucked his shirt, but hesitated, once more letting the others catch up with him. Justine put her hand up to her face to cover her smile as she saw Bill staring to slide his shirt off.

Mark slipped his shirt from his shoulders, letting it drop to his chair behind him. Bill stopped and from her right, Justine heard Evelyn let out a sharp breath. Mark's white tank top revealed the enormous demonic tattoos that covered both arms, shoulder to elbow. The right, facing her, was an evil rendition of Pan, the Celtic devil, horns, hooves and red eyes glaring. The colors were so vivid Justine could imagine the eyes staring at her. On the left arm, Justine knew was a rendition of the Pale Rider from Revelation, a skeletal figure on a huge black war horse.

Even underneath the dark colors of the tattoos, Justine could make out the muscles rippling in Mark's arms as he made a show of carefully hanging his shirt on the back of the chair. Turning back to face the table, Mark added a final touch. Reaching down he pulled the bottom of his shirt from his pants. He then leaned over and wiped the sweat from his face with it, exposing his tanned chiseled stomach. Justine risked a glance at Evelyn and was barely able to contain a laugh at the look on her face. The look told her that Evelyn was wet from something other than sweat, and she didn't blame her. Evelyn didn't escape Mark's attention.

"It's hot in here, isn't it Miss Jacobs?" He gave her a playful wink.

"Umm...it certainly...is," Evelyn stuttered.

"Then perhaps you should take that jacket off."

Evelyn blushed, and saving her from embarrassing herself, Justine spoke up, "Mr. Phillips, behave yourself, haven't you had enough trouble down there in Providence?"

"I was only..."

"Of course you were," Justine finished for him.

"Of course," Mark repeated, putting on a sheepish grin "I'm sorry, Miss Jacobs."

"Oh please, don't be," Evelyn said then catching herself, blushed even more.

"Damn, Mark," Roger said. "That's some ink."

"So your nickname is well earned," Justine added. "Now are you going to sit down, or do you plan on posing for the rest of the meeting?"

Again Mark came up with a properly abashed expression as he sat back down in his seat. He did however, make it a point to lean forward and fold his arms on the table. Justine looked to see that although Roger and a couple of others had removed their shirts, Bill had kept his on. Looking over at Mark, she saw he was staring directly at Evelyn, watching her try to avoid looking at him. Justine rolled her eyes. He was supposed to be watching her. He had gone from one game to another.

"Well," she began as she stood up. "I admit to being selfish with my decision, as I am far too overdressed in this stifling temperature."

Justine slowly removed her blazer, making a point to push her chest out a little more than she had to. She kept her head down, feigning interest in folding the jacket and giving the men table a chance to take in sight of the tight top straining against her full chest. Dropping the blazer to the floor next to her purse, she glanced up quickly, and caught them all trying to look away. She looked at Mark who was not looking at her, but was watching the others. Justine wasn't offended in the least; the game was watching the reaction of the others. Besides, it wasn't like Mark hadn't seen everything she had to offer.

Acting like she didn't notice them looking, she raised her arms behind her head. Fumbling with the clip in her hair, she noticed Bill and a couple of others had given up pretense of not looking. At the moment their eyes were focused on where her shirt had ridden up to expose the ruby pendent hanging from her navel. Let them think she was a prude now. Undoing the clip, Justine let her long auburn hair fall down past her shoulders. Tossing her head back, she made a show of shaking her hair out. Closing her eyes briefly, she allowed herself to enjoy the feeling of her thick soft hair falling across her bare shoulders and back. In reality her hair would make her warmer, but she was going for the full effect. Lowering her arms, she looked down as if just realizing her shirt had come un-tucked, and slipped it back into her skirt.

"I'm sorry, gentlemen," she said quietly.

Right on cue Mark said, "Oh please don't be."

There were a couple of snickers that were quickly silenced as Justine shot him a convincing dirty look. Mark looked down, fighting to keep himself from laughing. Shaking her head in mock disgust, Justine decided to really play it up. Stepping away from the table, she walked towards the bar along the far wall. As she made her away across the room, Justine could feel the eyes on her. Although the skirt she was wearing was not improper, it was a couple of inches above the knee. Taking into consideration she rarely wore skirts to work, this was more of her legs then most of them had seen.

Legs were something Justine had in spades, standing five nine, they were long, well shaped from exercise, and were well displayed, in the heels she was wearing. Justine reached the bar, and took her time pouring herself a glass of Coke. Turning, she sauntered back to her seat. She hadn't offered anyone else a drink, and it didn't seem as if anyone cared. When she reached her seat, she imitated Mark by folding her arms on the table. Leaning forward, she looked at Roger, Who was staring straight down her shirt

"I'm sorry Roger, please begin."

"I…" He looked up quickly. "I'm sorry I was just…"

"Roger?" Justine asked.

"Yes, Miss Bates?

"My eyes are up here."

As several people laughed, Justine sighed, picked up her soda and sat back in her chair. Sometimes it was just too easy.

Chapter Two

Justine entered her office with Mark behind her, and once he closed the door slipped her blazer back off and tossed it onto the small couch along the wall. Continuing to her large cherry wood desk, Justine sat down in the leather chair behind it. Mark went over to the small bar to make her a martini and pour himself some Jack Daniels.

The rest of the meeting went by much faster. Although there were several more topics being discussed, Justine found the game of watching them all stare at her made the time pass more quickly. That and watching Mark flirt with Evelyn. Evelyn was married, with a couple of kids, but Justine knew she wasn't happy with her husband. She wondered if, given the opportunity, if she would fuck Mark.

When the last report had been read, Justine stood, and thanked them all for coming in on a Saturday. Again, she resisted the urge to smile as they all remarked it was no problem and they were glad to come in and do their part. They also vowed to come up with something new for her, thanking her for the second chance. Even though the game had been between her and Mark to tease each other and the others around them, they were now more motivated than when they had come in. All over getting to see some cleavage, and her pierced naval. As Paul, who was one of the last to go, wished her a good weekend, Justine wondered what they would do if she showed proof she was a true redhead

Mark came over and after handing her the martini put his glass down on the edge of her desk. He stood looking around the large office, His eyes lingering on the small couch, before drifting to down at her well organized desk. Intuitively knowing what he was thinking, she asked, "Couch or desk?"

Mark didn't hesitate. "Desk."

"Go ahead then."

Justine sipped at her Martini, which was perfect as always. Mark had bartended his way through school and hadn't lost the touch. Sliding her heels off, she sighed and settled further back into the chair. Things would be getting pretty wild soon enough and she was enjoying the anticipation. While she sat there, savoring the thought of what was to come, she watched Mark clear off most of her desk.

Removing her laptop, he placed it on the floor next to the desk along with the pictures of Justine's sister Debra and her two teenage nieces. Can't have the girls seeing this, she thought with a grin. Ten minutes out of the meeting and she was feeling much more like herself. That was because this was now going to become the day it should be. When Mark had pushed the remaining few items off to one side of the desk, he removed his shirt again, and sat down in the small chair opposite her.

Justine pushed her chair back enough to swing her long legs up onto the desk. Mark had a foot fetish, and no sooner had her bare feet rested on the edge of the desk, his hand reached for them. His fingers had almost reached the sole of her right foot, when he stopped. Justine playfully wiggled her toes at him, and whispered, "Good boy."

"May I?"

"No," Justine said simply. "You get away with enough as it is. Can't have you getting too cocky can we?"

"No, My Lady," Mark said softly, while still looking longingly at her toes with their blood red nail polish.

"My Lady?" She raised her eyebrows.

"My Mistress."

"That's better." Justine finished her drink in one long swallow and sighed. "Instead, my dear Lovecraft, perhaps you can explain why we're doing this here rather than in front of the others."

Sitting back in his chair, and taking a sip of his own drink, Mark said, "I don't feel it necessary to demean a sister in front of the group. I..."

"Aurora broke the rules and if I'm not mistaken it's my enforcer's job to show her the error of her ways."

"And I shall."

"Privately?" Justine asked, cocking her head at him.

There were rumors throughout some of the groups that her legendary enforcer had a tendency to go soft on some of the ladies of their group. Justine knew there was nothing soft about Mark. He always did what he needed to, but that didn't mean she couldn't egg him on.

"No," he replied calmly. "In front of her Mistress, so you know it was properly dealt with."

"And why exactly are we cutting our newest sister a break?"

"Because I think it would be embarrassing to her to..."

"Of course it would be!" Justine put her hands out. "Isn't that the point?"

"With all due respect, Justine I think ..."

Swinging her legs from the desk, she leaned forward.

"First of all, we're discussing the Circle, and you'll refer to me by my proper title. I'm not Justine to you right now, Lovecraft."

"I'm sorry, Mistress Scarlett, but..."

"And as for humiliating?" She pointed at her chest. "Humiliating is having the master of the Las Angeles Circle call to tell me his brother was sorely disappointed with the gift I bestowed upon him."

"I..."

"No, you let me finish," Justine said heatedly.

She hadn't thought much on the reason they were here today until now. Their newest member, The Lady Aurora, had made her look bad. The Lady Scarlett would allow no one to do that to her.

"Our brother, Alexander, traveled here for business. His days in the group are numbered and Master Ramses asked if I'd provide him with entertainment." Justine spread her arms. "I figured what better gift than being pleasured by the newest member of my group? Alexander gets a special evening and Aurora learns how to defer to an older member."

"She was probably not the best choice," Mark replied.

"Are you questioning my judgment, Lovecraft?" she asked, her voice rising. "Don't think for a second you're above being punished."

Mark looked away, but not before Justine noticed his eyes darken slightly. When he spoke however, his voice was still calm. "Alexander has a reputation as being very demeaning. Many Masters and Mistresses do not allow him with their ladies, unless they enjoy that treatment."

"Again, you're questioning me?"

In the beginning of the conversation, Justine had been teasing him, but now he was starting to piss her off.

"The Lady Aurora is new, and still quite proud. Sydney comes from money, she's a fucking debutante. She'll learn proper behavior, but having her first time out being with someone like Alexander was a mistake."

"Proper behavior is to be taught during an initiation," Justine countered softly, refusing to show him he was getting under her skin. "At the moment of breaking, all pride is forgotten." She smirked. "Isn't that right, Lovecraft?"

Mark's eyes darkened further, and his jaw clenched. Justine smiled pleasantly at him.

"Problem?"

"None whatsoever," he replied in a tone that said everything but. "But you make my point. When a member is truly taught humility these issues don't arise."

"So you fault her initiator?" Justine asked. "You think Orion was soft on her?"

"I know he was." Mark shrugged, and leaned forward. "But, then again we all know some initiations are softer than others. Based on the pledge's personality and how bad we want them."

"You're correct." Justine nodded. "I knew she wouldn't respond to an all out assault." She grinned. "That's why I didn't give her to you. Orion has a different approach."

"A soft initiation creates lack of proper respect." Mark paused, and looking her straight in the eye finished. "*Now* I'm questioning your judgment."

"How dare..."

"This problem was created by her not being taught correctly; hence your embarrassment is of your own doing."

Justine frowned as she considered his words. Mark was right. When her high Lady Felicia had come to her about Sydney Stone, she had decided then and there she wanted her for the group. Stone was a successful erotica author, having penned some of the most brutal femdom stories she'd ever read. Felicia had learned Sydney's stories were written from a wealth of firsthand experience. The woman was as hardcore as they came, and had somehow managed to keep her bedroom activities secret. But Felicia had suspicions and there was no information the Circle was not privy to.

Justine had Mercedes send one of the young doms from her club for a 'chance' encounter with Sydney, to see if she could handle him. She had broken him so badly he had lost confidence and Mercedes was currently retraining him. Sydney was beautiful, wealthy, talented and vicious, exactly what she needed to fill the empty seat at her table. The drawback was Sydney came from an affluent family. Couple that with her supreme dominance in the bedroom, and it was a problem.

Many members of the Circle joined for the chance at professional advancement as much as they did for the endless sex games. Most had tasted success, but not to the level the Circle could create for them. Sydney had that already and the initiation was not an easy sell to her. There was nothing in her that would submit. After all, what could the group offer she did not already have?

Justine and Felicia had pushed the game aspect, the fellowship. A place of equals where she could share her exploits in an outlet other than her stories. Sydney had agreed to an initiation and although it was Mark's turn, Justine knew he would be too hard on her. Sydney was from old money; Mark a poor foster child who had made good. He would have enjoyed breaking her for more than just the good of the group. Yet now here it was not six months later, and he was going to get his chance anyway. Taking a deep breath to calm down, she nodded.

"Your point is proven. But it still doesn't answer my question of why we're not doing this before the group."

"You said Ramses told no one else of this and instructed Alexander to do the same right?"

"Ramses and I have a history, and he wouldn't want to see me lose face. He didn't tell High Mistress Persephone as he should have."

"Then no one at the group is expecting to see anything."

"I want her humiliated, Lovecraft, even though others don't know, *I* know."

"Mistress, if you were afraid a harsh initiation would scare her off, what do you think my tearing into her in front of the group would do?"

Justine didn't answer. He was right and she knew it.

"We do it this way," Mark continued. "She gets punished, but we tell her how much worse it could've been. We're giving her a second chance."

"Punishment tempered with mercy." Justine nodded.

"Precisely. She could still walk out on us here, but the chances are better this way to keep her." Mark sighed. "Scarlett, we're already down a member with Cerce stepping down. Do you want two empty seats?"

"I suppose you're right." She sighed "For the record, what makes you convinced she'll be okay with this?"

Mark smiled wickedly, and Justine felt her heart miss a beat, she loved that look, he was excited about something.

"Because if we can get her started, by the end she'll enjoy it."

"Enjoy her punishment?"

"Yes." Mark nodded. "She'll end here the way she should've in her initiation, by breaking and being damn glad she did. She'll be getting off on it. A punishment that, when we're through, will seem like a reward."

"You base this on your arrogance? You think every woman bends to your will?"

"I base it on what I saw in Orion's sham of a performance," Mark replied with a smirk.

Justine rolled her eyes. Orion, Alex Warner to the rest of the world, and Mark had been best friends for close to twenty years, yet at the same time never passed up an opportunity to dig at each other. Over the years, those digs had led to feuds and even the occasional brawl. The two were constantly trying to one up each other, and not for the first time, Justine had to admire Mark's ability to keep a secret. If Alex, who had been after her for years, ever found out Mark shared her bed, he would be beside himself.

"Tell me what I missed then, because she looked properly pissed off to me and the others," she said.

"There were three or four instances where Orion really pushed her, before backing off. Each of those times I saw her eyes start to shine. She was still being defiant, but there was a totally different look on her face. Every time I thought if he just kept going she would've broken, and been begging for more."

"You saw it in her eyes?"

Mark nodded.

"No one else did."

"They were watching her suck cock and get on all fours. The guys were looking at her pussy, and the women were too caught up in 'look at the slut get hers' and they missed it."

"But you don't miss anything do you, Lovecraft?"

"Never," he replied seriously, causing her to shake her head.

There was conceited and there was convinced, there was no doubt which Mark was.

"Better than that, while everyone was watching the video, I was watching her watch herself. She was getting worked up."

"Is this one of those every strong woman wants to be submissive things? "I hope you know better than that."

"I do, but she really does. She's been writing about and living the part of the top for years. That initiation gave her some curiosity about the bottom. She'll get into this, and thank us in the end." He smiled. "Sincerely."

"You're wrong," she said simply, and then smiling back at him raised her eyebrows. "Wager?"

"Yes," he said with no hesitation.

"Hmm, let's see." Justine thought for a moment, "If you're wrong, you give your latest pet, Stephanie, to Orion for a night."

She sat back, pleased with herself. Mark was extremely selective with his pets. He picked young inexperienced girls who needed help through school and offered to help pay for their education in exchange for anything he wanted. He was notorious for never sharing them, and had been bragging about this one for months.

She waited for him to back down, but with no hesitation he said, "Deal. What I want is a full night with you."

"You've had many of those."

"On top." Mark smirked.

Justine shook her head, he'd put the ball back in her court. He began to smile smugly.

"Fine," she said quickly. "But not tonight, and within reason. Keep your leashes for your pets."

"Why of course, My Mistress, I'll be nothing short of respectful."

"I'm sure. I..."

They both jumped at the sound of the phone on her desk buzzing. Hitting speaker, Justine called out, "Yes, Brenda?"

"Sydney Stone is here to see you."

"Send her in, and Brenda?"

"Yes?"

"You can go home for the day. Miss Stone is an old friend and we'll be leaving together from here."

"Thank you, Miss Bates, enjoy your weekend."

Justine thumbed off speaker, then looked at Mark and grinned.

"Orion's favorite color on a young girl like Stephanie is white; do be sure she has something in that color."

As Mark shot her a dirty look, Justine rose from her chair and walked around to the front of the desk. Mark had risen as well, and walked over to the side, taking the chair with him, so it would not be in the way later. The door opened and Brenda held it as Sydney Stone entered the room. She thanked Brenda, and then turned to face Justine, as the door closed behind her.

"Good afternoon, Justine," she smiled "I have to say, what a pleasant surprise, your inviting me to lunch."

Sydney had started forward, but stopped when she noticed Mark leaning against the bar. He didn't address her, just simply stared.

The smile left Sydney's face.

As she returned Mark's stare, Justine took a moment to take in her Circle's newest member. There was no doubt Sydney was qualified to be in the group. In addition to the wealth and dominance, she was absolutely beautiful. Although not quite as tall as Justine she was taller than average, with a pair of legs that seemed to go on forever. Those legs were currently being shown off in the short white sundress she was wearing. Sydney's tits were on the smaller side, but were pushed up quite well. She was deeply tanned and the dress accentuated her bronzed flesh. Sydney's long blonde hair was currently up due to the heat, but when it was down fell almost to her waist.

"Good to see you, Mark," she said quietly. "I didn't know you'd be joining us."

"It's Lovecraft from this point on, and I think you should've been expecting me Aurora."

Turning to Justine, Sydney took a couple of more steps towards her.

"I'm sorry, Justine, I thought the meeting was tonight, why are we…"

"If your brother is calling you by your title then I believe you should try readdressing me."

Justine was looking into Sydney's blue grey eyes and saw a flash of anger, before she took a breath and said softly, "My apologies, My Mistress, I was unaware we'd be conducting business here today."

"As Lovecraft said, I believe that you should've been expecting this..."

"I'm not sure I…"

"Don't play coy, my sister," Mark said, still leaning against the bar. "You know exactly what this is about." He grunted. "Surely you wouldn't think our Mistress would actually want to spend time with a disgrace like you."

Again her eyes flared, but she wisely bit back a response. Turning back to Justine she asked, "Mistress Scarlett, have I done something wrong?"

"Really, Aurora?" Justine asked. "Did you think word of your embarrassing behavior wouldn't reach me?"

Crossing her arms, Sydney sighed, "You're speaking of my night with Alexander. Mistress, I assure you I was there to please him."

"That's funny, he didn't seem pleased when he called Master Ramses," Justine pointed out. "In fact he was quite put out."

"Because apparently you don't know how to put out," Mark said. "Just like those useless sluts you write about in those crappy books of yours." He grunted. "No wonder they're in the clearance bins."

"And are we in high school now?" Sydney asked him. "Throwing around cheap insults?" She sighed. "I suppose I should let it slide, considering where you came from."

Mark's reply was a nasty smirk, and Sydney turned back to Justine.

"Mistress Scarlett, I don't understand the issue here."

"That in itself is an issue," Justine told her. "My lady, I was told the evening didn't start out poorly. That you were cooperative."

"I was quite playful, Sydney replied. "Just as High Lady Felicia instructed me to be."

She paused and watched nervously as Mark walked up behind her. Justine knew she wanted to turn around, but wouldn't give him the satisfaction.

"For a time you were. Then Alexander requested something didn't he?"

"He requested many things," Sydney replied coolly.

"And he was to be given every one of those things. He is not only a long standing member, but time was granted to him. He was entitled to enjoy his sister, every bit of her."

"I refused him my ass, yes," she admitted. "I drew the line there."

"It wasn't up to you to draw the line," Mark slowly walked around to the other side of her. "You were his for the evening."

"I'm not a possession."

"You were that night."

"Aurora, the Circle will not allow its members, male or female, to be unduly used." Justine explained. She hadn't wanted to speak this much, but was enjoying watching Sydney's unease while Mark stalked around her.

"Granted time is meant to be playful," she continued. "However the member given the time is always the top. You're the bottom, and you didn't fulfill your role, Aurora."

"Mistress, I was told specifically by the High Lady my initiation would be the only time I'd ever have to do something against my will, that there would not be..."

"Anal sex is not against your will," Mark commented from behind her. "From what we know it's very much in your repertoire, so to speak."

"It's my body and my choice."

"What is this, a pro-life discussion?" Mark asked, coming around in front of her so quickly she stepped back, causing Justine to smile. "For that night it was his body, and what he chose."

"I won't be rented out like an average whore!" Sydney pointed at Scarlett. "I will...ow!"

She cried out in surprise, as with unerring accuracy, Mark reached out and flicked his finger hard against her right nipple.

"You don't raise your voice! Is that understood?" he asked. Sydney stared angrily at him, but nodded. "And you're not even an average whore; at least they satisfy their masters."

"Understand one thing," Justine said, cutting her off before she got Mark going even more. "We'll never ask you to do something you've never done, but Lovecraft is right. We know all about you, Aurora, and you're not above that act."

"I didn't like his tone. He didn't ask, he demanded. I politely refused, and he became irate, telling me I was his to do with as he pleased."

"He was right." Justine shrugged.

"This isn't fair, My Lady. I..."

"Was disobedient and brought shame upon my Circle and me personally," Justine snapped. "This is not a debate, Aurora. You broke the rules. You were proud when you should've been demure, and now you'll answer for that."

"I am to be punished?"

"Why do you think Lovecraft is here?"

"No, this isn't right." Sydney shook her head. "He broke the rules as well; he wasn't supposed to be like that and..."

Mark put his finger to her lips.

"My Lady, there's something to be said in your favor for that. He shouldn't have pushed, but again he shouldn't have had to." Removing his finger he continued, "There's a reason you're here now Aurora, and that's to give you a second chance."

"What does that mean?"

"Punishments are supposed to be done in front of the entire group. The last lady who was punished for refusing a higher member was subjected to a merry-go-round by all six male members. It was quite a show."

Sydney's eyes widened slightly and Justine tried to signal Mark to stop, that had not been done in the Circle in years. Mark was trying to scare her, but she was afraid it would push Sydney away.

"But you see, my proud whore, our mistress has decided to take mercy on you. I feel you were treated too softly in your initiation, so this may not all be your fault. So we're going to offer you a second chance to make a first impression."

"And if I don't?"

"Three choices, my lady: this punishment, a proper one in front of the group, or you simply quit."

"You'll ask me to leave after you sought me out?"

"I never sought you out," Mark said. "I argued against your very presence in our group. I knew you'd be a disgrace," He snorted. "I can smell a poser a mile away. Your failure was inevitable."

"Try again," Sydney said. "I know this game, I'll not be dared."

"Then do me the favor and leave," Mark replied calmly. "Take your worthless ass back to your mansion and go back to amateur hour with the boys. They're all you can handle anyway."

"I won't waste my day arguing," Justine said. "The choice is yours, Aurora. Leave and miss out on what you know you'll truly enjoy over stubborn pride, or prove to me you can properly please a brother of this group."

Justine locked eyes with Sydney's and watched the struggle within them.

"Just be warned, you're also making up for my embarrassment to not only a fellow Master, but a dear friend. Lovecraft is not here to be kind."

"Obviously, I'm here to be bored," Mark shook his head. "So be honest, who writes those scenes in your books? Can't be a fraud like you."

Sydney stared over at him, her lip twitching, and then looking back at Justine, put her head down and said softly, "I'll submit to the will of my Mistress."

Justine felt a surge of excitement. Sydney had spoken properly, but she could still see the steel in her eyes. She was going to force herself to go through with this.

"Step back," Mark said.

Sydney hesitated, and then cried out as Mark, again demonstrating his uncanny speed, caught her tit with another flick of his wrist.

"Yes, Master," she whispered.

"I'm not your master; I'd be ashamed to be," he snapped. "Go to the middle of the room."

Justine slid up onto the edge of the desk and watched him. Turning his back to Sydney for effect, he slipped off the tank top. Mark's entire back was covered with a tattoo of a half man half goat creature sitting in a circle full of mystic symbols. The detail was incredible, and as with the tattoo on his arm, Justine could envision the eyes of the goat staring at her. Above the circle and going across his shoulders, were the words "Lex Talionis."

Mark tossed the shirt to the side and turned back to face them. Justine felt her pussy begin to heat up. Mark's eyes had darkened to the point they appeared black and his muscular chest and stomach were glistening with sweat. More than that had changed; he somehow seemed bigger, stronger, and even more confident. The person standing in front of her was no longer Mark Phillips a pretty, smooth talking attorney. No before her now stood her enforcer, Lovecraft of The Circle. She turned to see Sydney staring wide eyed at him. She was trying to maintain her calm, but Justine could smell the fear on her. Mark walked slowly over to her, stopping a foot in front of her.

"Lex Talionis, an eye for an eye," he began softly. "Let the punishment fit the crime. Your crime is pride and refusing to give what your brother wanted. You'll now give to me what he wanted, and do so willingly."

Justine wiped at her face, she was flushed and it was no longer from the heat. Mark hadn't discussed what he would do. The thought of watching Sydney taking that cock in her ass was enough to make her want to masturbate right there on the desk.

"Strip," Mark ordered her as he slid his shoes off.

Sydney paused and looked at Justine, who said, "I advise you do as your brother says. He's not known for his patience."

"The dress hits the floor, or your ass takes the door, slut," Mark snapped. "Now take your fucking clothes off, or I'll do it for you."

Sydney untied the dress from behind her neck and let it fall to the floor. The dress had padding and she was not wearing a bra. Her small tits were high and firm, the left one pierced with a silver loop. Justine noticed her nipples were erect. Maybe Mark was right.

"Keep going," Mark said. "Hopefully the bottom is better than the top; I saw bigger tits in middle school."

Sydney flushed red, but obeyed. Hooking her fingers into the sides of her white thong, she began slowly sliding it off, shaking her hips as she exposed her shaved pussy. Mark stepped up to the side of her and dealt her ass a slap that sounded a like a gunshot in the office. Sydney cried out in pain and would have fallen over, had Mark not grabbed her by her hair.

"I said strip, not pose!"

"I won't...." Sydney started, and then yelped when, Mark yanked her head up to face him.

"Then don't." he hissed. "Just pick up your clothes and go."

"I...I'm sorry, My Lord."

"Yeah, sorry was the word I had in mind." He snorted. "Sorry excuse for a lady of the Circle that's for damn sure. Now get on your knees."

Sydney's hesitation was barely more than a second, but Mark's hands flashed out, caught her nipples in his powerful fingers and twisted them hard. She squealed, and the pitch of her voice sent a surge of wetness through Justine. She could feel the thin strip of her thong soaking between her legs.

"Y...yes my..."

"Now!"

Mark feigned going for her tits again, and she dropped to her knees so hard she winced when they hit the floor. Sydney swallowed hard, and then reached for his zipper. Mark contemptuously slapped her hand away.

"Did I tell you to touch me?"

"N...no, Sir." She said, looking at her hand.

"Then why did you?"

Sydney paused, and Justine could see her thinking, trying to guess the right answer. Mark reached down towards her tit and she blurted out; "To please you, My Lord."

"The only way you could truly please me is to leave," Mark said. "However, our Mistress has chosen to be merciful and give you a chance I wouldn't. So you'll begin by properly worshipping her."

Mark gestured toward Justine, and Sydney began to stand. She was stopped by Mark yanking hard on her hair, pulling it from the clip and bringing her back to her knees.

"Crawl."

Mark let go of her hair, and shoved her in the back. Sydney caught herself with her hands, and stayed there. She looked at Justine, who beckoned her with her finger.

"Come here, my little pet."

Sydney's eyes hardened and Justine smiled to herself, enjoying the struggle behind that glare. She was so intent on that look she jumped at the sound of Mark slapping her ass again. Sydney's breath hissed out between her teeth, but she did not cry out. Mark drew back his hand again, and she began to slowly crawl on all fours towards her mistress.

If Justine had been wet before, she was close to dripping now. It was an effort to maintain her aloof expression watching Sydney coming towards her, naked and on all fours. As good as her small breasts hanging down and her tight tanned ass up in the air looked, what had Justine's heart racing was the look on Sydney's face. It was a mixture of anger and humiliation, yet behind that there was still a look of stubborn pride, as she tried to tell herself this was still on her terms somehow.

Reaching her, Sydney lowered her head and kissed the top of her right foot. The touch of her lips sent a charge through Justine, but the contact was quickly broken when Mark again delivered a sharp slap to her ass.

"Since when do you touch without permission?"

"I...you..." Sydney sputtered, trying to keep the anger out of her voice. "You told me to worship her."

"You never touch your Mistress without permission." Mark snorted. "Don't you read your own shitty books?"

Sydney lifted her face to Justine, swallowed hard and whispered, "Mistress may I please have the privilege of kissing your feet?"

Justine paused, reveling in the look in her eyes. The longer she hesitated the angrier Sydney appeared.

"Although your words are proper, Aurora," She began quietly, "I doubt their sincerity. I don't appreciate that haughty look on your face. But then again that's why we're here is it not?"

"Yes, Mistress," she answered evenly.

Justine took Sydney's chin in her hand, lifting her face and looking into her eyes. Sydney held her gaze, her grey eyes blazing. Justine nodded, let her chin go and said,

"Lovecraft, change her tone."

"My pleasure, Mistress."

Mark grabbed Sydney by the shoulders and pulled her up onto her knees. Sliding his hands further down her arms, he squeezed hard and with a wrench of his powerful shoulders yanked her up and off of her feet. Sydney cried out in surprise as Mark lifted her higher so her feet were at his knees. Justine took a moment to admire his muscles bulging from the effort, before focusing on their prey.

Justine took in Sydney's naked body being presented before her and took the silver hoop between her fingers. Sydney took a deep breath, bracing herself for the pain. Instead, looking her in the eye, Justine let the hoop go and slid the tip of her nail across her swollen nipple. A shudder went through Sydney's body and a soft gasp escaped her lips. Justine brought her other hand up, cupping Sydney's small tit and using her thumb, stroked that nipple as well. Again a small sound of pleasure came from her. Better yet the look in her eyes changed slightly. Not much, but it was a beginning.

"What, no thank you?" Justine asked.

Sydney's response turned into a yelp, as Justine twisted the hoop and gave her the pain she had, a moment ago, been expecting. Mark was right; Sydney couldn't follow the same game she made her pets play. That was okay, they would teach her.

"Th...thank you, Mistress, you're too kind."

"Too little, too late, My Lady."

Justine looked up at Mark to tell him to continue. Before she could speak, he jerked his head to the side. Justine hopped off the desk and walked around to the other side. She heard a bang, followed by Sydney grunting in pain. Justine didn't have to be look to know Mark had thrown her over the desk. She turned to see she was right; Sydney was now bent over the desk with Mark standing directly behind her.

Sydney had an expression of naked fury on her face and pushed up onto her arms, trying to stand up. That was a mistake.

"I will not be..." she started.

"I will do as I choose to you, whore!"

Mark slid his arms under hers and spread them wide, knocking her hands off of the desk. Sydney fell forward, turning her head away so it wouldn't hit the hardwood surface of the desk. As it was her head was still going to. Justine was ready to call out to Mark to stop. Rough was one thing, assault was another. Sydney cried out first, as her head was stopped inches from the desk, by Mark who had gotten his hand around quick enough to catch her by her hair. Justine relaxed, for a moment she had worried he was losing control.

"If you move again, you'll be tied down."

"Yes, sir." Sydney gasped out.

Justine nodded in satisfaction. There had been no edge whatsoever in that response. Mark was scaring her. Stepping back, he looked down at the floor.

"Up on your toes."

Sydney didn't move and Mark dealt her a backhand slap across her ass that caused Justine to wince. Without waiting for her to move, Mark grabbed her by the cheeks of her ass and lifted her higher onto the desk. Mark took a couple of steps back and began removing his belt. Justine became aware of a wet feeling on her thighs as she knew where Mark was going to target first. Mark whipped the belt off and, stepping forward, flicked his wrist. The tip of the belt whistled past Sydney's ear and struck the desk with sharp crack in front of her face. Sydney's eyes widened and Justine took in the look of fear in them. She lifted her head and looked as if she was going to speak, but Mark cut her off, "Try again, whore."

"Thank..."

"Not a thank you, an apology!"

Mark punctuated his words with another snap of the belt. This one so close it passed through her hair.

"I'm sorry, My Mistress!" Sydney called out. "I'm sorry I disgraced you!"

Justine looked down at her. It was the most sincere she'd sounded. Still, there was a price to be paid, not to mention Justine was greatly anticipating her punishment.

"You're only saying that to save your ass, Aurora," Justine chuckled. "Literally." Looking over at Mark she smiled. "Lovecraft, I'd like a little more sincerity."

With no hesitation Mark lashed out with the belt. He aimed low below the desk and Sydney let out a high pitched yowl as he struck the tender sole of her foot with the belt. The second he struck, he expertly whipped his wrist around and flicked the belt back out. Sydney cried out again and Mark shouted, "Put your foot back on the floor!"

For emphasis, the belt flew out and struck her left ass cheek. Justine felt a surge go through her at the sound. Sydney pushed up to her arms.

"I'll not be whipped like a dog!" she snapped.

"Then fucking quit!" Mark snarled behind her. "Go ahead, you fucking spoiled bitch, put on your clothes and walk out! This is the only thing in your life that hasn't been handed to you and you can't handle it!"

Sydney stopped and looked down at the desk, her breathing was heavy and she was trembling in rage as he continued, "Even your fucking initiation was sham. Orion's a rich fucking poser just like you and he went soft, well now you're paying for his failure." He laughed. "But then again, that's all you do is pay for things right? Buy everything in life; well the Circle cannot be bought. Now get up and get out."

Sydney stayed where she was, her head down, hands clenched into fists on the desk. Justine wanted nothing more than to move the blonde sweat soaked hair that hung around her head so she could see the look on her face. This was the moment of truth. They would keep her or lose her in the next moment. Justine looked up at Mark; Sydney's decision would also mean his Stephanie could be on her way to a very memorable trip to New York. Mark was standing there, the belt coiled around his left hand. He was also staring intently at Sydney, but as always there seemed to be no doubt in his eyes.

Sydney proved her smug enforcer correct again. Looking up at her, Sydney whispered. "Again I am sorry, Mistress. Not just for my affront to you, but that the group doesn't feel I earned my place." Swallowing hard, her grey eyes looking up demurely through her lashes, she added, "Please allow me the opportunity to prove them wrong."

Even in submission, she was showing defiance, but of the proper kind. Showing she had the steel to take what was put to her and earn her keep. Justine felt relieved; they would not lose a member today. The next thing she felt was a wave of lust flow through her as extending her arms, Sydney crossed her wrists in front of her, inviting Justine to take them. Justine grabbed her forearms and pulled her towards her so she was lying flat across the desk.

Justine looked at Mark, who was doing a good job of keeping that ever present smirk off his face. His job wasn't done yet, they had gotten her to agree, but she was far from broken. Justine paused, trying to think of another way, but he was on the right track. Sydney had always been a top and had never been subjected to pain and humiliation; it would have to be this way. Justine would turn him loose and hope he was right. Meeting Mark's eyes, she winked.

"So be it, Aurora," he said quietly. "I've broken far prouder than you."

Mark snapped the belt down low again; Sydney gasped in pain, but stayed still. There was another crack of the whip for the other foot, and the same reaction. Mark whispered, "Good girl."

He nodded in approval, a small sign of respect shown to his sister. Drawing the belt around, he paused, took a deep breath, and tore into Sydney with a vengeance.

Snapping the belt out, he quickly drew it back and, immediately lashing out again, Mark began methodically working the length of her body. The office was filled with a series of sharp cracks followed by yelps and small cries of pain from Sydney. With each blow, her body jerked, and she emitted a sound of pain from between her clenched teeth. Justine saw her bite her lip to try not to cry out and admired her effort. She was stronger than Justine had thought she would be. Taking her eyes from Sydney's face, Justine watched a master at his craft.

Mark was playing the belt up and down, and side to side. Justine had seen this many times and knew where the blows were landing. First the left then right foot, the next two blows were to the soft skin behind the backs of her knees. From there he would strike the inside of her thighs, before targeting her ass. Justine was tempted to walk around and watch. Mark was amazingly accurate, the blows to the inner thighs would be no more than an inch from Sydney's pussy, and the first set of blows to the ass would be at the very tip of the cheeks.

Mark struck higher, catching her in the back, just below the shoulder blades. Sydney's body jerked and she squeezed her eyes shut against the pain. Mark went back and started at the bottom again. Justine's breathing was heavier than Sydney's. God, she was fucking hot right now! Her pussy was dripping and her nipples so hard they were aching. There was no way she was making it until after the meeting without taking Mark. Speaking of, as good as Sydney's squirming looked; Justine tore her gaze away to watch him

He looked nothing short of demonic. His torso was covered in sweat and the muscles in his arms and shoulders rippled underneath the enormous tattoos as he whipped the belt around again and again. But it was his face that had Justine's pussy flowing. Mark's once perfect hair was sweat soaked, and hanging in his face just over his eyes, and his eyes! They were as black as the night and so bright they appeared as if they were glowing from within. He had a nasty smile on his face, and his lip curled each time the belt struck home.

Justine's eyes went back to Sydney and took in the series of small red welts on her back. Mark was only striking with just the tip, and the marks were not much larger than a dime. Justine shook her head in amazement as she noticed all the welts across her back were in one line, and inside her thin tan lines. Mark had over two decades of martial arts training and anything in his hands could become a weapon. Justine licked her lips at the sight of the small red marks on the top of her ass, and then returned to her face to see how she was holding up.

Sydney's eyes were shut tightly and there were tears streaming from them. She had stopped biting her lip and was no longer yelping, but moaning. Justine listened closely and wondered if it was her own high state of arousal or were those moans starting to sound as if there were some pleasure mixed with the pain? Her body however, was jerking harder against Justine's grip with every blow and the moans were quickly becoming whimpers.

"Try again, My Lady," she said softly.

Opening her eyes, she gasped out. "I...I'm sorry, Mistress." The belt struck low again and no longer trying to hold back, Sydney sobbed. "Oh please, please forgive me."

She sobbed again and Justine drew her fingers across her throat. Mark coiled the belt back around his hand, and then tossed it to the floor. Justine knelt down so that she was looking into Sydney's tear streaked face and said softly, "That was much better, my pet; perhaps you've learned your lesson. Now we shall see if this had made you more willing to please."

Justine nodded to Mark, who coming up behind Sydney, grabbed her long blond hair and tugged back on it. He did not pull hard, but she instantly slid off of the desk and onto her knees for him. As Justine walked back around to the front of her desk, Sydney remained kneeling, her head down.

"What are you waiting for?" Mark asked.

"For direction, My Lord," she said softly.

"Good answer," Mark said quietly. "Perhaps I judged you too quickly, but that still remain to be seen."

Justine smiled to herself, another small encouragement thrown her way. Mark had truly mastered the game. She once again sat on the desk and let her bare feet dangle off the floor.

"Now, show your Mistress proper respect," Mark told her.

Sydney turned and leaned over so that she was on her hands and knees again. This time however, she lowered herself to her forearms, putting her tits on the floor and raising her well tanned and quite red ass into the air. Looking up at Justine she asked softly, "Mistress, may I have the honor?"

"You may," Justine answered.

"Thank you, you're too kind."

There was no sarcasm in Sydney's reply and lowering her head she kissed the top of Justine's left foot. Like before, she felt a thrill go through her at the feel of Sydney's lips. This time the thrill continued, as Sydney started planting soft kisses along the length of her foot. When she reached the end of her toe, she flicked her tongue out, licking the tip of it. Justine held back a moan as she felt her toe sucked into Sydney's warm wet mouth. She looked down to see her looking up at her, and again had to fight to appear unimpressed.

Sydney swirled her tongue around her toe, then sliding it from her mouth went to the next one. As she sucked that one into her mouth, Sydney's eyes rolled in pleasure. Unable to repress it, a shudder went through Justine's body. Women were not generally of interest to her these days. In fact it had been several years since she had slept with one. Here and there she had played a little, but really had no great desire. That was beginning to change at the moment as she watched Sydney's pink tongue and soft lips work their way across her foot.

She hadn't expected this. A sincere kiss to each foot was all she had required, but she was certainly not going to stop her. Sensing movement, Justine looked up to see Mark had moved to the side of the desk so he could watch. The look of desire on his face set Justine's heart beating even quicker. Her eyes dropped to his crotch and both her mouth and pussy watered at the sight of the enormous bulge in his pants. She looked back up to see him watching her. Their eyes met, and with a smile he indicated Sydney at her feet.

Justine looked away before he smirked at her, and was glad she did. Sydney had finished her toes and went to her other foot. She had not asked permission, but Justine was going to let that slide right now. She watched, getting hotter by the minute as Sydney sucked on each of her toes. When she finished she gave Justine an extra thrill by ducking her head and sliding her tongue along her instep.

"Mistress, please raise your foot for your pet," Mark whispered.

Justine did as he said. She knew damn well it was for his benefit, but had to admit the way Sydney's tongue ran across her foot from heel to toe was driving her wild. Once Sydney reached her toe, she ran her tongue along the top of her foot, and started up her ankle. Justine remained silent as Sydney's tongue trailed up the inside of her calf and wondered how far she would go. The Circle had found no evidence Sydney was bisexual, was she? Or was she playing the part to the hilt? Resisting the urge to find out, Justine said, "Well done, my pet. Now let's see if you've learned to please your brother."

Sydney removed her tongue from Justine's leg and, rising to her knees, turned to Mark.

"May I, My Lord?"

"I wasn't overly impressed with the work you did on our Mistress's feet," Mark lied. "I've watched dogs lap water out of the toilet with more skill than you have, but I'll let you try."

Credit where it was due, Mark never broke character. That remark also brought a brief flash to Sydney's previously demure look. The game might not be over yet, he was going to keep pushing.

Reaching up, Sydney undid Mark's slacks. She pulled them down, and stopped and stared at the huge bulge in his black boxers. Justine was staring as well, especially at the large wet spot that had formed where the head of his cock had been dripping. Sydney grabbed the sides of his underwear and pulled them down quickly, causing his cock to spring free.

"Oh," she whispered as she took in the sight of his cock inches from her face.

Mark had the largest cock Justine had seen, at least ten inches. It was not only long, but thick as well. Justine recalled many of Mark's videos where he would tear into young girls, causing them to wail in pain as their tight young pussies were stretched far beyond what they were used to. Justine was no young girl, and had more than her share over the years and there were times he could still make her cry out.

"What's the matter slut?" Mark asked. "Never seen a real one before?"

"My master is quite the man," Sydney said quietly while wrapping her hand around it.

Justine noticed that her fingers did not quite make their way all the way around his shaft, and again felt her body responding in anticipation of what was to come. Sydney slowly pumped his cock while staring at it, as if wondering if she could handle it.

"I can give myself a hand job!" Mark snapped. "Go ahead and suck it. Pretend you're back in your slutty little sorority, blowing some rich frat boy."

Sydney slid her mouth over the head of his cock. She went down a couple of inches, then rising up higher on her knees managed to take him about halfway down before stopping. Justine saw her force her mouth open wider to get a little further. After a brief pause, she started bobbing her head, going down on him in a slow steady rhythm. Sydney started sucking faster, now using her hand as well, and jerking him off as she blew him. Mark remained silent, the expression on his face completely indifferent, as if he were watching traffic pass rather than receiving a blow job from a stunning woman.

"Is she pleasing you, Lovecraft?" Justine asked, eagerly awaiting one of his patented nasty remarks. As always he did not disappoint her.

"I think she should consider herself lucky all Alexander complained about was her refusing him something. They must be easy to please out West."

Sydney's eyes flared and Mark saw it. "I'm sorry, Aurora. Should I be rolling my eyes and begging for more of your mediocre mouth? Sorry, I'm not one of your Daddy's rich friends' sons." He sighed dramatically. "Fuck, I'm standing here having a conversation, you can't even get me to moan."

Sydney went further down his cock and began to suck faster. She added her second hand, caressing his balls as she worked his massive cock. She seemed to be doing just fine to Justine, but Mark rolled his eyes.

"Oh for Christ's sake!" he snapped. "Here, let me."

Grabbing the back of her head, Mark slid his cock part way from her mouth, then drove it in to the hilt. Sydney made a sound that was a cross between a squeal and gagging, and Mark pulled his cock all the way out. She gasped for breath, and grabbing his cock, he slapped her hard in the face with it.

"That's the best you can do? No wonder you stick with the kids. Here, try again."

Mark shoved it back into her mouth, but this time more slowly and he had pulled her head back, changing the angle. Justine watched, resisting the urge to stroke herself as Mark fed Sydney his cock inch by inch. Sydney's mouth opened wider and she gurgled around him, but he managed to push it all the way in. Holding her hair tightly in his fists, he started slowly fucking her mouth.

Sydney groaned as he pushed his dick so deep Justine saw her lips touch his balls. Mark began to pick up speed, pumping his cock faster. He was drawing it out almost to the head before shoving it back in. Sydney was trying to move her head with his rhythm, but he was holding her still. After several more pumps, Mark said, "enough practice, let's see you take it like you know what you're doing."

Mark drew back his hips and thrust forward hard. Sydney let out a muffled squeal as his cock was slammed down her throat. Her hands came up and pushed against his hips, slowing him up as he thrust into her again. Sliding off the desk, Justine stepped up and grabbed her hair, wrapping her hands in it just past Mark's.

"You don't resist your brother," she hissed, giving Sydney's hair a good hard tug.

Mark released her hair and, grabbing her wrists, pinned them together. Gathering them in one of his large powerful hands, he yanked them above her head. Sydney cried out in pain as he pulled her up so that her knees lifted off the floor. She moaned around his still pumping cock as her shoulders bore her weight. Justine let out a breath at the sight of Mark's muscles bulging as he held her up, and continued to fuck her mouth. Justine was standing so that her thighs were pressing into Sydney's back and Mark was pushing his cock into her face.

The two of them were not much more than a foot apart and staring into each other's eyes. Looking down to make sure Sydney couldn't see, Justine leaned in and kissed him. Her tongue shoved against his lips and he opened his mouth, allowing it access. Their tongues played across each other and Mark released a small moan into her mouth as he kissed her while face fucking Sydney. Justine broke the kiss and pulled back, breathing hard.

"Stay still," she hissed.

Mark stopped moving his hips and Justine began pulling Sydney by the hair, shoving her mouth down onto his cock, before pulling it back.

"You like this, Aurora?" she asked. "Do you? Imagine this being at a meeting, with every man at that table in a circle using your mouth just like this!" Justine lowered her head until she was whispering in her ear. "That's right, every man using your mouth while the women take turns holding you like I am. Round and round from one to the other, and they take a long time to come, My Lady. That's what we could've done to you. So be grateful and enjoy the privilege of your brother's beautiful cock."

Sydney squealed something and unable to resist, Justine nipped her earlobe, her teeth digging into the soft flesh. She yelped around Mark's cock and Justine knew then and there she was going to need to come and soon. Standing, she looked down to see Sydney's eyes were watering as they continued to force his cock down her throat. Looking back up at Mark, she nodded towards the desk. Letting go of Sydney's hair, Justine went back around to the other side of her desk and watched as Mark let go of her arms and yanked his cock from her mouth. She fell forward onto her hands and knees, gasping for breath, her long hair plastered to her face with sweat.

"Fucking useless," Mark said. "I've gotten better head from my pets."

"I...I'm sorry I disappointed you, My Lord."

"Don't worry, I was expecting it."

Mark again grabbed her by her shoulders and, hauling her to her feet, pushed her towards the desk. Sydney stumbled and caught herself by her hands. Mark came up behind her and, placing his hand in the middle of her back, pushed against her.

"Time to make amends my whore."

Justine had a perfect view of Sydney's eyes widening as it dawned on her what Mark meant.

"No," she gasped. "I…"

"It's too late for that," Justine grabbed her wrists, yanking her towards her. "You chose to stay and take your punishment, my disobedient pet. Take the consequences for your actions and this will be forgotten."

Again Mark saved her face from hitting the desk by holding her hair. Justine held her arms pinned to the desk and, looking into her eyes, saw nothing resembling defiance. The breaking was inevitable, now it was a matter of Mark being right about her enjoying it. Sydney let out a priceless whimper as he started slapping his cock against her ass.

"Aurora has redeemed herself somewhat, Lovecraft. Get it wet first."

"As you request."

Grabbing her hips, Mark drew back and drove hard into Sydney's pussy. She cried out as he continued to push his massive cock all the way inside her, and groaned as once he had, he remained there.

"Oh," she whispered. "Your cock is…"

"Better than you deserve," Mark said and, drawing back, started fucking the shit out of her.

There was no other way to describe it. He was pulling his cock all the way out to the tip before plunging hard back into her. Justine watched transfixed by the site of his huge prick pounding in and out her. There was no doubt Sydney was not as put off as she had pretended as Mark's cock was glistening from her obviously wet pussy. In fact she was so wet that Justine could hear his cock sliding in and out of her. Oh, she was enjoying this, the little slut. Justine could also hear the sound of Mark's flesh slapping against hers as he was fucking her with everything he had.

Sydney was moaning continuously as now that she had begun getting used to him, she was enjoying the sensation of being so completely full. Justine knew that feeling well, and couldn't wait to know it again. Looking down she asked, "What you don't…"

"Oh thank you, My Lord!" Sydney cut her off, desperate not to get punished further. "Thank you for showing me what it's like to be with a true Master!"

"Oh don't get excited," Mark replied. "I'm only fucking you because I was tired of that poor excuse of a blow job you were giving me."

Justine looked up as he had spoke. Although he was trying to sound casual she could hear it in his voice that he was beginning to feel the effects of fucking Sydney. Justine was in the same position; her pussy was so hot it was throbbing between her legs. She looked up at Mark who was breathing noticeably heavier and had started to slow down his assault on his disobedient Sister of the Circle.

"Well, My Lady," Justine began, "Here's your chance. How would you like to please your brother?"

Sydney looked up, her grey eyes meeting Justine's unblinking gaze. There was a question in those eyes, and Justine nodded. Yes she was going to make her go through with this. Looking back over her shoulder at Mark she spoke, "My Lord, it'd be my privilege for you to have me in any way you choose."

"Better than that!" Mark snapped, slapping her across the ass. "Tell me like the fucking classless whore you are!"

"I'd love it if you'd take that beautiful cock and fuck me in the ass."

The words had come out rushed and Justine could hear her voice trembling as she finished.

"You'd love that wouldn't you?" Mark asked, as sliding his cock from her pussy he placed the tip higher up against her asshole. "You like it in the ass, you little pig?"

She groaned as Mark began to push the head of his cock into her ass. "I want to be your whore, My Lord. Please use me as you will."

Sydney turned back and began to put her head down. She stopped part way and, with a sigh, looked up into Justine's face. Justine whispered, "Good girl" then watched, pussy oozing as Mark slowly forced his long thick cock into Sydney's ass.

"Oh, ohhh it hurts," Sydney moaned as he went deeper into her.

Sydney whimpered as he continued to stretch her asshole with his huge dick. With a quick thrust that caused her to squeal, Mark shoved himself completely into her.

"How does that feel, My Lady?"

"Oh, it's I…" Sydney looked up at her and groaned. "It's an honor to have my brother want me this way."

"Good that you know that." Justine nodded. "Lovecraft, make our contrite sister sing for her Mistress."

"It would be my privilege," Mark said, smiling wickedly.

Mark drew back and, with a savage thrust of his hips, sent his cock plunging into her ass. Sydney screamed. Her mouth opened wide and she howled as Mark began fucking her hard and fast. The sound of Sydney's cry sent a surge of wetness through Justine and she began to breathe through her mouth, she was so worked up. Sydney let out another long, loud wail, and let her face drop to the desk. Justine looked down to see that she had grabbed the edge of it and was squeezing it tightly, her knuckles turning white as Mark tore into her ass.

Justine knelt down to look into her eyes and saw that again there were tears running down her face. Seeing her looking at her, Sydney gasped. "T..thank you, My mistress, thank…." Her words turned into another squeal as Mark started going faster. Again Justine could hear his flesh striking hers and she could imagine the fiery pain of Sydney's ass being spread further than it ever had before. Sydney let out a long shuddering moan and, unable to resist doing it, Justine leaned in and kissed her.

Sydney squealed against her lips and she opened her mouth to capture that delicious sound. She plunged her tongue into her mouth and, to her delight, felt Sydney's tongue dart into hers. Justine let go of her arms and, sliding her hands underneath Sydney, found her nipples. They were as hard as hers felt. Justine couldn't hold back and released a soft moan into Sydney's mouth. That moan was met by first another squeal of pain, then a moan identical to her own as Justine felt Sydney's lips push against hers, kissing her back as hard as she had kissed her.

Justine opened her eyes to find they were inches from Sydney's. Those grey eyes, which for most of her time here had alternated between defiance and rage, now had a different look to them. They appeared to have changed colors, no longer grey, but so bright they were more a shade of silver. They were also beginning to glaze over into a look Justine knew well, a look of pure animal lust. Her squeals were changing pitch as well. They were sounds of pain, but as had happened when Mark had been tearing into her pussy, there were hints of pleasure mingled in.

Justine started to pull her head back, and Sydney whispered, "Oh please, Mistress, please let me…"

She trailed off into a disappointed whimper as Justine pulled her lips from hers and stood up. Justine looked up at Mark and smiled at the sight of him. He was drenched in sweat, every muscle in his body standing out, as he held Sydney's hips and pounded her ass every bit as hard as he had her pussy. His eyes were wild and he was breathing like a bull. Justine swallowed hard and made a decision. She could no longer wait, she needed to come, and Sydney's desire for her had let her know exactly how she wanted to.

"Flip her over on the desk!"

Sydney groaned as, removing his cock from her ass, Mark yanked her into a standing position by her hair. Justine hiked her skirt up to her hips and quickly slid her red thong off. Mark had spun Sydney around to face him and with a rough shove sent her onto her back on the desk. Grabbing her ankles, he spread her legs as far out as he could and plunged his cock back into her ass.

"Oh fuck!" she cried out. "Oh, oh yes!"

She was screaming at the top of her lungs, but that was okay, Justine could fix that. Climbing up on the desk next to Sydney's head, she called out. "If your tongue is going to keep flapping at least put it to good use!"

Swinging her knee over Sydney's head so that she was straddling her shoulders, Justine shoved her red haired pussy down into Sydney's face. With no hesitation, she plunged her tongue deep into Justine's soaking wet pussy. Throwing her head back, Justine cried out and began grinding her hips, sliding Sydney's tongue through the soft wet folds of her pussy. Mark had stopped as Justine had gotten into position, but now resumed driving his cock into Sydney's ass.

Justine cried out again at the sensation of Sydney screaming into her pussy. Leaning forward, Justine braced her hands on Mark's shoulders and started bouncing up and down, plunging Sydney's rigid tongue in and out of her dripping slit. Justine moaned in pleasure as Sydney's arms came up and wrapped around her thighs, pulling her down into her flickering tongue. Oh who could have seen this one coming? Grabbing the back of Mark's head she pulled his face to hers and kissed him hard. Mark returned the kiss, and moaned as their tongues probed each other's mouth.

"She can't see us." she whispered,

Mark reached behind Justine's head and, grabbing a handful of her long red hair, stopped and whispered, "May I?"

"Oh, you're so well trained," Justine purred in his ear. "Yes you may!"

Mark yanked her hair back hard enough to make her moan as a wave of pain laced pleasure flowed through her scalp. Leaning forward, Mark kissed her neck, gently at first then harder. Justine yelped as Sydney's tongue had stopped probing the depths of her pussy and had worked its way up to her swollen and sensitive clit. Justine yanked Mark's hair back and, darting her head forward, caught his ear as she had Sydney's and bit down hard. Mark's breath hissed as she bit down harder and tasted blood.

Mark pushed her away from his head, then in a move that caused her pussy to gush into Sydney's eager tongue, grabbed the sleeves of her shirt and yanked them down her shoulders. Her bra was next, and as he pulled the cups down, her large tits sprang free. Mark immediately lowered his head and Justine groaned as his mouth fastened onto her aching nipple. She shoved her tit hard into his face, and moaned as his tongue swirled across her swollen flesh. Sydney's tongue was busy as well, moving in deliciously slow circles around her clit. Mark had slowed his thrusting, but as he switched to her other nipple his excitement caused him to start slamming her hard and fast.

Sydney squealed again into her pussy, and her finger nails started to dig into the soft flesh of Justine's thighs. The pain added to her pleasure and she started to grind her hips harder into Sydney's talented tongue.

"Fuck her harder!" Justine shouted.

Shaking the sweat from his eyes, he removed his cock from her ass, then after a brief pause drove it in again. The scream Sydney released into Justine's pussy caused her to cry out as well. She was already close to coming, but slowed her hips up as she called out. "Oh you're loving this aren't you, you little fucking pig?"

"Hmm-mmm," Sydney groaned into her dripping pussy.

"Oh, you're a little whore aren't you, Aurora?"

Sydney moaned her agreement, and her tongue sped up on Justine's clit.

"Are you enjoying your brother's cock in your ass, My Lady?"

Sydney stopped sucking long enough to call out a muffled, "Oh yes! Oh thank you! And thank you, Mistress, for allowing me to taste you!"

"Oh what a good little pet you are!" Justine cried out. "I think I shall even reward you!"

Justine reached down between Sydney's legs and her fingers found her clit, her hard swollen clit. Sydney's body jerked beneath her as she started rubbing in fast hard circles. Justine moaned with her as her action caused Sydney to begin to suck her clit into her mouth. Mark was driving into her harder than ever and Justine reveled in Sydney's struggle to work her clit while yelping from his painful thrusts. Justine could feel her thighs beginning to tremble and knew it would be any second now.

Between her thighs, Sydney was also ready to go off, her squeals were higher in pitch and her back was arching off the desk. Sydney was now pushing her hips into Mark's thrusts, plunging even deeper into her now more than willing flesh. Justine stopped rubbing and, taking Sydney's clit between her fingers, gave it a hard pinch. That pinch set off a chain reaction of pleasure.

Sydney screamed into Justine's pussy as her orgasm crashed through her. She began bucking so wildly Justine had to wrap her arms around Mark's shoulders so she wouldn't be thrown off of her. Sydney's convulsions were enough to start to send Justine over the edge. She gasped loudly, and knowing her as well as he did, Mark bit down hard on her nipple. Justine threw her head back and screamed out her pleasure as her own orgasm tore through her body. Her hips began grinding harder onto Sydney's tongue which was still playing across her clit. Justine felt her thighs lock up and her orgasm seemed to pause, a moment later her body convulsed and she cried out again as she felt her pussy gush into Sydney's mouth. Mark let go of her nipple and began moaning and fucking Sydney even harder.

"Yes," Justine gasped. "Give it to her, come all over your whore!"

Beneath her, Sydney cried out as Mark began fucking her so savagely Justine again had to lean forward to not be thrown off.

"You want your brother to come for you, my little pet?"

"Oh please!" Sydney cried out from between her thighs.

Pulling his cock from her ass, Mark squeezed it tight around the base of his shaft. Grabbing her ankle with one hand he yanked her down from the desk. Sydney yelped as she landed hard on the floor. Stepping forward, Mark grabbed her hair, tilted her head back and pumped his cock into Sydney's face. Justine had leaned over the desk to watch as Mark sprayed his cum into Sydney's face and wide open mouth. Sydney grabbed Mark's cock, took it into her mouth and proceeded to pump it herself, jerking him off into it.

"Oh, ass to mouth," Justine cooed, "Oh you are a dirty little thing aren't you, My Lady?"

Sydney groaned around Mark's cock as she continued to suck on it. He moaned and his eyes rolled back as Sydney sucked every last drop from him. Mark groaned again and, pulling his cock from her mouth, leaned against the desk where Justine was on her hands and knees looking down at Sydney's cum splattered face. Sydney was gasping and her eyes still had that bright silvery look Justine had first noticed when they were kissing. Justine looked at Mark who had sunk to his knees next to Sydney. His eyes were closed and he was still breathing hard. With an effort, she forced herself to pull her bra and shirt back up and, sliding off the desk, came around to face Sydney.

Before she could speak, Sydney began, "Thank you Mistress," she panted. "Thank you for giving me a second chance to prove myself to you."

"Thank you for proving yourself," Justine said softly.

"And thank you, My Lord," Sydney continued, looking at Mark. "For teaching me my place."

"My pleasure," Mark replied as he stood up and walked over to the bar. "I think one more thank you is in order however."

Turning back to Justine, Sydney smiled through her cum covered lips. The sight was enough to make her want to come again.

"Thank you for allowing me the honor of pleasing you."

"Well I couldn't let Lovecraft be the only one enjoying himself."

Mark returned with a towel and, kneeling down next to Aurora, began gently wiping the cum from her face.

"So, My Lady," he said, "Do you feel you learned your lesson?"

"I do.' Sydney nodded. "Although between pleasing the both of you, and cumming myself, I feel as if I've been rewarded."

"My Lady," Mark said, flashing a smug smirk at Justine, "that's an excellent answer!"

Fifteen minutes later Justine was walking Sydney out to the main foyer where she could take the elevator down to the first floor. She had offered her to use the shower in her private bathroom, but Sydney had declined, saying her hotel was only a few blocks away. With a nasty little smile she had added that this way she could smell her mistress on her face that much longer. Justine felt a sense of relief flow through her. Not only was Sydney staying, but Justine felt convinced she would be just fine from this point on. Especially when just as they reached the elevator, Sydney turned to her and said, "Mistress, if you'd allow it, I'd like to contact Alexander and offer to fly out to LA and make this up to him."

Justine smiled at the offer, but shook her head.

"I appreciate that, but Alexander is known to hold grudges and I'd rather not go that route. However, I'm thrilled you offered."

"I am sorry I made you look bad," Sydney said. "I really didn't think it worked like that and…"

"It's in the past, Aurora," Justine told her, putting her arm around her. "And I will have you know this'll be forgotten. You accepted your punishment and it'll never be mentioned again."

"Thank you, Mistress."

"Also know that Lovecraft didn't mean the things he said. I hope you know it was all part of the game.."

"He's damn good at the game besides," Sydney shrugged. "On the bright side, how many can say they had the pleasure of being mistreated by a man as fine as him?"

Justine laughed and kissed her on the cheek, "My Lady, you're going to be just fine. You're one of us, no doubt about it."

Sydney laughed and waved as she stepped into the elevator. Justine headed back to the office smiling at the thought of Mark waiting for her there. She had come incredibly hard, but was far from satisfied. It had been fun playing with a woman for the first time in a while, but at the end of the day, what Justine needed was a good hard cock. She entered the office and frowned as she saw Mark had his pants back on and was holding his shirt.

Closing the door behind her, she said quietly, "Did I tell you to get dressed, Lovecraft?"

"No, but…"

"Then why did you?"

"I just thought that…"

Justine raised her hand.

"Are you here to think or to serve?"

Putting his head down, Mark answered softly, "As always, I'm here to serve my mistress."

"Good thing you know that," Justine said. Reaching around, she unzipped her skirt, letting it fall to the floor. "Now take off your clothes and go ready the shower." She smiled. "Because trust me, your work here is far from over."

Chapter Three

Justine opened her eyes and squinted at the alarm clock, wondering if she were seeing it correctly. According to the red numbers that slowly came into focus, it was eleven a.m. How long had it been since she had slept this late? College? Speaking of college, Justine couldn't help but grin at the mostly empty bottle of Southern Comfort on the nightstand. Last night had been a wild one! She wasn't sure exactly what time her and Mark had finally fallen asleep, or more accurately passed out, but she had seen the clock hit four a.m.

She was lying on her back and turning her head to the left, found herself face to face with the evil looking goat tattooed on Mark's back. The eyes were level with hers and she wondered if hers were as red at the moment. As surprised as she was to have just woken up, Justine was shocked to find Mark was not awake. Normally he arose by six a.m., even on the weekends. She turned her head to stare at the ceiling and allowed herself a satisfied smile; it was quite an accomplishment to wear out the normally insatiable bad boy attorney.

Lifting her arms over her head, Justine arched her back and stretched. Her entire body ached, but it was a pleasant pain, like the kind after a good hard work out. That would pretty much describe yesterday's festivities. After the session with Aurora, Justine had greatly enjoyed having Mark wash her in the shower before turning him loose and letting him fuck the shit out of her against the wall. All that had done was leave her hungry for more and Mark had made damn sure she had gotten her fill.

The meeting itself had, as always, been amazing. Loki had started things off by telling a hot story about a couple he had been taping as part of his job as a high end private investigator. The couple was mid-forties professionals who went around seducing young girls of barely legal age and tearing them apart. Loki had shown a half hour clip of their latest victim that was so incredible, Mephisto had pointed out if they weren't married, either could be Circle material. The main entertainment, as always, had been exquisite; A sixty minute video featuring The Lady Felicia dominating and humiliating a cocky young bartender, who by the end was thanking her for the privilege of jerking off on her feet.

When the meeting adjourned at midnight, Justine had prepared to go up to her room to wait for Mark. She lived only blocks away from the Crown Royal hotel where they'd had the meeting, but knew she was going to drink quite a bit at dinner and rented a suite. She didn't want Loki or the Lady Lexi, who also lived in Boston, to go by her place and see Mark's car there. Justine had been dripping all night while staring at him, then at Aurora who smiled every time their eyes met. The entire night, her mind kept replaying that scene in her office, picturing Aurora screaming between her thighs as Mark fucked her ass. Yes, she had been more than ready to go when the meeting ended.

To her surprise, Mark suggested going out to a club. At first she refused. She'd spent the last few hours worked up, had a nice buzz, and wanted to fuck. Mark managed to talk her into it and they went down the street to a club where Justine figured she would humor him, and stay for a drink or two. They ended up staying until the two a.m. last call and Justine had an amazing time. They'd played pool, drank and then Mark dragged her out onto the dance floor with him.

Initially she'd protested, but when he wrapped his arms around her waist from behind and started grinding on her, she couldn't hold back and the two of them had put on quite a show. Justine was still wearing the short tight black dress she'd chosen for the meeting and was reveling in looks she was getting from the young men around her. Mark was getting more than his share of looks as well from the pretty little coeds from BU that were there. At one point he talked her into dancing with a couple of the guys and as she ground her ass into their hard cocks she thought she was going to gush right there on the floor.

Mark had decided to show off with a couple of the girls and Justine loved watching them melt for him. Although not nearly as much as she enjoyed being the center of attention of a roomful of boys half her age. When the club closed they returned to the hotel where Mark talked the bartender at the restaurant, which was closed, into letting them sit and have a couple more drinks. When they had finally gotten back to her room, he had produced the bottle of from under his jacket and they did a couple of quick shots before tearing into each other.

Justine sighed contentedly. Mark always seemed to know what she needed and last night had been a perfect example. She'd been working hard even by her standards lately and hadn't been playing much at all. She hadn't had a night like last night in longer than she cared to remember. It wasn't just the sex; she could always get that. Last night was about fun; Justine had felt like a young girl again. A great dinner, even better company, pool, dancing, amazing sex, it was the perfect night.

That night had now turned into a perfect morning. She had slept late, and was lying naked in a comfortable bed next to a gorgeous man. Justine took a deep breath, closed her eyes and released a satisfied purr, the room reeked of sex. That smell caused her to slide her hand down her stomach and into the cleft of her pussy. Her pubic hair was damp to the touch and the soft folds of her flesh still moist from last night. Justine exhaled as her fingers rubbed across her clit which was sore, yet ready at the same.

Bringing her fingers back to her face, she inhaled deeply, taking in her own musky scent. Although it was in vogue to have a shaved pussy, Justine let hers grow in, and had never heard any complaints. If anything, men and women alike loved the patch of fiery red hair between her legs. The hair also served to cause her pussy to smell stronger, and the scent drove her wild. Sucking her fingers into her mouth she felt her nipples stiffening against the sheets and began to think about something else stiffening.

She glanced over at Mark's muscular back and the sight of the long red scratches that were visible even through his tattoos made up her mind. It was time to make it an even better morning. Justine rolled onto her side, slipping her arm around Mark's waist and sliding close to him. Her hard nipples pressed into his back and, nuzzling her face into his neck, she placed a kiss just below his ear. Mark made a soft little sound in his throat and burrowed his head into the pillow. Justine smiled; who would ever think Mark could be cute?

She repeated the kiss and let her hand slide down his chest to linger on his hard flat stomach. Mark sighed, but still didn't appear to be waking up. Justine decided to be patient for once and, laying her head on the pillow next to his, relaxed and enjoyed the sensation of being close to him. She lay there feeling the rise and fall of his breathing against her hand and for a moment could understand why most women yearned to marry and have this every morning. The ironic thing was most married people lost this closeness over the years and strayed into the arms of others. Justine had realized at a very young age, she had no desire to ever commit to one man.

For the first time since the meeting with Sydney, Justine's thoughts turned serious. What exactly was she doing with Mark? The answer, from the standpoint of Mistress Scarlett, was abusing her position in the Circle. Granted time was not common amongst members. It was reserved for mostly rewards, or to provide entertainment for high ranking members who were traveling. The rules could be bent by Masters and Mistresses; there was nothing wrong with using the power of the position to enjoy the charms of one of their Circle.

Yet repeated encounters with favorites, Circle Pets as they were referred to, were frowned upon. It not only established a feeling of superiority in the member, but weakened the authority of the Master. That's not to say it didn't go on. Justine herself had been a favorite of the prior leader of the group, Lazarus, in the last year before he had to step down. That had only been several times and most of those nights after sex, they would sit and Lazarus would teach her the ins and outs of the Circle he was grooming her to run.

Mark was a different story. Justine had first let him share her bed as a way of making up for what she had done to him at his initiation. A year later on the night she had ascended to Mistress, Justine had taken him for her celebration. After that she found she greatly enjoyed his company and not just in the bedroom. Mark was one of the most intriguing men she'd ever met. On one hand arrogant, ruthless, even dangerous, yet on other occasions he could be charming and sweet. There were times she, amongst many others, wondered if he were bipolar.

As Justine got older and she moved up the corporate later, it was becoming increasingly difficult to find men to toy with. That was a double standard in the Circle and in life itself. The men could show up with women half their age and all their indiscretions were met with shrugs and "boys will be boys." But if it was discovered a woman in Justine's position enjoyed not only fucking men of all ages, but totally dominating them, all hell would break loose. The Lady Mercedes owned a BDSM club in New York and would send subs to Justine as well as other members of the Circle all over the country.

These men and women were not only trained to please, but to keep their mouths shut, under pain of severe punishment by Mercedes herself. Even then some members, like Victoria Redding, who as a successful model had a lot to lose, would still either blindfold them or herself wear a mask. Justine had been getting weary of the game, and on a whim a couple of years ago invited Mark back to her place after a meeting. She had been in a bit of a funk and the game that night was there was no game. They were just two attractive professionals going at it like the animals they really were. After the initial tearing into each other, the next time was slower and playful.

Justine had enjoyed everything about that night and since then Mark had more and more often spent the nights of the meetings with her, either at hotels or his place when the meeting was in Providence. Many nights Justine would tell herself she wouldn't the next month, but always caved. Things then took another turn three months ago when Justine had been feeling particularly horny and called him on a Friday, after which he had ended up spending the weekend. That was the first time she noticed how much she enjoyed his company beyond sex.

There was no doubt there she was feeling an increasing amount of affection towards him. The best way to describe it would be friends with benefits which would be fine if not for the group. As it was, Alex suspected them, constantly fishing during meeting nights, asking Mark what he was up to afterwards, even inviting him out to go hunting as they put it. Alex had also tried playing twenty questions with her. Justine knew he didn't care in the sense she was abusing her position, as much as his arrogant ass couldn't fathom why she didn't want him.

Her thoughts were interrupted by Mark moving, rolling over onto his back. His head turned to her and she saw his eyes were barely open and what she could see of them was as red as her hair. Mark put his arm out and closed his eyes again. Justine moved back next to him, putting her hand on his chest, and resting her head on his shoulder. Mark brought his arm up so it was around her shoulders and she thought, yes this was getting to be a problem. She could stop it easily. Never once had Mark asked, it was all her doing.

In the end, she always came down to why should she care? The Circle was about doing and taking whatever you want. She had been in the group for over seventeen years, starting at a time when the ladies were treated as nothing more than glorified whores. There were nights she had been bent over the table and taken by the Master himself or whatever member he was rewarding in front of the entire group. She had complained once and been whipped bloody by the sham of an enforcer they'd had. Justine had wanted to quit, but Lazarus, who was the diplomat then, had taken her and the other ladies aside and said that he was going to force a vote. In exchange for their votes, he promised change. The ladies would be revered and respected as they should be.

Justine and the others had trusted him and not only had Lazarus changed their Circle, but others had noticed the difference and followed suit. The Lady Persephone from the Chicago Circle, who was now High Mistress, had changed the nature of the Enforcer position to be a protector as well as a rule keeper. The new enforcers defended their sisters and dealt out fierce justice against any male member who misused a lady. But it had not happened overnight and Justine had paid her dues. She deserved to get whatever she wanted from the group. Right now what Justine wanted was laying next her, and she had waited long enough.

Using her fingernails, Justine lightly traced her way down the middle of his chest, to his stomach. Mark sighed softly as, flattening her hand; she began caressing the inside of his thigh. Justine flicked her tongue out, swirling it around his nipple. Mark's breathing picked up and his hips twitched when the edge of her hand rubbed along his semi hard cock.

"Hmm, good morning," he whispered.

Lifting her head from his chest, Justine kissed him.

"You smell like my pussy," Kissing him again, she opened her mouth, letting her tongue play lightly across his lips. "You taste like me too."

Mark's answer turned into a moan as her hand left his thigh, wrapped around his thick cock, and gave it a squeeze.

"Now this is a good morning!" Justine laughed.

Mark smiled at her and his now completely open eyes showed the amazing green gold of his irises.

"You really are beautiful, Justine," he said quietly.

"You have to say that," she told him. "I'm playing with your cock." She gave him another squeeze. "But it still sounds damn good."

Mark kissed her again, but this time it wasn't quick, but slow and sensual. Justine closed her eyes and slowly stroked him as their lips parted and their tongues darted across each other. His arm tightened around her shoulders, pulling her closer against him. Justine could feel her nipples pushing into his side and began rocking, causing them to slide across him. Still pumping his cock, she slid her lips from his and began to trail her them down his chest. Lifting his leg, Mark kicked the covers off, and Justine felt her pussy begin to flow at the sight of his huge throbbing cock in her hand. He pulled at her shoulder, trying to roll her over, but she resisted, whispering, "Just lie back, and let me show my appreciation for an amazing evening."

"As my Mistress commands," he replied.

"No mistress," Justine said softly in between kissing his chiseled stomach. "Just you and I having fun."

Even as she said it, her mind went back to this being a problem, but with her mouth inches from the swollen dripping head of his cock, she quickly pushed it aside. Drawing her legs up, Justine rolled over onto her knees next to him. This way he could watch as her tongue darted out and playfully ran along the head of his cock. Mark moaned softly and his hips twitched as, ducking her head, she swirled her tongue around his balls, while giving his cock a hard squeeze. Her hair had fallen across her face and, taking it in her hand, she offered it to him.

Mark took her hair and, wrapping his fingers into it, placed it on the back of her head. Positioning his cock so that it was standing straight, Justine took just the spongy head in her mouth. Angling her head so that her blue eyes were staring straight into his, Justine slowly caressed his hard flesh with her tongue. He closed his eyes and sighed as she sped her tongue up. His eyes opened and he gasped when she gave his cock a hard suck. Justine moaned in her throat as she was rewarded with a squirt of his precum in her mouth.

Deciding she wanted to give him an even better show, Justine sat up and, rolling over on top of him, quickly slid down between his legs. She felt her nipples slide down his chest and his hard cock rubbed along her thigh. When she was lying directly between his legs, she propped herself up on her elbows and, taking his cock between her lip's winked at him before taking the entire length of it down her throat.

"Oh goddamn," Mark moaned.

"Hmmm," Justine groaned around his cock, loving the sensation of having her mouth and throat stuffed with his hard flesh. She could feel his sticky precum dripping down her throat and her eyes rolled in pleasure. She loved how much he was enjoying it, even in the Circle; few were the women who could deep throat him at all, never mind so easily. Giving him an extra thrill, she forced her mouth open wider, slid her tongue out along the base of his shaft, and licked his balls.

Sliding him from her mouth, she smiled, "Better than The Lady Aurora?"

"Oh hell yeah," he answered. "Better view too."

"Aren't you sweet?" She kissed the tip of his cock. "Well you know what they say flattery will get you."

Justine again took him down to the base of his shaft. She shook her head back and forth; causing him to moan then began bobbing her head in a slow steady rhythm. Justine removed her hands from his shaft and placed them on his thighs, now using only her mouth to pleasure him. She picked up the pace slightly, showing off how easily she could handle him. She began sliding him all the way to the very tip before going halfway down then back up before going down to his balls.

Mark worked his hands down between them and started playing with her nipples. Justine closed her eyes and moaned softly around his cock. They were tender from last night's marathon, but his touch was soft, his fingers teasing lightly across her swollen flesh. She slowed up on her sucking, taking her time and savoring every sensation. In addition to the delightful feeling of his cock sliding between her soft full lips, Justine could taste herself on him. More than that, when she had him all the way down and her face was buried between his legs, she could smell her pussy. Even his thighs smelled like her.

His fingers stopped their light teasing and, taking her nipples between them, started twisting them back and forth. They were sensitive and the hint of discomfort heightened the overall feeling of pleasure. Justine started sucking faster, and sliding her hands up, returned the favor, caressing his nipples with her finger nails. They both sighed at the same time, and she would have smiled had she not had his cock buried in her throat. For as much as she loved the games and the control, Justine was enjoying these slow playful encounters more and more.

She opened her eyes to see Mark watching her, taking in the show of her working his amazing cock. Knowing how much he liked it, Justine bent her legs up so that he could see the bottoms of her feet and started kicking them back and forth. His gaze went to them and she bent them far enough so he could see her red toenails. Mark smiled and, slipping his hand from her tit, placed it on the back of her head, wrapping it into her long red hair. He started to push and pull to match her rhythm. He was not forcing her, but guiding her and again the softer touch made her desire him even more. Justine began sucking hard and fast, fully showing off her oral skills as she took him deep again and again.

Mark's breathing became heavier and his hips began to rock back and forth matching the movements of her mouth. Justine became aware of her own hips rocking, grinding her pussy into the soft sheets. Still sucking him, she slid her knees up underneath of her and, grabbing her tits wrapped them around his cock. Mark's hand tightened in her hair and his hips began to thrust harder, fucking her full breasts as she tongued the sensitive tip of his dripping prick.

Justine sucked hard on the head, causing him to gasp, and sending another spurt of his salty fluid down her throat. She released his cock as she was still sucking, causing a wet popping sound and eliciting another groan from him. Putting her hands down on the bed, Justine began to crawl back up the length of his body. Her eyes locked onto his, enjoying the look of desire in them as he watched her make her way up to him. She was holding herself low enough so that her large heavy tits were dragging across his stomach and chest, her hard nipples teasing themselves against his equally hard flesh. When her hands were on the bed over his shoulders and she was over him, she pushed up and swung her tits back and forth in front of his face. They were just out of the reach of his tongue and he tried to sit up. She shook her head. "Hmm-mm."

Mark put his head back on the pillow and remained still as she lowered her tits and started teasing him with her nipples. He opened his mouth and she leaned over, allowing him to take her swollen nub between his lips. Justine let him suck on it for a moment before switching off and offering him the other tit. Mark's hands were sliding up and down her back and ass, and she could feel his hard cock pressing against the back of her thigh, inches from her pussy. Lowering herself onto her elbows, she nuzzled her face into his neck.

She started nibbling on his ear as she rocked her hips up and down, sliding his hard cock through the wet folds of her yearning pussy. Mark was breathing heavy in her ear, and she could feel him tensing beneath her. She was teasing both of them, but enjoyed knowing that he would not enter her without permission. Even though he knew they weren't playing the game, Mark still gave her full control. Raising her hips higher, Justine placed her pussy against the head of his cock and, lowering herself, allowed him to penetrate her. Mark grunted as she stopped with barely more than the tip inside her. His hands were on her hips and she could feel them trembling as he resisted shoving her down onto him.

"Spread me open," Justine whispered as she nibbled his ear.

Mark's hands moved down to the cheeks of her ass, and she cooed in his ear at the sensation of him spreading them, causing her pussy to open wider. Justine paused, and then quickly let her weight go. Mark's breath hissed in her ear, and she cried out as she impaled herself onto his huge dick. She stayed down, holding him inside her and feeling her pussy stretch around his thick cock. Sliding her hands beneath his arms, she started rocking her hips, only removing a couple of inches of his cock, before taking him back inside.

Picking her head up, Justine kissed him softly. Mark's hands slid up and wrapped around her shoulders, holding her face to his as their tongues probed each other's mouths. Justine began rocking further back and forth; letting more of him slide out and driving back down harder than before. He moaned into her mouth as one of his hands began sliding up and down her back, caressing her smooth skin as they continued to kiss. Justine stopped moving and he took over, pumping his hips and thrusting in and out of her. She was so wet, she could hear him entering her and she broke the kiss to moan softly.

She looked into his eyes to see he was staring at her, a soft smile on his lips. She smiled back, and then kissed him again. She began rocking once more, and now the two of them were moving in perfect rhythm. This was what brought her back to Mark time and again, this familiarity, the comfort of knowing she didn't have to put on a show. He kissed her neck and, as he began gently sucking on the soft skin between her neck and shoulder, Justine wondered if this is what people considered making love.

That thought caught her attention, and in reaction to it she pushed herself up, and sat back so that she was straight up on top of him, straddling his hips. She gasped as that maneuver drove the entire length of his cock deep inside her. Reaching down, she placed her hands on his chest and began sliding back and forth. Mark grabbed her hips and started pushing and pulling on them, helping her ride him. Justine didn't need any help and, knowing a better place for his hands, grabbed them and brought them up to her tits.

She moaned as Mark squeezed them hard, before finding and playing with her nipples. Pushing on his chest, Justine began lifting herself up and down, plunging his throbbing cock in and out of her. Mark gasped and began driving his hips hard into her descending pussy. Justine cried out and, removing her hands from his chest, leaned backwards. Reaching behind her, she found his ankles and grabbed them. She was now bent backwards, grinding her hips into his cock. Mark groaned and pumped her harder. His cock was now at an angle and this position would make it harder for him to come. As always, Mark knew why she had moved and his left hand dropped from her tit, and between her legs.

"Oh, yes!" she cried out as his thumb pressed against her swollen button.

Mark's thumb started tracing slow circles around her clit as she continued to grind into his thrusting cock. Justine leaned back and, balancing herself on one arm, started playing with the nipple he had abandoned. Her clit was sore from over stimulation as were her nipples, her entire body ached from last night, yet she drove herself hard into both his thumb and cock, completely caught up in the need for more.

"Faster," she moaned to him as she ground her hips against his touch. "I want to.... No!"

Justine cried out as he removed his thumb from her clit, and stopped fondling her tit.

"What are you... hey!"

Mark sat up, causing her to land on her back between his legs, she moaned as she felt his cock slide from inside her. That moan turned into a surprised yelp, as sliding his hands under her ass, Mark lifted the lower half of her body off of the bed, bringing her pussy up to his face.

"Now this is a good morning," Mark smirked, flicking his tongue across her clit.

"Damn straight it is." Justine laughed.

She raised her legs, draping them over his shoulders and, bracing herself on her elbows, watched as Mark buried his face between her legs. Even though she expected it, Justine still moaned at the sensation of his tongue plunging directly into her hot pussy. Mark started rocking his head, tongue fucking her as she moaned and squirmed on his face. Justine let her arms go so that she was lying on her back looking up across her body as Mark slid his tongue teasingly through the lips of her pussy.

"Don't tease," she panted, as his tongue barely caught the tip of her clit. "I need it."

Mark obeyed, swirling his tongue in hard fast circles around her aching clit as his hands squeezed her ass. Justine's fingers found her nipples and she squeezed them hard, using the pain to bring her closer to the edge. She yelped as Mark sucked hard on her swollen clit causing a surge of pain.

"Easy," she gasped. "I'm sore, I..." She laughed. "Oh screw it, just make me cum!"

Mark started sucking her clit hard, again causing her to yelp, but even as she did, she could feel her thighs beginning to tremble. Although a part of her would have loved to lie there and let him tease and take his time, Justine just wanted to come, get fucked and maybe even go back to sleep. God what a glorious morning! Mark had moved one of his hands to the small of her back and, sliding the other down her ass, slipped it up between her legs. Justine moaned as she felt his finger slide inside her and started bucking her hips into his swirling tongue.

'Oh yes," she moaned as she felt her orgasm building.

She started twisting her nipples harder as she took in not just the sight of Mark's face buried in her red haired pussy, but the way his arm bulged as he held her up with one hand. She began grinding even harder into his face, and moaned with frustration. She had come so many times last night that her overworked clit was holding her right on the edge.

'Oh, please make me come," she begged

Mark's eyes lit up at the sound of his Mistress pleading. Pulling his finger from her pussy, he slid it back and, drove it into her ass. Justine went off like a rocket, throwing her head back into the mattress, she screamed as the orgasm smashed through her. Tightening her legs around his head, she began wildly bucking her hips, forcing him to plunge his finger in and out of her ass. Mark managed to keep his lips fastened to her clit and continued sucking, keeping her coming as long as possible. Justine twisted her nipples hard and howled again as another wave of intense pleasure slammed into her. Arching her back so that even her shoulders were off the bed, she felt her body tense, and with a loud cry, felt her pussy convulse and gush onto Mark's face. Justine went limp on the bed, gasping for breath as her heart pounded in her chest.

"Shit, did I come hard," she breathed, "That was... oh fuck!"

Mark had lunged forward and, slamming his cock deep inside her, proceeded to fuck the shit out of her.

"Oh fuck yeah!" she screamed as he tore into her, driving his huge prick into her so hard she could feel his balls slapping against her ass.

Her legs were still on his shoulders and, leaning over so that his hands were on the bed, he had her all but bent in half. Justine's feet were next to her head and she could feel her ass lifted off the mattress. She let out a long, loud squeal as Mark started driving into her even harder, pumping her hard and fast. Justine placed her hands on his chest and dug in with her nails, squeezing hard as he caused her to yelp with every thrust of his powerful hips. Although she was no inexperienced young girl, Justine caught herself whimpering under what could be more accurately described as an assault on her sopping wet pussy.

She was so wet she could feel her cum squirting out of her as he plunged into her. Her thighs were dripping and, looking between her legs, she could see his shaft glistening with her juices. Mark leaned forward, bending her further back and started slamming her faster. He was breathing like a bull and moaning in between. Justine realized that like her, he had come so much last night he was having a hard time finishing. Placing her nails on his shoulders, she dug in, and then ripped them savagely down his chest.

Mark cried out in pain, but at the same time she felt his body tense and after several more vicious pumps, he pulled his cock from inside of her. Justine cupped her tits, holding them up for him, and groaned as he sprayed his thick hot cum all over them. Despite how much they had fucked, Mark managed to do a good job of painting both of her tits before, with a tired gasp, he fell onto the bed next to her. They both lay there on their backs panting and staring at the ceiling. Justine winced as she straightened her legs. She was going to be limping around the office tomorrow for sure. She looked over at Mark who was lying there with his eyes closed.

"See," she said. "Sometimes it's worth sleeping in."

Mark opened his eyes and, gave her a tired smile. His eyes then narrowed as he looked past her.

"Shit," he muttered. "It's after twelve, checkout's one right?"

"Yeah." Justine sighed. "It is."

Sitting up, Mark reached down next to the bed and, using the towel that was on the chair, began wiping the cum from her tits. She winced as the towel passed over her nipple. Damn they were sore. Watching as Mark tossed the towel back on the floor and looked longingly at the bed, she asked, "You still tired?"

"Believe it or not yeah, I could go right back out."

"Me too," she said.

Mark started to get up, but realizing she wasn't ready for the morning to end, she spoke up.

"Hey, Mark, did you even bother getting a room?"

"No."

"Awfully presumptuous these days aren't we?" she asked. But then again why wouldn't he be?

"Well, if you didn't want to," he grinned. "I'm sure I could have found some company at the club."

"I was only kidding." Justine patted the bed "lay back down, I know the manager; I'll get us a late checkout."

"Yeah?" Mark asked. "That'd be great." He gave her a wicked smile. "Then when we wake up, we'll shower together before I have to head back."

"I do like how you think." She laughed. "Settle back in, I'll be right back."

Getting up, Justine went into the main room and grabbed her cell from the coffee table, wincing at the aches in her legs and shoulders. She sat on the couch as she dialed.

"Crown Royal, this is Victor."

"Victor, this is Justine Bates, room two twelve. I'd like to request a checkout time of three please."

"I'm sorry, Miss Bates, we can't do that we..."

"Victor, is Roger Bennett at the desk with you?"

"Yes ma'am, but he's with someone. Do you wish to..."

"What I wish is to have a three o'clock checkout. Do be a dear and tell Mr. Bennett."

There was a moment of silence then Victor came back on. "Mr. Bennett said the room is yours for as long as you need at no additional charge."

"Thank you."

Justine ended the call and walked back into the room to see Mark lying on his back, looking at his phone. Seeing her enter, he put it on the nightstand. Justine walked over to his side of the bed and, laughing, rolled over on top of him to get to her side. Mark rolled over with her, and they finished on their sides, her back against his chest and his arm around her waist.

"Thank you for last night, I had a great time."

"It was my pleasure, my lady," he answered. "It was a privilege to..."

"No, Mark, seriously thank you. I really needed last night. The club was a great idea, and it's been awhile since I had that kind of fun."

"Good," Mark said, pulling her tighter to him. "You deserve it."

"Do I?"

"Everyone deserves to be happy, just not everyone realizes it."

"Wow," Justine laughed. "That's a very inspirational thought from a Satanist."

"Satanists are happy too. We just don't need everyone else to tell us what makes us happy."

"And are you happy Mark?" she asked.

He was quiet and Justine frowned, hoping she hadn't triggered something. Mark had a dark past and was prone to mood swings.

"Not completely," he said quietly.

Changing the subject, Justine took his hand that was around her waist, and whispered, "And thank you for keeping this quiet. You know it's not that I can't defend my position, but..."

"No worries, Justine. I want to honor your reputation." He laughed softly. "Besides dirty little secrets are more fun when they're kept secret."

"That's a good one," Justine nodded. "Something tells me you have your share of those."

Mark sighed. "You don't know the half of it."

"I'm always here for more than sex, Mark, you know that," Justine offered, already knowing the response.

"I'm tired." He kissed the back of her neck. "And so are you, get some sleep."

"Good night, Mark," she said rolling her eyes.

Justine lay awake for a few minutes, trying not to be annoyed Mark wouldn't confide in her. There were things about his past she knew, but knew there was a lot more. There were times she swore she could see something strange behind those beautiful eyes, but could never quite put her finger on it. As she drifted off, she reminded herself of the expression be careful of what you wish for, because you may just get it.

Chapter Four

Justine's eyes flew open at the sound of someone shouting. Lifting her head from the pillow, she listened. The bedroom of the suite was too far from the corridor for it to be someone out there. Maybe someone was yelling in the next room over. Letting her head fall back, she closed her eyes. They immediately opened again when Mark jerked violently next to her.

"No please!" he cried out.

Justine was still lying in the crook of his arm, and started to sit up to try to look at him.

Mark sat up so violently she was thrown off of his arm. She fought to catch her balance, but lost the battle and fell off the bed onto the floor. She grunted in pain as she landed hard on her side. Immediately getting to her feet, Justine saw Mark was sitting up, his head in his hands; he was gasping and muttering something. Sitting on the edge of the bed, Justine leaned over and put her hand on his shoulder.

"Mark!" she called out, giving him a shake.

"I'm sorry." he whispered. "I'll be quiet I promise."

"Mark, wake up!" She shook him harder, grabbing his wrist to pull it away from his face.

"I'll be a good boy."

This was uttered in a pathetic whimper and Justine tried to put her arm around him.

"It's okay," she whispered. "It's...Mark!"

"Don't touch me!" he snarled, ripping his hand from her grasp.

Before Justine could react, Mark's hand flashed out and caught her by her throat, his fingers squeezing just under her jaw. That however, wasn't what caused Justine's heart to pound. That reaction came from the look on his face. He had pulled her towards him, and his eyes were bulging and so dark they appeared black. In those eyes, Justine saw nothing short of raw violence. His lip curled up, baring his teeth in a snarl and the veins in his neck were standing out. He looked insane.

"Mark, it's only me."

Fighting the urge to panic, she spoke softly, forcing the words out of her constricted throat. Mark blinked, but his lip curled up further. She could feel his fingers trembling against her throat. She knew how strong those hands were and knew what she would have to do. Moving quickly, Justine swung and slapped him in the face, as she shouted "Lovecraft, cease!"

Cease was the safe word he gave all of his pets as well as anyone in the Circle he had dominated. Mark's face snapped to the side from the force of her blow, and as he turned back towards her, she braced herself in case he was going to swing. Instead, his hand fell from her neck and when he looked at her, he seemed to appear normal again. Well not quite, now he looked terrified.

"Justine, I'm..." he put his head back in his hands. "I'm sorry."

Breathing a sigh of relief, Justine touched her neck. It wasn't tender so he hadn't squeezed that hard. Sliding onto the bed next to him, she put her arm around his shoulders.

"Are you okay, Mark?"

"No, I'm not okay. I...I'm..." he put his hand to his eyes and Justine saw it was shaking, in fact his entire body was trembling. "I'm fucking pathetic."

"No you're not," she said quietly. "You've just been through a lot, its okay."

Justine opened her arms to him. "Come here, Mark."

"I'm not a kid, Justine, I'll be okay I..." he stopped speaking and she could see him looking longingly at her.

"Come here, baby," she said quietly. "Let me help."

This was not the first time this had happened and for whatever reason, Mark responded to that name. He looked as if he were continuing to struggle against himself, and then with a sigh leaned into her. Justine put her arms around him, and began running her fingers through his thick black hair. His arms had gone around her waist and he rested his head on her shoulder.

"Just relax," she said in his ear.

"I feel like a..."

"Shhh," Justine whispered in his ear. "No worries, we've known each other for a long time. Now just let it go and stay right here, there's no need to talk right now."

Mark sighed and she felt him relax into her. They remained silent, and as she continued caressing his hair Justine found a spot just over his temple where the skin was slightly raised. Her finger traced the three inch scar that was there. That was the part of Mark's past she knew about. Although even that had come second hand from Alex the one time she had put her foot down and demanded some answers from him.

When Mark was a young child, his mother had given him and his older sister, Megan, up because she claimed she was unfit to raise them. The two of them were separated, but the plan was to find a home they could both live in. The state lost track of them and they would not be reunited until years later. In the meantime, Mark had bounced around until he ended up in the care of a drug addicted monster named Max Thompson.

Max was an animal and beat Mark constantly, most of the time for making noise. Somehow, despite missing a lot of school, and when he did go it was covered in bruises, Mark remained with Max for three years. He was finally taken away, and literally, in an ambulance, when he accidently knocked over a plate Max was doing lines of cocaine off of. Max had become enraged, hitting Mark in the side of the head with the plate hard enough to fracture his skull. Mark had spent close to a week in a coma before waking up, miraculously with no brain damage.

After the years with Max, Mark never spoke to anyone and kept to himself. It left him vulnerable at the group homes; until they realized that when cornered he became violent and had sent several of the other boys to the hospital. Mark was destined for a training school when, through an act of kindness that was certainly due to him, fate intervened.

Mark's sister had been adopted at the age of eleven and her new parents had tried to find her brother. The two siblings had different last names and the mother was uncooperative. A month before he was due to be transferred to the training school, the social worker who handled Mark's case made the connection and contacted his sister's family. A week later the state awarded Mark into the custody of his eighteen year old sister and her parents.

From there, Mark's life had completely turned around. Intelligent to the point of being gifted, he excelled at school as well as sports and martial arts. He had gone from tragic tale to all American boy. At eighteen, he was awarded a full scholarship to PC university and from there one to Suffolk Law. From there, Mark's success should have continued uninterrupted. However, fate once again intervened and this time not for the good.

Playing pool in a bar one afternoon, Mark ran into Max who had been released from prison the previous year. The story Alex had told her was that Max did not recognize Mark. Seeing the animal who had beat him had caused him to snap. Mark befriended Max, hanging around with him at the bar until he earned his trust, then luring him back to his apartment where Mark came within seconds of killing him. Alex did not know all the details, but knew that somehow Mark's sister had shown up and managed to stop him. Mark was arrested and sent to jail.

Megan had gone to Alex looking for help. He admitted to Justine that he was not going to, the case looked cut and dried and the level of violence Mark had used on Max was horrific. Supposedly Mark had bitten a piece of his face off and broken over a dozen bones, including his kneecap. When he refused, Megan spent over an hour telling him the things Max had done to Mark, including gagging him and locking him in closets for days at a time. Alex had given in and, with the help of his father's attorney, Max's long criminal past, and in the end an expensive bribe to the judge, had gotten Mark off.

The reason Justine had finally pushed to get that information from Alex was because of what had occurred at Mark's initiation. Back in the beginning, The Circle had been leery of Mark. He was beautiful, successful and one of the fiercest dominants anyone had ever seen. On the other hand, he was erratic, a loose cannon with rage issues and had been seconds away from taking a life. Mark drank and on occasion still fought like an animal, walking a fine line between remaining a successful attorney, and losing everything if he lost control. He was also only twenty-seven, three years younger than the minimum age of thirty.

As Orion the Hunter, Alex had fought hard to get Mark in, citing his charisma and his occult background. The Circle was comprised of a variety of personalities and types. Many members were like Alex himself, playboys and debutante's from wealthy families whose lives had been nothing but success. Other's came from nothing and had scratched and clawed to get into a position where they attracted the notice of the group. Amongst some of those were some truly dark personalities. These were highly valued, as when the Circle originated centuries ago in Europe, many members were of mystical backgrounds.

The Lady Persephone, a woman who came from a long line of witches, had joined the Circle three years prior and had already given the Chicago table the reputation as being the most powerful. Mark, Alex insisted, would be the East's Persephone. The Circles were extremely competitive and Alex had planned his argument well. At the mention of Persephone, Lazarus became interested. At the time, Justine was High Lady, and already being groomed to be the next leader of the group. She and the enforcer, Tartarus, were dead set against Mark. Especially Tartarus, whose job it would be to take Mark out if he did indeed get in and get out of line. Tartarus was an ex green beret who was as dangerous as any man Justine had ever met, but Mark held belts in three disciplines of martial arts and was prone to blackout rages.

But Alex kept pushing and, intrigued, Lazarus decided to take the first step and send The Lady Cerce to administer a test. She met Mark in a bar, and initially he played along. Although cocky at first, he eventually began saying and doing all the right things to show Circe he was completely smitten and would do anything to be with her. They went back to his place where within minutes, Mark flipped the switch. Before she knew it, Cerce was being totally dominated by him. By the end of the night, Mark had her calling him sir and groveling at his feet. When Justine and Lazarus spoke to her, she had said that Mark was the most powerful personality she had ever encountered.

Alex's argument was gaining momentum and Lazars decided to give him a chance. That was when the next debate began, who was going to handle his initiation? Alex further pushed things by suggesting a soft initiation. Mark had been studying the occult for years and his mind and will were his own. He had also had a violent past and pain meant nothing to him. In the end, Alex said Mark could never truly be broken. The first and most obvious choice was the Lady Morrigan, herself a witch of some repute, originally from Ireland. Morrigan was one of the most feared women in the Circle and enjoyed inflicting pain. After some debate, Lazarus decided that she would not be the proper choice, too much potential for things to turn ugly. He then began saying Alex could be right, perhaps a soft initiation would suffice.

Tired of listening to this arrogant street punk in a suit being referred to as if he were beyond them, Justine demanded to be given the initiation. After a vote amongst the group, she was granted the right. The night before Mark was due to meet her at a small cottage in the north end of Boston, Alex came to see her. He told Justine he had been telling Mark he needed to cave in order to get in, even if he had to fake it. As Justine sat there becoming increasingly angry, Alex said Mark told him no one could take him. He would earn his place by being stronger than their best. To Justine, the gloves were now off. Looking Alex in the eye, she told him not only would Mark break, but it would be legendary. Unfortunately, Justine's words turned out to be prophetic.

The initiation started on Friday night and as of Sunday morning Mark had not broken. She had done everything she could think of and still he held fast. Justine was not one to inflict much pain, but had whipped him bloody on Saturday. When he continued to mock her, asking when she was going to 'put some effort into it' Justine had lost her temper and, going into the kitchen, came back and threw salt into the cuts on his back. Mark had screamed in pain, causing Justine to drop the whip, and become upset at how far she had gone. Domination was one thing, cruelty another. She started to ask him if he were okay, when his moans turned into an evil laugh. Looking up at her from his knees, he asked her to do it again.

Knowing early on that Mark was an incredible physical specimen, her plan had been to wear him down any way she could. Not only did she force him to fuck her over and over, every time feigning complete disinterest in his efforts, even though his cock was nothing short of amazing, but wouldn't let him eat or drink. Justine had cranked the heat up past ninety to help dehydrate him, and drank in front of him, telling him he could have some if he would show her proper respect. Mark continued to resist, until knowing she would have to give in before he passed out, Justine offered him a drink. Fastening a leash to him, she made him crawl on all fours to the toilet. She told him to drink out of that or simply kiss her feet and call her mistress. To her disgust, Mark stuck his head in the bowl, and lapped up the water like a dog.

By Sunday morning Justine herself was exhausted. Her pussy hurt from the constant fucking from the biggest cock she had ever seen and she was running out of ideas. Refusing to lose, she called Lazarus and received permission to take it to an even higher level. Leaving Mark tied to the bed, Justine went back home and picked up the shock collar she used to punish her pets. When she came back, she fastened the collar to his neck and they started over. Anytime Mark disobeyed her, she would send the current through him.

Tying him back down, she proceeded to stroke him, attempting to get him hard again. She doubted he would be able to; she had lost count of how many times she had made him perform for her. As she expected, his cock was not responding and with a smile she asked if he was ready to admit he couldn't handle anymore. Mark returned her smile, closed his eyes, and to her dismay his cock began to stiffen in her hand. Keeping the surprise from showing on her face, Justine climbed on top and began to ride him. She still held the remote and began shocking him every time she drove herself down onto his raw cock.

Mark winced each time, but also thrust his hips up into her. After one particularly vicious pump, Justine, whose pussy was so sore she was not enjoying this at all, cried out in pain. Mark smiled at her and asked if she wanted to quit. Enraged, Justine dug her nails into his chest, and began slamming herself onto him as hard as she could despite the pain it was causing her. Mark was gasping in pain and beginning to make small whimpering noises as his chaffed and exhausted cock strained to come.

Hopping off of him, Justine began violently jerking him off, yanking his cock hard and slamming her hand down on it. She demanded he come, and told him she would keep stroking him until he begged for her to stop. Somehow, within seconds, his cock twitched in her hand, and he cried out in more pain than pleasure as a few drops of cum dripped from his spent cock. Frustrated, Justine climbed off of him and setting the collar on a five minute timer, showered and left to go get food and figure out how she was going to end this.

If she couldn't break him soon, she would have to let him go, as it was becoming obvious he would let himself suffer permanent damage before he would quit. Justine decided to stay out for a couple of hours. Lounging in a chair on the beach near the cottage, while Mark was being repeatedly shocked, she closed her eyes and tried to get some rest. The timer on the collar would make it impossible for him to sleep, which meant at this point he hadn't had any in almost forty eight hours.

When she returned, she stared down at him, shaking her head. He was covered in sweat which had to be burning the cuts on his back as well as the scratches and bite marks she had left on his arms and chest. His eyes were open, but glazed over, and he was alternately gasping and moaning. She watched long enough to see the collar zap him twice. Both times his body jerked and he whispered something she could not make out. All in all Justine was sure that he was not completely coherent at the moment.

Justine nodded to herself, this was the end. She would be able to get him to say enough to consider him broken. Or so she thought. When she looked back down at his face, she saw his eyes were now focused and staring at her. They were bloodshot, but were extremely bright, as if lit from within. He smiled tiredly at her and whispered, "I'm ready when you are."

Justine's eyes widened; he was hard again. Alex had been right. Mark was nothing short of a freak of nature. As she glanced around the room trying to come up with something, Justine heard Circe's voice in her head saying that Mark was the most powerful man she had ever met.

Her eyes landed on the small bag she had left next to the bed. There was a ball gag in it that she hadn't used yet. She doubted being gagged would bother him, but he was panting though his mouth. The gag would affect his breathing, weaken him even more. Letting her dress drop to the floor, Justine removed her thong, and as she bent over, picked up the gag. While there she noticed the salt shaker, and quickly poured some into her right hand. Cruel yes, but Justine was not here to lose. Keeping it behind her back, she climbed up onto the bed and straddled him. She bit her tongue to hold back the moan of discomfort as her aching pussy was once again filled by his relentless cock. She saw him wince as well, and began to slowly ride him.

Their gazes met, and Justine could see the pain and exhaustion in his eyes. They were both hurting, yet still going, each stubbornly refusing to admit they'd had enough. Justine leaned back so that she was sitting straight up, impaling herself further onto his cock, and staring down at him, forced a cold smile. "Well, my arrogant little whelp, it looks as if we're starting again, but this time I've decided to at least spare myself the annoying sound of your voice."

Justine slapped her salt covered palm down on the scratches she had left on his chest. Mark screamed in pain and, moving quickly, she brought her hand from around her back and shoved the ball into his mouth.

That was when all hell broke loose.

Mark screamed behind the gag and bucked so violently, Justine was thrown off of him. She fell off the bed, hitting her head on the floor and laid there for a moment as her vision swam. Above her on the bed, Mark was screaming continuously into the gag as if someone were torturing him. Rolling to her knees, Justine looked at him, wondering if this was some kind of weird trick. One look at his face told her it wasn't. Mark's eyes were bulging and every muscle in his body was taut as he strained against the ropes around his wrists and ankles.

Justine reached for the gag, but had to lunge back when with a loud crack, Mark succeeded in snapping the post off of the headboard. The wood whistled past her face, close enough for her to feel it passing through her hair. The wood hit the bed, and Mark tried to bring his hand up to his face. Realizing that he would strike himself in the head with the wood, Justine grabbed his arm to hold it down, while she again reached for the gag with her other hand. Mark screamed and yanked his arm from her grasp.

Taking a chance he wouldn't strike her before she could do it, Justine leaned over him and ripped the gag from his mouth. The scream he released sent a chill down her spine. It wasn't the rage she expected, but was a wail of pure fear. Justine tried to speak to him, but he continued to scream. Not sure what else to do, Justine slapped him in the face, trying to stun him back to reality. Again the reaction was immediate as well as frightening.

Mark stopped screaming and cried out, "Please, don't hit me!"

Fighting to remain calm, Justine said his name softly and told him no one was going to hurt him.

Mark whimpered like a child and began begging, "No please, I'll be a good boy, I promise."He had stopped fighting and, in an effort to calm him, Justine leaned over and untied his other hand. Mark simply let it fall limply to the bed, and continued to plead.

"I'm sorry I made so much noise," he said.

He appeared to be looking at her, but she could tell his eyes were seeing someone other than her. Justine also realized with a start that he was crying. She put her hand to his face and again spoke soothingly, telling him everything was okay. At her touch, Mark jerked up to a sitting position, causing her to flinch away from him in fear he was going to attack her. Instead, he buried his hands in his face and began crying. Justine reached out and, taking his wrists, gently pulled his hands away from his face. He didn't resist and she started to try again to tell him he was safe.

She stopped, stunned at the look of sheer terror in his eyes. Looking up at her he whispered, "Please, Mistress, please don't hurt me anymore."

He had barely gotten the words out, when he began to sob uncontrollably. Not knowing what else to do, Justine wrapped her arms around his shoulders and drew him against her. Not only did he not resist, but he collapsed into her, his head on her shoulder, and continued to sob like a small child. Justine whispered in his ear, saying his name over and over, trying to bring him back. She was trying hard not to panic. If he didn't come around, she would have to call for help. Justine could just imagine what the police would think. Mark tied to a bed, scratched and whipped bloody, crying like a baby. Things would not look good for her, at the least it would be a severe blow to her career, and if Mark had somehow snapped for good, she could be looking at criminal charges.

Justine closed her eyes and started playing with his hair, trying to calm him. Noting that he was acting like a child, she stopped saying his name, and started calling him baby, telling him she was there for him. She had been grasping at straws, but it seemed to have an effect. Mark's sobbing subsided, and his body stopped trembling. She continued to hold him, stroking his back as well as his hair, continuing to tell him it would all be okay.

After what seemed like an eternity, Mark lifted his head from her shoulder and looked at her. His eyes had lost that wild look, and he seemed as if he were just realizing where he was. Justine asked him if he was okay, and he nodded slowly. Justine got him a bottle of water and helped him hold it in his shaking hands as he drank. Eventually Mark came around and was totally humiliated, apologizing to her over and over. Flooded with relief, Justine apologized to him just as much; she should have never hurt him like that.

Mark tried to get up, but she made him stay on the bed, telling him to rest and they could talk about it later. He had resisted at first, then gave up and, leaning back against the headboard, closed his eyes. Justine went into the other room and, grabbing her cell phone, called Lazarus. All initiations were taped and the cameras hidden about the room had caught everything that had happened for the last two days. When he answered, she gave him a quick version of what happened. He told her to come see him that night, and said he would call Alex and have him go meet her. Alex had been Mark's best friend for years and it would be good for him to take over so Justine could get out of there. Justine agreed, but told him to have Alex give her at least an hour, she wanted things to be okay between her and Mark.

When she went back into the room, Mark was sitting there looking more asleep then awake. Without a word, she slipped into the bed next to him and put her arm around him. He rested his head on her shoulder and within minutes fell asleep. Justine slipped away a few minutes later and, calling Alex, told him to give her more time. Mark slept for a few hours and when he awoke was nothing short of embarrassed. They talked for awhile and Justine, hoping it would make him feel better, welcomed him to the Circle, god knew he had earned it. Mark had tried to say forget it, but she insisted he join, that was the point of all this after all.

Eventually Mark agreed to join and Justine asked if he wanted to tell her what happened. He refused and she didn't push. A couple of hours later, Alex arrived and took Mark back to Providence where he spent the night with him to make sure he was okay. Justine met with Lazarus and they agreed to edit the end of the tape, fixing it so it would end with Mark looking at her, and calling her Mistress. The only people who would know the true story were he, Justine and Alex.

The week after the initiation, Justine had gone to visit Alex at his condo in New York and had demanded to know what was wrong with Mark. After some initial resistance, Alex told her the story of Mark and his foster father, Max. He told Justine that even he had heard all of it second hand from Mark's sister. She told him everything so he would help Mark in court. Alex said Mark still battled night terrors on a regular basis, but would never seek help. The only person he would talk to and could help him was his sister, Megan, who Justine would later discover had also been a victim of abuse.

Justine was pulled from her thoughts by Mark moving from her embrace. She had a moment of déjà vu when she saw that same humiliated look on his face as he had that night.

"Sorry," he said quietly.

"Never be."

Mark leaned into her with a sigh and, not for the first time Justine was amazed at how child like he seemed sometimes. A far cry from his image as the perennial bad boy he was known as in and out of the Circle. Mark sat back again and she asked, "Mark, are you taking the medication to sleep like you're supposed to?"

"No."

"Are you talking to anyone?"

"No."

"Mark you should get some…"

"I'm fine," he said; with a stern tone his voice.

Biting back the response that he didn't seem fine, Justine simply nodded and said, "Maybe you should give your sister a call."

"My sister's in Chicago. She has her own life, and I'm not going to call her every time I have a nightmare."

"Okay." She shrugged.

"Well, now that I fucked up the morning, I think I'll get going," He said, beginning to get up

"Hey," Justine said, grabbing his shoulders. "Not so fast, you owe me that shower."

"Yeah, you still want to?"

"Of course I do!" She laughed. "It's my last time to tell you what to do for awhile. After all," she winked. "I owe you the next night, remember our bet."

Mark nodded. "That's right."

Putting her head down, Justine pushed her lip out into a pout and, looking up at him through her eyelashes, whispered, "I'll be all yours, Sir."

Mark laughed and Justine smiled at him, glad he had moved on from the nightmare. Standing, she reached out to take his hand, planning on leading him into the shower. Mark went to take it, but stopped at the sound of a knock on the door in the other room.

"Who the hell is that?" he asked.

"I don't know, I asked for the late checkout." Walking over to the chair, she picked up the short red silk robe she had brought with her and slipped it on. "I'll go check. Don't you dare get dressed."

Looking up through his eyelashes, Mark said softly, "Yes, ma'am."

Justine left the bedroom, shutting the door behind her and, loosely tying the robe, approached the door. She had just reached it when the knock came again.

"I had asked not to be disturbed," she said through the door.

"Sorry," a muffled male voice spoke from the other side. "I have something for Miss Bates, compliments of the manager."

Roger had probably sent her up a Bloody Mary along with breakfast. As she undid the latch, she looked down to see that the robe didn't even reach down to her mid-thigh, and she was showing quite a bit of cleavage. She started to open the door, planning on standing behind it to just take the tray. Then, remembering the fun she had showing off for the boys at the club, she decided to give the young attendant a little thrill. Opening the door wide, Justine stepped back to give him a nice long look at her. She began to smile, but stopped. Standing there, holding a covered tray and smiling like the Cheshire cat was Alex Warner.

Chapter Five

Justine stared hard at Alex as he stood in the doorway grinning at her. What the hell was he doing here? The answer of course was spying on her. Justine had been under the impression Alex had suspected her and Mark and the last few meetings had seemed overly interested in how she spent those Saturday nights.

"Well good morning, My Mistress." Alex said, his flawless smile growing wider. Giving her a blatant up and down "looks as if it were a pretty good night as well."

Glancing down the corridor, Alex pointed to her with his free hand.

"Not that I mind the view Justine, but there's some kids coming, you may want to close the robe, or let me in."

"Or slam the door in your smug face," Justine replied as she stepped to the side of the door. "What the hell are you doing here?"

Alex paused as two teenage girls and a boy walked past. They did indeed look into the room, and seeing her, the boy stopped dead in his tracks, his mouth dropping open. Justine closed the door partway, until he passed.

"Yeah, he was young even by your standards," Alex grinned. "Bet he hasn't even..."

"Unlike you and some others who think they need young lovers to make themselves seem experienced, I'm quite content to be with men, not boys."

"Oh?"Alex raised his eyebrows, "That's good to know. I happen to know of a..."

"You didn't tell me why you're here," Justine reminded him. "And if you don't, I'm closing the door the rest of the way and going back to bed."

"Bed? Oh, so you're very lucky guest is still here?" He grinned. "Then again, I suppose he'd have to be. Why else would you have asked Roger for a late checkout?"

He was looking into her eyes and Justine carefully kept her expression blank. Behind her calm gaze her mind was spinning. First she was hoping to hell Mark wouldn't come out of the room looking for her, but more than that was what to do right now. If she told Alex to screw off, it would add to his suspicions. If she let him in however, she was risking Mark coming out, and at the least would be wasting her last couple of hours talking to Warner.

"So can I come in?" he asked, forcing the decision on her. "I brought Bloody Mary's."

Justine continued to stare into his eyes, which were nothing short of amazing. Credit where it was due, Alex was a good looking guy who had the bluest eyes she had ever seen. The color of the ocean, they were so bright they seemed electric, and she could see where most women could get lost in them. But Justine was not most women.

"Fine, get your ass in here. You look like an idiot standing there with that damn tray."

"Not the invitation I was hoping for, but what the hell an in is an in." Alex laughed as he entered the room.

"Sums up your sex life at least," Justine quipped as she closed door behind him.

"My aren't we testy?" Alex asked, grinning at her. "Did I interrupt something?"

"If you did, I'm sure it's exactly what you had in mind."

Justine walked past him heading for the recliner in the center of the room. Stopping at the coffee table, she bent over to pick up her cell. She could have reached it just by leaning, but this caused her robe to rise, and she knew damn well Alex was staring at her bare ass. Justine didn't care. Like all members, The Mistress was expected to show videos of her sexual exploits at the meetings, so it's not like everyone hadn't seen her body already.

Truth be told, she liked him looking. Justine was proud of her still impressive form as she approached fifty. Besides, it would distract him while she sent Mark a text.

"Alex is here, stay in the room."

Justine turned and sat down, gesturing for Alex to sit on the couch across from her. He set the tray on the table and, removing the lid, handed her one of the two Bloody Marys' before taking the other and leaning back into the couch. As Justine took a sip, the phone vibrated in her hand.

"Nosy little prick, let me know when he's gone."

Justine looked up to see Alex staring at her. She could imagine how she looked; her long red hair had been down all night and was hanging unkempt about her face and shoulders. When she had gone to the bathroom earlier, she had noticed her mascara and eye shadow were smeared around her eyes, but hadn't felt like washing it off. She could tell just by the way they were stinging, her own blue eyes were as red as hair. Overall, she was sure she was giving off the impression she'd had quite the night. She also knew Alex, like everyone else in the Circle, had sex on the brain and most likely found her disheveled appearance exciting.

Justine had pretty much flopped into the chair and her robe was open and hiked up around her upper thighs. As she watched Alex's eyes work over the length of her body, Justine took another sip of her drink and took him in as well. Once you could tear your eyes from his, the rest of Alex's face certainly was not a letdown. He was easily as good looking as Mark, but in a different manner. Where Mark had high cheek bones and smooth pretty features, Alex was more on the rugged side, with a square jaw and features that gave him an intimidating look. Despite those features, Alex had an amazing smile and showed it often, especially if there were women around. Justine always felt her age when she considered him a better looking version of Tom Selleck without the mustache.

Alex was forty-two and, like Justine, had kept himself in damn good shape with a body that belied his age. A former golden gloves boxer in college, Alex was a workout freak and his broad shoulders and huge biceps strained the fabric of the white polo shirt he was wearing. In addition to flattering his build, the white shirt looked damn good against his deeply tanned skin and Justine had no doubt he took that into consideration when putting it on. But who was she to talk? Narcissism was definitely something she was more than guilty of.

"Thank you for the drink," she said, breaking the mutual appreciation session. "They have the best Bloody Mary's in Boston."

"Honestly, these are from Roger," Alex replied. "I saw him at the desk and asked if you had checked out. When he said you were staying late, I mentioned I was going to go see you and he sent these." Alex laughed. "No, let me be more specific, he took me to the bar and made these himself."

"Roger is a good friend,"

"Not sure about that, but you must've really treated him well the night you and he hooked up."

Justine felt a surge of anger go through her.

"And exactly how do you know I spent time with Roger?"

"Come one, Justine, Roger and I go all the way back to college. Hell our fathers went to Harvard together," he shrugged. "We were fraternity brothers, we talk about everything."

"Apparently, you're still frat boys," Justine said disgustedly. "Immature little boys who still kiss and tell."

"Come on, we...."

"So do you still talk about girls who blew you twenty years ago? Old conquests?" She grunted. "Pathetic, and I'll tell you this, if Roger had any hopes of a second night with me, they're gone now. In fact I'll be sure to tell him that on the way out today."

"Hey easy." Alex put his hands up. "It's not his fault. We were discussing some mutual friends and your name came up. I could see by the look on his face he was taken with you and I asked." He grinned. "He did deny it at first, but after a few drinks...."

"I don't like being discussed by anyone." Justine pointed at him. "And my sex life sure as hell better never again be a topic of any of your conversations." She paused and added, "In or outside of the Circle."

"Calm down, Justine," he said. "It's not a big deal, it's...."

"It's the point, Alex, you seem just a little too preoccupied with how I spend my time lately, especially on meeting nights."

"I ask everyone what they do." He shrugged. "It's fun to know what my brothers and sisters are doing for entertainment."

"And I'm sure not all of them tell you. Somehow I can't see the Lady Mercedes telling you anything but where to go and what to do when you get there."

"You're right, some don't." He sighed. "Mark for instance, used to tell me everything, but he seems awfully vague the last few months, doesn't even want to go hunting with me."

"I don't blame him, from what I hear your hunting is more like buying." Justine smirked as she knew she had hit a nerve.

"Christ." Alex rolled his eyes. "Pay for a couple of escorts and I never hear the end of it."

"A brother of the Circle shouldn't be paying for his women, he should be claiming them." She shrugged again. "Unless you're losing your touch."

"Back to Mark," Alex said. "Last meeting I brought along a pet just for him." He smiled. "Just his type, you know the goth look? Long black hair, ghost white skin? He turned me down." He shook his head. "Damn strange, even stranger is he never brings his pet when the meetings are here or New York."

"Alex, why are you here?" Justine asked softly. "Is it just to spy and talk in circles?"

"Well no, I need to talk to you Justine."

"And you couldn't have talked to me last night? Between dinner and the meeting, we spent close to eight hours together."

"I didn't find out my news until a couple of hours ago, so I..."

"I have this you know," Justine held up her phone.

"I wanted to talk in person. I...."

"Wanted to see who I was with, pure and simple."

"No, I do have something important to discuss with you," he insisted.

"Why Alex?" she asked. "Why does it matter to you who I'm with?"

"Let's forget about that." He waved his hand and, reaching under the tray, pulled out a manila folder. "I want to...."

"I'll decide what's discussed here, Orion," Justine said firmly. "And what I choose to discuss is your latest obsession with my personal life. And I say latest because this isn't the first time you've expressed interest in my choice of partners."

"Justine...."

"Did you not hear me address you as Orion, or is your hearing going along with your manners, and common sense?" she asked pointedly.

Alex regarded her for a moment before bowing his head, "My apologies, Mistress Scarlett, I didn't think this was a formal conversation."

"It is now, and since it is, you'll tell me why it matters who I share my bed with."

Alex stared at her and she could see his wheels spinning. Out of the Circle, Alex was as shrewd of a business man as one could find. Having taken his father's small chain of home electronics shops and turning them into the international company, Orion software. He had accomplished this by designing the ultimate antivirus software called "Orion the Hunter." A program so efficient it rivaled Norton. In the Circle, Alex currently held the position of diplomat, the liaison between their Circle and the others. In every facet of his life, Alex was a consummate politician and game player, but here, faced with a direct question, he appeared confused with how to answer.

As she waited for him to realize there was no way out other than the truth, she decided to make things more difficult on him. Sliding down further into the comfortable chair, Justine put her left foot on the coffee table, while letting her right leg rest against the chair. Right on cue, his eyes dropped and narrowed as they stared between her legs, hoping for a glimpse.

"Well this is a switch," she said. "Normally I have to tell you to stop flapping your gums, but now I can't get you to speak."

"Fine." Alex nodded. "I want to know if you and Mark..." he caught himself. "Lovecraft, are hooking up."

"You have no right to even wonder that." she replied evenly. "But I'll indulge you and ask why it'd concern you if I was."

Alex paused and Justine rolled her eyes as she saw he was still staring intently between her legs. She had done it as a distraction, but was now becoming annoyed. Answering her without looking up he said quietly, "It's not so much as who you're with as it is who you're not."

"Meaning?" Justine asked even though she knew damn well where this was going.

"Mistress, I'm simply wondering why we've never had any time together." He put his hands out. "Am I not attractive to you?"

"Oh please,." Justine shook her head. "You're head can barely fit through the door. You know you're attractive, all men of the group are. That has no bearing on who I choose to be with."

Well not exactly true as there were times Mark could make her melt like a teenager. Shaking that thought, she continued, "but to respond to your question with one of my own, why should I have spent time with you? I haven't spent time with many over the years."

"But…."

"I'm your Mistress. My body is mine to be given to whom I choose. Only High Mistress Persephone herself could command me otherwise."

"But you've not always been Mistress," Alex began, finally looking up at her. "Before you ascended we shared the table for close to ten years."

"Your point?"

"I…. well I'd always thought we would have our time," he said simply.

"Orion, there are members who've served together for their twenty year duration who've never shared time. Or maybe they have. The rule is, no one is ever supposed to tell. Remember?"

"I know but…."

"And time is rarely granted."

"I…." Alex sighed, and Justine realized he was having a hard time admitting his frustration. "I'd thought for sure you would've chosen me as your celebration the night you ascended."

"You thought wrong." She shook her head. "Why would you have thought that in the first place?"

"Because I…. I had asked Master Lazarus for time with you twice and both times he said you declined. I thought perhaps you were waiting for that night."

"No, I turned down the time because I simply didn't want to. No offense, but I started back when the ladies of the Circle were passed about the table like bottles in a drinking game. Sometimes to more than one member in a night." She paused to make sure she was looking him in the eye. "Sometimes to more than one at a time."

Justine gave Alex a chance to let that visual sink into him. As she did, an image formed in her mind of her on her knees sucking the cock of one member while Lazarus's predecessor, Poseidon, was behind her, alternately using her pussy and her ass. Standing around the bed were two more members, waiting their turn with her. It was the event that had driven her to quit until Lazarus had come to her and made his proposal. Speaking again, to dispel that from her mind she continued, "So trust me, Orion, my days of being requested like a cut of meat from a menu were over."

"Except for Lazarus," Alex replied. "You had no problem being his Circle Pet."

"How dare you!" Justine snapped. "How fucking dare you speak to me like that? Are you looking for an hour in Mercedes dungeon, Orion, because she'll be happy to give it to you. And believe me there'll be many at that table who'd love to see the video I'd play as further punishment for you not knowing your place!"

"Are you denying it?" Alex asked, remaining calm. "I mean no disrespect, Mistress, but the story came from a reliable source. And I'm not saying it in front of anyone else."

"You shouldn't be saying it at all." Justine spoke softly this time, trying not to let him get the better of her. "But in honor of Lazarus's reputation, let me clarify something. When our former Master requested my time, it was not as a Master looking to sample one of his ladies, but as a man who wanted to enjoy my company. Each time he asked, he told me I could refuse. Once I did, to see if he meant it and he was fine with it. Another thing you don't need to know, but I'll tell you is there were a couple of nights we didn't sleep together, we simply talked and enjoyed each other's company. Unlike his predecessors and members like you, he appreciated his sisters for more than just their pussies."

Alex remained quiet and with a sigh she asked, "So is there a point to this, Orion? Do you have some reason other than our time in the group together that makes you think you should be able to add me to your trophy case?"

"That's not how it'd be, it would...."

"No?" she asked "It's exactly what it'd be! Look at you and Roger, forty year old successful men sitting at a bar talking about pussy! The Circle is about bedroom games, but outside of the group."

"Some circles are more lenient with time granted and...."

"That's not my Circle, Orion; sorry if you think I should imitate New Orleans and have a yearly Secret Santa sex swap."

"It is a great tradition." Alex smiled. "I...."

"Then move to New Orleans."

"Mistress, please, I..."

"At my table we're equals not conquests, or challenges! The fact we don't share is the paradox of the group. We're all people who've had anyone they want, anytime and in any way they want. Yet in the group, we sit across from the most desirable people we've ever met and we can't touch. It's called control Orion, something you sorely lack."

"That's not true, Mistress." Alex said. "I'm not asking for free reign, I'm simply saying that in twelve years...."

"Two, twelve or twenty, there's no rule saying you're entitled to..."

Justine trailed off as she saw Alex's eyes dip down between her legs again. Case in point, she thought, then seeing a game forming, snapped, "Oh, for Christ's sake here!" Picking her right leg up, she swung it over the arm of the chair, spreading her legs and exposing her pussy.

"Here, Orion, take a good look at it, you've been peeking at it during our entire conversation!"

"I...." Alex stopped and simply stared at her fiery red pussy.

"You act like you've never seen it before. How many of my video's have you seen over the years?"

Pausing to take a breath Alex whispered, "My Mistress is much more impressive in person."

"Good answer." She smiled, beginning the game. "Here, let me give you a better look."

Reaching down with her left hand, Justine slid her red tipped fingers through the still damp lips of her pussy, before spreading it wide for him.

"How's that? Is that better, my pet?"

"My...." Alex started to repeat, then stopped as, putting the now empty glass down on the chair, she put her other hand between her legs and started stroking herself. "Yes, Mistress," he managed to breathe out.

"Yes? You getting a good look at the pussy you've been after for over a decade? The pussy that has eluded you?"

"It's a beautiful pussy," he whispered, his eyes fixed on her wandering fingers.

"It is isn't it?" She smiled. "The carpet matches the drapes no?" running her fingers down through her lips, she dipped her fingers inside and released a soft moan for his benefit.

"And still wet from this morning." She sighed. "Oh, yes your Mistress's pussy was quite well taken care of earlier."

Removing her fingers she slipped them into her mouth.

"Hmmm," she purred as her eyes rolled back in her head. "Damn I love tasting myself." She winked. "It's even better off a nice hard cock."

Alex's eyes were wide and she could see him beginning to breathe heavier. She was sure if she lowered her gaze she would see an impressive bulge in his pants. Taking her fingers from her mouth she put them under her nose and inhaled. Leaning forward she extended her arm across the table. Alex started to move, then catching himself asked softly, "Mistress, may I have the pleasure of sniffing your fingers?"

"How can I deny such a sincere request?" she asked him, smiling.

His eyes still locked onto her pussy, Alex leaned forward and, placing his nose just over her fingers, breathed deeply.

"You like?"

"Your scent is divine," he answered.

"Divine?" She laughed. "I like that. Wonder how you'd describe a taste?"

"I'd describe it as a privilege."

"Oh, another nice answer. The Lady Morrigan broke you in quite well all those years ago didn't she?"

Alex blinked, but remained silent and Justine held back a smile. Morrigan had totally humiliated Alex in his initiation and it was still talked about amongst members of her age.

"My lady taught me my place," he replied.

"And where is that place, Orion?"

"Wherever my Mistress wishes it to be."

"And don't you forget that." She smiled at him. "But good behavior should not go unrewarded. I think I'll let you have a taste."

"Thank you Mistress."

Alex opened his mouth and had just flicked his tongue across her fingertips when she pulled her fingers away.

"Who said you had to settle for my fingers?"

"I..." Alex paused to get control and answered. "I'd never seek to presume that you'd give me the honor of tasting your pussy."

"And because you didn't presume it, then I shall allow you to." Justine beckoned him with her finger. "Come lick your Mistress's pussy, my pet."

Alex was so excited he didn't even blink at the pet reference. Putting his drink down he made to stand.

"Stop," she said firmly. "Is that how a pet approaches his Mistress?"

This time, his eyes did flare. Justine waited to see the delicious battle of lust versus pride, but to her disappointment Alex quickly dropped to his knees and, going to his hands, began to crawl around the table towards her. Her disappointment was replaced by a warm feeling between her legs. This was why Justine preferred to toy with men and not boys; there was nothing more exciting than watching a man of his status take to their knees for her. Alex had reached her and, pausing to push the table away, knelt between her legs.

Justine swung her other leg over the chair so her pussy wide open. Spreading her lips, she tapped her now swollen clit with her finger. "You want that, my pet?"

"Yes Mistress."

"Lean in close."

Alex obeyed and her pussy flowed as his face was inches away.

"Take a nice deep breath, Orion, savor your reward."

Alex closed his eyes and inhaled deeply. He sighed in pleasure, and then as he released the breath, blew on her clit. His warm breath felt good on her sensitive clit, and she fought to keep her hips still.

"Go ahead and taste," she whispered.

Alex bent his head and, placing his lips at her clit, opened his mouth.

"No, that's a lick, I thought you wanted to taste."

Alex looked up at her and, sliding her fingers down, she opened herself wide

"Inside, my pet. Shove that eager tongue into my pussy; get a nice mouthful of your Mistress."

"It'll be my pleasure," he said softly.

Alex cheated a bit, putting his tongue just under her clit and sliding it down through her lips. Justine felt a shiver run through her as he did and decided to indulge herself a little.

"Slide it back up and do that again."

Alex did a good job of not smiling like she knew he wanted to and returned his tongue to just under her clit.

"Go ahead, just a couple of quick licks,"

Alex swirled his tongue around her hard flesh and she fought back a moan. Justine allowed herself the thought of how he would feel if he knew Mark's face had been there not two hours ago. Alex licked again and she let him as her mind wandered further, envisioning Alex licking her as Mark slid his cock into her mouth. She felt her pussy beginning to drip as she took the image further. The three of them on the bed together, the two of them all over her, but she would be in total control. Telling each of them where to lick and touch, where to put their cocks, and how fast or slow they could fuck her. Totally dominating them as they strived to compete to see who could please her more.

"Stop," she said, more sharply than she had intended.

Damn, last night and this morning had left her sex drunk, she hadn't had thoughts like that in quite some time. Between her legs, Alex had obediently stopped and was resting his head on her thigh looking up at her.

"What a good little puppy you are." She smiled and ran her pussy drenched fingers across his lips. Alex didn't open his mouth and she nodded. "Very nice, now go ahead and spread me nice and wide, and take that taste you're dying for."

Placing his hands on her thighs, Alex spread her open and began to lean in.

"Just to warn you," she said, working hard to keep a smirk from her face. "I do enjoy the feeling of a man coming inside me, and I haven't yet showered." As Alex stopped she added, "And we did just fuck not long before you stopped by."

The battle not to smile became harder as she saw him frown. He hesitated, his eyes locked on her gaping pussy.

"But, hey if you don't mind a creampie." She said softly. "I'm more than willing to indulge you."

Alex took a deep breath and after licking his lips, leaned in anyway.

"Then again," she said offhandedly. "You and Lovecraft have shared women before so who knows? Maybe you've tasted him before?"

Alex froze and from between her legs whispered, "Mark?"

"Lovecraft, yes." She nodded. "You were right, I've been with him. But that was earlier, now are you going to take me up on my most gracious offer, or are you going to decline?"

Alex put his head down, and Justine was getting ready to swing her leg back over the chair, when to her surprise, he brought his face to her pussy and she felt his tongue graze her lips.

"Oh you're fucking pathetic!" she snapped, grabbing his hair and shoving his head back. "You really are more pet than master aren't you?"

"What are you…?"

"Get out from between my legs and go sit down, you sorry excuse for a man," she said disgustedly, twisting his hair hard enough to make him wince, before letting it go.

Alex shook his head, and looked as if he were going to speak. Instead he turned and made to crawl back to his seat.

"Oh get up will you? Seeing you crawl would only be a turn on if you had something to offer afterwards. Just get up and go back to where you were."

This time there was a look of anger in his eyes, but he stood and walked slowly back over to the couch. Justine swung her legs back down to the floor and, picking up her phone texted Mark, *"I'm done with this game, give us a couple of minutes and come out. Just make it a proper show."*

"Mistress, with all due respect...." Alex began. "I don't...."

"Have any respect due to you." She shook her head. "See that little game, Orion? That's why you'll never have me! You're too much of a grabby little boy whose sense of self entitlement makes me sick. Never mind how pathetic you just made yourself look."

"Pathetic?" he asked. "I shouldn't desire my Mistress?"

"You crawled like a dog, for a taste."

"As I should," he told her. "As we're trained to do."

"It's in the manner you did so. Worse, you were willing to taste another man, to get a taste of me?" She smiled. "And don't say I demanded you to. I gave you an out."

"And if I refused, it would've turned into me being an ingrate who turned down your offer," he said with a tone. "Don't forget, Mistress, I've been playing this game almost as long as you."

"Yet who's under who, dear Orion?" She smiled. "Besides you just thought of that now. You were willing to do it just to get me, hope you'd do a good enough job for me to let you have more." She laughed. "I even told you it was Lovecraft you would've tasted and you were going to do it." She made a disgusted sound. "All to tongue me for a couple of minutes."

"Is it so bad to desire you?" he asked, still sounding testy. "And, I'm aware everything here's a game, and I know you made that up about Lovecraft, just so you could use it against me."

Justine smiled as in absolute perfect timing, she heard the door to the bedroom swing open. As she heard Mark approach her from behind, she had to stifle a laugh as Alex looked up and his mouth opened.

"Good morning, Alex," Mark said softly as he reached the chair.

Alex didn't answer; instead he looked at Justine and back at Mark. She looked at Mark to see that like her, he was maintaining a neutral expression on his face. Justine knew he was thrilled she had let Alex find out he had been sleeping with her, but out of respect for her position, was not going to gloat. Mark had indeed come out to make an impression and a fine one. Wearing just a pair of black jeans, he was not only showing off his build, but the bites and scratches she had left on him last night were in plain sight. The jeans were unsnapped and the fly down, exposing his pubic hair and the fact he was not wearing underwear. Damn Alex! She should be in bed still enjoying that body.

"Well good morning, Mark!" Mark said. "Nice to see you."

Turning to Justine, he dropped to his knees next to the chair and kissed her on the cheek.

"Thank you for allowing me the honor of your bed last night, My Mistress, I hope I entertained you properly."

"I have no complaints, My Dark Prince, know that your Mistress went to sleep and woke up quite satisfied."

Turning her head, she kissed him quickly on the lips.

"My Mistress is too kind," he said softly while looking her in the eye.

She noticed his eyes were red, and he seemed tired. She wondered if he was completely over the nightmare.

"Unfortunately, I do need to get back to Providence to meet with a potential client. With your permission, I'd like to shower before I take my leave."

"Of course." She nodded, cursing Alex again for costing her that shower.

"Oh, cut the shit!" Alex snapped. "Don't act like this is some formal occasion, you two have been...."

"Are you questioning our Mistress, Orion?" Mark asked softly as he stood up and turned to face him.

"Oh, stop posing Lovecraft; I'm not afraid of you."

"You'd think you would be by now," Mark said smirking.

"Lovecraft, go shower and leave Orion to me, the two of us need to have a little chat."

"As you wish," Mark said, giving her a slight bow, then, with a wink to Alex, he turned and left the room.

Alex watched him leave and she knew he was taking in the claw marks on his back.

"I'm really not your type, Orion, trust me. We've all seen how you handle pain," she said quietly

"Whatever," Alex said quietly as he stood. "I did need to speak with you about something else, but I'll call you tomorrow."

"No, Orion, you'll sit and talk to me today, but not before we straighten out your little issue of jealousy, understood?"

With a sigh Alex sat back down. "As my Mistress commands," he said with a complete lack of sincerity.

Justine sat in silence. When it became apparent he wasn't going to speak on his own, she cleared her throat. "Why so quiet? I thought you'd be gloating." She smiled. "After all you were right; Lovecraft has been my entertainment several times in the past months."

Alex's reply was a simple nod as he looked off into space. Justine glanced down at the folder in his lap and wondered what was in it. Well she would know in due time, but right now she needed to straighten this out. Justine had wanted to keep it secret between her and Mark, but Alex had egged her on and she felt it was worth it just to wipe the smug look from his face. Justine knew he wouldn't tell anyone, if for no other reason than to save his own bruised ego that he was not her choice. Speaking of said ego, now that he was upset she would need to find a way to appease him before he left. Games were games, but her job was to keep her Circle strong which meant spending a lot of time trying to keep everyone happy.

"Or," she continued into his silence, "did this become a case of be careful of what you wish for?"

"I don't understand," Alex said with a sigh. "Why Lovecraft?"

"That's not really your question is it? The real question is why him and not you. Isn't that right Alex?"

"What happened to Orion?"

"I was formal to get to the bottom of your game and now that I've wiped that smirk off your face, we can speak as friends."

"Is that what we are?" he asked quietly.

"Oh, stop being dramatic!" she snapped."We've known each other for twelve years, and serve together in the Circle. Of course we're friends."

"Point taken." Alex gave her a rueful grin. "I'm being a baby."

"Bitch was the word that came to mind." She grinned back. "But baby will do."

"Well thanks," he laughed. "With friends like you…." He trailed off then shook his head, "But fine, why him and not me?"

"Mark does it for me, you don't."

"That's it?"

"For the most part," she put her hands out. "I like it rough and Mark can deliver that, but still never forget his place. He's also a switch. He's able to submit to me without even a hint of pride. You, on the other hand are not rough, nor do you like to bottom."

"I would for you and you know it," he grunted. "I think I just proved that a few minutes ago."

"Honestly Alex, what you've proved here today is why Mark has had the privilege and you don't." She paused, waiting for him to ask.

Alex knew she was waiting and held back for about a minute before rolling his eyes.

"And what was that Justine?"

"You, Alex, are an impatient, grabby little boy. No matter what you have, it's never enough."

"Isn't that what the Circle is all about?" he asked. "Excess? To quote that crap Mark slings all the time, we take what we want."

"And again, part of the Circle is being with those we cannot take. In the Circle, we wait and hope for what we want, and may never get it. It's a test of will, something you don't possess."

"That's not…"

"Oh please," She waved her hand at him. "You were so busy trying to get a peek of my pussy you couldn't even look at me when we were talking."

"My Mistress," Alex started. "Is…."

"Don't give me that crap. I'm a woman, I have a pussy like any other, and I'm sure you've lost count of how many you've seen. Yet you sat here like a teenager trying to see up his girlfriend's dress!"

Alex started to speak again, but she continued, "You're not only an attractive man, but a wealthy one. You've had any woman you've ever wanted and that was before the Circle. Through the Circle, you've been with some of the most amazing women in the world. Women most men wouldn't even be able to speak to without stuttering, and yet you act like the idiot frat boy you always were."

"Aren't we a little above name calling?" he asked.

"Shouldn't you be above kissing and telling?" she asked pointedly. "You got Roger drunk to find out if he slept with me. And you sit here with that sense of entitlement that pisses me off! I don't care how long we've been in the group together; you have no more right to be with me than the newest member at the table."

"That's not true," he said quietly. "I'm an exemplary member. I'm one of the most respected diplomats in the group, and I've recruited two of the strongest members of our Circle." He pointed down the hall where Mark was in the shower. "Mark's the most feared enforcer in the country and Loki is so amazing with the video's he has been requested to do them for members of other groups. You wanted neither of them. I talked you into it both times."

"And that entitles you to share my bed?" she asked, enjoying baiting him.

He nodded. "I feel I've earned a reward, yes."

"You've always been quite well rewarded, Alex. When you kept the Lady Circe from leaving because of a problem with another Circle, you were rewarded by Lazarus with The Lady Felicia who was new and I had sworn I wouldn't let anyone have time with her right away. I let my word as High Lady be broken by you, and she almost left because of it."

"I was very soft with her," Alex put his hands up. "And we're very close now."

"It was the point. You were also rewarded by Lady Morrigan for discovering Mark, because she was one of the few who were dying to see him get in. And if memory serves me, oh poorly treated one, finding Loki got you a night with Mistress Aphrodite from New Orleans." She shook her head. "I'm pretty sure there's not a man in any Circle who wouldn't be envious of that. Yet instead of appreciating what you've had, you sit and whine because you're not my choice for a lover."

"The pleasure of a mistress is the greatest reward one can earn," Alex said.

"And as I just stated you received that."

"My own Mistress."

"I'll be sure when I see Aphrodite next that I tell her she wasn't considered a fit reward for you."

"I don't mean it like that."

"I do. Alex, you're an immature fool. It probably kills you that you can't tell anyone in the group you were with her. Trust me, if I ever did think of you, that reason alone would be enough to deter me, you'd tell someone."

"No, I...."

"And that brings us to Mark," Justine cut him off. "You've been his best friend for almost twenty years and he never told you he was with me. That's why he is. Mark has achieved as much in the Circle as you have, probably more. Yet he looks for nothing. Do you know when he became enforcer by beating the shit out of Tartarus when he whipped Felicia, she offered him a night with her and he declined?"

"I...." Alex frowned. "Why would he...."

"Because he told her defending her honor after that disaster was reward enough. It was a privilege to defend his sister."

"Oh please," Alex snapped. "That was a line. He may not have gotten it from Vicky, but that would've set him up with others. He knows what he's doing."

"Exactly." Justine nodded. "Better than you do. Alex, it's as simple as good things come to those who wait. Mark loves the Circle and appreciates everything about it. He's never requested time with a lady of our group or any other." She shrugged. "And because of that, they request him constantly."

"That's because of the lame ass Dark Prince routine of his."

"That and his ten inch cock." Justine nodded. "But it's about the respect he gives them. He never doms them Alex, he plays with them. Sure he's rough if they want it, but if not he just enjoys them. He ends each time with telling them it was his privilege. He's a ten year member, and he told a pledge that last year, treated her as if she were a High Lady. They also know he never says a word." Justine laughed. "You think it's upsetting that he's been with me? You'd be beside yourself if you knew some of the women Mark has had time with."

"I don't care about the others." Alex let out a deep breath. "But okay, I'm a frat boy and because I'm eager I'm off the list."

"Eager and desperate are two different things, dear." Justine smiled.

"On a different note, Justine. Circle pets are frowned upon. Next time Mark asks...."

"First off, if a Master or Mistress chooses a pet so be it. Frowned upon it may be, but against the rules it's not. And so you know, Mark has never asked to be with me once. Even now that it's been a regular thing between us, he never takes it as a given we'll spend the night together."

"Still unwise, Justine. If others find out."

"And how would they? By getting you drunk and asking you?" She shook her head. "Besides, Alex, things are quite different for the ladies of the Circle then the men and you know that. Mark can get drunk and party like an animal and the press eats it up. The bad boy attorney strikes again. But a woman of my stature? How would it look for me to show up with a twenty year old on my arm?"

"Good for you?" Alex laughed.

"To some, but to most it wouldn't. As for the bedroom? You think I dommed Roger? I can't risk that. I can only cut loose with men Mercedes or other group members can trust or take chances. I choose not to take chances. Mark is beautiful, caters to my every whim, appreciates being with me, and is at my beck and call." She shrugged. "There are no airs between us and we have fun. That's something I sorely lack in other areas of my life."

"Besides, Alex," Justine said softly, trying to spin it another way. "You know Mark better than anyone. Underneath the persona and the bad-ass attitude, there's something wrong with him, and it's more than his childhood. He goes into depressions and needs someone to watch out for him."

"He's not a child," Alex shook his head.

"You've known him for years. You know what I'm talking about. You can also pick on him all you want, but you know you're like a brother to him. When you were in Providence, you used to keep an eye on him. Try to get him out of those funks."

"Yeah, I suppose," Alex said.

"Alex, what's wrong with him?" she asked remembering this morning's nightmare.

"Got all day?" Alex asked wryly. Then after a pause said, "Justine I have no idea." He frowned. "Even what I told you I got from his sister. There's more than just the abuse, I know there is. There's times he's just off and seems like a different person. Megan's the only one who knows and she's not telling."

"She also moved to Chicago a couple of years ago. You went to New York and now he has no one. So I spend time with him. He gives me what I need and his time with me makes him feel like he's special in the group."

"I don't think he needs help there," Alex said.

Justine sighed, and leaning over, reached out and touched his cheek.

"Listen to me, Alex. You and Mark are my boys. Both of you. In life you're one of my best friends as is Mark, he just happens to be one with benefits. Within the Circle, you two are my right and left hands."

"I suppose," Alex took her hand and gently kissed the back of it. "I wouldn't mind getting the benefit package however."

"You'll get more than that." Justine said removing her hand and sitting back.

"What do you mean?"

"Alex, you and I have discussed what'll happen when I step down in two years. There'll be three people who have the ten years to qualify to take over. You, Mark and Amado. Mark could never be Master, he's too erratic and is the best enforcer in the group. Amado isn't serious enough, and wouldn't be a good choice."

"You've said that before."

"And I mean it. Alex you're a perfect diplomat and you'll be an excellent Master. Mark will stay as enforcer, meaning your lifelong friend will be the one to have your back against any who oppose you. Amado will become diplomat and, with his family connections and charm, will be as good as you."

"Your circle will be in good hands Justine," Alex said seriously. "I mean it, we won't let you down."

"I like that you said we." Justine nodded. "I want to take care of you and Mark. So yes, he may get the pleasure of sharing my bed but, Alex, you're going to be the Master of The Eastern Circle. You'll have the best enforcer at your side, The Circle's most beautiful High Lady in Felicia and Mercedes is as feared as any enforcer. It's a strong group Alex." She smiled at him. "Or should I say Master Orion?"

"I do like the sound of that." He nodded. "I guess I'm just being...."

"Immature," Justine finished for him.

"Agreed."

Justine smiled to herself. She'd humiliated him, laid into him, and now given him some hope. It was time to make him an offer that would guarantee she would get what she wanted from him.

"But remember, Alex, nothing in the Circle is free. There's no guarantee you'll become Master. Two years is a long time and this conversation reminds me of my one issue with you taking over."

"And that is?" he asked.

"I don't want you treating the ladies of the table as your personal harem, and I fear that you would."

"So you want me to say I'll never partake of any of the ladies?"

"You're being childish again," she pointed out. "I'm not saying ever, but with discretion. You don't need to be doling out rewards for yourself. Keep in mind that once you're Master, when you travel, the other heads of the groups will provide you with entertainment. You don't need to sample your own Circle."

Alex nodded. "Fair enough."

"I want you to know this is nothing personal," she pointed out. "I'd have this conversation with Mark or Amado as well. I'm one of the last women in the Circle who remembers the old days. I want to be sure the East continues the respect for the ladies that I, and others around the country, have instilled in the last fifteen years."

"You have my word Justine," Alex bowed his head his head.

"I'm sure I do for the moment. In the next two years, I'll be watching you closely. Things like spying on Mark and I, asking Roger if he's slept with me and haunting me for time with the ladies need to stop. If it doesn't, I'll give Amado the chance that should rightfully be yours." She shrugged. "It'll be up to you."

"I'll rein it in." Alex told her.

"I hope so." She nodded. "And to give you further incentive, I have a deal for you."

"A deal?"

"On the night I step down, I'm entitled to pick from the men for a proper send off. You, as ascending Master, may pick one of the ladies as a celebration."

"I'll abide by their natures," Alex said. "I know Felicia has her once in a lifetime rule and wouldn't ask her to break it. And Mercedes." He shrugged. "Well I wouldn't take any chances." He frowned. "Or am I to waive that right?"

Justine rolled her eyes. The Lady Felicia claimed a night with her was a once in a lifetime experience. Literally, as she claimed to have never slept with the same man twice.

"In a sense, you'll be waiving your right to the women in the group," she said, smiling. "However the reason you won't be choosing from them, my dear Orion, is because I'll be choosing you as my send off."

Alex stared at her as if waiting for the other shoe to drop. After a moment he asked softly, "we'll celebrate together?"

"Yes we will." She gave him a wink. "You'll finally have what you have so desired, but only if you behave accordingly." She pointed at him. "Just know that Master or not, you'll not be in control."

"Of course not!" he said without a hint of sarcasm.

"But I believe you'll have an enjoyable time nonetheless." She reached across the table. "Do we have an agreement?"

Taking her hand, he kissed the back of it.

"Of course, My Lady, it's a more than fair proposition."

"Good," she said as she sat back in the chair. "Now that we have that cleared up, what did you need to see me about that was so urgent?"

Alex flashed his high wattage smile and laughed, "Only fitting that after our conversation I'm able to follow it up by showing you why you'll be making the right choice in me."

"Oh really?" she asked unable to help smiling back at him. "Do tell, oh humble one. What's in your folder that has you so excited?"

"Not what," Alex passed the folder across the table. "But who. Justine, in that folder is the woman I believe will be the next member of our Circle."

Chapter Six

Justine felt her heart begin to beat faster. Their Circle had not been complete in months. The Lady Morrigan had stepped down last January and they had not found a replacement in time. Sydney joined in March, but a month later, The Lady Circe, stating personal reasons, had left abruptly in April. After a visit during which Justine begged her to reconsider, Circe admitted to her she had fallen in love with a long time friend with benefits.

Although she was not geared towards love herself, she had no issue with someone being happy. Unfortunately that had left her table short again. The annual conference was coming in October and it would reflect poorly on her if the East was short a member. High Mistress Persephone had called her last month to ask her if she'd had any luck yet. Although she had known Persephone for years, there was something about her that still made her nervous. She didn't want to risk the high Mistress deciding on a whim that Justine should pay a price for being shorthanded.

If Alex had indeed come through yet again and found someone, Justine might very well be finding him a reward despite their recent conversation. She sat back in the chair and after a look up at Alex, who was grinning from ear to ear, opened the folder. She was looking at a close up of an extremely attractive brunette with a fair complexion and a pair of full lips that were pushed out into a playful pout. What caught Justine's eye however were her eyes. They were emerald green and as electric as Alex's, practically leaping out of the photo.

"She's gorgeous," she said softly.

Flipping the photo over, Justine took in the next one. The woman was standing in a bar and dressed to kill, wearing a black mini skirt that exposed a long set of shapely legs, red stilettos and a tank top barely containing a more than ample set of tits. The next pictures were even better. Taken through the window of what appeared to be a very small apartment, the woman was sitting topless on a bed. Justine took a moment to take in her indeed very large breasts, before looking at the main attraction of the photo. Down on his knees at the foot of the bed was a young man who couldn't have been more than twenty. He had his hands behind his back as the woman held her bare foot in front of his face. Her toe was in his mouth and he had a look of adoration on his face as he stared up at her.

Following this was the same young man lying on his back on the bed. His hands were over his head and the woman was kneeling between his legs. Her mouth was open and her tongue no more than an inch from his hard cock. She was looking up at him and there was a look of desperation on his face. Justine could see his arms weren't tied, yet appeared to be straining from the effort of stopping himself from touching her. Justine smiled as she imagined his legs trembling anxiously and his young body tense as he yearned for her to put his cock in her mouth.

Her eyes drifted back to his unbound arms. Although Justine would bind men, it was more for show in the videos. Leaving them free to move was the true sign of control. When a sub was bound it proved nothing. They couldn't move even if they wanted to. Leaving their hands free gave them the choice to obey or not, taught them the only way they could get a reward was to learn control. If they stayed still, they were at their Mistress's mercy, but to move was to lose all hope of pleasure. The last photo was even better. The man was back on his knees on the floor and jerking off onto her feet. Justine assumed he had misbehaved at some point and that was all she would allow him. Closing the folder she looked at Alex.

"Nice technique," she said quietly. "She knows the game."

"She does."

"Are all her men little more than boys?"

"From what I have been able to find out, yes."

"So who's our hot little Mrs. Robinson?"

"Allison Saunders," Alex answered. "I've been watching her for the last few weeks. Last night was the first time I saw her really exert control, Loki sent me these via courier this morning."

"Why so long?" Justine asked. "We usually move a lot quicker and why didn't you tell me?"

"As for telling you, I wanted to be sure first," Alex began. "As to why so long? That's part of why she'll be perfect. She's been working that kid for the last two weeks. She doesn't go back to their place the first time. She shows up and toys with them a few times. Then puts out in grand style. No control, no games, just blows their minds."

Justine nodded. "Hooks them."

"Exactly. Second time she starts getting them to ask for what they want. Third time they're all but begging. By the next time she's in total control. These pictures were from the third time. The first couple I let go because she wasn't trying to control."

"Background check?"

"Clean, no crime, no drugs. Short of a couple of speeding tickets, she's a model citizen."

"Right age I take it?"

"She just turned thirty."

"So what does Miss Saunders do for a living?" Justine asked, getting more excited by the minute.

"Advertising exec. I heard of her through someone who met her at a networking function. He hit on her and she blew him off, but was quite taken with his nephew who he had brought with him. He told his uncle some interesting stories that my frat boy friend was nice enough to share with me." Alex laughed.

"Where is she in her career?"

"Right where we want her to be; stuck behind the boys club. She works hard, does excellent work, but the partners swoop in and take the clients. She's better than any of them and with a few breaks could be running the agency."

"So I take it she doesn't, shall we say, cater to the boys club?"

"From what I've heard she won't sleep with the partners or the clients. She wants to earn it. She's hot and she's dominant, but she's no whore. And she's hungry, Justine. She's driven and she's pissed at where she is. The Circle is made for people like her."

"Have you had contact with her?"

Despite the fact he had started by pissing her off, she could kiss him right now. This woman sounded perfect.

"I met her at a charity function about a week after I talked to my friend." He smiled. "She's even more beautiful in person."

"Who is?" Mark asked from behind Justine.

She turned in her seat to look at him. Mark was wearing the black jeans along with a grey sleeveless t-shirt that left his heavily tattooed arms bare. His black hair was slicked back, but he hadn't shaved, leaving the five o'clock shadow he had grown in since yesterday. The men were required to be clean shaven at the meeting, but this morning Mark was back to flaunting the bad boy look and doing it quite well.

"You're just in time," Justine handed him the folder. "Alex appears to have done it again."

Mark walked over and sat on the arm of the couch next to Alex and, opening the folder, whistled, "Damn."

"I knew you'd like her," Alex laughed. "Just your type, long black hair and damn near white skin."

"Nice lips too." Mark nodded. "I love a woman who can pout."

"Yeah I know." Alex said. Then smirking added, "kind of reminds me of someone we know doesn't she?"

Mark shot him a look. "Fuck off, we straightened that out years ago."

"Of course we did." Alex laughed. "That's why you know exactly who I'm talking about."

Justine rolled her eyes. She had no idea what they were talking about, nor did she care. Mark and Alex had an endless amount of private digs between them and she didn't bother asking anymore. Mark glared at him for a moment before flipping through the pictures. Closing the folder, he swung it at Alex who without looking, snapped his hand up and blocked it.

"Nice try, slow poke."

His hand flashed out to grab the folder, but yanking it away; Mark swung it around and caught him in the back of the head with it.

"Never was good at seeing past a feint were you?" Mark laughed as he slid off the arm of the couch to sit next to Alex who elbowed him hard enough in the side to make her wince.

"So what do you think?" Justine asked, ignoring their idiotic behavior.

"Nice technique, no bondage," Mark said.

"So what happened when you met her, Alex?" Justine picked up where they had left off

"She knew who I was so she started out nicely, looking for a lead. I asked her some work related questions, then started flirting and gave her the 'we should talk about it over a drink sometime.'

"And?"

Alex grinned. "She told me no offense, but she preferred her men much younger. I made a crack about having a lot more to offer than youth and she replied 'I prefer men who earn it over those who pay for it.'"

"Wow, she had you pegged from the start." Mark laughed.

"That's a good reaction though." Justine nodded approvingly. "We don't want women who whore themselves."

"And she obviously has standards," Mark added with a smirk.

"Coming from a guy who fucked forty year old housewives to pay for his text books, I won't take offense to that," Alex countered.

"Enough," Justine said quietly. "Save your insults for when I'm not around. So any contact after that, Alex?"

"Knowing I was going to have my answer on her sexual nature last night, I planted the seed by calling her Friday and asking her to throw me together a proposal and have it ready next Saturday. If I have your permission I'll try to recruit her.

"You going to play the game with her?" Mark asked.

"I'll see where it goes, but most likely. If she holds off it'll be a good sign. If she caves, I'll back off and use the game as a segue. One way or another it'll lead me where I need to go."

"You think she'll bite?"

"I think the idea of advancement will get her over the sexual aspects. I also have an ace in the hole with her career. Think how much Victoria could do for her."

"And if not, can she be trusted not to go running and telling stories about what you tell her?"

"If she is adamant she has no interest, I'll warn her of how easily we could ruin her. But she doesn't seem to have many friends, and keeps to herself. I doubt she'd say anything. I feel she'll want this." He paused then asked, "So shall I try to reel her in, Justine?"

Trying to keep the excitement out of her voice, Justine said, "Yes, follow your plan for next Saturday and let me know immediately so we can set up the initiation for as soon as possible."

"Speaking of which," Mark said. "I believe it's my turn to receive the initiation."

Justine frowned and looked over at Alex who had also stopped smiling. Mark looked at Justine.

"Why yes, Mark," he said. "It's your turn."

"Mark," Alex began. "I'm not so sure you're the right choice here."

"And why not?" Mark asked, already getting a tone in his voice.

"Allison's been playing the game for a long time. She's pretty strong willed and from everything I've seen, has never submitted."

"That's the point of the initiation, to teach her how to. The same way we were all taught."

"I think that a hardcore session may backfire here," Alex said. "She may be the type to say fuck this, use the safe word and leave."

"Then we don't need her," Mark shrugged. "You can't prove you can humble yourself to a member, you don't belong at the table."

"Thing is, we do need her," Alex pointed at the folder. "The conference is coming up and our Circle needs to be complete. We've been looking for months and she's the first viable candidate. We can't take a chance on her."

"So what are you suggesting?" Mark asked him. "A soft initiation?"

"I'm thinking that may be the best approach." Alex nodded. "She'll have to defer and play the part of sub, but it doesn't need to be a true breaking we…."

"I don't perform soft initiations."

"Then perhaps you won't be performing this one then," Alex shrugged.

"What?" Mark asked, his voice rising. "Are you fucking kidding me?"

"Listen," Alex turned to face him on the couch. "Try not to get upset about this, it's just…."

"Its bullshit is what it is!"

"Don't take this personally, but we…."

"Initiations are a rare honor," Mark continued, ignoring him. "Two years ago Mercedes should've been mine, instead she was given to Mephisto."

Alex looked at Justine, his hands up as if saying 'some help here?' With a nod she took over.

"That was my decision and you know why. Mercedes was too hardcore, too experienced and strong willed. You would've pushed and she would've pushed back until things got ugly." As he shook his head she went on. "If you remember, that's why we avoided having Morrigan handle yours."

"Yeah, and that stopped things from getting ugly didn't it Justine?" he asked, staring into her eyes.

Justine held his gaze briefly before looking away.

"That was an accident Mark," she said softly.

"Point is, it was ugly," He spread his arms out. "But okay I see the point with Mercedes. What about when Sydney came along? Again I was passed over, this time for Alex."

"We needed Sydney," Alex said. "We were shorthanded and she was tough to even talk into the group let alone an initiation. Sad to say, we needed her more than she needed us at the time. A brutal session would've caused her to safe out and walk away, so I did what I had to and went soft on her."

"And I'm sure you didn't enjoy a minute of it." Mark made a disgusted sound. "I get bumped so his lame ass can get a reward like that."

"Considering where you spent last night, I wouldn't make comments about rewards," Alex snapped.

"So I suppose that's the story with this woman," Mark said quietly. "She's strong willed, always been in control, and if I push she'll quit."

"And we really need her," Alex told him. "The conference is in three months. If we're short, it looks bad for Justine. Persephone is unpredictable; she may punish her for it."

"I doubt it," Mark said simply. "I have some sway with her. Being we go to the same church so to speak."

"No one has sway with Abigail and you know it better than anyone," Alex said softly. "The last Mistress who didn't fill her group in time for the conference was used as a pledge by the New Orleans enforcer, and quite roughly."

"No one will touch my Mistress without going through me," Mark said quietly, his eyes darkening.

"You won't have that choice. Persephone makes the rules remember? Point is, Justine could pay a price if we don't land Allison."

"So I should step aside again for the sake of my Mistress?"

"Exactly!' Alex clapped him on the shoulder.

Mark remained silent and Justine noticed his head was cocked slightly to the side and his eyes seemed unfocused. Alex had told her that he had done this all of his life. His sister called it 'going away' and it was a by-product of spending years not speaking to anyone. He would fog out and 'talk' to himself on occasions. Justine had come to notice when he did this, he was usually plotting something. Alex noticed as well, and tapped him on the shoulder.

"Hey, Mark, you in there?"

"Or perhaps," Mark began as if he had never stopped speaking. "I should initiate her properly to avoid our Mistress being punished even more harshly."

Justine's eyes narrowed. She had the feeling Alex had said exactly what Mark had wanted him to.

"What do you mean?" Alex asked.

Turing to Justine, Mark revealed his game.

"Justine, with your permission I'd like to tell Alex what transpired with Sydney yesterday and why."

"What happened with Sydney?"

"I'll let Justine tell you," Mark answered while staring at her. "Or should I?"

"I think what you should do is keep your mouth shut," Justine replied, fighting to keep her voice down. "You talk me into handling her punishment privately, and then you choose to speak of it?"

"I talked you into not doing it in front of the group," Mark shrugged."But I believe Alex should know, especially because if things go bad at the conference it could be his ass in the sling as well yours."

"What the hell are you talking about?" Alex asked, staring at Mark.

Mark was watching her, and Justine remained silent. Taking his opportunity to push on, he looked over at Alex.

"Long story short, your little initiate exhibited some embarrassing behavior during her granted time with Alexander."

"Really?" Alex asked. "I spoke with Ramses last week and he said all was fine."

"Because he and Justine go way back, and he kept it between them instead of reporting it as he should've."

"What'd she do?"

"It's what she didn't do, Alex. She didn't submit completely and he didn't leave happy."

"Why would she...."

"Because the little whore was still proud because she was never properly broken that's why!" Mark snapped. "Because you went soft on her so you could put her ass in the seat."

"I was told to go soft," Alex snapped back. "Don't put this on me."

"Whose fucking idea was it to go soft?" Mark asked.

"Mine actually," Justine replied.

"We had that conversation earlier," Mark said without looking at her. "No need to have it again."

"Watch your tone," she warned him.

"Thing is, Alex, yes you were told to go easy and as always, your lemming ass did exactly as it was told."

"And since when do we disobey our Mistress?"

"When you see what's in front of you." Mark shook his head. "Shit, Alex, you had her! There were a few times that you were close, I could see it in her eyes and you pulled back! Had you went further, she would've broken!"

"I had a job to..."

"Our job is to have a strong Circle, not a bunch of fucking posers!" Mark said loudly. "Let me tell you something, Sydney broke and damn quickly did she not Justine?"

"Yes," She said quietly. "You were right, Mark, but...."

"Know why? Because she wanted to!" Mark said throwing his hands in the air. "I broke her because the little slut wanted to be broken, because she was at that point we all were at one time."

"What are you getting at?" Alex asked.

"I'm getting at what a true breaking is all about. No matter how hard it was on us, we all reached that moment that as much pain as we were in, as humiliated and degraded as we were feeling, there was a moment when we wanted to succumb, to let go, to cry out to our tormentor." He pounded his fist into his palm "To break!"

"What does this have to do with Allison?" Justine asked. "We all went through our time. We know what you're saying."

"What I'm saying is since when did the Circle become a free pass?" Mark asked. "Alex and I got it put to us and I can't imagine what the initiations were back when you started."

"The word rape comes to mind," she said with a sigh. "I understand what you're getting at and maybe the next one we'll get back to the way it should be."

"Next one?" Mark asked. "Well hopefully that's not for a long time, but..." He shrugged. "Something tells me Allison could be over before she started and we'll be back to square one, with you learning the hard way this time."

"That's the second time you mentioned me being in trouble, Mark," she pointed out. "Care to elaborate?"

"How bad would this have been had Ramses gone to Persephone?"

"Much worse of course," Justine answered.

"Damn straight, you'd have been humiliated, Sydney would've had to have been punished in front of the group, most likely causing her to walk, and Persephone may have decided to call the initiator to task for being soft." He looked over at Alex.

"Well, we got lucky," Justine said.

"Let's take this a step further," Mark said adopting the tone he would use in court. "Let's say we do what you're suggesting, Allison gets in on a cake walk, a little groveling, a lot of sucking, a token spanking and she's in." He paused and smiled. "Everything's great right? Full table and we'll have Allison to offer as a pledge at the conference."

"I know where you're going with this," Alex said. "You're going to ask what if something goes wrong and she fails to please the person she's granted to."

"Exactly." Mark nodded. "What...."

"We'll make sure it's an older member who'll be more playful than forceful. That's how most are in those situations anyway," Justine explained.

"But, there are no guarantees. What if she gets an attitude like Sydney did? What if she refuses something asked of her or has an air of pride? What then?"

"We...." Alex started, but Mark waved him off.

"What'll happen is that member goes to their Master or Mistress who goes straight to Persephone." He shook his head. "Can you imagine what would happen? How upset she would be that at the biggest day of the year, a pledge insulted a high member because she wasn't properly trained?"

Justine looked over at Alex to see him staring back at her. She could tell he was thinking what she was, 'what if?'

"Persephone will be beside herself. Most likely Allison would simply be dismissed and she'd turn to you." He pointed at Justine, then at Alex, "And maybe you." Pausing to let his words sink in, Mark began speaking quietly. "Persephone is known for her brutality in these matters. The last Mistress who caused her a problem at a conference was tied down on a bed and fucked in the ass by several members. She was bleeding and begging by the end of it. Right into Persephone's pussy, because that's where her face was shoved the entire time."

"That wouldn't be allowed to happen now," Alex said quietly.

"Really? This was three years ago."

"But...."

"And the last Master to displease her?" Mark made a disgusted face. "Bent over and pegged by Persephone wearing a ten inch strap on. He was crying by the end as well. And that was done in front of over two dozen members." He looked over at Justine. "Wasn't it, My Mistress?"

"Yes," she said softly.

That had taken place at Persephone's club the Black Flame five years ago. The Master had been so humiliated he had stepped down a month later. She shook her head to shake the image of him screaming in pain as Persephone drove the huge dildo into him repeatedly, smiling as she did.

"See where I'm taking this? You think there could be a problem if this girl walks? Not half of what'll happen if she's not properly broken."

"We'll have three months to tell her about the conference and what's expected of her. She'll be ready," Alex said.

"It'll only be words," Mark countered. "What'll she have to worry about? She'll think we're soft, because that's what we are these days."

"That's not true," Justine said.

"Yes it is! This will be the third straight cakewalk you've granted and you saw the result yesterday." Leaning forward he lowered his voice. "Please, Justine, let me do this the right way. Our Circle will be weakened if we keep doing this, and I don't want to see things go bad at the conference."

"Mark," she sighed. "I'm not saying you're wrong, but you're...." she paused trying to think of the right way to say it. Coming up empty she shook her head. "Mark, you're erratic and I don't...."

"You don't trust me?" he asked, his eyes wide.

"You get a little out of control, and this is a big deal. You force her to safe out, it's over."

"I know how to play the game." He said quietly. "You have to trust me. The other Circles watch and they know I've been passed over. They'll begin to wonder why and the answer will be I'm what? Too harsh, that the east has gone so soft, their enforcer's on a leash. That initiations are no more than walk throughs?"

"Perhaps you're right," she said.

"Justine, we can't risk this now," Alex said. "It's too close to the conference. We'll let her in easy then we'll prepare her for being a pledge."

"Or I do it right and there'll be no worries. Not only that, but recent initiation videos are shown at the conference," he smiled wickedly. "So all the Circles will see the East is not weak."

"Justine," Alex began. "No one thinks we're weak, he's...."

"Yet," she said. "But we would be if Ramses didn't honor our friendship."

"So we do it my way?" Mark asked.

Justine took a deep breath and rubbed at her eyes. Alex still had a good point, but Mark had put her on the spot. The initiations had been soft and in that light, Sydney's transgression was almost not her fault. But Mark was capable of losing control. She saw he was fighting to keep the smirk off of his face. He knew he had her.

"Okay, Lovecraft," she began quietly. "I'll grant you the initiation, but on one condition."

"Name it."

"Seeing you're using the threat of punishment to back your argument, know this. If you fail me, then it's you who'll be punished, by me personally." Staring him in the eye she added, "And remember, I know how to punish you." Mark's eyes widened as she continued. "And if we go to the conference shorthanded I'll make it a point to tell Persephone it was your doing and we'll see what she comes up with for you."

Mark cocked his head and appeared to be listening to his thoughts again.

"Well, My Dark Prince?" she asked. "Are you still so sure?"

Mark's eyes slid from their light golden green to a shade of dark brown. Smiling, he whispered, "So be it."

Part Two

Chapter One

Allison Saunders looked up from the portfolio and rubbed her eyes. It was six o'clock and she'd been in the office since seven this morning and her vision was beginning to blur. Picking up her mug, she frowned when she saw it was empty. She thought about asking Cindy to get her another cup, but she'd been drinking coffee all day and was a night owl as it was. Glancing back down at the book in front of her, she turned a couple of more pages, looking at several more photos of male models. There wasn't one that really jumped out at her and as it had several times today, the thought she was wasting her time anyway, came into her mind.

In general Allison tried to remain positive and although the client she was meeting for dinners account wasn't a large one, the more clients she had the better it looked. No, she thought disgustedly, the better it was supposed to look. In reality the only thing the top executives looked at where she was concerned was her non professional assets. Closing the portfolio she hit Cindy's extension.

"Yes, Allison?"

"Cindy, I'm going to change for my meeting okay?"

"Sure, I'll call you if anyone wants to see you."

"Thanks, hon, and once I'm dressed you can go home, you've stayed late all week."

"I was hoping you'd say that, I have plans with Bill for eight," Cindy said. "Do you need me tomorrow morning?"

"No," she answered. "I'm meeting with someone, but it's at their office." With a laugh she added, "Feel free to include breakfast in your plans with Bill."

Cindy laughed and disconnecting the line, Allison pushed her chair back from the desk and stood up. Fridays were casual and, having no meetings scheduled, she was wearing a pair of jeans and a Red Sox t-shirt she wore to piss off the Yankee fans in the office. Slipping off the plain black sandals she was wearing, she walked over to the small closet and looked at the clothes hanging there. The outfits ranged from professional to things she would wear when meeting up with one of her pets. She looked at a black blouse paired with a knee length grey skirt, but shook her head. Who was she kidding?

Ted Miller was as big of a dog as there was. He would be hoping for something sexy and Allison would oblige him. She would never sleep with a client for an account, but was smart enough to use what she had to keep them hoping, and in the meantime giving her work to have an excuse to keep trying. Stripping the t-shirt off, Allison shimmied out of the tight jeans and paused to look in the full length mirror inside of the door.

Never one for modesty, Allison loved checking herself out. Especially when naked or, as she was now, dressed in only a blood red thong and matching lace bra. Allison was gorgeous, and if she ever doubted it, there were men everywhere who would line up to tell her. Her long lustrous raven black hair fell to just below her shoulder blades and was a sexy contrast against her ivory complexion. Her two best attributes in her mind however, were her full lips which despite her age gave her a slightly bratty appearance, and a pair of devastatingly bright emerald green eyes.

Allison knew that behind her back the catty bitches in the office claimed she dyed her hair and wore contacts. Much to their dismay however, Allison's beauty was all natural, from those devastating eyes, right down to her large firm tits. Letting her eyes roam from her face down her body, Allison smiled and, putting her arm against the door, struck a seductive pose. Again she had no problem admiring what she saw. At five foot six, Allison considered herself just right, not short, but not too tall. Likewise, although her lush figure sported a delightful set of curves, she would never be considered chubby.

Not for the first time, Allison thought she was the type of woman all men wanted and most women hated. Allison went to turn away, but stopped halfway to admire how good the red thong looked from behind, exposing the well rounded cheeks of her ass. Just above the thong, on the small of her back was a tattoo of a pair of cat's eyes, the exact shade of green as her own. Tossing her head she watched her black hair cascade across the creamy skin of her back. This time she did force herself to turn away before she began to get worked up.

Reaching into the closet, she selected a black mini skirt that barely went more than halfway down her thighs and a tight red blouse with a plunging neck line. Standing on her toes, Allison reached up and grabbed a pair of red stiletto heels and after slipping them on, went back over to her desk. Removing the folding mirror from her drawer, she placed it on the desk and took her time applying her makeup. Once finished, she put the mirror away and, removing a silver anklet from her purse, slipped it onto her left leg. She had just straightened when her phone beeped. Thumbing speaker, Allison answered, "I'm all set, hon, you can get going."

"Ben Watts is here to see you."

Allison rolled her eyes. Ben was a senior executive who'd been with the firm for years and whom she had worked for at one point. He was the epitome of the boys club, mid forties, not overly good at his job, but with a top position nonetheless and despite being married, hit on anything in a skirt. When she had worked for him, he had propositioned her repeatedly until she had gone to the president of the company. Instead of Ben being written up, she was transferred to another department and the two clients she had found while working for Ben had been given over to him.

She had been upset enough to look for another job, but the industry was competitive and she had already been at A&S for five years. So she stayed and continued to work twice as hard as the men for half the results. Twice in the last year she had brought in large clients only to be told the firm felt the client was too big for her and one of the more experienced partners would be taking over. Last year Allison had done fairly well, making over sixty thousand, but that was working sixty plus hour work weeks and by having a large stable of clients the boys club let her have because they were too small for them.

Allison thought about the proposal she had put together at home this week for Orion Software. Alex Warner had called her on her cell, rather than her office and she hadn't mentioned to anyone in the firm she was trying to land him. If she could, things would be different this time. She would get it in writing from Edwin Blake, the president of the company that Orion was hers, if he didn't agree she would pull the proposal.

"Allison?" Cindy's voice cut into her thoughts.

"Send him in," she replied, keeping her voice carefully neutral.

This idiot was the last thing she needed tonight. Normally Friday and Saturday nights were the time she played with her pets, but the client had insisted on tonight at eight, essentially taking up the evening. Now this loser wanted to see her and she would spend the next few minutes watching him blatantly stare at her. The door to her office opened and Ben entered. Like her, he was dressed casually in a pair of jeans and a New York Jets t-shirt. Unlike her, Ben was nothing to look at. Only a little taller than Allison, his brown hair was beginning to thin and he combed it accordingly, trying so hard to hide the fact he was calling more attention to it.

Ben was losing the battle of the bulge as more and more of his stomach seemed to be hanging over the jeans he wore on Fridays. He strolled up to her slowly, a confident smile on his face as if he were giving him time to check her out. She realized she probably was staring at him, but doubted her eyes showed anything resembling desire.

"Hey, Allison, hear you're going to pitch Ted Miller tonight."

"That's the plan," she said. "Unless you'd like to do it for me."

"Nah." Ben laughed. "Ted's all yours. I don't have quite as much to offer him as you do." He gave her a wink. "Professionally of course."

"Of course," she said with no hint of a smile on her face.

"Oh, come on, Allison," Ben said, sitting down in the chair across from her. "Let's face it; Ted's more interested in what his reps look like than what they offer. Nothing wrong with using what you got." Looking blatantly down at the considerable cleavage she was displaying he grinned. "And you have it, that's for damn sure."

"I suppose, you're right. I don't know why I'd think you'd pitch Miller."

"Right, I...."

"You'll just wait to step in and take the account when the work's done."

The smile left Ben's face.

"What are you trying to say?"

"I don't think I'm *trying* to say anything Ben." She smirked at him. "I think I was being pretty direct."

"Back to this again?" He rolled his eyes. "Look Allison, yes there have been a few instances where the partners...."

"You being one of them," she cut in.

"Decided the client was important enough to require the full attention of one of our top people. You received your commission."

"A percentage of it," she said. "I know you think all women are stupid, but I can add and you screwed me."

"That's not true."

"Funny, because Bob in payroll thought so as well, but when he went into Mr. Blake's office, he was told I was forgetting I was splitting my commission with you." She laughed humorlessly. "I think I forgot because I was never told. It must be nice to make money without working."

"Okay, look...."

"Who was the last legitimate client you brought in, Ben?" she interrupted.

"Is it that time of the month, Allison?" He shook his head. "I came in here to talk to you about a chance to get some more work and you give me this?"

"Time of the month?" She shook her head, refusing to let him bait her. "Your wife must be the envy of the neighborhood landing a smooth talker like you."

"Enough, I..."

"Let alone how loyal you are and how you go out of your way to be nice enough to put the picture of her in a drawer while you're fucking an intern."

Ben stared hard at her, and Allison returned his gaze calmly. She had no right to speak to him that way, but he knew damn well he had screwed her over and would let her get away with it.

"And just so you know, whether it's that time or not, if tonight's account hinges on Ted getting more than dinner from me, call and cancel now." She smiled. "I know he called you first and you set this up. This'd be the type of business you'd give me."

"Ted has a fair sized business, it's not like this is a waste of time. And from what I can see, you're dressing the part, so don't act like you don't know the game."

"I'm aware of the game, Ben," *and many others*, she thought, "He can sit across from a hot woman and hope people around him think he's going to get some. Personally I'd imagine most of those people would think he was paying me. However, the game ends after dessert pure and simple."

"You've made that abundantly clear in the past," Ben said.

"Yes, and almost lost my job over it." Allison glanced at the red Movado watch she had saved up for over a year to buy. "Speaking of Mr. Miller, I need to get going soon, I want to get there early and make sure our reservations are all set." Looking up at him, she put her hands out. "You said you wanted to talk about me landing some more work?"

"Right." Ben nodded. "Let's start over. First just keep this between us because there's been no announcement made yet."

"Okay."

"Peter's going to be leaving us. His father in law is offering him a fantastic position at his company and he's going to be moving to Dallas next month. That's going to leave a few choice accounts up for grabs."

"Really?" Allison asked, her interest peaked. "He does have some good ones."

"That he does, and he does good work so they'll expect more of the same."

"So how'll they be decided?" she asked, then with a frown added, "Divided up between you and the others I suppose?"

"Well that's what Blake's thinking, he does like to take care of his top earners."

"Boys club."

"Shall we stop here?" Ben asked.

May as well, she thought, but deciding to hear him out just in case, she nodded.

"No, go on; just understand I don't have a lot of confidence in my chances here."

"Well, Allison, your attitude doesn't instill confidence either, but I believe in giving you your fair shot here."

He paused as if waiting for her to thank him. She deliberately looked down and began straightening her desk. If he wanted a thank you, he was nuts. As she picked up the portfolio she'd been looking through, she saw the small tape recorder she used to practice her proposals to clients. Quickly putting her hand over it, she thumbed it on. If this went where she was thinking, it could be interesting.

"Anyway," he continued, "Bill Westcott from Harper Vineyards has expressed interest in your work, and it is your work as Bill is..." He grinned. "Let's just say he plays for the other team."

"What's that mean?"

"You know, he's..." Ben paused, "He's a fag."

"Oh." Allison nodded, fighting the urge to smile.

"He saw some of your work and asked if you could take him on."

"And you said?"

"That I had to see if you had room in your schedule."

"You know I do."

"You do?" he asked. "So how does next Friday night work for you?"

Allison's eyes narrowed, was he really offering her this?

"If it's not already clear I'll cancel what I have. Is he coming here or am I driving to Jersey?"

"Neither." He reached out and put his hand on hers. "Friday night I have a suite at the Hilton booked and I figure you can show me you're willing to finally get on board."

Sliding her hand from his while carefully keeping the recorder hidden under it, she shook her head, "Let me get this straight," she said softly. "You're telling me I can have this account, but only if I show my appreciation by getting on my knees."

"You don't have to be that crude about it. Come on, Allison, it's not like it won't be fun. I'll be good to you."

"Oh how nice of you!" she exclaimed. "Will you even put a pillow on the floor so I don't get rug burn on my knees?"

"There's that attitude again." Ben pointed at her. "When are you going to figure it out? Blake has known me and the others for years, goes golfing with our fathers and takes care of us. The only way you're going to get up to where you need to be is to just relax and play the game."

"That's all huh?" she asked. "Just let you fuck me and all of a sudden I'm making the income I should be."

"It won't happen overnight, but it'll start with Westcott and we'll add things as time goes on."

"Maybe even let me keep my own clients?" She smiled. "How magnanimous of you!"

"If you want to pass this up, it's your choice, but it's one night and if you relax we can have fun."

"You'd have fun, I'd be filing my nails after the three minutes you'd last. And it's more than just that night."

"No, really I just want...."

"It'll be every time you find me a new client, but more than that, by Saturday morning every man here will know you had me because you'll tell them."

"I swear I won't. My wife...."

"Just like you said nothing about Shirley, and Joanne, and Tammy." She shook her head. "All of them are still working here and being told that if your wife finds out there goes their job."

"Allison..."

"So simply put, Ben, I sleep with you I get the account. I don't, I get passed over until I do."

"Simply put." He sighed. "Yes, a fun night between co-workers and you'll be doing much better here."

Allison nodded and thumbed off the recorder in her hand.

"Thank you, now can you do me a favor?"

"What's that?"

"Get your two timing sleazy ass out of my fucking office."

"What did you just say?" he asked, his eyes widening.

"You heard me. I'm done with your bullshit. You and those other dogs have been drooling over me for years. This is the third time you've blatantly propositioned me and it'll be the last, understood?"

"You watch your mouth, Allison," he said his face reddening. "I could have you fired."

"Based on what?" she asked. "My sixty hour work weeks, perfect attendance and quality work?"

"Don't forget who you're talking to."

"I know exactly *what* I'm talking to." She replied keeping her voice calm. "A cheating slug who should've been fired for sexual harassment years ago, and if you don't get your sorry ass out of here that's exactly what'll happen."

"Oh really?" He gave her a nasty smile. "What are you going to do, go to Blake?"

"I made that mistake before and almost lost my job, because you have him conned into thinking you're a decent guy." She smiled at him. "No this time I think I'll go straight to an attorney."

"Good luck with that! I...." he stopped in mid sentence as she held up the recorder.

Thumbing the rewind button Allison waited a couple of seconds before hitting play.

"So simply put, Ben," her voice said from the device. "I sleep with you I get the account."

Thumbing it off, she said quietly, "Now you listen to me. Unlike you, I've worked my ass off for everything I have. I've earned every bit of what I own and will continue to do so. What I won't do is fuck a limp dicked cheating prick like you to get ahead. All I want is to be left alone to do my job and be treated fairly." Holding up the recorder, she added, "And from now on I *will* be or you can explain to Blake why he's being sued, and trust me I'll get the other women who work here to stand with me."

"Think about this, Allison."

"I have thought about it. Not only will you end up losing your job, because trust me in lieu of a lawsuit, Blake will forget all about who your daddy is, but your wife's going to walk away with the kids, the house and whatever else she wants."

Allison was whispering, in an attempt to keep the anger from entering into her voice. She had never planned this, but there was no backing down now.

"So you turn around and get out. I'll deal with the other partners, the ones who're smart enough to leave it at just staring at me. And from this point on, any client who comes my way stays with me. Understood?"

Ben swallowed hard and looked down at his hands, which she noticed were trembling. Taking a deep breath, he looked up at her and spoke quietly, "Okay, Allison, I'll leave and keep my distance, but understand this is the end of you. Think you get no leads now? I'll see to it nothing comes your way and if you go out and find leads without company approval it'll be your job."

Allison felt her stomach tighten as she thought of Warner.

"You better start looking for another job, because your days here are numbered. In a few months you'll be working twice as hard just to get your hands on the crumbs we'll throw your way. I'll start by having my father and his friends calling around until they find someone who knows your current clients and convince them you should no longer represent them."

"And this goes to the labor board as well as my attorney," she said, trying to remain confident.

"Blake has a half a dozen attorneys on retainer, and all you have is part of a conversation. No one knows the before or after and I doubt the rest of the girls will back you up. But for now I won't put Blake through this. You sit on that or use it, it's your choice. Either way, you'll be the one going down." He grinned. "And wishing all the time you had gone down, that's all it would've taken, Allison, spreading your legs just like you did for Jim Pearson back when you started here."

As she tried to keep a neutral expression, he laughed.

"What, you think no one ever heard about that? Why do you think I keep trying?" He laughed harshly. "Fucking slut, sitting here on your high horse saying you'll never take anything you haven't earned. Well I suppose maybe you earned the right to keep your job bent over Jim's desk, but I'm sure that's not what you meant."

Standing up, he began to walk towards her door. Turning he gestured around her office.

"You're only here because you used what you had, what you're probably best at. If you were smart you would've done it again, but oh well." He shrugged. "Enjoy the rest of your time here and you may want to rethink what you're willing to do, because you'll be starting at the bottom again soon enough."

He walked to the door and as he opened it stopped and again turned to face her.

"You're always telling people how proud your father is you went to college and got yourself a good job. I heard you even sent him a picture of this office when you got it." He smirked. "Did you send him a picture of you on Jim's desk?"

"Get the fuck out!" Allison snapped, losing her temper.

"I'm going; you enjoy dinner with Ted and hey, keep this conversation in mind. I'm sure if you fuck him he'll give you the account, most likely the last one you'll ever get."

After he slammed the door shut behind him, Allison let out a deep breath and put her head in her hands. What the hell had she just done? She'd put up with Ben and the others' games for years. Why had she picked tonight to make a stand? Now even the Warner account might be taken from her. Odds are Ben knew Warner or someone close to him. Maybe she should call him and cancel. It would be better not to bother than to see someone else land Orion's account.

She looked down at her cell phone and shook her head. No, she had been telling herself for the last five years, ever since she had slept with her former boss to keep her job, that if she just kept working hard and doing the next right thing she would catch her break. When Warner had called her out of the blue, Allison felt he was that break. She'd never quit anything in her life, she wouldn't start now. She would go through the motions with Miller tonight and pitch the hell out of Warner tomorrow morning. Beginning to calm down, she allowed herself a small smile. She had done the right thing sticking up for herself and tomorrow was going to be a big day for her, she could feel it.

Chapter Two

Déjà vu all over again was the thought going through Allison's mind sitting across from Ted Miller. Not that she'd expected anything less than to be hit on under the guise of doing business, but after the ugliness with Ben, it was bothering her more than it should have. Watching Ted devour the rolls in front of him as if he hadn't eaten in a week, Allison wondered why the hell she hadn't cancelled. Even before tonight's drama, it's not like there was a chance that it could end in her favor.

Miller owned a men's clothing line specializing in big and tall sizes and had come to A&S looking for an ad that could push his company to the forefront. Right from the beginning it was obvious what he was after. Initially, Allison had pushed him off on another rep because she knew all Miller would be interested in was her. The rep she had sent him to was a guy and Miller point blank told him he wanted a woman's touch.

Allison knew the touch he was looking for and again deferred him, this time to a new rep named Janet. Miller came out and said he was looking specifically for Allison. She had tried to say she was too busy, but Miller had called Ben who had been kind enough to inform him she would certainly make time for him. After an initial consultation, during which Allison dressed purposely professional, wearing slacks and a loose fitting blazer, they discussed what he wanted and she promised to come up with something.

She had put together what she considered a pretty good campaign and that's when Miller's new game started. No matter what time during the week she tried to schedule a meeting, Ted was never available. Each time she offered to stay late or meet him on a Saturday, Miller would say nights and weekends were for fun not business. Finally he suggested a Friday night dinner and Allison, seeing this as the only way to get it over with, agreed. She had at least succeeded in sending the proposal over to his office so he could look it over and hopefully speed things up at dinner.

Things hadn't started off well. Arriving at the restaurant a few minutes early, she discovered Miller had already been seated. Thinking not waiting for her told her something about his character or lack thereof, Allison followed the waiter to the table. To his credit, Miller did stand when she arrived. The credit was rapidly lost when he gave her a long slow up and down look he made no effort to conceal.

"Allison, you look amazing!" he exclaimed, coming around the table to take her hand.

"Thank you, Ted." She smiled. "It's Friday night after all."

She made to pull her hand away, but he held onto it as he gave her a kiss on the cheek. His palm was sweaty and he already reeked of scotch. Making an effort to keep the smile on her face, she stood, waiting for him to pull her seat out, but instead he went back to where he was sitting. The waiter looked at her and made a show of pulling the chair out. As she sat she also noted him looking at her legs. Taking a closer look, she pegged him for early twenties. He had dark hair, blue eyes, and an engaging smile. Allison ordered a watermelon martini and Ted another seven and seven. When the waiter, whose name was Michael left, Allison made a note to perhaps come back here some Friday night and check him out a bit more.

Ted, on the other hand, was nothing to look at unless one was using him as the before in a make-over campaign. Ted was only forty-two, but aging badly. His hair was receding and he was a good hundred pounds overweight. His complexion was as red as the tacky shirt he was wearing and Allison could see the beginnings of a whiskey bloom around his nose. He had already developed jowls and was working on his third chin. Despite that, he seemed to have an air about him as if he thought he were something.

Michael came back with the drinks and, as Allison took hers, she let her long red nails slide across the back of his hand. When he glanced at her, she gave him a wink and a coy smile. His eyes widened, but he gave her a huge smile in return. After collecting himself and removing his eyes from Allison's chest, he asked if they were ready to order. Before she could speak, Ted cut her off and placed his order for a king cut prime rib with double mashed potatoes and extra gravy. Allison ordered a Cobb salad and handed her menu over, again making contact with his hand.

"Guess that's how you keep that stunning figure of yours," Ted said as the waiter left.

Biting back the response that she could say the same for him, Allison turned to business.

"I made the changes you suggested and honestly, for your budget, I think I've done about as much as I can."

"I did see the changes." He nodded as he buttered a roll, the third he'd had since she'd sat. "Not a hundred percent sold on the model, he doesn't seem as sexy as I'd like."

"Honestly, Ted, you've been looking at a lot of women's clothing campaigns and in general men are not as eye catching as women. As a woman I'm all for the male form, but reality is, women are easier to market sexually. So unless you want to go the route of a woman wearing one of the shirts as a night shirt, I'm not sure I can sex up the campaign any more than I already have. Aside from that I'm not really sure what you would be looking for."

"Well, tell you what, Allison," he said around a mouthful of bread. "I did like what I saw in the revised proposal and as far as what I'm really looking for I have that now as well."

Here we go, she thought. Well at least he wasn't beating around the bush.

"Oh, and what do you mean by that?" she asked, smiling sweetly.

Waste her Friday night? Well seeing as she might be on borrowed time at work, she may as well enjoy this. He smiled back at her, showing off a set of nicotine stained teeth.

"What I mean is seeing I have to leave town tomorrow afternoon I don't have a lot of time and I think we both know how this game is played."

Allison regarded him silently as she sipped her martini. The audacity of this man was incredible. She would probably need a GPS to find his cock and he was expecting her to put out. Compared to Miller, Ben Watts was a stud. Well she'd had enough and was playing with house money. It was time to show Ted a different game.

"I'm not sure I know what you mean. Why don't you explain it to me? I'm still a little wet behind the ears when it comes to dealing with big clients."

"I doubt behind the ears is where you'll be wet later, honey."

Allison paused as Michael came and put their food in front of them. Once he had set the plates down, Allison couldn't resist dropping her napkin. As she knew he would, he kneeled down to pick it up which left his face level with her legs. Allison moved her right leg out, giving him a quick view of her upper left thigh, before quickly crossing her legs. After dropping the napkin again he stood up, muttered something and walked away.

"How charming!" she began "You must be quite a hit at the singles clubs." She paused and smirked at him. "Or do you pay extra for them to agree with anything you say?"

Ted stopped in the middle of raising his fork to his mouth and stared at her. "I'm sorry, Allison. I thought we were on the same page. You know how this works; you have to give a little to get a little."

"Very little is what you have to offer, Ted. No offense, but your account isn't worth wasting a Friday night so you can drool over me."

"Don't be hasty," Ted said, giving her a look she supposed he thought was intimidating. "It's not just this company. I'm involved with others and know quite a few people. Let me tell you, sweetie, I can open a lot of doors."

"I'll take my chances," she replied, and then figuring she would be leaving within the next five minutes finished her martini.

"You're that sure huh?" he asked. "Come on, it's not just about the deal, we could have some fun too." He gave her a smile that was supposed to be enticing. How the hell was this guy so full of himself?

"Really?" she asked, flashing him her best smile "You have something good for me?" she batted her eyes. Too stupid to notice she had shifted gears, Ted gave her another smile.

"Oh, my dear, I have something very special for you."

"Well let's see then."

Slipping her shoe off, Allison lifted her leg under the table and placed her bare foot onto his crotch. She held it there for a moment, enjoying the shocked expression on his face before removing it and slipping it back into her shoe.

"Well, Ted," she said. "It appears your cock, much like your account, is too small to hold my interest." Before he could respond, Allison continued, "I think were done here. Thank you for wasting my time with that pathetic offer."

Picking up her purse, Allison stood.

"Where are you going?" he asked. "What about my ad?"

"You can ask Ben to finish it for you," she said calmly. "Now if you'll excuse me, I'm going to go give a little to get a lot."

Leaving him to wonder what she was talking about, Allison turned and walked through the restaurant. On her way towards the door, she saw Michael and, going up to him, smiled. "Hey, blue eyes, I need to leave." She gave him a pout. "The man I was with was very rude to me."

"I....I'm sorry to hear that, Ma'am."

"Allison," she said. "You'd never be mean to a lady would you?"

"No, ma....ummm, Allison," he stuttered.

"Good." She put her hand on his shoulder. "So do you ever work the bar, sexy?"

"I...I wait on the tables there on Thursdays."

"Well maybe I'll see you Thursday then?" She gave him a wink and, turning, walked slowly away from him, letting him take in her legs and ass. Who said Allison couldn't play the game? She just liked younger players.

Chapter Three

As Allison waited for the valet to bring around her red Mazda, she was surprised to find herself in a good mood. In the last two hours she had painted a target on her back at work, and hadn't just tossed away a client, but insulted him and dared him to tell her boss. Despite that, she felt pretty good. She had Warner to meet with tomorrow and still felt optimistic about it. Her brief encounter with the cute blue eyed waiter had also steered her mind away from work to more pleasant thoughts.

Allison lived by two mottos. The first was work hard, play hard and second was if it feels good, do it. Both of those mantras were running through her mind as she realized that it was only nine o'clock and she was dressed to kill. Tonight had been a tough one and she needed to be sharp for tomorrow morning. It was time for a little fun to relieve the day's stress.

The best way to do that would be by having her needs catered to by someone much more her type than the pompous ass with whom she had spent the last hour. Yes, that's exactly what she needed, someone who knew their place. Allison took her cell phone from her purse and, after scrolling through several numbers, decided on Jeff, the newest of her young playmates. After several rings Jeff answered, "Yes, Mistress?"

He sounded winded; better not have one of his little girlfriends over.

"Why did you take so long to answer?"

"Sorry, I'm at work."

"I see, and what time will you get off work?"

"Eleven, my Mistress."

Allison could hear the excitement creeping into his voice. *As it should be,* she thought, Ted already fading from her mind.

"No, that's much too late. I'll be at your place at ten o' clock."

"But, Mistress, my boss..."

"If I have to ask twice, I'll never ask again. I have a phone full of young men who'd be more than happy to service me this evening. You, however, were my first choice. A poor one apparently."

" Please don't hang up! I... I'll be there!" he stammered.

"That's better. Don't be late."

Allison hung up and, approaching the valet, handed him the ticket for her car. Maybe there was still hope for the evening.

* * *

Although she had said ten, Allison arrived at Jeff's apartment at 9:40, so she could set the tone for the evening by saying he was late. Leaving her car in the parking lot across the street so he wouldn't see it, Allison walked around to the back and let herself in with the key he had been more than happy to give her. Jeff was twenty-one and worked as a bus boy at night, while attending New York State during the day. The three room apartment he lived in was in a decent neighborhood so she had no worries about waiting in the hallway.

Reaching the third floor, Allison removed her compact from her purse and reapplied her bright red lipstick. She then pushed her lips into one of her best weapons, an adorable little girl pout that belied her forceful personality. Putting the compact away, she slung her purse over her shoulder and struck an impatient pose, leaning against the railing at the top of the stair case. Allison had been seeing Jeff for three months and had him pretty well trained. Well enough that she had paid part of last month's rent for him, as she had caused him to miss a few nights of work. Jeff had protested, but she explained to him that he should enjoy the fact a hot older woman was willing to pay him to fuck her.

Hearing the downstairs door open she glanced at her watch. 9:50. He must have driven like a maniac to get here. Jeff came around the corner and had just started up the landing. He froze when he saw her leaning there. As Allison watched, two looks crossed his face: the first was an oh shit look, he knew she wouldn't be happy she was waiting. The second one she liked even better, it was pure lust.

"Mistress," he said softly as he came up the stairs "You look amazing."

"Resorting to compliments to mask your tardiness, Jeff?" She asked "You should know better than that."

"I'm sorry! I tried, but you said ten."

She cocked her head at him, "When I say ten that means you should be here before that to properly greet me at your door. Speaking of which, are you going to let us in or shall I stand here like one of your pathetic little coeds?"

"Forgive me, Mistress, I was distracted by your outfit and forgot myself."

Allison rewarded this try with a small smile. "That was much better than your first attempt, I'll give you that. Now shall we?"

Jeff unlocked the door and hit the light switch as they entered the apartment, which was small with the typical mismatched furniture of a college student. Jeff shut the door behind them and approached her.

"May I?" He asked, leaning towards her.

Allison turned her head to the side and allowed him to kiss her cheek.

"Thank you, Mistress."

She looked at him after he kissed her. Jeff was only slightly taller than her, with dirty blond hair and brown eyes. He was usually clean shaven, but tonight…

"You're scruffy!" She exclaimed, rubbing her cheek.

"I'm sorry; I was in a hurry to get to work tonight."

"It's your loss." She shrugged. "Because I hope you don't think you'll be putting that rough face between my thighs tonight."

"Of course not." He put his head down.

Allison thought for a moment. She never planned things, just went with whatever her mood was.

"You know, Jeff, I've had a very long day, and at the end I thought, you know what would be nice? Having my good looking young man take care of me, and if he did, then how could I not be good to him in return?" She sighed. "But here you are late, unshaven and having not even asked me what I'd like this evening. Maybe I should just go home and play with myself. At least I know I wouldn't be disappointed that way."

"No, Mistress," he said. "Please give me a second chance tonight."

"Why should I?" she asked, enjoying the look on his face.

Three weeks ago she had walked out on him, and then told him she had gone out and picked up another guy to play with. To add salt to the wounds, Allison had lay there and told Jeff how good William, one of her other playmates, had fucked her, while making him rub her feet and suck on her toes.

"Because I haven't had the chance to properly please you in some time and I ..." He paused and said quietly, "I don't want you to have to go elsewhere."

"That'd bother you?"

"Yes, Mistress."

"Why is that?" she asked. "You certainly don't believe this pussy is yours, do you?"

"Of course not, I'm fortunate to have what time you give me."

She nodded. "It's good you know that. I'll tell you what; because it's late and I'm in sore need of some attention, I'll give you a second chance tonight."

"Thank you, Mistress. How may I serve you?"

"Well seeing as how you asked for a second chance, I think I'll leave it up to you to impress me. Just know the second I'm bored I'll leave."

"Thank you, Mistress. May I leave the room for a moment?"

"You'd choose to leave me alone now?" she asked.

"If it pleases you, I'd like to prepare a hot shower. You did say you had a long day."

Allison paused to consider it. "That's a very good start, Jeff," she said. "Be quick about it."

"Right away, Mistress," he said as he entered the bathroom.

Allison kicked off her shoes, then removed her watch and tossed it on the coffee table. When Jeff came back she put her hands up over her head, "Undress me and be sure to keep your hands to yourself."

Jeff came up behind her, grabbed the bottom of her blouse and gently pulled it up over her head. He then unhooked her bra and slid the straps off her shoulders. Jeff was careful not to touch her tits with the sides of his hands as he slid it off her arms.

"Good boy," she said softly.

Jeff had come a long way from being the grabby, impatient young man he had been three months ago. Allison removed the clip from her hair, allowing it to fall down across the ivory skin of her back. Jeff got down to his knees and unzipped her skirt, letting it fall to her feet and leaving his face level with her ass.

"Do you like looking into my pretty green eyes Jeff?" she asked, referring to the tattoo she knew he loved.

"Oh yes," he breathed as he put his hands up to remove her thong.

"I'll take that off." She said.

Hooking her fingers through the sides, she slowly slid the thong off, bending over in Jeff's face in the process. From this angle her pussy was inches from his nose. Allison stood up and turned around so that he could see her pussy from the front now. She loved the look of absolute desire on his face as he took in her body. He was still fully clothed and it excited her to be totally naked in front of him. His eyes wandered from her pussy to her large firm tits with their light pink nipples, the silver barbell in her naval gleamed as it caught the light of the lamp.

"Do you like my body, Jeff?"

"My Mistress is perfect in every way," he whispered, his eyes glazed over with lust.

"Far better than that skinny little girlfriend of yours."

"Far better," he agreed

"And far better than you deserve," she told him.

"That goes without saying, Mistress."

"Good answer. Shall we go to the shower?"

She turned and walked to the bathroom, knowing he was following close behind, unable to take his eyes off her.

"Fix the water please," she told him as they entered the steam filled bathroom. She sighed as she waited while he adjusted the temperature. The hot air was making her sweat and feel a little drowsy.

"The water's perfect, my Mistress," he pronounced.

"We'll see," she said, stepping in as he held the curtain aside for her.

He was right, the water was just fine.

"May I wash you?"

" As long as you wash and not fondle."

Jeff stripped down to his boxers. When he went to remove those Allison stopped him, "Leave those on. I don't want your cock touching me in the shower. After all it's for my benefit not yours."

"Yes, Mistress."

Jeff entered the shower behind her and grabbed a bottle of body wash off the shelf. Pouring some into the soft sponge he had picked up, he began slowly rubbing it across her shoulders and back, Allison smelled raspberry.

"That smells nice, Jeff."

"Thank you, Mistress; it's my favorite on you."

Allison leaned back against him and he reached around to begin washing her stomach, slowly making his way up her chest. He paused with one hand just under her right breast.

"May I?"

"Yes, but just to wash."

Jeff gently lifted her tit so he could wash underneath. As he did Allison, put her arm up behind his neck, leaning her head against his. She liked the scruff, but why tell him that? He switched to her left and she lifted that arm as well.

"This is really nice Jeff!" she cooed happily while giving him a kiss on the neck.

"Thank you," he replied with a small smile before dropping to his knees and washing her legs.

Allison turned to face him and put her right foot up on his shoulder. After washing the top of her foot, he continued up her leg, his eyes fixated on her pussy. Allison switched legs, when he finished, he hesitated.

"Go ahead," she said softly.

Allison spread herself open and Jeff gently rubbed the sponge across her pussy, which was wet from more than just the shower. She let him do it several times and it felt incredible, but she wasn't ready to cum just yet.

"Enough."

Jeff stood up and took a bottle of shampoo from the shelf.

"May I wash your hair?

"Yes. I'd like that."

Jeff took his time lathering her hair, running his fingers through it, massaging her scalp. He was doing an excellent job tonight. When he had rinsed her hair, Allison turned to face him.

"Now wash yourself, you smell like food."

"Of course, Mistress."

He began soaping himself up and she had to resist the urge to do it for him. Rub his shoulders and chest, feel his muscles beneath his skin. Jeff wasn't big, but he worked out and his young body was lean and hard, which speaking of hard.

"You may remove your shorts now and clean yourself."

Jeff stripped then began washing himself. His cock stood at full attention.

"Stroke your cock for me," she whispered.

He began sliding his soapy hand up and down the length of his shaft. It looked incredible, after a moment she stopped him, "That's enough. I wouldn't want you wasting it in the shower. Now turn off the water."

Jeff obeyed then, stepping out of the shower, held up a towel.

"May I?"

Allison stepped out and turned her back to him as he began to dry her off.

"Easy!" she snapped "You don't rub me like a dog, you pat me dry gently."

"I'm sorry, my Mistress" He began to pat her softly.

"That's better. Remember, I'm much softer than you."

Jeff finished and dried himself quickly. "May I take you to my bed, Mistress?"

"You've been good so far, so yes."

She began to walk out in front of him, but he stopped her.

"Mistress, you shouldn't have to walk across the floor after you have just been cleaned."

"You do have a point there, and what would you do about it?"

"May I?"

She nodded and, putting his left arm around her waist, he bent down, put his other arm under her knees and effortlessly lifted her.

"Oooh," she cooed as he carried her towards his bedroom "This is a very nice touch."

She turned her head into his chest and began tonguing his nipple. She could feel him shudder.

"Thank you, Mistress," he breathed.

He turned sideways to get through his door, and then gently laid her on his bed.

"Would my Mistress like to roll over so that I may rub her back?"

"I'll allow it," she said, rolling over onto her stomach.

Jeff took a moment to light a couple of candles then grabbed a tube of lotion from the nightstand. For the next twenty minutes he massaged her from the bottom of her feet up to her neck. His hands were strong and firm and he was taking his time. Allison lay there thinking she should be pampered like this every day. It felt so good she could have fallen asleep, well almost. She was also getting quite wet.

"I'd like to roll over now," she said softly.

He moved to the side and she lazily rolled onto her back and smiled at him, "You're being a very good boy tonight, Jeff, I'm glad I gave you a chance." Allison stretched, watching as his eyes devoured her lush body.

"Thank you." He was positively beaming at this point.

"How do my tits look?" she asked, stretching her arms over her head. Allison had very pale pink nipples which, on her ivory skin were almost invisible.

"Fantastic, Mistress."

"Lean over and tongue them, just a minute each."

Jeff eagerly leaned over and she began breathing heavier as she watched his tongue flicking over her swollen nipples.

"Okay stop." She paused, and smiling sweetly at him, asked, "Do you have my favorite toy?"

Jeff leaned over to the nightstand and removed a silver bullet vibrator from the drawer. Allison put her hand out and he handed her the remote. Slowly spreading her legs, and loving the look on his face as she exposed her smooth pink pussy to him, she reached down and opened herself.

"Kneel between my legs." She took the egg and placed it on her clit. Allison switched it on low, she didn't want to cum quickly. "Now place the tip of your cock at my pussy, but don't put it in."

Jeff obeyed and Allison could feel him throbbing right at the edge of her pussy. She raised her legs and put her feet on his chest.

"Now ease in an inch."

He did as told, moaning softly as the head of his cock pushed into her soft, warm pussy. She turned the control up a bit more.

"A little deeper," she said.

He eased in a little more, and she could feel him twitching inside of her. Allison contracted her pussy around his cock, causing him to moan.

"Your little girlfriends can't do that can they?"

"No, Mistress," he breathed

"All the way in. slowly," she commanded.

His body trembling with the effort to take his time, Jeff pushed himself inside her. He was not large, but damn was he hard!

"Back out just as slow." She turned the vibrator up a bit more while he did as she said. "Now give me a few good hard pumps," she whispered.

"Oh yes!" she breathed as he slammed his hard young cock into her several times then obediently stopped. "Mmmm," she groaned. "You like that don't you?"

"It's a privilege to be inside of you."

"That's right and the best part is how nice and soft I am. Not at all like those bony skanks you fuck."

"They're young girls, you're an amazing woman."

"That's a good answer! As a matter of fact you've been very good tonight. I think there may be a reward for you if you make me cum nice and hard."

"Your cumming will be my reward Mistress."

Damn, Allison thought, he's on tonight. "That's right, it is, isn't it? Now put it all the way in."

Slowly, inch by inch, Jeff slid the length of his cock deep into her wet pussy.

"That's right. Push that vibrator into my clit. Oh yes." She moaned turning the bullet all the way up. "In and out, but slow."

Jeff began gently pumping her, pulling his cock out only about halfway each stroke. Every time he pushed in, he would grind the bullet into her clit. Allison licked her fingers and began playing with her nipples. The look on Jeff's face gave her almost as much pleasure as the movement of his cock inside her pussy.

"Oh that's sooo nice!" she purred as she got closer. She pushed her feet against his chest, loving the way her bright red toes looked on his tanned chest and how it forced him to strain to stay inside her. Allison could see the muscles in his arms bulge. "Yes right there," she said. "Just a little faster."

Allison emitted a yelp that sounded like a hiccup as she began to cum. Her hips bucked and the muscles in her thighs spasmed. She threw her head back and let out a long shuddering moan. She arched her back off the bed, shoving her legs harder into Jeff as waves of pleasure crashed through her body. She let out another loud cry, deliberately louder than normal. Jeff had been good and he loved hearing her cum. Shutting the vibrator off, she went limp, dropping her legs from him.

"That was very good, Jeff," she said when she had caught her breath. "That was just what I needed at the end of a long week."

"Thank you, Mistress. I hope you enjoyed that," he said, removing his cock from her pussy and the toy from her clit.

"I did." Allison reluctantly forced herself to sit up. Damn she was relaxed. "Now to show you that I keep my word, I think I owe you something special." Lowering her head, she looked up through her eyelashes at him."Would you like a little treat, Jeff?"

"Only if you feel I'm worthy." He was sitting back on his knees as he spoke, and not only was his cock standing at attention, but was glistening from her pussy.

"Yes or no?" she asked, batting her eyes "Would you like a treat?"

"Yes, Mistress."

"Yeah?" Pushing her lips into a pout and using her best little girl voice she said, "You want your Mistress to be good to you?"

"Oh yes," he said smiling.

By going from demanding to playful she was showing him he had done a good job tonight and a little reward would guarantee Allison more nights like this.

"Well then why don't you bring that nice big hard cock over here?" She tapped the side of the bed "And let your Mistress give you something special." She slowly licked her lips.

With a look of anticipation Allison loved, Jeff hopped off the bed and came over to her. Sitting up, she turned sideways and stretched herself out on her stomach, propping herself up on her elbows. Her face was at the edge of the bed and Jeff's throbbing prick was level with her face.

"You were a very good boy tonight, Jeff." She blew gently on the tip of his cock.

"Thank you Mistress," he whispered, his eyes fixed on her mouth that was no more than an inch from his cock. Allison grabbed it and squeezed.

"Oooh! Look at that!" she cooed as his cock began to drip.

Reaching out with the tip of her tongue, she licked it then slowly pulled her head back. A string of his precum trailed from his cock to her tongue before dripping off. Jeff moaned, his thighs shaking as Allison smiled up at him. Leaning forward, she placed just the tip in her mouth. He moaned again, louder this time. She was going to have to get him off or he wouldn't last thirty seconds fucking her. That was okay, he'd earned it. Allison would usually let him fuck her, but her mouth was reserved as a special reward.

Slowly, a little at a time, Allison took him all the way in, until her lips touched the base of his shaft. God, she loved the taste of herself off of a hard cock! Allison flicked her tongue around, enjoying his trembling, then just as slowly, worked him back out. She took him in again, but a little quicker this time. After teasing him a couple of more times, Allison began to bob her head, all the while keeping her eyes fixed on his. After only a minute, she knew he was getting close, but she wanted to play a bit more.

Allison stopped with just the tip in her mouth. He groaned as she began to take it a little further. When he pushed his cock all the way into her mouth, she paused, keeping her mouth still, waiting to see what he would do next. Jeff slid out part way and then back again. Allison didn't fight it. Rather she let him go one more time to let him think it was okay. This was the part of the game she loved. She had been tough in the beginning then let up on him, but now Jeff needed another lesson. After one more pump she pulled her head back.

"Are you fucking my mouth?" she asked angrily.

He froze. The look on his face was priceless!

"Mistress, I...." he paused, he knew he was done.

"I can't believe you!" she snapped and rose to her knees on the bed "How dare you? I was trying to give you a reward and you misbehave like that?!?"

"I'm so sorry, Mistress! Allow me...."

"Allow what?" she asked. "You can't possibly make this up to me. Fucking my mouth like you were even worthy to be there in the first place! Treating me like I was one of your little college sluts!" She looked hard at him. "Get me the other toy!"

Jeff reached back into the drawer and removed a six inch purple vibrator. She took it from him and assumed her former position, lying on her back.

"Get back between my legs, but at my feet!" As he did, Allison reached down between her legs and slid the vibrator inside her pussy. "You see that?" she asked as she began sliding it in and out, "That could have been your cock fucking that pussy! Couldn't it?"

"Yes, Mistress," he whispered.

"That's right! Nice long hard strokes for as long as you could do it! And you would've done it a long while, you know why?" Jeff shook his head. "Because I was going to suck you off so you'd last awhile!"

He made a whimpering noise in his throat.

"I was going to let you cum and was going to take every drop in my pretty little mouth. But no, you misbehaved, acting like an impatient little boy, but that's what you are, isn't it?"

"Yes, Mistress."

"Well now you can watch me cum."

Jeff nodded sadly. He looked as if he were going to speak then stopped. Allison removed the vibrator and looked at him.

"What?" she asked "Don't tell me you expect to be able to cum tonight?"

He looked at her helplessly.

"Please, Mistress," he begged "I was very good earlier and I..."

She laughed. "Oh, because you were good for part of the time you should get something?" She shook her head. "I think I'll leave now, I don't even want to cum, I'm so disgusted! Maybe it's not too late to find someone who knows how to follow orders."

"Oh please!" He was practically whining.

She was going to get up, and then thought of something better. "Okay, Jeff, you know what? Maybe you're right! Since you were good part of the time I'll let you cum."

"Thank you, Mistress!" He exclaimed, a look of relief on his face.

"But don't think I'll be involved, you're going to jerk off. It's all you deserve."

He paused then said, "Yes, Mistress. Thank you."

Watching him begin to stroke his cock Allison thought *what a waste*, but rules were rules.

"Come up between my legs," she told him "I want you to cum on my pussy." He eagerly knelt between her thighs, the tip of his cock inches from her. "Right here." She reached down and spread herself open. "I want to feel it running down my pussy."

It only took Jeff a few more strokes and, with a loud groan, he came. With an effort, Allison held back a moan of pleasure at how good his hot cum felt hitting and dripping down her smooth pussy. Jeff had it pointed right at her clit and she could feel each spurt. Her thighs began to tremble with the need to cum again.

"That's a lot of cum!" She said. "What a shame. Imagine that all could have been in my mouth, and I would've swallowed every drop!" Shaking her head disgustedly, she sighed. "You've made a mess of my pretty pussy, Jeff."

He swallowed hard. "I'm sorry! Here let me clean you off!" He leaned down and reached over to grab a towel.

"You'd wipe me with something from the floor?" she raged. "Something you probably wiped your ass with in the shower? I don't think so! As a matter of fact, just for that I think you'll clean it with your tongue."

He gave her a distressed look. "Mistress, I can't..."

"Not true. You have a tongue so you can. Sounds more like you won't! If you don't that's fine, but you'll never see me again. Now, do I clean myself or do you accept your punishment?"

God that cum dripping on her pussy was hot, she was getting wound up again. In the meantime, Jeff was staring at her. At first his eyes seemed to harden as if he were going to refuse. Allison returned his stare steadily, her unblinking emerald eyes boring into his. After a moment she cocked her head and smiled slightly. With an almost audible snap, Jeff's will broke.

"As you wish." he said softly.

With a delicious look of resignation on his face he lay on his stomach between her legs and began to gingerly lap up his own cum.

"Just think that should have been in my mouth, not yours!"

Allison began to squirm. She was close to cumming, but was so wet she couldn't quite get there. She grabbed Jeff's hair and started grinding her cum soaked pussy into his face, forcing him to lick harder. Allison looked down and caught Jeff just as he finished a lick, his cum was dripping from his tongue and his cheeks were covered with it, but it was the helpless look in his eyes that pushed her over. Allison wrapped her thighs around his head, drawing his face even deeper into her cum smeared pussy.

This time she came even harder, arching her back so far she could feel it crack and letting out a cry she was sure Jeff's neighbors could hear. The entire time she was cumming she had his hair in her hands and was grinding and smearing his own cum, now mixed with hers, into his mouth and tongue. With one more twitch of her hips, Allison lay back, panting. "That was very good, Jeff! I came much harder that time! You can wipe us off with something now."

"Thank you, Mistress," he said, not sounding too happy, but it wasn't about him anyway.

Grabbing a towel, he gently wiped her pussy off, then his face.

"Will my Mistress be leaving or would she like to rest?" he asked. "Maybe spend the night?"

Allison smiled to herself. This boy had just licked his own cum off of her and he was asking her to stay. Truly one of the best she'd trained. However, she couldn't let on.

"Now you know better than that! Even when you behave, you're not worthy of waking up next to me. But I'll take a nap so set your alarm for an hour from now."

After he did he looked at the bed."May I join you?"

Allison looked at him, her eyes already half shut. Part of her wanted to tell him to sleep on the floor, but he had been humiliated enough. "Lie across the foot of the bed," she told him.

Jeff awkwardly lay across the bottom of the bed on his stomach and she stretched her legs out, putting her feet on his back. Once again, she relished the half disgusted; half smitten look on his face as he turned his head to face her. Perhaps she would do something nice for him before she left. After all, a pet this controllable was rare indeed. Sliding her feet across his back, Allison opened her legs so that he would be staring directly at her pussy.

"Tell you what, Jeff," she began drowsily. "You don't move down there and let me sleep perhaps I'll let you fuck me..." Jeff started to say something, but she continued. "Not for your benefit, but thanks to your screw up I really didn't get much, and why should I be denied a good fuck?" She smirked. "Or in your case a mediocre one."

"My mistress is too kind," he forced himself to reply.

"Well that remains to be seen." Allison closed her eyes and sighed contentedly. "Sweet dreams, Jeff."

Chapter Four

Allison opened her eyes and, turning her head to see the alarm clock, saw it was ten a.m. With a sigh, she reached out and turned it off. She had set it for ten thirty, but figured if she fell asleep again, she would feel worse when it went off. Taking a chance, she closed her eyes for another minute, basking in that delightful drowsy feeling she so loved. If not for her meeting with Warner, Allison could easily stay in bed until early afternoon.

She opened her eyes and rubbing the sleep from them caught the scent of her pussy on her fingers. Sliding her hand under her nose, she inhaled deeply and smiled. She had woken up around seven and after going to the bathroom, was wide awake, her mind beginning to spin. She thought of last night's run in with Ben and the possible consequences followed by her telling Miller off. From there she started worrying about the meeting with Warner. Knowing it was far too early to stay awake; Allison forced her mind to focus on the best part of yesterday, her night with Jeff.

No sooner had his name entered her mind, Allison recalled the look on his cum covered face as he licked her pussy. Within moments, her hand had slipped down between her legs and begun to rub her clit. She came quickly and surprisingly hard, then rolling over, immediately fell back to sleep. Now smelling her fingers had gotten her thinking again. Drawing her leg up, Allison kicked the sheet off and looked down along the length of her body, admiring the way her fair skin looked against the black sheets. Allison had slept in just a pair of black lace boy shorts and, sliding her hand down, reached into them and moaned as she found her swollen clit.

While her fingers rolled her excited flesh between them, Allison's left hand drifted up and began playing with her nipple. Closing her eyes, she thought of how after she'd awoken from her nap, she had Jeff worship her feet. She had laid there dripping while he worked all ten of her toes, alternately licking them and sucking them into his mouth. When she couldn't hold back any longer, Allison told him to slide up between her legs and fuck her.

Jeff had been more than happy to oblige and as he knelt between her legs, Allison placed her feet on his shoulders and told him to go ahead and fuck the shit out of her. Grabbing her thighs, Jeff tore into her, driving his hard young cock into her repeatedly while she stroked her clit and moaned. When Jeff turned his head and started licking her foot again, Allison threw back her head and came like an animal. Screaming harder than she had in a long time, Allison bucked and writhed beneath him as her pussy contracted around his cock. Unfortunately he couldn't last long giving it to her like that, but she forgave him as she enjoyed the sight of his hot cum spraying onto her stomach and thighs.

Allison gasped and, sliding her hand down, spread herself open and added another finger around her clit. Straightening her legs, she tightened them around her hand and whimpered as a deliciously slow orgasm flowed though her. With a satisfied purr, she let herself go limp on the bed and laid there with her eyes closed. Damn that had felt good! The only thing that could make it better would be to go back to sleep again. Allison had spent entire Sundays like this, rolling around in bed, sleeping and playing with herself.

But not today, she sighed and cleared her mind of all thoughts of fun. Today was a big day for her. Alex Warner was a big fish and she had never needed a client so badly. Sitting up and leaning against the headboard, Allison wondered for the hundredth time since it happened why she had picked last night to challenge Ben. She should have just rolled her eyes and blown him off as she always did. Now even if she landed Warner, she may lose him. No, no ifs. She would get Orion's business. Allison's ideas were better than what his current firm was putting out there and although he was rumored to be difficult, Warner had a reputation as going with nothing but the best.

She would bring the contract she had drawn up from home with her and wouldn't leave until he signed it. Allison would refuse to accept no for an answer today and would do anything it took. She stopped at that last thought. Anything? Back to sex again. Warner was good looking, wealthy and a notorious lady killer. It was hard for Allison to imagine him not hitting on her. Granted not every man was like that, although recent experience seemed to refute that idea. Warner however, had flirted with her at the charity dinner a couple of weeks ago. She had a buzz and not thinking clearly, blew him off, which made it more surprising he had called her. The fact he had contacted her on her cell had made her wonder if he was looking for a rematch.

Sad to say in her current circumstances, Allison was going to have to consider it. Her roommate of the last four years, Jennifer, had moved out four months ago to live with her fiancé and the rent for the two bedroom Manhattan apartment was more than she could handle comfortably. Each of the last few months she had dipped into her savings to make the full amount. Allison had known Jennifer since college and didn't like the idea of trying to find a roommate. She liked the idea of moving even less so the only alternative was to make more money and quickly. Warner was still under contract, but because he was launching a new product, had decided to shop it around. With the budget he was proposing, Allison, doing some quick math, figured her commission to be close to five thousand, which would be enough to give her a cushion for the next few months.

So if push came to shove, Allison was prepared to do what she said she never would again, and that was use sex to get ahead. Hopefully Warner wasn't a kiss and tell fool like the jerks she worked with. She thought of one of those jerks: Jim Pearson. Allison shook her head disgustedly. That had been a tough pill to swallow, hearing Ben bring that up last night. All these years Allison had assumed no one had known. Despite her love of sex, there had only been two occasions Allison had slept with someone to get ahead.

The first one she didn't regret because it had indirectly led her to discover her dominant side. Allison's father couldn't afford to send her to college, but because of her excellent grades, she had landed a scholarship to the University of New York. She had also been accepted to Florida State which was a better school, but as a Florida resident she would have had to stay living at home. Allison desperately wanted to get away from Florida and her older brother, Jack, who hated her, and live her own life. She had also always wanted to see New York so the choice was fairly easy.

Her scholarship, which included living on campus, was contingent on her maintaining a certain grade point average and in her sophomore year, Allison was having a difficult time with English. By the time of her midterm, despite working her ass off and doing extra credit, she was still looking at a C. The midterm exam would be a third of the grade and if she could get an A it would pull her up to the B she required. Professor Stafford was in his forties and as far as Allison knew, single. He had worked with her after class several times and had never given her the impression he was into fooling around with his students, but she decided to try.

Allison sat in the front of the class and, for the week leading up to the midterm, had worn short skirts and revealing blouses. By the third day there was no mistaking he was staring at her. When they were working in their notebooks, she would look up and catch him looking. He would always look quickly away, but a couple of times Allison had managed to give him a wink. The day before the exam she had worn a t-shirt a size too small that made it painfully obvious to Stafford she wasn't wearing a bra. It was obvious to everyone else as well and Allison had been wet all morning, watching every guy that passed stop to stare at her. She had no boyfriend and had developed a rep as girl who was a damn good time and was hit on left and right, but at the moment Stafford was her only target.

He couldn't keep his eyes off of her, and once, when Allison was sure the students around her were all reading, she reached up and lightly ran her fingers over her hard nipples for him. Approaching him after class, Allison simply smiled and asked him if there was anything he could do to give her some last minute help with the midterm. Stafford had stared at her nervously, desperately trying to keep his eyes on her face. Finally in a shaky voice he said he had to attend a department meeting in five minutes, but if she didn't do well on the following days test, perhaps they could work something out for her to get some extra credit during the rest of the semester.

Allison had given him a huge smile and said okay, but when she walked away had no intention of playing teacher's pet for the rest of the year. She would get her grade the next day. The day of the test, Allison wore the shortest skirt she owned, the same one she wore at her part time waitressing job. Sitting in the front, she watched until Stafford looked up at her, and opened her legs to show him she was not wearing panties. His mouth opened and Allison closed her legs before other students noticed him looking.

The test was three hours and Allison, who had been studying her ass off, sweated through it, doing the best she could, but knowing damn well it wouldn't be enough to get an A. When the test ended Allison made sure she was the last student up to the desk so her test would be on top. She walked out of the classroom with the other students, and then stayed near the door. When her classmates had made their way down the corridor, Allison quickly slipped back into the classroom and, closing the door, locked it behind her.

There was no window to the classroom door and as soon as she turned around, she slipped her blouse off, then her bra. Stafford had sat there speechless, his mouth open as Allison sauntered slowly over to him, giving him as much time as possible to take in her bare tits. Walking around his desk, she grabbed the arm of his chair and, turning him to face her, cupped her left tit and placed her nipple at his lips. Stafford swallowed hard and in a barely audible whisper asked, "A....Allison what are you....?"

"I'm trying to earn some extra credit sir," she answered, giving him a huge smile and pressing her tit against his cheek. "You said you'd be willing to work with me." Leaning over, she whispered in his ear. "And, Mr. Stafford, honey, I'm willing to work very hard to not *blow* this grade."

Straightening, Allison again presented her tit to him, and with an air of a drowning man going down for the last time, Stafford opened his mouth and allowed her to shove her nipple inside. He eagerly sucked on it, and Allison released an exaggeratedly loud moan. Stafford's hands came up and began to fondle her tits as his tongue went back and forth between her nipples. Allison's hand dropped down into his crotch and rubbed his cock through his pants. As Stafford had continued to suck on her tits, Allison reached over to the stack of papers, removing hers and putting it in front of him. Backing away, she dropped to her knees and, quickly undoing his zipper, reached in and pulled his cock out.

"Oooh," she cooed. "Mr. Stafford, is this all for me?"

"Yes," he managed weakly

Grabbing the sides of his pants she tugged and, lifting his hips, Stafford allowed her to pull his pants down.

She smiled up at him. "This is my after school project?"

His reply was swallowed up by a loud moan as, ducking her head, Allison swirled her tongue around his balls. He groaned even louder as she sucked on them while stroking his cock. Sliding her tongue slowly up his shaft, Allison swirled her tongue around the head before giving it a kiss. Allison wrapped her tits around his throbbing dick and started sliding them up and down, tit fucking him. Bending her head, she placed the tip of her tongue into the slit of his dick and came away with a trail of his pre-cum.

"Oh, God," Stafford groaned, his hips twitching.

Looking up at him, Allison said softly, "Mr. Stafford, honey, I really need an A on this test today."

"I..."

"I think I've been a good student, don't you?" Again, his answer turned into a moan as Allison took him quickly into her mouth and sucked hard on his cock. Removing it, she licked her lips and smiled up at him. "Do you think if I finish this project maybe I could get that A?"

Stafford had been sweating and she could see his hands trembling where they were resting on the arms of his chair. Taking a breath he said softly, "Why yes, Miss Saunders, I....I think that would be a fair exchange."

"Good," she said. "Because I'd love to show you what a good student I am." Allison took him briefly into her mouth, before giving him a pout. "Am I a good student, sir?"

"I daresay you're my favorite student, Miss Saunders," Stafford replied, with a slight smile.

"Oh good!" she purred. "Because this good student loves to be a bad girl."

Bowing her head, Allison went to work. This time she took Stafford all the way into her mouth, so deep she her lower lip was touching his balls. Stafford moaned loudly and his hips twitched as she held his cock there and began slowly shaking her head.

"Oh damn, that's good!" Stafford groaned.

Giving him a wink, Allison started to bob her head in a slow steady rhythm. She was taking him all the way down, sliding her full soft lips all the way back to his dripping tip before again deep throating him. He wasn't small, but Allison had been sucking cock like a sporting event since she was fifteen and was having no trouble handling him. Wanting to give him an even bigger thrill, she reached out and, grabbing his right hand, placed it on the back of her head. As she continued to suck, she felt him pushing and pulling on her head, not roughly, but gently guiding her.

"Hmmm-mmmm," she encouraged, sucking him faster.

Allison's hands were on his thighs and when they began to tremble, she sped up some more. When Stafford was moaning continuously and his hips began to rock back and forth, Allison removed his cock from her mouth. Stafford groaned and she said, "Mr. Stafford, please be a dear and grade my paper."

Stafford looked at her for a moment, and then moving so quickly he dropped his pen twice, marked her exam "A, your hard work has paid off, Miss Saunders!"

Laughing, Allison had immediately gone back to sucking his cock. Knowing she was going to be asking for more from him, she began to tease and let him enjoy it. Twice she removed his cock and went back to sucking on his balls, before finally, when his moans were turning into whimpers, taking him deep and sucking him as fast and hard as she could. Stafford cried out and his cock went off in her mouth, sending his hot thick cum down her throat. Allison moaned and it wasn't a fake one, she had always loved the taste of cum and the feeling of a hard cock twitching in her throat. Allison continued to suck, taking everything he had and trying for more. Stafford moaned as she sucked hard enough on the head of his cock to get a couple of more drops, then slumped back into his seat, panting as she opened her mouth, showing him she had swallowed every drop.

"Damn," he panted. "That was...." He paused and whispered, "You can't say anything, Allison, I'll...."

Standing in front of him so his eyes were level with her tits, she shook her head, "No worries, Mr. Stafford, all I want is a fair deal." She smiled. "And speaking of sir, I have another deal for you."

"You do?"

"Yes, sir. On my end I promise I'll study and do the best I can to pass, but at the end of this course I need an A."

Sitting on the edge of his desk, Allison hiked her skirt up and opened her legs, exposing her pussy.

"Jesus," Stafford whispered as she spread herself open for him.

"If I get that A, I promise you can have anything you want from me for a night." She winked. "I'll even pay for the hotel."

"How...how do I know you will?" he asked.

Allison slid two fingers into her pussy then shoved them into his mouth. As he greedily sucked on them, his eyes rolling with pleasure, Allison asked "Do I seem like a tease?"

Allison slid back down onto the bed as her mind wandered back in time. Despite having just masturbated, the thought of what transpired with Stafford at that hotel room at the end of the year, already had her pussy heating up again. Reaching over and opening the night stand drawer, Allison removed a slim purple vibrator and, placing the tip of it onto her clit, turned it on. Closing her eyes, she let her mind drift back to that eventful night ten years ago.

Allison continued to work hard, but was due to finish the class with a low B. That would be enough to keep her scholarship, but she had A's in every other class and was willing to honor her deal with Stafford. He wasn't a bad looking guy for his age, and hadn't hit on her between the day she blew him and the end of the class. On the day the final scores were posted and she saw she received an A, she went to his office and dropped a card with the name of a small motel on it.

Stafford met her there at eight and by eight thirty, Allison was laying naked on the bed, more than a little disappointed. Stafford had stripped immediately and gotten on the bed, Allison had followed suit and after sucking on him for a moment laid back and spread her legs, figuring he would take a good long time appreciating her young body. Instead, Stafford was like a teenager. After sucking on her tits, he slid between her legs and gave her pussy a few quick licks, as if her clit was a lollypop. Sitting up, he asked her to get on her knees. Allison rolled over and put her ass in the air for him, and grabbing her hips, he proceeded to fuck her for all of two minutes before he groaned and sprayed her ass with his cum.

Allison had rolled back over; hoping Stafford would go back between her legs, but instead he apologized for going off so quickly and went into the bathroom. When he closed the door behind him, she had laid there for a few minutes wondering what the hell was wrong with him. Surely that couldn't be it? Disgusted, she was going to leave, but had left her purse in the bathroom. Deciding to stay undressed so he could get one more look at what he could have had for the night; Allison sat on the edge of the bed facing the bathroom door.

When Stafford came out, he walked over to the bed and Allison felt her hopes rise when he knelt on the floor between her legs. Thinking he wanted to go down on her, she started to lean back to put her legs on his shoulders. Stafford grabbed her ankles, holding her legs down and looking up at her said, "You have very sexy feet, Allison."

"Umm....thank you," she replied.

He cupped her foot in his hand and, bringing it to his lips asked, "May I kiss them?"

"Sure." Allison shrugged. "If you want to."

She'd heard of foot fetishes, but hadn't been with anyone that had one. Stafford gently kissed the tips of each of her toes, before beginning to lick them. Allison gasped at the sensation of his soft wet tongue going across her toes. Stafford then sucked two of her toes into his mouth and began swirling his tongue around them. Allison let out a surprised moan and felt her pussy begin to moisten.

"You know," he said, looking up at her, "This would be a better game if you told me to do it."

Not sure what he was talking about, but not wanting him to stop using his tongue on her feet, Allison said, "Mr. Strafford, I want you to lick my feet."

"No," he said quietly. "I want you to tell me as if I'm being punished by you," He then gave her a smile that caused her pussy to become even hotter. "But yet as if it's a privilege for me to do so." He nodded. "Now try again, and call me Kyle."

Lifting her foot, he brought her toes to his lips, and teasingly by flicked his tongue along the top of her foot. A shudder went through her, and her nipples were so hard they were beginning to ache.

"Mr.... Kyle," she began, "Would you...." She stopped when shaking his head; he started to lower her foot. "Don't you dare put my foot down!" she snapped.

Stafford froze as did Allison, surprised at how harshly she'd spoken. As she looked down at him, she saw Stafford had a look of expectation on his face. When she didn't speak right away, Stafford helped her along. "I'm sorry, Allison, I...."

"You should be sorry!" she exclaimed. "Now put my toes back in your mouth and start sucking them again until I tell you to stop."

"Yes, Allison," Stafford whispered in a tone that sent a surge of heat between her legs.

Stafford put her toes back in his mouth and Allison began to breathe heavier and her heart was pounding. Raising her leg she told him, "Now the other."

"It'd be my pleasure," he said, grabbing her other foot.

"Damn straight it is," she said. "An old man like you getting to suck on my pretty little toes." She made a disgusted sound. "God only knows nothing here has been my pleasure."

The effect on Stafford was amazing. Putting his head down, he whispered, "Of course, Allison. You're better than I deserve."

He proceeded to suck on her toes as if they were the most delicious thing he had ever placed in his mouth. By now her pussy wasn't the only thing that was hot. Allison could feel her cheeks flushing and she was beginning to sweat, after enjoying him working her toes, another even sexier image leaped into her mind.

"Now lick my feet."

Stafford obediently removed her toes from his mouth and licked the top of her foot. It looked good and felt even better, but it wasn't what she wanted.

"Not like that!" She pulled her foot from his grasp and held it up in front of him. "Lick the bottom," He hesitated and she snapped, "Now!"

Stafford quickly ran his tongue along the length of her foot and Allison moaned. He moaned at her enjoyment and getting bolder, she continued, "Faster, like a dog." She laughed nastily. "Because that's what you are, aren't you? Look at you, giving away a grade so you can suck my toes. Nothing but a dog."

"Of course, Allison,." he said, pausing between licks. "I'm not worthy to even lick your feet."

He went back to licking and, unable to take it anymore, Allison's hand went between her legs; she needed to cum and began to stroke her clit while watching him. As she rubbed her clit, she thought it was a shame she had to get herself off. That thought was followed by another, why should she have to do it?

"You're enjoying that aren't you?" Allison questioned.

For emphasis she dropped her other foot onto Stafford's rock hard cock.

"Oh, yes." He panted as she rubbed her foot along his cock. She could feel his sticky pre-cum on her foot and on a whim, brought her foot to his face.

"You made a mess, clean it up." She had thought she was pushing it, but to her delight, Stafford grabbed her ankle and licked his own fluid from her foot. "Damn, you even like that." She shook her head disgustedly.

"I do," he began. "You have gorgeous…."

"Well that's nice that you want to lick my feet isn't it?" She cut him off. "That's what *you* want well this is about what I want and what I want is for you to lick my pussy."

Allison had no idea where that had come from, but it sounded good and damn was she getting worked up. Stafford didn't mind either, putting her foot down and spreading her legs he whispered, "Yes, Allison, whatever you wish."

He leaned in and began swirling his tongue around her clit, and forcing herself not to moan to show him she was enjoying it, said, "Damn straight whatever I want. What I really wanted was a good fuck, but since you can't seem to give me one I'll settle for you sucking me off instead."

"Of course, Allison," he answered, his eyes filled with lust.

Allison couldn't believe it, he was getting off on being humiliated and she loved doing it to him. His tongue was doing a much better job on her than it had earlier, but she was caught up now and kept going.

"Not that you deserve to taste that pussy after that sorry ass fucking you gave me." Moving as if she had done this before, Allison put her foot on his shoulder. She pushed him back hard enough to make him fall over and shook her head disgustedly. "You know what? You're terrible at that too so just sit back and watch me."

Allison began to play with her pussy, and when he sat up told him, "That's right stare at that pussy that you're no good at pleasing and while you're watching, get back to sucking my toes again. That way you'll at least be doing something, you worthless excuse of a lover."

Stafford did as she said, and no sooner had her toes gone back into his mouth, then she came harder and louder than ever before. When she finished, she made Stafford lie on the bed, and stroke himself, begging her to fuck him. She hopped on and rode him, stopping and starting and teasing him with her pussy until he was so frustrated he was whining and pleading with her like a child. Allison had slid up and, sitting on his face, made him suck her off, while she stroked his cock and told him he couldn't come until she did. When Stafford finally came, his cum spurted so hard he had cried out in pain.

From that day on Allison had been in control. The next boy she slept with she had lain on the bed and wouldn't let him touch her until he licked her feet. When he refused, she had thrown him out of her room. The next day he came back and agreed to do it. Allison had been playing the game ever since and it just kept getting better. She gasped and clamped her legs together as the image of Stafford lying on his back, begging to cum sent her over the edge and her third orgasm of the morning crashed through her.

No sooner had she shut the vibrator off then her cell began ringing. With a groan, she forced herself out of bed. Grabbing the phone from the bureau she looked at the screen, it was Ben Watts. Allison let it ring and when the phone beeped to tell her she had a voicemail, took a deep breath and listened to it.

"Allison, its Ben. I just met with Ted Miller, and he's not happy. Neither am I, and Blake won't be either when the two of us sit down with him on Monday afternoon. You better start packing your things because I don't think Blake is going to see this your way." There was a pause and he added, "And do bring that little recording of yours, because trust me, that's not getting you anywhere but fired. Blake knows all about your little promotion from Jim and that you're a little whore."

Allison put the phone down. Talk about a mood killer. Turning from the bureau, she sat on the edge of the bed. She didn't think Blake would fire her, she was good and he knew it. But he would let Ben do whatever he wanted to make things hard on her. She still couldn't believe Ben had known about her and her former boss all these years. That had been the second time she had used sex to get what she needed and this one did bother her.

Allison had started at A&S when she was twenty-two and, because of the abundance of reps at the time, had been stuck in an entry level position. The company was doing poorly and then department manager Jim Pearson went on a spree and fired more than half the reps. He then gathered Allison together with the two other people who were working with her and explained he was cutting back and only one of them could stay.

On the plus side that person was going to get a chance to do some real work. Pearson told the three of them he was going to give them a campaign to work on and he would keep the person who came up with the best ideas. Better yet, they would get to keep the client and become a rep. The only thing Pearson told them about what he wanted was it needed to be a sexy angle and was to be on his desk first thing Friday morning.

Allison was excited, but nervous. She knew she was better than the other two, but one of them was the nephew of a current ad exec and she was pretty sure he would have an edge. She expressed those concerns to another employee who had been there for years. He took her into his office and told her Jim was married, but fooled around and hired women who "played ball" as he put it. Allison said she wouldn't do that and he had shrugged and said it wasn't right, but might be her only chance.

After giving it some thought, Allison decided she would have to do it. She had very little money put away and if she lost her job might have to move back to Florida. Her father had been so proud of her when she got hired there, she didn't want to let him down. Nor did she want to return home a failure. That Friday Allison arrived early and talked the janitor into letting her into Jim's office under the pretense of setting up her proposal. When Jim walked into the office, Allison was lying naked on his desk. As he stood there wide eyed, she slowly lifted her legs and, letting them fall open to expose her pussy, whispered, "Is this a sexy enough angle for you, Mr. Pearson?"

Pearson had locked his door and fucked Allison hard over the desk, then told her the job was hers, but he wanted more. For the next month she let him fuck her several times, then one night he told her he had to be careful, because his wife was getting suspicious. He told her to just work as hard as she had been and she would do well at the firm. Six months later, he called her into his office to tell her he was leaving A&S. In a move that surprised her, Pearson told her he was promoting her before he left so her job would be guaranteed. She thanked him and he told her it was not just because she had fooled around with him, but because he felt she was that good. He added with a smirk he would have hired her without the sex, but he sure as hell wasn't going to turn it down.

That had been five years ago and Allison had worked her ass off, never hearing a word about what had happened between her and Jim until last night. All this time she felt everyone there thought she'd earned her keep and now here was Ben hitting on her because he figured it would be a matter of time before she would play ball again. Dropping the phone Allison walked out of the bedroom and over to her desk.

She looked down at the folders containing her proposals to Warner and wondered if she was prepared to give into the boys club again. Hopefully it wouldn't come to that, but if it did, Allison would do what she had to. Hell, she thought with a shrug, Warner was a good looking guy, but pretty full of himself, and probably never had to work to get a woman in his bed. Allison looked over at her reflection in the mirror on the dining room wall, taking in her large tits, and lush figure. She might have to earn the contract, but Alex Warner was going to have to earn her. She smiled at her reflection. Let the game begin.

Chapter Five

Allison arrived at the corporate office of Orion software at eleven fifty and after giving her name to the security guard, waited while he called upstairs to Warner's office. Orion occupied the top three floors of the modern glass office building and she couldn't fathom what it cost for rent. Then again when your company reported a fifty million dollar plus profit last year, rent was probably not much of a concern. Another security guard came from the small office behind the desk and said Warner had confirmed her appointment and he would escort her upstairs.

Standing in front of the glass doors of the elevator, Allison gave herself a quick once over. She was dressed in a black skirt that was short enough to show off her legs, but not enough to be considered inappropriate. For a top, she chose a short sleeve black blouse that buttoned halfway up. Underneath that was a tight red tank top with a lace neckline. Due to the heat, her legs were bare, and she was wearing red sandals with three inch heels. All in all, the look said sexy professional. If she felt the game was starting, she could remove the blouse and the skirt was short enough to allow a look up to her black thong if she opened her legs.

Allison felt a rare feeling of anxiety. Normally she was confident and if nothing else generally had the attitude things were meant to be, you did your best and hoped for the best. Today was different; her heart was beating faster than normal and her stomach felt tight. If she could bring Warner into the fold, it would make it difficult for Ben to convince Blake to fire her, but then again, he may just take Warner from her. First things first, she told her racing mind. The deal with Warner was the priority right now, without that there was nothing to do, but start packing, both her office and most likely her home. When the elevator reached the top floor, the doors opened and Allison found herself face to face with Alex Warner.

"Good morning, Allison," he said, flashing an engaging smile she imagined had helped to set up many of his female conquests. Standing aside as she exited, he continued, "I'm so glad you could make time for me on a Saturday."

"I'm glad to be able to have the time Mr. Warner," Allison replied as she turned the full force of her own not inconsiderable smile on him.

"Alex, please," he said as he took her hand and brought it to his lips, another calculated smooth move she was sure. "It's Saturday, I get enough Mr. Warner during the week." Looking over her shoulder he addressed the guard. "I'm all set, James, thank you."

James nodded and, as the elevator closed behind them, Alex's cell began to ring. Removing it from his side he frowned at the number. "I'm sorry, I have to take this, but it'll only be a minute."

Allison nodded and watched as Warner walked a few feet away and leaned against the wall while speaking. He was facing her, but looking down and she took the time to take him in. Warner was in his early forties, but looked damn good for his age. Although a bit on the shorter side his shoulders were broad and the muscles in his arms were pretty damn impressive, stretching the material of the plain black t-shirt he was wearing. Despite his large upper body, Warner had a narrow waist, giving him the triangular build of a weight lifter.

Warner's hair was short and thick, but still as dark as Allison's own, leaving her wondering if he dyed it. He was good looking in a rugged way, with a strong jaw and even features, but by far the main attraction was a pair of deep blue eyes that could best be described as electric. Coupled with that killer smile, Allison could easily see how he had bedded pretty much any woman he wanted. The fact he was worth upwards of fifty million didn't hurt either. Allison couldn't make out what he was saying, but his voice was deep and smooth, yet another weapon in a pretty impressive arsenal. Hanging up, Warner walked back over to her.

"I have to say, Allison, you're as beautiful as I remember from John's charity dinner."

"As are you," she replied, then taking a chance laughed, "But I think you already know that don't you?"

Alex looked at her and Allison thought oh, shit, but a moment later he burst out laughing.

"You do your homework don't you?" He shook his head, still smiling. "I guess I'm guilty of spending more than my fair share of time in front of a mirror."

"Sorry." She grinned at him. "I couldn't resist."

"No worries," he said. "I enjoy it when someone makes fun of me."

"You do?"

"Yeah, it makes me feel like one of the guys," he told her. "Think about it, how many people around here do you think tell me what they really think as opposed to what they think I want to hear?"

"Not many I suppose."

"Hardly any. In fact." He pointed at her. "You know how guys like me have yes men following them around? I'm going to hire a no man, just to keep me on my toes."

Allison laughed. "That'd be different."

"Different, but useful. It's good to be denied once in awhile." Giving her a wink, he continued, "Although I doubt you've been denied too often."

"About as often as you hear the word no." She returned the wink.

"I like you already, Allison," Alex said. "Now shall we?"

Allison followed Warner down the corridor and into a suite of offices. There was no one else working and, when Warner reached the waiting area where his office was, she noticed there was no receptionist at the desk. The two of them were alone in the suite. Allison sighed; this would be more than a business meeting.

"No one else here?" she asked.

"No, the only people who work up here are number crunchers. No need for them to be in on a Saturday, the sales departments and tech support are on the lower floors there are some people working there today." He shrugged. "That's why I like Saturdays. I get more done with no one bugging me. It's very relaxing. Which speaking of," he gestured down at the jeans he was wearing. "Pardon my appearance, I wear suits all week."

"No worries, it's your office," she replied, and the jeans were certainly more flattering than a suit would be.

Warner led the way around the desk and, opening the large oak door to his office, stepped aside. "After you."

Allison walked into the office and stopped, her eyes widening. She had never seen an office as large as Warner's; it had to be the size of her entire apartment. Directly across from her, in front of a huge window was an enormous cherry wood desk. Between Allison and the desk was a glass coffee table surrounded by leather chairs. Along one wall was a long bar and opposite of that, was a bookcase that ran the length of the office.

As Alex walked past her, she began to follow while looking at the large glass trophy case that was located next to the bar. Taking a couple of steps towards it, Allison saw several boxing trophies as well as many awards for scholastic achievements. As Alex walked over and picked up a folder that Allison recognized as the one she had sent him containing her proposal, she shook her head at the furnishings, the entire office breathed success.

"Have a seat at the table, Allison," He gestured towards the center of the room. "I'm going to make a drink. What would you like?"

Making her way over to table Allison said, "Just a Coke is fine."

"Oh, please," Alex said from the bar. "We're hard working people still working on a Saturday, have a damn drink."

"Okay." She laughed. "I'll take some Kahlua with just a little bit of Coke."

While waiting for Warner to bring the drinks, Allison looked at the two large oil paintings over the bar. There was a man in a suit and a woman whose blue eyes, even in the picture, appeared to be as bright as Warner's.

"Your parents?" she asked as he handed her the drink.

"Yes." He nodded as he walked around and sat in one of the leather chairs. "Now please, sit down."

Allison sat across from him, and marveled at how soft the chair was. Leaning back into it she said, "These are more comfortable than they look."

"They are," Alex said. "What would be the point if they weren't?"

As he took a sip of what Allison was pretty sure was scotch she indicated the picture again. "Do they still live in New York?"

"My father passed away eight years ago," he replied. "And I lost my mother when I was eleven."

"Oh, I'm sorry." Smooth, Allison, smooth. "My mom died when I was ten."

"I imagine that would be harder on a young girl," Warner said. Holding his glass out to her he said, "To our mothers."

Allison clicked her glass to his and took a sip. "Wow, this is perfect. Usually people don't get it right the first time."

"I've had a lot of practice. I was my old man's bartender whenever his friends came over."

He paused, taking another sip of his drink. Allison saw his eyes dart down to her feet and slowly work their way up. Putting the drink down on the table he said, "You really are quite attractive, Allison."

He gave her a smile, but it was different from the previous one. This one had something else behind it. It was the smile of a predator, a cat crouching and waiting to pounce. As he spoke his startling blue eyes stared into hers.

"Why thank you again," she replied, returning his stare with her own devastating emerald gaze. Time to feel him out. "You know what they say flattery will get you."

"Really?" he asked. "Well if I knew it'd be that easy we could've skipped this and done dinner instead."

Allison laughed, kidding or hitting on her?

"Yeah, but then there would be people around at a restaurant. We wouldn't be alone like we are now." She took another chance. "Coincidentally."

Alex finished his drink and put the glass on the table.

"And would you think if I was looking for more than business, I'd have a woman as beautiful as you, sprawled out on a couch or bent over a desk?" He winked. "That's more suited for young girls trying to advance themselves with men who are little more than boys."

Allison's eyes narrowed, he was sitting there smirking as if there was a joke there.

"Well," she began. "I'm glad to know I'd at least rate dinner."

"At least."

Allison was unsure of what was going on. She expected to be hit on, but not quite so blatantly. Shifting gears she began, "I see you received the proposal that I sent you."

"Three actually." He tapped the folder.

"I wanted to show you some different angles," Allison began, "The first one is…."

"I'm sure you'd look good from any angle, Allison."

Not taking his bait, she continued, "I do, but what we're discussing here is my proposal."

"Maybe I'm discussing mine," he replied quietly.

"Excuse me?" she asked as if she were offended.

"Oh, please. A woman with your looks gets this all the time." He shook his head. "Would you like it better if I used some cliché's? You know, give a little to get a little?"

"I'd like it better if we discussed what we're here to discuss."

She'd said it coolly, still feigning indignation. She may very well end up caving, but wouldn't make it seem as if she wanted to.

"Yes, but business is boring," he replied. "I'd rather talk about you. I like to get to know who I'm doing business with."

"Apparently you'd really like to get to know me." Sitting back in the chair and crossing her legs, she gestured towards him. "What do you want to know?"

"When I kissed your hand, the skin cream is it Mario Badescu?"

"Why yes it is," Allison said, surprised. "That's very impressive."

"I have great sensory recall."

"Well then maybe when you retire, you could get a booth at a carnival guessing scents instead of weight."

Alex laughed again, and she couldn't help but smile. His laugh seemed genuine and contagious. She could just imagine all his cronies at the country club laughing along with him.

"That was good!" He told her grinning. "But let me ask you, that cream is quite expensive no?"

"It is," she answered, wondering where he was going with this. "Why do you ask?"

While waiting for him to answer, Allison had slipped the sandal from her heel, letting it dangle from her toes and began kicking her leg slightly. The move was not lost upon Warner, whose eyes locked onto her legs.

"Well no offense, but it seems a little beyond your means."

"Again, excuse me?"

"Like I said, no offense meant. I just play little guessing games with myself sometimes. Please humor me. Was the cream a gift perhaps?"

"It was."

"From an upscale gentlemen, I'd imagine."

So that was where this was going, she thought.

"Actually it was a gift from a client."

"You must have been very impressive." He gave her another smug smirk.

"I always am."

"That's what I'm counting on."

His eyes were still focused on her legs as he spoke and Allison switched legs, opening them more than she needed to before crossing them and once again dangling her shoe from her toes. He was pretty much declaring what he wanted, so it was time to begin the game. If he wanted it, he would have to earn it. To her delight, Alex gave her an opening with his next question.

"So do you use the cream anywhere else?"

"I use it on my feet." She kicked her shoe off. "Would you like to taste it from them?"

Alex laughed softly, but his gaze was fixed on her now bare foot, which she was wiggling back and forth. "Do you always ask men to kiss your feet, Allison?"

"No." She shook her head. "Usually they're the ones asking for the privilege."

"Oh," Alex whispered, a strange smile playing about his lips. "I like that answer, I really do."

"I'll bet you do." Leaning forward, she placed her glass on the table and, looking Warner in the eye, began speaking softly. "I think we both know where this is going."

"Do we now?" he asked, again with that odd look on his face.

"I do," she told him. "It's down to the good old give a little to get a little." She smiled at him. "Normally I don't play that game, but tell you what, Alex, for you I'll make an exception."

"I knew you would," he replied, the smile turning into a smug smirk.

Kicking her other shoe off, Allison placed both of her bare feet onto the coffee table.

"So I'll tell you what, how about I sit back on your nice comfy couch, and you come over here." She indicated the floor in front of her. "And I'll let you start at my feet."

"Start at your feet?"

"Yes, and if you're a good boy and do a good job on my toes, maybe I'll let you work your way up to my pussy."

"I don't think so, Allison," Warner said.

He had spoken softly, but something in his tone caused her to narrow her eyes. Looking into his deep blue eyes, she saw they had hardened and the smile was gone from his face.

"Seeing I'm the one with something you want, I think you'll come over *here*." He made a show of pointing at the floor as she had done. "Get on your knees, and if you do a good job sucking, I may be nice enough to allow you to swallow it."

His eyes were still locked onto hers and his resonant voice had a hypnotic quality to it. Allison forced herself not to look away as she replied. "Apparently I have something you want as well, and you want it bad enough to have called me." She smiled. "You sought me out, Alex, remember that. Now stop posing like you do for those young escorts you pay and come on over here." Opening her legs, she hiked her skirt part way up. "I'll even let you look at my pussy while you suck my toes for a little inspiration."

"Keep talking like that, Allison, and I'll be fucking your mouth rather than you sucking on it, and instead of letting you swallow it, I'll be watching you lick my cum off this table."

Allison was taken aback. That was a lot harsher than anything she'd heard before. With a start, she realized they were alone and Warner was a large powerful man. Taking a deep breath, she told herself this was the same game she played, just a rougher version of it. Allison had never let a man control her and was not about to start now.

"That's crude, Alex," she said quietly. "I expected you to be classier that that." She gave him a nasty smirk of her own. "Or are you just mad because I'm not fawning all over you like those inexperienced little girls who think you're a man because you have money?" She laughed. "You'll get more from me with honey, so why don't you try again, with some manners this time."

"And I, my dear, am not one of those little boys that you play with, boys who barely know where their dicks are and fawn all over you because you know how to use your mouth better than their little girlfriends."

Young boys? How did he....?

"And as for my manners?" Alex continued, "You're right I'm usually not crude, but then again I'm used to dealing with women with class, not slutty little career climbing whores, who'll drop to their knees for a chance to land a decent client. You're not worth more than crude tactics, Allison. Pigs never are."

That got under her skin and, forcing her voice to remain calm she whispered, "I'm not a career...."

"Oh spare me!" He waved his hand disgustedly. "Of course you are! Why do you think I brought you here? Because your work's any good? You're mediocre at best, Allison. An average talent with an above average set of tits, and a pair of blow job lips."

Shaking her head Allison began, "I think that...."

"Don't think, it's not your strong suit. No, what you do best is what you're about to do." He gave her a nasty smirk. "And that is stand up, take your clothes off and come over here and suck my cock. You've put up your token fight, now just get on your knees and show me how you got that nice little office of yours."

While he continued to speak in that same soft yet intense tone, his electric blue eyes held hers fast, refusing to let her look away. Allison was aware that she was beginning to sweat and felt her breathing picking up.

"Besides, Allison, you know you'll enjoy it. After all when was the last time you got to fuck a guy who was decent looking? Of course I'll only fuck you if you give a decent blow job and thank me for letting you. Any more of that attitude and I'll just make you suck it twice, and again lick every drop from the ...." He smiled. "No not the table, since you're obsessed with feet perhaps you can lick my cum off of my feet, after you drool it out of your mouth."

To her surprise, Allison realized that she was getting wet. She imagined being naked and on her knees, sucking Warner's cock while he grabbed her hair and shoved her face into his lap. She imagined him exploding into her mouth and letting it spill out, down her chin and tits.

"And if you clean up every drop, then I'll be a nice guy and let you play with yourself in front of me and get off." He laughed. "God knows I wouldn't want to touch what half the city of New York has." He must have noticed her wavering as he smiled and began in an even softer tone, "Oh you like that, you little pig? You're getting turned on aren't you? Like the idea of lapping up cum like a dog? Tell you what, Allison, I'll give you a chance. Crawl over here like a good girl and say you're sorry and I'll even bend you over and fuck you, give you a real cock in that used pussy of yours."

Allison swallowed hard, her mind now filled with the image of Warner bending her over and fucking the shit out of her, his powerful hands digging in to her hips as he drove himself in and out of her. He would be rough with her, pulling her hair and spanking her, she would still be tasting his cum in her mouth and.... no. She wouldn't give in.

Moving quickly, Allison reached down and, pulling her thong to the side, exposed her pussy. Raising her right leg, she straightened it out across the table so her toes were inches from his face. Keeping her eyes on his she began speaking softly, "Nice try, Alex, but I'm not one of your little toys. I'm a career climbing whore am I? Well I have news for you, Warner; you're the one who wants this career climbing whore. I'm a pig? What are you for wanting me? I'll tell you what you are." She gave him a smirk as nasty as his. "You're nothing but a spoiled little brat who throws a fit when he gets told no, a poser who has to pay his girls to moan for him."

For the first time, Alex's smug smile faded and he blinked at her. "Enough!" he snapped. "I...."

"Will sit there and stare at that pussy you want so bad, that's what you'll do. The pussy you couldn't score at that dinner, the pussy you sought out and are trying to bribe with a contract. That's right, Alex, take a good long look at that nice pink pussy, the one you want to lick, the one you would love to fuck."

"Allison, this...."

He stopped as she pushed her foot into his face. She stifled a groan as she felt her toes graze his lips and kept speaking, "You think you're calling the shots, Alex? I don't think so. I'm a woman, not a store bought slut that gets paid extra to stroke your ego along with your flaccid cock. You sit there with that arrogant smirk on your face? Well hate to tell you poser, but underneath your suits and behind that money, you're nothing but a grabby little boy who hates to be told "no"."

That hit home, his eyes widened and his face turned red.

"I am not a boy and...."

"But that's okay, Alex, you know why?" She smiled. "Because I feel bad for you I'm willing to let you start over. So be a good boy and if you suck on my pretty little toes, I'll let you jerk off on my pussy while I get myself off. Because God knows a sorry excuse of a silver spooned Romeo could never fuck a woman the way she needs it." She shoved her foot at him again and hissed. "Now be good little puppy and open your mouth, because this is your last chance."

Alex was staring hard at her and Allison felt her pussy begin to flow when he lowered his head and gently grabbed her ankle, bringing her foot to his lips Alex softly kissed the top of her foot, sending a shiver through her. She held back a moan as he trailed his lips along the length of her foot and across the tops of her toes. Then to her surprise he lowered her foot to the table. Letting her ankle go, Alex looked up at her and burst out laughing. Confused, Allison sat there watching him. When he got control of himself she asked, "Am I missing something?"

"Not at all, Allison," he exclaimed. "In fact you're absolutely perfect!"

"Umm.... Thanks I guess," she said quietly, wondering if her were nuts.

"I knew you wouldn't disappoint me, I knew it!" He seemed more excited than he had when he was trying to have sex with her.

"Well I'm glad, but what the hell is going on?"

"Okay." Alex put his hands up. "I didn't really bring you here for business, I...."

"Whoa!" she exclaimed. "Hold on, what about my proposal?"

"Don't worry about that." He waved his hand. "We'll...."

"Don't worry about it?" she asked. "Are you kidding? I...."

"Oh, here," Pulling a pen from his jeans, he leaned over and, opening the folder, pulled the contract out and as she watched, her eyes wide with excitement, signed it. "Done," he said. "Someone from my office will call you on Monday to work out the details, now…."

"Thank you!" Allison blurted out. "Thank you so much, Alex, I won't let you down, you'll see."

"Oh trust me; you haven't let me down in any way. In fact you've exceeded my expectations."

"I… what are you talking about?"

"Tell you what, Allison," Warner began, standing. "How about I fix us another drink and you can sit and listen to my proposal."

Allison couldn't help but notice a very impressive bulge in his jeans and began to wonder if sex might still be on the table.

"Your proposal?" she repeated.

"Yes, I invited you here for a reason, but before we talk about it can you do me a favor?"

"Anything,"

"Can you please close your legs and fix your skirt?" He grinned at her. "Not that I mind the view, but it's a little distracting."

Chapter Six

Allison watched Warner walk over to the bar and took a moment to compose herself while trying to figure out what the hell just happened. Less than a minute ago, she'd been sitting, face flushed, and pussy dripping, fully prepared for some hot sex. Now she felt like an idiot after Alex broke laughing at her all out push to get him to give in to her. Lifting her hips, she pulled her skirt down and taking a tissue from her purse wiped at the sweat on her forehead. On the bright side, regardless of whatever Warner was up to, he'd signed the contract. Whether or not she would get to keep it was another matter, but she would most likely be able to hold onto her job.

Picking up the contract, she slipped it into one of the folders she'd brought with her, and looked up in time for Warner to hand her a drink. As he turned away from her to sit down, Allison quickly chugged half of it, closing her eyes as the smooth liquor warmed her throat and stomach. When Warner had sat down, he took a long swallow of his own drink.

"Okay, as I said, I didn't bring you here just to discuss business, and before I continue, let me apologize in advance if anything I bring up seems inappropriate."

"Little late for that," she said, shaking her head. "Career climbing whore?"

"I'm sorry about that," he told her. "And for being crude in general, but I needed to get you going and make sure I was right."

"Right about what? Alex, what the hell is going on here?"

Finishing his drink, he put the glass down and when he began speaking there was an air of excitement in his voice. "Allison, earlier I mentioned I wanted to discuss a proposal with you. That was not a double entendre. I brought you here to extend a special invitation to you."

"You already did," she said coolly. "I believe it was to lick your cum off the table."

Rolling his eyes, he sighed "Again, my apologies. It was all an act." He stopped and appeared to be thinking. A moment later he smiled. "No not an act, a game. One you're very familiar with."

"What are you talking about?" Allison asked, although she had the feeling she knew damn well what he meant. She hadn't forgotten that comment he had made about young men. It hadn't seemed like a guess.

"Please don't insult me. You know damn well what I'm referring to. You were a little too good during our exchange to pretend you've never dommed anyone before."

"Dommed?"

"Yes, dominate, control whatever word you use. You've been doing it a long time and quite frequently." He smiled. "Just last night as a matter of fact."

"Last night?" The sweat was once again returning, but for a reason other than excitement.

"Your little friend Jeff." Alex gave her a big smile. "And last Saturday it was Alan."

"How do you....?"

"So how many are you juggling these days? Three? Four?"

She paused and took a deep breath. There was no way to deny it. "How the hell do you know about them?"

"There's very little we don't know, Allison."

"Who the hell is we?" she demanded.

"We is what I brought you here to discuss. You see I represent...."

"I want to know how you know about Jeff and the others," she interrupted.

"I've been watching you for awhile," he began. "And I've loved what I've seen."

"You.... have you been following me?" she asked incredulously.

"Me personally?" He shook his head. "No, but I've had others do so."

"I.... are you kidding?" She threw her hands out. "Who the hell are you to be following me?"

"Allison, please calm down."

"Calm down?!" she exclaimed. "You're stalking me and I'm supposed to calm down?"

"I know it sounds strange, but you need to let me explain this to you." He spread his hands out in a disarming gesture. "Please?"

"You better explain," she told him. "Because this is bullshit."

"Right." He nodded. "I can see where this would upset you so I'll get to the point. Allison, I'm part of a very special group of people."

"Define special."

"Simply put, the group I'm here to tell you about is comprised of people just like us."

"Like us?" she asked. "I really don't see me as being anything like you."

"No?" he asked. "And why not?"

"Oh, I don't know." She laughed. "For maybe about fifty million reasons."

"I'll give you that, but aside from my wealth what separates us?"

"Success, power, social standing," She shook her head. "I don't know what you're getting at here. We're nothing alike."

"And why do I have so much more than you? Why have I achieved so much more?"

"You're part of the boys club," She told him.

"Good answer." He pointed at her. "And what do they have that you don't?"

"A cock between their legs."

"Now you're just being bitter," he chided her. "What does the boys club have you don't?"

"Alex, just come out and say what you need to."

"Allison, I just awarded you what is most likely one of the bigger contracts of your career, and before this is over you'll have the promise of much more."

That caught her attention. "How much more?" she asked.

Alex laughed and clapped his hands. "Have I told you you're perfect?" He sighed. "Let's just say more than you can imagine."

"I like the sound of that," she said. "But...."

"Answer the question," He stared at her and when she didn't answer right away he prompted her. "The boy's club?"

"Fine." She paused to think for a moment. "Connections."

"Exactly."

"Influence," she added.

"Again exactly," he agreed. "And that, not money, is what separates us. The money is a result of influence and connections. But also." He gestured towards his trophy case. "Hard work and dedication, not to mention being damn good at whatever it is they do."

"Not the one's where I work." She made a disgusted sound. "They're where they are because of who they know. God knows it isn't hard work."

"You're probably right, but I'm talking about us, Allison, not them."

"Back to us again, I'm telling you ...."

"When I mean us, I mean my group." He paused again, "Allison, are you familiar with the term Alpha?"

"I've heard the theory."

"It's not theory, its fact." Sitting up in his chair he leaned forward and, clasping his hands together, began to speak. "You, my dear, are one of them."

"I don't know about that."

"Oh please." He waved his hand at her. "Modesty is for fools, and you don't strike me as a fool by any means."

"I'm not," she replied, "But I don't know that I'm any better than...."

"Of course you are," he said simply. "Just as I am. Let me explain. You know the expression "all men are created equal"?"

"Yes."

"That was made up by underachievers to make themselves feel better about their mediocrity. Let's face it, Allison; some people are better than the rest. Look at you, you're absolutely gorgeous."

"Why thank you." She laughed.

"Seriously, think about it. You know my reputation. I've been with some beautiful women in my day and you're just as, if not more amazing, than any of them."

"You're just saying that."

"Hopefully you'll get to know me well enough to know I never *just* say anything." He grinned at her. "Come on, Allison, you know it's true. Men want you, women hate you."

"I tell myself that sometimes." She grinned back.

"As you should." He nodded. "And that's just your physical attributes. In addition to those is your intelligence. See we've done a lot of research, we know quite a bit about you."

"How much?" she asked.

Smirking, Alex asked. "How is professor Stafford these days?"

"Oh my God," she said softly. This was no longer even remotely amusing. "Alex who the hell is this group you're talking about?"

"I'm getting there," he said calmly. "On the subject of Stafford and school, you never had anything less than an A in high school and graduated NYU with a perfect grade point average." He smiled. "From what we could tell, you would've gotten through Stafford's class with a decent grade, but you did what you had to do because you wanted to be perfect."

"How do you know the damn details?"

"There's little we are not privy too," he said cryptically. "And even less we can't accomplish, but my point is: you have the brains to back that beauty, and coupled with those attributes is the drive to use them. You use your body to drive the young men wild, to gain total control of them, to enjoy the fruits of your sexuality under your terms."

"I'm not thrilled that you know that for the record," she told him.

"That tune may change and sooner than you think." He gave her another sly smile. "Yet for all of your sexual prowess, there's only been two occasions you've used it to get what you needed, and even then it was a last resort, which again demonstrates your intelligence. When seeing you couldn't succeed, you weren't so stubborn that you wouldn't use all of you assets."

"Twice?" She shook her head. "Let me guess, you know about Jim Pearson."

"Yeah, but nothing cloak and dagger there, I used to golf with him and when your name came to my attention I called him."

Rolling her eyes, Allison asked, "Does every man talk about every woman they've screwed?"

"He spoke very highly of you."

"I'll bet he did." She snorted.

"I'm talking about professionally. Jim said you were going to be one of the best." He laughed. "Said he would've hired you...."

"I've heard that fucking story before!" Allison snapped. "Thank you for giving me a chance to work for you. But as for whatever game you're playing? I'm not interested."

"Which brings me to number three, I...."

"Alex, if you don't stop talking in riddles and get to the point, I'm leaving."

"That'd be a mistake Allison."

"I'll take my chances." She began to stand.

He put his hands up. "You're right. I'm being a little too cryptic here. Please sit."

With a sigh Allison sat down "Go ahead."

"The group I represent is called The Circle. There are a dozen chapters of it around the country grouped together geographically. We're the eastern Circle and our members are from all over New England."

"How many members are there?" she asked, starting to become interested.

"Twelve. Six men and six women. We're currently in need of a woman to replace a member who recently left."

"And that's supposed to be me?"

"The Circle is the best of the best, Allison. It's comprised of people who dominate in every aspect of their lives. We're the wolves amongst the sheep, the people everyone says they hate, yet desire to be."

"Well I suppose I have the looks, but I...."

"The Circle isn't for everyone," Alex went on as he warmed to his subject. "We're quite specific in what we want. The first requirement is a certain age bracket. Members are to be between the ages of thirty to fifty, the age where you're peaking in every aspect of your life."

"So twenty years then out to pasture?"

"Many don't make twenty years."

"Well if it's so great, why not?"

"Some tire of the games, and some choose they want more from their lifestyle and choose to be with one person." He shrugged. "Fall in love."

"That's not allowed?"

"When you know more you'll see why, but yes, falling in love is not allowed. The member must be single and willing to stay that way."

"Don't think that'd be a problem." She nodded. "I don't know why I'd want to settle for just one."

"Again, perfect answer. Another rule is no criminal record and no bad habits. There are no cocaine addicts, thieves or murderers in the group. The only behavior allowed at our table that society frowns upon is sexual in nature. You obviously fall into the right age and your beauty speaks for itself."

"But what about....?"

"Allison, you wanted me to get to the point, so please let me."

Making a show of zipping her lip, Allison sat back and put her hands in her lap.

"Your record is clear, age and appearance established, so now we needed to know if the rumors we'd heard of your bedroom activities were true. That was when we started following you. One of our members is in surveillance and filmed one of your encounters."

"Are you fucking kidding me?!" exclaimed.

"No worries, I deleted the video after watched it." He smiled wickedly. "The look on his face when you made him suck his cum off your toes was priceless. Not a member at the table could have done better."

"I don't like being spied on, Alex, and certainly don't like the idea of someone watching me have sex."

"That'll change." He laughed as if he'd said something funny and went on. "So your dominance is there, which brings us to this." Leaning forward he tapped the folder. "You're excellent at what you do. If you weren't we wouldn't be interested."

"So you didn't give me this just to get me here?"

"Allison, from what you know of me, would I put my name on anything I didn't feel was the absolute best?"

Allison allowed herself a smile. "No."

"Damn straight!" Alex exclaimed. "And yes smile, because you earned this. I've looked at your previous work. If you weren't the best, you wouldn't be here. So you're exactly what we need."

"I'm not exactly wealthy," she pointed out. "And I'm only mid-level at A&S I...."

"Yet and for now,"

"Say again?"

"You're not wealthy *yet* and you're mid-level for *now*. You accept my invitation and things will change very quickly for you."

"How?"

"I've told you what we are; now let me tell you what we do. What the Circle is about is power and advancement. Every member lives to do anything in their power to help their brothers and sisters."

"Brothers and sisters?"

"Trust me; The Circle will become a second family to you. To some of us it's more of a family than our true families ever were. We share things with each other that our families would not be able to understand, not the least of which is our bedroom escapades. Now the members are quite different. Some of them are like me, born into some money and connections and have managed to do even more with it. For us, the group is more about the sexual aspects than..."

"What are the sexual....?" Allison trailed off as he gave her a look.

"Others are like you. You have the natural ability, but are being held back by those who, at the end of the day, are afraid of what you're really capable of. But like you, those members had done enough to catch our attention and once you join us you'll never be held back again."

"And why is that?"

Alex gave her a big smile. "There are more powerful groups than the boys club, Allison. When you're one of us, you'll be privy to every connection the group has. It'll be our duty, as well as our pleasure, to see that our new sister enjoys all the success she's entitled to. In no time, you'll be further along than you could've ever imagined."

"How far ahead?" she asked.

This time Alex didn't seem to mind her interrupting, and tapped the folder on the table. "Soon you'll be passing a contract this size off to an assistant because it won't be big enough to hold your interest."

"That's a stretch don't you think?"

"Not at all, especially considering there's a member in our group whose career could do wonders for yours."

"Who is it?" she asked eagerly.

"Sorry, rule is you only meet the full group after you join. Today I'm extending that invitation to you" His expression turned serious. "This is a once in a lifetime chance that you won't regret."

She considered it. The entire thing sounded far-fetched and part of her was waiting for him to start laughing again. Another thing nagging at her was what was involved in joining? Allison was no fool and knew nothing in life was free especially something like this.

"Allison?"

"So what about the sex part of this thing?" she asked. "What is it a sex club where we're all going to take turns humiliating each other?"

"No, it's not like…."

"Or," Allison continued as something dawned on her. "Will I be getting it put to me; because I'm the new girl in town is that the catch? I'm the club mascot?"

"To the contrary, the ladies of the Circle are treated with the utmost respect."

"Ladies of the Circle?" She had to admit she liked the sound that.

"All the women are addressed as lady and whatever their Circle name is. That name, before you ask, is something you choose. Most of us take our names from mythological or historical figures. There is actually little contact between members, but I won't say more on that. If I got into every rule, we'd be here all week. You'll learn as you go. Now before I go further, allow me to ask a question of you. Why do you keep your little playthings secret?"

"Because my life is my business," she said. "Especially my sex life."

"There's a little more to it though isn't there?"

"Why don't you tell me, Alex?" she asked. "You know where you want this to go so just take it there."

"You're worried about how it'd look."

"I suppose." She shrugged. "Guys like you do girls half your age it's expected. A woman like me does it and I'm Mrs. Robinson."

"Well maybe. But I didn't so much mean age. I meant the type of sex, the control, the humiliation."

"I guess the average person would think it was sick."

"Right, well let me ask you something else. How would you enjoy being able to talk about what you do?"

"Why?"

"You don't think it'd be exciting? Instead of keeping your games secret, you get to meet up with us once a month and share your adventures."

"So this group of superior beings gets together once a month to swap dirty stories?" she asked. "Seems a little juvenile."

"There's more to it than that, but close. Think about it, Allison. Think about what a turn on it'd be to have a table full of wealthy powerful people watching you torment your young lovers and instead of thinking, 'that's sick' we're thinking 'my god what an amazing woman!'"

"Watch?" She frowned. "What are you saying? I bring someone with me?"

"No, you tape your encounters."

"I'm sorry?"

"More on that when you join. I can't discuss everything here."

"But I get taped and then sit there and watch people watch me?" She shook her head. "Now that's sick."

"And making a young man lick his own cum isn't?"

"Touché."

"Think of it as simple voyeurism. If you can grasp BDSM you can grasp that. Allison, it's an indescribable turn on to watch others watch you. Just imagine a table full of people worked up over you. The men hard, the women wet, and you'll watch the other's and be just as excited."

"I don't know." She shook her head.

"You'll see I'm right." He sighed. "For right now let's talk about what means most to you. Your career will advance to a point that if you wanted to, you could be running your own agency and in less time than you would think possible." He grinned. "And it's already started with what I just gave you. It's a drop in the bucket, Allison, just the beginning of what's in store for you."

"It sounds too good to be true."

"I assure you this is the real deal. You think the boys club is running your firm?" He laughed. "Look around my office, I'm the boys club and I'll be doing everything in my power to help you earn your place."

"I want that more than anything," she said quietly. "I want what's coming to me, what I deserve, but all this sounds so good, my question is: what do I have to do? This can't just be as easy as I say "yes" and it's "welcome aboard."

"There's one catch, Allison."

Here we go, she thought.

"You'll have to go through an initiation to get in."

"Of course. How would I not have to fuck my way into a sex club?" She sighed. "So what would I have to do? Take you up on your kind offer of lapping your cum off the coffee table?"

"Well first off, it wouldn't be me. The recruiter can't initiate the candidate."

"You're starting to sound like the girls in the sororities during pledge week."

"I assure you this isn't going to be a college sex game."

"Whatever." She put her hands out. "So what do I have to do? Fuck his brains out to prove I'm worthy?" She shrugged. "I'm willing to do that, especially seeing you say all the guys are as attractive as you."

"No, Allison, it's not like that. The point of the initiation is to break you."

"I don't like the sound of that."

"Look, as I said everyone in that group is like you. They've been in control most of if not all their lives. And remain that way. However, because we're all dominate, in order to gain entry, we had to prove we could properly submit."

"Oh." She shrugged. "I can do that, if I have to. I can put on the pout and call him sir, and be good to him."

"No." He shook his head. "I mean truly submit, in a way you never have before."

"Cut the Hollywood drama, Alex." She was getting annoyed again. "I don't care who you De Sade wannabe's think you are, but I've been doing this far too long to "break" as you put it."

"Many of us thought that, including myself." He looked her in the eye. "I learned differently."

"So let me get this straight: you expect me to meet a total stranger and let him do whatever the hell he wants to me until he thinks he broke me?" She shook her head. "I don't think so."

"Allison, its one night, for a lifetime of...."

"Are there limits? Can he tie me up? Whip me, beat me?" She shook her head again. "No way."

"There's a safe word. If it goes farther than you want, you say it and it stops."

"That simple?"

"Of course." He raised his hands. "The member who'll be handling you is an attorney Allison, he's not a lunatic."

"So I say enough, and it's over?"

"Yes, but you don't get in."

"So in order to get in I have to take whatever he gives me."

"Until you break."

"And if I don't?"

"Everyone breaks. It's just a matter of how long it takes."

"And where does this happen?"

"He lives in Rhode Island."

"I'll be states away, in a stranger's house, getting treated like an extra in a bondage movie?" she grunted. "Thanks, but no thanks, I'm not crazy."

"Allison, think about who I am. Would I be involved in anything dangerous?"

"You won't be involved," she pointed out. "It'll be me and someone I don't know. Forget it."

She leaned over and, picking up the folder, said, "Thank you for this opportunity, Alex. I hope I can earn more of your business."

"You can, just go through with this, Allison. Join us."

"I...."

"Yes it may be unpleasant, but its one night and you'll never be asked to submit like that again."

"Then why do I this time?"

"To show you're willing to sacrifice to get what you want. You have my word any future encounter within the group will be fun. You can use your pout and be playful, but...."

"I can be playful now."

"It is what it is. The Circle will make you everything you want to be and more. If you can't sacrifice your pride for one night, then maybe you don't deserve the chance."

"Pardon me if I don't want to be raped by a stranger."

"Again, we're professionals in the real world, no one is being raped. Will you be treated harshly? That depends on your attitude, you know the game." He sighed. "One night, Allison. One night for the rest of your life, it's a small price to pay."

If all he was saying was true, it would be worth it. Besides, no matter what Alex thought, there wasn't a man out there she couldn't handle. She didn't mind sex with someone she hadn't met, but she wouldn't be controlled. She could turn it around on him the way she had with Alex. Then again, what if the guy was expecting to be able to hurt her? Taking a deep breath she said, "Let me think about it."

"The rule is: you don't leave without an answer it's yes or no."

"Then my answer is no. I won't be bullied in the office or the bedroom."

"Allison, you're making a mistake. If you go through with this the next time you see me, you won't be able to thank me enough."

"Oh please." She laughed. "Oh wait a minute." She snapped her fingers. "That's when I get to pout and be playful, when I have to crawl on my knees and say 'thank you, sir'?"

"A simple kiss on the cheek will suffice," he said quietly. "I told you it'll only be the one time."

"One time too many. I'm not playing slave to some rich suit. I may as well whore myself at work if that's what it'll take to get ahead."

Sitting back on the couch Alex rubbed at his eyes. With a sigh, he said, "Okay, I'll make a deal with you."

"Unless it's no rough stuff, there's no deal."

"We'll see." He pointed at the folder in her hand. "That contract is for a new product launch, which is how I was able to give it to you and not my current agency, correct?"

"Yes."

"My contract with Wilson and Thomas is up at the end of the year. You go through with the initiation; all of my business is yours next year."

"I…." She stopped unable to speak, her mind already trying to throw numbers together. That would be….

"I'd hazard to say that'd increase your income by at least a third next year if not more," he said as if reading her mind.

"How?" She took a moment to gather herself. "How do I know you'll go through with it?"

Standing, Alex walked over to his desk, speaking as he did. "I anticipated you wanting to join and had already drawn this up as a gift for you next year. In order to convince you, I'll give it to you now."

Returning to his chair, he placed a document on the table. Leaning over, Allison stared at it and felt her heart begin to pound. It was indeed a contract granting A&S advertising the exclusive rights to handle his product line next year.

"My signature is already on it," he said quietly. "The attorney who drew it up is your initiator. I'll send this to him. When the initiation is over, you'll sign it and he'll bring it back to me."

"How do I know this'll happen?"

"You're going to have to trust me at some point."

Staring at the contract, she frowned as something dawned on her. "Well I'm afraid there could be a problem here for me anyway."

"What do you mean?"

"I may not even be able to keep this contract, let alone another."

"Why not? That's your name there, you brought me the proposal."

"I'm having some trouble at work, Alex. They have a habit of swooping in and taking the big fish."

"Perfect." He slapped the top of the coffee table, causing her to jump.

"What the hell do you mean?"

"I'll tell you what, I'm going to let you walk out of here without an answer, and on Monday you're going to get two reasons to trust all I have promised you can and will be delivered."

"How are you going to do that?" she asked.

"First off, you're going to get a demonstration of the type of power you'll have behind you. Secondly." He stood up and, reaching into his pocket, extended his hand. "Take this."

Allison put her hand out and he placed a red coin the size of a silver dollar in her hand.

"Red Gold," Alex said as she stared at it.

Holding it up, Allison saw there was a design on it. Bringing it closer she saw it was a crest. A Circle with three Latin words inscribed into it and a banner across the bottom.

"The Crest of the Circle," He began. "Vis Virus, Luxus, Dapes, Dominatus. Power, lust, wealth and Mastery. I want you to put that in your purse and make sure you keep it with you next week."

"Why?" she asked, still staring at the ornate coin.

"Another member of the Circle is going to approach you. They won't discuss the group, but you'll know they're one of us. Once you see who it is and what they offer, you'll have a choice. If your answer is still no, keep the coin. If it's yes, give the coin to your visitor and your initiator will contact you."

"I thought this group is secret."

"It is."

"Then why would you give me this?"

"To show you I trust you." He sighed. "Besides at the end of the day, we could destroy you as easy as we could make you. We have no worries."

"Well that makes me feel better about things."

"It won't come to that, Allison, because I fully expect to have this coin back in my hand very shortly."

Slipping the coin into her purse, Allison shook her head. "You seem confident I'll say yes."

"I have complete faith in the person I'm sending your way."

"And I'll know who they are?"

He smiled. "Allison, everyone at your office will know who they are."

Chapter Seven

As she had been doing all morning, Allison jumped at the sound of her phone and felt her stomach tighten. "Yes, Cindy?" she answered.

"Jen's running out to Subway, you want anything?"

"Ummm," she hesitated. All she'd had to eat today was a yogurt and that had been hours ago. On the other hand her stomach was in knots and she wasn't sure if she could eat. "Just grab me a salad. You need money for it?"

"Nah, you bought yesterday, I'll get it."

"Thanks, Cindy."

Hanging up, Allison let out a deep breath. She was a nervous wreck and was pissed off for being that way. For what seemed like the hundredth time today she glanced at the time and wondered what the hell Ben was waiting for. That last thought pissed her off even more, she had no doubt Ben was stalling on purpose to make her sweat. Well it was two o'clock so it had to be coming soon.

Allison closed her eyes and took a series of long deep breaths to relax. When Ben called or came by her office to tell her it was time to meet with Blake, she wanted to appear calm and confident. Whether she could manage that or not, her outfit would at least give the impression. Not wanting to give Ben any ammunition as far as her style of dress went, she had chosen to wear a black blazer with a matching knee length skirt and a pair of plain two inch pumps. She had swept her long hair up, sporting an overall more professional appearance than usual.

Opening her eyes, she leaned back over her desk and looked down at the pile of computer magazines she'd had Cindy run out and buy for her. She had spent a good part of the day pouring through them, comparing Warner's products to the competition and looking at what the other companies were touting in their ads. As she had several times today, she flipped open one that had an article on Warner himself. One page featured a picture of him in a gym, wearing shorts and a tank top, his powerful arms slicked with sweat as he delivered a blow to a punching bag. As she eyed his body, she wondered what Saturday morning could have been like had she succumbed to him. Shaking that thought off, she went to close the magazine when she stopped.

"Orion delivers the knockout blow to the competition," she whispered.

She repeated it again, this time louder. It sounded corny, but it would work. Especially considering most tech geeks were males whose nerdy side still seemed to find things like action movies and over the top macho stars cool. Grabbing the scissors from her desk, she clipped out the picture to add to the vision board she was building for the campaign. It hadn't been her initial concept, but being the ego maniac Warner was, she couldn't see him objecting to something like this.

Her excitement faded and she tucked the clipping back into the magazine. It was yet to be determined if she would even be leading this campaign. That was the other reason she was dreading Ben's inevitable visit. She was waiting for him to swoop in and tell her that she most likely would need help with such a big account. Although she had kept her meeting with Warner secret and even drawn up the preliminary contract herself, the cat was now out of the bag.

At nine thirty this morning Allison had received a phone call from a Jill Walters. After introducing herself as Orion's VP of marketing, Jill spent over an hour on the phone with her, discussing a few minor changes she wanted to see in the proposal. At the end of the call, Jill said she would fax over the client application form Allison had left with Alex as well as a copy of the check for the deposit. Allison had spent the next hour filling out paperwork, then had Cindy bring it upstairs to the office for approval.

Allison figured word had begun circulating she had brought Orion Software into the fold within a half hour and Ben would be one of the first to hear of it. That had been around eleven thirty and she'd been waiting for the axe to fall ever since. Allison went back to perusing one of the magazines when her cell beeped telling her she'd received a text. Picking it up, she saw it was from Cindy and cursed under her breath as she read it.

"Ben is coming down the hall, you ready to speak with him?"

Allison had needed to vent and had told Cindy of what was going on. Although she appreciated the warning, she had no real excuse not to speak with him, and truth be told, needed to get it over with. She quickly texted yes back to Cindy, and seconds later her phone buzzed.

"Ben Watts, Allison."

"Send him in."

Placing the magazines in a neat stack on her desk, Allison turned towards her computer screen and began to edit an e-mail she'd been composing earlier. She heard her door open, and made herself count to three before she looked up. Ben was making his way over to her desk, and she felt her heart begin to pound when she saw him holding the purple folder she had turned the account in with. Fighting to maintain a neutral expression, she studied his face, expecting to see the usual smug expression that always made her want to smack him. To her surprise, he not only wasn't smirking, but seemed quite serious. Strange, she would have thought he'd have been grinning ear to ear.

"Good afternoon, Allison," he said quietly as reached her desk. Indicating her chair, he asked, "Mind if I sit?"

"Of course not," she replied, wondering what game he was going to play. "What can I do for you?"

Ben was silent and Allison wanted to kick herself for giving him such an easy lead in with that remark.

"Orion Software, Allison?"

"Yes." Forcing a smile, she added, "Not too shabby, no?"

"That's putting it mildly." He tapped the folder. "This is by far the biggest client you've brought in, most likely your best commission to date."

Yeah, if I can keep it, she thought. Out loud she said, "I believe it is."

"And a lot of potential, Orion's exclusive with Wilson is up soon." He gave her a smile that couldn't have been phonier if he tried. "You may have landed a big fish here."

"That's my plan," she said, still playing along. "I wow him with this campaign and he remembers us when it counts." Or, I go fuck a stranger and I get the business handed to me.

"Funny I don't remember you saying you were pitching Alex Warner." He shook his head, a thoughtful expression on his face. "I certainly don't recall him calling here to set anything up."

Now that the moment was here, Allison began to calm down. Giving Ben a shrug she replied, "He called me on my cell. I had given him my card at John Wexler's dinner."

"I see. I also checked with Bill and he didn't draw up this contract, at least not the original one Mr. Warner signed."

"Mr. Warner didn't give me much time to work on this, and other executives have done this in the past."

"Senior executives," Ben pointed out. "Long story short, you went around the proper channels and did this behind our backs."

Allison gave up and grunted disgustedly, "Well I guess that's you're out to take it from me right, Ben? Not only take it from me, but another thing to throw at me when we sit down with Blake."

Ben stared at her and she prepared for him to lay into her, but instead he took a deep breath and said, "To the contrary, I came in here to commend you for this."

"You...." Taken completely off guard, she blurted out, "What?"

"This took a lot of initiative, and it was smart not to involve the entire firm in case Wilson caught wind he was speaking to us. All in all, very well done."

"Thank you," she said simply.

"And as for what you just said, you have no worries. You reeled him in, and the account is all yours. As soon as we go through the formality of Orion's references, Bob will be cutting you your commission."

Ben's voice seemed strained and his hands were squeezing the arms of the chair. It was as if he were forcing himself to speak. Sensing something was amiss, Allison pushed further.

"Well thank you for letting me have what's mine," she said with a smirk.

Ben's eyes narrowed and she saw his jaw clench. "No need to thank me, you did the work."

"Okay Ben, what gives?" she asked. "What is this, a set up? You get my hopes up, then we go see Blake and you take...."

"That was the other thing I wanted to talk to you about," Ben interrupted her. "There's no meeting with Blake."

"Since when?" she asked. "You seemed to think there was going to be one when you left me that message Saturday morning."

"Yeah well." He sighed and when he spoke again, she swore he was practically choking on the words. "Allison, I owe you an apology. I was way out of line Friday night and it wasn't the first time. I had no right asking you to sleep with me."

Allison sat there wondering if she'd heard that right. She came close to asking him to repeat it, but the look on his face told her he might not be able to get the words out again. What the hell was going on?

"What about Ted Miller?"

"I spoke to Ted and told him he was out of line as well. He did like your work and I offered him to work with Rick on the pitch you made to him and...."

"My pitch?" she asked. "Well then...."

"You'll get the full commission on the campaign," Ben told her. "Rick will keep Miller as a client, but you get the initial money." He let out a deep breath. "Fair enough?"

"I.... yes, thank you," she said, unable to come up with anything better to say.

"Good." Standing, Ben extended his hand to her. "Again, I'm sorry. Perhaps we can start over from here."

Allison took his hand, and could feel it trembling. She had no doubt in her mind he was being forced to do this, but by who, Blake? Maybe because she had gotten Warner? Well, whatever it was, she was grateful for it and felt her heart racing with excitement. The commission would keep her afloat at home and.... realizing she was still holding Ben's hand; she resisted the urge to say something smug to him and played it safe.

"Apology accepted, and it'd be nice to be able to work together with no problems."

He gave her another forced smile. "I'm looking forward to it."

Ben put the folder on her desk and without another look back walked out of her office. Allison slumped back into her chair with a sigh of relief. After taking a couple of minutes to calm down, she reached for the phone to call Cindy and tell her what happened. Before she could, her cell beeped with another message. Glancing at the screen she didn't recognize the number, and picking it up checked the message.

"Get your apology yet?"

"Who is this?" she typed back.

"Answer the question. Yes, or no?"

Allison stared at the phone and typed, *"Yes, just now."*

"Excellent," the reply came back. *"Now check your e-mail."*

"Who are you?" she typed again.

Allison sat and waited for a response, but it didn't come. Putting the phone down, she turned to her PC and, shaking the mouse, brought up the screen. She had been in the middle of sending an e-mail and saw she had a new one in her inbox. The e-mail address was 'agift4you@yahoo.com'. Clicking on it, her eyes widened as she began to read it.

Dear Allison,

My brother and good friend, A.W., has asked me to help you with an unpleasant situation. It was my pleasure to do so, and allow me to say it would be an even bigger pleasure to be of service to you in the future. For now read the below e-mail that was sent to Ben Watts this morning. Please save this and feel free to use the attachment if ever another issue with Mr. Watts should arise. Sincerely, your future brother, Loki.

Holy shit, this was what Alex had been talking about yesterday when he said he would show her what he was capable of. She scrolled down further and saw there was a message to Ben that was forwarded with this one. That message was from the same e-mail address used to send to her and she felt her heart race at what it said.

Mr. Watts,

It has come to my attention you've been harassing a good friend of mine, Miss Allison Saunders. Your harassment has ranged from sexual, where you've repeatedly made lewd advances to her, to professional, as you've blatantly stolen her clients and cheated her out of what's rightfully hers. This behavior will stop today. From now on, not only will Miss Saunders keep all of the clients she brings aboard, you have until two o'clock this afternoon to apologize and assure her that she'll be treated fairly by you from this time forward. If Miss Saunders doesn't receive that apology, the attached pictures will be in your wife Elizabeth's hands by three thirty p.m. today as well as in each of her three e-mail addresses. I'll be in touch with Miss Saunders this afternoon.

Allison clicked on the attachment and gasped, "Goddamn!"

She was staring at a photo of Ben lying naked on a bed with a woman with long dark hair lying between his legs blowing him. There were more pictures and all showed Ben in various sexual positions with several different girls. She noticed it was always the same bed, and the girls were all young, most likely college coeds moonlighting as escorts. Closing the attachment, Allison went to save the e-mail to her personal folder, when she noticed she'd received another e-mail. This one was from Alex Warner. Clicking on it she saw only two words. "You're welcome."

* * *

Allison looked up from the magazine she was cutting into and was surprised to see it was almost five o'clock. After the e-mail from Alex, she had sat back and thought about his offer. Although it had kept trying to intrude upon her thoughts all day Sunday she kept pushing it back, focusing instead on worrying about what today was going to bring. Now that everything had been settled, in dramatic fashion no less, she had no excuse not to dwell on the bizarre proposal.

Every time she thought about it, she wanted to start with 'Dear Penthouse'. It just seemed far-fetched, a group of rich sexual deviants who ruled the boardroom as well as the bedroom. Things like the videotaping and dirty story swapping seemed immature, like some type of wild college party out of control. As much as Allison played the same games they apparently did, she considered herself a solo act. She had no desire to have someone tape her then sit around and act like an x-rated Siskel and Ebert, rating her performance.

The promise of advancement did have her thinking. Allison wanted to be able to earn everything she had, and didn't want handouts. Then again, connections were the only way to get ahead and all she would be doing is what everyone else above her did. If there were any doubt Warner had been making the whole thing up as a joke, they had been dispelled with what had happened with Ben. She wondered how they had gotten pictures of him with so many women. Had they been following him as well as her?

That thought caused her to sit straight up in her chair. That was exactly what they had done. Warner said he had been watching her. Had he known of her problems with Ben and foreseen he would need to do this at some point for her? Most likely he had, which again showed how serious he was about this. Never mind his 'demonstration' had already made a huge difference for her. The commission worked out to just under six thousand dollars, her next three months rent. Better than that, she would never have to worry about Ben again. All this just to prove a point.

She supposed if it were the only way to get everything Alex was offering, she could go through with getting taped once every few months. Alex had seemed genuinely excited when he spoke of how she had handled Jeff. As she thought about it more, she had to admit it would be something to see someone else play the game. On the heels of that thought was she certainly wouldn't mind seeing Warner in action. She had held her own in his office, but Allison had a feeling Alex had been holding back on her and kept wondering how much longer she would have held out. So maybe she could deal with some voyeurism, but the sticking point was the initiation.

She didn't like the word break, nor had she liked the way Alex had been so crude with her. If that had been him just trying to feel her out, how far would one of these freaks go in the bedroom to prove a point? Allison referred to herself as a velvet domme. She didn't hurt her pets, nor did she ever restrain them. For Allison, the game was getting them to do anything she wanted for the chance she would reward them with her body. She would be lying if she said the humiliation didn't get her going, but she would never resort to physical pain. Allison herself had never been on the other end of even a teasing game, never mind something harsh.

No, she couldn't go through with it. If these people were as powerful as she was thinking they were, they could get away with hurting her and what could she do? Allison was pretty sure they would want to tape what he did to her and then there would be.... she stopped. There would be a sex tape of her, one that could be used to blackmail her just as easily as those pictures of Ben. If she joined and did anything wrong, broke one of their rules, or even wanted to leave they could threaten her with it. Maybe that was why they all helped each other, they had to. There was no way she could risk that. She felt a chill go through her as she recalled Alex saying, "We could destroy you as easy as we can make you."

She couldn't accept his offer, even with all of his business next year being dangled in front of her like a carrot. From there, Allison pushed it from her mind and instead, focused on working on Alex's account. He'd said he always went with the best available work. If Allison could turn this into a lights out campaign, she could still have a chance to win his business next year. Picking up the magazine, she removed the picture of Alex hitting the bag and taped it to the bottom of her computer; she would contact Jill about that angle at the end of the week when she had something solid to present to her.

Allison had then immersed herself in the magazines, trying to familiarize herself with the industry. Now it was almost five and she began to debate if she wanted to stay and do some more work, or go home, relax and sleep on what she'd learned so far. All in all, it had been a very profitable day and maybe she would stop off at one of her boy's places and have some fun before she went home. Her phone buzzed and she figured Cindy was telling her she was leaving. Thumbing speaker phone she called out, "Night Cindy, see you in the morning."

"Allison, you have someone here to see you."

Cindy sounded odd, as if she were either nervous or excited. Allison glanced down at her calendar, and saw nothing scheduled. "I'm not expecting anyone," she said. "Who is it?"

"Umm.... All I can say is: it isn't someone you'd be expecting, but you really want to get out here."

She had been talking softly as if trying not to let anyone hear her, and picking up the phone, Allison asked again, "Cindy, who...."

"Allison, get your ass out here!" she hissed in her ear. "Victoria Redding is here to see you!"

"I.... what?" she asked, refusing to believe she'd heard her correctly.

Victoria Redding? One of, if not the most, sought after models in the industry? Realizing she was sitting there staring at the phone, she whispered quickly, "I'll be right out."

Hanging up, she stood and after taking a deep breath, walked around her desk and forced herself not to run to the door. She had no idea why Redding was here. Allison had reached out to her agent a couple of times, but had never gotten past the receptionist. Opening her door, she went through it so fast; she narrowly avoided hitting herself in the face, and hoped to hell Redding wasn't looking. She had nothing to worry about, after a quick glance at Cindy, who was staring at her with a huge smile on her face. Allison saw Redding had her back to her, looking at the framed posters of some of A&S's biggest campaigns.

Allison took a moment to take Redding in from behind. She was wearing a white dress that was short enough that Allison wondered what she would do if she dropped something. The legs the dress were showing off were long, well shaped, deeply tanned and ended in a pair of white sandals that laced around her legs, ending just below the knees. Redding's long curly honey blonde hair reached down past the middle of her back, but the dress was cut so low that Allison could see the smooth tanned skin down to just before the swelling of what Allison couldn't help but notice was a very well shaped ass. The reason she couldn't help notice was the dress was so tight she could see Redding was not only wearing a white thong, but must tan in a string bikini. Taking a couple of steps closer, she cleared her throat.

"Miss Redding?" she spoke softly, hoping she didn't sound nervous.

At the sound of her name, Redding turned around and Allison was blown away. To say Redding was gorgeous was like saying the sun was warm. Her hair was styled in the front so that blonde ringlets framed her face, and her wide baby blue eyes were even more beautiful in person than they were on the magazine covers. Redding's make-up was flawless and her red lips were as full as her own. Pulling her gaze from those flawless features, Allison took in the front of the dress which was just as revealing as the back.

The dress tied around the neck leaving her shoulders bare and the neckline plunged down low enough to expose the top half of her breasts. The dress was tight enough that Allison could tell her left nipple was pierced. What was even more eye catching was the middle of the dress was cut out in a diamond pattern leaving her stomach bare and showing off the diamond pendent dangling from her naval. Redding's stomach was flat and hard, and Allison recalled reading somewhere that she worked out two hours a day with a personal trainer.

"Why hello, Allison!" she exclaimed, coming towards her. "It's so good to see you!"

She had spoken to as if she knew her, but what caught her off guard and left her speechless was Redding s voice. It was soft, sultry and absolutely dripped sex, the voice of a phone sex operator. When Redding reached her, Allison extended her hand, and was taken by surprise by Redding hugging her as if they were old friends. Allison hugged her back awkwardly, and found her face buried in Redding's neck where she could smell her Chanel perfume. Redding leaned back, but keeping her hands on Allison's shoulders, stared at her and said softly, "You have the most amazing eyes I've ever seen!"

Allison felt herself blush as if she were a young girl, and stammered, "I.... well thank you! You have amazing...." She gave a nervous laugh. "Everything of course."

Redding laughed, "Thank you! I always take a compliment from a woman to heart. Usually all they do when I walk by is meow and hiss."

"I can imagine."

Redding was still holding her arms, and looking into her eyes. Allison stood there nervously as Redding's eyes left hers and wandered up and down her body. It was more than a casual glance, more like the appraising look a guy would give here. Then again, she had probably stood there gawking at her. One thing was for sure, Victoria Redding oozed sex, Allison could feel it coming off of her in waves. It wasn't just sex, it was confidence. Allison had heard the term animal magnetism, but this was the first time she had felt it. As Redding's eyes reached her legs and started back up, Allison wished she hadn't dressed so severe today. She certainly didn't lack confidence in her appearance, but standing in front of Redding she felt more than a little inadequate.

"So, what brings you by, Miss...."

"Victoria," she said, giving her huge smile. "No need to be formal."

Redding removed her hands from her shoulders and, waving at the posters, said, "I came by to discuss the possibility of adding my name to your portfolio."

"You…." Allison blinked and forced herself to continue without stuttering. "You're thinking about letting us work with…."

"Miss Redding!"

Allison turned to see Ben Watts approaching with Joe Perez, another of the senior executive's right behind him.

"Like vultures they circle," Victoria said softly, then out loud, "Why hello gentlemen, how are you today?"

"Honored, is how I am!" Ben exclaimed, extending his hand.

Victoria took it briefly then shook hands with Joe, who looked as if he were barely able to keep from drooling.

"So, did I just hear you right, Miss Redding?" Ben continued, "Are you considering allowing us the privilege of featuring you in some of our work?"

"Perhaps," Victoria answered, "That's what I am here to discuss."

"Well then why don't you come down to my office?" Joe asked. "I'll call Bill the VP of the company and he can join us as well."

"I came to speak with Allison," Victoria replied, gesturing towards her.

"Oh," Ben did a good job of not looking disappointed and said, "Well she'll come with us of course."

"No, dear," Victoria said, giving him an obviously fake smile, "You don't understand. I'm here to discuss business with Allison. If I decide to do some work for A&S it will be under the condition I work exclusively with her."

"Well," Ben looked at Allison, who had to bite her lip to avoid smiling at the look on his face. "If that's what you wish, then that's how it'll be. Allison is one of our best people. You'll be in good hands."

"Really?" Victoria asked. "Are your best people always relegated to small offices on the lower level?" She shrugged. "I suppose every company is different." Turning her back to Ben and Joe, she winked and said, "Allison dear, I don't have much time, shall we?"

"Pleasure meeting you, Miss Redding." Ben called out.

"I'm sure it was," Victoria said and Allison stifled a laugh as she saw her roll her eyes.

They entered her office and, walking behind her desk, Allison gestured to the chairs in front of it. "Please sit down."

"I really can't stay long." Victoria replied as she looked around. "Dear, you need a bigger office. We'll have to work on that." "We'll…?"

"Yes, when we work together, we'll make that a priority."

"I…" Allison shrugged. "I'm thrilled to get a chance to meet you Victoria, but I have to admit I'm confused. I've never even had a chance to speak to you in the past."

"No we haven't, but I don't understand why you'd be confused." Victoria continued, "Weren't you told to expect a guest?"

"Oh my god," Allison whispered. "You're from….."

"Colorado originally." Victoria nodded, giving her a wink.

"Oh." She felt like an idiot. "That's right it's a secret and…"

"That I'm from Colorado? No, I think that's common knowledge." She was smiling and Allison felt like an even bigger idiot. "I was speaking with Alex Warner yesterday and he was raving about you." She gestured towards her. "Went on and on about your credentials and I have to say I agree."

"Thank you," she said not knowing what else to say.

"And I'm sure your work is good as well." She laughed. "Well no, I know it's good. I spent most of yesterday researching you."

"You did?" She bit back the comment of asking if she had been following her as well.

"I did and Alex is right, you're excellent at what you do." She shrugged. "And if nothing else, if Alex recommends someone that's enough in itself."

"So," Allison paused to gather her thoughts. "Are you serious about working with me? I thought you were doing business with…."

"I'm exclusive with no one," Victoria said simply. "I refuse to sign that kind of deal and, quite honestly, no one will push me to. I do as I choose."

"Well I hope you choose to come here and…."

"If I'm not mistaken you're the one that has a choice to make."

"Oh." She put her head down, another carrot.

"So let me tell you what I was thinking," Victoria began. "You know Rapture perfume would love to have me as the face of their line?"

"I've heard that, but…."

"Honestly although I think it's a good product and do wear it from time to time, I don't care enough for it to give up some of my time to endorse it."

"I understand," Allison said. "But maybe…."

"Until now," Victoria said softly. "Allison, whoever can get me, gets Rapture, and I'm willing to let you contact them and tell them you're able to do so."

"You will?"

"I meant what I said in front of those drooling buffoons. Anything I do here will be through you. You have a client you can't land, feel free to dangle my name and as long as I feel the product suits me, I'll be more than happy to work with you."

"I… Victoria, thank you! You don't know how much that means for me!"

"Of course." Victoria pointed at her. "That's only contingent on us remaining close."

"Close?"

"Alex sent me to you and I do like you. In fact I'd love for us to begin to travel in the same *circles*." She emphasized the word. "And if we do, then how can I not do what I can for my new found friend?"

"And if we don't travel in the same…*circles*, I take it the offer is off the table?" Allison asked.

"I have very little time in my schedule and can't be expected to give that time to a stranger now can I?"

Allison nodded and, looking down, saw her purse next to her chair. This was it, she had to accept or decline, there wouldn't be another offer. Orion's contract, Rapture, no not just Rapture, but a goddamn supermodel in her back pocket. Alex hadn't been exaggerating, Victoria Redding could single handedly shoot her to the top of her profession. She picked her purse up and, putting it on the desk, rummaged around until her hand found the coin Warner had given her. Clenching it in her fist, she looked at Victoria who was regarding her calmly.

"Is that for me Allison?" She pointed at her hand.

"The initiation," she said softly.

"I'm not here to discuss, I'm here to collect something from you." She shrugged. "Or not, it's your choice. But I do have to get going."

"Victoria, is it worth it?" she asked, "It just seems...." Victoria sighed and Allison shook her head. "Sorry, I'm just...."

"Allison, six years ago I was very much like you," Victoria began quietly. "I was doing okay, but nowhere near what I could've been doing. I was just another model, more talented than most, but stuck in the middle of the pack." Pointing at Allison, she continued, "And like you. Part of why I wasn't getting the shoots I should have, was because I refused to let my auditions start on the casting couch. Then one day I was given an amazing offer, a chance to change my life. I took them up on it. Yes the initiation was a bit tough, but let me put it this way."

Reaching into her purse, she removed a rolled up magazine. "Before that offer, the best I'd done was a few back page ads in magazines hardly anyone read. Within a year of my joining this is where I was."

Unrolling the magazine, Victoria held it up for her to see. It was the Sports Illustrated Swimsuit Edition from five years ago; on the cover wearing a red string bikini bottom with her arms crossed over her bare breasts was Victoria.

"You tell me if it was worth it."

Putting the magazine back in her purse, Victoria put her hand out. "Now do you have something for me?"

Moving quickly, before she could change her mind, Allison placed the coin in her hand.

Part Three

Chapter One

"What's the matter honey?" a gruff voice said from behind her. "No one here can afford you?"

Allison looked up from the empty beer mug she'd been staring into to see a large man wearing a denim vest with no shirt beneath it, grinning down at her. He was sweaty and unshaven and when he smiled it exposed a set of teeth that would drive a dentist to drink.

"I'm waiting for a friend," she said quietly.

"Hell sweetie, I'll be your friend!" he exclaimed, and made to sit on the stool next to her.

Reaching into her purse, her hand closed on the small canister of pepper spray, and said, "I have enough friends, thank you."

"Oh really?" he asked, sounding annoyed. "Well I don't see any here bitch!"

"Shut up, Derek," the bartender said, making his way over. "You heard the woman, go back to playing pool, or get lost."

"What is she, your date, Mitch?" He snorted. "You makin' that much money these days?"

"How much money could I make with broke jokes like you hanging around? I know who she's waiting for and that's all you need to worry about."

Derek stared belligerently at Mitch who appeared to be in his sixties. He was tall and thin, his long grey hair pulled into a pony tail. Despite his age and the fact he was less than half the size of Derek, he stood there with an air of confidence that had Allison thinking he knew how to handle himself. Derek muttered something and, taking his beer from the counter, headed toward the back of the bar. Looking up at Mitch Allison said, "Thank you."

"Yeah whatever." He shrugged. "Mark doesn't like sloppy seconds."

Trying not to think about what that meant she asked, "You know Mark?"

"Kind of." Another shrug.

"Does he come here a lot?"

"Sometimes. He really don't fit in around here, but I guess he likes slumming."

"Is he always late?"

"Mark does what he wants when he wants."

He said that over his shoulder while walking down to the other end of the bar where a couple of more bikers were sitting. Allison let go of the pepper spray and, picking up her phone, grunted disgustedly, it was almost three thirty. She'd been sitting in this dump for close to two hours. She thought about calling Warner and telling him his mysterious friend had stiffed her and she was ready to forget the whole thing. Then again, this could be part of the game, making her sweat it out.

If that was the case, it was a little overdone. As it was she had been stewing over this all week. Within a half hour of Victoria leaving, Allison had received a text from another unknown number asking if she were Allison Saunders. When she had replied yes she had received the response, *Mitch's, 525 Broad Street, Providence RI. Be there at two p.m., this Saturday. Come alone, don't make me wait. Mark.*

One thing was for sure, they moved fast. She had replied, asking if she should dress a certain way or bring anything. There was no response. Allison tried to call and received a message saying it was not a working number. The week dragged and she spent it waffling again and again on whether or not she should go through with this. Several times she had the phone in her hand ready to call Warner and cancel. Whenever she got to that point she envisioned Victoria Redding telling Ben and Joe she would only work with her.

That would always cause her to put the phone away and she would be fine for a few hours, then start thinking again. She threw herself into the Orion presentation and on Friday received the green light from Jill to pursue the boxing angle. Another thing that had kept her in a positive mind frame was not only Ben and Joe asking her repeatedly about Victoria, but Edwin Blake had found his way down to her office to ask her about it. She had responded to Blake she had nothing set in stone yet, but fully expected to have another conversation with Victoria sometime after Saturday. Blake had been thrilled and told her landing Orion and having Victoria Redding on her radar, had him watching her closely and he would see to it her hard work would pay off very shortly.

Using that conversation to motivate her, Allison had gotten in her car at eight a.m. this morning to take the four-hour drive down to Providence, for what would be a hardcore S&M session with a man she'd never met. The only thing Warner had told her about Mark was he was an attorney. During the drive, she was alternately nervous, and then upset at herself for being nervous. She wasn't thrilled with the idea of submitting to someone she didn't know, never mind whose sole purpose was to try to break her.

Then again, she was confident in her looks and her own brand of control. Allison was far from the scared young girls this guy was used to handling. There was no way out of sex, but the type of sex was definitely still up in the air. Her plan was to be playful and demure, offer him a hell of a ride, and forget about all this "breaking" stuff. They could just be two attractive people enjoying each other.

She chose to wear a short red sundress that showed off her generous chest and long, shapely legs. Despite the heat, she was wearing her long, black hair down. She also sported her best slut-red lipstick which matched her finger- and toenail polish. The finishing touch was a pair of stiletto heels. This ensemble, coupled with her bright green eyes and her perfect, full lips pushed out in a little girl pout, would be more than enough to get her off the hook from the rough stuff.

Allison arrived at the Mitch's at 1:45 to find out it was a hole in the wall biker bar. At 2:30, she was still sitting at the bar, being ogled and pointed at by the half dozen or so Hell's Angels-types who were in there. She was hit on twice while enduring several "you must be slumming" remarks. Having no way to get a hold of Mark, she sat and did the best she could to ignore the stares and lewd comments. Derek was the latest to accost her, and had been the most aggressive. If this kept up she would have to leave. The bikers were drinking pretty steadily and she had no interest in being sexually assaulted.

"Here." Mitch's voice snapped her out of her thoughts as he put a drink in front of her. "This is from one of the guys playing pool."

Allison glanced over to the pool table in the far corner and saw Derek standing there with two other guys as big and nasty looking as he was. Another, smaller man, stepped out from between them and raised his beer bottle towards her. Allison returned the toast and took a sip. It was a Captain and Coke, with maybe a drop of Coke in it. He tipped his beer back and she looked him over. It was hard to tell much from the distance and the bad lighting in the corner of the bar, but she could see he was far better looking than the other guys and in much better shape.

At quarter to four she again went for her phone determined to call Warner and walk out. She stopped when she sensed someone next to her and looked up to see the guy who had bought her the drink, sit down next to her. She waited for him to say something, but he simply sat there looking at her. While he stared she gave him a quick once over and had to admit, she liked what she saw.

Unlike the rest of the crowd, he was attractive. Both arms, shoulder to elbow, were covered with huge tattoos of some type of demons, and there was a pentagram charm hanging from the black chain around his neck. He was well muscled and, despite a couple of days' worth of beard, she could see he had high cheek bones and his features were perfect, even pretty. What caught her attention most were his eyes. They were a beautiful shade of golden-brown, with greenish highlights. She'd never seen a color exactly like them before. If these were different circumstances, and if he was a few years younger, she might even take him for a ride.

"Thank you for the drink," she said breaking the silence.

Making a show of blatantly staring down her dress he replied, "Thanks for the view."

Allison gave another hopeful look at the door, before sighing and saying, "Sorry, I'm waiting for someone."

He smirked. "I've been watching you for an hour. You've obviously been stood up, so why not have some fun?"

She couldn't resist. "Oh, and do you think you could be fun?"

He flashed a surprisingly pretty smile and told her, "I can give you exactly what you're looking for."

Returning his smile with a perfect one of her own, she countered, "Sorry, but I like my men a bit younger, better dressed, and shaved." She turned in her stool to face the door.

"What, do you think you're better than me?"

Without turning, she replied, "No, hon, just out of your league." She picked up her cell phone to call Warner.

"You really are a proud whore, aren't you, Allison?" he said softly.

She stopped dialing. *Oh shit!* She turned to look at him. "Mark?" she asked, already knowing the answer.

"You drove a long way to insult me."

"You're um... not what I expected."

He gave her the smirk again as he signaled the bartender. "And what did you expect? Warner?" He snorted. "Some smooth talking fag in a suit?" Mitch came over and Mark said, "Three shots of Jack."

Allison looked at him and smiled sheepishly. "Let's start over. I'm..."

"A proud whore who needs to be taught some manners," Mark finished.

He was soft spoken and said it calmly, but there was something in his tone that gave her an uneasy feeling.

"Hey, Mark," she began, "I'm sorry. I really am."

"No, you're not. Not yet, anyways."

Allison sighed. She had played this game herself. Once the pet said something stupid, it was all over. She would have to try to play along for now. Mitch put the three shots down and Mark slid one over to her. As she picked it up, he did his two in rapid succession.

"Um... Cheers." She poured the shot down her throat. The bourbon burned, but she hoped it would settle her nerves.

"Ready?" he asked as he tossed a couple of twenties on the bar.

"Shouldn't we talk about this?" she asked, trying to stall.

"Trust me, Allison, you've said enough. I'm leaving. Either follow me, or take your sorry ass back to New York. Maybe Warner's good enough for you." He sneered the name.

"I thought you guys were friends."

"Warner's a poser. He doesn't master his women, he buys them. Let's go." Without waiting for a reply, he got up and walked out. "Thanks, Mitch," he called over his shoulder.

"Anytime, pretty boy," he answered. Grinning at her he winked. "Have fun sweetie."

Realizing she'd been played and Mitch had known Mark was there the entire time, she shot him a dirty look and followed Mark outside to where he was standing next to her Mazda.

"Get in your car. I'll be around in a minute."

"Yes, sir," Allison said with a tone.

Mark's smile sent another round of butterflies through her stomach. "I'm going to enjoy showing you your place, Allison."

He walked away, once again leaving her cursing at herself. She had to remember she was on the other side. The trick was to say whatever she would want her pets to say, not smart off. Although they had started badly, she was still holding out for a chance to get to him. A minute later, an old, restored, grey Firebird pulled up alongside of her, she noted with dismay that the license plate read DOMINUS. Mark made sure she saw him before driving away.

She followed him through the unfamiliar streets of Providence until they came to a building called The Promenade, where he turned into the garage with her close behind. He parked and waved her into the spot next to him. As she pulled in, he got out of his car and walked away, not even looking to see if she was following. She had to run to make the elevator he was standing in with no intention of holding it for her.

"Thanks," she said sarcastically. Realizing she had done it again, she added, "It's not easy to run in these." She bent her leg to adjust the strap on her shoe, giving him a great shot down her dress. It didn't matter. When she looked up, he was staring off into space. They got off and he walked down the hallway without looking back.

As she followed him, a sense of the surreal came over her. Was she really going to do this? It's not like she was a stranger to kinky sex by any means, but she was hundreds of miles from home, about to enter the apartment of a man she didn't know and had already pissed off. *Think of the contract,* she told herself, as she had dozens of times this week. The fact Mark lived in a luxury condo building settled her nerves somewhat. He couldn't be that much of a maniac. He stopped at the last apartment on the left and, after unlocking the door; opened it and stood aside for her. She took a deep breath and walked past him.

"Thank you, sir," she said softly.

The apartment was large and well furnished, with a huge eight-foot window overlooking the city. It was also quite cool. The air conditioning must be cranked all the way up, she thought. She walked over to look out the window, hoping Mark would check her out. Once again, however, he was looking everywhere but. Another standard trick, letting her think he had no interest. Okay, she told herself, it's just sex. Maybe a little rougher than she was used to, but still just sex. Walking over to the coffee table, she removed her watch and bracelet, putting them down on the table.

"Take your shoes off," Mark said quietly.

Allison bent over and slowly removed them, giving him another great shot of her full, milky-white tits. This time, she didn't look up to see if he was watching. When she finished, she kicked the shoes under the table and looked up at him. He was looking this time, down at her feet with their deep red nails. He wasn't just looking. He was staring. Foot fetish? Taking a chance, she playfully wiggled her toes. His eyes wandered up her legs to eventually linger on her tits. She raised her arms over her head, taking her long hair up with them. "All yours, sir," she said in her best little girl voice. "Would you like me to turn around?"

He nodded, so she turned in a slow circle. She gave her skirt a little flip, giving him a glimpse of the curve of her ass in her black lace thong. She turned back to face him and put her head down demurely. This was her chance.

"I'm ready when you are, sir."

"Then follow me." Mark walked down the hallway. They stopped in front of a door that had two symbols carved into it. "Pleasure and pain," he said softly. "They can both be found behind this door. It's just a question of which comes first." As he spoke, he stared intently into her eyes.

"Now," he began, "I'm required to tell you the rules. Once in that room, you'll refer to me as 'Master.' Any other response will lead to pain. Understood?"

"Yes." Pain. Butterflies again.

"The safe word is 'cease.' Say it, and it ends. You won't pass, but I'll stop. You can only say it once. We won't start over."

"Okay," Allison replied. A safe word! This was not sounding good.

"This continues until either you quit, or I feel you've been properly broken. Any questions? It's your last chance to speak freely."

She looked away from his eyes and gave him a shy smile. Reaching up, she put her hand on his arm. "Listen, Mark," she began, lightly running her nails up to his shoulder. "I'm sorry we got off on the wrong foot. I was just a little nervous."

"Understandable," he said, looking down at her tits.

Oh yes, she thought, *I can do this.* "I've never done anything like this before." She lowered her eyes, putting her lip out and trailing her nails back down his arm. "I have to say you're quite sexy." She squeezed his arm. Damn, it did feel good. "So, why don't we go into your bedroom, and you can lie back while this bad little girl makes it all up to you."

She moved her hand to his face. He leaned into it, closing his eyes as she rubbed his cheek.

"Yeah, that's it," she cooed, "just let me take good care of you. We can forget all this rough stuff and just have a good time. I'm so much more fun when I'm playful." She gave him the full power of her green eyes and pout. "Yes? Please, sir?"

She removed her hand from his face, lowered her head, closed her eyes, and waited. Mark's hand gently touched the side of her face. She opened her eyes and smiled at him as she rubbed her cheek into his hand. His hand quickly shifted from her cheek to her chin. He tilted her head up so their eyes were only inches apart.

"You're a very attractive woman, Allison. I'm sure to the frat boys, you're something special. But to me, you're just another proud whore who doesn't know her place."

"I'm willing to learn, sir," Allison began, "I..."

She stopped. His eyes had changed colors, they had gone from greenish gold, to a shade of so dark they appeared black.

"Y...your eyes," she whispered.

Ignoring her Mark squeezed her chin tighter. "Telling me you like them younger. Well of course you do. You like them younger because they're more controllable, because they've barely gotten their little cocks wet, and they melt when they see a woman who's older and knows how to dress. You love it because you think you're more than they can handle." The smirk came back. "Truth is they're all you can handle." He let her chin go and, stepping back; put his hand on the door knob. "Allison Saunders, do you enter this room of your own free will?"

Here we go. She took a deep breath and looked him in the eye. "Yes."

He pushed the door open, gesturing her in. With one final look into his eyes, trying to confirm that they really had changed, she stepped past him into the room.

"Goddamn, it's hot in here!" she exclaimed. "Where's the air?"

Mark pushed her in the back, sending her forward a step so he could close the door behind them. "Your comfort is of no concern to me. Go stand before the bed."

She turned towards the bed and took a good look at the room she had entered. "Oh shit," she whispered under her breath. Although it was daylight, the room was full of shadows. The only light came from two huge candelabras, one on each nightstand. The bed itself was an enormous four-poster, the columns of which appeared to have carvings similar to those on his door. As she approached the edge of the bed, she saw her reflection. The headboard was mirrored, and, as she stared, she could see her back, reflected in another mirror on the opposite wall over the bureau.

She saw him behind her. He was facing away from her, but she could see his face in the mirror. His eyes were closed, and his lips were moving as if he were speaking or, judging by the room, chanting. Looking up, she saw the ceiling over the huge bed was mirrored. Lowering her head, she could now see paintings over each set of candles. Both appeared to be visions of hell.

She had already begun to sweat.

"Turn around," Mark told her.

She did as he said and stood looking at his back. Allison noticed he was watching her in the mirror in which she could see his front, but her back was in the other one. The effect was confusing.

"Take your clothes off and sit on the edge of the bed."

She hesitated, but then slid the straps of the dress over her shoulders and let the dress drop to the floor. Looking in the mirror, she noticed he was looking down at something, not even watching her. She quickly removed her bra, then slid her thong off and sat on the bed.

"So much for foreplay," she said.

"Did I tell you to speak?" he asked, still not looking over.

"No."

"From this point on, you speak when spoken to, and when you do speak, it will only be to answer me. Understood?"

"Yes, sir."

"Yes, Master."

"Yes, Master." She put a little too much emphasis on the word 'Master.'

Mark then turned, and his hand moving faster than she could react to, pinched her left nipple.

"Ow!" she yelped.

"Mind your tone, whore," he told her, turning back to the mirror.

She watched him take his shirt off. His muscular back glistened with sweat. She would have thought it sexy if his entire back wasn't covered with an enormous tattoo of some type of half-man, half-goat thing. No, she knew exactly what it was. Back in college she had done a paper on Satanism for Psych class. It was a Baphomet. With a sinking feeling in her stomach, she realized this was a sick individual.

He kicked his shoes off and spoke. "Close your eyes."

"Yes, Master." She could feel him approach her, feel something slip around her neck.

"You're a proud, little whore, Allison, but I'll change that. Open your eyes."

She did and saw in the mirror the black leather dog collar around her neck. He stepped in front of her. Dangling from his hand was a chain-link dog leash.

"It's time you were taught your place." He clicked the leash to the collar and, taking a step back, pulled on it hard. "To your knees, slut."

Not that she had a choice; he pulled hard enough to yank her off the bed, and she fell to her knees. He stepped back up to her and stood, waiting expectantly. Knowing what he wanted, she reached out to unsnap his jeans. He reached down with both hands and pinched her nipples, getting another yelp out of her. "Since when does a whore not ask her Master's permission?"

Allison swallowed hard. Her hair was already sticking to her neck, and that last pinch had really hurt. *Just play along,* she told herself. "Master, would you allow me the privilege of removing your cock, so that I may please you?"

"Like you've ever pleased anyone other than yourself, but go ahead, I'll let you try."

She hesitated for a moment, making sure her tone would be right. "Thank you. My Master is too kind."

She unsnapped his jeans and began to unzip them, thinking that if she had to, well, then she would show him how good she was. She reached in to grab his cock, but he slapped her hand away and pulled it out himself.

"Oh, damn," she whispered.

To say she had seen her share of cocks over the years would be an understatement, but the one in front of her was easily the biggest. It was huge, long and thick, damn thick. She wrapped her hand around it. Her fingernails barely touched, and it occurred to her that this thing could hurt.

Noticing the look on her face, he smirked. "What's the matter? Been playing with the boys so long you forget what a real one looks like?"

"My Master is very impressive," she replied. She wasn't lying. She licked her lips slowly, then, remembering her part, said, "It would be my pleasure if my..."

"Oh, just shut up and suck it," he snapped, grabbing the back of her head and shoving her face forward.

She opened her mouth and took it about halfway down. He let her head go as she started sucking him in and out, as far as she dared. She wasn't sure if she could take him all the way. As it was, her mouth was full and there was plenty of him left. She kept her eyes turned down as she blew him.

After a couple of minutes, he sighed, "That's better."

She looked up, making a little noise in her throat, thanking him for his approval. It was the wrong move.

"That wasn't a compliment, you fucking slut!" he said. "It's just better than listening to your voice. Now stop playing and suck it, you know? Like you know what you're doing?"

She put her eyes back down, and, picking up the pace, also started stroking with her hand. After a couple of minutes, she began to wonder if he was even close to cumming.

"You're fucking pathetic. Do I need to do this myself?"

He roughly grabbed the back of her head and, holding it still, started fucking her mouth. She opened wider to take more of him, but he was pushing too deep. Afraid she was going to gag, she put her hands on his hips to try to stop him. Another wrong move. This time, her nipples didn't just get a pinch but a vicious twist that would have caused her to yell had her mouth not been stuffed with his cock.

"How dare you touch me!"

He grabbed her wrists and, pinning them in one of his hands, wrapped the leash around them several times. Mark pulled up, holding her arms over her head with one hand. With the other, he grabbed a handful of her hair close to her scalp, causing more pain. He tipped her head back while putting one of his legs up on the bed, forcing his huge prick down her throat at a deeper angle. He then shoved it all the way down. With her head at that angle and her mouth stretched wide, she was being forced to take him to the limit. He was fucking fast and hard, to the point she could feel her eyes watering, all the while holding her arms up so high, her shoulders were starting to hurt.

Oh god, please just cum!

"Look at you, you fucking pig!" he sneered. "On the floor, getting face-fucked and loving it. Don't let the boys do this, do you?"

She stared up at him through her watery eyes and tried to shake her head to answer.

"Did I tell you to fucking move?"

She shook her head again. *Oh fuck!* she thought as soon as she had done it. Tricked at her own goddamn game.

"Proud and disobedient." Mark let go of the back of her head. "Fine then, pay the price."

He pinched her nose shut. She froze. Her eyes bulged. Was he kidding? To make it worse, he started fucking her mouth again. *It's a scare tactic,* she told herself, but he had caught her before she could take a breath, and she was already starting to panic.

"Look at me!" he snapped.

She turned her eyes up to him again. She had no doubt she looked scared. He looked into her eyes, smiling coldly. She couldn't breathe; she heard a high pitched whine and realized it was her, whimpering. Her blood rushed to her head and her vision blurred. She tried to say 'cease' around his cock, but couldn't. He felt her try to speak, and letting her nose go, he also released her arms and pulled his cock from her mouth. "What was that?" he asked, his smile widening.

She fell forward onto her hands and knees, gasping. *That's enough! Nothing was worth this bullshit!* He could have made her pass out or worse. She looked up with every intention of saying the word, then telling him to go fuck himself. But then she saw the expectant smirk on his face.

"Were you trying to tell me something, whore?"

She stared at him, feeling her anger rise. Fuck him. Taking another couple of breaths, she looked him in the eye and spoke. "I was simply trying to thank you for teaching me a valuable lesson, Master."

He gave a slight nod, as if approving of her decision to continue. Reaching down, he un-wrapped the leash from her wrists and unhooked it from the collar. Then, grabbing her by her shoulders, he pulled her up to her feet.

Damn, he's strong!

He looked at her, shaking his head. "That was a good answer. Too bad your eyes weren't telling me what your mouth was. Oh no, Allison, that look won't do, not at all. Let's try again."

With no warning, he wrenched her shoulders, spinning her completely around. She tripped and would have fallen had he not caught her by the back of her hair. Another red hot stab of pain went through her scalp as he used her hair to turn her around and shove her into the bed. The bed was set high, and she was bent over just past her waist. She was now facing the headboard mirror and watched him step up behind her. Taking his cock, he put it on her ass, the tip stopping just shy of the cat's eyes tattoo at the small of her back.

"Nice tattoo," he said softly.

"Thank you, Master."

"The bright color looks good on your sickly skin. Don't you agree?"

She knew something was coming, but had no choice. "My Master is right, of course."

"Good. Then let's add some color." He reached up and brought his hand down in a vicious slap that sounded like a shot in the quiet room.

"Oh, god!" she cried out. Oh, that stung!

"See? Doesn't that look better?"

He pulled her by her hair, bringing her face up to look into the mirror. He stepped to the side so she could see her ass in the opposite mirror. Her right cheek was sunburn red, with a huge welt the shape of his hand already rising on it. She winced, not just at the sight of it, but at the fact that it was also still stinging. "Of course, Master."

"What? No thanks?" He whipped the same hand back around, catching the left side of her ass backhanded.

"Thank you!" she yelped.

In the mirror, she saw him roll his eyes. "Thank you, *Master*. Let's try again." He slapped her again.

"Thank ...oww!"

He proceeded to deal her a series of short, quick slaps. They came faster than she could count, each one stinging more than the one before and adding to the overall pain. After several of them, she began crying out, "Thank you, Master! Thank you, oh, thank youuuuu!" The last one ended in a whimper as he dealt her a particularly hard one. Finally, he stopped and she let her head drop to the bed. Panting, she could feel the cheeks of her ass throbbing. He grabbed her hair, pulling her head up again. "Did I say look away? Do I need the leash?"

"No, Master."

He began to slap his cock on her ass, hard enough to make it sting more. Then, taking it, he put the head at her pussy and pushed in just a little. "You don't seem that wet. Do I not excite you?"

"Of course! My Master is quite attractive I... oh!!!" she gasped as he slammed his prick all the way in.

"Don't bother; it just would have been easier on you if it were wet."

Oh my god, He was deep! Her pussy had never felt so full. He held it there, then once again, grabbing her hair, said, "Put your hands behind your back."

She did and winced as, when she put her hands back, she was being held up by her hair. He once again grabbed her wrists in one hand. Pulling back on her arms as well as her hair, he lifted her up off the bed so just her sore nipples rubbed on the sheets. Once in that position, he slid his cock most of the way out, paused for a moment, then began fucking the shit out of her. She tried not to make any noise, but couldn't help it. "Oh, ow!" His cock alone was hurting her, never mind her shoulders and the pulling of her hair.

"What? No thank you for allowing a filthy slut like you to have the pleasure of my cock?" he asked. Before she could reply, he let go of her hair to slap her ass again.

"Ow! Th.. thank you, M-Master!" she stammered as he started fucking her even harder.

He had pulled her higher by her arms so that he was entering at an even deeper angle. Was he ever going to cum? Trying a different tactic, she forced herself to start mixing in small sounds of pleasure in between the groaning and thanking him.

"Yeah, you like that big cock, don't you, you little pig?"

"Y-yes, Master. I'm glad my Master has chosen to fuck me with his beautiful... uh!" She grunted as he really reared back and slammed her.

"You think I want to fuck you? I'm only dirtying my cock in your disgusting pussy because I got sick of that pathetic attempt at a blow job!"

"I'm s-sorry, Master." she groaned, and then followed it with a moan, a real one this time. She was getting used to him at this angle, and, despite the pain in the rest of her body; she was beginning to enjoy his huge cock stuffing her. She had never been fucked this hard, and she couldn't believe his control. He was still showing no signs of even being close to cumming.

He pulled her back further, to the point she was almost standing. Facing the mirror, she could see he had leaned back and had one arm braced on the bureau behind him. He was at an angle, driving his hips up into her while holding her up. The muscles in both his arms were bulging impressively, and their bodies were slick with sweat.

She let out another moan. "Oh, thank you, Master," she whispered, almost meaning it.

"Yeah, you like that, my little whore?"

"Oh, yes!" she cried out. It made it easier to stay in character. "Thank you, Master."

"Well, that's no good! I'm supposed to be enjoying it, not you. Apparently, I'm not being harsh enough on you, and I haven't even cum yet, so you're sure as hell not pleasing me."

He pulled himself out of her and stepped back, taking her with him. As he held her, he reached back and grabbed something from the bureau. Letting go of her arms, he reached around. Watching in the mirror, her eyes widened, and she groaned to herself as he attached a set of wicked looking nipple clamps to her. He turned the screws until she let out a low whimper.

"Does that hurt?"

"Yes, Master," she hissed between her teeth. Then she yelped out loud as he gave the screws another turn.

"That's in case you were lying and this…" She cried out louder, as he turned them again. "Is for not telling me you're sorry when I said I wasn't pleased."

"I'm sorry, Master!"

"From this point on, anytime you act up, I'll give them a turn." He grabbed her by the collar, holding her head up so she was looking into his face in the mirror. "Understood?"

"Yes, Master," she answered immediately.

"Trust me, you'd be surprised how much they can be squeezed, so be a good little whore." He smiled coldly at her. "Now you're going to crawl up onto the bed and lie on your back for me. Think you can do that?"

"Of course, Master." She leaned onto the bed, putting one knee up to crawl across it.

"Hold on," Mark said. "I almost forgot something.

He reached up to the column on the right and pulled a small silver chain. There was a click as a small door located in each of the four columns slid open. As they, did a length of chain ending in a manacle fell out of each one onto the bed.

"Jesus Christ," Allison said softly. Then let out a cry that was close to a scream as he hauled off and gave her a wicked slap on her swollen ass.

"Never use that name in here!" he shouted at her. Reaching around her, he gave each screw a turn.

"Oh, I'm so sorry!!" she whined.

She was scared. During the time they had been here, as nasty as he had been, he had seemed calm and controlled. Now, looking at him in the mirror, he looked crazy. The candlelight reflecting in the mirror made his eyes look as if they were glowing.

"Now crawl your slutty ass onto the bed and roll over."

She hesitated. He was sick, really sick. If he chained her down, she would be helpless. He had already tried to suffocate her. She closed her eyes. It was just a game. This guy was an attorney, not a serial killer. It was for show. It...

"Crawl or quit." This was followed by another smack to her ass.

"Yes, Master." She got her other knee up and crawled across the bed.

"Good little slut."

She went up to the headboard and turned over onto her back, wincing as she let her weight go on her ass. He remained at the foot of the bed, looking at the chain nearest him as if measuring. Reaching out, he grabbed her ankles, pulling her down to the middle of the huge bed. He picked up the manacle, holding out his other hand. "Give me your foot."

She swallowed and, unable to help herself, whispered, "Please don't hurt me."

He rolled his eyes in disgust. "Typical poser. You love to make them beg, but can't handle much yourself." He held his hand out again. Once again, she hesitated, knowing she would probably pay a price for it. Instead, he said quietly, "This is what you make of it, Allison. Pain or pleasure, you'll endure only what you choose to." His voice was soft again, and he seemed calmer than before. Slowly, she lifted her leg and put her foot in his hand. He clipped the manacle around her ankle and tightened it. She placed her other foot in his hand without him asking.

"Good girl," he said softly.

Walking around the bed, he leaned over and, taking her right hand, put the cuff around her wrist. When he went for her left, she pulled it away, panicking suddenly. No." She shook her head. He twisted the screw on her right nipple.

"Nooo," she whimpered.

He stared coldly at her. "There's only one word that will result in anything but more, and we both know you want to say it. I told Warner you were a poser. Now prove me right."

She closed her eyes. Warner, Redding, thousands of dollars and the prestige she deserved. She opened them to see that arrogant smirk back on Mark's face and put her left hand out. He nodded as he attached the manacle to her wrist. He walked back to the foot of the bed and stood, looking at her with that smug look on his face again. "How do you look?" He pointed to the mirrored ceiling.

"Like an unworthy whore." She answered properly, while thinking, *piece of shit! Getting off on this!* She was here because she had to be; otherwise, she wouldn't as much as spit at him.

"Once again, good answer, Allison, but very insincere. That's okay; I can take care of that." He reached up to the left column and pulled another chain.

She gasped as she felt the chains pull her arms up and out as far as they could go. Oh my god! She was on a fucking rack! He smiled at the look on her face. Going over to the other column, he grabbed another chain. Her legs were then pulled to the sides. As he continued to pull, her legs kept spreading open even farther. She let out a groan as they were forced into a complete split.

"Oh please," he sneered. "Fucking skank like you should be used to spreading them."

She lay completely spread eagle, not only feeling totally helpless but, for the first time in her life, she felt ashamed of her nakedness. He bent his knees slightly and, from that position, jumped up onto the bed, landing on the edge, perfectly balanced. His cock, as it had been from the start, was rock hard. He walked across the bed, one leg on either side of her, and then dropped down, his knees just under her arms. He leaned over onto his hands, his cock pointed directly at her mouth. "Let's get it wet this time."

She obediently opened her mouth and with no hesitation, he started driving his cock in and out of her face. Once again, he was going all the way in, and, with her head against the bed, she had nowhere to go. At one point, she almost gagged. Balancing himself on one hand, he turned the screw on first the right, then the left nipple.

"Don't you dare," he said as she squealed around his cock.

After several more pumps, he pulled his cock out and backed up. He positioned himself over her pussy. He paused, looking into her eyes, then, entering her with one smooth thrust, began fucking the shit out of her.

"Oh, goddamn!" she exclaimed, unable to help herself as he pounded into her.

Her legs were spread so wide that he was going in right up to his balls. He held himself up over her, using his powerful legs and hips to slam into her.

"Oh th-th- thank you," she managed to get out as he continued assaulting her.

That's what this was. This wasn't sex, it was an attack. His head was just over hers, and their eyes were only inches apart. Even though he was fucking her relentlessly, there was no expression on his face. It was as if he wasn't enjoying it at all. With a start, she wondered if this was what it was like to be raped. Unable to control it, she yelped with each thrust, and this time, there was no hint of pleasure in it at all.

"Oh, does that hurt my little whore?"

"N-No, Master. Thank you."

"It feels good?"

"O-of course, my Master feels good."

He shook his head. "Then I'm being too gentle. It's supposed to hurt."

"Oh, please!" she gasped, and then yelped, as that got her another twist of the clamps, one at a time. "Please, Master!"

"Please what?"

"Easy, Master, please!" Allison begged. "It hurts!"

"Now it hurts?"

"Y-yes, Master," she stuttered. *Oh, how it hurt!* He was driving into her so hard she could feel herself sinking into the bed with each pump. This guy was a fucking animal!

He leaned over into her ear and whispered, "See, now I don't believe you. Guess we have to give it to you harder." He started lifting himself further out of her, all the way to the tip, then back down.

"Ohhh," she was whining and couldn't help it.

"Yeah?" he asked, looking in her eyes. "You don't like being taken? Too bad, because this is exactly the way fucking whores like you deserve it! Proud little cockteaser, playing with the boys, getting what you need, then kicking them out. Toying with them, then making them beg." He lowered himself to his elbows, still driving savagely in and out with his hips. He grabbed her chin and pushed her head up. "Watch yourself being taken!"

She stared up at the ceiling. Her legs were spread out, and she could see the muscles in his back and ass flexing as he slammed her. She was a mass of sweat, her hair stuck to her face, and she looked scared as hell. "Oh, please, Master! Oh, it hurts! It does!"

"I like that, Allison. Who's begging now? No fun when it's you and not the boys." He leaned over farther. Once again, he whispered in her ear. "Lucky for you, there's rules, or I'd have found a couple of your little playmates and let them come in and take turns on you. Have a nice little gang-bang, make you fuck and suck until you were so used up, you couldn't walk. Make you thank them for it."

This image must have gotten to him as, finally, Allison could hear his breathing start to speed up, and his arms were tensing. He was finally going to cum. He sped up even more, banging in and out of her. She was beyond even moaning. Instead, she made tiny little sounds in her throat. He grabbed her chin again and looked into her eyes. "Say it!" he snarled at her.

She knew even he couldn't hold back much longer, and, summoning up the last of her will, whispered, "Thank you, Master, for showing this unworthy whore what it's like to be taken by a real man."

His eyes widened slightly. He had thought he'd had her. Not only hadn't she broken, but he was going to cum, she could feel it. He was starting to let out a couple of small gasps of his own. Gaining a little confidence, she forced a pout and said softly, "Oh, thank you, Master."

He gave her several more hard pumps, then pulled out and squeezing his cock, he once again straddled her face. She opened her mouth, expecting to be made to swallow, but instead, he grabbed her mouth and forced it shut. "As if I'd let you taste it!"

He jerked his cock off into her face. The first spurt hit her directly in her right eye. She tried to turn her head, but he was holding her chin. First, she couldn't wait for him to cum, but now she wondered if he would ever stop. Spurt after spurt was hitting her face and going into her hair. She closed her eyes in time to avoid her other eye being hit. Finally, he stopped jerking and, taking his cock, started rubbing it all over her face, spreading the cum around even more, mixing it with the sweat she was already covered with. When he was finished, he leaned back and told her, "Open your eyes."

She did and looked up into the mirror. She had become a mess.

"Maybe we could get some pictures, send them to your parents. I'm sure they'd be proud." He got off the bed and stared down at her. He looked as if he were waiting for something.

Oh shit! She quickly spoke. "Thank you, M... Oww!" But she was too late.

He turned the clamps, shaking his head. "Give you the honor of cumming on you, and I have to wait for a thank you."

"Sorry, Master."

"Not yet, but we're getting there."

He walked around the bed, opened a nightstand drawer, and removed something from it. Making his way back to the foot of the bed, he released her ankles.

"Thank you, Master," she got out quickly.

Ignoring her, he knelt between her legs. As he did, she saw he had a small, silver bullet vibrator in his hand. Spreading her pussy open, he placed it directly on her clit.

"Close your legs."

She obeyed. Was he really going to let her cum? She was surprisingly horny, considering the way she had been treated. Was this how her pets felt? That mix of humiliation and lust? He grabbed her ankles and crossed them. Reaching down to the floor, he picked up the belt he had been wearing and wrapped it around her knees. He pulled it until she grunted, then fastened it. "Don't want that to fall out, now, do we?"

"Thank you, Master. I…" She let out a long moan as the vibrator kicked on. It was on low, but pressed tight against her clit. After only a couple of minutes, she could feel her body beginning to tense up. Not wanting to risk it, she immediately spoke up. "Oh, Master, may I please cum?"

He shrugged. "That's up to you."

"Thank you, Master!" she moaned again. *Oh, here it is!* She began to arch her back and… The vibrator shut off. She gasped.

He smiled wickedly. "Guess not."

He held up a small box. She recognized it as some type of remote timer. He walked over to her, placing the remote on the nightstand next to her.

"I have to go shower your stink off of me. Hopefully, this will keep you entertained while I'm gone." He walked away. As he opened the bedroom door, he stood there for a moment. "Damn it's cool out here." He swung the door back and forth, causing a slight breeze to reach her.

Oh, that air felt good!

He looked at her, smiling. "Don't worry, *hon,* I'll be back, maybe even tonight. Try not to wet the bed, will you?" Then he left, closing the door behind him.

She slumped into the bed, grimacing with disgust as some of his cum slid down her cheek. She closed her eyes. Between her legs, the vibrator began to hum.

Chapter Two

Lying in the oppressive heat of the room, her arms chained to the massive four poster bed, Allison let out a low moan. She felt the silver bullet pressing against her clit begin vibrating again. She tried squeezing her legs together even tighter and pushed her hips off the bed, desperately straining to cum.

"Oh, please," she whimpered, knowing she sounded pathetic, but unable to help herself.

She tried to work her thighs up and down to no avail. Her legs were tied together at the knees so tightly; she couldn't budge them at all. She gasped. However, as she began to feel the first welcome twinges of orgasm flow through her loins, her thighs started to quiver and she arched her back, wincing, as this caused the chains attached to the nipple clamps to pull tighter. *Oh, yes!* she thought. Despite the added pain, the vibrator was lasting longer and she was going to...

The vibrator stopped.

"Oh, no!" Allison moaned, pumping her hips in vain.

With a groan she slumped back into the bed. How long had she been left alone like this? That was at least the fifth time the vibrator had gone off. How long in between? Fifteen minutes each? She'd lost all track of time. She swallowed hard. Her throat was as dry as a bone, unlike the sweat-soaked sheets beneath her. The temperature in the room had to be close to a hundred degrees.

She pulled against the manacles that were holding her wrists, hoping the sweat would give her enough play to slide up a little. All this did was cause her shoulders to hurt more. At this point, the aching in her shoulders was in perfect time to the throbbing sensation in her ass. She'd been spanked so badly, she could still feel the stinging.

Opening her eyes–as far as they would, anyway, between the sweat dripping into both of them and what had been squirted into her right one—she looked up into the mirrored ceiling. She saw herself lying there and let out a groan. Her normally ivory complexion was flushed red from the heat, and her black hair was plastered to her forehead and parts of her cheeks.

Even in the reflection, she could see the bruising around her pink nipples from the clamps, as well as the twisting of them. She was chained with her arms as far out to the side as they would go, and her legs were wrapped together with a belt. Everything hurt, including her pussy, which had endured the hardest fucking she could have ever imagined; it had been more like an attack than a sexual encounter.

She knew this wasn't the end, not by a long shot. At some point, when he felt her will was worn down even further, Mark would come back, and the games would begin anew. As if that thought had cued it, the vibrator started to hum against her over-stimulated clit. She moaned loudly. Despite the pain and humiliation that she had endured, her body was being forced to want to cum.

She closed her eyes, trying not to push to cum, for it would do no good. What the hell was she doing here? More importantly, why hadn't she quit yet? It would be so simple. All she had to do was say one word and it would be over. She would be untied and could go home. Go back to being the one in control. Who the hell needed this? This wasn't fun. It was sadistic, trying to get her to break as she, herself, had broken so many boys. But she hadn't done it like this she...

"Ohhhhh," she whined as her orgasm once again approached just in time for the vibrating to stop. Slumping back, panting once again, her parched throat burning, she turned her head, thinking she saw something move. She realized it was a trick caused by the flickering of the half dozen or so candles that were lit on each side of the bed. She jerked her head as she realized she was starting to sink into a daze. She forced herself to concentrate, to remember why she was here and what was on the line for her and why she would not quit. Closing her eyes, she tried to take shallower breaths so she would stop panting, and let her body relax while it could before the vibrator kicked in again.

Her eyes remaining closed, she lay there, telling herself it couldn't last much longer. The vibrator started to hum again. She tried not to press for the orgasm she knew would elude her, even when her thighs started to shake again. This time, she barely sighed as it stopped. At least she was getting used to it. After what seemed like an eternity, she heard footsteps outside the door. She felt her heart begin to race. It was too many footsteps. More than one person was approaching!

She heard Mark outside the door, speaking. His words sent a sinking feeling into her stomach. "Okay, here's the rules, boys. It's one at a time, but you can go as many times as you like. If you don't think you can get it up again, just shove it in her mouth. She's a hell of a fluffer."

No! He couldn't do this! He said there were rules, there were…The door began to open. Mark's voice was louder. "Oh, and by the way, if she forgets to thank you, make sure you give her tits a good, hard twist."

The door swung open, and after entering, Mark stepped to the side as four young men came into the room, one after another, all staring hungrily at her, and all naked. Naked and ready.

"So, who's first?" Mark asked.

"Cease!" Allison gasped out as the first man; a tall, well-built blond who was hung like a horse approached the bed.

"What did she say?" he asked.

"She said, 'Please'," Mark told him. "Now get on the bed and fuck her like I'm paying you to."

"Cease!!!!" Allison wailed. "Oh, please…"

Allison's eyes snapped open and she jerked so hard on the chains she cried out from the pain it caused in her shoulders

."Oh, god!" she gasped, her heart pounding in her chest. She tried to catch her breath, but sucking in mouthfuls of the hot air hurt her already raw throat. She couldn't believe she had nodded off like that, but, thank god, it had only been a dream. He had threatened her with a gangbang, and she was borderline delirious at this point.

"Bad dream?"

Mark's voice caused her to start again. She forced her head up to look and saw him standing at the foot of the bed, or thought she did, as, when he stepped forward, he disappeared. She blinked and shook her head. It had been his reflection in the mirror. He must be behind or at the side of the bed. The room was so dark beyond the candles; she had no idea how big it really was.

"Over here."

He stepped out from the shadows, but only halfway. As if drawn perfectly down the middle, one half of his body was visible, the other shrouded in darkness. She wondered how long he had been there, and, on the heels of that thought, she wondered if she had yelled the word "cease" out in her sleep, which could mean this was over. All this would be for nothing. As though he could read her thoughts, he stepped out of the shadows and said, "Actually, to be dreaming, you have to be asleep. Your eyes were half open."

He was naked and his hair was wet, as was his skin, as if he had just taken a shower and not dried off. He held a bottle of water, and, as she watched, walked over next to her. He took a couple of swallows, and then placed the bottle on the nightstand next to her. She licked her dry lips. She wanted the water as bad as she wanted to cum. He walked away and, stopping at the foot of the bed, leaned over to undo the belt.

"Only three hours and hallucinating already," he grunted. "Hell, I went a day and a half before I started losing it. Then again." He smirked. "This room does have that effect on soft, little pretenders like you."

He removed the belt and put it on the edge of the bed. His cool, damp hands felt good on her hot flesh, and she found herself hoping he'd run them over her.

"And it is pretty hot in here," he said, before making a show of sniffing the air. "Fucking stinks in here, too. Smells like your nasty pussy."

"Sorry, Master," she managed to whisper.

"And did you cum, my little whore?"

"No, Master," she whispered hoarsely. Her voice was fading.

"Well, that's your fault. I gave you enough chances."

He reattached the manacles, then tugged on the chain, pulling her legs open again. He walked over to the side of the bed and picked up the remote. "No wonder," he said. "It was on low." He took his thumb and turned the dial all the way up.

"Ohhhh!" The vibrator kicked in much faster than last time. She began panting, eagerly thrusting into it. A moment later, it fell away, as her legs were no longer holding it.

"Nooo!" she moaned.

"No?" Mark gave the screws a turn, causing her to yelp. "It's my fault that it fell out of that loose pussy of yours?"

"O-of course not, Master."

He walked back around, got onto the bed, lying between her legs. Unable to hold it up for any length of time, her head went back onto the bed, but she could watch him in the mirror. He stopped with his face inches from her pussy. Spreading her lips, he leaned forward and blew lightly on her clit. She groaned as her hips twitched.

"Someone's close to cumming. Wouldn't take much would it?"

"No, Master."

"Mmmm." He sounded as if he were thinking. "Now isn't one of the games you play with your pets is that when you're close, you try to get them to keep you on the edge, and if you cum quick, they have to start over?"

"Yes, Master." Oh, why did this not sound good?

"When I was younger, I used to have an older woman do that to me, and if I screwed up, my punishments were a lot harsher than simply starting over. Needless to say, I became very good at it." He looked up into the mirror and winked at her. "Let's see if I still have the touch."

To Allison's chagrin, he still had that touch. For what seemed like an eternity, Mark lay between her thighs, alternately fingering, licking, and using the vibrator on her pussy. She was so close, her thighs trembled continuously. He would suck her clit several times, then stop and place the vibrator on her for a few seconds. It was everything she could do to hold onto enough pride not to whine. The several times she almost came, he stopped her just in time. Whenever he stopped, he would slide up and shove his cock in her mouth again. Her throat was so dry, it hurt every time. After that, he would just lie there, giving her body time to calm down before starting again. She was in a stupor, the heat, the pain, but also the lust, the entire room smelled of sex, her sex.

He was back to slowly licking her pussy. He had an amazingly soft, teasing touch with his tongue, and she could feel herself getting close yet again. She wanted to beg to cum, but the time before she had and had received another turn of the screws. However, being this close, she could not help moaning loudly, and her thighs trembled as she strained, trying to force the orgasm. She had never needed to cum so badly!

After she let out a long whimper, he stopped again. "What's the matter, Mistress? Don't like your own game?"

"I...oh" she gasped as he flicked his tongue across her sensitive clit.

"Isn't this what you do to your little boys, Allison? Tease the shit out of them?"

"Y-yes, Master," she groaned as he placed the vibrator on her again.

"You let them play with you, make you cum, then keep teasing. Use your pussy and your mouth, get them to the point they're begging, just like I'm doing to you. Isn't that right?"

Holding the vibrator to one side of her clit, he used his tongue on the other side. Her hips jerked off the bed. She had never had that done to her before, and in her present state... He pulled away and, reaching up, flicked her nipple with his finger, sending a wave of pain through her. "Did you just move?"

"I'm sorry, Master, I..."

"Isn't that what you do? Lay them back and use that pretty little mouth of yours, and when they lose control, like they always do, like they can't help at their age, you punish them, don't you?"

"Yes, Master," she whispered.

He sucked her clit into his mouth and swirled his tongue around it.

"Oh! Please, Master!" she moaned as, somewhere in the back of her head, the deviant side of her thought he really was fucking good with that tongue.

"Please, *Mistress,* is what they say." He looked up at her in the mirror and smiled. "And do you let them cum?"

Oh no! Oh please! At this point, she was even begging in her head. "Y-yes I..." She trailed off.

"But not all the time, isn't that right? Sometimes, they have to suffer, don't they?" He paused as their eyes met in the mirror. She let out a long whimper, knowing how this was going to end.

"Well?" he asked.

"Sometimes I don't let them," she whispered in resignation.

Mark nodded. "Well then, how does it feel, Mistress?" He made to push away from her, and Allison felt herself lose control.

"Oh, no, please, Master, please don't tease me anymore. Oh!"

He began quickly licking her clit, bringing her to the edge before stopping yet again.

"Nooooo!" She was practically sobbing. "Oh, please, Masterrrrr!"

"Why should I? Why should I have mercy when you had none?"

"Because I..." Allison started then, knowing there was no real reason, simply groaned. "Oh, because I need to, oh, please have mercy, Master, please."

"I have to say, Allison, that wasn't bad. You sound just like one of those pathetic little kids." He blew lightly on her clit. "Tell you what, the next time you get close, I want you to start thanking me. If it sounds sincere, maybe I'll let you. If it doesn't, I'll quit and fuck you again, instead. You get one chance."

He roughly shoved two fingers into her sore pussy and began pumping them in and out rapidly. As he did, he started sucking her clit in and out of his mouth in the same rhythm. *Oh yes!!* She could feel her orgasm rapidly approaching and started thanking him in advance. "Oh, thank you, Master!" she cried out. "Thank you for letting me cum!" The hell with pride!

He sped up as the strongest orgasm of her life began to flow through her. She arched her back so hard, her arms and legs tightened against the chains enough to lift herself off the bed. Her shoulders throbbed and the nipple clamps tightened, but the pain seemed to add to the pleasure. Between the power of the orgasm and the fear of him stopping in the middle, she was screaming as loud as her sore throat would let her.

"Thank you!!! Oh Master, thank you!! Thank...ohhh!!"

Wave after wave of pent-up pleasure crashed through her. She had never cum this hard! He continued to lick as she pumped her hips into him, not caring if she'd get punished for it. Another, smaller orgasm exploded after the first one. She tried to get out another thank you, but her voice was all but gone. When it was over, she went limp, collapsing back onto the bed, panting and so dizzy from the heat and the orgasm, she felt as if she were going to pass out. He got off the bed and, walking over next to her, picked up the bottle of water. He took a sip, then held it up to her. "Would you like a drink?"

"Yes," she croaked. "Yes, please, Master."

"Well, then, let me give you one." He took the bottle, poured some of the water onto his cock and, grabbing the back of her head, shoved it into her mouth. His cock was cold in her parched mouth, and she eagerly sucked the water off of him. He pulled his cock out most of the way and poured some water onto it, letting it run down the length of his shaft into her mouth. She was drinking from his cock and could care less how bad it was, all she knew was how bad she needed it. He took it away from her. "Want more?"

"Yes, please, Master."

"Here you go." He held the bottle up, pouring the water onto her face.

She sputtered as the water got into her eyes and nose, but she couldn't believe how good the cold felt. He took the last few sips himself, then smirked at her. "I get no thank you?"

"Master, I'm sorry I..."

"I'll show you sorry." He reached down and gave another turn to the screws.

"Oh god!" she cried out, "I'm sorry! I'm so sorry!"

He looked at her, shaking his head in disgust. "Sorry is right. Actually, a fucking mess is what you really are. You're stinking up my fucking bedroom, aren't you?"

"Yes, Master," she agreed.

"Dirty little slut. Now I'm going to have to clean you up."

Reaching down, he removed the clamps. Her breath hissed as the blood rushed back through her nipples. Moving around the bed, he released the cuffs from her. "Sit up," he told her.

Slowly, she sat up. She was sore, dizzy, and still reeling from the power of the orgasm. She was unsure if she'd be able to walk. He grabbed the leash from the end of the bed and clipped it to her collar. "Get on your hands and knees. We're going for a walk."

Allison stared at him. There was no fucking way. "Master, I don't want..."

"Don't want to?" He reached down with both hands and twisted her sore nipples, making her yelp again. "Let's try again."

She glared at him, shaking her head. She would not do this. He pulled on the leash and she held herself back.

He rolled his eyes. "The floor or the door, slut, it's your choice." He held the leash up again.

After staring briefly into his eyes, she let herself slide off the bed and onto her hands and knees.

"Let's go." With a tug, he began to walk.

With a whimper, she began to crawl next to him. Oh god, what the hell was she doing? This was too much. Just say the fucking word! Instead, she continued to follow him to the door. When they left the bedroom, the air conditioning struck her like a slap. God, that felt good! He tugged on the collar and walked her down the corridor. She could feel how red she was, crawling naked across the floor on a leash.

Mark stopped. "Up on your knees."

As she obeyed, he grabbed his cock. Taking her cue, she obediently leaned forward to suck on it. He became hard quickly and pulled his cock away. "Back on all fours."

He resumed walking down the corridor. "Good little puppy," he said. She crawled alongside him until they reached the bathroom. Mark pointed at the toilet. "Go if you have to."

He turned to the shower and started the water. Totally humiliated, but unable to help it, she sat on the toilet and quickly went, hoping he wouldn't turn around. Without looking, he said over his shoulder, "Don't bother wiping. I have to wash that filthy thing anyway."

She stood up as he gestured to the shower. When she got in, the water was shockingly cold. He removed the leash from her collar, grabbed her wrists, and wrapped it around them. He then reached up over the showerhead and placed the loop on a hook. He looked down to see she was still on her feet. He grabbed the chain again and lifted a few more inches so that she was on her toes, then locked it in.

"Owww," she groaned. Her shoulders hurt as well as her leg muscles from staying on her toes. He stepped in behind her and began washing her, not sensually, but roughly, with a harsh washcloth that hurt her skin as he scrubbed. She winced as he scrubbed her pussy, scratching her clit with the cloth. When he reached her tits, he was just as rough, giving each nipple a pinch through the cloth. He spun her on the chain to face him and, pulling her directly under the ice cold water, rinsed her off.

He then pushed her back away from the water, sliding the chain farther along the hook so her back was up against the wall. As she stood, straining to keep her toes on the floor to take the pain away from her shoulders, he got under the water and washed himself. He took his time, seemingly unaffected by the cold. Allison, on the other hand, was shivering badly. He finished rinsing himself, then reached down and grabbed her underneath her knees, lifting her up and onto his cock. She cried out as he began fucking her up against the wall, driving into her as hard as he could. Stepping back, he pulled her with him until her arms were stretched against the leash. He was fucking her almost sideways, easily holding her weight up.

"At least I can't get your stink on me like this, and you finally got that cum off your face," he told her. Then, leaning forward, he put his mouth on her incredibly sore right nipple and began to suck on it.

She moaned, then yelped as he used his teeth on her nipple and drove into her harder. He let her down and spun her around so her back was to him. Once again, he lifted her by her thighs and placed her feet against the wall so her knees were drawn up to her tits and entered her from behind.

"Oh my god!!" she yelled as he started to fuck her. Oh, he was fucking deep like this.

He pinched both her nipples again. "Stop your whining," he snapped in her ear.

He continued to slam her, then pulled out and let her drop back onto her toes, sending a searing pain through her shoulders. Shutting off the water, he reached up, unhooked her from the wall, then handed her the leash. Taking her cue, she hooked it back to the collar and got down on the floor, adding, "Thank you for cleaning me, Master."

"I did it for my own benefit. You were stinking up the bedroom."

He walked her back to the bedroom where he told her to get back onto the bed on her hands and knees, facing the mirror at the foot of the bed. In that mirror, she could see the reflection of her ass in the headboard mirror. It was still sunburn red. Getting on the bed behind her, he grabbed her wrists, put them behind her back, and wrapped them with the leash. Then he grabbed her ankles and tied them with the belt. Letting her go, he came around to the edge of the bed.

In this position, she couldn't hold her head up and was face down on the bed. He lifted her up by the hair and pushed his cock into her mouth. Holding her head still, he slowly pumped it in and out several times.

"Get it nice and wet," he told her. "It's for your own good."

He then pulled it away and got onto the bed behind her. He pulled on the leash just over her wrists, lifting her up to face the mirror. As she watched, he took his huge prick and put the tip directly against her ass.

"No," Allison whispered. "Please no."

She hadn't had anal sex since college, and that had only been a couple of times with a boyfriend. Now, as Mark was right there, she realized he had not touched it at all, hadn't wanted to stretch it out. Between her being tight and his size, she knew it was going to…"Oh that hurts," she moaned as he pushed it in a couple of inches.

He looked at her in the mirror. "Then say it."

"Please, Master, just not this. Anything, but…oh."

He slid his cock all the way in. She tried to put her head down so he couldn't see her face, but he was holding the leash. Her eyes were all but bugging out of her head. Oh, that hurt so badly! She could feel herself tearing. She bit her lip so she wouldn't say it.

"That hurts?" he asked her.

"Yes, Master." She winced as he started to work it back out.

"Well, then, this will really hurt." He pulled his cock out almost the entire length, then slammed it in so hard that, had he not held the leash, she would have gone off the bed.

"Oh fuck!!" she screamed. "God, that hurts! Stop, please!"

He kept fucking her. Not as hard as that first thrust, but fast enough, as if it was her pussy. With each pump, she squealed and whimpered. Oh, she couldn't take this!

He pulled on the leash so she was looking at the mirror. His other hand grabbed a handful of her sweat-soaked hair. "Look at yourself," he whispered. "Tell me, whore, are you still something special?"

"No, Master," she got out between gasps.

He started fucking harder. She was whining, one continuous whimper as he was pounding in and out. He let go of her hair and reached onto the bed. A moment later, she felt something between her legs, and gasped as she felt the vibrator turn on.

He pulled her hair again. "The banner over the mirror, read what it says."

Allison looked where he said. There was a large tapestry across the top of the mirror that looked like old parchment. Across it in gothic lettering it said…

"Read it out loud!" he snapped, slapping her ass.

"It is always by way of pain," Allison gasped out, squealing between each word, "one arrives at pleasure."

"Marquis De Sade," Mark told her. "Now enjoy the journey."

He completely let loose, brutally slamming his cock into her. She howled in pain. Her ass was on fire, and tears were running down her face as he tore into her, full force.

"No more!" she cried out.

He continued, ignoring her. She wailed in pain again, and started to say it. "Ce- ce-" She looked up to see him smirking again. She froze, staring back at him.

He reached down, and, after turning the vibrator all the way up, started ripping into her again. Despite the pain, she could feel her clit beginning to respond to the toy, and even his pounding into her started feeling different.

"What was that whore?" he asked, smiling at her.

She closed her eyes. She had not allowed herself to be walked naked on a leash to quit now. No, he wouldn't get the satisfaction, not like this, anyway. She looked into his eyes.

"Go ahead, slut, I'm listening."

Allison felt something snap inside of her. "Oh yes!" she screamed. "Yes, Master! Oh, thank you, Master!!"

As she yelled, he started fucking her even harder, but as the pain increased, so did her body's desire to cum. She could feel it starting in her loins. Her thighs shook. *Pleasure and pain,* she thought. As her orgasm approached, she continued to cry out.

"Thank you for showing me my place, Master! Thank you for fucking this unworthy whore, for treating me like the fucking pig I am! For showing me my place! Oh, oh, oh!"

She began to cum, and she couldn't believe how good her ass contracting around his cock felt. It must have felt good to him, as well. He began to groan as he continued to fuck her. As her orgasm continued to send spasms throughout her body, she watched him in the mirror. Mark was quite a sight, the muscles in his chest and arms were flexed out with the effort of slamming into her, and he was glistening with sweat. More exciting was the look on his face. He was completely caught up in lust. Her screaming was like music to his ears, and Allison sang some more.

"Oh, god, yes!! Thank you for wasting your beautiful cock on this ungrateful slut! Please cum for me! Please cum all over this filthy whore!"

That put him over the edge. With a loud moan of his own, he pulled his cock out, and, squeezing it so he wouldn't cum immediately, he rolled her over on her back and, kneeling over her, pushed his cock into her mouth, squirting shot after shot of cum. Not caring it had just come from her ass, Allison sucked hard, taking every drop, desperately hoping it was all he had left.

When he finished, he sat back onto the bed, panting. For the first time since this had started, he seemed tired. She lay there moaning. Her ass was on fire, her tits hurt, everything hurt, she was dripping sweat, her breath coming in gasps. They stayed like that for several minutes, before he rose from the bed, grabbed her shoulder and rolled her onto her stomach. Walking over to the side of her head, he grabbed her hair so that she faced the mirror. "What do you see, Allison?" he asked.

She hesitated, knowing the answer would be very important, because she couldn't take anymore.

"I see a whore," she began as she stared at her reflection. She was a mess, with her hair plastered to her forehead, eye shadow everywhere, and tears on her cheeks from when he was fucking her ass. "I see a once proud whore who now knows her place."

"Good answer."

He reached over, removed the cuffs from her wrists and untied her ankles. She simply let her arms and legs go limp. She didn't think she could move. He returned to her, putting his still semi-hard cock right in her face she groaned inwardly. He can't want more. He seemed to be waiting. She knew once again she had to be exactly right.

"Does my Master wish me to please him by sucking his cock again?"

"What do you wish to do, Allison?"

"I have no will of my own," she whispered, looking up at him. She was pouting, but for real, her lip trembling. "My only desires are my Master's desires."

Closing her eyes, she opened her mouth and waited for him. His cock was not put into her mouth, and, after a few seconds, she opened her eyes. Mark was on his knees in front of her. With surprising gentleness, he took her face in his hands. "That's a very good answer, Allison," he said quietly. Leaning forward, he kissed her on the lips softly, almost lovingly.

"Welcome to the Circle, my lady."

Chapter Three

Allison awoke to the pleasant scent of strawberries. As her mind slowly became aware of her surroundings, she felt the delightful sensation of her body surrounded by warm water. She opened her eyes, and stared up at the black and red tiled ceiling of Mark's huge bathroom. Her head was resting on a pillow placed in the corner of the tub, and she sighed contentedly at how good the water felt around her aching flesh. Her arms were along the sides of the tub, and moving her right; she gingerly touched her nipple and winced at how tender it was. Allison also became acutely aware of a rather unpleasant burning sensation in her ass. The cheeks of her ass still hurt as well and there was a dull throbbing in her shoulders. Swallowing also hurt, her throat still tender from being repeatedly force fed his enormous cock.

She began to feel her eyes start to shut, and forced them open. The heat of the scented water had her feeling comfortably drowsy and her body could certainly use some more rest. The room was dark except for several candles, which added to the feeling of comfort, but she had no idea how long she had been asleep. Stretching, she winced at the various aches and pains in her arms and legs. Forcing herself to sit up straighter against the tub, she wondered if Mark would eventually check on her, or if he would leave her alone. Speaking of Mark, Allison couldn't believe the change in him, the second he had welcomed her to the group.

Once he had given her what could only be described as a sweet kiss, she had stared at him unable to speak. Her ass had been on fire and between the brutal pounding and the powerful orgasm he had given her during it, she was borderline incoherent. She had also been overcome by her own response at the end, screaming like a porn star and loving every minute of him hurting her. The one thought that cut into the daze she were in was that Alex had been right, she had indeed broken.

"Allison, are you okay?" Mark had asked, pulling her from her stupor.

"I...." she fought to get her breathing under control. "That's it? I....I made it?"

"That's it?" He flashed her that perfect smile he had at the bar. "I must be getting soft."

"Oh no," she said in between gasps, "You're not soft, I'm sorry if...."

She stopped when he started laughing, and like the smile it was a surprisingly pleasant one. "I was joking," he said, "You passed the test Allison. You're now officially a Lady of the Circle."

"So now what?" she asked, trying to summon up the energy to sit up. "Do I just go home?"

"I don't think you'd get too far."

Standing, he slid his arms under her shoulders and helped her into a sitting position. Turning away from her, he reached over to the bureau and handed her a bottle of water.

"Drink?"

Allison started to take it, then remembering him pouring it all over her, hesitated. Mark held it for a moment, and then laughed again.

"No tricks, Allison. I told you it's over."

Allison took the water and started to drink. Her hand was shaking so badly, Mark put his over it and held the bottle to her lips as she chugged the entire thing. When she finished, she took a deep breath and whispered, "I'm so tired."

Mark picked a pillow up from where he had them piled on the floor and put it on the bed behind her. "Here, lie down for a little while."

She stared at him, unsure of whether or not she wanted to stay. Everything in her told her she should get up and get out in case there was more to it, and he was screwing with her. What her mind said however, was being ignored by her body, which didn't seem as if it could respond.

"Just lie back, Allison. Trust me, you're safe."

"This from the man who has a rack for a bed," she said softly.

Mark laughed again, and she noticed his eyes were once again that odd mix of colors. Placing his hands on her shoulders, he gave her a slight push. He wasn't rough, but in her weakened state she let herself fall back onto the bed.

"Ow," she moaned, "Damn my ass is sore."

"Try this," he said and, slipping his arm under her back, lifted her up high enough to slip a pillow under her ass. "That better?"

"A little." She realized her eyes were closing and forced them open.

"Don't fight it." Mark said. "Get some rest. I'll come get you in a little while."

Without waiting for a response, he turned and walked away. Stopping near the door, he adjusted the thermostat. "I'm putting the air on, and I'll leave the door open partway so it'll be cool in here in a couple of minutes okay?"

Her eyes were closed again, and not trying to fight her exhaustion she whispered, "Okay."

She had gone right out, because next she knew, Mark was calling her name, and she opened her eyes to see him standing over her. Once again his hair was wet, and he was wearing a pair of jeans and a plain black t-shirt. There was something red slung over his shoulder, but she was not sure what it was. Noticing his clothes made her aware she was still lying there naked. Feeling like a fool for doing it as it was pretty damn late for modesty, she crossed her arms over her tits and her legs at the ankles.

"It's a sin to cover up such a beautiful body," he said with a grin.

"I don't feel beautiful," she replied.

"Well let's see if we can get you to feel that way." He extended his hand to her. "Come with me."

With a groan, she forced herself to sit up.

"Where are we going?"

"To get you cleaned up."

She shook her head. "Sorry if I don't want to shower with you again."

Mark shook his head and sighed. "Again, you have nothing to worry about. Now come, my sister, let me show you how a Lady of the Circle should be treated."

He put his hand out again, and now intrigued; she put her hand in his and swung her legs off the bed. He helped pull her to her feet, and then held up the red robe he had been carrying.

"Thank you," she said softly as she turned and let him slip it onto her and tie it around her waist.

Taking her hand again, Mark began to walk towards the door and she slowly followed. She noticed that it was indeed much cooler and was thankful for it, but she still felt lightheaded and after several steps she noticed her legs were trembling.

"Hold on," she stopped and leaned against the doorway. "Wow, I'm out of it."

"Allow me."

Putting her arm across her shoulders, Mark slipped his arm around her waist, then stooping down swept the other arm behind her knees and easily lifted her into his arms. Turning, he began walking through his apartment towards the bathroom. Allison was too tired to protest and had to say, the feeling of his powerful arms against her wasn't necessarily a bad thing. She let her head rest on his shoulder and let her gaze wander across his muscular chest.

"I take it you work out," she said.

It sounded lame, but her eyes wanted to close and she was fighting to stay conscious.

"Two hours a day."

"Goddamn," she muttered "Well it shows."

"Thank you."

They had reached the bathroom and she noticed the shade was pulled down and he had lit candles. The room smelled strongly of strawberries and, as he placed her on her feet, she saw that he had drawn a bath

"Wow, isn't this nice," she said softly.

"A lady should be pampered at all times, should she not?" He asked from behind her.

"From your lips to Gods ears." She laughed.

"I don't speak to God."

"Oh, sorry I...."

"May I remove your robe?"

His hands had reached around her waist and were holding the tie to the robe. Allison was surprised to feel a thrill go through her. He had asked in the exact tone she taught her pets. God I'm sick, yet even as she thought that, she raised her aching arms up and said softly, "Yes please."

Mark undid the robe and slid his hands up to the top to remove it from her shoulders. As he did, the edge of his hand rubbed along her stomach and grazed the side of her breasts. Another charge went through her, and as she had many times in her life, she wondered if there was something wrong with her. Horny was the last thing she should be feeling right now.

"Allow me to help you in."

Taking her arm, he slipped his other arm around her waist, steadying her as she stepped up and into the tub. When she was in, he held her arm as she slowly slid down into the tub.

"Oh, this is perfect," she purred as she slipped into the warm soapy water.

Mark had knelt down beside her and, giving her a smile, nodded."Glad you're pleased, now just close your eyes and soak for awhile. Stay as long as you want, I'll be out there." Reaching into his pocket, he produced a red cell phone and placed it on the floor beside the tub. "If you need anything call me. My number is in there."

"Whose phone is that?" she asked.

"Yours, my lady," Mark said. "That phone is only to be used for the group and the numbers are to be under our Circle names. Right now the only number in there is mine. The others will give you theirs at your first meeting."

"I...when is that, and...."

"Later, Allison," Mark said as he reached out and, leaning her head up, slipped a small pillow behind it. "I'll answer all of your questions later, for now rest."

"Thank you," she said softly as he gently removed her hair from her face and tucked it behind her head. Again she felt a pleasant tingling sensation within her. She couldn't believe what a soft touch he had. Mark hung the robe behind the door and then left the room, closing the door quietly behind him. As exhausted as she was, Allison quickly picked up the red phone. It was an iPhone similar to hers and finding the contacts she looked at the name there, "Lovecraft."

Looking down, Allison saw the phone where she had left it and, picking it up, was surprised to see it was eight o'clock. Shit, there was no way she was going to drive back home tonight, she would have to get a hotel. As much as she hated to do it, she lifted the lever to drain the tub. Standing, she pulled the shower curtain closed and turned the shower on to rinse off. Stepping out of the tub, she dried off and towel dried her hair as best she could. She didn't want to rummage around to see if he had a hair dryer, and sure as hell wasn't going to walk out there with her hair in a towel.

Grabbing the robe from the door, Allison uncovered the full length mirror behind it and winced at the sight of her badly bruised and swollen nipples. Turning to the side, she saw that her ass was covered with welts. Tying the robe, she opened the door and stepped out into the hallway. The corridor was dark, but she saw a light coming from the other end and, following it, came out into the dining room. Mark was sitting at the table, flipping through a magazine. He didn't look up right away, and Allison noticed he was now wearing a wine colored dress shirt and black slacks.

"Feeling better?" he asked, without looking up.

"You have good ears," she said, walking up to the table.

"No," he replied as he closed the magazine, "I have a good sense of smell and strawberry is my favorite."

He lifted his head and Allison couldn't believe how different he looked. He had shaved and his features were nothing short of perfect, not only that, but with his high cheek bones, and olive complexion he really was nothing short of pretty. His thick black hair that was tousled and hanging in his eyes earlier, was brushed back and she could tell he had used gel in it. Again however, it was his eyes that really caught her attention, once again that mix of gold and green and she swore there were flecks of blue in them.

"You okay?"

"Damn you're beautiful," she said, then instantly felt like a fool.

"Why thank you!" he exclaimed, flashing a delighted smile. "I do what I can."

"You do plenty," she said, then realizing she was blushing, put her head down. "Sorry, I sound like a fool."

"Not at all," he told her. "There's nothing wrong with acknowledging when someone is attractive. If that makes people fools then you must be surrounded by idiots."

"Thank you," she smiled. "That was pretty smooth for being on the fly."

He spread his arms wide. "Well I am an attorney after all." Gesturing towards the table he said, "Please, have a seat, I have something for you."

Allison sat down across from him and watched as he moved the magazine, which she noticed, was dedicated to martial arts, and uncovered a folder. Opening it, he removed a pen from his pocket, and slid both over to her. Turning it to face her, Allison saw it was the contract from Alex's office making A&S his new marketing company next year.

"Oh my God," she whispered as she picked up the pen.

"Just sign and it's a done deal Allison," Mark laughed. "You earned it."

"That I did. My ass hurts just sitting here," she remarked, as, her hand trembling with excitement, she signed the contract.

"That's not how you earned it," Mark replied. "You earned it by being damn good at what you do, and so much better than those around you that you attracted Alex's notice."

"You know, I'm really not sold on this 'better than' mentality."

"You don't have to be, because we are," he told her with a shrug. "You'll see what I mean soon enough. It's not as arrogant as it sounds. Some of us are just more gifted than others."

"I suppose." She nodded, thinking Mark was pretty damn gifted.

He slid the contract away from her and closed the folder. "I'll send this back to Alex. It'd look a little funny if he handed you everything before you handled his first campaign."

"I didn't think of that."

"That's okay, I think of everything," he said with a smirk.

"You have no problem with lack of modesty I see." She laughed.

"And should I?" He smiled wickedly. "I have a mantra: Every woman wants me, every man wants to be me."

"And you believe that?"

"Absolutely, and because of that others do too." He tapped his chest. "Law of attraction, Allison, expect the best, and that's what you'll receive."

"Not sure if that's what I received today."

"It's what you'll receive from now on. Trust me."

"Easier said than done."

Mark laughed and, sitting back in the chair, crossed his arms. His sleeves were rolled up, and Allison stared at his muscular forearms. Raising her eyes to his face, she saw he was looking down at his phone, and again marveled at how damn attractive he was. He certainly had Warner beat, and Allison had more than her fair share of thoughts about him over the week. Something told her she might have a few of Mark in the days to come, but certainly not about what he had done to her. Then again, not only had she cum while he had been all but raping her, but it had been one of the strongest orgasms in her life. Never mind the one she'd had with him going down on her. Amazingly, she felt herself beginning to get worked up at the thought of him lying between her legs.

"Allison?"

"Sorry. I was just...."

"Doesn't seem real does it?"

"I...." With a laugh, she shook her head. "Yeah, I feel like I'm in the twilight zone. A secret group, some guy sending my boss blackmail photos, coming down here and....I just can't believe a couple of hours ago I was chained to your goddamn bed and you were...." She paused. "Doing whatever the hell you wanted to me."

"Well that's part of...."

"You were acting like a fucking psychotic, and looked like one," she continued. "Then you do this Jekyll and Hyde thing. You draw a bath, look like you walked off of GQ and you're being nice to me." She laughed. "And then have me a sign a goddamn contract that's going to make me twenty grand next year. I don't know whether to like you or hate you."

"Just like your pets feel about you," he said softly. "You torment them, and they swear it'll be the last time, that you're a fucking bitch. Then you come back and oh, how they fawn over you in hopes you'll be good to them." He put his hands up. "Self loathing over powered by lust."

"I suppose that's what I seemed like to you isn't it?' she asked. "A pet?"

"Of course not."

"I don't see how you wouldn't. Alex talked about the ladies being revered, but I can't see how you'd see me that way." She sighed. "And as much as I love having that contract, I feel like I whored myself. It was just to a higher level of the boys club."

"Oh no, my lady, you couldn't be more wrong." Leaning over the table he grabbed her hand and, lifting it to his lips, gave her a soft kiss. "I assure you, Allison, that you have nothing but my utmost respect."

"Nice try, councilor," she replied, ignoring the shiver the feel of his lips sent through her. "But I can't see how that's possible."

"Listen to me," Mark began. "First of all, you were at a disadvantage coming down here and you know that."

He had lowered her hand back to the table, but was still holding it in his own. Allison didn't make an effort to pull away. She not only enjoyed his touch, but her ivory hand was a hot contrast to his darker complexion. Her mind was filled with the image of him over her on the bed, driving his huge cock into her helpless pussy, his powerful sweat soaked back and ass flexing as he ravaged her. With an effort, she forced that visual from her mind and focused on his voice.

"When you faced off with Alex, he told me he was impressed. You were under the impression you had to fuck him for his business, but you were still trying to force him to ask for it." He grinned. "To beg for it, he told me there was a moment when your foot was in his face he could see himself caving. That's a hell of an accomplishment, Allison. Alex has been at this a long time."

"Are you his friend?"

"Of course I am," Mark replied as if he didn't know why she was asking. "He's like a brother to me."

"You sounded like you didn't like him, at the bar."

"All part of the game. I wanted you to think I hated him and was planning to take it out on you. Now tell you what, you can ask me anything you want later, let me finish this point."

"Sorry," she said feeling stupid yet again.

"Don't be." He squeezed her hand. "Now when you came here, you weren't allowed a fair chance, you were here to do what I asked." He gave her another of those resolve weakening smiles. "Still didn't stop you from trying though, you and your good little girl routine."

"Fat lot of good it did." She sighed. "You let me think I might have a shot, then started calling me names."

"Again the game, but so you know, Allison, I'm a sucker for a good pout and that was one of the best I've ever seen."

"You mean this one?"

Putting her head down, she pushed her lower lip out and looked up at him through her eyelashes.

"That's the one. Tell you what, not many women who are as strong as you can still pull that off. Makes it even hotter."

"No effect though."

"Nope, had to do what was needed. And, Allison, you put up one hell of a fight."

"Didn't seem like it." Before he started again she asked, "Did you want me to pass?"

"Of course I did, but the right way. What you didn't know at the time was that initiation was decided when I pinched your nose shut."

"Yeah nasty little trick by the way. Scared the shit out of me."

"It was meant to, and I played dirty. I knew you'd say the word, but knew you really couldn't because...."

"My mouth was full," she rolled her eyes.

"But when I backed off you had your chance. When you first looked up, I figured you were going to say it, and if you were going to quit that easily I would've been fine with you doing so. But when you saw me expecting it, the look you got in your eyes told me you were going to make it then and there. It was just a matter of taking to the limit and showing you where pain stops and pleasure begins."

"I.... have to say I was surprised," she grunted. "I can't believe the way I got into it."

"It's called breaking, and we've all been there."

"Even you?"

"I wouldn't be here if I hadn't."

"Can't see anyone getting to you. Something tells me there isn't any pain you couldn't handle."

"We...." He frowned as if remembering something unpleasant. "We all have our weaknesses."

"I'd like to meet the woman who could break you."

"You will, she's the mistress of our group."

"Mistress?"

"I'll explain later. Just know you have nothing to be ashamed of."

"Speaking of later, I'm going to need to get dressed and get going."

"You don't want to know about the Circle?" he asked, surprised.

"I do, but its eight thirty and I'm not going to New York, so I have to find a place to stay."

"Then look down the hallway, I have another bedroom. You think I'm going to have you stay in some hotel?"

"I.... really? You don't mind?"

"My pleasure."

"Well, then let me take a run out and grab some dinner, because I'm starving."

Removing his hand from hers, he shook his head. "Damn, you really did come a long way to insult me didn't you?"

"Well...."

"Do you really think that I wasn't planning on taking my beautiful new sister out for a fabulous meal in historic Federal Hill?"

"I...I'm sorry, I guess I didn't know what to think."

"Then don't. Just sit back and let me show you a good time. We'll go to a great place, have a few drinks and I'll answer all your questions, then you stay here tonight, okay?"

"Okay. But I take it, that this'll be a fancy place?"

"One of the best in the state." He smiled. "As befitting the occasion."

"I didn't bring anything with me, and I'm not sure that sundress will cut it."

"No worries, I have it all taken care of. Just...."

"I know, trust you, right?"

"Exactly."

"Let's see." Lifting her hand, Allison began raising her fingers one by one. "A member of a secret group, a rack for a bed, a Satanist and to top it all off, a lawyer." She shrugged, "Sure. What's not to trust, right?"

Mark tried to look put off then began laughing. "Alex was right, you're going to fit in just fine."

Chapter Four

Despite the fairly late hour for dinner, The Blue Grotto was crowded and Allison could certainly see why. Located in Federal Hill, which was the one area of Providence Allison had heard about, the restaurant was one of the most elegant she'd been to. The food was amazing, and the wine delicious. A little too delicious as she looked down at her empty glass and debated refilling it. She'd already had three, which normally wasn't too much for her, but in her exhausted state she was feeling it more than usual.

What she was also feeling, and not for the first time today, was a sense of the surreal. Mere hours after being treated like Justine in a hundred and twenty days of Sodom, here she was feeling like Cinderella at the ball. Complete with a gorgeous dress, given to her by a supermodel. When she had first entered Mark's guest bedroom, Allison's eyes widened at the sight of a dress on the bed. As she held it up, she realized that with the exception of the stomach not being cut out, it was a red version of the dress Victoria had been wearing when she came to see her. She also noted that it looked as if it would fit perfectly. She laughed as, underneath the dress, was a red lace thong, and a pair of red heels, also the right size.

Removing her robe, Allison slipped on the thong, then the dress, noting the reason she hadn't been provided a bra was the front of the dress had cups sewn into it. Very different from Victoria's which had been so flimsy it was close to transparent. Sitting on the edge of the bed, Allison put the shoes on the floor to slip them on and noticed a note under them.

Allison,

If you're reading this, and I have no doubt that you are, then congratulations! You are now officially a Lady of the Circle. So allow me to be the first, aside from Mark, to welcome you to our group! I greatly look forward to spending a lot of time with my beautiful new sister, but in the meantime allow me to bestow the dress upon you as a welcoming gift. I will be coming by your office this week so we can call Gabrielle at Rapture to announce our partnership. In the meantime, enjoy your evening with my Dark Prince, and fear him not, as fierce as he is, he is just as sweet to his sisters. Victoria.

Calling Rapture together! Allison had stared at the card and smiled. This was too good to be true, Orion Software and Rapture perfume in the same week? Her smile widened as she imagined the look on Ben's face when she announced she had landed another huge client.

"You're awfully quiet." Mark's voice cut into her thoughts. "Getting tired?"

"No," she said with an embarrassed smile. "I just....I still can't get over all of this!"

"It's all good though isn't it?"

"Hell yeah!" She laughed. "Damn, after Victoria helps me land Rapture, I'll be guaranteed to double what I made this year!"

"So today was worth every minute?"

"If you said I had to do it again, I'd…" She gave in and picked up the wine bottle. "Get drunk and let you do it again!"

"This is just the start Allison. You have no idea how much is still to come."

"Then here's to more!" She laughed, holding up her glass.

"Now that's what I want to hear!" Mark exclaimed, lifting up what Allison thought had to be his sixth Jack and Coke. "That's what we're all about, my lady!"

He gave her a huge smile and she was again amazed at how pretty he was. Easily the best looking man she'd seen. He had added a black tie to the shirt and a suit jacket that, from the way it fit, she was sure was custom tailored. They tapped glasses and as she drank, it occurred to her she couldn't remember the last time she's gone to dinner with a man who wasn't a client. Allison never went anywhere with her boys beyond a local bar for a couple of drinks, and she was surprised at how much she was enjoying his company.

She was also amazed they had not yet discussed anything about the Circle. When they had first left, she was full of questions, but had wanted to wait for dinner. Once they had arrived at the restaurant however, Mark began asking her about herself. Allison had mentioned that she'd grown up in Florida and how she had wanted nothing more than to come to the big city to succeed. Mark told her some things about Providence and over dessert she discussed her career. He listened intently and asked her a lot of questions. She enjoyed the conversation. Outside of Cindy at work and her ex-roommate Jennifer, she didn't have a lot of friends. It was nice to have someone interested in her for more than her appearance. Mark killed his drink and, signaling the waiter for another before he had even put the glass down, said

"So, I've enjoyed learning about the advertising world, but I figure you must have some questions?"

Putting her glass down, she nodded.

"Well before you ask, I have a question for you." Pointing at her he asked, "So, my lady, what'll your circle name be?"

"Well:, I hadn't given a lot of thought to it, but when I did, I kept coming up with Pandora." She shrugged. "Is that okay? It's not taken is it?"

"No, and I'm surprised," he told her. "It's very good actually." He grinned. "I'm all about unleashing sin upon the world."

"One girl at a time?" she asked with a wink.

"Sometimes more than one." He returned the wink, "So any particular reason?"

"Yeah, I guess there's a story behind it, but…" She shrugged. "You don't want to hear it."

"Of course I do," he said. "I want to get to know you, Allison,"

He reached out and took her hand as he had earlier. And just as it had then, his touch caused a warm feeling to go through her. This time however, the wine already had her feeling quite warm, and, looking down at her hand in his, it dawned on her she was more than a little attracted to him. Allison began to wonder if there was more than just being nice behind his offer for her to stay the night. Looking up into his amazing eyes, she gave him her best smile, "Yeah, you want to know all about me?"

"Whatever you want to tell me."

"Even if it's….kind of dirty?"

"Especially if it's dirty,"

He gave her a wicked smile and this time the warm feeling was located between her legs. Was he flirting with her, or was he just enjoying being with his new sister, as he referred to her?

"I'll tell you and it's something I've really never told anyone." She laughed. "I guess maybe I trust you after all."

"Said Red Riding Hood to the wolf." He gave her another evil smile that sent her heart pounding. Damn he was something.

Allison began to reach for the wine bottle, but stopped. She was feeling pretty damn good as it was, but her real concern was she was more than a little horny and if she got drunk, she wouldn't trust herself not to make a move on him. Noticing her hesitation, he picked up the bottle and filled her glass.

"You trying to get me drunk, councilor?"

"No, I just don't believe in denying the flesh what it wants." He laughed. "Indulgence over abstinence, it's one of the Satanic principles."

"I don't know anything about that." She picked up the glass and held it up to him. "But I always say if it feels good do it, and this wine is pretty damn good."

"Well said," He told her, lifting his fresh drink to toast her. "I'm a pretty firm believer in that one myself."

"Really?" she winked, "We'll have to see about that."

Mark's smile appeared to falter, sliding his hand from hers; he took a long swallow from his drink and said, "No more stalling, my dear Pandora. Where's my story?"

Allison took a sip of wine and cursed herself for pushing it. Mark wasn't one of her lust addled boys. Hell, he spent time with Victoria Redding. To him she was just another attractive woman who was fawning over him. *Talk about role reversal,* she thought as she put the glass down.

"All right, I guess it doesn't really start out sexy, but the fact I lost my mom to cancer when I was ten is a big part of it."

"I'm sorry to hear that," Mark said softly.

"After that it was just me, my dad and my older brother, Jack. Dad was pretty old fashioned and I think he may have dated here and there, but never brought a woman into the house, out of respect for my mom."

"That *is* old school. Good for him."

"The other part of being old school is he was pretty damn clueless about what to do with a daughter." She sighed. "I remember the first time I got my period. I was at school and when the nurse called him, he showed up with my aunt so she could deal with it. Good old Aunt Becky, anytime anything girlie was involved she got the nod."

Allison paused at the memory of having her aunt help her get ready for her first dance while all the other girls Mom's helped them. The wine was getting to her and all her emotions were close to the surface. Shaking her head, she continued,

"Well the one thing aunty never covered was sex. Now damn straight my dad wasn't touching that one, and the only thing my brother ever told me about boys was if one bothered me to let him know. So when I was younger I was kind of shy. I was pretty and boys did ask me out, but I always said no." She shrugged. "I didn't even know what I was supposed to do with them."

She stopped and watched Mark drain his drink and, putting it down; he began looking around for the waiter. *How much can this guy drink?*

"One day I'm in Jack's room looking for notebook paper, and I find his dirty movies. I didn't know what they were; I just thought they were movies. I took one into my room and found myself watching this woman playing with herself." Pausing to take a sip of the wine, she took a moment to enjoy the knowing smile that was playing about Mark's lips.

"I wasn't really sure what she was doing, but knew I'd been feeling kind of funny down there sometimes and when I would rub, it would feel good. So I locked my bedroom door and..." She laughed. "Pulled my pants down and imitated her. I came pretty quickly and I still didn't really know what happened, but knew I liked it and it became my new hobby."

"If it feels good do it." Mark laughed.

"Like a sporting event! There were weekends my damn hand had cramps. I watched all of his movies and most of them were all fucking and I started wondering what it would be like to be with a guy."

"Something tells me you were able to find that out with no problem."

"Pretty much." She grinned. "One day when my brother had to work, I had a kid named Jamie come over to do some homework. He'd come over before and I was pretty sure he liked me, and I was noticing he looked pretty good. All I had to go by was porn so when we're sitting on the couch, I look at him and say, "Hey, Jamie, wanna fuck me?"

"You...." Mark burst out laughing and Allison put her hands up.

"Hey look, what did I know?"

"You knew the magic words we all want to hear, that's what." He wiped at his eyes and waved his hand at her. "Sorry, go ahead."

"He looks at me like I'm kidding, so I stand up, take my shirt and bra off and ask if he wants to suck my tits. Nervous or not, I didn't have to tell him twice and I'm sitting there wet as hell watching him licking my nipples and decide I want to do some licking myself."

"Wish my first girl was like you."

Allison stopped as the waiter sat a couple down on her left. Sliding her chair around the table so that she was closer to him, she continued softy, "So I tell him to sit on the couch and I get between his legs and..." Making sure she was looking into his eyes, she whispered, "I pull his cock out, put it in my mouth and just start moving my head. I wasn't sure if I was doing it right, but he's saying my name over and over and next thing you know I got a nice mouthful of...."

"Spit or swallow?" he asked; that nasty little smirk on his face again.

Leaning over, she whispered in his ear, "Swallowed every drop and sucked for more. I sucked so hard, he was pulling on my hair asking me to stop."

Turning his head to face her he whispered, "Bad girl."

"Oh, no I was a very good girl, and because I was, I wanted some fun too. I got on the couch and pulled my skirt and panties off and told him it was my turn. Well he dives in, and I suppose he really didn't know what he was doing either, but every time his tongue hit my clit, I wanted to scream. So I put my fingers down there and helped him get me off. By then he was hard again and I put my feet on his shoulders and told him to fuck me."

"Not very romantic for a first time," he said.

"The hell with romance, this girl needed to get fucked."

"Have I used the word 'perfect'?"

"So he slips it in and it hurts for a minute, but then it was..." She sighed into his ear. "The best thing I'd ever felt, the way his cock was stretching me open and how he looked fucking me, hmmm" she purred. "Before he was done I knew I'd be wanting as much of this as I could get. He didn't last too long and he pulls it out and cums all over my stomach. I sat up, took him in my mouth, sucked him hard and made him fuck me again."

She fought back a smile at the faraway look in Mark's eyes as he was no doubt picturing her as a young girl, greedily sucking her lover so she could keep getting what she needed. Watching the expression on his face, it occurred to her it may very well indeed be exciting to hear others tell stories like this. Warner was right she was going to enjoy every aspect of this group.

"From that point on I was off to the races." She shook her head. "Within a month I became the most popular girl in school."

"I can imagine."

"I didn't have a lot of girlfriends, because they were catty and called me a whore. I'm sure the guys were saying some nasty things too, but all I cared about was getting laid and enjoying every minute of it. Any guy I saw that I wanted, I pretty much said 'let's go'." She laughed. "And whether they had a girlfriend or not, I don't ever remember being turned down."

"Can't see you being turned down now either," Mark told her.

Biting back the remark, 'That's what I'm hoping' she returned to her story. "By senior year, to say I was out of control was an understatement. I remember a Saturday I had three guys, one in the morning, one after a lunch date, and a guy from Florida State I met at an under twenty-one club that night to top it off."

"Ever run a train?" he asked softly.

"Funny you should say that," she said. "I never did that, but near the end of senior year, I ended up with two of my brother's friends."

"Do tell."

They were turned in their chairs while they were speaking and leaning into each other. Allison was aware of the couple behind Mark staring at them, and she loved it. Sliding her chair even closer, she put her hand on his thigh as she spoke into his ear.

"They came over looking for him, but he worked Saturdays with my dad. I told them he was out and they were disappointed. They had a case of beer and were hoping to have fun. They asked if I wanted to have a couple of beers with them, and I said hey, why not."

"Famous last words."

"You know where this is going. A couple turns into six and I'm buzzing and we go into my room. They have me sitting between them and their hands and lips are all over me. They said they heard I loved to have fun and they wanted to have fun with me."

"I'll bet."

"They felt great! They were both three years older than me and played football for a local college. They were hot and sexy and damn were they good to me." She put her forearm on his shoulder and, resting her cheek on it, closed her eyes, and lowered her voice to a sultry whisper. "They weren't rough at all, and they weren't just looking for me to do them. They took turns going down on me while I sucked the other off, then we started fucking. I was on my knees taking it doggy style while sucking the other. They kept switching and the taste of my pussy from their cocks was driving me wild. I was so caught up in that, every time one of them was ready to cum, I had them shoot it into my mouth, I had to taste it!"

"Damn," he said softly.

Looking up at him through her eyelashes, she could see his beautiful eyes were beginning to glaze over, and not just from the effects of alcohol. If there was one look Allison had come to recognize in a man, it was lust. Mark was fully caught up in the visual of her being doubled up by two hot older guys.

Her hand was still resting on his thigh and she was dying to slide it over to feel the hard-on she knew he had, but held back.

"We fucked all day," she continued. "I swear to God I was sex drunk. There wasn't a moment there wasn't a cock or a finger or a tongue between my legs, and every time they went soft I sucked them hard again. At one point I was lying on my back with each of them sucking on my tits and their fingers between my legs. I remember looking up at the ceiling wondering how the hell anyone could see anything wrong with this. I was so into it the last time they fucked me. I let one of them put it in my ass. I was so far gone it didn't even hurt."

"So you ever do anything like that again?"

"I...no."

She stopped speaking and closed her eyes against the memory of what that had led too. She felt that familiar feeling of sadness that was the reason she always avoided thinking of her brother begin to creep in and again cursed herself, she should have stopped drinking.

"Allison, you okay?"

She opened her eyes to see a look of concern in his. "Yeah, I just.... that day had some pretty serious consequences and...." She took a deep breath. "Let's just say a real mood killer, let's just...."

"You can tell me," Mark said quietly. "I don't judge."

"I....I've never told anyone." She sighed. "Then again, I really don't have anyone I'm close enough with, or who would care."

"It's your choice," He put his arm around her shoulders. "I know Alex played up the fun and professional aspects of our group, but know this, Allison: the people around that table will become the best friends you'll ever have. For many of us they're more like family." He grinned. "A dysfunctional one, but family nonetheless, so if you want to tell me, I would consider it an honor. But if not, it's fine."

Allison lifted her head up from his shoulder, but made no move to pull away from him. His arm felt good around her and at the moment not in a sexual manner. She could feel that air of confidence about him that she had felt in Victoria. Although she hardly knew him, and considering what he had done to her earlier, she felt a sense of safety being close to him. She still couldn't shake the after events of that day and decided to continue.

"That was Saturday and when I went to School on Monday the story had gotten out. Apparently one of the guys had told his younger brother, who went to my school. So there were some nasty comments and more dirty looks from the girls and smirks from the guys than usual, but that was no big deal. What was a big deal was when my guidance councilor called me into her office." Allison picked up her glass and finished the rest of it.

"She told me she had caught wind of the story and I needed to think about my future. I was up for a scholarship along with some other kids and she explained they looked at everything. Wild sex and, more importantly, underage drinking were not going to go over well, so I needed to think about that."

She put the glass down and, reaching for the bottle, was surprised to find that it was empty. Seeing her looking at it, Mark raised his hand and, catching the waiter's attention, pointed at the bottle, and then tapped his own glass which was empty again. The waiter nodded and hurried away.

"Well that put a scare into me. My Dad was so proud of my schoolwork and it looked like I was going to get to go away to a good school. I couldn't disappoint him, so I promised myself I'd behave. But when I got home the real shit started."

"Excuse me, sir?"

Allison looked up to see the waiter standing there.

"You can't see we're speaking?" Mark asked.

"Sorry, sir, but the manager says you've reached our limit. We have policies on alcohol consumption, for the safety of our guests of course."

"That's okay." Allison nodded. "We...."

"I appreciate your concern for my well being," Mark interrupted. "However, what I would like is for you to tell Mr. Baccala, that Mark Phillips has yet to begin to defile himself."

"Ummm," the waiter shrugged nervously. "Yes, sir, I'll do that right now."

As he walked away, Allison said, "No big deal Mark, and you're driving. Maybe you've had enough."

"I never get enough," he said quietly. "Of anything. And I always get what I want." He paused and with a smirk nodded his head towards the back of the restaurant. "See?"

Allison looked up to see the waiter coming back with a bottle of wine and another drink. Right behind him was an older man in a black suit.

"Your drinks, sir," the waiter said.

Allison watched the waiter put Mark's down then pour her a glass of wine before heading away.

"Mark, how are you?" the older man asked, putting his hand out.

"I'm good, Joe," Mark replied, shaking his hand, indicating the wine bottle he added, "Thank you."

"Of course." Joe nodded. "I'll get you a cab if you need one, okay?"

"I won't, but again, thank you."

"And who's your beautiful companion this evening?" Joe asked, turning his attention to her.

"Allison Saunders," she replied, extending her hand.

Joe took her hand and brought it to his lips. "A pleasure, Miss Saunders."

"This is Allison's first visit to Rhode Island, so I wanted to make an impression and what better way than to bring her to the best restaurant in town?"

"I am honored, my dear." Joe smiled down at her while still holding her hand. "I hope you're enjoying our city and that I'll see those beautiful eyes here again some night."

"I'm sure you will." She smiled back at him.

"Oh, and by the way, Mark, it's on me tonight," Joe said as he released her hand.

"No way," Mark said, raising his hand. "You want to cover a couple of drinks fine, but you have a business to run."

"A business that wouldn't be here without your help a couple of years ago," Joe said quietly. "So drink up and shut up okay?"

"If you put it that way." Mark laughed. "Thank you, Joe."

"Anytime and, young lady." Leaning closer, he made a show of whispering in her ear while speaking loud enough for Mark to hear. "Don't let Mark fool you, he acts a little crazy, but in reality, he's even crazier."

As Mark rolled his eyes, Joe clapped him on the shoulder and walked away. Picking up his drink, he drank half of it and handed Allison's glass to her. She took a couple of sips and closed her eyes as the room began to blur. Damn she'd had a lot.

"I'm sorry," Mark said. "I didn't mean to interrupt, but you looked like you could use another one." He laughed. "I know I always can."

"Speaking of drinking," she said quietly. "Before I go further, I have to tell you that my brother, Jack is an alcoholic and he was already drinking heavily back then. He was twenty-one and had been in trouble for fighting, and stealing, with a couple of drunk driving charges thrown in. He'd done a couple of months in prison and was living with us under the pretense he was getting help. My dad thought he wasn't drinking. I knew otherwise, but didn't want to see him thrown out and never said anything."

"Okay." He nodded, then to her amazement chugged the rest of his drink, and held up the glass to the waiter. Allison began to wonder if he had a problem himself.

"I get home and Jack's there and he's drunk and pissed." She sighed. "The whole thing was a set up. His friends told him everything. What I didn't know was he had done something to one of them, and they weren't his friends anymore. They knew my reputation and did it to get back at him. They told him all about how they fucked the shit out of his slutty little sister."

"I take it things didn't go well with him."

"He..." she paused to take a deep breath before continuing. "He started screaming and swearing at me, calling me a fucking whore. I tried to say I was sorry and he..." She put her head down and said quietly, "He hit me."

"He hit you?"

"Yeah, and it wasn't a slap either, he punched me in the face." She swallowed hard against the tightening in her throat. "Broke my nose, and then he hit me again. I ran and he tried to chase me, but he was drunk and fell. I locked myself in my room and he was screaming he was going to kill me and trying to kick the door down. I climbed out the window and ran to the neighbor's. They wanted to call the cops, but I called my aunt instead."

"What about your dad?"

"He was a truck driver and this was before cell phones. He would check into work a couple of times a day, but he was hard to get hold of. My aunt came and took me to the hospital. I begged her not to call the cops and she said she wouldn't, but damn straight dad was going to know."

She stopped and wiped at her eyes, afraid they were beginning to tear. In front of her, Mark was watching her, an expression of disgust on his face.

"I hope your brother got what was coming to him," he said softly.

"And then some," she replied. "Aunty kept calling home until dad answered. He'd been worried about me, and my aunt brought me home. Jack wasn't there, but I saw where he cleaned the place up. Aunty told dad what happened. By then my nose was swollen and my eyes were both black and blue. Dad told her he would take care of Jack and told me to go rest. When my brother came home, he called me out of my room so Jack could see what I looked like then started screaming at him. Jack started yelling back, telling my father what a whore I was and how did he like his little girl being the school slut?"

"Piece of fucking work," Mark muttered, his eyes darkening.

"My dad lost it, and..." She looked longingly at the wine glass, but held off and went on. "He started hitting my brother. Not just hitting him, but beating him. My dad's a big guy and he had worked his ass off on the docks. He was a lot stronger than my brother and my god, did he beat him. I started trying to get him to stop, but instead he literally threw my brother out of the house, right through the window and told him to never let him see him again. The cops came and dad spent a night in jail. My brother spent two days in the hospital, and he never came back home after that."

"Good for your father."

"I guess, but it was my fault. If I hadn't done that with those guys...."

"It would've happened another way." Mark stopped her. "I know a thing or two about addicts, and violent behavior. Sooner or later he would've snapped on you." He paused and, looking away, said quietly, "Addicts always hurt who they're closest to."

"I know that now. As for back then, after dad came back from the police station he talked to me and told me how disappointed he was in me, for doing that with those guys, the drinking as much as the sex. Told me I had a chance to get the hell out of that shithole town and make something of myself. I started to cry and then he blamed himself for being a bad father and not knowing how to take care of his daughter."

The tears were beginning now and she finished quietly. "He couldn't have been a better father, and I swore after that I'd never disappoint him again. As much as I love sex and play games I promised myself I'd never use it for anything but fun. That anything I had I'd earn." She gave in and took a couple of sips of the wine. "That's why I wrestled with going through with today. I do feel like I whored myself."

"People whore themselves every day," he said quietly. "But if we don't do what we need to sometimes, then where would we be?"

Allison nodded and, picking up her napkin, dabbed at her eyes. "I'm sorry," she said.

"Don't be." Mark was silent for a moment then asked, "What happened with your brother after that? You see him at all?"

"I saw him a few times after that, but it was usually when he needed something. He got married a few years ago and I have a three year old niece I've never seen back home."

"He doesn't allow it?"

"No, he says he doesn't want his daughter around a whore. That's still what he calls me. His wife went to school with me. She sends me pictures all the time and puts me on the phone with Amanda when he's not around." She sighed. "He's still drinking and life isn't easy for her, so I send some money when I can."

Mark rubbed at his eyes, and looked down, a frown on his face.

"I'm sorry Mark," she said as she dabbed at her eyes again. "Talk about a mood killer."

"No worries," He squeezed her shoulder, "That's what brother's are for."

"Brothers?"

"Allison, you'll see soon enough that not only myself, but the other men you haven't met yet, will all become brothers to you, and far better than the sack of garbage that was born as yours."

"Thank you, Mark." She kissed his cheek. "That means a lot."

"You know, if you want to see your niece I can make it happen."

"You…" She blinked, he had said it so matter of factly. "How?"

"There's a group in Florida. I can see what they can do."

"There's no visitation rights for anything but parents, there aren't even grandparent rights out there. My dad has never seen his granddaughter. I've tried."

"Then we go the other route and make it worth your brother's while to let you see her."

"You mean bribe him?" She laughed. "I suppose he's for sale, he…"

"I mean going down there and explaining why he needs to do the right thing." He gave her a chilling smile. "I can be quite persuasive."

"I…." She sighed. "I don't enjoy violence. Let it be. If I ever decide I need to do something to help her, I'll come to you."

"Fair enough."

"Anyway, sorry to kill the mood."

"And again, don't worry about it. Although some members of the group are like Alex and have never had anything but success, for many the path to the Circle hasn't been an easy one."

"Was yours?"

"Not at all," he said quietly. "But, I think we've talked about enough real life."

"Now, that's not fair," She said quietly. "I open up to you, and I only know your last name because you just said it."

"You volunteered."

"And considering how intimately, you got to know me already, I think I'm entitled to know a little bit about you, my brother."

"Maybe another time, Allison," he said. "The point of dinner was to discuss the Circle."

"And you said that first and foremost these are my new brothers and sisters. So tell your new sister something about you."

"My new sister," Mark repeated.

"Yes, your new little sister." Smiling at him, she pushed her lips into a pout "Come on. Mark, be nice to your sister."

"I..."

Mark stopped and Allison's eyes narrowed as his seemed to lose focus. He appeared to be looking past her rather than at her, and she wondered if the drinks had finally made an impact on him. Mark cocked his head slightly, and then said softly, "I'm always nice to my sister."

"Sisters, you mean," She pointed out.

Mark blinked and with a grin said, "There's only one here now. So what do you want to know?"

"I don't know. Do you have brothers or sisters? Real ones I mean."

"I have a sister named Megan. She's a couple of years older than me."

"Mark and Megan." She laughed. "Slightly Irish parents no?"

"I guess, I don't know my real parents."

"Oh," she said quietly. "I'm sorry. I'm batting a thousand tonight."

"It's okay. I never met my father, but he was a lunatic, very dark individual and violent."

"Nothing like you." She laughed.

"I'm nothing like my father," he snapped, his eyes flashing, and his lip curling. "My father was an animal, an abuser of women, and a pariah to all who knew him."

"Whoa." She put her hands up. "I'm sorry, Mark. I didn't know it was a bad subject."

He looked away from her and she saw him take a deep breath and slowly let it out. He nodded slightly as if he were agreeing with his thoughts and when he looked back at her he seemed calm again.

"No, I'm sorry. I do have a lot of his traits, but I'm not him. Before you say anything, I know after what I did to you, it seems odd to call someone out for being abusive, but understand everything I do is consensual. Any woman who steps into that bedroom knows what she's getting into and can stop whenever she wants. My father, like your brother, saw fit to use women as punching bags. I despise anyone who picks on anyone weaker then themselves." He smiled unpleasantly. "And on occasions when I run into them, I show them what it's like."

Picking up his drink, he downed the last of it, but didn't signal the waiter again. By now the restaurant was beginning to clear out, and Allison was glad it looked as if he were going to stop drinking. They could talk for awhile and hopefully he would be sober enough to get them home.

"Guess I'm a paradox," he continued "But many of us are. My father got locked up for murder, and my mother, who I barely remember, dropped us off at the pound when we were around six and four."

"The pound? That's awful."

"At the time they had nowhere to put both of us, so put us in separate homes. It was supposed to be temporary, but they lost track of us and we bounced around the system. We both ended up in some pretty ugly homes, until she was taken in by some good people who adopted her."

"What about you?"

"I stayed in the bad homes, then ended up in group homes. I had a lot of problems, and no one wanted a teenager with issues. I was fighting a lot and they were going to send me to a training school. Just before that, a social worker realized I was the brother Megan's family had been trying to find and called them. Megan was eighteen then, and I was released into her custody. The last time I saw her she was six with a missing tooth. Next time I saw her, she was a beautiful young woman." He paused and his eyes seemed to drift off again. "But I knew it was her, I could feel it when I saw her."

"So you guys close now?"

"As close as we can be. She moved to Chicago a couple of years ago."

"Oh, for work?"

"Sort of, she's an artist, she can paint anywhere, but she had a girlfriend who was moving down there for a fresh start and Megan thought it'd be good for her as well."

"Fresh start? She get divorced or something.?"

Mark went silent and seemed to be thinking before he spoke. When he did speak, it was little more than a whisper. "Because you confided in me, I'll do so for you as well. Much like your brother, Megan had some serious issues with drinking and drugs. She spent her twenties in and out of rehabs and was involved in some pretty tough things. I did what I could for her, when I could, but she had to be the one to stop. Finally she did a few years ago, and she has been doing very well for herself."

"I'm glad to hear that."

"But as you can imagine, it's different when a woman has an addiction. They'll do...." He looked away. "Certain things. There were a lot of bad memories for her here and she decided she would be better off leaving. It was the right move, but tough on the rest of us."

"You miss her?" Allison asked.

"I wouldn't be where I am today without her. I had a lot of issues when her and her foster parents took me in. She was the only person I trusted and she helped me get my shit together. She was my big sister and looked out for me. To this day, we look out for each other, but she's my best friend as much as she is my sister." He sighed. "I miss her. We went through a lot of shit most people don't understand."

"You still see your foster parents?"

"Yeah, but according to my foster mother, not nearly enough, and Megan's father insists I'm as ungrateful as any real kid could be." He shrugged.

"I get the impression there's a lot you're not telling me. That story about my brother and my mom is the extent of my baggage I guess." She shrugged. "In general I'm pretty happy go lucky. But something tells me you've been through a lot."

"Happy go lucky is a good thing." He smiled, ignoring her last statement. "We have some serious sorts at the table, we could use more fun."

"Something tells me you're one of those serious sorts." She smiled at him. "At least on the surface." With a laugh she asked, "Are you one of those sensitive bad boys?"

"Sensitive bad boys only exist in cheap romance novels. What I am is just a bad boy," he told her without a hint of a smile. "One of the worst you'll find, but never to my friends."

Squeezing his thigh and trying to get the playful mood back, she again gave him the voice. "Well then your new sister is going to have to make sure she stays on your good side."

He picked up the wine bottle and poured some into his glass. After drinking some of it, he looked at her and gave her a smile that seemed forced. "Well, my lady, seeing as we've gotten to know each other, and somehow managed to go from a hot story to real life shit...."

"My fault," she said.

"No problem, but for now, let's order some coffee and get back to what we're here for." He smiled and this time it seemed sincere. "Let's talk about the Circle and how much fun you'll have."

"Sounds good to me,"

"So before I just kind of go on," Mark began, "Any specific questions?"

"Your name." Allison pointed at him.

"What about it?"

"Not exactly befitting your nature." She shrugged. "I was expecting, oh, I don't know, something demonic."

"I've heard that before." He nodded. "Lovecraft was my favorite author, lived in Providence, and the name does have a sexual innuendo to it. But, the main reason is the name has significance to me and someone close to me, so that's why I chose it." He gave her an evil grin. "Those who have mocked it haven't done so for long."

"I can imagine. So what are the other names there? What's Victoria call herself?"

"You get that at your official introduction."

"Okay, so when's that?"

"Two weeks from tonight is the August meeting. They're always the first Saturday night of the month, and short of health issues or urgent business, you're never to miss one."

"So where's the meeting?"

"Not sure yet. Victoria's hosting. A couple of days before she'll call and tell everyone. It's in New York so your first meeting is in your home city."

"Where else are they?" she asked.

Mark waited to answer as the waiter brought coffee. He went to remove the second bottle of wine, but Mark stopped him. "I might have more."

The man nodded and walked away. Allison thought about asking him if he'd had enough, but let it slide she'd talk him into a cab if she had to.

"All over New England, but you make out pretty well. You're the fourth member from New York, so a third of the year you're home."

"What do I do when I get there?"

"Don't worry about that. As your initiator I get the honor of escorting you to your first meeting, and introducing you to the Circle."

"And what do we do at these meetings?" she asked as she took a sip of her coffee, which like most of the evening was perfect.

"Honestly, Allison, I think that's something I'd rather you see firsthand. It ruins the fun if you know in advance."

"Oh, come on!" she exclaimed.

"Nope." He laughed.

Leaning into to him, she rested her chin on his shoulder and batted her eyes. "Please? I want to hear all about the fun stuff!"

In addition to the pout, she put her hand on his chest, running her fingers down his shirt. She saw the woman at the next table roll her eyes, but could care less. The woman was just jealous because she had no desire to paw all over her boring husband, who was busy staring at his cell phone.

"Don't be a brat, Allison," He was trying to sound stern, but she could see him fighting not to smile.

"But I'm good at it!" she declared then, turning the little girl voice into a sexy purr, added, "I'm good at all kinds of things."

"That you are." Mark nodded, and dipping his shoulder, slid out from under her chin.

Allison swore at herself again. She was acting like an overheated schoolgirl. She was getting more of a reaction out of him being playful then throwing herself at him. She needed to slow up, and just let it happen, because she had no doubt that it would, she would see to it. Picking up the bottle of wine, she poured a glass and, taking a sip, handed it to him.

"Share one with me?" Mark took the glass and, as he took a long swallow, Allison went in a different direction. "You didn't seem like you thought I was good at anything earlier."

"What?" He blinked at her and she smiled. He wasn't following along quite as well; the ridiculous amount of alcohol he had consumed was getting to him.

"I said I was good at things and you said I was and…." She waited.

"Oh." He took another sip of the wine and passed it back to her. "Right and glad you said that because I should've said this before now, but I hope you know I didn't mean anything I said earlier it was all part of the show."

"So I don't give a lousy blow job?" she asked, and seeing the woman looking at her again, but not caring, slipped her tongue and slowly licked her lips.

"You give a hell of a blow job." He laughed. "And it was a pleasure to take you."

A shiver went through her at those words. Take her. Damn she wanted to be taken again. Not anywhere near as hard as the first time, but she would be more than happy to let him have his way.

"Sorry if I can't say the same," she told him. "But I guess if you're into being torn apart, you're pretty good."

"I can be more fun when I'm playful too," he said, and then caused her to burst out laughing as he gave her a poor attempt at a pout.

"Stick to being a bad ass okay?"

"Thanks." He rolled his eyes then sighed. "But really, Allison, you," Taking her hand and giving her a smile that sent a wave of heat through her whispered, "Are one of the most beautiful women I've ever had the pleasure of having in my bed."

Then I'll have to give you that pleasure again, she thought, but instead, giving him a soft kiss on the cheek said, "Thank you, Mark."

He looked at her, and as she smiled at him, saw he had an odd expression on his face. He was weakening, she could feel it. As if proving her point, he let go of her hand, picked up the wine and after draining the glass shook his head. "Where were we?"

"You were going to tell me what happens at the meetings," she prodded.

"No I wasn't," he told her. "I know Alex gave you basics like the standards and age requirements, that there are twelve of us. So let me tell you about what some of the member's roles are."

Frowning, she raised her finger to stop him and voiced one of the concerns she'd had from the beginning. "Mark, no one's going to hurt me, are they?"

"Why would anyone hurt you?" He looked confused.

She paused, embarrassed for asking. Then again she was sitting next to a man who hours ago had walked her through his house on a leash. "This is a group based on dominance right?"

"In every facet of life."

"I...I've gone to that website, you know, Inner Sanctum?"

At the name Mark rolled his eyes, but she continued. "And they have those parties and they take the initiates and do things to them like you did to me, but a bunch at a time and it's like...." She shrugged at him. "I...I'm not going to be the group pet am I?"

"You have anything to worry about," he told her reassuringly. "Members are treated equally and although there may occasionally be something..." He paused searching for the right word. "Live shall we say, it might involve someone's pet, or a sub, and they'd be blindfolded."

"I'm not going to like watching what you did to me, I know that," She sighed.

"Allison, you're going to love watching everyone else watching that video. Back to what you asked, no one will force you to do anything or hurt you. First off, because that's not what we're about, and second of all, if anyone did, they'd answer to me."

"Because you initiated me?" she asked. "Am I like.... Yours?"

"No and I'll get to why if you'll let me finish."

"Sorry, sir." She pouted at him.

Mark gave her a smile. "I do like that pout."

"Good," she said and poured them another glass of wine. She was really feeling it and knew he had to be drunk, but wanted keep him nice and relaxed for later. "Now go ahead, I promise I'll be a..." She batted her eyes at him. "Very good girl."

"We'll see about that," he grunted.

Allison smiled, knowing damn well she planned on being very good later on.

"So there's four positions out of the twelve members. Aside from the four, your rank is by your time at the table."

"So I'm low man on the pole?"

"Yes, but rank really only counts in things like who'd take charge in granted time."

"Granted....?" She stopped as he shot her a look.

"And no offense, but hopefully you stay the newest member. It's a good thing when people stay for long stretches, not good when we're always looking for new people, looks bad for the group."

"I can't see why people would want to leave if it's...."

"Allison?"

"Sorry." She sighed and took a sip of wine.

"So of the four seats of power within the group, the first and foremost is obviously the master or mistress of the group. Currently we're under a mistress."

"Sorry, but how do they get to be in charge?"

"By vote, but usually when someone's ready to step down, they start grooming another to take over and it's usually a lock. They can technically be opposed and voted out, but that's pretty rare."

"You said our mistress is the one who initiated you?" she asked.

"Yes, and before you ask it, lasted over two days, now can we move on?"

She whistled. "I can't wait to see what she looks like."

"She's an amazing woman, and as beautiful as ever."

"You have to say that."

"I don't have to say anything except one thing and that's stop interrupting me." Without waiting for her to respond, he continued. "Next is the diplomat. Their job is to deal with the other groups. If a member from say, Florida needs a favor of a member of our group, it goes though the diplomat. Granted time is also initially handled through that person."

"Back to this granted time thing again."

"We'll get there," Mark said then paused to take the glass from her hand and take a couple of sips. "You've already met our diplomat."

"Alex?"

"Yes, and now that I think about it, you've met three out of four."

"So what do you and Victoria do?"

"Victoria is the high lady. She is the longest tenured lady other than our mistress and is sort of the big sister for the rest of the ladies. If you need anything, you usually go to her; she'll take you under her wing and teach you the rules."

"I thought you'd be the one to do that," she said with a feeling of disappointment. She had looked forward to spending more time with him.

"Why?"

"Well I...."

"My job was to break you. Victoria will help you with whatever you need to know."

"Break me." She rolled her eyes. "You sound so casual about it."

"You will too someday." He killed the last of the wine, and then blinked. "Damn."

"We'll get a cab," Allison said.

"Yeah right." He laughed as if she'd said something funny. "Well that brings us to the Enforcer."

Allison laughed. "Sounds like the damn mafia!"

"Shhh!" Mark put his finger to his lips. "There's a few of them here."

"Oh, please," she said. "Why, because it's an Italian restaurant?"

"No, because Joe is the head of one the local families."

"Oh." She looked around, nervous now.

"Yeah, he got in some trouble a couple of years ago and I managed to find a way to blame someone else so he didn't take the fall. It's a long story."

"So you...." She shrugged. "Are you a crooked attorney?"

"I'm a good one. I dance with whatever devil suits my needs at any given time."

"All right then." She frowned. "So the enforcer does what?"

"What it sounds like. I enforce the rules. Someone breaks one, I decide the punishment and either carry it out myself or get another member to do it."

"What are the punishments?" she asked nervously.

"Depends on what rule is broken. Some of them are more embarrassing than anything else. For instance we had a member who met a mistress from another group and didn't kiss her feet, which is an insult. So next meeting he has to crawl around and worship the feet of every lady at the table" He grinned. "I think you would've liked that one."

"Sounds hot." She paused then let out a breath. "Okay, tell me one I wouldn't like."

"Last year a lady didn't properly satisfy a member of another group. He wanted her to swallow, and she didn't. Again quite embarrassing to our mistress."

"So what did you do?"

"I took her to a college party, brought her into a bathroom stall and made her suck off three guys through a glory hole."

"Oh, that's nasty." She shuddered.

"She won't refuse a request again now then will she?" He sighed. "Hell of a turn on, seeing a powerful woman degrading herself like that."

"I guess."

"I also handle trouble. If any member is having an issue with someone, I take care of it."

"How do you do that?"

"Usually through connections, blackmail." He shrugged. "You know, dirty pool. Other times if it comes down to it, I get physical."

"You look like you could handle yourself."

"Over twenty years of martial arts. I had a chance to compete nationally when I was younger, but…." He stopped and frowned. "Shit kind of happened."

"So if Victoria is the big sister, you're going to be my big brother?"

"Exactly!" Mark exclaimed, and to her delight put his arm around her shoulders. "I'm there to take care of you, anything you need."

"Be careful with that." She laughed.

"Seriously." He rolled his eyes. "It's my job to look out for the ladies and it doesn't mean just trouble. You ever have a problem and you just need to talk, pick up the phone. Maybe I can help, or…" He shrugged. "Maybe all I can do is listen, but you can bring anything to me, I don't judge."

"So, nothing like my real brother," she said disgustedly.

"I can assure you, I'm nothing like him." He squeezed her shoulder as he spoke.

"I don't think I'll need any help. I'm not the type to get in trouble."

"Yes you are, but you've been lucky so far."

"What do you mean?"

"Let me tell you what I tell all the ladies who enjoy young men like you do. What happens if you pick the wrong one?"

"I'm not sure what you're getting at."

"Come on, Allison, you tease the shit out of these kids, fuck with them. What happens if one of them really gets pissed off?"

"I get to know them pretty well first and…."

"Not enough. You never know what could happen. One minute you're teasing and controlling, next minute you're being raped. It can happen and I always worry when one of my sisters has those tastes."

"I think I'm a pretty good judge, and I don't really like aggressive or bad boy types." She pointed at him. "You at twenty I'd have no interest in."

"We have a woman in the group that loves my type. She also loves to have more than one at a time." He frowned. "And likes it rough. She's dominant in her career, but loves to be degraded sexually. She lets these guys fuck the shit out of her and get rough." He sighed. "She scares the hell out of me."

"So what do you do, tell her she can't have what she wants?"

"No, just try to get her to be careful, find a couple of regulars. If nothing else, another of our ladies owns a BDSM club." He laughed. "Hiding in plain sight. She'll send subs or doms to any member of the Circle for entertainment and they're all trained to not speak of whom they're with."

"So if some guy gives me a hard time, you'll kick his ass big brother?" She gave him a playful kiss on the cheek.

"The last man who hurt one of the ladies of my group still walks with a cane."

"Damn, Mark, that's....."

"He was a member of our group at the time, but one of the old school members, thought his sisters nothing more than pets. I taught him differently."

"But you said a cane," Allison pointed out. "You broke his leg?"

"Amongst other things." Mark's eyes darkened and he said softly, "No one hurts my sisters"

"No worries, baby." Trying to lighten the mood, she smiled and lightly touched his cheek with her nails. "You're new little sister won't cause any trouble for you okay?"

Mark reached for the wine bottle, then shifting his hand, picked up the coffee and after drinking some said, "And speaking of trouble, although Victoria will cover a lot of things, it's my job to go over the two biggest rules."

"I think Alex mentioned them," she said, also passing on the wine in favor of the coffee which was now luke warm.

"I'll mention them again. Number one, you cannot be in love with someone." He shrugged at her. "I think the reason for this is fairly obvious. We're not real big on monogamy and you're required to indulge in the sexual aspects of the group."

"What happens if someone does fall in love?"

"Then you leave the group. The woman you're replacing left for that reason. After years in the group she fell for a long time friend and decided to leave."

"I can't see that happening to me." She laughed. "I doubt I could ever be a one woman man, I like having fun." She shrugged. "Plus I just think the whole thing is overrated."

"Most of us start that way, but you'd be surprised at how many do fall."

"Fall?"

"If a member falls in love we say they're fallen."

"So it's a bad thing?" Allison asked.

"It's bad as in they leave the group, but we fault no one for wanting to be happy. Fallen does have a negative connotation to it. In general, many consider those members weak."

"Do you?"

"No." He shook his head. "Life's all about being happy and if one person does that for you, then good for you. Now disgraced is a bad thing and you have to fuck up pretty bad for that one."

Allison nodded as she stifled a yawn. "Excuse me."

"I'm losing my touch." Mark grinned. "I usually manage to hold a woman's interest."

"Sorry, it's been a long day, and a lot of wine." She gave him a playful smile. "But I'm sure you could recapture my interest if you wanted to."

"Now if you leave the group in good standing," Mark went on, ignoring that remark. "The connections you made will always be there. The Circle doesn't turn its back on its brothers and sisters. But if you're banned, then you lose all of that. Depending on why you're banned, there could be serious consequences such as those connections turning on you."

"What would be that bad?"

"Victoria can handle that one." He closed his eyes and let out a deep breath. "Getting tired myself. The next rule is the big one and the one that can cause problems."

"Is this the no sex amongst members thing?" she asked, trying to keep her expression neutral.

"Absolutely," he said. "I know it sounds crazy, a group based partly on sexual dominance and its hands off, but there are reasons. The first and foremost is…."

"Alex said it teaches control."

"It does, but I think discipline is a better word. Up until the group, none of us have really ever been denied and certainly not been told look but don't touch."

"Well we have, but we just don't listen." She sighed. "I lost a few girlfriends in college over that one."

"Exactly." He agreed. "But here it really is hands off, well for sex anyway, there are some exceptions to have some fun, but …."

"I'll learn those later." She rolled her eyes.

"Yes. The other reason, aside from control, is plain old human nature." He sighed. "The high school bullshit the privileged still suffer from rather than out grow. 'Well she fucked you, why won't she fuck me?' that stupidity. Besides, I think it adds an aura of mystique to the group. We all wonder what it would be like to, but may never find out."

Allison's interest perked up at that last comment. "May never? That sounds like there's a chance."

"Right, that'll bring us to granted time. But first I want to point out something else."

"You're killing me!" She laughed. "You've mentioned that a few times, now you're stalling." His arm was still around her and snuggling into him she asked. "Or are you just dragging it out because you like the company?"

"I can never spend enough time with a beautiful woman." He winked.

"Smooth, councilor." She rolled her eyes.

"Well I think you won't mind this stall tactic, because you get to find out something I think you'll enjoy thinking about."

"And what's that?"

"First off, understand that even without granted time, there are some at that table that have been with others. For instance, I initiated you, so obviously all will know we've been together."

"That wasn't together," she grunted. "That was a pretty one sided affair."

"True, but it counts. The guys will wish it were them and many of the women wouldn't mind being you."

"If you say so."

"Now for the part you'll like."

"I get revenge someday?" she asked laughing.

"You got it."

"Wait….what?" Had she heard him right?

"As a reward for going through an initiation, there's a payback night."

"I am liking this," she told him, smiling.

"I thought you would." He laughed. "So one year from tonight, I show up at your door, completely at your mercy."

Allison closed her eyes for a moment and let his words play through her mind. 'At her mercy'. She would treat him the way she did her pets, totally humiliate him. Just the thought of it caused her to squirm in her seat. When she moved, Mark removed his arm, but as she turned to face him, made no effort to remove her hand from his thigh. His voice brought her wandering mind back from envisioning him tied to her bed.

"This was put into place not only for a reward, but as a way to remind the initiator to be careful, because what comes around goes around."

"I guess you're not worried," she said.

"The Circle is a privilege and new members need to be properly broken. There are no free rides and if I've now set myself up for a pretty rough night, so be it." He put his hand over hers. "It'll also give you the chance to show us what you have. Putting me in my place will be a lot harder than handling your boys."

"I think I'll manage just fine," she said, tossing her hair dramatically.

"I'm sure you will, and since it's a payback it, like your experience today, it'll be taped." He laughed. "So you have a year to wait, but you'll get your time."

Allison smiled and nodded, all the while doubting she would be waiting much more than another hour.

"Now that falls under granted time, by the way. For granted time itself, that's pretty self explanatory. Rule is: we don't engage in sex with each other, but the second part of that is without permission. You can ask for time with a member of the group."

"Something tells me there's more to it than that."

"No, it's that simple, but there has to be a reason other than just wanting to. For instance, let's say a member of the group does something exceptional for you, a huge favor. You can go to the mistress and request time with them."

"What are the odds of a yes?"

"Not great honestly, some groups have different standards. Ours believes in adhering to the control factor. Now if by some chance it is granted, it's to never be spoken of. No one knows and it adds to the fun. You look around the table and you envision different people together and you wonder, have they?"

"Have you and Victoria?" she asked. "Hmmm? Because damn the two of you together would be something."

"Maybe," he said with a smirk.

"I think you have."

"Think what you want." He shrugged. "Now that's granted time within the group. There's granted time with members of other groups and that's more frequently given."

"So how does that work?"

"If a member from say, Texas, is up in New York for business, they may check out what we have to offer so to speak, and decide to have their diplomat ask Alex if one of the ladies may be available." He squeezed her hand again. "Maybe they take an interest in a certain hot ad exec for example."

"So I say yes and just meet him and fool around?" She frowned. "I do get a choice don't I?"

"Technically yes, but why would you say no?"

"Well I…."

"You don't strike me as a prude, Allison." He laughed. "Or did we peg you wrong?"

"No, I just don't want to be picked off of a menu," she said removing her hand from his leg.

"You can pick off of the menu as well if you travel."

"So I say yes, how does it work?"

Mark paused and looked away. "Well I suppose you'll have an issue with this, but if the member has more time than you, you're to submit."

"Screw that!" she snapped. "You and Alex said my initiation would be the only time for that!"

"It's not rough like that," he assured her. "But they have seniority so it's up to you to please them." She frowned and he continued. "But it's playful, like you tried earlier with me, the pout, the yes sir. You're there to please, but trust me, you'll have a good time. He'll enjoy you as well. If nothing else there's pride, a man of the Circle would want the lady to remember him fondly so you'd be happy, I'm sure."

"We'll take it as it comes," She said shaking her head.

"Victoria would be the one to discuss it with you and if she thinks the member wouldn't be a good match for you she'd tell you to say no. You can trust her."

"So back to this rule, if you're caught having sex with a member?"

"You can get thrown out," Mark said. "At the least severally punished."

"Care to share?" she asked.

"A lady from New Orleans got one of her brothers drunk and took advantage. Her punishment, since she seemed to want her brothers so badly, was to be gang banged right there at the meeting by all six men in the group, and it was not made to be...." He hesitated. "Enjoyable."

"They raped her." She shook her head. "That's bullshit Mark!"

"She was given a choice, she chose to accept her punishment."

"And would you do that?"

"I...." He thought for a minute. "I like to keep it one on one. Every group is different, and we're not usually that harsh."

"Usually," she said. "That's comforting."

"Allison." Reaching out, he turned her face towards his and, leaning forward, kissed her cheek. "Like I said, most of the rules are minor and the punishments more like jokes. Serious punishments are pretty rare. The Circle is about advancement, dominance in all that we do, but also a hell of a lot of fun." Looking her in the eye, he again gave her that perfect smile. "You're going to have a lot of fun, Allison. You like to have fun don't you?"

"I love to, but I...."

"Then think about the fun." He put his arm around her again. "Think about going out with Victoria and the other ladies, and toying with men. Think about one of your sisters maybe even sending you some hot young boy toy to fool around with."

"Yeah?"

"Yes, and think about the meetings. I had to leave out the fun stuff, but you'll see it all in two weeks." He put both his hands to her face, and as his amazing eyes stared into hers, whispered, "Trust me, my sister, you'll have fun. Okay?"

Allison nodded as she allowed herself to get lost in those eyes. The wine was hitting her hard and she could feel her face was flushed, but knew it was from much more than the wine. Although he had just stressed to her that they were not supposed to be together, Allison knew she was going to have him. Despite his words, he seemed damn taken with her, and had been affectionate all night. The thought occurred to her this could be some kind of test, but she didn't care. This time when they went back to his place, it would be her game, not his.

"I'm so ready to have some fun," she said softly.

"Good, well I don't know about you, but I'm about ready to call it a night."

"Sounds good to me."

"Then we'll get going," Reaching into his jacket he took out his wallet and, removing a fifty, put it on the table for the waiter. "I'm glad you seem happier now, I knew fun would get your interest."

"Oh, it did." She smiled.

Fun was definitely what Allison was thinking about and was glad he was thinking of it because she was planning on showing him just how much fun his new sister could be. As he stood and offered her his hand, she smiled and thought, *rules be damned, I want him.*

Chapter Five

During the short ride back to Mark's condo, Allison sat back in the leather seat of the Lexus, a delicious feeling of anticipation flowing through her. The wine had her relaxed, but beneath was the familiar twinge of excitement just before a new game began. Turning her head, she took in Mark's perfect profile as he expertly guided the car through the late night traffic of downtown Providence. Allison had been concerned about his driving considering how much he had to drink, but he appeared to be fine. Again she felt that aura of confidence emanating from him, that feeling that even when he appeared not to be in control, he was still calling the shots.

Allison was about to change that. Mark was a far cry from any of the young boys, or grabby older men, she'd seduced in the past. In fact, he was probably the only man she'd met who didn't seem completely taken with her. Despite the fact he'd been with women who were just as, if not more, attractive than her, Allison could sense he was into her. She'd seen it in the way he had looked at her several times. He had enough experience and control not to feel the need to make a pass at her, but she was convinced she could get through to him.

She was also pretty sure Mark's stressing how members of the group not being allowed to have sex with each other was as much for his own resolve as it was to instruct her. If there was one thing she'd learned over the years, it was that rules were made to be broken. Allison refused to believe a group of people who always got what they wanted would let a rule stop them. Well it wouldn't stop her. Earlier today Mark had his way with her. She'd been forced to submit to anything he chose to do to her, and she felt fair was fair and she should get to have her way with him. Allison smiled at the thought he most likely wouldn't mind her way. All she wanted was for the two of them to have fun. They reached the Promenade and Mark parked the Lexus between her car and his Firebird. Getting out, he quickly came around and opened the door for her.

"Thank you, sir," she said softly, putting her right leg out onto the ground, but pausing before getting out. "You're quite the gentlemen for such a bad boy."

She spoke very slowly and with a slight slur to the word sir. She had done it deliberately, letting him think she was drunker than she was. Mark stared down at the length of her leg, before looking into the car.

"You coming, my lady?"

"Sorry," she whispered, extending her hand. "I think the wine's caught up with me."

"Not just the wine." Mark took her hand and helped her from the car. "You had one hell of a day."

And it's far from over, she thought as she stood up and made a show of shaking her head. "Wow, I'm feeling a light headed."

Mark slipped his arm behind her, his hand resting on the small of her back, and turned her towards the elevator at the far side of the garage. Leaning against him, Allison allowed him to guide her along, smiling at how sometimes the old tricks were the best ones. Sliding her arm around his waist, she rested her head on his shoulder and enjoyed the walk to the elevator. Once inside, she sighed. "These shoes are killing my feet." Bending her leg at the knee, she removed the shoe her and handed it to Mark, while she removed the other.

"We still have to walk down the hall you know."

"I know, but it has a nice carpet and I bet it'd feel good on my feet." She laughed. "If it feels good do it, right?"

"Right," he agreed. "I never think of little things like that."

"Well you should," she chided him. "There's fun in everything we do, you just have to be willing to look for it."

"I can see why you're in advertising." He laughed. "You're very motivational."

"In every way, baby." She giggled.

The elevator opened and although she had removed her shoes for the purpose of Mark being able to stare at her feet, Allison had to say the soft carpet did feel good. As they walked down the corridor, an older couple was coming down from the other end and she noticed them looking distastefully at Mark. When they passed, the man spoke to his wife loud enough for them to hear.

"There goes another one."

"At least this one looks like she's out of high school," the wife replied.

"Bingo must have let out late at the home tonight," Mark replied over his shoulder.

"Your fan club?" she asked as they reached his door.

"Jealousy is an ugly emotion," he said while unlocking the door. "They look at me with scorn, but fact is, they're bitter they settled down, bred at an early age and missed out on the life I so freely enjoy."

"Bred?" She laughed. "Not one for kids I take it?"

"I'm not one for anything that involves donating my time to anything but my own causes."

Opening the door, Mark stood to the side to allow her to enter in front of him.

"We really need to work on your sunny disposition," she told him.

Walking past him into the condo, it was not lost upon her how different this was from earlier. This afternoon she had entered with a feeling of dread and fear. Those feelings were now replaced with lust and desire. Allison walked into the living room and stopped in the center of the room, waiting to see where he would go. Mark passed her and, entering the dining room, removed his suit jacket and draped it over one chairs. Loosening his tie as he walked into the kitchen, he went into the fridge and came back to her, holding a bottle of water.

"Drink this," he said. "This way you don't dehydrate and won't wake up with a headache."

"Pro at this, huh?" she asked as she took the bottle and chugged half if it.

Mark slipped the tie from its knot and left it hanging around his neck. She felt her heart begin to beat faster. Allison could picture young girls and bored housewives falling for Mark's scruffy bad boy look. For her, seeing him clean shaven and dressed up, driving the expensive car, and telling managers what they were going to do for him, had her hotter than the bad ass look ever could. Handing the bottle back to him, she asked, "So what now?"

"Seeing how it's after one in the morning and you can barely walk, I'd say bed is next."

"Sounds good." She laughed and, wrapping her arms around his neck, looked into his eyes. "Lead the way."

"You don't remember where it is?" he asked. "You that far gone?"

"Playing dumb doesn't become you Mark," she said quietly. "You know what I mean." Allison had planned on being more subtle, but now that the moment was here, she decided to, as Mark had stressed, earlier take what she wanted.

Mark regarded her silently for a moment before saying, "And what part of 'members aren't allowed to engage in sex,' didn't you understand?"

"I'm not a member yet," she replied, still holding his gaze. "I haven't been officially introduced to the group."

"You were a member the second you broke, Allison." He tried to step back from her. "You're buzzed and tired, and you're not thinking straight. Just go to bed."

"Oh, I'm thinking just fine." She held on tightly to his neck so he couldn't move. "I feel great, we both look great, now how about you forget about these stupid rules and we have a good time?"

"The rules aren't stupid."

He, grabbed her forearms, and gently tugged on them.

"Fine, the rules aren't stupid. But it's only breaking them if someone knows, and I'm not going to tell, are you?"

She grabbed her right wrist in her left hand, making it difficult to move her arms without forcing her. He stopped tugging and shook his head. "I'd know, and you could get in a lot of trouble."

"You'd know?" She smirked at him. "And since when does Mr. Indulgence over abstinence care about rules?"

"When it's my job to enforce them he said. "If anyone found out…"

"I don't kiss and tell." She winked and, standing on her toes, whispered in his ear. "Or suck and tell, or fuck and tell."

She flicked her tongue out, giving his ear a playful lick. "Come on, Mark, show me what a bad boy you are."

She heard him take in a breath as her tongue traced the inside of his ear, and pulling his head to the side said, "Enough, Allison, we can't do this."

He pulled on her arms harder this time, and she let go, allowing him to pull them from his neck. She placed her hands on his chest and, frowning, asked, "Don't you want me? Don't you think I'd be fun?"

"I'm sure you would be," he said, putting his hands over hers to stop them from wandering.

"Doesn't seem like it," she told him, looking up through her eyelashes. "Seems like you don't want me."

"Can't always have what we want."

"I thought we took what we wanted?"

"Allison…"

"And I want you." she told him.

"Because you can't have me." Grabbing her wrists, he pulled her hands away from him and snapped, "Now go sleep it off!"

Allison laughed at him. "Don't try it, Mark, that shit won't work with me." She gave him a big smile. "I'm not a coed, try again."

He rolled his eyes. "Yeah, okay, you're right, but forget it."

"This isn't fair." she told him, placing her hands on his arms.

"Rules usually aren't."

"Not the rules, but this whole thing." She gave him the pout. "You got to be mean to me and do whatever you wanted. Now here I am, looking for some fun and you tell me no." She used the voice. "Not fair at all."

"Allison...."

"Come on, baby," she whispered, "We did it your way, now let me show you my way." She stepped away from him and, reaching around behind her neck, untied the dress. "Like I said earlier, I am soooo much more fun when I'm playful." Letting the tie go, she raised her arms over her head, letting the dress drop to the floor. "Don't you want to come play with me?"

Mark's eyes dropped down with the dress, and she smiled as they worked their way up her body. She was afraid he would have simply turned and walked away. That's all it would take and the fact he didn't told her he wasn't as adamant as he was letting on. Allison cupped her large breasts and held them up.

"Sorry they're all bruised, but someone was mean to me earlier." She pouted again. "Want to make it up to them?" She stepped towards him, and he took an almost comical step back.

"My lady," he began.

"I'm not your lady yet, but what I will be is your very good girl." She gave him a wink. "Or your bad girl if that's what you want, a bad girl who breaks the rules, and makes you break them too."

She took another step and this time he didn't move. Giving him a playful smile she again put her arms around his neck. Leaning into him, she sighed as her tits pressed into his shirt. She began rocking back and forth causing her hard nipples to slide across his chest. She winced at how sore they were, but that little bit of pain was nothing compared to the aching need she felt between her legs. She went to kiss him, but at the last second he turned his head. Undaunted, she placed a soft kiss on his neck. Before he could react, she opened her mouth and gently sucked on the skin just below his ear.

"Allison, don't." He grabbed her arms again, but didn't seem to be trying to move them.

"Mark, can I ask you something?" she whispered in his ear. Without waiting for his response she asked. "Do you ever have sex without it being a game?"

"I..." He hesitated.

"I haven't since college," she said softly. "Because until now I never met anyone I thought was worth giving myself to." Removing her head from his neck she looked into his eyes. "Let me enjoy you, Mark, let yourself enjoy me. No rules, no control, no game, just two beautiful people having fun."

"You are beautiful, Allison," he said. "You really are, but I can't do this."

Allison maintained her composure. He wasn't pulling her arms away, and hadn't moved when she kissed his neck. His eyes were glassy, and she realized as she was sobering up, he was finally succumbing. Remembering the way he stressed how it was his job to take care of the ladies of the group she gave him her best pout, the one where her lower lip began to tremble.

"But I thought you were supposed to be good to your sister?"

"I...." He blinked, "What?"

"You said your job is to be good to your sisters."

"It is," he said softly.

"Then be good to your new sister." She gave him a sweet kiss on the cheek. "Your little sister."

Mark's eyes, began to lose focus again as they had earlier. "My little sister."

"Your sad little sister." She turned on the pout again. "The sister that doesn't want to sleep in a bed all alone." She batted her eyes at him. "The sister who wants to be oh, so good to her big brother."

Mark took a deep breath and squeezed his eyes shut as if he were trying to focus. Burying her face in his neck again, she pressed her lips to his ear. "Please let me good to you honey, let your new sister show you how much fun she can be."

She kissed his neck and felt a thrill go through her as a soft moan escaped his lips. She kissed him again harder and, moving her hand, ran her fingernails though his thick black hair. Mark sighed and, to her delight, his arms slipped around her waist and his hand started sliding across the smooth skin of her back. Taking her time, Allison opened her mouth and started sliding her lips across his neck. His hand made its way up through her long hair, and she moaned as his fingers wrapped themselves in it. Removing her face from his neck, Allison smiled. "Yeah, Mark, you going to let your sexy sister be good to you?"

His answer sent a wave of heat through her pussy. Bending his head, his lips found hers. At first he kissed her softly, tentatively, as if he was still fighting it. She didn't force it, just allowed his lips to caress hers. A moment later, he became more forceful, holding the back of her head and engaging her in a long deep kiss. She moaned in her throat as their lips slid across each other. He backed off and started moving his lips teasingly across hers and, unable to hold back any longer, Allison opened her mouth and pushed her tongue out. Mark's lips parted and his tongue reached out meet hers.

She began grinding her hips into his and groaned at the feeling of his hard cock pressing into her stomach. That amazing cock that was going to be in her mouth and between her legs in a matter of minutes. Mark broke the kiss, and whispered, "I don't think we can...."

"Yes we can," she answered calmly. She hadn't gotten this close only to go to bed horny. "You're going to show your new sister just how good her big brother can be. No more rough stuff, just you being good to me."

She ran her fingernails down his cheek, just as she had done earlier today. Mark reacted the same way he had as well, leaning his cheek into her palm and closing his eyes. This time however, he didn't pull away, instead he sighed, and opening his eyes said softly, "You're beautiful, my new sister."

"And you're the most beautiful man I've seen." She smiled. "My beautiful brother."

Mark blinked again and his head cocked slightly. His eyes, which had remained unfocused, seemed to come back to the here and now, and she noticed they seemed to have gotten darker. He started to speak then stopped.

"What is it?" she asked.

"You.... remind me of someone."

"Really?" she asked. "A fun someone?"

"Yes," he answered in a faraway voice. "A lot of fun and beautiful."

"Ohhh," she cooed. "Well I can be a fun someone, all you have to do is let me."

She began unbuttoning his shirt and felt a surge go through her already dripping pussy when he didn't stop her. Reaching the bottom, she yanked the shirt from his pants and, undoing the last button, ran her hands along his hard flat stomach and muscular chest. Pulling the shirt to the side, Allison swirled her tongue around his nipple, before beginning to suck on it. Looking up at him she stopped and asked, "You ready to have some fun with your new sister?"

This answer was even better than the last one. Mark cupped her tits, his fingers finding her swollen nipples and giving them a light pinch. Allison cried out in a mixture of pleasure and pain and whispered, "Easy, honey they're sore."

"This better?" he asked as his fingers started gently sliding across her throbbing tits.

"Oh yes!" she gasped, "Oh hell yes!"

Throwing her arms around his shoulders, she kissed him hard, this time shoving her tongue into his mouth and greedily sucking on his while his large strong hands began to squeeze and fondle her tits. Mark groaned into her mouth and then gasped as her hand dropped down and squeezed his huge cock through his pants.

"Like I said when we started," she said in his ear. "Lead the way."

He gave her a wicked smile that told her she had indeed gotten what she wanted. "How about you go first, so I can enjoy the view?"

Laughing, Allison turned and walked slowly towards his bedroom. She was putting some extra swing into her hips and, looking over her shoulder, saw his eyes glued to her ass. Reaching the door, she tapped the runes. "All that better be in here this time is pleasure."

"Of course," he said, taking her hand. "I have to show my new sister a good time don't I?"

"That's right." She pouted. "You owe me!"

Mark opened the door and stepped aside for her to enter first. The candelabra's were still lit and now that she was less nervous and could see them more clearly, she realized they weren't flames, but small light bulbs set to flicker like candles. Reaching the foot of the bed, she stared at her reflection, trying not to notice the purple swelling around her tits. Behind her Mark slid his shirt off, and she smiled at him in the mirror. Coming up behind her, he slid his arms around her and, cupping her tits, began to caress her nipples. Leaning her head to the side, she moaned as, taking his cue, Mark leaned in and began kissing the soft skin of her neck.

Allison started grinding her ass into his hard cock, and felt him moving his hips, pushing against her. Turning in his embrace, she sat on the edge of the bed and, grabbing his pants, quickly undid them and pulled out his huge cock. "All for me?" she asked as she gave it a squeeze.

"All of it," he groaned as she started pumping it in her fist.

Reaching the tip, she squeezed hard, causing his hips to twitch and some of his pre-cum to squirt out. Leaning forward she placed the tip of her tongue into the slit of his dick and pulled it back, along with a trail of his sticky fluid. Looking up into his eyes, she bent her head back to his cock, making a show of sucking the trail back into her mouth. When she reached the head, she parted her lips and, taking just the tip into her mouth, sucked hard on it. Mark gasped and Allison rolled her eyes in pleasure at the feeling of his juice squirting into her mouth.

Opening wider, she took him deep into her mouth and began bobbing her head slowly. As he moaned his appreciation, Allison grabbed the sides of his pants and underwear and yanked them down as she continued to blow him. Wrapping her arms around his waist, she grabbed his perfect ass and started sucking harder and faster. Mark's hands began caressing her back and running through her hair as she sucked him deeper and deeper into her warm wet mouth. Taking a deep breath, she opened as wide as she could and slowly, an inch at a time, managed to take him all the way down. When she felt her lips touch the base of his shaft, she shook her head from side to side while swirling her tongue around his hard flesh.

Working her way back up just as slowly, she kept her tongue pressed against his shaft as her soft full lips caressed his long thick cock. Reaching the top, she removed it from her mouth and looking up at him pouted. "Is that better? You said I was bad at it before?"

"Much better," he breathed as she brought her right hand around and began stroking him again.

"Told you I'm more fun when I'm playful."

Mark's reply turned into a groan as she ducked her head and began licking his balls while jerking him off. Sucking one of his balls into her mouth, Allison began lightly trailing her fingers along his shaft, teasing him. His hands tightened in her hair as she trailed her tongue along the length of his cock before swirling around the head and sliding down the other side. Bringing her other hand around, she cupped his balls and, still stroking him, took his cock deep into her mouth. This time she took him all the way much easier and, after a brief pause to allow her mouth to get used to him, began sucking him fast and hard.

She moaned around his cock, as his hands came around and began toying with her nipples. Looking up through her eyelashes she saw him staring down at her, his eyes on her mouth devouring his amazing cock. At first she was only going to get him worked up, but the taste of his pre-cum sliding down her throat had her hungry for all of him, and she began sucking as fast as she could. Mark's breathing picked up and his hips began to move. Allison stopped her sucking and, holding her head still, groaned her permission around his huge dick.

"Hmm-mmm."

Mark started to fuck her mouth, but slowly this time. Allison moaned and began to grind her hips, rubbing her throbbing pussy into the mattress. The sensation of his long thick cock sliding between her lips and down her throat was driving her wild. Grabbing his hips, she urged him to go faster. Mark picked up the pace, and she began to bob her head, matching his rhythm. Maybe it was the drinks or the fact he wasn't trying to put on a show, but Allison could already feel his thighs starting to tremble. Letting go of his cock, she slid her hand up his chest and, as she began bobbing her head as fast as she could, she gave his nipple a hard twist.

Mark gasped and plunged his cock hard into her mouth. Allison moaned as his cock twitched telling her he was almost there. Giving his balls a gentle squeeze, she again twisted his nipple as she drove her mouth down on his cock taking him all the way into her mouth.

Mark cried out as his cock exploded. Allison squealed in pleasure at the sensation of his hot cum gushing down her throat. She moaned continuously as he filled her mouth. Like earlier, it seemed as if he would never stop. Unlike earlier however, she didn't want it to. When he groaned and stopped fucking her mouth, Allison grabbed his cock and started pumping it, greedily wringing every drop she could from him. When his moans began to sound desperate, and her best efforts couldn't illicit any more cum from his cock, she let it slip from her mouth with a loud sucking sound. Looking up, she made a show of swallowing and opening her mouth to show it was empty.

"Damn," Mark gasped as he placed his hands on the edge of the bed to hold himself up.

"So am I good new sister Mark?"

"Oh, yeah," he panted. "Damn you do love that don't you?"

"Damn straight, and it's not like I can let the boys get away with that." She gave him another pout. "My turn?"

Moving so fast she let out a surprised yelp, Mark grabbed her around the waist and lifted her off the bed. Allison wrapped her legs around his waist, her arms around his neck, and gave him a long hard kiss as he effortlessly held her up. Pulling away from her lips, Mark tossed her onto the bed. She laughed as she landed and bounced, but the smile left her face, as kneeling at the edge of the bed; Mark took her right foot in his hand and brought it to his lips.

"Oh yes," she purred as she felt his tongue begin to swirl across her toes. "Oh how I love that!"

Mark winked at her and sucked her toe into his mouth. She sighed contentedly, as one by one, he worked her toes in and out of his mouth, alternately licking and sucking on them. He took his time with each one and, lying on her back, Allison watched with her heart pounding and her pussy dripping as he devoured her foot. Leaving her toes, he slid his tongue along her instep before licking the bottom of her foot. Lifting her other leg, she pushed her foot at him. "This one is jealous."

"Can't have that," he said taking that foot and beginning at her toes again.

Allison smiled as she watched him close his eyes as he enjoyed sucking and licking. Goddamn it was a turn on to have a man that fine worshipping her feet. Spreading her legs wider, she reached down and pulling her thong to the side, exposed her smooth pink pussy.

"I think you should work your way up."

Mark opened his eyes and, removing her foot from his mouth, smiled. "That is a pretty little pussy isn't it?"

"But it's a lonely little pussy, now come up here and give it some attention."

"Yes, Mistress." Mark laughed.

Allison began to laugh, but instead breathed, "Oh damn does that look good."

She was looking in the mirror and watching Mark crawl onto the bed and slide up between her legs. Bending her legs, she lifted her hips and, sliding the thong down, playfully kicked it off and onto his back. She went to put her legs back on the bed, but grabbing her ankles, Mark placed her feet on his shoulders. Sliding all the way up, he stopped with his face directly in front of her pussy and, spreading her open, lightly blew on her clit. Allison moaned and her hips twitched. She'd been wound up for hours and needed to cum badly.

"Please don't tease me," she moaned. "Your little sister needs her new big brother to make her cum."

"I always take care of my sister," Mark replied and, leaning in, plunged his tongue directly into her sopping wet pussy.

"Oh fuck!" Allison cried out as he began moving his head, sliding his rigid tongue in and out of her hot wet flesh.

She grabbed his hair and started grinding her hips, helping him tongue fuck her. Wrapping his powerful arms around her thighs, Mark's tongue slipped from inside of her and teasingly began to make its way up through the soft wet folds of her pussy, towards her throbbing clit. Allison yelped as his tongue flicked across her swollen button, but then began sliding back down her pussy.

"Please don't!" she moaned. "You teased me before, I need it!"

She squealed in ecstasy as, fastening his lips around her clit, Mark sucked it into his mouth and started swirling his tongue around it. Letting go of his hair, Allison let her head fall back onto the bed, and groaned at the sight of him lying between her thighs in the mirror. His tanned muscular body looked incredible between her ivory thighs and, lifting her legs, she started sliding them back and forth, caressing his back with her soft feet. Mark moaned softly between her thighs as she did and bending her leg, she shoved her foot into his face. He left her clit to quickly lick the bottom of her foot. She removed her foot and cried out as this time when he went back to her clit, he shoved two fingers deep into her pussy.

Allison moaned as, like her nipples, her pussy was sore, but the overwhelming feeling was that of pleasure. That pleasure increased as his fingers began to thrust in time with her clit being sucked into his mouth. Her pussy was so wet she could hear his fingers sliding in and out, and reaching up to her tits, she started rolling her nipples between her fingers.

"Oh, yes," she moaned. "Oh, yeah honey, just like that, oh you're being so good to your new sister."

She let out a long moan as Mark began working his fingers and tongue faster and harder. Bracing her feet on his back, Allison began to pump her hips off of the bed and into his fingers. She let out a small gasp as she could feel her legs shaking and the orgasm she had been waiting all night for began to build up within her. "Right there," she panted. "Oh, don't stop. Please don't stop! I'm going to…oh!"

Allison screamed as Mark drove a finger deep into her ass while sucking hard on her clit. The initial pain immediately gave way to a feeling of intense pleasure as her orgasm crashed through her. Throwing her head back, Allison opened her mouth and wailed as her body convulsed against the waves of pleasure coursing through it. Arching her back, she bucked her hips wildly into Mark's still moving fingers and tongue and screamed again as the orgasm took her to even further heights. Allison began to relax when her body tensed up and a second orgasm slammed though her. She howled again, and closed her thighs, pinning Mark's face to her gushing pussy as she writhed and squealed, delirious with lust. After one last, slow tremor went through her pussy, Allison gave a long shuddering moan and collapsed, panting, onto the bed.

"Oh," she groaned. "Oh my….. Oh fuck!"

Moving quickly, Mark had risen to his knees, lifted her legs and drove his once again hard cock deep into her still twitching pussy. Allison yelped as he began thrusting hard and fast.

"Yes," she cried out. "That's it, fuck me! Oh fuck yeah!"

Grabbing her ankles, Mark spread her legs wide and continued to slam the shit out of her. Allison lay there helpless to do anything but yelp each time his massive dick plowed into her aching, yet delighted pussy. She could feel herself stretching around his hard flesh, but unlike earlier, loved every minute of it. Looking up, she felt her pussy gush around his cock at the sight of his sweat slicked muscular torso as he pounded the shit out of her. "Come down here," she gasped, reaching out with her arms.

Letting her legs go, Mark leaned over and, wrapping her arms around his neck, she engaged him in a long, passionate kiss. Their lips parted and she squealed into his mouth as he slowed down and was now pleasuring her with long, slow thrusts. Catching sight of the mirror again, she took in the muscles in his ass and back as they flexed while pumping her over heated pussy. Wrapping her legs around his waist, she began driving her hips up in time with his thrusts all the while playing her tongue across his as she moaned into him. Seeing him on top of her in the reflection made her sex crazed mind wonder how the reverse would look and breaking the kiss, she whispered, "Roll over, I want to ride that fucking cock."

"You are a romantic." He laughed in her ear.

"Nothing's changed," she panted. "This girl still needs to get fucked."

She yelped, as wrapping his arms around her, Mark wrenched his hips to the side and rolled them over, so she was on top of him. Allison sat up and, lifting herself from his cock, paused before driving her hips down as hard as she could. They both cried out as she impaled herself onto his long, thick cock. Allison remained still. Gasping at how deep he was, then bracing her hands on his chest, began to rock back and forth, slowly riding him. Mark pulled her down far enough to capture her nipple in his mouth and she groaned as he began sucking on it.

Allison began to bounce up and down, each time sliding more of him out before dropping back down on top of him. Each time she drove herself onto him she yelped and he gasped around her nipple. Mark released her tit and, pulling her down, wrapped his arms tightly around her, pinning her to his sweat slicked chest. Holding her still, he began pumping his hips, violently plunging his cock into her helpless pussy.

"Oh hell yeah!" she squealed into his ear. "Oh my god, is that fucking deep!"

Mark wrenched his hips again, flipping them back over and, sitting back on his knees, draped her legs over his shoulders and began fucking her, but more slowly. Reaching down between her legs, his thumb found her clit and began rubbing it in hard fast circles.

"Oh yes!" she cried.

Mark started fucking her faster, while his thumb stroked her clit harder. Allison lay back with her hands by her side, moaning and squirming against his finger. She was so tired she couldn't raise her hands to play with her nipples, yet as exhausted as she was, she could already feel her body beginning to respond. Reaching out with his free hand, Mark caught her left nipple and gave it a pinch. Allison cried out and the yelp became a long, loud wail as her pussy convulsed around his cock.

"Oh, I'm cumming!" she gasped as she felt her pussy contract around his thick cock.

Mark pinched her clit between his fingers and Allison screamed and drove her hips into his thrusting cock. Her pussy tightened around him even more, causing her to scream even louder. Allison stopped as her body seemed to gather itself, then with a loud cry she felt her pussy release and felt a surge of wetness spurt out around his cock and down her thighs. "Oh my fucking God!" she gasped.

Mark started fucking her hard and fast again, and she could tell by his breathing he was getting close.

"Stop," she panted, "I want to roll over, I…hey!"

Again he surprised her by grabbing her hips and, with a twist of his powerful shoulders, rolled her onto her stomach. Grabbing her hips, Mark pulled her up onto her knees and drove himself so far into her pussy she felt his balls slap against her clit.

"Holy fuck!" she howled.

Mark squeezed her hips harder and started slamming the shit out of her. Allison screamed and, looking up, found herself face to face with her reflection in the headboard mirror. Her normally fair skin was flushed from both heat and passion and her sweat soaked hair was stuck to her cheeks. Her eyes were wide as his cock plunged into her and her mouth was open as she yelped and squealed. Behind her, Mark was moaning with each thrust. The moans were becoming more desperate each time he drove into her and, looking up at him in the mirror, she encouraged him.

"Oh, oh," she gasped. "Oh cum for me, baby, cum for your sister, show her how much you love it!"

Mark gasped and began to fuck her even harder. Allison was aware of a high pitched whining sound and realized it was her. She was so far gone she couldn't even beg him to finish. Mark cried out and, after a couple of more savage pumps, he pulled out and Allison whimpered in pleasure as she felt her back being sprayed with his hot sticky cum. Collapsing onto her stomach, she lay there groaning as he continued to cum on her, painting her back with another huge load. Mark released a soft whimper and fell onto his back on the bed next to her.

Lying on her stomach, Allison tiredly turned to look at him. Mark was staring up at the mirror, his chest heaving as he fought to calm down. She closed her eyes as the room began to spin and forced herself to take several long deep breaths through her mouth. Her eyes opened as she felt movement next to her. Mark had sat up and, getting off the bed, stood there swaying on his feet before he shook his head. "I'll be right back."

"Oh, I'll be here," she whispered.

She closed her eyes again, then opened them as she felt something on her back. Looking up into the head board she saw Mark wiping her off with a towel. The towel was cold and wet and she sighed at how good it felt.

"Roll over," he said softly.

With a groan, Allison forced herself to roll over onto her back, then cooed delightedly as Mark gently ran the other end of the cool towel across her face and neck.

"That feels nice," she managed to say.

Mark tossed the towel aside and held up a bottle of water. Taking it from him, Allison took several long swallows, then handed it back. Mark finished the bottle, then slid in next to her. He pulled the black sheet up to their waists and let out a deep breath.

"Damn."

"Damn is...." She was still breathing heavy and had to wait to continue. "I mean....wow, I...." She laughed. "The goddamn room is spinning. Holy shit I've never been fucked like that before."

"Like I said," he began. "Every woman wants me every..." He stopped and laughed. "Oh, whatever, that was damn good."

"Tell you what." Allison shook her head. "You can be as cocky as you want to be, because that was fucking amazing." She sighed. "I've never been so tired in my life." She giggled then added, "Or satisfied."

"So I made my sister happy?"

"You made your sister, veeery happy," she purred.

"Good, now come here." He extended his arm to her.

With an effort she slid over and he slipped his arm underneath her. Resting her head on his chest, Allison put her arm across his waist. She sighed as he put his arm around her shoulder. Damn he felt good. Allison tried to remember the last time she had spent the night in someone's bed. With a start, she realized it might have been as far back as college.

"Funny," she said quietly. "You didn't strike me as the afterglow type."

"And should my sister go to her room like a pet?" he asked.

"Well when you put it that way." She sighed. "Damn I'm tired."

"Look at us," he said pointing at the mirror. "Are we not beautiful?"

Allison looked up and, as arrogant as his remark sounded, she had to say they looked damn good lying together. "I guess so," she told him. "But I..." She yawned. "Have to go to sleep before I pass out." She noticed his eyes were still wide open. "Aren't you tired?" she asked as her eyes began to close.

"I'm going to sleep." He kissed her forehead. "Good night, my beautiful new sister."

"That it was," she replied just before she fell into sleep's warm embrace.

Chapter Six

Allison opened her eyes and winced as a searing pain went through them, causing her to close them again. Her head was throbbing, her throat was dry, and she wondered why the hell she was awake at all. Opening her eyes, but only partway this time, she jerked her head back against the pillow as she saw someone above her. The sudden move caused another blinding wave of pain to pass through her skull, but she felt a sense of relief when she saw it was her reflection in the mirror over the bed.

She closed her eyes, and told herself to relax. Most likely she'd woken up because she was unaccustomed to sleeping in a strange bed. She turned her head to the side and nuzzled her face into the soft pillow. Now that she was resting and not fucking like an overheated animal, the room was pleasantly cool. Either her or Mark had pulled the silk sheet up over her tits and the material felt amazing. Allison decided when she received her commission from Orion's account she would treat herself to a set of red silk sheets.

The pounding in her head began to recede and she smiled. Her body still ached, but it was a happy ache. Between her legs she could feel her pussy was still moist. Damn, Mark had given it to her good. Laying there on her back, it occurred to her she must have rolled away from him at some point, and thought about curling back up to him. Her tired mind still racing, rather than sinking back into much needed sleep; it dawned on her it really had been years since she'd spent a night in a man's bed. She never stayed the night with pets, and damn straight she wouldn't let them know where she lived.

The couple of times Allison had slept with a man around her age, it was at hotels and she always made it a point to leave as part of the game to make them think they had barely held her interest. Mark had definitely held her interest. For the first time in her life, Allison felt out of her league. Even on her terms, Mark had simply taken her, and damned hard. Not that she'd minded, she had been looking forward to that fucking all night, but even after the blow job she had given him, he had still been calling the shots. Then again, Allison's had gotten him to break his rules, she had succeeded in seducing him, and that had to count for something.

Allison felt her mind start to settle down and again rubbed her face against the cool pillowcase. She felt sleep beginning to creep up on her again. She had just begun to drift off when she became aware of a feeling of being watched. Opening her eyes, she saw Mark on his side, propped up on one elbow watching her. She blinked a couple of times to get her tired eyes to focus and noticed his weird shifting eyes were quite dark. Mark was facing the candelabra behind her and the flickering light was reflected in those dark eyes, giving them the illusion they were glowing.

"Don't you sleep?" she asked softly.

"Very little," he replied.

"I can see that."

"You pout in your sleep."

"What?" she asked.

"I've been watching you and..." His fingers brushed her lower lip. "You pout in your sleep."

"I didn't know that."

"It's adorable," he said. "Makes me want to do this."

He kissed her softly, just on her lip where his fingers had been. His hand began lightly caressing her cheek and Allison could smell her pussy on them. Between that and the look of desire in his eyes, she felt her nipples stiffen against the sheet.

"You truly are beautiful, Allison," he whispered.

She began to tell him he was as well, but her response was cut off by his lips once again finding hers. This time, it wasn't a quick peck, but a slow teasing kiss, during which he playfully flicked his tongue across her lips as his mouth caressed hers. Allison parted her lips, further inviting his tongue to enter her mouth, and sighed as he accepted. The kiss picked up in intensity, their tongues playing across each other. Allison moaned as she could taste her pussy on his lips, and could feel her nipples pressing against his chest through the sheet. In the past, she had always mocked the Hollywood kisses that left people breathless. As Mark continued to kiss her, she could feel herself melting beneath him, willing to let him do whatever he wanted to her.

Allison slipped her arms around his shoulders, trying to pull him down even closer. As soon as she did, Mark's lips pulled back slightly and started sliding them back across hers, barely brushing them. His tongue darted between her lips, teasing her and, with a moan, she opened her mouth wider and pulled on his shoulders. Mark began kissing her harder and his hand left her cheek to begin to run through her hair. Again his lips withdrew from hers, and she made a sound of protest that quickly turned into a delighted purr, as nuzzling her head to the side, Mark began to kiss the soft skin of her neck.

His hand left her hair and, sliding down, pulled the sheet from her tits. Allison groaned at the feel of his hand on her inner thigh and opened her legs for him. Instead of sliding between them as she'd hoped, his hand worked its way back up and gently caressed her stomach. She opened her eyes, and took in their reflection in the mirror. Mark had tossed the sheet off of them and the sight of his dark hand trailing across her ivory skin, while he continued sucking on her sensitive neck, sent a thrill through her. Not as big of a thrill as she felt when his hand made its way up and started to fondle her tits.

Mark's fingers lightly rubbed across her tender nipple, before working across her chest, to play with the other. He slid further down the bed, and she gasped as his soft tongue began to trace slow circles around her swollen nipple. Letting her tit go, as he sucked on it, his hand trailed back down her stomach, and this time did not disappoint. Allison moaned at the feeling of his strong fingers slipping through the soft wet flesh of her pussy, where they began to slide up and down between her lips.

Allison's hands began wandering as well, sliding down his back and arms, enjoying the feeling of his muscles bulging beneath his tanned flesh. Mark's mouth left her nipple to once again begin teasing her mouth with those soft playful kisses. She moaned softly into those kisses as his fingers teased across her clit, before sliding back down the length of her pussy. His touch, like the kisses, was surprisingly gentle and driving her crazy. Allison whimpered in her throat, and began pumping her hips, against his hand, hoping he would slip his fingers inside. Mark stopped kissing her and, after trailing his lips under her chin and down her throat, teasingly flicked his tongue across each nipple.

Allison pulled against his shoulders, trying to hold his face to her yearning nipples, but bracing his hand on the bed next to her, he pushed himself up. Her sound of protest turned into her breathing, "Oh, yes," as he pushed up on his other arm and rolled over so that he was between her legs, holding himself above her. Looking down along the length of her body, Allison saw his huge, hard cock pointing directly between her legs.

"Oh damn," she whispered, "What are you waiting for?"

Mark lowered himself down to her, and as their lips met, slowly entered her. His cock easily slid into her and she moaned as he sank deep into her welcoming flesh. Still kissing her, Mark let his weight go, sliding his arms beneath hers and pulling their bodies close together. Nuzzling her head so she arched it back, Mark began placing a series of gentle kisses along the soft skin of her exposed throat, all the while using long slow strokes that felt incredible. They were teasing yet as impatient as she usually was, Allison felt so good, she found herself in no hurry to get him to speed up. Turning her head to invite him to begin kissing the side of her neck, she purred. "Oh, Mark, that feels soooo nice!"

His reply was to turn his head and begin planting those teasing kisses on the top of her shoulder. He was still using those slow steady strokes, but had slid up a little higher, changing the angle as he did. His shaft was now stroking her clit on its way down into her pussy and she felt a shiver go through her each time it did. Allison wrapped her legs around his waist and moaned as that brought him even deeper inside of her. She began running her fingernails lightly across his back and through his hair, causing him to make a soft whimpering sound in his throat that seemed strange coming from him. Allison slid her fingers down the length of his back, and smiled as she was rewarded with another of those oddly cute noises.

She then made a noise of her own, as pushing himself up slightly, Mark bent his head to her right nipple and sucked it into his mouth. She sighed and closed her eyes as he switched to the left, before bringing his lips up to meet hers. He began to thrust harder into her, not faster, but hard enough to start to really begin to stroke her clit.

Allison moaned into his mouth and wrapped her arms around his neck, pulling his mouth harder into hers. She started running her fingers through his hair again and received a soft moan from him. Mark's control was amazing. He had not slowed or paused once, but just continued that deliciously slow rhythm. She started moving her hips as well, not quickly but in perfect time with his. Her hands drifted from his neck and began slowly rubbing her hands up and down his arms, loving the feel the muscles rippling in his arms and forearms. All the years she'd been having sex Allison couldn't remember a time that she had taken the time to enjoy someone's body this way.

She could feel an orgasm beginning to build deep inside and rather than speeding up so it would crash through her, she continued to let Mark go slow and easy, letting it take its time. She found that rather than being a tease, the slow build up felt damn good. Taking her hands, she placed them on either side of Mark's face and, pushing him up from her neck, looked up into those strange eyes and flawless features thinking he really was beautiful. Allison parted her lips for him and Mark lowered his mouth to hers and shared another long passionate kiss. She had never kissed like this, so slowly and sweetly.

All her life whether it was an older guy or a young pet, a boyfriend back when she used to date, or a one night stand, Allison had never gone soft and easy. Not that she had ever wanted to, as she had told Mark earlier, all she ever wanted to do was get fucked. Making love was something they did in chick flicks and was vastly over rated. Or so she had thought, because this felt damn good. She still couldn't believe how sweet he could be, especially after the animal like encounter she'd suffered through earlier today.

Her mind stopped racing as her body took control. The orgasm she had been teetering on the edge of for such a delightfully long time was about to reach its conclusion. Normally when Allison was at this point, the orgasm would just crash through her, yet even now, knowing it was right there, her body stayed on the edge awhile longer. Her thighs started to shake and, breaking the kiss, she started moaning each time his cock stroked her clit, her hips twitching harder into his. Mark sped up as well. He was still going nowhere near as hard as he had before, but was going fast enough and now using short strokes that were rubbing her clit harder and faster.

"Ohh," she gasped looking up into Mark's eyes. She squeezed her fingers into his arms and gasped again. The orgasm was starting, but was flowing slowly through her. Instead of a rush it was more of a slow steady stream of intense pleasure.

"Oh, Mark," she moaned. "Oh that's so good it's...."

Allison let out a series of long moans that got louder as Mark sped up even more. He was breathing heavier as he finally closed in on his own climax. The orgasm finally reached its peak and exploded through her. Wrapping her arms and legs tightly around him, she bucked her hips into his. Allison let out a long drawn out groan as the orgasm lingered, sending a continuous wave of intense pleasure through her. She squeezed her legs around his sides and arched her back into him as her body convulsed beneath him.

Mark moaned in her ear as his body tensed up and he began pumping her harder and faster. Allison groaned as the last of the orgasm flowed though her and as he thrust harder into her, urged him on.

"That's it, Mark," She moaned, "Go ahead. Let me feel it."

Mark came hard, his cum exploding deep inside of her as he continued to thrust in and out. He moaned in her ear as he continued to cum. Allison gasped as she felt his cock twitching inside of her, filling her with his cum. She couldn't remember the last time she let a man cum inside of her, and was amazed at how good it felt, at how good he felt. Every muscle in his arms and back were flexed and Allison thought that he was cumming even harder than she had. They both moaned as he continued to spray the walls of her pussy with his hot cum. Mark gave her one last hard pump, then let his weight go, resting on his forearms. His chest was pressed tightly to hers and she could feel his heart beating rapidly.

Allison smiled up at him and whispered, "That was.... amazing."

"As are you." He said softly.

He kissed her then nuzzled his face into her neck. Allison closed her eyes and held him close to her, enjoying the feeling of his cock beginning to soften inside of her. A moment later, her eyes snapped open as she realized she was starting to fall asleep. She felt Mark jerk against her and figured he had been falling asleep as well. Mark rolled over onto his back, and Allison rolled over with him. She thought she'd been exhausted and satisfied earlier, now she felt like she could sleep for a week. She had no idea where that had come from, but wouldn't mind more of it. Despite how tired she was, Allison was already beginning to think about what the morning would bring. Sliding her arm across his waist, she whispered, "Mark, can I ask you something?"

"Anything," he said as his arm wrapped around her shoulder and his hand started running through her hair.

"So which one are you?"

"What do you mean?"

Allison looked up at the mirror and saw him staring up in to it, using it to watch her. "Earlier once you started being good to me, I thought he's like Jekyll and Hyde, but now, I think it's more like Beauty or the Beast." She kissed his chest and asked, "So which one are you really?"

"I'm whichever my sister needs me to be." he answered, giving the top of her head a kiss.

Nuzzling her face into his chest she closed her eyes and sighed, "I think I like beauty better."

If he replied she didn't hear it, she was already falling back into a deep satisfied sleep.

* * *

The sound of music startled Allison out of a deep sleep. Propping herself up on her elbows, she looked around the room, her heart pounding in her chest. Mark was no longer next to her and the bedroom door was shut. The music sounded again to her left and she recognized Heart's *If Looks could Kill.* Turning her head, Allison saw a red phone identical to the one Mark had given her, on the night stand. Curious, she reached out and picked it up as she listened to Ann Wilson belt out, *"You'd be lying on the floor, you'd begging me please, please, please, baby, please don't hurt me no more!"*

Very appropriate considering this must be a member of the group. *Her group,* the thought dawned on her. Looking at the screen she saw the name Scarlett. She didn't answer and a moment later the music stopped. She put the phone down, leaned back against the pillows and looked up into the mirror. She smiled up at herself and, kicking the sheet off, stretched out, admiring the way her ivory skin looked on the black sheets. She pushed her tits out, and playfully cupped them, offering them to her reflection. The bruises on her nipples were even darker than they had been last night, but they didn't seem quite as sore.

Spreading her legs, she slid her hand down her stomach and watched as it dipped between her legs. She let out a deep breath as she felt her still damp pussy. The sight of her touching herself was a hell of a turn on, and she removed her hand before she slipped her fingers inside. As much fun as it would be to watch herself get off, it would be much more fun to get Mark to do it for her. The room was still fairly dark even with the candelabra's flickering and she wondered how early it was. Glancing over to the nightstand on the right, she was surprised to see it was just after eleven. Damn she had gone out like a light.

Allison forced herself to get up from the huge comfortable bed. She stretched again and it occurred to her she had no idea where her clothes were. Allison supposed Mark wouldn't complain about her walking out of the room naked, but thought it would be sexier to have something to strip off. There was a door off to her right she assumed was a closet and smiled at the thought of putting on one of his shirts. She started to walk over there, but stopped when she noticed a black robe hanging from a hook on one of the bed posts. When she removed it from the hook, she smiled delightedly when she felt that, like the sheets, it was silk and quickly slipped it on.

As she tied it, she looked around the room, frowning in distaste at the huge murals that depicted various scenes of hell. Curiously, she walked over to one of the tapestries to see if he had hung it over the window. Pressing against the velvet material it felt as if there was a wall behind it. She was turning away when she noticed the there seemed to be a depression in the wall. Reaching out, she tapped it and was surprised to feel that it was glass. He had painted the window black.

"Weird," she whispered.

Turning, she walked towards the door to go and find her weird but gorgeous host and see if he wanted to make her breakfast, then maybe get something to eat! But before that, she would get him to shower with her. The thought of running her hands over that hard body, in a nice steamy shower, sent a pleasant shiver through her. Leaving the room, Allison glanced into the dining room and, not seeing Mark there, padded quietly down the hallway to use the bathroom, rolling her eyes at the thought no one ever had to pee in the movies. When she finished, she stopped in front of the mirror and took a moment wash her face, rinsing the smeared make up from her eyes, and then went looking for Mark.

She walked down the hallway, enjoying the feeling of the soft carpet beneath her feet and, entering the living room, saw Mark sitting in a black leather recliner. His back was to her and she slowly approached him. He was facing the large flat screen TV on the wall, but Allison noticed that it wasn't on and wondered if he were asleep. Moving as quietly as she could, she came around to the front of the chair and saw he was awake. He was shirtless and wearing a pair of jeans that she noticed was unsnapped. Allison could see the edge of his pubic hair through the open jeans, God how she loved that look.

Mark didn't seem to be aware of her. His eyes were focused on the television as if he were watching something on it. For a moment Allison wondered if he was sleeping with his eyes open, after all it would fit with his bizarre bedroom motif and obvious occult background. Mark's legs were up on an ottoman and his arms resting along the sides of the chair. Allison noticed he was holding a glass in his left hand that appeared to have whiskey in it. Shaking off the memory of her brother Jack drinking first thing in the morning, she sauntered up to the chair. She was planning on leaning over and kissing him, when without looking at her, he spoke, "Good morning, Allison."

He put his feet down on the floor and seemed as if he were going to stand. That move worked out perfect for her.

"It's a very good morning." Quickly stepping between his legs so he couldn't stand, she began to sink to her knees. "But I think I can make it an absolutely glorious morning."

"Allison, stop." he said, closing his legs to prevent her from getting down on the floor. "We can't."

"Oh, I get it." She rolled her eyes. "New day, and back to the rules right?"

"That's…." He began, but stopped as, grabbing the tie to the robe, she undid the knot and let it fall open to expose her tits. Shaking his head, he whispered, "No."

"Oh please?" she asked. "Please give your new sister a proper send off?"

Allison started to slide the robe from her shoulders, but reaching out; Mark grabbed the edges of it, and pulled it closed. "I mean it, Allison, forget it."

"Oh, come on, Mark." She laughed, pulling back from him. "You fucked me twice last night."

"That was last night and I…."

"Had a pretty damn good time, so let's have some more fun." She gave him a sexy smile. "I think you should shower with me, but be a little nicer than you were in there yesterday."

"Allison…."

"And I'll be very nice to you," she purred, as she opened and closed the robe, playfully flashing him.

"We can't keep breaking….."

"But we did," she said with a sigh. She was starting to get annoyed. Why the hell did this have to be a game? "Look, Mark, we broke the rules last night and I haven't left yet, so just consider it one continuous rule breaking okay?"

She let the robe drop open and, stepping up to the chair, placed her foot onto the arm of it. Reaching down she spread her pussy open. "Come on, baby, you know you want that pussy, show me again how goddamn good you are with that tongue of yours." She put on the pout. "Don't you want to be good to your sister?"

"Enough!" Mark snapped

Allison yelped in surprise as, grabbing her ankle, he yanked it off the chair. Losing her balance she started to fall forward. Mark caught her shoulders and stood up quickly, keeping her on her feet.

"Hey!" she exclaimed.

Letting her arms go, Mark again grabbed the robe and pulled it closed. "Listen, Allison, you got what you wanted last night."

"Oh, only I wanted that?" she asked, taking a step back from him. "Just me, huh?"

"No, I…." He appeared to be making an effort to stay calm. "You played your game last night and you won. You're beautiful and playful, and seductive and…." He sighed. "You got the better of me. But that was last night."

"So what now?" she asked. "You're back on your game so nothing?"

"Now?" Mark shrugged. "Now you go home."

"I go…." She started.

"Yes, home." He pointed at her as he spoke. "You came down here to be initiated into the Circle. Be proud of yourself, because not only did you make it, but you ended up getting a lot more than you should have. You shouldn't even still be here."

"I shouldn't?" She was becoming more than a little annoyed.

"No, the rule is not to spend the night even with granted time. Now it's almost noon and you have a long ride. Your clothes are hanging in my closet, so go ahead and shower and…."

"Who the fuck do you think you're talking to?" she demanded, her voice rising. "What do you think I am one of your pets? You're done so…" She wiggled her fingers at him. "Run along now?"

"It's not like…."

"Fuck you, Mark."

"Nice." He nodded ."Are we twelve now?"

"No, usually guys don't get that arrogant until they're older, you know, your age?"

"Like I said yesterday." He gave her that cocky look he'd had during the initiation, "That's why you like them young, you can handle them."

"Really?" She returned the smirk. "Seems like I handled you pretty well last night, Mr. Keeper of the rules."

Mark stared at her coldly, and she smiled at him. "Maybe that's why *you* like them young."

"I gave you credit, Allison," he said quietly. "You did play your game." The smirk returned, "But I played mine as well."

"Oh really?" she asked. "And when was that? When you were fucking who you shouldn't have been?"

"No," he shrugged. "You got to me, but I figured while I was there I may as well have tried something new."

"Something new?"

"Sure," he replied as he snapped his jeans. "I always wanted to give that slow sweet shit a try." He flashed a smug smile. "Seemed like you enjoyed it."

"You…"

"See I can't do that with the young ones, they'll read something into it." He shrugged. "Then again, you seemed like you might have too." He laughed. "I prefer beauty," he said in an exaggeratedly breathless tone that sent her over the edge.

"Now you can really go fuck yourself, you arrogant jerk!" she snapped as, following his example she tied her robe. Sex was as far from her mind as it could be right now. "How stupid do you think I am?"

"What do you mean, stupid?"

"Oh, please!" She waved her hand at him. "Trying to tell me that was a game?" She laughed. "You forget something, Mark, you and your rich playmates sought me out because I know something about games myself, so don't sit here and try to cover last night up." She grinned. "I think you were pretty into it, and now you're pretending it was a game." she made a disgusted sound. "Give me a break."

He looked away from her and she continued in a quieter tone. "Hey look, Mark, you were tired and drunk, and said I reminded you of someone. So maybe you had someone who was more than a game, and it caught up with you." She shrugged. "Whatever, it was new for me and I enjoyed it, but that's it. So don't sit here and try to pretend you didn't."

"Yeah," he sighed. "You're right, I should know better than to play you." He spread his arms out. "I just figured I'd toss that out there in case you…."

"I what?" she raised her eyebrows.

"You read something into it." He laughed. "You know, like it meant something."

"Are you kidding me?" she asked, her voice rising again. "You're worried I was going to what? Fall for you?"

"Well." He winked. "I am pretty…."

"Fucking full of yourself!" She shook her head. "You're a damn good looking guy and one hell of a lay, but don't flatter yourself!"

"Well you were…."

"For Christ's sakes, I wanted to have a great night, and we did, but I'm sure as hell not looking for a boyfriend!" She sighed and said quietly, "But breakfast would have been nice."

Mark frowned and didn't reply. Allison tightened the robe and began to walk past him.

"I'll get dressed and leave, I'll shower at home, I wouldn't want to over stay my welcome."

"Whatever you want," he said softly.

Allison started to leave the room, when she turned and, staring at the huge tattoo on his back added, "Well I guess all that talk about how revered the Ladies of the Circle are is just a bunch of shit. And if you're the one looking out for me, I think I'll take my chances, because you have no clue how to treat a lady, Circle or otherwise."

Turning around, she walked quickly down the hallway to his bedroom and headed for the closet. She opened the door and found the red sundress she had arrived in hanging there. Grabbing it, she turned and let out a startled yelp, as Mark was standing right behind her.

"Damn, you really are creepy you know that?" she asked him, her heart pounding.

"Allison, I'm sorry," he said, taking her hand. "You're right; this is no way to treat the Circle's newest lady."

"I don't know what your problem is Mark," she said, removing her hand from his. She was not going to fall for the smooth routine again.

"Come sit with me for a second." He gestured towards the bed. When she didn't move right away he added, "Please."

Allison walked over and sat on the foot of the bed. Mark sat next to her and turning to face her, began speaking softly. "Allison, last night was a huge mistake."

"You really need to work on your apology skills." She rolled her eyes.

"You don't understand," he said shaking his head. "I wasn't kidding at dinner. Next to falling in love, sex between members is the most important rule there is and I broke it."

"We broke it," she pointed out.

"No, Allison, I broke it. I've been in the group almost ten years, I know better, you didn't." He shrugged. "You were tired just like I was and had a lot to drink and was overwhelmed."

"There's that modesty again."

"I don't mean it that way," he explained. "But yesterday was a lot and you know it. And not trying to sound arrogant, but many times there is an attraction to the one who breaks you."

"Here we go..." she started, but he raised his hand to silence her.

"It happens a lot, Allison, and it usually fades pretty quick."

"Oh, it faded all right."

"But it was there. I'm like no one you've ever met, just like you're like nothing those young men have ever seen. So between that and your exhausted state, it was a given you'd want to play."

He paused and, tapping his chest continued, "That's why it's my fault, I know better and I should've held off, but you..." He reached out and touched her cheek. "There's something about you, Allison and I'm not just saying that. I let myself think I'd just play a little and..." He shook his head. "I couldn't stop myself. I overestimated me and underestimated you. Then this morning I just...I had to stop you so I pissed you off."

"That you did," she agreed.

"Allison, no one can ever know what happened."

"Okay."

"I mean it. I don't just mean now, but even down the line, you can't...."

"I said I won't!" she snapped irritably. "You want me to pinky swear it?" She sighed. "What's the big deal?"

"The big deal is you can't think it happens all the time. That was why it's a big mistake for me."

"What do you mean?"

"I tell you the rule is we can't. I break the rule. So now maybe some night, Alex calls you and invites you out to some networking thing or just for dinner with his sister. You get hot and bothered and figure, hell I got to Mark I can get to him too."

"I wouldn't...."

"But say you did. Now Alex is wondering why you'd think you could. Even if you don't say anything, he's going to think something's wrong. More than that, if he went to the mistress and told her you tried to seduce him, you'd be punished."

"This seems overly dramatic, Mark," she told him.

"It's what'll happen, and if you were to say something right away?" He put a hand on her shoulder. "Then everything you went through yesterday would be for nothing."

"You mean they'd throw me out?" she asked.

"Yes. Me they'd punish, and I'd lose a lot of respect. But you they'd ban. And you'd lose everything you could get from the group."

"Everything?"

"Everything, no member is allowed to associate with or help a disgraced member. It'd be over before it started, Allison, and that's why I was so upset this morning. My weakness could cost you dearly."

He was staring intently into her eyes and Allison could tell he was serious. She would have never said anything anyway, but until now had thought perhaps there could be another time for them. Maybe a little friends with benefits thing, a chance to be with someone more her age who could give her what she wanted once in awhile, an equal. A feeling of disappointment went through her. Allison had always been able to have any man she desired.

No sooner had that thought passed through her mind, than she recalled Alex telling her that was the reason members didn't get together. It taught control to people who had never had to exercise it. Looking at how upset Mark was she took his hand and said softly, "I understand, Mark and I'm not mad." She squeezed his hand and added, "It's too bad though. Desiring someone should never be a mistake."

Mark looked down at her hand, then back up. He had that faraway look in his eyes that he'd had a couple of times last night and whispered, "It all depends on who you desire."

Chapter Seven

Friday afternoons at A&S were generally pretty relaxed. The dress code was casual and most of the reps were completing paperwork and putting the finishing touches on what they had worked on during the week. If they had nothing to finish, most were at their desks allegedly cold calling prospective customers. Allison always threw in the word allegedly, because more often than not they were making one call per every ten minutes of facebook updates. The lead by example partners like Ben Watts and Joe Perez were normally wandering the halls, bullshitting with the other established reps who no longer seemed to feel they had to put in a full week's work for their over inflated salaries.

In her six years there, Allison had always worked right up to the last minute. Granted, after five o'clock or so she might take a few minutes to decide which of her pets she was in the mood for. Once she had played out a few fantasies, she would give the winning candidate a call to tell them they were going to get the pleasure of her company for the evening. After that, she would generally go back to work for another couple of hours while everyone else in her department ran out the door.

This Friday was far from relaxed and it was all because of her. As she had promised last week, Victoria had arrived on Wednesday and together they had called the president of marketing at Rapture perfume, Gabrielle Williams. Victoria had stated she was more than happy to represent their fine product, but the campaign would have to run through A&S advertising and more specifically, Allison. As she sat there trembling with excitement, Williams scheduled an appointment to meet with both Victoria and Allison at her office next Wednesday. When they had hung up Victoria, who unlike last time, had arrived dressed in a conservative black pantsuit smiled and said, "This is just the beginning, my sister, you and I are going to make a lot of money together."

Laughing, Allison had replied, "You already have a lot of money."

"But one can never have enough, dear," Victoria replied seriously.

Once again Victoria's arrival caused quite a stir, and when the two left her office to go to lunch, Ben, Joe and a couple of other higher ups were hanging around the corridor. This was under the pretense of Joe wanting to officially welcome Victoria aboard and perhaps they could have some lunch to celebrate their new partnership. As much as she didn't want that to happen, Allison said nothing and looked at Victoria, leaving it up to her. Taking a step back, Victoria leaned over and spoke in her ear, "When I put my arm around you, you flash them the sexiest smile you have, the 'I just saw a twenty year old bartender with your name all over him' smile."

Keeping her hand on her arm, Victoria turned away from Allison and, leading her along, walked up to Ben and the others and began speaking, "Well, gentlemen, that's exactly what Allison and I are off to do, grab some lunch and celebrate *our* working together."

"Well perhaps we could come along, Miss Redding," Ben said. "Allison won't be working alone on something this big and we feel that…."

Putting her arm around Allison's shoulders, Victoria leaned in, and pressed her cheek against Allison's. Knowing she was doing the same, Allison did indeed flash her best smile, but this one was not inspired by sex, but the look on the faces the men.

"Sorry, Mr. Watts," Victoria purred in that sultry phone sex voice. "But no boys allowed."

Victoria dropped her hand down to the small of Allison's back, and guided her along as they walked past Ben. They had taken several steps when Allison gasped in surprise as Victoria's hand slid down, cupped her ass, and left it there.

"Do the same, dear," she whispered.

Trying not to laugh, Allison reached around and placed her hand over Victoria's round and, she noticed, very firm ass. They stayed like that until they made it around the corner. Removing her hand, Victoria turned to her and, giving her a playful kiss on the cheek exclaimed, "Allison, we're going to have a lot of fun together, the men around us will never stand a chance!"

When Allison had gotten back from lunch, she immediately had gone back to her office, pretending not to hear Ben Watts calling her as she walked past Cindy. As soon as she entered, she told Cindy to tell Ben or anyone else she was on the phone with Orion and couldn't be disturbed. Allison went to her desk and, kicking her shoes off, leaned back in the chair and, swinging her feet up on her desk, closed her eyes. From the time she had left for lunch and, even during, Allison had felt a familiar nagging sensation at the back of her mind.

It was an exciting feeling because she knew it meant she had an idea, but it hadn't risen to the surface yet. Whenever that feeling arose, Allison would close her eyes and relax. Many times her best ideas had come in the moments before she either fell asleep or had first awoken, when her mind was relaxed and hadn't started racing yet. Nothing was coming and she let her mind drift to the fabulous lunch she'd had with Victoria. Allison had tried to ask her about the Circle, but Victoria had told her since she had not been officially introduced yet, they couldn't discuss it.

Allison had asked her if everyone took all the rules that seriously and Victoria had told her the group was based on rules, some fun, some not. The Circle was all about games within games, but the rules were to be followed at all times. She had then told Allison she would bend them just enough to ask her what Mark had told her the two most important rules were. Allison had answered that love was off the table, and then as Victoria looked at her expectantly said members are never to engage in sex without permission. Victoria had smiled and said she had no doubt Mark would have told her that, but wanted to be sure.

After Allison had nodded, trying not to envision Mark giving her the best sex of her life, the conversation turned into simple girl talk and Allison loved it. Victoria told her about her two brothers and sister out in Colorado and spoke of her teenage niece who was already starting to break into modeling. Allison avoided any talk of her own family. Victoria sounded like she came from the Brady bunch and Allison didn't want to talk about having no mother, and a brother who had disowned her. When Victoria had been speaking of her niece, who was also her god daughter, Allison had felt a pang of sadness about her own niece.

She thought of Mark confidently saying he could make it so she could see her. Maybe someday she would take him up on that offer. Her mind began to drift down that unwanted path, but she let it. Allison envisioned herself being able to be a real aunt and going to see Amanda, taking her out for the day and having some girl time. The kind of time she used to have with her mom. When Allison was young, every Saturday her father would take Jack out and mom would take her, so they could spend some time together, no....No boys allowed!

Allison's eyes snapped open as she heard Victoria purring those words in her ear. During the brief discussion earlier, Williams had mentioned that they wanted to use Victoria to help launch their as of yet unnamed line of new skin care products, which included scented bath oils. Closing her eyes again, Allison was struck by the vivid image of Victoria in a spa, wrapped in a towel and sitting with two other gorgeous women. They would be applying the products to themselves as they laughed and smiled, the catch phrase would be no boys allowed.

Maybe, if Victoria was all right with it, the ad could be sexed up, have the women rubbing some of the cream on each other's shoulders or legs. Nothing sold better to men than hot lipstick lesbians. They would be buying gift baskets for their women, just because they were located under a picture of Victoria Redding having her shoulders rubbed by another gorgeous woman.

Allison opened her eyes and, dropping her feet from the desk, had grabbed a pen and started jotting down ideas. When she was finished, she realized that in order to get something done by the time Williams came in next week, she would need help. A couple of interns at least, plus someone to help her set up a quick photo shoot. They would have to look for models then have them come in for an audition. Reaching for the phone, she caught herself beginning to dial Joe Perez, and then quickly hung up. Joe was her supervisor who in turn answered to Ben. In the past she had found Joe easier to deal with and he'd never been inappropriate with her. Joe did however go to Ben with everything and pretended he didn't know what she was talking about when she complained she was being screwed.

Victoria had made it clear she would only work with Allison, but the company policy was if you had to bring in help from other departments and supervisors, the account could become a house account and she would have to give up total control of the campaign. Tapping her red nails on the phone, she thought about the things Alex and Mark had told her. She had more potential than the others around her and it was time to take what she wanted. Picking up the phone, she dialed the office of Edwin Blake.

"Mr. Blake's office, this is Jean."

"Hi, Jean, this is Allison Saunders, may I speak with Mr. Blake?"

"He's in a meeting right now, Allison. I'll let him know you called."

A glance at the time told her that it was four p.m. The meeting Blake was in was him sitting around with his cronies and bullshitting. Blake left right at five and never scheduled anything important after three.

"I need to discuss an important matter with him."

"Well, as I said I...."

"Jean," Allison interrupted. "Tell Mr. Blake I just met with Victoria Redding and there may be a problem."

"I'll try," Jean told her.

The music had just begun playing in her ear when Blake's deep resonant voice came on.

"Allison, what can I do for you this afternoon?"

"Well." She stopped and swallowed, trying not to sound nervous. "As you know, I met with Miss Redding today."

"I heard, very impressive, but I understand there's a problem?"

"Not quite a problem, Mr. Blake, but I believe I'm onto something and may need some help." Blake was quiet and Allison went on, "I think that it'd look great for us if we...."

"Allison?"

"Yes Mr. Blake?"

"I have some time before I leave. Why don't you come up here and we'll speak in person."

"Ummm, okay," she said, surprised.

"Good," he replied. "You're starting to make a lot of noise down there and I'm eager to hear what you have to say."

"I'll be right up."

Five minutes later, Allison was standing in front of Jean's desk trying not to look nervous. In the six years she had works at A&S, Allison could count on her fingers how many times she had spoken with Blake and most of them were brief conversations at office parties. Ben and the boys pretty much kept the rest of the employees from seeing him to help protect their monopoly on things. The fact he had requested to see her, she knew should be a good thing, but she was worried nonetheless.

"Go on in Allison," Jean told her.

"Thank you."

Allison walked up to Blake's huge oak door and after a quick knock, entered and frowned. Blake's office was similar to Warner's in that he had several leather chairs and a small table in the center of it. Ben Watts was sitting in one of the chairs. Across from him was Joe Perez and Jack Roberts, another senior executive. Blake was sitting behind his massive desk, and waved at her.

"Come on over, Allison, we were discussing you."

"Good things I hope." She laughed as she walked over to his desk.

"Of course! I was telling the boys here that I don't know how you managed it, but Alex Warner and Victoria Redding in one week?" Blake whistled. "Damn impressive."

"I'm pretty sure I know how she managed Warner." Ben said softly as she walked by.

Allison refused to look at him or the others, but as she walked by she could feel their eyes on her. She was wearing a red skirt that was on the shorter side and knew they were staring at her legs. Blake stood up and gestured for her to sit. Allison smiled when he didn't sit down until she did. Edwin Blake was in his late sixties and had a reputation as a gentleman. Blake had also earned a lot of respect for being a good family man who had been married for forty years and still adored his wife.

Allison had found it odd he would tolerate the behavior of men like Ben and the others. Then again, Blake had never witnessed their antics and had gone to school with Ben's father. Any time anything came up, Blake always took their word on things. Before Allison had come there, Blake had been much more active in the company, but after Jim Pearson left, he had pretty much turned the reigns over to Ben and the rest. Once she'd sat, Blake nodded at her and, as he folded his tall thin frame back into his chair, he put his hand out to her. "So, what is it that you need to discuss, and how does it involve Miss Redding?"

Glancing over her shoulder, she saw all three men staring at her. Jack and Joe seemed curious, but the look on Ben's face was nothing short of disgusted, as if just her being in the office was offending him.

That look sent a wave of anger through her. Grabbing hold of that anger and using it to lend confidence to her voice, she began. “As you know, Mr. Blake, Victoria Redding and I called Gabrielle Williams at Rapture today and set up a meeting next week to discuss how we can represent her new line of skin care products.”

“I wasn’t aware they sold skin creams.” Blake said.

“Well no one does.” She shrugged. “Hence new products.”

“Allison, watch your mouth,” Ben Watts snapped behind her.

“Oh, knock it off, Ben.” Blake laughed. “She’s right, she got me good.” He sighed. “Getting old these days.” With a disarming smile he told her, “Go on, dear.”

“I’m pretty sure this’ll be a lock for us. Victoria signed an agreement allowing us to use both her name and face for the campaign and Rapture has been dying to have her represent them.”

“Excellent. Now I sense a but?”

“Here’s the thing.” Allison leaned forward in the chair. “The meeting’s next Wednesday and we’re only supposed to be talking over some ideas and getting a feel for each other.”

“Is there a point to this?” Ben asked.

Pausing to keep her voice steady, Allison continued, “But I have come up with an idea I think will work, and rather than just tell her about it, I thought how good would it make us look if when she shows up, we have an actual presentation ready to go?”

“That’d make us look very good.” Blake nodded. “I’m still not seeing the problem.”

“In order to get something done that quickly I’d need to get some help and I can’t do that without authorization.”

“Why is that?” Blake asked. “Seems like we should all be working together out there.”

“We make the reps go through proper channels to make sure the labor cost is justified and the right people are working on the right things,” Ben spoke up quickly.

“Oh,” Blake replied. “Makes sense. We can’t be going over budget.”

“Which brings me to why you’re up here Allison?” Ben asked. “Since when do you go over your supervisor’s head to get what you need?”

She felt a tremor in her stomach at his words, then recalling what she had gone through with Mark, she spoke over her shoulder. “Well, Ben, I thought that since Victoria Redding is going to be such an asset to this company, Mr. Blake may want to hear how important this is in person.” She raised her hands and added, “Sometimes it seems there are breakdowns in communication and Mr. Blake gets left in the dark.”

She’d turned her head towards Ben and, as soon as she finished speaking, winked. Ben shot her an evil look, but she noticed Jack smirking.

“Regardless,” Blake said. “Allison’s here now, so before I sign the farm away on some over budget emergency presentation we don’t necessarily need, let’s hear it.”

Taking a deep breath, Allison went on to describe her concept, including the image of the three women rubbing the lotion on each other to sex things up and pitching Rapture to call the line “No Boys allowed.” Blake listened intently, but when she finished, sat back and rubbed at his jaw. “Hmmm, I’m not sure I like the sexual overtones.”

“I assure you, Mr. Blake that it’s not as….”

“I’ve been in the industry long enough to know sex sells, but we’ve always tried to keep our ads a little less racy.”

"It's three women in a spa," she told him. "They'll have towels on. We've done lingerie campaigns that show more."

"It's that lesbian angle." He shrugged. "I don't want to appear I'm implying that type of thing."

"I agree," Ben said. "It's not our style and it's misleading. Plus you know those damn church groups."

"I go to church every Sunday, Ben," Blake replied calmly. "Perhaps you should try it sometime."

"Mr. Blake," Allison began, refusing to let it go. "The campaign is simply three women relaxing at a spa, they're putting on lotion and one puts it on the other's shoulders. Their hands aren't under the towels and nothing inappropriate is going on at all."

"But the perception will be..."

Allison cut him off. "That's the key, perception. Some people will see it as some attractive women having a fun girl's day out, others may see it as that fun day out heading for more, but that's not the ad's fault. That's people's dirty minds and we can't help that."

"Valid point." Blake nodded. "But why risk it? What does doing it this way get us? We have Victoria Redding. Her face alone, or perhaps her in a spa alone would..."

'"I'll tell you what it gets us!" Allison exclaimed, slapping the top of his desk. "It gets us the men's money not just the women's."

"Forget it, Edwin," Ben said. "You're right, we..."

"No, I want to hear this," Blake cut him off. Pointing at her he said "Go on, tell me how."

"Victoria Redding will get us exactly what we will already have, the women. Yes, she'll get us more women than a no name model, but still mostly women. Now Rapture has a great reputation and odds are this line will pretty much self itself, but again to the women."

Turning around in her chair she pointed at Ben and the others. "But what we want is to go beyond the target audience, we want them!"

"And how will we get them?"

When Allison turned back to him she noticed a slight smile playing about Blake's lips. Unsure whether or not he was mocking or encouraging her, she pressed on excitedly. "Victoria by herself will get some guy's attention, especially with a strategically placed towel. Guys will see the poster and say 'Victoria, yeah she's hot' and keep walking."

She paused as her eyes landed on a bottle of hand cream on his desk, reaching out; she squirted some into her hand while speaking. "But three women together?" Standing, she turned and walked towards the guys as she spoke, "Guys see three hot women; they're going to stop and look. Isn't that right Jack?"

Allison had picked Jack because he had never seemed as bad as the other two, and she had chosen right as he nodded. "Absolutely."

"Right!" she said. "And once they stop and look, they're going to see this." Putting her leg up on the arm of Jack's chair, Allison started slowly rubbing the cream up and down her calf.

"That's right," she continued, looking at Blake as her hand made its way down to her foot. "I'm not looking at them and I know they're looking at me. Now picture that it's another woman rubbing my leg, imagine the attention that would get!"

Allison put her leg down and walked back over to Blake whose smile appeared to be widening.

"Now, how does that benefit Rapture? I'll tell you!" Pointing back at the guys she said, "They see a poster like that, they're going to walk right over to it and gawk at it!"

"Most likely," Jack agreed.

"Not most likely, definitely!" she exclaimed. "And under that poster is going to be the product those women are using, gift baskets and sets, creams and lotions. The guys will smell the samples and in their minds that smell with remind them of Victoria and the other models. And now they'll buy it!" Turning, she again indicated Ben and the others. "Rapture is expensive so sitting right there is your audience. The money we can find for Rapture with that ad is guys who have no clue what to get their wives or girlfriends, but now they do, they'll buy Rapture!"

Caught up, she started pacing back and forth as she went on. "Birthdays, Valentine's day, Christmas, anniversaries. This'll become their default expensive, thoughtful gift. And it's a gift for them as well, because I know how men think. Their wives will put that cream on and the men will smell it and..." She smiled. "Think of Victoria Redding rubbing it into some cute woman's shoulders. The smell will be like Pavlov's dog, they'll think of that ad every time they smell it and will love their women wearing it! Now we're getting men's money on a women's product. We can double their market!"

"I suppose that's a good point," she heard Joe say. She had no doubt that remark had just earned him a look from Ben.

"And one last thing," she went on. "Even though again, it's not the angle you're looking for, the appeal to the lesbian market is pretty obvious. This ad will make the girls go out and by this for their favorite girl."

"Sexy line right there, 'their favorite girl'," Jack remarked.

Allison stopped and let her breath out. Her heart was racing and she could feel the adrenalin pumping through her. Blake was sitting back stroking his chin, still with that odd smile on his face, she asked, "So what do you think?"

"I'm still not sold on being that racy." He pointed at Ben. "What do you think, Ben?"

"I think it's too risqué for your image, Edwin."

"Of course you do," Allison said disgustedly, not caring if Blake heard her.

"Joe?"

"Umm." Joe looked at Blake, then Allison and finally to Ben who was shaking his head. "I'm not..."

"Oh for Christ's sake!" Jack snapped. "I don't know what the hell you guys are thinking about, but I can see it!" He looked at Blake. "Edwin, this is a great angle"

"Thank you Jack," Allison smiled at him.

"In fact." Jack pointed at her. "Taking what you said a little further. When you were mentioning the men envisioning Victoria and the models when they smell that? Well guys have different tastes and there are different scents I'd assume so..."

"So we get two models that are totally opposite Victoria!" Allison exclaimed delightedly, that was exactly what she had envisioned, but let Jack feed it to the guys.

"Right!" he agreed. "So maybe a brunette and a...."

"Better than that!" Allison cut him off. "Not just hair color, but skin tone as well. We get an African American model or a Hispanic model with a dark complexion and hair, Victoria's tanned and blonde. We get a red head with fair skin and we have three completely different types. Something for every man's taste."

"And women's, don't forget." Jack winked.

"Only if they perceive it that way though, right?" Allison winked back at him.

"Of course, that's what I meant." Jack laughed. "Damn perverts."

Looking at Edwin, Jack put his hands out. "What do you say, Edwin? It's time to follow what the others are doing!"

Blake looked at Allison and began to speak. "Honestly, still a little unsold, but I'll let you run with it. You said the meeting is Wednesday?"

"Yes, sir," she said, trying not to smile.

"Well, tell you what, you get me something together by Tuesday for me to look at, and if I like it, you pitch it at that meeting fair enough?"

"That's not a lot of time," Jack pointed out.

"I'll make it happen," Allison said quickly. "I just need some..."

"I'll get you what you need," Blake said, "Jack, can you spare some people?"

"Damn straight, I can," Jack said. "I'll pitch in myself if she needs me." Shaking his head he added, "About time we had some fun around here."

"Thank you, Mr. Blake!" Allison exclaimed. "I won't let you down."

"I just want you to know one thing Allison," Blake said. "I'm not letting you do this because I'm overwhelmed with the concept. I'm letting you do this because I've never seen someone that passionate about a pitch and that's what this place needs, some new blood."

"Thank you again, Mr. Blake."

Leaning over his desk, Allison extended her hand to him. Taking her hand, Blake smiled at her. "Call me Edwin, something tells me I'll be seeing a lot more of you in this office."

"Okay, Edwin." Allison gave him a huge smile, which he returned and, turning, walked towards the door. Stopping to put her hand on Jack's shoulder, she said, "Thanks, Jack, I appreciate the help."

"Anytime," he told her. "Just let me know what you need."

"You know," Joe spoke. "This was supposed to go through me, and it should be my people who...."

"Well I'm glad it didn't," Jack said softly so Blake couldn't hear. "Or it would've been you handling it and fucking up."

"Watch yourself, Jack," Ben said quietly.

"I don't think I'm the one who's going to be looking over his shoulder soon," Jack said, and with a nasty smirk added, "Guess you shouldn't have screwed me out of the Walters account, now should you?"

Although she wanted to listen to them bicker, Allison walked away and headed for the door. She let herself out and had just passed Jean's desk when she heard Ben's voice behind her.

"Allison, hold on."

She turned and waited until he had walked up to her to speak. "You didn't have to come out here and congratulate me." She smiled sweetly at him.

"I don't know who you've been fucking lately to get Warner and Redding." He smirked, "Unless of course it was Warner, although you're a little low class for him, but....."

"I think you should watch your tone, Ben," said quietly.

"Or what? Your friend who sent the pictures is going to send them to my wife?"

"No, you should watch your tone, because pretty soon your sorry ass may very well be answering to me."

"I doubt that. Don't let this go to your head. And don't you dare sneak around behind my back like that again."

"I wasn't sneaking, Ben,"

"Oh, no?" he asked. "Then what was it?"

Giving him a cold smile she told him, "It was me doing what I'm going to be from now on, taking what I want."

* * *

"Allison?"

She snapped her head up at the sound of Cindy's voice and blinked at her.

"What?" she asked.

"I called you twice, were you dozing?"

"I..." Allison shook her head. "No, but maybe zoning a little."

"I don't blame you." Sitting down at the table across from her, Cindy tapped the pile of modeling portfolios in front of her. "You've been staring at these for the last four hours."

"Well we found our dark, we got our classic blonde, but I still haven't gotten our elusive red head yet." She sighed. "Victoria and Miranda are coming on Monday for the photo shoot, I need to find this girl today."

"I have red hair!" Cindy made a show of flipping her auburn hair back.

"I know, but we can't have Victoria not being the hottest woman in the shoot."

Cindy laughed and clapped her hands together. "Wow you said that with a straight face!"

"You're very pretty, Cindy."

"Yeah I guess, if you like freckles and a few extra pounds." Looking closer at her face, she said, "Allison why don't you go home, you're exhausted."

"No, I need to...."

"Take the books home with you and look through them later, call the girl tomorrow when you find her."

"Too short notice," Allison pointed out. "Even today is..."

"To be in a shoot with Victoria Redding? Shit, you could call an hour before and any model would come running."

"True."

"You were here until nine the last two nights and already have people coming in with you half the day tomorrow. It's Friday, go home and get some rest. Or..." She winked. "Have some fun."

Allison leaned back in her chair and looked around the photo studio she had commandeered for the project. There were a dozen people bustling around, working on art, layouts, shooting pictures of the product she'd had Williams overnight to her and working on blurbs that might work with the ad. Everyone was busy, including Jack, who was sitting at a table across from her looking through the previous day's sketches. She was tired, but seeing everyone working this hard, made her not want to leave. She recalled how Alex had told her that soon the initial contract he had given her would seem small. That had only been two weeks ago, and Rapture would greatly eclipse what his contract was worth.

"You're drifting away again," Cindy told her. "Go home Allison, I'm sure if you ask Jack he'll stay late tonight."

"You think?"

Cindy smirked. "I think he'd stay all night for you, if you know what I mean."

She looked at her and shrugged.

"Oh come on, he's into you." She grinned. "He's single."

"I don't shit where I eat," Allison replied, adding to herself that he was twenty years older than her type.

"Whatever, but you can take advantage of his raging hormones and get him to cover while you go get some sleep."

"I'll think about it, but I'm staying at least until five."

"I'll go get you some coffee then."

Allison went back to flipping through the portfolios, but after a minute gave up and rubbed at her eyes. Sitting back in the chair, she watched the people around her work on her campaign. That thought was not going to get old. She looked up to see Cindy hurrying back and noticed she didn't have any coffee with her.

"Decide I didn't need the caffeine?"

"No, when I went down to the coffee room, Jen came and got me and said someone was looking for you."

"Who is it?"

"Amado Rosario." Cindy smiled as if the name should mean something.

"Rosario." She tried to get her mind to focus.

"Rosario Enterprises!" Cindy exclaimed. "Shit, Allison, they're into everything from a Spanish food line, to goddamn government contracts!"

Allison sat up in her chair. Was this another.... Before she could finish the thought she heard a ringing from her purse. She grabbed her cell, but when she glanced at it, there was no call. The ringing continued and she saw the red phone Mark had given her was lit up. Grabbing it she said, "Hold on, Cindy."

"I'm going to go wait with him before Ben shows up like he did with Victoria." she smiled. "Besides, goddamn he's gorgeous."

As she hurried away, Allison answered the phone. "Yes?"

"Where are you, my dear?" A soft voice with a European accent asked. "I've come to take my new sister out for a drink."

"I...." laughed. "I'll be right there."

"Do hurry," the reply came. "It'll be a matter of time before my presence draws the wolves and I have only come to see you."

He hung up and Allison stood up and walked around from behind the table. Looking down at herself, she shook her head. It was Friday and she was wearing a white t-shirt with a picture of a black cat on it. The cat's eyes were the color of hers and had been a gift from Cindy. In addition to that, she was wearing a pair of black jeans and the black Nikes she worked out in, when she could push herself to get to the gym. She was wearing very little make up and her hair was in a pony tail. At least she had looked good when she met Alex and Mark. Heading quickly across the room, she realized she was leaving everyone unattended and veered off towards Jack. He saw her coming and walked over to meet her.

"Jack, I have to...."

"I know, Cindy told me." He smiled. "Rosario, Allison?"

"Do you know him?"

"I know of him, and I met his sister out in L.A. a couple of years ago. Tried to get a meeting with her, but didn't get anywhere."

"What do they do?" she asked. "I'm going to look stupid."

"It's more like what don't they do. They're completely diversified, have their hands in everything." He shook his head. "Warner, Redding, this guy. I don't know what you stepped in, Allison, but do me a favor and go rub your foot on the rug in my office, because I want some too."

"Can you....?"

"I'll keep an eye on everyone, no worries."

"Thanks, Jack," she said.

"Anytime, just remember me when you're running this zoo okay?"

"Deal." She laughed and hurriedly left the room and headed down the hall towards her office.

When she rounded the corner, she saw Cindy standing there laughing and blushing. In front of her, sitting on the edge of her desk was a tall Spanish man dressed in a white polo shirt and Dockers. He was looking at Cindy, whose face seemed to be getting redder by the minute. From the side, all Allison could see was that he was clean shaven and had an olive complexion. When she got closer, Cindy pointed at her and, sliding off of the desk, he turned to face her.

"Good afternoon, Allison," he said as she approached him.

Holy shit, where did they find these guys, she thought as she extended her hand. Rosario was every bit as beautiful as Mark, in fact maybe more so. His features were soft to the point of bordering on feminine, and his smile was nothing short of perfect. The smile lit up a pair of large, expressive brown eyes Allison could easily see a woman getting lost in. Cindy certainly seemed pretty far gone. His curly black hair was slicked back, and he was wearing a diamond earring that looked as if it cost more than Allison's car.

He was tall, at least six feet and, although not rugged, Allison could see the muscles in his forearms and could tell by how snug his shirt fit there wasn't an ounce of fat on him. Her inspection stopped as, taking her hand, he brought to his lips, while locking his eyes onto hers.

"A pleasure, my lady," he said softly.

"I think the pleasure's mine."

"A mutual pleasure then," he said, a sly smile playing across his lips. "Nothing wrong with mutual pleasure now is there?"

"Most men wouldn't know that," Allison replied.

"I am not most men." He winked. "So shall we speak in your office?"

"Oh, of course." She shook her head. "My bad, you have me at a disadvantage. I wasn't...."

"That would be a change no?" he asked, still smiling. "I would imagine it's usually you who have the advantage when meeting a man for the first time."

"Not lately," she replied, "Especially not last week."

Rosario laughed and, glancing over at Cindy, Allison saw her mouth the words, "Oh my God!"

"Cindy, can you go back and help Jack?"

"Okay," she said, a look of disappointment on her face.

She started to walk past them and said, "Nice meeting you, Mr. Rosario."

"Please, it's Amado," he took her hand, kissing it as he had Allison's. "Mr. Rosario is my father. I'm too much fun to be a Mister."

"I...I'll bet," Cindy stammered out.

"You never did tell me, my lovely, is Cindy short for Cynthia?"

"Yes it is."

"I see." Amado was still holding her hand and looking into her eyes. "Pardon my saying, but Cindy reminds me of the little blonde in the Brady Bunch. It does not become a young lady of your beauty and playful nature."

He cocked his head and appeared to be thinking, then flashing a smile Allison knew was causing more than Cindy's face to get hot said, "I think Cyn would be much more appropriate, short and sweet, but." The smile widened. "Sexy as well, much like you."

"I....okay," Cindy breathed as she stared into his eyes, looking like a dear in headlights.

"So next time I drop by, may I call you that?"

"You can call me anything you want." She gushed.

"Careful, my dear," He raised his eyebrows at her. "The last time a woman told me that I ended up calling her a cab." He paused to wink at Allison. "Two days later."

"I...oh," Cindy froze her face now beet red.

"Careful, Amado," Allison said. "Cindy's engaged." She paused, "Aren't you Cindy?"

"Y....Yes I am actually," She stammered.

"Of course." Amado made a show of shaking his head sadly. "All the beautiful ones are taken. Well, my sweet Cyn, all I can say is I hope your fiancée appreciates the fine beauty he has, because there are others who will."

"Thank you." Cindy sighed as Amado released her hand. "Well, I hope I'll see you around here again."

"I think you will." He smiled and, giving her a slight bow, looked at Allison. "Shall we speak more privately?" he asked as Cindy reluctantly walked back down the hallway.

"I thought we were going to go get a drink?"

"Eventually we will." He nodded as he gestured for her to lead the way. "But understand if we just leave, it looks as if I'm simply swinging by to take a lovely woman for a drink." He smiled. "But we chat in your office for a bit, it looks like you're getting business, gets your superior's attention."

"Is everything a game with you guys?" she asked as she opened her office door and waved him in.

"First off, it's not 'you guys,' it's us, and..." He laughed. "To answer your question, yes, life is a game and everyday brings a new one."

Allison closed the door behind them and, walking around Amado, went over to her desk, she pointed at the chair in front of it. "Have a seat."

"I prefer to stand," he said. "I really can't stay long and would love to take you across the street for a quick drink."

"Oh, okay."

Amado nodded and turned his head, looking at the posters of advertisements on the wall. As he did, Allison took a moment to take him in again. Damn he was something, and like Alex and the others, she could feel the confidence coming off of him in waves. Turning, he saw her looking and cocking his head asked, "What is it, my lady?"

"Are you all so goddamn beautiful?" she asked. "First I get Alex, then Mark with that pretty bad boy thing going, and you're..." She shrugged, "Damn fine!"

"The Circle is the embodiment of the best of the best, every man and woman at that table is beautiful."

"I guess so."

"And you, Allison, are just as beautiful."

She laughed at him. "Okay, look, smooth is one thing, but you need to warn me when I'm going to need my boots. I look like I'm going to the Laundromat!"

"Your eyes alone are enough to stand out in a crowd." He then grinned. "And the jeans aren't fancy, but fit quite well. I enjoyed the view on the way in."

"Well thank you."

"I am looking forward to your video."

Allison frowned. "Is everyone really going to see that?" She shook her head. "I'm not thrilled with being filmed period, but what he did to me was..."

Amado held his hand up, giving her a rueful smile. "We need to stop, Allison, I'm stretching the rules by meeting you before your introduction as it is."

"Rules again." She shook her head. "But you're breaking them, and so did Victoria and...." She caught herself just before she mentioned Mark.

"Alex has a lot of pull in the group and gave me permission to stop in for a quick hello. He wants to see you elevated professionally as quickly as possible." He frowned distastefully as he looked around her office. "And I see why, this office is hardly more than a closet."

"Gee thanks." She rolled her eyes. "This is what happens when your daddy doesn't own a million dollar business and you have to work for a living."

"I'm sorry, I meant no disrespect."

"And I'm sorry, but the whole better than routine doesn't sit well with me. I don't have a lot, but I've earned it not had it handed to me, and that means I appreciate it more than most. I'm proud of what I've done. Sorry if I'm the black sheep of the group at the moment."

The words came out in a rush, and she instantly regretted them. She wasn't better than, but hadn't meant to come across as bitter either.

"Your fangs are showing, my lady," Amado said quietly. "And again I apologize, you've done as much as you can, but many doors have remained locked to you. Alex, along with myself and others, are going to unlock them for you, and are proud to able to do so."

"I didn't mean to...."

"Just as it's not your fault your family was not well connected, it's not our fault we were born into wealth. The Circle is about helping our brothers and sisters. I'm blessed to be able to do so and all I ask in return is you make the most of those opportunities."

She sighed. "I'm sorry I sounded like a brat, I'm just touchy."

"No worries, my sister. I've heard more than enough of the poor black child routine from Mark over the years. You're nowhere near as annoying as he is."

Allison laughed and he continued. "He may have come from the streets, but the only time he goes back is when he gets in one of his weird moods for trashy women."

"Speaking of moods and women," she said pointing at the door. "Were you really making a play at Cindy?"

"Not at all. I did see her ring, and at the risk of sounding..." He laughed. "Well let's face it, I am vain, she's not quite my usual standard. I do however, enjoy making women smile."

"And want you."

"And desire me, yes." He grinned. "I enjoy knowing that she'll be thinking of me while she goes down on her fiancée tonight."

"Crude, but I get it."

"Of course you do. You know you've flirted with men you don't want just to watch them get hot and bothered."

"So Cindy was just a game."

"They're all a game. For people like us, the world is a buffet and we have our choice of meals."

She went to reply when her door opened and Ben Watts entered, closing it behind him. "Mr. Rosario," he began as he walked over already sticking his hand out. "Allow me to introduce myself, I...."

"Am in need of some manners," Amado said looking down at Ben's hand distastefully. "Do they not knock in this establishment?"

Ben looked down at his hand, then working hard to keep a neutral expression said, "Cindy wasn't at her desk, so..."

"You could have used her phone, Ben." Allison said, trying not to smirk at him.

"I figured I wouldn't be interrupting anything."

"You were interrupting our conversation," Amado replied.

"I heard you just arrived, so I thought I'd come down quick before I..." He shot Allison a look. "Interrupted anything more....personal."

"And what does that mean?" Amado asked.

"He's just busting my balls." Allison quickly walked around the desk to get between them. Ben was being a prick and she didn't want Amado to know how she had been treated here.

"Sounded like he was insinuating you sleep with your clients."

"He was, sort of," Allison said putting her hand on his shoulder. "I do it to him too, it's a running joke."

"I see," He gave her a dubious look, before turning back to Ben. "So you don't knock and make sexual comments about your female co-workers? Interesting first impression, Mr. Watts." He gave him a cool smile. "Care to try again?"

Ben nodded his head, "My apologies, Mr. Rosario. I was excited to hear you'd dropped by and wasn't thinking when I barged in." He looked at Allison as he finished. "Allison and I go way back, and I do tend to be a little too comfortable with my language in front of her. I think she knows I'm kidding."

"Sure," Allison put on a fake smile. "No offense, except I thought we agreed to keep it between us."

"Sorry." Looking at Amado, he put his hand out. "So let me try again, it's a pleasure to meet you, Mr. Rosario."

This time Amado shook his hand. "Good to meet you as well. Are you a junior, by chance? I believe last time I golfed with Edwin, there was a Ben Watts with him."

"Yes," Ben smiled. "That'd be my father. So you know Edwin well?"

"Pretty well, before he founded this agency he did some freelance work for my father."

"Then may I ask why we're not allowed the opportunity to represent any of your fine endeavors?"

Amado shrugged. "My father likes to keep things local out in L.A., and my sister. Anna, the current VP of Rosario enterprises, has been happy with the people who represent us."

"Well if I may be so bold...."

"However," Amado continued. "While having lunch with Alex Warner last week, he mentioned Miss Saunders and how she came up with an excellent campaign for his new software and I thought I'd speak with her." He smiled. "My sister is set in her ways, but personally I like to spread the wealth."

"That's good to hear!" Ben exclaimed. "You know your timing couldn't be better. Every Friday Edwin meets with the senior execs. Why don't you come upstairs and speak with us? I'm sure Edwin would be delighted to see you. You guys can catch up and we can discuss what A&S can do for you."

"That's exactly what I came here to do," Amado nodded.

"Excellent! I'll..."

"As a matter of fact, before you barged in, Allison and I were about to go get a drink and discuss how she and A&S can benefit my company."

"How Allison can..." Ben repeated.

"Allison was recommended to me, more so than the company, so it stands to reason that it'll be her representing my account."

"Of course." Ben took a deep breath and gave her a nasty look.

"Problem, Mr. Watts?" Amado asked.

"No, I'm sure you will be in very capable hands."

"I am as well."

"Amongst other things," Ben muttered, beginning to turn away.

"Excuse me?" Amado asked.

"Yeah, hands, and mouth and whatever else she's been using lately."

"Ben, knock it off!" Allison snapped.

"Oh give it up!" Ben exclaimed. "You're a mid-level rep at best, then you meet Warner and a who's who of the Fortune Five Hundred come in here with your name on their lips." He laughed harshly. "Guess you must have let Warner leave something on your lips to get that kind of..."

"That's enough!" Amado raised his voice. "How dare you insult a lady in front of me?"

"I'm sorry, Mr. Rosario, but we don't cater to women who whore themselves to their clients we...."

"And now she's a whore?" Amado demanded, his formerly soft brown eyes hardening. "I know for a fact she's not, Mr. Watts, because if she were, she wouldn't have this closet for an office. Do you think I don't know your reputation? I'm sure you'd have no issue if she were whoring herself to you."

"With all due respect, Mr....."

"Respect?" Amado grunted. "I doubt a crude dog like you knows the meaning of the word, but I believe it's time you learned it."

"Amado," Allison began. "It's not a big deal, he's just jealous and..."

"It is far from all right."

Amado pulled out his phone and, after looking through his numbers, dialed and put it to his ear.

"Who are you calling?" Ben asked.

"You'll see soon enough," Amado told him. "Just stay where you are. I.... Edwin?"

"Edwin," Ben repeated.

"Edwin, it's Amado, how are you?"

"Oh Jesus," Allison whispered.

"I'm doing well," Amado spoke into the phone. "Yes my father is as well, he's currently back home in Barcelona." He laughed. "Yes my sister is running the show as always, Anna is certainly more suited to it than I am."

He paused and listened then said, "Well funny you say that Edwin, because I'm currently in your building and I'm having a serious problem with one of your employees. I came by to talk shop and well.... I'm in Allison Saunders' office and I think you should come down here." Amado listened again and shook his head. "No, you'll come to me. I've been insulted and shouldn't have to come to you. If you want to disgrace the name of your firm, that's your business, I'll take my leave and.... Yes, thank you Edwin, I'll wait here."

Hanging up the phone, Amado looked at Ben. "I hope your resume is updated."

"Oh please." Ben waved him off. "You can take your money and walk, I run this place."

"You run your mouth my friend," Amado replied coolly. "And not very well."

Ben rolled his eyes and took a couple of steps towards the door, but stopped and stood, waiting for Edwin. Allison whispered, "Amado, let this go, I'm getting the last laugh, he..."

Turning to her, he whispered, "Never will a lady of the Circle be insulted in my presence."

Allison was taken a back at how angry he sounded. She nodded, resigning herself to the ugly scene that was coming. She knew Amado had connections, but Ben was Edwin's boy and had protected him in the past. There was a knock on the door and as Allison called out 'Come in' Amado muttered, "Even the damn owner of the firm knocks."

Edwin came in and, after looking at Ben, spotted Amado and walked quickly over to him. "Amado," he began. "It's been a long time. You look fantastic."

"Thank you, Edwin," Amado replied, shaking his hand. "As do you."

"You're lying," Edwin said grinning.

"It's called diplomacy. Men never look old and women are never overweight."

Edwin burst out laughing, clapping Amado on the shoulder. "So you finally going to throw your old friend a bone?" he asked. "Your sister is a tough nut to crack."

"I did in fact come here looking to speak to Allison about some opportunities."

"Allison is one of our best," Edwin said. "She's definitely on the rise here."

"I can see that by this sham of an office you have her in." Amado shook his head. "But that's something we'll rectify soon enough. In the meantime, a problem has arisen and sadly, I may not be able to do any business here."

"Why, what's wrong?"

"Apparently your right hand man seems to think it's sporting to refer to Allison as a whore."

"Excuse me?" Edwin asked, looking over at Ben. "What's he talking about?"

"It's nothing, Edwin, I made a joke and Allison got all worked up and...."

"No, you lying fool," Amado interrupted speaking heatedly. "Miss Saunders didn't get upset because, sadly she's used to your neanderthal behavior. I'm offended for her."

"What is going on here?" Edwin asked. "What joke did you make that...."

"It wasn't a joke. Mr. Watts came out and boldly declared Miss Saunders obtained Mr. Warner's business by performing sexual favors."

"Oh for God's sakes, Ben!" Edwin rolled his eyes.

"It was a joke!" Ben repeated. " I...."

"And was your crude comment that I'd be in good hands as well as mouth with Miss Saunders a joke? Is it funny to demean not only your co-worker, but her client as well?"

"I didn't insult you...."

"You insulted myself as well as Alex Warner by saying we'd sell our business for sexual services. That I was basically going to go get a blow job in an alley in exchange for my contract, and Alex had done the same. You called Allison a whore in no uncertain terms, and I won't stand for that."

"And who the hell are you?" Ben demanded angrily.

"I'm not only a large client that this firm will never see, but one who has a lot of influence with other clients. Orion for example."

Oh, no, Allison thought, grabbing Amado's hand she whispered, "Please drop this."

Ignoring her, Amado stared as Edwin looked at Ben, a frown on his face.

"Ben, did you say those things?"

"Not really, I...." Ben put his hands out. "Come on, Edwin, who are you going to believe? Christ you were at my communion."

"And my father knows Edwin as well, as does my sister who's running Rosario Enterprises." He smiled coldly. "Sorry, Mr. Watts, that game will not help you here. Edwin knows I was raised with integrity and won't lie. I have no reason to."

"Ben," Edwin began. "This isn't the first time I've heard of something like this from you. In the past I took your word for it, but Amado and his family have a reputation as being quite fair. So I'll ask again, did you say those things?"

"Yes, but...." He rolled his eyes. "Look, Edwin, I was a little pissed off and she, well she does have a reputation for...."

"Hard work from what I can see," Edwin said.

"Fine, Edwin." Ben nodded. "I said it and know what? I pretty much meant it. Allison had no big time clients, meets with Warner behind our backs and now is lighting it up. Warner's a dog in heat and Allison ...."

"And now you insult my best friend?" Amado snapped. "Edwin this is unacceptable!"

"You're right. Ben, I want you to apologize to Allison and I think a week's suspension will be in order."

"Come on, Edwin!"

"And I want you to enroll in those sensitivity classes that were offered here during the sexual harassment seminar."

"I..." Putting his head down, Ben sighed. "Fine, Edwin I'll...."

"Not enough," Amado said.

"What do you...." Edwin began.

"I want him terminated, right now."

"Amado, don't," Allison said quietly. "This is enough."

She stopped as he squeezed her hand hard before letting it go. "Edwin, this man's behavior is a disgrace. He treats women as if they were whores and in your very presence insulted a current and future client. I demand you fire him."

"I think that's bit harsh don't you?"

"You stood here and admitted he's done this before. You let it go and look where we are. It's your company and your choice. However, I'd be sorely disappointed if you allowed this swine to continue to make a mockery of your business."

"I think you're blowing this out of proportion," Edwin said.

"Let's put it this way, how much is this over paid liability worth to you? Enough to lose the opportunity to do business with me?"

"We've done no business yet." Edwin pointed out.

He looked as if he was getting pissed and Allison felt her stomach twist. How the hell had this gone so bad? Standing his ground, Amado continued speaking. "Edwin, much like you, my father has gained the reputation as not only a respected businessman, but a church going, god fearing man of character.

Knowing this, I cannot in good faith, go to him and recommend your services. I'll see it fit to mention to Alex Warner, a man who's like a brother to me, that your top executive thinks he thinks with his libido and not his business savvy. I doubt after that conversation he'd want to continue doing work here."

"But that'd hurt Allison as well, Amado, and that's hardly fair."

"No, Allison will be just fine Edwin, and do you know why?"

"I'm sure you'll tell us," Ben said.

"Shut up, Ben, you've said enough," Edwin snapped.

"Allison will be fine, because since I see she has talent, I'm sure my sister could get her a job at your competition. With better pay, and certainly a better office."

"I don't like being put into a corner," Edwin said.

"Mr. Watts put you in this corner. So what'll it be? The loss of future and current business, as well as watching your up and coming rep go to the competition? Or will you do what you built your name on, the right thing?"

Edwin looked at Ben, then back at Amado and finally Allison. She returned the stare as calmly as she could. He sighed then spoke. "Allison, when you came to me a few months ago and said Ben was inappropriate, and he said you were making it up, I take it you weren't?"

"No, Mr. Blake," she said quietly. "In fact I have something on tape."

"Oh. For the love of…." Ben began, but Edwin raised his hand.

"Ben, you have the weekend to clean out your office."

"What?" Ben asked, his eyes wide. "Are you kidding?"

"Do I look like I'm kidding?" Edwin shook his head. "You're done here, Ben. I'll speak to accounting about your severance package. And if you try anything litigious I will take the tape Allison says she has and send it to my lawyers."

"But my father…."

"Would be appalled by your disgraceful behavior, so out of respect for him, I won't tell him what happened here, but I will if you don't leave quietly."

Ben stood there for a moment staring at Edwin, then pointed at her. "You happy, you fucking whore? You found the right cock to suck and now you're on top of the world? What comes around goes around bitch."

He stormed out of the office, slamming the door so hard the glass cracked. Allison let out a deep breath and sat on the edge of her desk. Speaking calmly, as if nothing had happened, Amado said, "Edwin, I'd assume Mr. Watts had a much more spacious and better located office than Miss Saunders?"

"Yes, he has a corner office."

"Then when next I visit to discuss business, I shall find Allison in that office?"

"Amado," she started, but Edwin spoke up.

"If you indeed are going to give her some work, consider it done." Edwin took her hand. "Allison, I apologize for this ugliness and not listening to you before. I guess I didn't want to believe it."

"It's okay," she said.

"No, not really. Tell you what, Monday you come see me. We're going to talk about a salary increase as well as a higher commission percentage, how's that sound?"

"Sounds damn good to me!" She laughed in relief.

"Good, can't have you wandering off now can we?"

Letting her hand go, he shook Amado's. "My apologies and thank you for setting this straight."

"Thank you for doing the right thing."

Edwin nodded, "Well I'm going to go make sure Ben's not causing a problem. Do tell your father I said hello."

"I'll be happy to."

Edwin left and, glancing at his Rolex, Amado shook his head. "It appears I'll have to take a rain check on our drink. I have to meet with someone in a half hour."

"No problem." She let out a deep breath. "Thank you for that, but you didn't have to get him fired."

"Allison, listen to me and please don't be offended at the first part of what I say okay?"

"Okay."

"You're a strong independent woman, but despite your sexual mastery, you're still lacking the confidence you should have in the professional world. That's not your fault. Due to the games the men in control play, you've been conditioned to accept men like Ben's behavior. Your first reaction was to let that slide. That was fear. Fear you'd lose what you earned. Fear you'd look like the whore. That's why you didn't want me to defend you. Isn't that right?"

"Yes," she said quietly.

"That will change. The Circle will teach you you're entitled to everything you desire. You'll also grow in confidence. I'm sure you feel that in myself and the others you've met. We enter the room and the room stops. You'll get there, Allison."

"You think?"

"I know. But in the meantime, you're new to the group and are..." With a smile he put his arm around her shoulders. "Our little sister and all of us will be looking out for you until you gain that confidence. I was thrilled to handle that fool for you."

"I do feel kind of bad," she admitted. "He lost his job and...."

"Mercy is for the weak. That man was not innocent. He brought this down upon himself." He shook his head. "Even in front of me, he wouldn't stop trying to degrade you. Things will be very different going forward for you here."

"They already are."

"Mark has an expression that at some point he'll subject you to."

"Every woman wants him every man wants to be him?" she asked smiling.

"No." He laughed. "The man isn't conceited he's truly convinced."

"Just him?" she raised her eyebrows.

"Touché. No he says takers take until they're taken. Ben Watts was a taker and today he was taken. We're the takers Allison. That doesn't mean we're cruel people, but it means no one takes us, and that's a lesson Mr. Watts learned in spades today."

"Looks that way," she agreed. "And he had the nerve to say what comes around goes around."

"That's right, he did."

Amado reached into his pocket and removed a red cell phone identical to hers. "Right after he called you a fucking whore, if I recall."

"Yeah pretty much."

"Glad you reminded me of that," he said as he dialed.

"Why?"

"Hello, my brother," Amado said, holding his finger up to her. "I need you to do something for me. I need you to take the photos of Mr. Watts and send them to his wife." He paused. "Send them as a gift with ...." Looking at Allison, he smiled. "A green bow on it."

Part Four

Chapter One

The shrill sound of her phone's alarm pulled Justine from the comfort of her much needed nap. Without opening her eyes, she spoke softly, "Stop." The alarm kept going and she tried again, but louder. When it continued, Justine's eyes snapped open and she shouted, "Stop!"

The phone stopped, and she sighed. The voice activated features on new prototype still had some bugs. No matter how close one was to the phone it still responded to nothing short of yelling. The designers claimed they would be able to work out all the kinks by the big Black Friday launch, but Justine wasn't so sure. Maybe she would give one of the prototypes to Alex to fool around with. Phones were a little out of his realm of expertise, but underneath all his playboy bullshit, the man was a genius.

"That's enough of that," she said softly.

Justine had spent the last four days down at a conference in Florida and had been sleeping, eating and breathing work. Now she was back home, soaking in her tub and less than an hour away from some damn hot sex. Although she had wanted to see Mark as soon as she had gotten back, her flight didn't get in until ten last night and she was exhausted. It was Friday and she'd taken the day off from the office, but Mark had court and the earliest he could arrive was six. It had definitely worked out better this way. Justine had slept in until ten, gone to the spa, and an hour ago decided to set the alarm and take a nap in a nice warm bath.

Inhaling deeply, she took in the strong scent of strawberry and smiled, knowing it was Mark's favorite. After all, she did owe him a night and that was before the initiation. Loki had sent her the video of Mark's breaking of Allison, and she had masturbated three times during it. To say his performance was amazing would be an understatement. Truth be told, Mark was nothing short of magnificent. There was no doubt he'd been out to make a point and the results were like nothing Justine, or anyone else in the Circle, for that matter had seen in a long time. It was certainly one of the harshest in quite some time. There were several occasions Mark had come very close to breaking some of their rules, but he had pulled back each time before crossing the line.

Allison had been impressive as well. Despite the delicious look of fear on her face when Mark had held her nose, she had shown her resolve. Refusing to cave several times and, even gaining a small victory over Mark as she goaded him into cumming when he had thought he'd broken her. Everything about the video was nothing short of perfection, especially that incredible bedroom. There was no doubt a portion of this would be played at the conference.

Justine smiled at what the reaction would be amongst the other masters and mistresses. Mark had been right, this old school initiation would show the other Circles the East was a force to be reckoned with. For Justine it would be a feather in her cap that many of the higher-ranking members knew she was the woman who had broken him. For Mark it would cement his reputation as being one of the darkest, most feared members and would assure him a long list of women begging for time with him that weekend.

Speaking of begging, a warm sensation began to build between her legs as Justine recalled Allison's weakest moment during the initiation. The way she had looked up at Mark when he was cuffing her to the bed and whispered 'please don't hurt me' had sent Justine's fingers to her clit and she had rewound it three times. As her mind replayed Allison's ordeal, she remembered Mark's comment about her being fortunate there were rules or he would have had her gangbanged.

Her smile faded as Justine recalled her own initiation. There were no rules to speak of back then and she had in fact been taken by several men. It had started with her and her initiator, but Justine, like Allison, had been in control for years, but unlike Allison could handle her share of abuse. When it became obvious to her tormentor, which Justine always felt was a more fitting term, realized he didn't have what it took to break her, he involved others.

Justine had been forced to kneel on the bed with her hands tied behind her back and her ankles cuffed as well. Three men then came in and proceeded to run a train on her, one by one fucking her in the ass. By the time the last man came, the first was ready again. All the time she was enduring this, her face was in her initiator's lap, her mouth stuffed with his cock. She was told to keep sucking and anytime she stopped he would simply fuck her mouth. He came twice in her mouth as she was repeatedly fucked and she still had to suck him. Justine was told the only time she could remove his cock from her mouth was to either quit or to call him master and admit what a shameless fucking whore she was, and mean it.

She held out as long as she could, long enough for him to blow a third load in her mouth, most of which drooled back out as her throat was too sore to swallow. By then her back was covered in three men's cum, her jaw was throbbing, and her ass burning. The men were demeaning her the entire time, calling her names, spanking her ass raw and grabbing her hair to force her master's cock in even deeper. When he told one of the men to lie on his back so that he could make Justine straddle him and take all three cocks at once, her will broke and, removing his cock from her mouth, and sobbing, said she was a worthless whore, and to please have mercy on her..

Back then there were no payback nights and for three years she'd been subjected to that asshole's jeers and insults. That was until Lazarus took control. He had told every member who voted for him he would grant them one favor. Both Justine and The Lady Morrigan, who had joined two years after Justine, and endured an equally horrific initiation, demanded payback to their initiators. Lazarus was good on his word and the men were told to allow the women revenge or leave the group.

Justine had greatly enjoyed sitting back', her legs spread, while her former tormentor screamed into her pussy while Morrigan fucked him with a strap on. Justine had forced him to wear women's lingerie and repeatedly beg to be fucked in the ass like the closet faggot he was. Justine had placed a cock ring on him that was so tight he remained hard even while having his ass taken. She then took her turn fucking him while he fucked Morrigan. Reaching around and removing the ring, she told him she would keep fucking him until he proved how much he loved it by cumming all over Morrigan's ass. He came screaming, more in pain than pleasure, which was when Justine leaned forward and shoved his face into Morrigan's ass and made him lap up his own cum.

They then made him shower both of them, letting him think his ordeal was over then switched off and made him fuck Justine while Morrigan went at him. One of the strongest orgasm's of Justine's life was when she came from his licking his own cum off of her clit while whimpering as Morrigan tore into him. The next weekend the two of them did the same to Morrigan's initiator, except Morrigan, who had been subjected to a merry go round featuring four men at her initiation, added the additional treat of allowing two men to come in and jerk off in his mouth while she fucked him. He had tried to quit, but the rule was anything went and if you didn't like it you had to leave the group.

Justine took a deep breath and pushed that image from her mind. Not that envisioning those two dogs getting theirs wasn't a pleasant one, but Mark was due in an hour and she had been horny all day. She supposed she could play with herself now, come nice and quick which would make him have to work harder for her to cum later, but she wanted to cum as hard as possible for her dark prince. Her smile returned at that thought. Never before had that nickname been more fitting. Mark had used his satanic beliefs and gothic bedroom to full effect, even adding the beautiful touch of pretending to be enraged when Allison had used the name Jesus.

As if of its own accord, her hand did slip under the water and find its way between her legs. Justine released a low moan as her fingers found her hard clit and caressed it. Knowing it was a losing battle; Justine gave in and, lifting her leg from the water, stretched it out along the edge of the tub. Closing her eyes, she stroked her clit while imagining her fingers as Mark's skilled tongue. He wouldn't be showing that skill however, until Justine had demonstrated her own. She began breathing hard as her fingers sped up to the thought of how she was going to lie him back and give him a long slow blow job, that would have him begging to cum.

She licked her lips in anticipation of tasting him, of feeling his long thick cock filling her eager mouth. Justine gasped and began rocking her hips, already feeling her legs trembling as the orgasm she had been denying herself all day approached. She envisioned him cumming, his cock twitching and his hot fluid painting the back of her mouth before slowly dripping down her throat. Justine arched her back and let out a loud cry as the orgasm tore through her, causing her to buck her hips into her dancing fingers as waves of pleasure filled her pussy.

"Oh goddamn!" she gasped as the orgasm finished having its way with her.

Slumping back into the tub, she sighed and smiled up at the ceiling. Damn she was looking forward to tonight. She'd been pissed when she had found out they needed her at the conference the same week as the initiation. She had received the video via e-mail from Loki on Sunday night and had been thinking of nothing but getting her hands on Mark since. She had called him Sunday to tell him how thrilled she was, but he hadn't answered. He did call her back on Monday while she was at the conference, and she finally spoke to him Monday night. He sounded oddly subdued, even when she told him to be at her place for Friday for a celebration.

He sounded even worse last night when she called him to set up a time. She recognized that tone and asked if he was sleeping and he said he hadn't been. She wasn't sure how after such an amazing session with Allison, and the promise of an even hotter night with his mistress, he could sound so down. Then again, Justine remembered his nightmare in the hotel room and knew they came in stretches. *That was okay,* she thought, as she used her toes to flip the lever to drain the tub, she would give him a fantastic night, then hold him close and he would sleep just fine.

As she stood up and waited for the tub to drain a bit, Justine frowned. It was one thing to fuck, but the level of affection between them was increasing. Turning the shower on to rinse off, she shrugged the thought away. Granted they were more than Mistress and pet, but they were not more than friends with benefits. They both engaged in sex with others, but were unable to express any affection with their pets or conquests, so they enjoyed some closeness when they were together. So what? No, that wasn't true; it had been awhile since… "Enough for now," she told herself aloud.

After taking her time under the hot water, Justine stepped out of the shower, dried off and, slipped on a short red silk robe. Mark loved wet hair so she left her long red hair down and didn't bother drying it. Justine had a closet full of lingerie, but decided to just go with the robe. Red was his favorite color, it showed off her long shapely legs and to Justine there was nothing sexier than simply untying a knot and letting it fall away from her naked body. Tonight would be all about simple and fun.

Taking a minute to mist some strawberry body spray on her neck, Justine went into the bedroom and lit several candles. Leaving the bedroom, she entered the kitchen, poured herself a glass of red wine and, taking the bottle and a second glass into the living room, sat on the couch to wait for Mark. Sipping at the wine she smiled, she hadn't felt this excited in a long time. The downside about always getting what you want was you forgot how much fun anticipation was. Stretching her long legs out so her feet were resting on the coffee table, Justine looked down at her red toes and pictured them against Mark's chest as he fucked the shit out of her.

Pushing her mind from Mark for the moment, Justine thought of Allison and a satisfied smile touched her lips. She was going to enjoy watching Allison advance to where she belonged. Years ago, Justine had been in Allison's shoes. Mid-level management, Justine had gone to her supervisor with two lights out ideas to promote Speakeasy. Both times those ideas appeared under the name of that supervisor, who had blatantly stolen the credit.

Justine was frustrated and had considered quitting, but it would mean starting over and she knew she could put Speakeasy on the map. One night while at a bar, Justine was approached by a man named Marcus who ran an investment firm in Boston. They had drinks and she knew he was into her. She could also see he was arrogant and used to getting his way. Justine had been domming men since her and her girlfriends had gone to an S&M club in New Orleans on spring break and had no desire to be anyone's toy.

However he was hot and she decided to go back to his hotel room with him. He immediately told her to strip and she responded by telling him the word please would be the only word she would acknowledge. She had told him he could practice by asking if he is he could please kneel at her feet. They had gone back and forth and Justine felt herself beginning to lose the battle. Marcus was not only attractive, but his confidence went beyond arrogance. She could feel his will as he stared into her eyes and she realized that, like her, he was into control. After a few more exchanges, he stated he would be willing to say please as long as it was 'Justine would you please suck my cock?' With that he had sat down in the arm chair and pointed at the floor.

Justine could see the bulge of his hard cock in his pants and before she knew it she had begun to kneel. At the last minute, she snapped herself out of it. Whipping her leg up, she placed her foot on his shoulder, hiked up her skirt, pulled her thong to the side and told him that a true gentlemen allowed the ladies to cum first. Her pussy gushed as, leaning forward, Marcus placed a soft kiss on her clit. He then gave her a huge smile and told her to go sit down on the other chair because he had a deal for her. Justine had been confused, but did as he asked. Marcus then explained the Circle to her and invited her to join. It sounded good except for the initiation, but Justine figured *how bad could it be*, and had accepted.

Sitting there on the couch, Justine recalled approaching Marcus at her first meeting, and telling him the next time he tried to recruit someone to not use the word initiation, but call it for what it was, rape. That had earned Justine the pleasure of being bent over the table and fucked by Marcus in front of the entire group and threatened with worse if she didn't learn her manners. Closing her eyes, Justine let out a deep breath thinking it was amazing the group had managed to keep any of the women who had joined.

That reason became apparent two days after her intitation. Justine was sitting in her office when the VP of marketing called her and told her he wanted to see her. Justine got up, wincing from the pain in her still sore ass and, limping down the corridor, entered his office. He told her to lock the door behind her. Justine had begun to get nervous, but that quickly faded as he began to speak. He told her he had received a package in the mail that contained proof her supervisor's last two proposals had been stolen from her.

Justine listened as he told her not only had her supervisor been fired, but she was going to be replacing him. The promotion came with a twenty thousand dollar a year raise plus commission on the new product line her ideas had helped get into production. Justine was also told to bring anything she came up with directly to him and he would see to it she received proper compensation. Two years later, Justine herself would become the VP of marketing, and in another three years reached her current position of regional manager of the east coast. That position had grown along with Speakeasy and last year Justine had earned close to a quarter of a million dollars in salary and commission.

So yes, her humiliation and pain had been worth it, at least initially, but had it continued, Justine knew she would have quit. Three years in the group and she was still being passed around like a cold to members of their group as well as others. But things were different now and Allison's brutal ordeal at Mark's hands would be her last. She would be a pledge at the conference, but Justine would make sure it would not be with someone rough. In fact….Justine smiled to herself. Allison would become her gift to Ramses, a token of her appreciation for him not making a production of Sydney's misbehavior.

She sighed contentedly at how everything had fallen into place. They had bent several rules for Allison, letting her leave Alex without an answer, then letting Victoria meet her. Justine also knew of Alex's bribe of a year's worth of his business and then Victoria dangling her services. Justine had thought both were going too far, but Alex had said that they would need it; the sexual aspects of the group would not be what landed Allison, only advancement.

Alex had been right, as had Mark about the initiation. Despite their constant bickering, the two of them had the Circle's best interest at heart and Justine felt better than ever about leaving it in their hands. Justine was startled out of her thoughts by the buzzer telling her Mark was downstairs. All but jumping up from the couch, Justine quickly made her way to the door and hit the intercom.

"Mark?"

"It's me."

"Oh, how I've been waiting for you," she purred into the intercom. "Come on up, baby, because this girl is dying to give you something special."

She had spoken using her best attempt at a simpering young girl and had thought he would have replied excitedly, instead he simply said, "Yeah, well we'll see about that."

Justine frowned, and then laughed as she realized he was going to play her, make her beg for him. "Yes we will, sir," she replied, hitting the button to let him in. "You'll see your little girl can be very good to you."

Justine stood there waiting for him to make it upstairs. She looked at herself in the mirror over the mantle and laughed at the big smile on her face. She felt positively giddy, as if she were waiting for a date for the prom. She so needed this after a week of business. She'd had a couple of chances in Florida, but both times decided it wasn't worth it. One was a cocky young bartender she would have spent the night training and another was a guy her age she figured was most likely married and wouldn't be able to keep up. No, she was better off avoiding games and masturbating, and what she had masturbated to was due to arrive in…

There was a light knock on the door and Justine started to reach for it. She stopped, not wanting to look as if she were hovering, and took a few steps to the side to shut the main light off, leaving the room in the dim glow of the one small lamp next to the couch. Walking back over to the door, she loosened her robe until her tits were all but falling out. Opening the door part way, she playfully peeked around the side of it.

"Why hello, sir, I'm so glad you could make it."

Her smile faded as Mark stepped in and she saw his face. There were dark circles around his eyes, and his eyes themselves were not only as red as her hair, but appeared swollen.

"Damn, baby," she said softly, putting her arms around his shoulders. "When was the last time you slept?"

"I…" He shrugged. "A little last night I think."

"Well trust me, baby," she cooed in his ear as she kissed his neck. "You'll sleep tonight."

"Justine, listen," he started.

"What no hello kiss?"

Before he could respond, she grabbed his hair and pulled his face to hers. Mark seemed to resist at first, then succumbed and pressed his lips to hers. Justine groaned as she pressed her tongue into his mouth and her tits against his hard chest. He was wearing a plain black t-shirt and jeans and as they kissed, she let her hands slide down his arms. Justine felt a thrill go through her as she squeezed his hard biceps and, dropping her hand down between his legs, sought another hard muscle. Just as her hand found his cock, Mark broke the kiss and stepped away from her.

"Justine, stop."

"Why?"

"Because we can't right now, I need…."

"Oh, I see." She nodded. "That's going to be your game tonight, Mark, hard to get?"

She undid the belt of her robe.

"You going to make me seduce you?"

The robe parted and she cupped her large tits, presenting them to him.

"You going to pretend you don't want these?"

"It's not a game," he said quietly, dropping his hands as if afraid he was going to touch anyway. "Justine, I need to…"

"To make me beg I guess," Dropping to her knees, she looked up at him, pushed her lip out and whispered, "Please, sir, please let your naughty little girl be good to you?" She reached up and started pulling his zipper down, her mouth watering in anticipation of sucking his huge cock. "Come on, baby, let me have that nice big….hey!"

Mark grabbed her shoulders and, lifting her to her feet, snapped, "Justine enough! It's not a game!"

"Mark, what's the matter with you?" she asked, reaching out to touch his cheek.

"We…we need to talk."

"Hey listen," she began, stepping up to him and putting her hands on his chest. "You're tired, Mark, and I can tell you're having one of those bad stretches. So tell you what, how about you and I go into my bedroom and have some fun, and then we can talk okay? We'll just lay there and you can tell me what's wrong, I'll send for food and ...."

"It can't wait."

"Of course it can." She smiled. "Now come on and let your grateful Mistress show her appreciation for that amazing initiation."

"That's what we need to talk about Justine." He looked away from her. "It might not have been as amazing as you think."

She felt a sinking feeling in her stomach at how serious he sounded. "What do you mean?" she asked.

Taking a deep breath, Mark's red rimmed eyes met hers. "Mistress Scarlett, I have something to confess to you."

Chapter Two

The sinking feeling in her stomach turned into a slow twisting one as Justine stared into Mark's burnt out gaze. "Okay," she said quietly. "Let's go sit down."

Tying her robe as she turned and walked over to the couch, Justine's mind began to race. *What the hell could he have done?* Maybe he was on one of his weird kicks and he thought he screwed up, or perhaps he was in one of his moods and was rude to Allison afterwards. Justine reached the couch and, sitting down, saw that rather than sit next to her, Mark had sat in the recliner across from her.

"Okay, Mark," she told him as he looked at her like a whipped dog. "What do you think you did wrong?"

"Not think, Mistress, know, and you should be addressing me by my title." He sighed. "While I still have it."

Justine paused before answering. Mark was not one for being melodramatic, why the hell would he say that? "No, I'll call you by your name, Mark," she said. "You're obviously upset and even if it pertains to business we'll speak as friends. Now tell me what happened, because from what I could see everything went perfectly and Victoria said when she saw Allison this week she was thrilled."

"Yeah, well it's what you didn't see."

"What didn't I see?" She paused. "You didn't get out of line with her later did you? Get in one of your asshole moods?"

"Oh no." He shook his head. "That wouldn't have been an issue, I was supposed to break her, I could get away with rude."

"So what did you...."

"I slept with Allison."

"You...." She had to have misunderstood that. "Of course you did, it was part of the initiation, right?" She'd added the last part, in hopes that what he'd said hadn't been as obvious as it sounded.

"No, Justine, this was after that, we...." He shook his head disgustedly. "I fucked her Justine, twice and she....she spent the night in my bed."

"I...." She was speechless. This couldn't be right, there was no way in hell Mark would break the most important rule in the group. "Please tell me this is a joke, one of you and Alex's screwy little games or..."

She trailed off as his eyes met hers. He was a mess and she now knew why. In fact she was willing to bet he had been a mess last weekend when he'd met Allison, when he'd .... fucked her.

"You're serious?"

"Yes." He nodded. "I'll accept whatever…."

"Mark," she stopped and, leaning forward, picked up the glass of wine and drank the rest of it, before continuing. "I…." She took a deep breath, trying to stay calm. "How the hell did this happen?"

"The how doesn't matter," he began. "It's the point that…."

"I'll decide what matters!" she snapped.

Putting his head down, Mark began speaking softly "Allison was going to get a hotel for the night and I told her she could stay the night guest bedroom."

"That's breaking the rules right there," She interrupted. "They're to leave afterwards, or if you want to go out for a drink fine, but they're not to come back and you know why, don't you?"

"Because many times the initiate ends up looking for more," he said quietly.

"Which seems to be what happened here," she pointed out. "Then again, someone was supposed to explain the rules to her."

"I did explain the rules."

"When?"

"Over dinner. I took her out and we talked for awhile and she had a lot to drink. We went back to my place and I told her goodnight and she came on to me." Looking away, he finished, "I told her no, but she kept going and I… I gave in and I took her into my bedroom."

"Please tell me this is a joke," she whispered.

"It's not. We fucked and fell asleep, I…I woke up and fucked her again."

"No, no, no."

Justine shook her head as she repeated the word and the consequences of what Mark was telling her dawned on her. She put her head down and took a long breath, trying to reign in the anger growing within her. She should have known this had all gone too smoothly, should have known bending this many rules would lead to trouble, but she had never seen this one coming. Losing the battle with her temper she snapped her head up.

"What the fuck, Mark!" she shouted at him. "How the hell did this happen?"

"You already asked that," he said quietly.

"And I'll fucking ask it again!" she snarled. "And don't you get smart with me, you…you fucking disgrace!"

"I deserve that."

"Oh, we haven't even gotten to what you deserve yet! Now answer my fucking question! How the hell does a member of this group, my enforcer no less, let some common whore seduce him?"

"She's not some whore, Justine, she was chosen for…"

"At that time she was no more than any other bitch in heat who wanted you and you succumbed to her like a pathetic dog!" she snapped. "Jesus Christ, even Alex has more control than that! Fuck, our newest members know better!"

"Justine, I…."

"And know why they do? Because it's what's drilled into their head by their recruiter and more importantly their initiator! You don't fuck another person at that table and if you do The Enforcer will punish you or you will be banned!" She waved her hand disgustedly at him. "That's when he's not busy fucking breaking the rules himself!" She paused and tried to calm herself down. "But go ahead, Mark, tell me how it happened, tell me how this nobody managed to get herself into the bed of her initiator."

"I told you."

"Tell me again! Tell me how you gave in Mark! Tell me what was so fucking special about this woman!"

"I had a weak moment."

"Bullshit!" Justine shouted, pointing at him. "You've turned down time with Victoria Redding! Now Allison pops up and she's irresistible? Weak moment my ass. Now tell me what happened."

Mark sighed and rubbed at his eyes before speaking. "We went to dinner and before we started going over the group we talked about ourselves. Allison started telling me this hot little story, the kind perfect for around the table, but it led to her remembering something painful and she was pretty close to tears."

"Over a story?" Justine shook her head. "Or was she playing you? Setting you up to be soft on her?"

"Justine, she'd been put through a lot and had drank quite a bit. The story just hit her hard. It was about her family and a brother who disowned her. I assured her she now had new brothers, ones that would never let her down."

"Ones that will hold them close and give them a little peck on the cheek, and lead them on right, Mark?" she asked, raising her eyebrows.

"I was trying to comfort her. I told her some things about my past and...."

"You never talk about your past. I've asked you many times and get nothing." Justine was upset, no more than that, jealous. Who was this woman that he would share something with he wouldn't tell her?

"Well..."

"Anything I do know of your past came from Alex," she cut him off. "He's your best friend and even he got it second hand from your sister." She made a sound of disgust. "Guess Allison is really something, an irresistible pussy and a great shoulder to cry on."

"As I was saying, we shared something's and I..." He sighed. "I could see her looking at me in that way. She made a couple of leading comments and I ignored them. I saw where it could end up going."

"Exactly where it went, right into your room."

Ignoring her, Mark went on. "So I steered the conversation to the group and the last thing I covered was the rules."

"Guess neither of you were paying attention. Just get to the point."

"We get to my place and she made a play and I tried to back her off, then she...."

"She what Mark?"

"She kept going and she....caught me off guard with something and I...." He put his head in his hands. "I failed you, Justine, I caved to her and...."

"What did she catch you with?"

"Just something, and like I said I had a weak moment and as soon as I gave her an in it was all over. She's not a woman off the street. We chose her for a reason, and she knows how to get what she wants."

"From twenty year olds and horny married men! But from you, Mark?" She grunted. "And weak isn't the word, I think pathetic is what you are."

"You're right."

"Damn straight I am!" she snapped. "Let me ask you a question. How long have you been having trouble sleeping?"

"A few days."

"Don't lie to me!" She pointed at him. "You had a nightmare in the hotel two weeks ago. You weren't sleeping before the initiation were you?"

"No."

"And you were having the nightmares?"

"Yes." He was starting to sound annoyed, but she could care less.

"So you were in one of your funks, exhausted, strung out and you went through the initiation anyway."

"I was fine during…."

"That meant you were taking a chance of losing control and crossing the line. You could've really hurt this woman, you know how you get and you didn't care."

"I was…."

"Going to prove me wrong for not trusting you." She nodded. "So now it's over, and you're even more tired than you were. You take her out and…" She laughed humorlessly. "You called out her drinking, how much drinking did you do? I would say far more than you should have."

"I…. yes I had a lot to drink."

"So now drunk and a mess, you go back and this hot little thing comes onto you and you can't help yourself can you?"

"Apparently not."

"Mark, I swear I'll whip you raw if you take that tone again," she warned him. "So what did she do, Mark? Did she pout for you? Call you sir? Give you that fun little girl routine you teach all your pets?"

"Does it matter?"

"Everything about this matters!" Justine yelled at him, slamming her palm down on the coffee table. "I want to know what it was about her! I've seen you consume enough alcohol to supply a frat party and still function. It wasn't just booze, Mark, I want to know why you caved!"

"She just…."

He stopped as snapping her fingers, Justine cut him off. "That day in the hotel, Alex asked you if she reminded you of someone and you got pissed off at him. Who was she Mark?"

"He was just busting balls."

"And you snapped at him," she reminded him. "So who was she that Allison brought back to you? Was she a former love, some girl you loved who was smart enough to run away from your fucked up ass?"

"There was never anyone like that," he said, looking away.

"You're lying again!" she yelled. "Tell me the truth; was there someone you fucked up with? Maybe she was sweet and you fucked her in the ass in one of your moods. Maybe she didn't like your satanic bullshit? I want to know!"

"Why?"

"Because you don't fucking tell me anything!" She tried to stop yelling, but couldn't. "You don't tell your friends anything! You spend your life walking this tight rope, going from having it all too almost losing everything. People want to help and you don't let them. Then shit like this happens and I find out you're telling your life story to some whore you fucked in the ass!"

"Are you jealous, Justine?"

She stopped and stared coldly at him. Even as screwed up as he was, he didn't miss a damn thing. Taking a second to get herself together, she said softly, "No, I'm disgusted that people like me and Alex who are as close to family as you have are kept in the dark, yet you bare your soul to a slut with cat's eyes and blow job lips. You obviously don't want help which means you enjoy wallowing in self pity. You'll get no pity from me, Mark, ever again."

She had been staring into his eyes, and he blinked and looked away from her. "One more time, Lovecraft, and this is as your Mistress. Who was she, because I have a reason for asking now."

"She...." He swallowed hard and cocked his head slightly, his eyes closed, and when he opened them he finished. "Someone I wanted to be with a long time ago, but it couldn't be."

"It couldn't be." She rolled her eyes. "How melodramatic. So poor fucked up Mark sees a dead ringer for his lost Juliette and falls for her." She smirked. "So you think of your unrequited love while fucking Allison?" He stared at her and she went on. "Because I just realized this was going to happen before you got drunk, that little kiss at the end of the initiation was awfully sweet, a little too sweet. You were already thinking more than you should've been. Isn't that right?" She laughed. "Did you tear into your past love as well, tie her up and use her?"

"I'm here to tell you I failed my Mistress, and my Circle," he replied. "Not to tell you my life story. Punish me as you see fit, or ask me to step down." He lowered his head. "I'll do as my Mistress desires."

"You think this is just about you?" She felt her anger rising again. "This is about the integrity of the group!"

"And I..."

"You fucked up is what you did!" she yelled again. "You fucked up worse than anyone has since I took over. Goddamn it, Mark! You fucked a new member, showed her our rules are jokes, that the group is a free for all, that all we're is about sex!"

"That's why I came to you," he said quietly. "I wanted you to know what I...."

"I wished to hell you hadn't!" Her voice was rising as she went on, but she no longer cared. "I would have been better off not knowing! We all would have been! But no, not only do you fuck up, but now you have to feel bad and say something!"

"Would you rather I didn't?"

"I think that's what I just said. Are you that fucking pathetic you can't even follow the conversation?" she demanded. "Or do I need to be a green eyed brunette to get you to pay attention."

"I wanted to show you I'm loyal to you, that I can't..."

"All you showed me was why I can't trust you! I didn't want to give you this initiation, Mark, you know that. Your behavior has become more and more erratic and I was afraid you'd hurt this girl. But I felt I owed you something and let you." She threw her hands in the air. "And look how you reward my faith! Compared to this I wish you had hurt her, it would have been easier to deal with."

"She said she won't...."

"She said she would obey the rules as well when you told them to her, I'm sure. Her word to me means as much as yours right now."

"Justine, she...."

"Do you have any idea how serious this is? Do you realize what you've done?" She slammed her hand down on the table again.

"I broke..."

"You just got Allison thrown out of the group before she even started you fucking idiot!" She was screaming now, her face was flushed and she could feel her heart racing. "You made her go through all that for nothing!"

"You don't have to do that, it was my fault."

"It was your fault, but I do have to do it because you frigging told me! I can't turn my head to this; I can't just punish you and be done with it. She needs to be told she's out!"

"Justine, please think about this."

"There's nothing to think about! On the night of her joining, she broke the most important rule. She has to go and I have to ask Alex to do it, because God knows you'd end up between her legs again."

"That's not true," he snapped. "She came looking for more Sunday morning and I pushed her away, told her what we did was wrong and we couldn't speak of it." He pointed his finger at her. "I told you it was a weak moment. I denied her the next day."

"How sporting of you! After you got what you wanted! And again you're not listening, because I just said that I can't trust you anymore."

"I'm speaking of her now, and...."

"You're not getting it, Mark! We broke rules even before you did! She not only has met Alex and yourself, but she knows Victoria is a member. Victoria is our most public figure and has maintained a clean image. If its leaked she's in a sex group she'll lose a lot of money."

"She..."

"And fucking Amado went sneaking in today to meet her. She's seen four of us Mark, and now I have to hope to hell when Alex tells her she's done he can sufficiently threaten her to keep her mouth shut!" Justine paused and took a deep breath. Picking up the wine bottle, she poured herself another glass and noticed her hand was shaking. She couldn't recall the last time she had been this angry. "Of course it should be my enforcer threatening her, but all you'd threaten her with is a good fuck, which is apparently all you're good for these days."

"Justine, think about this," He began. "Yes she came on to me, but it was up to me to say no. It's on me not..."

"You explained the rules, Alex even touched on them. She's a thirty year old woman, not a teenager, and I doubt she was as drunk as she appeared to you. She put her game against yours and won."

"Only because I...."

"We can't let this go. If I did, what happens when she goes out to dinner or a function with Amado, or Alex, or Eros? What happens when she decides she wants them and figures she got you so she'll get them?"

"She promised that she wouldn't say anything."

"Of course she did. But we both know lust does things to people like us. She gets it in her head she wants them she'll try. What am I to do then?"

"Pretend you didn't know. They won't know what happens after they tell you. Just like Sydney, we dealt with it ourselves."

Justine drank some of the wine as she listened to him. Part of her wanted to think there was a way out of this, it was his fault, but the potential for trouble here was extreme.

"Sydney's issue was disrespect, if it somehow got out it wouldn't have been that terribly embarrassing. This is different and you know it. There is no way around this. Allison will be told to leave." She shook her head. "She'll have to be threatened. I'll have Loki begin looking for some of her pets and gathering...."

"No."

"No?" she asked incredulously.

"She doesn't need to be banned and she certainly doesn't need to be threatened for my weakness," Mark told her. "No one will know Justine."

"If you wanted no one to know then you shouldn't have told me this."

"I'm telling you because I...." He rubbed at his eyes again, and she saw him wince as he did. "I can't lie to you, Justine. I wouldn't be able to see you and not tell you. I'm sorry if that's making it worse. Plus I know Allison is in jeopardy and it would be better for you to know, so I can...."

"What, talk me out of doing what I need to?"

"Justine, please listen to me."

Despite her anger, he sounded so upset she nodded as she drank the rest of the wine.

"She won't say anything. I told her what she could lose if she does. Alex's business, Victoria's help. You should've seen the look on her face." He put his hands out palms up in supplication. "She comes from nothing, the advancement is what sold her on us, and she'd never jeopardize it."

"I'd truly like to believe that, Mark. Don't think I want to see this woman go through that for nothing. But it's a huge chance. She slips, people will put it together and they'll wonder if I knew."

"I know it's not an easy call, but...."

"And what of you?" she asked. "I'll have to worry about you with her. And even if you're right, that this was a slip, she may think she can get you whenever she wants and why wouldn't she?"

"I don't think she'd want to even if I offered," he told her.

"And why is that?"

"I was pretty rude to her the next morning, basically told her to run along after I turned her down. She got pissed and I made it worse, made it sound like I was worried she wouldn't be able to get enough of me."

"So you were in asshole mode."

"I followed her and did apologize, told her I shouldn't have disrespected her, but then got into the rule again, about all she could lose. Justine, she's not looking for a hook up, when I was acting like an idiot she point blank told me it was sex, that was it. She had a fun night and wanted a fun morning before she left. She's not hung up on me."

"But what of you with her?"

"That was a...." He grunted. "You have no reason to believe what I say, but it won't happen again."

"I can assure of that by banning her."

"No, because then I could go and find her and do whatever I wanted, she'll no longer be a member. If I wanted her I'd be better off with her out."

"You're a lawyer, you'll spin this whatever way you think will work for you."

"I don't care about me, I fucked up. I don't want to see her punished for that."

"I don't see a way out. Not one that doesn't involve breaking more rules. I...."

She stopped as, sliding from the chair, Mark crawled on his hands and knees over to her. Kneeling in front of her he leaned over and placed his cheek against her bare foot.

"Please show mercy to her, My Mistress, it wasn't her fault. I accept full responsibility."

"It's not about that," she said quietly, looking down at him. "If she speaks of this, it won't matter what was done to you."

"Please trust me, she won't, it means too much to her. She has no real friends and not much family. She's thrilled to be part of this and she'll do well in the group. Alex hasn't been wrong yet."

"Yes he has, Mark," she said softly. "He was wrong with you. You're no longer who you were and it's becoming a problem."

"I'll leave if you wish me to," he replied, looking up at her with those painful eyes.

"Sit up," she said.

Mark got to his knees and Justine stared at him. Looking into his eyes, she felt a mixture of anger and pity. He was a mess. He was broken in a way she couldn't understand, but he had broken a rule that could cause a lot of trouble if not handled just right. In all the years it had existed, the group had never been exposed. He was most likely right about Allison, but it was a gamble. Justine only had a year and a half left and shouldn't have to deal with these issues, it should be all games at this point.

She felt the anger begin to outweigh the pity. All she had wanted tonight was fun. This was her own fault, she had been getting too close to him and this was the lesson to teach her it was wrong. There should be no hesitation about her punishing him. But when? He was a wreck, not only exhausted, but she could feel how hot his face was when he had pressed it to her feet. His body was worn down as was his reasoning. This wouldn't be the time to deliver a severe punishment. She would send him away, which in itself would be cruel, make him wait and wonder what she would do. No, that was wrong as well, his weakness shouldn't determine her actions.

Closing her eyes, she again imagined her initiation, and some of the things done to her and other members. There was no mercy back then. When rules were broken, the punishments were severe, even to the male members. Back in the hotel, Mark had mocked her, saying the Circle was getting soft. Perhaps it was time Justine showed him not only was her Circle not weak, but she was as strong as ever. Justine was survivor of the harsh days of the group, a true Mistress. This was where she would show him that from this point forward, that was what she was to him, his mistress. After all, he refused to confide in her all this time so perhaps it had been her being weak in thinking they were close all along. She would now show him that was not the case.

"I won't ban you, Lovecraft, that'd be too easy. I want you to sit at that table and know your shame. Especially the next time someone breaks a rule and I publicly declare someone other than you will handle it. Perhaps Mercedes might make a better enforcer. I know I'll never have to worry about her going soft. But for right now, I want you to go into my bedroom, strip and kneel on the floor at the foot of my bed and await me."

"As you wish," he whispered.

"And while you wait, take a good long look at my bed because it'll be a cold day in hell before you ever see it again."

Chapter Three

Justine stood in front of the open refrigerator letting the cool air strike her naked body. Reaching in, she grabbed a bottle of water and drank deeply. Placing the bottle against her sweat soaked forehead, she leaned on the edge of the door. Her shoulder was throbbing painfully and, reaching into the freezer, she grabbed an ice pack and placed it there. The cold caused her to shiver, but she held it in place, trying to settle down the fire in her muscles. Slung over her other shoulder was the cause of her pain. Grabbing the whip, she stared at it, and then tossed it onto the table. She wouldn't bring it back in with her, she'd gone too far with it already.

It was not a sign of control when you whipped someone so hard, you could barely lift your arm. Closing the fridge, Justine walked into the living room and, putting the ice pack against the back of the recliner, sat down and leaned against it. Closing her eyes, she took several deep breaths. The cool air felt good and she held the last breath as long as she could. Releasing it, she contemplated what had just transpired. As was her style, one that Mark had adapted himself, she had cranked the thermostat in her bedroom over ninety when she entered, then left him kneeling there, his hands cuffed behind his back.

When she'd entered again, the room was stifling and she could see Mark's entire body glistening with sweat. Walking past him, Justine went to her closet and removed the locked suitcase containing her nastier toys. Slowly manipulating the combination lock on it, she slowly opened the case. Justine removed her whip, and then stared at the rest of the contents. The ball gag was tucked into a corner and her hand strayed towards it. She stopped, unsure of whether or not she would go that far.

Walking around behind him, Justine snapped the whip a couple of times, measuring the distance between them. She whistled a couple just passed his ear and frowned when he didn't flinch. Justine reared back and delivered a solid blow to the middle of his back, which with the exception of a hiss of breath, got no reaction from him. She struck him twice more, and again not so much as a gasp from him.

"Fine," she said. "Think you can handle it? Good, because that means I get to really cut loose."

Coming up behind him, she reached down and, releasing one of the cuffs, told him to stand. Mark obeyed and, moving past him, Justine got onto her bed and, standing up, gestured with her finger. Head down, Mark walked up to the foot of the bed and waited. Justine removed the hanging plant from the hook and, placing it on the bed, said, "Put your arms up over your head."

Mark obeyed and, grabbing his wrists, she closed the cuff back on him and pulled the chain to the hook. He came up a few inches short which was perfect.

"Up on your toes."

Mark raised himself up and she slipped the hook through the links in the middle of the chain and, stepping off of the bed, put the plant on the floor, before walking back over to the suitcase. Looking around, she chose a stainless steel cock ring that released with the touch of a button. Approaching him, she looked down to see his toes were barely touching the floor and the muscles in his calves were bulging. She swung her foot out and swept his feet out from under him. He grunted and she watched the muscles ripple in his arms as he held his weight up. She looked up at the hook and nodded. The plant was only there to give her an excuse to have a hook in the ceiling of her bedroom, this was its true purpose. The hook was screwed through the ceiling and anchored to the two by four of the floor above. It could easily held the weight of two and would shortly. Reaching around his waist and grabbing his cock, began to stroke it.

"What, you're not hard for your Mistress?" she whispered into his ear. She stuck her fingernail into one of the welts and scratched the length of it. "I asked you a question"

"I...didn't think I was to enjoy this," he answered.

"You're not, but I plan to, and these days this cock is all you have going for you. Now get hard or I'll put a strap-on over your head and ride your face."

Mark's breathing began to pick up and she could feel his cock thickening in her hand. As she continued to stroke him, she thought of what a waste this was. This was not how she had planned on enjoying him tonight. That thought brought her anger back and she began pumping his cock furiously. "I said, fucking get hard for me!" she snapped. "Just think of Allison that should get you nice and ready shouldn't it?"

His cock was fully erect and, after giving it a couple of more hard pumps, Justine reached her other hand around and clamped the cock ring behind his balls. When it felt tight, she squeezed it harder until he groaned, then locked it in place.

"There, we don't want you losing interest now do we?"

"No, Mistress," he whispered.

Going back to the suitcase, Justine selected another cock ring, this one with a bullet vibrator attached to it. Approaching Mark, she slipped it over his cock and pushed it down to the base of his shaft.

"I figured it was either this or wear a black wig, but I like this better. I get something out of it this way." Glancing down, she made a clucking noise at how swollen the head of his cock was. "That's really tight, can't see how you'd be able to cum with that on." She laughed. "But then again that's the point right? Besides you came plenty last week, and in the worst possible place."

She thumbed the button, turning on the vibrator and started stroking his cock again. "That vibrator feels good doesn't it?" she asked. "It won't when that pleasure becomes frustration though will it?"

Shaking her head disgustedly, she continued, "And to think you could've been cumming all night long. Anywhere you wanted. My mouth, my pussy, on my feet." She shrugged. "I was so excited I would've let you have my ass. But no, you went ahead and had sex with your little playmate didn't you?"

"Yes, Mistress." His voice was already sounding strained and she could see the muscles in his arms beginning to tremble.

"So tell me, oh Lovecraft of the Circle. Where did you cum when you fucked her? Did she blow you? Did you cum all over her face, those nice big tits?"

Mark was silent and, stepping back, she pulled him forward, taking him off his feet and holding him by his cock. He moaned in pain and she pulled him further back, her own arm straining with the effort.

"I asked you a question. If you don't answer, I'll tie your cock to the bed post and leave you like this."

"I...she blew me and s....swallowed it, then I came on her back."

"Oh, what about the next time around? You said twice."

"Inside of her."

"You came inside of her?" she asked. "Aww, how sweet." Frowning she said, "You were sweet to her the second time weren't you, Mark? You woke up and saw that precious little pout next to you and went nice and easy didn't you?"

"I...oh," he groaned as she tugged him back a little further.

"Were you seeing Allison then, or were you so drunk and fucked up you saw your little mystery girl?" She smirked. "You gave it to her nice and easy didn't you? Loved her the way you wanted to..."

"Shut up," Mark hissed at her. She looked up and saw his eyes had darkened. "Do as you will, but I won't endure your taunts."

"You'll endure anything I want you pathetic excuse for an enforcer. Now how about I go find something to tie to your cock and leave you suspended by it for awhile?" Mark closed his eyes and let out a whimper as she tugged him back even further. "I'll give you one more chance. Tell me, my disgraced prince, did you love her or fuck her that time?"

"I...I made love to her," he whispered, his eyes still closed.

Justine let his cock go and watched him swing back to the floor, his feet desperately trying to find purchase to take the strain from his arms. "Well, she must be something then," putting her hands on his shoulders and rising up on her own toes, so that her lips were close to his she said softly, "Go ahead, kiss me the way you kissed her."

"What?"

"You heard me. I want one of those sweet kisses. Come; show your mistress how much you adore her. Better yet, show Justine how much she means to you." Leaning into his ear she whispered, "Tell you what, if it's a nice sweet one, the kind you gave to her, I might just let you go. I might forget the whole thing. But it has to be a good one." Placing her lips to his she kissed him softly. "Go ahead, and let me feel it."

Mark didn't try to kiss her and, reaching down, she grabbed his balls and gave them a squeeze. He moaned and she squeezed harder.

"I didn't think I was so terrible to kiss," she said, and then closing her eyes, parted her lips. When she felt nothing, she squeezed again. No sooner had she started to apply pressure, she felt his lips graze hers. "Better than that," she told him, releasing her grip on him.

Mark kissed her again and his lips gently slid across hers. She kissed him back and opened her mouth wider. His lips worked against hers, sliding back and forth gently. She opened her eyes as she felt nothing, but the mechanical act of his going through the motions.

"Well I guess I'm just not that special to you am I?"

As she asked the question she realized she was hurt. Mark had told Allison things he wouldn't volunteer to her, and had been sweet and gentle to her. Not that she was really looking for that, but she had felt there was more than just sex between them. She stopped and let that hurt turn to rage. What the hell was wrong with her? Mark was right, she was acting jealous. Behaving like a teenage drama queen. In her mind she heard Alex speaking of why Circle pets, although allowed, were frowned upon .Enough was enough. Grabbing the whip from the bed, she walked behind him and, after taking several steps, whirled around and, bringing her arm back, delivered a hard blow to the top of his back.

His body jerked, but there was no cry of pain. Remembering Mark's punishment of Sydney, she lashed out again, this time striking the sole of his foot. Mark cried out and his foot jerked off the floor. Expertly sending the whip back around, Justine caught the other foot, and then proceeded to go from one to the other, causing him to dance from one foot to the next.

"You feel that don't you?" she panted, as the heat and exertion were affecting her breathing.

"Yes, Mistress," he gasped.

"Good, because this is just the beginning, Mark. Tonight I'm going to prove that you're no different than anyone else. That your reputation is bullshit." Aiming higher, Justine caught the back of his right knee, getting another cry of pain from him. "I broke you once you animal and I'll break you again. This time in much less time, know why?"

"W...why?" he moaned out as she caught the back of his other leg.

"Because you're a shell of yourself, you're living off your reputation in the Circle, you're a broken down basket case!"

Justine spun herself around and grunted as she swung with all her strength. The blow stuck him in the back and this time he did cry out from the pain. "A fucking disgrace who can't keep his cock in his pants! Who can't say no to some piece of fluff he just met!"

Justine delivered another vicious blow to the back of his shoulder. Spreading her legs wide and bracing herself, she began to lash out as fast and hard as she could. Justine played the whip up and down his body, striking his feet, his knees and his thighs. His body jerked and writhed with each blow and the muscles in his arms were shaking form the effort of holding himself up. Aiming higher, Justine delivered a blow to his right bicep, causing him to cry out again.

"Fucking pathetic you are! More pathetic than that grabby frat boy Alex ever could be!" she snarled. "You said you were worried about me being punished if we gave her a soft welcome?" She hit him on the back of the neck and he let out a high pitched yelp. "What kind of punishment would I get if Persephone found out my members helped themselves at the table? She'd probably let every Master in the group have me and all at once!" She began just striking at his back now. "They'd fucking rape me, just like they did at my initiation and it'd be because of you, you fucking failure, because you can't admit you're a fraud at that table!"

She hit him again and again as images of her initiation began to flood through her, cock after cock plunging into her ass, them calling her names and pulling her hair, fucking her mouth. Being taken on the table by two men at a meeting. Being forced to kneel on the table and be fucked in the ass while face to face with Morrigan, who was having the same done to her.

"That won't happen to me again do you understand?" she demanded as she struck him again

"Y...yes, Mistress," he gasped.

Justine struck again, and felt a fiery pain go through her shoulder. She lashed out one more time and had to bite her tongue against the pain. When she pulled the whip back, she coiled it around her hand and stood there gasping. She looked at Mark and saw that blood was running down his back. She bent over and placed her hands on her knees trying to not only catch her breath, but calm down. Where that had all come from she wasn't sure, but knew she needed to put the whip down. Placing it next to her foot so she would remember where her range was, Justine walked around to face him.

Mark's eyes were closed and the sweat was pouring down his face. His breath was coming in short gasps and he was shaking. Reaching up, she ran her hands along the powerful muscles of his arms.

"Hope you're not getting as weak physically as you are mentally, Mark." He opened his eyes, and shook his head. "Good." She nodded as, untying her robe, she let it drop to the floor. "Because I'm going for a ride on that cock."

Putting her arms around his neck, Justine leaped up and, wrapping her legs around his waist, smiled as he cried out at the pain of holding the two of them up. Keeping one arm tightly around his neck, Justine reached down and, guided his engorged cock to her pussy. She eased herself down onto it just enough so the head was pushing between her lips, then bringing her arm back around his neck, let her weight go. Mark groaned as she impaled herself on his cock and, began lifting herself up and down, riding him as he hung from the hook. Mark's breathing was coming in painful gasps and his arms were shaking badly as she began rocking faster.

"There you go," she said. "That's what you're good for. That cock really is your only redeeming quality. Maybe I'll take you to the conference and put this cock ring on you and tie you to a bed, let any lady who wants to, ride you for a couple of minutes, just leave you there to be used, and you won't cum. Any lady who somehow manages that will get punished." She laughed as she drove herself down harder. "Hey you can take two at a time. One can be on your face while the other rides you. It'd be quite the attraction."

Mark didn't answer, his eyes were closed and his neck bulging as she rocked harder onto him. Descending all the way to the base of his cock, Justine sighed as the bullet struck her clit.

"Ohh, that's nice," she purred as she started grinding her hips hard into him, working the bullet against her swollen clit. Pushing herself up, she shoved her tit in his face. "Here make yourself useful will you?" Mark obediently opened his mouth and his tongue flicked out across her nipple. "Oh better than that!" she snapped and pushed her nipple into his mouth. "Just pretend its Allison's tit."

She paused and moaned as the vibrator against her clit coupled with his massive cock buried deep inside of her was beginning to cause a very pleasant sensation deep within her. Grabbing the back of his head, she forced her tit further into his mouth and began grinding harder into him, working the vibrator across her swollen button. Mark managed to begin to suck her nipple hard into his mouth and she gasped and started rocking back and forth, moving on his cock, but keeping the bullet in contact with her clit. "There you go, suck that tit! How's that pussy feel? Not as good as hers I'll bet!"

Mark moaned and she felt his cock begin to move within her as, bracing on his toes, he started pumping his hips as much as he could. "Oh you like that?" she asked. "Or you just trying to get me off?" She laughed. "Even if I cum who said I'm going to stop? And you can't cum can you? No I could just keep riding and cumming and...."

Justine's words were cut off as her hips twitched and she could feel her pussy contracting around his cock. Wrapping her arms around his neck again, she started grinding her hips as hard as she could. Mark whimpered at the strain of holding them up and the noise sent her over the edge. She cried out in his ear, as she felt the orgasm explode through her. Justine bucked her and moaned at the sensation of her pussy convulsing around his enormous cock. Mark whimpered again and she could feel his body trembling under her. His cock was twitching within her and she knew he was trying to cum as he fought to hold them up. Justine sighed as the last of the orgasm passed though her and smiled at him.

"You do have your uses don't you? You know I think Mercedes is looking for a well hung sub for some of her female customers. Maybe that could be your new job." Easing herself off of his cock, she stood in front of him. "Well thanks for the ride, Mark, sorry you couldn't cum, but you probably didn't want to anyway. I'm not good enough for you." She sighed. "I'm going to go cool off; you just hang around in here okay?"

Walking passed him; Justine saw the whip and picked it up. Turning she saw him slumped, hanging limply from the hook, gasping. She reared back and, despite the pain in her shoulder, struck him behind his knee. Mark jerked and cried out and she hit the other knee. "Didn't want you to miss me too much," she told him, before leaving the room.

Justine shifted in the chair, wincing at the ache in her shoulder. The cold had helped some and she felt more in control of herself. Looking at the clock, she figured she had left him alone hanging there for about fifteen minutes. Taking a deep breath she stood up and prepared herself for the next round. She couldn't lose control this time. She had to block out her emotions and handle him the way she used to the guys at the club who had paid her way through college by giving her a hundred dollars an hour to hurt and humiliate them. Mark was just another pet to be punished.

Walking over to the fridge, Justine removed a pitcher of ice water and, after filling a glass, walked back into the bedroom. The heat slapped her in the face as soon as she entered, and she took one last breath of cool air before she closed the door. Mark had no choice but to be exactly where she left him. His toes were back on the floor and she could tell that he was just hanging there, letting the pain settle in his shoulders rather than his legs. Standing in front of him, she took a long sip of the water and, reaching out, placed the glass against his cheek. His eyes opened and she winced at how red they were.

"Drink?" she pushed the glass to his lips.

He regarded her for a moment, probably thinking she was going to take it away from him. He parted his lips and she tipped the glass to allow him a couple of sips before removing it.

"Thank you, Mistress," he said softly.

Looking down at his cock, which was so swollen it was purple, she poured some of the water down on it. Mark's breath hissed as the cold water struck his aching flesh. She grabbed his throbbing cock and began stroking it. He moaned in a mixture of pain and pleasure as she started stroking it faster.

"Good to see you can't go down, because I'm not done with you yet."

Letting his cock go, she placed the glass of water on the floor and climbing back onto the bed, reached up and, with an effort, lifted the chain off of the hook. Mark immediately dropped to his knees, his arms hanging as he moaned in relief. Bending over, Justine released the cuffs then picking up the glass, she looked down at him. "Here, cool off."

She threw the water in his face and as he sputtered, tossed the glass onto her bed. Going over to the suitcase, Justine removed a leather leash, her hand hovered over a leather dog collar, but shifted and instead picked up a metal pronged training collar. Coming up behind him, she slipped the collar over his head and fastened it snuggly around his neck, the prongs just poking into his skin. Attaching the leash, Justine took a couple, of steps and yanked hard on the leash. Mark winced and began to start to crawl towards her. His tired arms gave out and he fell on his face.

"Oh, how pathetic." She shook her head. "Get up, dog, I'm not done with you yet." Mark placed his palms on the floor and, with a groan, pushed himself back up onto his hands and knees. "Good doggy." She nodded then with a hard yank, forced him to crawl around the room with her.

She circled once, then pointing at the floor a couple of feet in front of the foot of the bed, said, "Stay." Sitting on the edge of the bed, she spread her legs. "Come lick my pussy."

She yanked on the leash as she spoke and he crawled towards her. Kneeling between her legs, he leaned forward, but she tugged upwards on the leash, stopping him. "Hands down by your sides, you lift them, I'll cuff you again. You just use your tongue, like the dog you are."

"Yes, Mistress."

Again he leaned into her pussy and again she stopped him. "Ask."

"Mistress, may I please?"

"No." She smiled. "Call me Allison when you ask." Mark shook his head, and then cried out as she yanked savagely on the leash. "You do not refuse me!" she snapped. "Ask your new sister to lick her pussy. I want to hear how pathetic you sound."

Mark took a breath and whispered, "Allison, may I please lick your pussy?"

"But, Mark, the rules!"

Mark stared at her and she started to bring the leash up. Putting his head down, he continued, "Please, Allison?" He looked up at her through his red eyes. "Please I...." He closed his eyes. "I don't care about the rules, please let me make you cum."

"Ohh I like that," Justine cooed. "Okay, Mark, come lick your sister's pussy."

Mark slowly leaned forward, waiting for her to pull again. She didn't and, pressing his face between her legs, he slid his tongue into and out of her pussy. Justine sighed as he swirled his tongue around inside of her. She let him go for a minute then began speaking. 'Oh, I knew you'd take care of me, Mark, I knew I'd get to you." She laughed. "Say my name again."

"Justine I...ow!" Mark's scream turned into a gurgle as the collar dug into his throat.

"You know what I want to hear!"

"A....Allison, I...I love licking your pussy."

"That's better. Good thing you wear ties at work." she told him while staring at the red cuts on his neck.

Mark returned to her pussy and Justine sat back and allowed him to work his tongue through the wet folds and begin swirling around her clit. Bringing her feet up, she placed them on his shoulders and pushed against him while pulling on the leash. Mark gasped into her pussy, but continued to lick and suck on her clit.

"Good boy," she whispered. "Bet you licked her pussy good, didn't you? Made her cum damn hard. Show her how good you are." She sighed as he started sucking her clit in and out of his mouth. "Did you think of her, Mark? Your little girlfriend, whoever she was? And who are you thinking of now? Allison? You wishing that were her smooth little pussy?"

Mark shook his head into her pussy, but continued to lick. Justine could feel her thighs starting to tremble and started rocking her hips into his face. She could have forced him to make it last, but it was getting time to finish this and she wanted to cum for him one last time.

"Look at me," she told him. Mark looked up at her and she stared into his ruined eyes as he continued to trace his tongue in fast circles around her clit. "Ask her to cum,"

Mark stopped licking and, still keeping his eyes locked on hers, asked, "Allison, will you cum for me?"

"Of course, my brother, I'd love to cum for the man who said he'd never fuck me."

Mark sped his tongue up on her pussy and Justine started breathing harder, and thrusting her hips into his soft tongue. Dropping her feet from his shoulders, Justine closed her legs around his face and, letting her legs dangle, found his cock and wrapped it between her feet. Mark whimpered into her pussy as she started jerking him off with her feet. She couldn't imagine how sensitive his cock was right now. She started twisting her nipple and gasped as Mark began sucking her clit hard. Justine thrust her pussy into his face and, throwing her head back, cried out as she came. Mark moaned as she tugged on the leash, tightening the collar, but continued to lick, keeping her cumming for as long as possible.

Justine groaned and shoved her pussy harder into his face while pumping her feet along his tortured cock. He was whimpering and she could feel him thrusting his cock against her soft feet. Letting out one more long moan, Justine lay back onto the bed panting. She still had her feet in his lap and started lightly rubbing one foot along the length of his shaft. He was moaning into her pussy and she loved it. Sitting up, she looked over at the suitcase. It was time to get this over with and give him the punishment she knew he craved. That was the real reason he had told her and she knew it. He was a switch and had fucked up, he needed to be punished. Now it was up to her to make him sorry for what he wished for.

Justine pushed herself off of the bed and, walking over to her bureau, pulled the small wooden chair away from it and pointing at it, said, "Crawl over here."

Mark nodded and, turning away from the bed, began to crawl over to the chair. Walking past him, Justine hurriedly reached into the suitcase and, removing the gag, held it behind her back. Turning, she saw Mark kneeling in front of the chair. Picking up the cuffs she said, "Sit on the chair and put your arms behind it."

Justine got behind him, pulled his wrists together and put the cuffs back on and placed the ball gag on the bureau behind the chair. Stepping around to the side, she swung her leg over his and sat down hard, again driving herself down on him. Mark whimpered as she began riding his helpless cock.

"You want to cum don't you, Mark?"

"I..." He moaned as she ground her hips into him. "I...I'm not worthy to."

"True but if you ask the right way, I may let you."

"Mistress," he began, but stopped as she shook her head.

"Now what game have we been playing?" she asked, then moaned herself as she started bouncing up and down on him, using her legs to raise herself as high as she could before dropping down on him.

"Allison," he began. "Please let me cum."

"You want to cum?" she smiled. "Deep inside of me like I'm your girlfriend?" She pushed her lips out into a pout. "I'd really like that! But you have to ask me again!"

"Justine, please," Mark whispered.

"Ask!" she snapped, yanking the leash. "Ask that little whore to allow you to cum! Beg her the way you probably begged her that night!"

Justine sat down hard on his cock and started sliding back and forth. Mark whimpered again, then gasped, "Allison, please let me cum inside of you, I....oh I need to!" he whimpered.

"Oh that was nice." Justine moaned as she began riding him again. "I like that, truly pathetic!"

Justine stood up and Mark groaned as she removed him from inside of her. "Now here's the deal, Mark, we're going to play a game. First I'm going to make things easier on you."

Reaching down between his legs, Justine slid off the vibrating cock ring and then, sliding her hand under his balls, thumbed the release on the other cock ring. Mark moaned as the pressure left his cock and then groaned loudly as she grabbed it. Swinging her leg back over him she again sank down onto his hard flesh. Mark sighed as she started rocking back and forth.

"That's better isn't it?" she asked. "Makes it nice and easy for you to cum now no?"

He nodded and whimpered as she started gently moving up and down on him.

"Well now here's the hard part. I want you to prove to me you're still as good as you were back when I initiated you, when this cock would get hard no matter what. So now that I made it so you can cum, let's see how you handle a little adversity." Reaching behind him, she picked the gag up in one hand, then with the other found one of the raw whip cuts. Digging her nails into it, she ripped down hard. Mark screamed and, moving quickly, she jammed the ball into his mouth.

Mark screamed behind the gag and bucked so hard he almost threw her off of him. He began to thrash back and forth in the chair, but she was sitting on his lap and he was exhausted, even desperate, his body no longer had the strength to fight.

"Stop your whining!" she snapped and tugged hard on the leash. Mark continued to shake his head back and forth, and letting the leash go, Justine grabbed two handfuls of his hair and forced his head still. "Stay still!" she shouted into his face.

Mark moaned pathetically behind the gag and Justine fought to keep her eyes focused on his as they bulged in fear. Between her legs she could feel his cock softening. "You better not lose it, Mark," she whispered. "Because this gag is staying on until you cum for me. Right up inside like you came for her."

Mark cried out behind the gag and tears began to flow from his eyes. Justine looked away and took a deep breath before looking back at him.

"You want that gag out, you fuck me. You get nice and hard again and you give it to me! It won't take long. You know you need to cum. All you have to do is get hard and I'll do the work." She forced herself to smile. "Or I can just sit here on your flaccid cock and watch you ball like a baby."

Mark screamed behind the gag and she could make out the word please. Still holding his gaze, her mind raced. This was going too far, he wouldn't be able to and she would have to let him go. Shaking her head she kept pushing.

"Back when I broke you the first time you were getting up no matter what I did to you. You were impressive back then, not a pathetic dog like you are now." She squirmed on his now soft cock. "For Christ's sake your inside of me and can't keep it up!"

Mark wailed behind the gag and she caught herself starting to reach for it. Stopping her hand, she grabbed his chin and pulled his face to hers. "Just pretend I'm Allison again, that'll get you nice and hard. Pretend you're fucking that precious little whore. The one you couldn't say no to. The one that you'd risk our group for. The one you'd see me punished over."

Mark shook his head in her grasp and he began sobbing behind the gag. "Or just fuck me, Mark," she said. "I thought you enjoyed me." She sighed. "Guess not. All you have to do is show me you want me. Get that cock nice and hard and let me ride you."

Mark closed his eyes and began whimpering. "Guess we just sit here then." She sighed. "I should've left the ring on at least then I'd be able to...."

She trailed off as Mark went quiet. His head turned to the side and his breathing began to slow down. She felt his body tense up and between her legs she felt his cock twitch. Mark took a deep breath and she could feel him getting hard inside of her.

"There you go, that's..."

She stopped as his eyes snapped open and she saw they were almost black. She started to speak, but yelped as he violently thrust his hips up into her, driving his now fully erect cock deep inside of her. Justine let go of his hair and, bracing her hands on his shoulders, started to ride him again. Mark's hips thrust upwards to meet her descending pussy and she cried out again at how hard he slammed into her. She bit her lip to hold back any more yelps as she stopped moving and sat there, letting him savagely drive his cock into her.

Their eyes were locked and she saw no panic whatsoever in them. What she saw was rage. Even as he fucked her, Justine felt a surge of fear go through her. She had sent him over the edge, except now he wasn't scared, he was violent. Mark gasped behind the gag and he began thrusting even faster, pounding his massive cock into her. Trying to maintain her part, she egged him on.

"That's it, fuck me! Show me you're still worth something. Show me what you're good at, the only thing you're good at." Mark was breathing even harder and his hips were pumping furiously, fucking the shit out of her. "Oh, you must be thinking of Allison aren't you?" she gasped as she began driving back down into him to get him to finish. "That long black hair, that white skin, those lips. She looked like the one that got away didn't she Mark? The one that....oh!"

Justine cried out as he gave her another savage pump and exploded inside of her. She gasped and stayed still as he thrust into her, each pump ending in another spurt of cum. Mark whimpered behind the gag as she felt his cock twitch one more time sending the last of him spilling into her pussy. Justine paused to catch her breath then looked up as Mark began to sob again. She saw his eyes were back to their normal color and were staring into hers, begging her. Stepping off of him and, ignoring the feeling of his cum dripping down her legs, Justine reached forward and grabbing the gag yanked it from his mouth.

"Oh, I'm sorry!" he cried out. "I'm so sorry, Mistress!" Seeing he no longer looked violent, she reached behind him and released the cuffs. Mark fell onto his knees and put his head in his hands "I'm sorry, Justine," he moaned. "Please no more! Please! I'll quit, I'll...." He stopped trying to talk and sobbed into his hands.

Justine stared down at him and put her own hands to her face. What the hell had she done? What she had to, and she had to continue to do so. "It's over, Mark," she said, struggling to keep her voice steady. "You've been punished and I will see to it Alex takes care of Allison."

"No, she...I...."

"We won't speak of this again."

Justine stood there and closed her eyes, listening to him whimper and fighting the urge to kneel beside him and tell him he would be okay. To hold him and make sure he would be okay. That had gotten her into this mess in the first place. She stood still and, after what seemed like an eternity, his whimpering subsided. She opened her eyes to see him sitting there staring off into space. She winced at his bloody back and told herself again it was how it had to be.

"If you've pulled your pathetic ass together, then we're done here," she said softly.

Mark nodded, but stayed where he was.

"I said we're done," she repeated.

"Yes, Mistress," he breathed out and, with a groan, managed to get to his feet. He looked around and, seeing his clothes, started to go to pick them up.

"Go shower first, it's a long ride back home and you're a disgusting mess, go clean up. I'll leave your clothes on the couch and you can see yourself out."

"As you wish." He nodded and started to move slowly towards the door.

"And just in case you haven't figured it out," she began. "You better start lining up some sluts for the meeting nights, because you'll no longer be spending those nights with me."

"Yes, Mistress."

"It's for the best," she told him. "I wouldn't want you to start thinking you were anything to me other than a good fuck."

Mark put his head down and she looked down as well, glad he couldn't see her face. "And one more thing Mark," she was whispering, not trusting her voice as she could feel her throat tightening up. "You better think of a good lie as to why Allison ended up not making it, because I'm making you responsible to tell everyone."

"Of course." With his head still down, he left the room, closing the door behind him.

Justine sat on the edge of the bed and, after trying to fight it by taking several deep breaths and telling herself she did the right thing by the group, gave in and began to cry.

Chapter Four

Her head in her hands, Justine fought to stop the tears from coming. She hadn't cried since she was a teenager and didn't want to now. It was a losing battle. Not only were the tears streaming down her face, but despite her best efforts to hold them back, an occasional sob broke through. She'd gotten through the brutal session with Mark by using a combination of telling herself she was the Mistress and had to do it, as well as recalling some of the things she had gone through. She had called up those memories to feed her anger and to justify what she was doing. Justine had been forced to endure just as bad if not worse, why shouldn't he?

Back then, and even now, the women were punished in a sexual manner, forced into some degrading, humiliating act. The only rule in place now was it could not be an act of sexual violence. The men however, as it had always been, were punished more in the form of pain mixed with sexual torture. That was what she had done to Mark and she was within her rights to do so. He had broken the group's biggest rule and cost them a new member. Justine kept trying to tell herself this even as another sob tore through her. Why couldn't she stop crying? The answer was simple: She was crying because she had been wrong.

Mark had fucked up royally, but he didn't deserve that. Justine knew him well enough to know if she didn't punish him, he would have become even more upset, but she had gone too far. There was a difference between discipline and torture, and she had not only crossed that line, but leaped across it. Tonight she'd been as cruel as any of the sexual sadists who ran the group's years ago. Tonight she'd gone against not only everything her master Lazarus had taught her when he groomed her to take over. Let the punishment fit the crime when possible, but in the end the punishment must be tempered with mercy. The point of punishment was to make the offender pay, but keep them loyal to the group and its leader.

In essence the Circle had gone from taking pages straight out of the works of De Sade and entered the modern BDSM era of safe sane and consensual. Tonight Justine had taken it back to the dark ages. Wiping at her eyes, she knew it was more than that. Although she was upset at abusing her authority, the fact of the matter was she had just hurt someone close to her. Mark was not just a member of the group, he was a lover as well as one of the few close friends she had. Years ago she'd crossed the line and all but sent him to a nervous breakdown. Despite how badly she had hurt him at his initiation, he'd come to trust her. Tonight she betrayed that trust.

As Mistress Scarlett, Justine had to punish Mark, but because she'd followed that school of thought, she'd almost pushed him over the edge. He had come to her stressed and exhausted. She had whipped him, worn him down, and then deliberately scared the hell out of him. This was why the rule of not engaging in sex was in place. This was why it was frowned upon for the leaders to have pets within their group. It made it hard to separate business from pleasure. Justine looked down on the floor and seeing the gag near her foot kicked it across the room.

Fact was, part of why she had torn into Mark was she had forced herself too. Justine had tried to prove he truly was no more than a fuck buddy to her. The question was why? Because Mistress Scarlett had to do what she had to do? That was bullshit! What did she owe the group at this point? She'd been a member for eighteen years and always abided by the rules, at least the major ones. As Alex, Mark and even Amado had stressed to Allison many of them because of their lifestyles were not close to their family and had few friends which was why they considered themselves family. Except for her sister and her two nieces back home in Dallas, all Justine had was the group.

Over the last few years, she'd begun to become weary of the game. Justine had felt herself drawn more to fun and comfort than training and breaking men. Mark had filled that need and then some. She realized it that morning at the hotel a couple of weeks ago. There was more between them than casual sex. Mark had no one except his sister who had moved away a couple of years ago. That was his choice to a degree, he chose not to let people get close, but Justine knew he needed her. There were many times he had been in one of his funks and she had brought him out of it. Part of her anger earlier had been the fact she was jealous. Mark chose not to share things with her and she was okay with it, but to hear him say he had shared with Allison, then gone sweet on her had pissed her off.

She would not be jealous if he were not so much more than a member of the group to her. Even though Mark had come to her looking to be punished, deep down he had come to her as a friend. He was upset and needed to be told it would work out. Justine had torn into him as if he had hurt her personally. All in the name of The Circle. Justine only had two years before she was to step down. Should she have no attachments until then? She grabbed the edge of the sheet and wiped at her eyes. She could hear the shower running down the hall and stared longingly at the bedroom door. As Mistress she should do what she said. Put his clothes on the couch and not see him until the next meeting. But Justine needed to try to make this right, show him she was sorry and hope she hadn't done irreparable harm to their relationship.

Standing, Justine walked slowly over to the door. As she opened it, she looked over on her bureau at a picture of her and Victoria that had been taken at a Christmas party last year. Her eyes lingered on Victoria. There could be a way for Allison to stay. It would require asking a huge favor of Victoria, but it could work. Her high lady was fiercely loyal to her and still felt she owed Mark. Victoria would make this right if she asked her. Allison would listen to a warning from Victoria rather than a threat from Alex. Nodding, she made the decision. She would not punish Mark further by laying the guilt of Allison being banned on him. She would roll the dice on her high lady.

Justine left the bedroom and, reaching the bathroom, gently turned the knob, hoping he hadn't locked it. It turned freely and she entered as quietly as she could. The bathroom was full of steam and Justine could barely make out Mark behind the glass doors of the shower. Justine grabbed the edge of the door and gently slid it open. Mark had his back to her, his arms folded against the wall and his head resting on them as the hot water struck his back. Even through the dark ink of the tattoos Justine could see the large red welts from the whip and winced at the red cuts from the collar.

Entering into the shower, Justine slid the door closed. She stepped under the water, knowing he would realize she was there as soon as the water stopped hitting his back. She let the hot water strike her own sore shoulder as she waited for him to turn around. He didn't move and she began to wonder if he had fallen asleep leaning against the wall. Justine reached out to touch his back, when he startled her by speaking. "I'm sorry I'm still here, I'll leave now." He stood straight, but before he could turn around, she slid her arms around his chest. Hugging him tight, she placed her cheek against his wet back.

"Don't leave," she said quietly.

He didn't move, but she could feel how tense he was, standing there only because she'd told him not to move. Proving her point, he replied, "As you wish, My Mistress."

Justine felt the tears beginning to flow again and, pressing her face tighter against him, tried to say something, but all that came out was a muffled sob. Mark remained motionless as she continued to cry silently against him as she realized she had succeeded in pushing him away from her. Justine lifted her head and began to withdraw her arms, when Mark placed his hands over hers and held them to him. She felt his body relax and she again pressed her face to him.

"I'm sorry, Mark!" she choked out. "I'm so sorry!"

He let her hands go and, turning within her grasp, put his arms around her. Burying her face in his chest, Justine started crying harder and holding herself to him. Mark started rubbing her back, then slid his hand up through her wet hair and cradled her head to him. Justine tried to stop crying, but his holding her made her feel even worse. She had treated him horribly and here he was comforting her. Gradually, her tears subsided and she selfishly allowed herself to relax into him. The hot water felt good beating on her back, but nowhere near as good as his arms felt around her.

Even as it occurred to her she needed to get a grip on herself and take care of him, another part of her was relishing the fact she could be weak and someone was there for her. Justine forced her head from his chest and saw him staring at her sadly. Again she winced at how swollen his eyes were and cursed herself for being such a bitch.

"I am sorry," she began, "I..."

"No, Justine, I'm sorry," he cut her off. "I fucked up with Allison and..."

"That was no excuse for what I did. I should have never taken it that far."

"I've had worse."

As soon as he'd said it, Justine envisioned some of the things Alex had told her Mark's foster father had done to him, and felt the tears returning. How could she have done this to him? "From an animal and...." She put her head down. "One that I'm no better than."

"It's okay, Justine." Mark put his hands on her face and lifted it to look at him. "I'm okay and I started this. If I didn't screw up it wouldn't have come to this."

"I crossed the line, Mark, I hurt you and I could have done worse, you...."

"Okay," he said. Stopping her with a finger to her lips he said, "I screwed up, you screwed up, so how about we start over from here?"

"Do you..." She struggled to keep her voice steady. "Forgive me?"

He shrugged. "You did what you had to..."

"No, I did what I wanted to and for the wrong reasons. And yes, you screwed up, Mark, but nothing like what I did to you."

"Well as you said, we will speak of it no more." He removed his hand from her face and rubbed his eyes. "But I'm going to go while I can still see to drive."

He began to slide past her, but she stopped him with her hand on his shoulder. "Please stay with me tonight," she whispered.

"I thought I wasn't allowed that privilege anymore."

"That's what Scarlett said," she told him, kissing his cheek. "But I've had enough of that bitch tonight and Justine would love you to stay."

* * *

The pattern on the ceiling created by the flickering candles changed slightly as one of them began to sputter. Justine turned her head to watch the tiny flame struggle to survive before finally winking out. Her eyes then wandered over to the clock and saw it was nine fifty. They had come into the bedroom at just after nine and she was still wide awake. She shouldn't be, she was physically exhausted and emotionally drained. After Mark had told her he would spend the night with her, they had remained in the shower and washed each other. Mark had already showered and had just been letting the hot water work into his throbbing muscles, but let Justine wash him again.

They had then switched and, in addition to taking his time lathering and rinsing her, Mark had also washed her hair for her. They didn't play, in fact, neither of them was aroused. It was more like they were using the shower to convince each other everything would be okay. Justine gently caressed his skin, trying to make up for hurting him and she knew Mark was taking his time to comfort her. When they finished, Justine led him to her room, but again there was nothing sexual in the act, she wanted him to rest.

Telling him to lie on his stomach, Justine massaged his back and shoulders, trying to ease the tension out of his muscles. After awhile he did seem to relax and, rolling over onto his back, had said he thought he could sleep. Justine lay down next to him, and had been staring at the ceiling ever since. Her bare shoulder was touching his and she fought the urge to roll over and put her arm around his waist. She told herself that was so as not to wake him, but she knew the real reason was she was afraid of him rejecting her. Why should he want to be close to her?

Justine closed her eyes and tried to match her breathing to Mark's slow deep breaths. She tried to relax and tell herself to sleep. The real reason she couldn't sleep was she wanted to talk to him, but after all she had put him through wanted him to sleep. She could wait until morning, well obviously not, but she would. She could feel the length of her soft leg pressed against his and thought disgustedly this was not how she had envisioned him in her bed tonight. They should have been fucking and playing all night, then collapsing close together and sleeping until they could start again the next morning.

"Can't sleep?" Mark spoke next to her.

"How did you know I was awake?" she asked, turning her head towards him. "I haven't moved."

"I could sense it," he replied as he turned to look at her, then with a grin added, "Besides, you usually snore when you first fall asleep."

"I don't snore," she told him indignantly.

"Of course you don't. You just breathe heavy."

Justine rolled her eyes and prepared to reply, but he spoke first. "Do you want to talk?"

"I do," she admitted. "You really do know me better than anyone."

"Then why not talk?"

"I wanted you to try to sleep, did you at all?"

"No." He sighed. "It's been like this for a week. My eyes are stinging, my body feels like it's ready to shut down, but..." He shrugged. "Thing with insomnia is, the more tired you get the more wired you get."

"So you don't mind if we talk?" she asked.

"Not at all," he said and, using his elbows, pushed himself higher up onto the pillows. "On one condition."

"What's that?"

"You don't apologize again."

"I…,okay," she agreed. "You either."

"Fair enough."

Rolling over on her side, Justine propped herself up on one elbow. As she did, the sheet slid away and she felt her right breast resting against his chest. She saw his eyes drift down to it and linger there. She still wasn't in the mood, but it was good to see him noticing.

"Mark I…" She paused to make sure she took her time and picked her words carefully. "I'm already going to go against my words and apologize." He rolled his eyes and she put her hand on his chest. "Because I want to explain why I'm sorry. When I punished you, I got carried away, not because I was that mad at what you did, but because…." She looked down. "You were right."

"I don't think anything I did was right with…"

"You were right when you said I was jealous of Allison. That's why I got so upset. Not only was I jealous, but I was angry you saw it."

"Why would you be jealous of Allison?" he asked. "You have a hell of a lot more going for you than she does."

"I was jealous because you shared things with her. You just met her and were telling her things about your past."

"Justine." Mark rolled over onto his side so he was facing her. "I didn't go into details with her, I just pretty much told her I had it pretty rough and really had no family growing up. I've told you as much."

"No, Mark, I've heard it from Alex, who's your best friend, and heard it second hand from your sister. You volunteered this to her. Then proceeded to not only break the rules, but…." She took a breath as she prepared to admit more to him than she would have had tonight not happened. "When you said you were sweet with her, it upset me."

"I…I wasn't myself," he told her. "And why would that bother you anyway? I didn't think you were the loving type."

"Well I…." She hesitated, then seeing no way around it, just went ahead. "There've been times I feel I wouldn't mind it. Then I get pissed at myself for wanting it, then pissed that I was pissed."

"Funny, I never pegged you for over thinking things."

"I never used to, because I always knew what I wanted. Now sometimes, I'm just not so sure." Putting her hand on his chest, she looked into his eyes as she continued. "I've felt that we're more than friends, Mark, and sometimes even more than lovers. I feel very close to you at times and….I know you have pets sometimes and do whoever you want, but being that way with Allison just got to me."

"You are special to me, Justine," Mark said softly, putting his hand over hers. "But I was never going to say it. You've always made it seem that any time we're together could be the last and I've just gone along."

"Thank you for saying that."." she told him. "It makes the next part of what I'm going to say easier." She looked down again before going on. "You've been the only man I've slept with for the last six months. The last person I was with before you was the kid I picked up at a bar to use for my entertainment video."

"I…why?" he asked.

"Because as I get older, it's not about the chase or kill for me anymore and the game is getting old. I'm forty eight and have been dominating men for thirty years. I find myself wondering where Scarlett ends and Justine begins. In two years, I'll find out for sure, but for right now I'm both and I find I enjoy being with you more and more as Justine."

"I know what you mean," he said softly. "There's times, even with pets, I feel like letting up and catch myself and keep going with the game, like I'm letting myself down. I like that we don't always play the game, but never said anything because I didn't know how you'd take it."

Speaking of how he was going to take it, Justine reversed her hand in his so she could hold it and leaning closer to him whispered, "Mark, I really care about you." He started to speak, but she went on quickly. "I know tonight was a terrible way to show that, but I want you to know I consider you more than a lover, you're very dear to me."

Mark looked away from her and she hoped to hell she hadn't made a fool of herself. Bringing her hand up, Mark kissed the back of it and, holding it to his cheek, said quietly, "Thank you for telling me. I… I haven't heard that from too many people."

"The reason I'm telling you this, is because…" She sighed. "Mark, you need help. You've been having a lot of these bouts lately, more nightmares and your behavior is….sometimes I swear you're two different people."

"I'm okay, Justine, I'll sleep sooner or later and…."

"You screwed up badly with Allison, but that was a mistake within the group. What happens if you screw up a client's case, or worse if you lose control?" She squeezed his hand again. "Mark, you can be dangerous when you're like this and you know it. You aren't a kid anymore. You got a second chance after Max. You fuck up now, and you're done."

"I know what I'm doing, Justine," he told her. "If it gets…."

"If it gets bad enough you'll what? Work from home like you did a couple of months ago? When you were so on edge you were afraid to be around anyone? Hell, Mark, you avoided Stephanie for a week because you were afraid you were going to hurt her."

He looked away from her and she realized her voice was rising. Lowering it, she continued. "Mark, please promise me you'll go talk to someone. I know you get that woe is me attitude, but I just told you how I feel. Alex is like a brother to you and I know he's worried too. Victoria, Amado, the rest of the group, you have a lot of friends, you don't have to battle your demons alone." Mark sighed and nodded. "I mean it, and I'm going to say one thing that pertains to the Circle, then let it go."

"Go ahead."

"I step down in two years. If you're still this erratic, I'll have you step down before I do. I won't leave it to Alex to have to make that decision. It wouldn't be fair to him and I doubt he could do it."

"But you can."

"If need be." Taking her hand from his, she placed it on his cheek. "But I want you to be okay because I care and never want it to come to that. Please, Mark?" she kissed him on the cheek. "Promise me you'll at least look into medication."

His eyes seemed to darken, but he nodded. "Okay, I'll call my doctor. I promise."

"Thank you and please know you can talk to me."

"I'm sorry, if I hurt your feelings, Justine," Mark began. "I just don't tell people my baggage, I don't want pity."

"A friends help is not pity," She pointed out.

"Okay." Taking her hand again he kissed it and said softly, "What would you like to know? I'll tell you."

"You don't have to," she protested, even though she immediately knew what she wanted to ask.

"Going once, going…."

"Who was she?" she blurted out.

"Why do you…" Mark stopped as he caught himself getting defensive again and, rolling over onto his back, folded his arms behind his head and stared up at the ceiling. Justine didn't speak as she watched him stare at the flickering candle light as she had done. In a moment he started speaking softly. "I won't say her name, but I'll tell you the story."

"You know you really don't have to if it's that painful."

"I met her when I was a teenager and we were attracted to each other from the beginning," he began. "I had a lot of issues and was afraid to speak to anyone, but she was patient and had some issues of her own. When I did start speaking, we'd talk for hours. We began to get close."

"How old were you?"

"Sixteen when we met, but by the time I began to realize how I felt about her I was almost eighteen. After a while I began to feel more and more towards her. There was one particular time I remember we looked into each other's eyes and I knew I was in love with her."

He paused and Justine waited with mixed emotions. She knew this was something he didn't like to speak of, but excited too, after all this time, finally here was something about his past.

"Was she in love with you?" she asked when he still hadn't spoken.

"I…I thought so. I didn't say it just in case and wondered if she felt the same. We carried on awhile longer like that. Spending a lot of time together, doing everything a couple would do, except sleeping together. She had been sexually abused at one point and had issues with men, so I'd never pushed. But eventually I decided to make a move and find out once and for all."

"What did you do?"

"I'd still been living with my foster parents who, because of certain issues, wouldn't have approved of her."

"Did your sister like her?" Justine interrupted.

"Megan…" He stopped and she saw he was getting that going away look in his eyes. "She encouraged it, yes."

"Well you said she looked out for you, so this girl must've been good to you."

"I was totally enamored by her. I'd been working at a bar and there were a couple of burned out apartments over it. To make some extra money, I helped the owner fix them up to rent them. I talked him into renting one to me.

"I didn't tell her about it. I wanted to get moved in then take her out and surprise her. Just as I was finishing the place up, I got a letter from Suffolk saying if my grades stayed what they were in my final year of PC, I was guaranteed acceptance with a full scholarship. So I told her we were going out on Friday night to celebrate. I told her to dress nice because I was taking her somewhere special and had another surprise for her."

Justine felt herself already feeling bad as she knew this was obviously not going to end well.

"So I dressed up in my best suit and when I picked her up she was wearing this gorgeous black and red dress, my two favorite colors on her."

"What did she look…." Justine caught herself as soon as she began, as she remembered how they had gotten here in the first place.

Mark turned his head to look at her. "Really Justine?"

"Sorry, I was getting caught up in the story."

"Picture a young Allison with blue eyes," he said before once again turning his gaze to the ceiling. "I took her to the best restaurant in the state. It cost me a week's pay, but was worth every cent. Here we were two kids, hell I had to use a fake ID, and we were sitting there dressed up surrounded by all these older people, who were staring at us all night. We ordered prime rib and drank wine and talked about our futures."

Justine noticed he began to smile and his eyes seemed out of focus as if he were not seeing the ceiling, but looking back into the past.

"Everything was perfect, especially her. She'd always been beautiful, but that night she was just... stunning. And the way she was looking at me, I could see it in her eyes she felt the same way about me."

Apparently not, Justine thought as he paused.

"They had a big dance floor and we went out there and showed off. Even the way we danced was perfect. The way our bodies moved together. They played a slow song, and we held each other close and...." He laughed softly. "There's that corny expression about getting lost in someone's eyes, but damn if it wasn't true.

"I leaned in and kissed her. I could feel it, I could feel how much we wanted each other. We left the restaurant and drove back to my new place. The entire ride, she was curled up next to me and I was so excited."

He stopped and she noticed the smile was gone from his face.

"I was going to show her my place and tell her it could be our place, she could move in and...." He sighed, "But obviously that didn't happen. Instead...." He stopped and Justine put her hand on his chest.

"You don't have to finish, I can kind of figure that...."

"I show her the place," he spoke up. "And she seems thrilled. I had bought some champagne and we had a drink and then I took her into my bedroom." He closed his eyes, but continued to speak. "I came up behind her and moved her hair, kissed her neck, those perfect creamy white shoulders. She relaxed against me, and I undid her dress and let it fall."

Justine realized her breathing was getting heavier as she envisioned Mark as a good looking young man, slowly stripping this gorgeous girl and not to fuck her, but to be loving and affectionate, to claim the woman he had so desired. To her surprise, she felt a very familiar warm sensation between her legs.

"I kissed her back and got on my knees, then I kissed her thighs and the small of her back, her perfect little ass and she was moving her hips and breathing heavy. I stood up and she turned into me and we started kissing. Just like on the dance floor. I was so happy, I was finally going to have her the way I wanted to. She was going to give me the chance to show how I really felt, then...."

Justine leaned in closer to him and could feel her now erect nipple pressing into his side. She wondered if he had stopped because of that, but saw he had a pained expression on his face. She was going to tell him again to stop, but he spoke and as he did, she could hear he was fighting against the emotion he felt.

"To this day I don't know why, but she backed off, said we couldn't. That she'd bring me down and cost me my future. She put her dress back on, kissed my cheek and told me she'd go downstairs and call a cab to take her home."

"You didn't take her home?"

"I offered, well after I pretty much begged her to stay with me. I didn't care about money or a career, I just wanted her." He opened his eyes and Justine saw they were moist. "But she was adamant and I could see tears in her eyes. I knew she loved me, but was convinced she was somehow saving me from her problems." He sighed. "A year later I came within an inch of going to jail for attempted murder, so she really spared me."

"That kiss at the end of the initiation," Justine said as she began to lightly trail her nails across his chest. "You were thinking of her weren't you?"

"Yeah, I was going for a quick peck, but I... when I felt her lips, I just went soft and enjoyed it a little too much."

Justine didn't respond as she struggled to hold back her body's responses. She was amazed she was turned on, but there was something about picturing Mark that young and vulnerable. The way he had mentioned taking her the way he had wanted, and not the kind of taking they were used to doing had sent a shiver through her. She envisioned him with his sweetheart, not rough, but soft. Her legs were closed and she could feel how wet she was.

"I knew it was a mistake telling Allison she could stay with me. I was setting myself up to fall. Then at dinner, she got upset and I comforted her and she..." He let out a breath. "She's beautiful and I played right into her. When we got back to my place I knew if I didn't walk away from her it'd be all over, but I just stood there. I wanted her to seduce me. I was so tired and drunk and..."

"Let it go, baby," she said softly as her hand trailed down his stomach.

"When we fell asleep and I woke up, I was so out of it and I saw her next to me and I thought of that night, about what I wanted to do with ..." He trailed off.

Justine stopped moving her hand and, pressing closer to him, kissed his chest. "Thank you for sharing that with me."

"Not the type of story we would tell around the table, that's for sure."

"We're not at the table, Mark." She kissed his chest again, and then looked up to see him staring off. She could feel he was still tense and decided to put him at ease. "I've decided not to ask Allison to leave."

Mark's eyes snapped back into focus as he turned to look at her. "Thank you, Justine," he said and, bending his head, kissed her cheek. "She'll be fine and...."

"What I am going to go to do is tell Victoria what happened."

"Why?"

"Allison will need to be warned. If it comes from me, she'll think I went soft on her. I'm going to tell Victoria to tell her that you were upset and went to her. She'll deliver the warning to and it will seem as if I didn't know."

"Will she?"

"Victoria still feels she owes you for what you did to avenge her. She offered to thank you and you turned her down, and I have to admit even I never understood that."

"She was ready to leave," Mark reminded her. "And not just over what that prick did to her. She felt betrayed because she's been pledged several times, then punished when she complained and her punishment was out of line. So even though she offered her body as a reward, I didn't want her to think it was all we wanted her for, so I passed."

Justine smiled and fondly touched his cheek. "And that's why you've been honored to be with some of the women you have. You understand the game isn't just played in the bedroom. You get more waiting than chasing. That's the Mark I know and want to see back again."

"So she'll do it?" he asked again.

"Victoria is loyal to both her Mistress and the Circle. And," She smiled. "She's already taken quite a liking to Allison. They're in the same industry and work close by. Victoria's dying to go shopping and have lunch and drive the guys crazy with her. She'll take care of this." She sighed. "However, she's shrewd and there'll be a price, but I'll meet it."

"Again, thank you, Justine."

"I think I punished you enough, and I didn't want you to be responsible for Allison. You've put it on the line for the group many times, the least I can do the same for you."

Mark nodded and, looked back up at the ceiling. Justine could feel him relax and saw he had closed his eyes. As much as she wanted him, she knew she was being selfish. Justine knew she really wanted him so she would feel better. She wanted to know he would still desire her and want to enjoy her. She had never been one for patience, especially when it came to sex, but seeing his eyes closed and knowing how bad he needed to sleep, she told herself could wait until morning.

In fact, as she reached out and put her arm around his waist, she realized it would mean even more, if after what she had just done, he could trust her enough to fall asleep with her. Mark opened his eyes part way and turned to look at her.

"You can't sleep?" she asked, thinking so much for that last thought.

"Not yet."

Mark put his arm out along the pillows and patted his chest. Justine hesitated, but only briefly. Sliding down, she rested her head on his chest and sighed as he put his arm around her shoulders and pulled her close. She kissed his chest and thought again about how damn good he felt, and how there was now no denying there was more between them than either of them seemed to want to admit. Or was it they were afraid to? On her end, she was the Mistress. She also had no clue what love or real affection felt like. But Mark did know, he may have been little more than a kid, but he had known love, meaning he would recognize it again. That gave him an advantage between them and...she stopped on the word advantage, there she was thinking everything was a game.

Justine forced herself to stop thinking about it. She would definitely have to sort this out and decide what she wanted to do. It was coming down to either back off from Mark, or take it to another level, one that she had never been interested in before. But for tonight all that mattered was they were in her bed and from his breathing he seemed to be asleep. In the morning she would take her time and they would play and enjoy. Then he would go home and she would have a big decision to make.

Chapter Five

With a sense of relief, Justine saw the exit that led to Madison Avenue where Orion Software's corporate office was located. Although she'd started her drive from Boston at six am, it was now one o'clock and her nerves were on edge. The initial part of the ride had been enjoyable. There was hardly any traffic and Justine had the top down on her 2010 black Porsche Boxster and had aired it out, doing over ninety. She'd felt like a teenager, enjoying her long hair blowing behind her, as she weaved in and out of the lanes.

Halfway though Connecticut, the traffic started. By the time Justine had finally made it into New York she ended up in dead stop on the GW Bridge and her mood had darkened. She'd had to put her hair up, due to the heat, then eventually succumbed and put the top up so she could turn the air conditioning on. By then, no longer able to help it, she began to dwell on the reasons for her trip to see Alex in the first place.

The first was for him to look at the phone. Although she had taken today off to go see Alex, she had called in and tech was still saying they were having a hard time working out the audio bugs. In order to have the phone into mass production and in stores for Black Friday, they had two weeks to figure it out and Justine was taking no chances. The second reason was she needed to talk to him about what she had found out about Mark on Friday night.

After they had fallen asleep in each other's arms, Justine had woken up and having to use the bathroom, reluctantly slid from his embrace. He had started to wake up, but she sat next to him and lightly ran her fingers through his hair until he turned his head into the pillow and gone back to sleep. Justine had left the room and walking naked through the apartment, went into the bathroom. On her way back, she stopped in the living room and, as was her habit, checked her phone for e-mails. They were doing a lot of business overseas and she would get messages at all hours of the night.

She sat on the edge of the couch scanning through several messages and, after sending off a couple of quick replies, put her phone down and started to get up. Mark's phone then began to ring on the coffee table. The ring tone was Evanescence *My Immortal* and out of curiosity she picked up the phone to see who was calling him at one a.m. His phone was set up with a picture to identify the caller and as her eyes focused, she let out a surprised breath. She was looking at the woman Mark had told her about. It had to be her, the woman, who appeared to be in her thirties, had long black hair, skin so fair it was close to white and a pair of stunning crystal blue eyes. She was smiling and Justine noticed that her lips were large and full. Except for the eyes and a thinner face, she could be Allison's sister.

The song stopped and Justine started to put the phone down, when she caught the missed call message on the screen. Megan. Justine felt her stomach clutch and continued to stare at the phone. Mark's sister. Looking over her shoulder to make sure he wasn't coming out of the room looking for her, Justine went into his phone and, bringing up Megan's name, stared again at the photo. There was no doubt who she was, she resembled Mark quite closely, especially the cheek bones, and the number had a Chicago area code. Putting the phone down, Justine thought of the song, *My Immortal*, she had the CD somewhere and recalled some of the lyrics.

When you cried I'd wipe away all of your tears
When you'd scream I'd fight away all of your fears
And I held your hand through all of these years
But you still have
All of me

She couldn't remember the whole song, but another stanza came to her.

You used to captivate me
By your resonating light
Now I'm bound by the life you left behind

"Oh my God," Justine whispered. Mark had been, or maybe even still was, in love with his sister, had been since he was a teenager. As soon as that thought struck her, she replayed the story he had told her and an even more disturbing thought entered her mind. Mark had tried to seduce his sister that night at his apartment.

As Justine took the exit that led her into the heart of New York City, her mind kept dwelling on that thought. Mark had mentioned his foster parents would have had issues with his being with her, well no wonder, it was their daughter. It also made sense Megan had backed out when Mark had tried to seal the deal with her. They were siblings and would have been caught. From what little Justine knew of Mark's sister she had been heavily addicted to drugs and alcohol as early as her later teens. That explained the end to Mark's story, even if his sister was in love with him, he was heading for Suffolk and she was going downhill fast, she cut him loose.

She shook her head as she stopped at a red light and wondered if there was something still going on there. Mark hadn't been right since his sister had gone to Chicago. Alex had pointed out the two were close and watched out for each other. Close was not the word. Although she tried not to dwell on it, Justine kept wondering if Mark hadn't filtered his story. What if the two of them were having sex? No, she told herself for the hundredth time, he hadn't crossed that line, but not for lack of wanting to. Besides, Mark would have followed her to Chicago if he were truly still in love with her. God only knew The Lady Persephone would kick a member out of her group to make room for him.

She was snapped out of her thoughts by the ring of her Circle phone. Justine managed a smile as *"You're so Vain"* played. Victoria had been appalled Justine had picked that song for her, which of course meant that she would never change it. "Hello, My High Lady,"

"Good afternoon, My Mistress," Victoria's sultry voice purred in her ear. "I was calling to see if you're still planning on being here for three."

"I am. Got stuck in traffic, but Alex doesn't have a lot of time, so I'm sure I'll be there."

"Good, because I'm having my masseuse come by with one of her best people. I figure a massage, a soak in the hot tub, and then we can discuss business and grab some dinner. I made reservations at Balthazar for seven."

"I appreciate that, Lady Felicia, but after all that, I'm not going to be in any shape for a six hour drive home."

"Then you can stay and leave in the morning."

"Leave when, at three a.m.?"

"My Mistress works hard and could use a day of being spoiled. You can go in late on Tuesday," Victoria responded.

"I don't know."

"Please?" Victoria purred. "I'd so enjoy some time together. We've had very little of late and I'd love to treat you to a good time."

Justine paused. Maybe she would take her up on that. She could use it with everything going on and work was about to start getting crazy again. As she thought, Justine idly imagined Victoria purring into a man's ear like that. Her voice alone could weaken the knees of any man, never mind her looks. "Okay," she said into the phone. "I'll take you up on your most gracious offer. Thank you, My Lady."

"Thank you, for allowing me. I'll see you at three."

Justine hung up and sighed, two difficult conversations back to back. She had originally thought the one with Victoria would be tough, but now she was going to ask Alex if he knew anything about Mark and his sister, and if he did what the hell should she do about it.

* * *

Alex was waiting for her when she stepped off the elevator and greeted her with his trademark big smile and a kiss on the cheek. Justine gave him a forced smile in return and, putting his hands on her shoulders he said, "You look tired, Justine, everything okay?"

"Unfortunately no." She shrugged. "Or maybe. I'm not sure yet."

The smile left his face and he nodded. Taking her arm, they walked down the corridor and through the waiting area of his office. She noticed several people looking at them, and had no doubt they were thinking she was his latest fling. For her to still look good enough at her age to be considered an interest of a renowned playboy was fine with her. They entered his office and, after walking her over to one of the comfortable recliners in the middle of the room, Alex went over to the bar. A moment later, he came back, handed her a martini and, sitting across from her, took a sip of scotch.

"So, I take it this is a business meeting,"

"I need to discuss a couple of things," she replied after sipping her drink. "One, I suppose is a Circle favor, the second's technically business as well, but I want it off the record."

"Fair enough."

"First the favor." Reaching into her purse, she produced the prototype phone and held it up.

Alex's electric blue eyes widened. "Is that?"

"It is," she leaned forward and handed it to him across the table.

"This is nice," he said hitting the touch screen "Fantastic resolution."

"Well it's yours for a few days, but it's a prototype so don't pull it apart unless you can get it back together." Alex was staring intently at the phone, going through the options. As he did, he began to smile and she swore he was fondling the keyboard. "Need a minute?"

"Sorry," he said still not looking up. "Guess I'm just a geek at heart."

"Good, because I need you to try to fix something on it."

"What's that?"

"Call Alex," she said in a normal tone. When nothing happened, she repeated herself a little louder. The third time she shouted and a moment later his phone began to ring on his hip.

"I see."

"The tech guys haven't got it working yet and we have two weeks to not fall behind on production."

"I don't see where it'd be hard." He shrugged. "It has to work on the same principle as speech to text software. The volume sensor just needs tweaking." He looked up at her. "Will anyone's voice activate it?"

"Nope just the owner's." She smiled. "It needs a voice code to unlock; no one aside from the owner can get it to work, so if it gets lost no one can use it. Unless they can imitate your voice, even a hacker can't jailbreak this thing."

"Want to test that?" he asked. "Once I'm done with it I can give it to Loki. If he can't get in, no one can, and if he can, he'll tell you how."

"Okay, what about the bug with the voice?"

"I'll give it back to you at the meeting. Or maybe even earlier." Getting up, he walked over to his desk and, going into the bottom drawer, brought out a small metal box. "You want to come over here and talk, while I fool around with this?"

"Can't wait can you?" she asked as she stood and making her way over to the desk sat in one of the leather chairs in front of it. "You know they said it would take days."

"They also want job security," Alex said. "If tech fixed everything quickly, they'd be afraid they wouldn't be needed, plus they like drama. I wouldn't be surprised if your team doesn't already know the problem."

"I don't know about that. If they miss the date I've told them they won't have jobs."

"They'll solve it with a day to spare and look like heroes." He laughed. "Trust me I know these types."

He had opened the box and, removing a small adaptor, connected it into the phone. He pulled out a small device that looked like a calculator and plugged the phone into it, then hooked that into his laptop. "So what else did you want to talk about?" he asked as a bunch of codes appeared on the laptop.

"I'd really like your full attention on this, Alex."

"You'll have it. The diagnostics will take awhile to run."

"What is that?" She pointed at the small device. "I'm sure my tech guys have one."

"No they don't." He smiled. "I designed this and its one of a kind.. That is until I unleash it next year and try to sell it to the military."

"Yourself, or will you let Amado's family do it? They have government contacts."

"I'll try myself first." He grinned. "Although I'd love to meet Amado's sister again."

"Behave yourself, Orion," Justine told him. "Family members are off the table."

"Of course."

The word family brought her back to why she was there and, taking a long swallow of her drink, Justine sighed. "Alex I need to talk to you about Mark."

"Oh, for Christ's sake, what the hell did he do now?"

"It's not so much about now as before. You know Alex; you broke a lot of rules getting him in the group."

"Just the age."

"No, his record."

"I didn't hide that. What I did was explain the circumstances and say it was an aberration."

"You left out he had a sister. One that had a history of serious drug abuse."

"Not my fault the vetter's couldn't find that out." He shrugged.

"You knew they had different last names, and his mother didn't put his father on the birth certificate. You knew and didn't say anything because he wouldn't have gotten in."

"That's a bullshit rule," Alex said. "So anyone who has a family member who's been in trouble can't join? That shouldn't be a reflection on the candidate."

"It's a rule because those fucked up family members have access to the member's households and could find out things about other members. That's why the rule exists."

"Whatever." He put his hands out. "Are you going to toss Mark now over it? He's been in for almost ten years." He frowned. "Unless you feel you need to. What the hell did he do?"

"Back at the hotel a couple of weeks ago, when we were discussing Allison, you made a crack at Mark, asked him who she looked like."

"I remember." His eyes narrowed and Justine knew his wheels were already spinning.

"Well I want to know who it was."

"Oh, no one." He waved his hand. "I was just fucking with him, you know how we are."

"It got a pretty good reaction out of him and you commented it was funny how he knew who you were talking about."

"Just some old flame he had." Alex laughed. "He was soft on someone once and I like to make…."

"I'm going to ask again, but this time I'm going to add that I already know the answer, so one more time Alex, who is she?"

"If you know, then why are you asking?" He raised his eyebrows. "I'm not that easy, Justine."

"I'm done playing games." She pointed at him. "It was his sister Megan you were talking about. Wasn't it?" Alex blinked and she knew she was right. She waited as she saw him thinking and felt her stomach sink. He knew something and was going to try to cover it up. "Well?"

"Yeah, it's his sister." He sighed. "Why are you asking this?"

"You know Mark and I spend a lot of time together."

"I do." He rolled his eyes.

"Oh, get over it." Justine snapped. "I was upset the other night because he never tells me anything about his past."

"The other night? This an every week thing?"

"None of your business," she replied. "He's been having trouble sleeping and he's not himself. So we got in an argument and I told him I felt he didn't trust me. One of the things I'd asked him was who the girl Allison reminded him of was."

"Why?" Alex asked. "Nothing went wrong at the initiation did it?"

Justine cursed at herself for walking into that one. This was Alex's game, make a couple of comments to get you annoyed then wait for you to screw up.

"There's a moment at the end where he welcomes her that I found odd. He kissed her and there seemed to be more behind it than there should've been. I remembered your remark and asked. He didn't answer and that led to the fight."

"A lover's spat?"

"Alex, I'll share my bed with whom I choose. It's not my fault you're a better politician within the group than a lover."

"Ouch," he said simply. "Of course, you've never given me a chance."

"I've seen your videos." She smirked. "I'm not missing out."

Alex grunted and looked back over at the computer screen which had stopped running numbers and typed something into it. There was a beep from the phone and the codes began running again. "So he tells you a story," he prompted.

"He tells me about this girl he fell in love with. Claims she loved him as well, but when he tried to make it official, she backs off and tells him they can't."

"And you think this was his sister why?"

"Because it started with him saying she looked just like Allison, but with blue eyes. Later on I get up and his sister's calling. I look down and there's a blue eyed brunette that could pass for Allison. It became pretty obvious. What really disturbs me is I keep wondering if there was more, and he was watering it down, I wonder if he...." She paused, "Crossed the line."

"You think Mark was having sex with his sister?" Alex shook his head. "Really, Justine?"

"It was her, Alex. And he's been a wreck since she left."

"That's because they've always been close and she understands him. Now he feels alone," Alex pointed out.

"So then who was this girl?"

Alex sat back and, after glancing over at the computer again, frowned and shook his head. "Okay, I'm going to tell you a story now."

"I'm listening."

"Back when Mark almost killed Max. I.... I thought he was fucking his sister as well."

"Why did you think that?" she asked, surprised he was giving up this easily.

"I always thought the two of them were too close. When we would go out and drink, she'd get pretty wasted and start hanging on him." He shrugged. "It didn't seem right. I swore there were times I'd see him checking her out."

He paused as the computer beeped again and, using just his left hand, he began typing as he continued to speak. "Remember, they didn't grow up together. They were separated as kids and next time he sees Megan she's eighteen and she's gorgeous. He also admitted to me at one point that she'd sleep in his bed sometimes when he had nightmares."

"You said you thought he was, as in you found out differently?" She felt her stomach settling down, she wanted to believe she was wrong, but couldn't see how.

"When Mark lost it and went crazy on that animal, he was put in an institution for a week. His sister had talked me into helping him. I wasn't going to, I mean...." Alex let out a breath. "Christ, Justine, he bit piece of the guy's face off."

"Jesus," she whispered.

"But Megan told me everything Max had done to him, and when she saw me undecided, she even tried to offer me sex."

"And you didn't take it?" she asked, raising her eyebrows.

"Please, I'm not that bad. Anyway I agreed, but couldn't do anything because he wouldn't speak. Finally we go see him together and she gets him to start speaking. I posted bail and I had him come stay with me for the trial, keep him away from the press and out of trouble."

"Smart." She nodded.

"Now he would he'd only talk to Megan. It was crazy, the lawyer would ask a question he'd stare at him. Megan would ask the question he'd answer. So I decided to have her stay with me as well. I had enough room and Mark needed her."

He stopped and frowned at the computer screen. He started typing again, and Justine snapped, "Forget about the phone, Alex!"

He typed for another few seconds then turned back to her. "I was always a night owl, so two in the morning, I'm still up watching TV. A few times Megan comes out of her room and seems nervous when she sees me. Sometimes she sits and watches TV with me, sometimes goes to the bathroom and back to her room. I figured something was up. It's not like I would've cared if she went in to check on him."

"So you thought there was something going on?"

"Yes, and I set her up. I decided to go to bed early one night. Sure enough, I come out at one and she's not in her room. I go over to his door, but don't hear anything. I'm thinking maybe she's laying down with him, like when they were younger, trying to comfort him. So I go to bed, then get up at five to go jogging."

"Bed at one, jogging at five?" She shook her head.

"Hey I've worked hard for this body." He laughed.

"Oh, jeez." She waved her hand at him.

"I thought I'd see if Mark was up. I'd been trying to get him to do something besides sleep and stare off into space. I go to knock and I stop when I hear…moaning."

"Moaning?"

"Yes, and that kind of moaning. I listen closer and I swear I hear her squealing, but muffled, like maybe in a pillow. I stay there and a few minutes later the door opens and she starts to come out, when she sees me there she goes white as a ghost."

"Did you ask her what she was doing?"

"I did and she's stuttering and I know, Justine." He put his hands out. "Her robe is barely closed and her tits are all but falling out. She's sweating and she's scared as hell. I keep pushing and she says they were wrestling. I ask if she always wrestles with nothing on under her robe and she's really flustered, starts to cry. Then Mark comes out and starts in on me. I start to say something and realize he's talking. So I back off and I go jogging thinking big sis snapped him out of it by fucking him."

"God, this is sick."

"Now he's back to normal, working with the lawyer and we're trying to figure out how he is getting out of this. We decide Mark is going to say he didn't know who Max was, that his mind was so traumatized he blocked him out. Problem is they'd want him to take a polygraph. My lawyer gets us into his office late at night and we're going to practice. Well it's not going well. Mark couldn't so much as lie about the color of his eyes without that thing going off."

He stopped as the computer began beeping again. Justine rolled her eyes and waited for him to type something into it. This time he spoke as he looked at the screen.

"The lawyer's ready to call it quits, but Mark wants to keep trying. The lawyer goes outside to have a smoke and I suggest we try it with just me. Maybe he'd be more relaxed. So I start asking him things and all the lies are showing up. Then I start playing games, I ask him if he's ever kissed his sister."

"And his answer?"

Alex laughed. "He said, 'of course, she's my sister.' Even back then Mark was a good game player." He stopped typing and shook his head as the computer beeped angrily at him. Turning back to her he went on. "I ask if he slept with her and he said yes when he had nightmares. Meantime Megan is getting nervous and starting up with me."

"Mark's pissed, which is how I want him. I lower the boom and point blank ask if he's fucking his sister. He flips out and almost swings at me. She's crying and I think I got them. Then he sits down, stares at me and tells me he has never fucked his sister. The needle doesn't budge and he goes into a laundry list of sex. 'I've never fucked my sister; she has never sucked my cock.' He's going right down the line and everything's normal."

Justine looked down and felt herself relaxing. She'd been wrong or at least partially, maybe he had been in love with his sister, but he hadn't been sleeping with her.

"I feel like an asshole, and then Mark jumps up and attacks me, we fight and if his sister wasn't there to get between us, I think he might've killed me." He shook his head. "Mark really is nuts, Justine. It's buried further these days, but he can be flat out dangerous."

"So if Mark couldn't lie through the test, how did he get off? He must've failed the polygraph when they gave it to him."

Alex paused and seemed confused. He thought, then with a shrug said, "The reason he got off is the judge was crooked, knew I was involved and had my lawyer approach me about a bribe." He sighed. "I got Mark off for attempted murder, which he was guilty of, for ten thousand dollars."

"Okay," Justine nodded. "Alex, I don't want to believe that about Mark, but there's one problem here."

"Which is?"

"How the hell does someone fall in love with their sibling in the first place? More so, do you think it's still going on? His feelings I mean?"

"Justine, Mark was very sick back then. He was delusional. He had a psychotic break when Max put him into that coma, wouldn't speak for months after he came out of it. He was lost in his own head. It happened again after he almost killed Max. I don't know what it is, but I know he has a prescription that he takes. He gets it under another name and I can't find out what it's for. But you've seen him even now do that going away thing."

"So you think he's sick?"

"I think he goes off the meds from time to time and he still has night terrors and insomnia." Alex sighed. "Mark is brilliant, Justine. He's the best lawyer on the east coast, and he's tested at a gifted level his whole life, but he's fucked up. His sister is the only person he responds to when he's like that. I doubt there's anything there beyond her being his security blanket, which is now living a thousand miles away from him."

"I just…." She shrugged. "It hit me really hard Alex. That'd be pretty twisted and you know with the group, I'd have to…."

"He's not, Justine, and I doubt he ever did. He might still have some kind of unrequited love for her, and when he gets into his funks it might bring it up, but I know for a fact he wasn't committing incest."

Justine nodded and let out a deep breath. "Thank you Alex. I needed to hear that."

"No problem. He looked at the computer and, as he started typing, asked, "You didn't say anything to him did you?"

"No. I… pretended everything was okay and we fooled around in the morning and he stayed Saturday and went home Sunday. It was killing me, but I wanted to be sure first. I'm glad I did."

"All weekend?" He sighed. "Pays to garner pity I guess."

"And jealousy will never pay out," she replied. "I told him to get some help and I want you to go to Rhode Island and meet up with him and suggest it as well."

"He'll be fine, Justine," Alex told her. "He always is."

"I hope you're right." Looking at her watch she saw it was already two fifteen. "I have to get going, I'm meeting Victoria at three for some girl time as she calls it."

"Can I see pics of that?" He laughed.

"Victoria's not into women, and I haven't been in quite some time." Although she hadn't minded Sydney's tongue on her clit a couple of weeks ago.

"Well have fun and I'll see you Saturday." He smiled. "Allison's first meeting, I can't wait to see the video and see how she reacts."

"It'll be fun." She smiled back at him. "I have a little surprise as well. Something special in celebration of our new lady."

"Plus its Adonis's anniversary," Alex pointed out. "So who's taking care of him?"

"That's only for me to know." Standing she pointed down at the phone. "I'll see myself out, you have fun with that."

"Oh," Alex said as he continued to type. "Can you do me a favor before you go?"

"Of course."

Removing his cell phone from his hip he typed on it then turned the screen to face her.

"Can you read that for me?"

Taking the phone from his hand she read out loud. "Dial Alex now." She jumped as his phone began to ring in her hand.

Chapter Six

Justine released a contented sigh as she lowered herself into the hot tub. Once sitting, she slid over in front of the warm jets of water that were set at different levels. The next noise she emitted was nothing short of a moan as the water struck her lower back, as well as her calves. Stretching her arms out along the top of the hot tub, she sank down further and cooed delightedly as the highest jet found the back of her neck. This would have been relaxing under any circumstances, but considering this was the follow up to an hour long massage, she could already feel her eyes beginning to close.

Her masseuse, a young blond girl, had been amazing, easily the best she'd ever had. So good Justine booked an appointment with her for the Saturday of the next New York meeting and planned on making it a habit. Justine had lain there, naked except for a towel covering her ass, and let her mind drift as the girl's talented hands worked over every muscle in her back and legs. Alex had taken a huge burden from her by clearing up the Mark situation. Granted it was still disturbing, but more in the tragic sense than the appalling situation she had thought it was.

Alex's fixing the phone had also taken a lot of pressure off of her. Before she had left, he gave her a disc to pass on to the development team and told her if they claimed they couldn't work with it, to fire them and he would send her people. Right now all seemed well in the world. She felt she finally knew something about Mark, although it had become close to a 'be careful of what you wish for' situation. The only stumbling block left for her now was her impending conversation with Victoria. At that, Justine had turned her head to see Victoria lying on her stomach on the table a few feet from her as her masseuse rubbed her lower back.

Victoria's eyes were closed and she appeared so peaceful, Justine had wondered if she had fallen asleep. Justine took a moment to marvel at how beautiful she truly was. Victoria was thirty-six and could easily pass for a decade younger. Four months ago, Victoria had created a stir by having her face on a magazine cover wearing no makeup at all. The photo was a close up and the reviews had been outstanding, with many people saying she was the greatest natural beauty since Elizabeth Taylor. That comment had made Victoria more insufferable than ever, but no one could really argue the point.

Justine always found it hard to believe Victoria had never shot a nude, or done anything more risqué than a string bikini shot. Part of her success however, was based on that fact and Justine had to laugh whenever she heard Victoria tout her 'family values.' This was a woman who'd Justine once seen make a young man suck another man's cock, for the reward of licking her pussy. As her eyes left Victoria's flawless features and made its way down to the smooth tanned skin of her back, Justine frowned.

There was a three inch long scar that ran at an angle across her shoulder blade. That scar had been left by Tartarus, the former enforcer, when he had whipped her for a minor transgression. The scar was thin, but because of her deep tan, was quite visible. Whenever Victoria posed or went out wearing anything backless she wore cover up over it. Turning her head to the other side, so she would not again go down that path of guilt, Justine closed her eyes and enjoyed her massage.

When the massage was over, Justine had sat up, keeping the towel around her, but when Victoria had sat up, she simply let the towel fall away from her. She had been facing the two girls, and Justine noticed the blonde who had rubbed her down, was staring at Victoria's tits with a poorly masked look of desire on her face. There was a knock on the door and now, wrapping the towel around her, Victoria told them to come in. Her personal assistant, Lauren, had popped her head into the room and told Victoria she had a call from her agent who said it was important.

Turning to Justine, Victoria had told her to change and she would meet her in the tub in a few minutes. Keeping the towel around her, Justine had stood and, as Victoria left the room, walked over behind one of the two partitions in the room and changed into the red and black bikini she kept here for when she went swimming in the Olympic sized swimming pool located a couple of floors above her suite. Justine must have indeed nodded off as she jerked her head up at the sound of the door opening. Victoria entered wearing a short white robe and, walking over to the Jacuzzi, smiled down at her.

"And is My Mistress relaxed?"

"I swear I couldn't move if I wanted to right now," Justine told her. "That girl was amazing."

"That she is, they all are, and their spa is the best in the city."

Turning away, Victoria removed the robe to reveal she was only wearing a white string bikini bottom. Justine took in Victoria's extremely firm, perfectly shaped ass and the well toned backs of her legs. One of the other rooms was a private gym where Victoria worked out for close to two hours a day. Justine got an even better glimpse of that ass when Victoria bent over to lay the robe over the top of the chair. The bikini was so small, the thin strip of material between Victoria's legs barely covered her and Justine could see the material riding between the lips of her pussy.

Victoria straightened and turned around and as she slowly climbed down into the Jacuzzi, Justine stared at her tits. Like the rest of her, they were perfect, not very big, but firm and high, with a silver loop through each of her rose colored nipples. Justine noted she had no tan lines, and wondered if she went to a tanning salon or sunbathed topless. Victoria emitted a satisfied purr as she slid down into the warm water across from her. She didn't slide down as far as Justine, which left her tits just above the water. It had been years since Justine had a full out encounter with a woman, and didn't think about them much anymore, but had to admit those well tanned, perfectly shaped tits, were more than a little distracting.

"Not modest at all are we?" She laughed.

"Why should I be?" Victoria asked, as she put her long blonde hair into a bun to keep it out of the water. That move lifted her tits to an even better angle and Justine made it a point to look at Victoria's face as she added, "If you've got it flaunt it no?"

"Yes, but your flaunting them to me," Justine pointed out.

"It's not like you haven't seen them before. My Mistress has now seen how many of my videos?"

"Forget the videos, you whip them out at the meetings half the time."

"Hey, it keeps the guys' spirits up."

"Not just their spirits."

"And I love that they look and can't have." Victoria smiled wickedly. "The nicest tits they'll ever see and it's hands off."

"That's the point of the rule."

"Except for Amado and Alex, but I think after this many years, they'd want them all over again."

Justine sighed. "Will the Lady Felicia ever let that go?"

"No," Victoria said simply, and then smiled. "But whenever I bring it up, you're bothered by it, which makes me feel better about things."

"Glad I can help." Justine muttered.

Victoria finished her hair then slid down further into the water, mercifully submerging her tits beneath its surface. "You should take your top off," she told her. "The water feels soooo good on the nipples."

"There's not much to the bikini." Justine pointed out.

"That's like saying a cock feels the same through a condom." Victoria nodded over to her. "Take your top off and enjoy, I locked the door in case Lauren tries to come in."

"I can't believe your assistant stays with you on your day off."

"She keeps it my day off, and she's due to go home in a half hour." Victoria pointed at her. "Now stop changing the subject, take your top off." She grinned. "Or are you getting proper in your advanced years?"

"Watch yourself, My Lady,"

"Besides, they're gorgeous," Victoria went on. "Age and gravity has been kind to My Mistress."

"Again, Felicia, mind your tongue."

"Very few would ever mind tongue." Victoria laughed. "Come on, Justine, relax." she lowered her voice to an even sexier pitch. "Please, My Mistress, please show off those amazing breasts of yours, the most beautiful at the table."

"I'm not easy like the boys," Justine shook her head.

"Oh, for Christ's sake, stop being an old lady!" Victoria told her, then laughing said, "I dare you!"

"Oh, well in that case." Justine laughed and figured what the hell?

Leaning forward, she reached behind her and, untying the top, slid the straps down her arms and removed it, allowing her full breasts to pop out. Leaning back, she sighed as the water did indeed feel good on the sensitive skin of her nipples. So good in fact she could feel them hardening.

"Well, you'll never have to worry about drowning with those things." Victoria laughed. "Feels good no?"

"Yes it does."

She propped herself up a little more so her tits were half in and half out of the water and noticed Victoria's eyes were lingering on them and wondered if she were... Probably not. Victoria had always been a one way street. Then again, as a model, Justine was sure Victoria had some appreciation for the female form. Speaking of which, Justine was not self conscious in any way and if anything a bit vain about her looks. But as good as she knew she looked, Victoria made her feel out of her league. Victoria's stomach wasn't just flat, it was hard and everything about her body was perfectly proportioned. Across from her, Victoria's eyes had begun to close and she spoke. "I do need to talk to you, My Lady."

"Wait until after we soak," she replied drowsily.

"With all due respect, Felicia, I'm..."

"Very relaxed and you should stay that way." She sighed. "We'll soak for awhile then we'll slip on some nice soft robes, have a cup of tea and talk."

"It's important."

"So is this. We work our asses off, Justine," Victoria said softly, her eyes closed. "Today it's play first, then business, okay?"

Justine was going to push then decided not to. Leaning back, she closed her eyes and sank down lower. The water did feel amazing on her bare breasts and she was delightfully drowsy. She was just nodding off when she jumped, feeling something against her leg. She realized it was Victoria's foot which slowly slid up her thigh before it came to rest on top of it. Looking over at her, she saw Victoria's eyes half open. "Sorry, I like to stretch out."

"No worries," Justine answered and closed her eyes again.

Victoria other foot found its way along her other leg and Justine began to feel warm for a reason other than the water. Victoria was moving her feet back and forth slightly, just enough for Justine to feel how soft they were. She wondered if Victoria was screwing with her, but she stopped moving and a moment later, Justine could tell by her breathing she had fallen asleep. Justine stretched her own leg out so it was up against the length of Victoria's, enjoying the contact, but telling herself to knock it off. Victoria was as big of a game player as anyone at the table and insisted she could seduce anyone, including women, even though she had no interest. Despite that, the last thoughts she had before she drifted off were of wondering what those feet would feel like on her shoulders.

* * *

Justine sat across from Victoria in her living room, sipping a cup of herbal tea she had brewed for them. Although it was a warm summer day, the hot tea was delicious, and even though she had napped in the Jacuzzi, Justine felt as if she could curl up on the soft chair and sleep all night. Victoria was sitting in a similar chair just across from her, looking at her expectantly. Justine leaned forward, putting her tea down, it was time to get this over with. Shifting in her seat, Justine pushed the short white robe that was identical to Victoria's further down from where it had ridden up on her thighs and began. "As much as I'd like to say I came up here for fun, I do have something to discuss with you."

"As Victoria or the Lady Felicia?"

"This is business, although a lot of what I'm asking will be counting on our friendship, and not just ours, but yours and Mark's as well."

"Mark?" Victoria asked. "What about him? Is he okay?"

"Lovecraft is fine. Well as much as he can be these days. He hasn't been himself lately."

"Insomnia?"

"And then some, you know how he can be."

"I don't understand why." Victoria shrugged. "People would kill to have his life."

"We don't have to understand why," Justine countered. "All we need to know is it happens and when he gets like this, he sometimes needs help getting out of it."

"Is that what you came to ask?" She grinned. "You want me to cheer my brother up?"

"Not exactly, although your help today would do that."

"You look very serious, my dear Scarlett."

"It is serious. Most people in the group think Mark just gets depressed. It's more than that. He suffers from horrific nightmares that keep him from sleeping and when he gets strung out, he avoids people because he's afraid he'll hurt someone."

"I was only joking. No need to get carried away. I saw firsthand what my brother's capable of when he snapped Tartarus's leg in half.. If memory serves me, he was smiling when he did it. Having said that, if Lovecraft is in need of his High Lady's help, then ask what you will of me."

"I appreciate that." Justine nodded. "The favor is in a way more for me though."

"And the same shall go for you, Mistress." Victoria bowed her head. "But I can't help if you don't ask."

"True." She looked down. "Victoria I'd like to drop the formalities here. There's a reason this can't be official, plus to be honest, I'm getting tired of the cloak and dagger routine."

"Whatever you wish, but if that's the case just call me Vicky. Victoria's my work name; it's always been Vicky to my family."

"Since when?"

"I've been lightening up a bit I guess." Vicky laughed.

"All right, well the problem is Mark, he screwed up royally."

"When?"

"He broke a rule during Allison's initiation."

"Really?" She shrugged. "When I saw Allison Wednesday she seemed fine. I'm telling you, she's perfect for us. Very playful and we need more of that, we have too many serious people these days."

"I'm glad you like her."

"Are you kidding? I'm thrilled! I plan on spending a lot of time with her."

"Well hold onto that thought, because you may not be able to."

"What does that mean? What the hell did Mark do?"

"Mark slept with Allison."

Victoria looked at her for a minute, and then grinned. "Okay, who put you up to this? Loki?"

"Do I look like I'm kidding?"

Vicky shook her head. "No, you've got to be mistaken, or I misunderstood you."

"Neither. Mark fucked Allison after the initiation. She spent the night in his bed."

"I....what the fuck?" Victoria blurted out.

"That was pretty much my reaction." She sighed.

"How the hell did that happen?"

"The initiation was perfect. I saw the tape, Christ it had me killing the batteries in my bullet all week. I get back and Mark comes to see me and he tells me after the initiation he told Allison she could stay in his spare room, rather than drive to New York."

"Violation right there," Vicky pointed out. "You definitely want to smooth things over before your pledge leaves, but they need to leave." She shook her head. "Then again, Mark's the only member that uses his own house for this."

"Hard to get the bed and mirrors into a hotel I suppose." Justine sighed. "So he switches gears and becomes Prince Charming, let's her rest in his bed, draws her a bath and takes her out to dinner."

"Dangerous. Many times the pledge is sex drunk and will look for more." She sighed. "Not in my case of course."

"Knock it off, Victoria, at least you weren't gang raped!" Justine snapped. "You think you had it rough only because your proud ass had never submitted."

"Perhaps we should make this an official meeting then. That way I won't speak out of turn," Vicky replied coolly, her normally wide blue eyes, narrowed.

"I'm sorry," Justine said quietly. "This is a big deal and I'm tired of hearing about how you're still bitter about things. That was years ago, the Circle put you on the map and I feel I have more than made amends to you."

"I'm sorry as well." Vicky bowed her head. "Go on, I won't interrupt again."

Vicky crossed her legs and Justine watched the robe fall away to reveal her leg all the way to the hip. Her eyes lingered for a moment on her deep red toe nail polish, before she continued. "Mark admitted he hadn't been sleeping and he was strung out, probably should've pushed the initiation back, but he had something to prove and..."

"May I ask why he felt that way?"

"When Alex came to my hotel room to talk to me about Allison, Mark was there. Alex wanted to give her a soft initiation and Mark argued, saying we were getting to soft. Too many cake walk initiations and the other Circles were noticing.

"And Mark was in your hotel room why?" Vicky asked with a smirk.

Walked into another one, Justine sighed to herself, she really was getting tired of this. Staring into her eyes, she replied, "Because he spent the night with me and that's all my right and no one else's business."

Victoria nodded, then meowed and slashed outward with her long red nails.

"Again, point taken." Justine rolled her eyes. "But it's... a long story."

"And truly your business, you're the Mistress and you have the right to enjoy a member if you so choose."

"That's nice of you," Justine said, and ignored Vicky as she meowed again.

"So Mark nails the initiation, to the point they'll be playing this at the conference. But when he takes her to dinner, he's already exhausted as is she and he proceeds to drink himself into a stupor."

"That's a lot of drinking."

"Allison is overwhelmed by the entire day and she drinks a lot as well. Mark said he explained the rules to her, but when they get back to his place she makes a move and he falls. He fucked her more than once before they passed out"

"Are you fucking kidding me? Victoria grunted disgustedly. "What the hell does Allison have? He's the only man who ever turned me down and she just waltzes into his bed?"

"Regardless of how it happened, it happened." Justine sighed for effect. "Now you know what needs to be done."

"Mark needs to be punished and it needs to be pretty severe."

"Done." Justine said softly.

"Already?"

"That night he told me. I was.....I was furious, Vicky, I should've waited. What I did to him...." She shook her head. "The masters of old would've been proud of me."

Vicky frowned, but nodded. "You did what you had to."

"And then some, but the second part of the solution is..."

"To tell Allison she can't join," Vicky finished. As she spoke, her eyes widened and she shook her head. "Justine, I know the rules, but that would be unfair. Mark's was supposed to deny her."

"I know that. He said he talked to her the next day and told her that if anyone found out she'd lose everything. Allison, like we did, is joining for advancement, not sex. He said she looked terrified at the thought she could lose everything. He said she understood."

"Like he made her understand the rules?" Vicky shook her head. "We probably can't trust that. But I just hate to see it happen to her. She's perfect and she was so excited when I took her to lunch." She sighed. "She already came up with a lights out campaign for Rapture, her work is amazing."

Vicky frowned and, putting her elbow on her knee, rested her chin in her hand. She appeared to be genuinely upset, which was what Justine was hoping for. Now to finish it off.

"The biggest problem is me knowing. If Mark hadn't told me, I wouldn't have to do this."

"But if you pretend you don't know and no one says anything, she could try it with another member. So she'll have to be told to leave." Vicky nodded. "That's the favor isn't it? You want me to tell her."

"No. Alex would have to tell her, he recruited her. By rights it should be the enforcer, but I can't trust Mark to handle that."

"And it'd be bullshit. He helped her get into this mess." Vicky paused and then played right into Justine's hand. "Is there no other way? Maybe she could get a warning from you."

"I can't know," she pointed out. "Think about that. The Mistress finds out she broke our biggest rule and she gets a free pass. She'll have no respect for the rules. Not only that, but if she tells people I knew, I myself could be punished."

"That's true."

"With less than two years left, I'd step down before I would subject myself to Persephone's cruelty. I have no desire to be forcibly taken by who knows how many men in front of an audience."

"I'll tell her instead of Alex," she said softly. "I'd rather her hear it from me." She sighed. "It was going to be a hell of a campaign."

"And if you walk away, she loses Rapture and a lot of face," Justine added. "Her career will take a huge hit and Alex's contract will only be for this year. She'll be back at square one."

"She's going to take this hard. Especially if Mark was as hard on her as I imagine he was. It's not fair."

"There *is* a solution, Victoria, and that's the favor."

"A favor to keep her with us?" Her eyes narrowed. "What is it?"

"It's going to require lies on all of our parts. What I propose to you is that you go to Allison and give her a warning about what'll happen if she speaks of what happened with her and Mark."

"So now we're all involved in this?"

"No, I can't know. You'll tell Allison that Mark came to you, not me. He didn't want her thrown out so he went to the high lady, who is also a close friend, for help. You deliver the warning: if a word is spoken by her, she'll be banned and you'll walk away from her. Also tell her that her initiation tape is in our hands should she ever think to say anything about us. However, she keeps it quiet there are no worries, it never happened."

"Interesting," Victoria said softly.

Justine could see her mulling it over and hoped she had played her cards right.

"The problem is, if I warn her and it gets out and she says I kept it quiet and since Mark was involved, it'll be serious enough that Persephone would hear of it. Then it'd be me being punished."

"I give you my word that should it come to that, I'll take full responsibility. I won't let you be hurt, Vicky."

"I believe you gave your word to me when you recruited me that my initiation would be the only time I'd have to submit."

"Back to...."

"I was pledged at the conference to a master who was less than kind," Vicky continued. "Then passed around like a cup to Alex and Amado. My complaining got me scarred for life and your method of fixing it led to a man having to use a cane for the rest of his life." Vicky looked over at her. "Or am I just being bitter again?"

"Vicky, I can only apologize so many times. I was high lady when you came in and had nothing to do with the conference. I took over and it's not like Alex or Amado was harsh on you."

"No, but I had to please them, 'yes sir, no sir, oh please let me blow you sir.'" Vicky snorted. "All a game to those rich assholes, then they could run around and say they fucked Victoria Redding."

"They're sworn to secrecy as we all are. And both of them, especially Amado, have done many favors for you since. The fault was mine, not theirs."

"And here you are asking me to cover for Mark breaking the most important rule we have."

"Victoria," Justine said calmly. "You can either help Allison stay and help Mark, who'll be guilt ridden if she leaves, or you can hold onto an old grudge against me and refuse. It's your choice. I'm through apologizing for the past and I won't beg."

"I wouldn't ask you to. I'm just pointing out that my agreeing to this won't have anything to do with your word. I'll be doing it to help my brother, my new sister and of course My Mistress, but I'm doing it because I choose to."

"So you'll do this?"

"I will," Vicky replied. "But as you well know, nothing in the Circle is free."

Victoria had reached up and taken her hair out of its bun and, with a shake of her head, sent her long honey blonde hair cascading down her shoulders. Justine fought to try to keep the sense of relief out of her voice as she asked, "Name your price, My Lady, if it's within my power, you shall have it."

"Oh, it'll be well within your power." Vicky gave her a wicked smile. "But before I ask I'll tell you something: that, like the rest of this conversation, never leaves this room."

"You have my word," Justine said, and then wanted to smack herself.

"Well, on this I'll take that from you," Vicky said with a wink. Sitting back, she stretched her long legs out and, folding her arms across her chest smiled. "I have a bit of a dirty little secret to share with you, Justine, one even the Circle hasn't discovered."

"And what would that be?"

"A few years back, about a year after I joined the group and made it onto Sports Illustrated, I was invited on a month long tour of Europe. While I was in Spain, I met this beautiful model who I worked with on a shoot. We went out for a few drinks, and then the next day when we were in the dressing room, she completely strips in front of me. I remember looking at her and going to look away, but couldn't, there was something about her."

Victoria was smiling and Justine thought back to an hour ago when she found she was having a hard time looking away from Vicky's tits.

"I had never seen such a perfect body. She saw me looking and gave me a big smile. Later that night, she invited me out and we went to a club. We were drinking and she came up behind me on the dance floor, put her arms around me and started sliding around on me. It was the most erotic thing, her hands were running up and down my body, and she was breathing on my neck. I could feel myself getting wet right there on the dance floor. As you can imagine, we went back to her place and she showed me the finer points of the softer sex."

Victoria had said that last part in her trademark purr and Justine had to admit the visual of her with a woman was a hot one.

"Since then I have, on occasions, indulged myself. I'm still mainly into men, but there are times when I crave the touch of a woman. To feel their tongue on my body, to let myself lay back and be treated by them and then return the favor." She sighed. "And the taste." she rolled her eyes. "Delicious! The feeling of their wet flesh beneath my tongue, so good."

She stopped and Justine blinked. Hearing those things described in that sultry tone had her feeling more than a little warm. She waited for Vicky to continue, but saw she was staring at her. Justine noticed Victoria seemed to be breathing heavier as if she had gotten herself going.

"Well your secret is safe with me," Justine told her. "Now seeing as you're telling me this, I take it your favor involves someone of the female persuasion?"

"That it does."

Justine smiled knowingly. "You want time with one of the Ladies of another group?"

"No. I enjoy women who don't often indulge. I like it being a treat for both of us. Besides, I like that no one knows. That when I sometimes bestow a playful kiss on one of my sisters, they think it's just me trying to work up the men."

"Then what is it you're asking for?"

"What I desire as a reward for my loyalty is the privilege of having my beautiful Mistress in my bed."

Justine stared at her, trying to gage if she were kidding or not. There was no hint of it in Vicky's blue eyes as they stared into hers. She had been turned on by Vicky earlier, but still, before that brief experience with Sydney, it had been several years since she had been with a woman.

"You're asking a very high price,"

"You're asking a huge favor. No I'll rephrase that, you're asking for a huge cover up. I feel the reward justifies the deed."

"It's been a long time for me, I no longer...."

"It'll come back to you." Vicky smiled and added. "Justine, you are by far the most beautiful woman at that table, and I've cum many times to the thought of sliding my tongue through that red haired pussy."

That sent a shiver through her and as she sat there, thinking about it, Vicky untied her robe and, opening it, draped her right leg over the arm of the chair exposing her smooth pussy, which even from a distance, Justine could see was wet. She swallowed as she could feel herself beginning to heat up. It must have shown on her face, as smiling, Vicky reached down and slid her red fingernail through the lips of her pussy. "I wouldn't think I'd be such a bad choice of lover."

"You're perfect," Justine whispered.

"Then what's your answer, My Mistress? Will you allow me the honor of hearing you cum for me?" Vicky asked as she spread her lips, exposing her wet pink flesh.

"You were planning this weren't you?" Justine said softly, refusing to look as if she would cave so easily. "Topless in the hot tub." she smiled. "Getting me thinking?"

"I knew you needed something from me and I've been thinking of this all weekend," Vicky replied as she began teasing her finger along her swollen clit.

"You are shrewd, My Lady and I'll grant your desire, but with a condition of my own."

Vicky's eyes narrowed and, smiling, Justine lifted her robe and spread her own legs, exposing the red hair between them. Vicky's eyes widened as Justine slid her hand down and rubbed it. Vicky licked her lips as Justine briefly spread herself, giving her a quick peek, then closed her legs.

"Name it," Vicky said softly.

"After tonight, you're not to bring up the past. By bestowing this privilege upon you, I'm making amends. Your complaint was that I shared you. I'll now share myself with you. But it ends here."

Vicky nodded. "More than fair, My Mistress." Then tapping her clit, purred. "Now come seal our deal with a kiss."

Chapter Seven

Justine lay on her back, panting. She was sweating and her legs were stretched out and pressed tightly together. Her back was arched off the bed as the silver bullet vibrator sped up and she moaned as her over stimulated clit strained to cum. She was right on the edge, and her nipples ached for her touch, unfortunately her hands were tied over her head, making that impossible. Kneeling next to her, the remote to the vibrator in her hand, Vicky smiled and began to tease her tongue along Justine's swollen nipple.

"Oh yes," she groaned as Vicky turned the remote up and began sucking her nipple hard into her mouth. "Oh, just a little more…."

Her back arched until she heard it pop and she began to feel the welcome relief of what would be her fourth orgasm in less than an hour. Vicky leaned over so that her nipple was just over Justine's lips. She sucked it into her mouth and moaned around it as her legs began to shake. She yelped as Vicky gave her nipple a nip and started pumping her hips as the orgasm began to…..Vicky shut the vibrator off and pulled it out from between her legs.

As Justine groaned in frustration, Vicky sat up on her knees and shook her head. "You're really taking a long time, Justine, I guess maybe you're done for the night."

'No," Justine panted. "I….I need to cum again."

"Awww." Vicky pouted at her. "You need to cum again, well you know, you've been taking so long, now I do again too!"

Turning around, Vicky swung her leg over Justine's tits and. sliding backwards, lowered her pussy to her face. Justine obediently shoved her tongue into Vicky's dripping pussy and began to swirl it around. She moaned as she received a mouthful of sticky fluid, Vicky had already cum twice as well and her pussy was dripping.

"Inside." Vicky whispered. "Tongue fuck me."

Justine tried to do it, but with her arms over her head and Vicky lying on her chest she could barely move her head.

"Keep your tongue still." Vicky pushed herself up until she was sitting on her face and began rocking up and down, guiding Justine's rigid tongue in and out of her pussy. "Oh yes," she purred over her. "You're so good at that."

Bracing her hands on Justine's thighs, she started raising and lowering herself, sliding Justine's tongue along the length of her pussy. When she felt her hard clit against her tongue, Justine tried to suck it into her mouth, but Vicky kept sliding around, rubbing her pussy into her face.

"What's your hurry?" Vicky asked. "If you can take a long time, I can too."

Justine moaned and her hips twitched as Vicky started flicking her tongue across her clit. Justine spread her legs, giving her better access and then started licking faster, trying to get her to speed up as well.

"Hmmm," Vicky sighed into her pussy. "Is that it, Justine? You want to race?"

She sucked Justine's clit into her mouth hard enough to make her cry out, then laughed. "Okay, I'll play, we both go at it and if you come before me fine, if I cum first, you're stuck." She emitted an evil giggle. "And you know I cum awfully quick."

Vicky then fastened her lips around Justine's throbbing clit and began sucking it in and out of her mouth. Justine moaned and began licking, but not as fast as she could. She had to get off before her, or Vicky would tease her for who knew how long. Vicky stopped sucking long enough to say, "No cheating!"

With a groan, Justine started swirling her tongue faster and thrusting her hips into Vicky's skilled tongue. Vicky had stopped sucking and was tracing her clit in hard fast circles and Justine strained against the rope, desperately wishing she could use her arms to pin Vicky down to her and force her face deeper into her pussy. Justine gasped as Vicky slid her hand down between her legs and slipped a finger into her pussy. She started bucking her hips harder as she continued to suck on Vicky's hard clit.

"Oh damn!" Vicky groaned.

Justine whimpered when she felt Vicky's legs begin to tremble. She started bucking her hips harder as she tried to beat Vicky to it. She moaned again as her own legs began to shake. Vicky got her closer by adding a second finger inside of her and pumped them into her thrusting pussy. Justine heard a high pitched whining sound and realized it was her as again her desperate clit yearned to cum. Her entire body was shaking and she could feel the orgasm slowly building deep within her.

Vicky started rocking her hips back and forth and Justine could feel her moaning against her clit as she was also closing in. Oh, just a little longer, she was right there. Vicky cried out into her pussy and her legs clamped tightly around her head. Justine gasped into Vicky's convulsing pussy as she continued to try to lick and drive her hips into Vicky's fingers. Between her legs, Vicky was groaning into her clit while still using her tongue, but her orgasm was slowing her up. Vicky's hips were grinding into Justine's face faster and harder, smearing even more of her juices across her face, but all she cared about was her own orgasm. She was seconds away when she felt Vicky sigh into her pussy and start to relax, her tongue began to slow, and in desperation, Justine lifted her legs and, clamping them around Vicky's head, pinned her face to her pussy.

Vicky cried out, but ignoring her, Justine drove her hips up and down, grinding her aching pussy into Vicky's face. Her tongue had picked up speed again and her fingers began pumping her furiously. Justine threw her head back and screamed as the orgasm she had been on the edge of for the last half hour exploded through her body. Between her legs, she felt Vicky moaning as well as her tongue continued to work her clit. Justine cried out as her pussy contracted around Vicky's slender fingers and she felt herself gushing into her face. Justine let out a long shuddering moan as the last of the powerful orgasm made its way through her pussy and she collapsed, gasping, onto the bed. She relaxed her legs, but Vicky stayed down there for a moment, licking along the folds of her pussy and Justine groaned as she lapped up as much of her juice as she could. Sitting up, Vicky looked at her, panting. "That wasn't very nice." She laughed as she wiped at her glistening face.

Justine looked up at her unable to speak. The room was spinning and her heart was still pounding. She wasn't so out of it however, that the sight of Vicky didn't send a thrill through her. Like her, Vicky was sweating, her long blonde hair plastered to her cheek and her shoulders. Her face was flushed and not only was it glistening, but dripping from Justine's pussy exploding onto it. Justine lowered her eyes and stared, transfixed by the sight of Vicky's sweaty tits heaving as she also tried to catch her breath.

Justine sighed and let her head fall back onto the pillow. All she could smell and taste was Vicky's pussy and she wasn't complaining. Vicky lowered herself down and kissed her. Justine opened her lips and they explored each other's mouths, tasting themselves separately and together. Breaking the kiss, Vicky slid down further and started sucking on her right nipple. Justine moaned, and finally able to speak whispered, "Untie me now?"

"Nope," Vicky said. "That was a dirty trick Justine, so I think you owe me one more."

"Vicky, please," she groaned. "Untie me and I'll..."

"My night, my rules." Sitting up, she picked up the bullet and again placed it between Justine's legs, directly onto her clit. "That's okay, you can cum again too."

"I can't," Justine moaned.

"Well you better, or it'll be an uncomfortable night sleeping like that."

Justine's reply was lost in a whimper as Vicky put the bullet on low. Crawling between her legs, Vicky sat down then, laying on her back, slid one of her legs under Justine's, while draping the other over her, so that her foot was resting on her tit. Justine swung her leg over Vicky so their legs were scissored. Justine moaned as Vicky slid up into her, pressing her pussy against hers and pinning the bullet between their clits. Vicky moaned softly and laid back, her head resting on Justine's leg. Picking up the remote control, she spun the dial and Justine cried out as the vibrator thrummed against her sensitive clit.

"Oh, oh that...." She stopped as Vicky turned it down low, but then ground her pussy into hers.

"Hmm." She smiled. "We're going to take our time with this one." She licked her lips. "You look good tied up, I never thought I'd see the day, and I love how it lifts those tits up." She sighed. "You smell good on me."

Lying back again, she turned the vibrator up slightly. Justine stared up at the ceiling, trying not to squirm against the bullet. If she moved Vicky would stop. She was out to get her to beg and sooner or later she would. Laying there whimpering, she closed her eyes and tried to control her breathing. Vicky was going to make this last as long as she could and trying to get herself to not focus solely on what was going on, Justine played back the last wild hour she and Vicky had shared.

* * *

When Vicky gestured to her, Justine had stood and, walking over to the chair, stood in front of her. Untying the robe, she let it fall open exposing her large tits with their hard pink nipples. Vicky had sat up and licking her lips looked up at her, "You're gorgeous Justine, absolutely perfect."

Vicky slid her arms inside the robe, wrapping them around Justine's waist, and placed a soft kiss on her stomach just over her ruby pendent. The kiss sent a shiver through her and she ran her nails through Vicky's long blonde hair. Vicky sighed and began licking and sucking Justine's stomach, working her way up. Sliding her hands around to the front, she cupped Justine's tits and held them up.

"Damn they're beautiful," she purred in that phone sex voice.

"As are you Vicky," Justine whispered. "In every way."

Vicky smiled up at her, then turning her head, flicked her tongue across Justine's swollen nipple. Justine let out a sigh as Vicky began swirling her tongue around her swollen flesh. Sliding her hands through Vicky's hair one more time, she reached down and cupped Vicky's small, firm tits. Vicky moaned around her nipple as Justine grabbed the hoops between her fingers and started gently twisting them back and forth. Vicky switched to her other nipple and Justine started to rock back and forth as her pussy was already yearning for her high lady's touch. Sensing as much, Vicky's hand left her right tit and slid down across her stomach before dipping between her legs.

Justine moaned as Vicky's fingers probed the soft wet folds of her pussy. Removing her hand, Vicky brought it to her face and inhaled deeply. She closed her eyes and groaned at her scent. Opening them, she said, "Turn around for me."

Justine turned and felt Vicky stand behind her. Turning her head, she saw Vicky slip her robe off, then grabbing the shoulders of Justine's robe, slowly slid it from her.

"Such beautiful skin," Vicky whispered as she placed a gentle kiss between her shoulders.

Justine stood there, breathing heavy as Vicky's hands traced their way up and down her back and shoulders. She would sometimes use just her nails and Justine sighed, enjoying the gentle touch. Vicky kissed the back of her neck, then began placing soft kisses on the tops of her shoulders before trailing them down her back. Reaching up, Justine undid her hair and let it fall down across her back.

Behind her, Vicky had gone to her knees and was now kissing the small of her back as her hands caressed the backs of her legs. Justine could feel her legs getting weak as Vicky's soft touch was driving her crazy. Grabbing her hips, Vicky began kissing her ass, moving cheek to cheek and going lower and lower. Justine gasped as spreading her cheeks open; Vicky slid her tongue through her ass. She felt Vicky push against her hips and, leaning forward, Justine rested her hands on the coffee table, so she was bent over.

Again Vicky spread her cheeks and Justine cried out in surprise as she shoved her tongue into her ass and began licking it. She began breathing heavier and could feel herself getting wetter as Vicky's tongue probed her ass and her right hand slid up her thigh and started rubbing her pussy. Vicky's tongue left her ass and plunged deep inside her.

"Oh fuck that feels good!" she groaned as Vicky swirled her tongue around inside of her.

Removing her tongue, she trailed it through her lips until it teased across her clit. Justine started rocking her hips as Vicky's soft tongue traced slow circles around her swollen button. Vicky began playing with her ass and Justine groaned as she pushed a finger into it. Vicky began sliding the finger slowly in and out as she started sucking her clit into her mouth. Justine could feel her legs already starting to tremble and groaned as Vicky slid her tongue from her ass and sat back. "I think I should get to cum first tonight don't you?" she asked.

So much for no games, Justine thought as she straightened up and turned around. Any retort she had was lost as she took in the sight of Vicky sitting back down in the chair with both of her legs slung over the arms, her glistening pussy wide open and calling to her.

"Of course you should," she whispered. "I'm at your mercy this evening, my gorgeous High Lady."

"Oh, careful with that," Vicky cooed as she pointed at the floor.

"Yes, My Lady," Justine said softly as she gladly sank to her knees.

She took Vicky's face in her hands and kissed her. Vicky's soft lips pressed into her own and began to slide back and forth. Justine parted her lips and slid her tongue out. Vicky's mouth opened, allowing her entrance and Justine moaned at the taste of her pussy on Vicky's lips. Vicky's tongue darted out into her mouth and they both sighed as the kiss deepened and their nipples pressed against each other.

Justine sank to her knees and eagerly sucked Vicky's left nipple into her mouth as her hand began fondling her inner thigh. Even her thighs were tight, Justine noticed as she could feel the muscle beneath Vicky's tanned skin. Her hand made its way between her legs and Justine groaned at how wet she was. Vicky let out a low moan as Justine eased a finger into her. Justine switched to sucking on the other nipple and Vicky begin running her hands through her hair. Justine sighed as Vicky started caressing her back as she fingered her and sucked on her tits.

Justine went from one to the other, thoroughly enjoying those perky perfectly shaped tits. Vicky was moaning softly and rubbing Justine's back harder. Her hips began to rock into Justine's fingers and, looking up into Vicky's baby blue eyes; Justine left her nipple and trailed her tongue down her hard flat stomach.

"Oh, how I've thought of this," Vicky breathed.

Justine sank all the way to her knees and began kissing the insides of her thighs. She breathed deeply, taking in the scent of Vicky's pussy. Gently spreading her lips, she blew softly on her clit and Vicky's hips twitched in anticipation of her mistress's tongue. Justine placed a soft kiss on her clit then slipped her tongue into Vicky's pussy and sucked hard. Vicky gasped and Justine received a mouthful of Vicky's sweet juices. Justine's eyes rolled as she continued to tongue her pussy. It had been a long time and now she was wondering why.

Vicky released a soft whimper that sent a thrill through her and she started pushing her tongue harder and deeper into her. Vicky's hands wrapped themselves in her hair and her hips started rocking into her face. Justine removed her tongue from her pussy and replacing it with her finger, fastened her lips to her clit and started gently sucking.

"Oh Justine," Vicky moaned. "That's so good."

She then let out a soft squeal as Justine added a second finger inside of her and started swirling her tongue around her clit. Vicky lowered her right leg from the arm of the chair and rested it on top of Justine's thigh. As Justine began lightly flicking her tongue across her clit, teasing her, Vicky's foot slid across her thigh and Justine gasped as she felt the top of it rub against her wet pussy. Vicky began to rub it back and forth and Justine opened her legs further as her toe found her clit. Sucking Vicky's clit into her mouth again, Justine started sucking fast and hard. She started thrusting her fingers harder and Vicky moaned her appreciation.

Justine was moaning as well as Vicky's soft foot was sliding across her clit and she was wiggling her toes against it. She began rocking her hips into Vicky's foot and to her surprise felt her thighs starting to shake. She had never cum like this before, but it felt damn good. Closing her legs, she pinned Vicky's foot to her pussy and started sucking harder on her clit. Vicky whimpered again and started letting out a series of small gasps. Justine was letting out small sounds of pleasure as well as Vicky's toes were pressing hard against her clit and Justine ground her hips hard, riding her foot.

Vicky cried out and began to pull her hair as her hips thrust into her face. Justine felt her pussy contract around her fingers and Vicky let out a long loud wail as she began to buck up and down in the chair. Justine continued to lick despite the fact she could feel her own orgasm racing through her. Vicky's foot began moving even faster as her entire body jerked as she moaned and squealed. Justine let out a loud moan into Vicky's pussy and felt her toe press hard into her clit. Justine squealed as her own orgasm slammed through her. Justine rocked and twisted her hips, grinding them into Vicky's wiggling foot as she screamed into her pussy.

Vicky had stopped moving and was moaning softly as Justine's orgasm continued to have its way with her. Justine let out a long sigh and, lifting her face from Vicky's pussy, rested her head on her thigh. She moaned as Vicky slid her foot out from between her legs and said softly.

"I've never come that way.'

"I haven't cum that hard in a long time," Vicky panted then added, "Oh look at that."

Vicky held her foot up and Justine saw it was glistening from her pussy. On a whim, Justine grabbed her ankle and licked the top of it.

"Oh that's so hot!" Vicky moaned.

"Yeah?" Justine, winked at her. "Then enjoy a once in a lifetime show."

Justine slowly licked the top her foot clean. She wasn't just doing it for Vicky, Justine enjoyed tasting herself and to do it like this was an even bigger thrill. Vicky moaned loudly as Justine began to suck her toes clean one at a time, playfully flicking her tongue around them and getting her to let out a surprisingly cute giggle. When she finished, she looked up to see Vicky watching her, a look of absolute lust on her face. "Climb up here," she said, patting the arms of the chair.

Standing, Justine placed a knee on each of the arms and, leaning on the back of the chair, sat there spread eagle, her pussy wide open. Sliding down to a sitting position on the floor, Vicky wrapped her arms around Justine's thighs and began to suck on her clit. Justine moaned as Vicky wasn't licking her pussy, she was devouring it, sucking so hard on her clit that her lips were making smacking sounds. Justine folded her arms across the top of the chair and rested her head on them, whimpering as Vicky worked over her clit with her soft tongue and lips. Despite the fact she had just cum, she could feel her legs shaking and her pussy heating up.

Vicky was moaning between her legs, completely turned on by sucking and licking her and it was driving Justine crazy. *Fuck work*, she thought, *I'm spending the night for sure.* She gasped as she felt the orgasm beginning to race through her. She felt Vicky's hand slide down and around then let out a startled yelp as she plunged a finger deep into her ass.

Justine went off like a rocket and, throwing her head back, screamed, "Oh fuck yeah!" as her ass clenched around Vicky's finger and her pussy convulsed in her face. Justine started bouncing up and down on the chair, driving Vicky's finger in and out of her ass as sent her pussy into her swirling tongue. Justine released a long sigh and groaned as the orgasm passed through her. She jerked her hips as Vicky gave her clit another lick. Sliding out from between her legs, Vicky stood up and extended her hand to her. "Well now that the edge is off, let's go have some real fun.

Real fun consisted of a long slow sixty nine that was one of the most enjoyable experiences Justine could remember. Justine laid there with Vicky on top of her, her legs slid under her shoulders and her perfect pussy in her face. The two of them took their time, licking, fingering and teasing. Neither was in a hurry to cum, but both were out to please. Knowing from her videos that she loved it, Justine slid her tongue from Vicky's pussy and shoved it into her ass. Vicky moaned and whimpered as Justine teased and licked around her ass. Vicky started moaning louder and bringing her hand back started stroking her clit as she continued tonguing her ass. Vicky came, howling at the top of her lungs with Justine's tongue buried deep in her ass and that had set Justine off, her third orgasm exploding through her as Vicky sucked her clit while driving her fingers into her gushing pussy.

They laid there for a few minutes, enjoying their faces buried between each other's legs. Then rolling off of her, Vicky had stood and, moving over to the head of the bed, climbed up next to Justine and looked down at her. "Damn I love those tits, show them off for me." She smiled. "Stretch for me, push them out there." Laughing, Justine stretched her arms out, arching her back off the bed and pushing her tits up. "Thank you." Vicky smiled down at her.

Moving quickly, she leaned down and grabbed Justine's wrists. Before she could react, she felt something slip over them and tighten. Craning her neck around, Justine saw a red rope around her wrists. The other end was tied to the headboard.

"You did say you were at my mercy." Vicky laughed, and reaching into the nightstand drawer, had produced the bullet.

* * *

Mercy was what Justine was about to cry out for as she was brought back to the present by Vicky cranking the bullet up again. She tried to remain still, but as soon as Vicky started grinding her pussy into hers she couldn't help herself. Moaning, she pushed back as hard as she could, trying to force the orgasm. Her clit was to the point it was sore, but her body still yearned for release. She felt herself getting ready and tried not to groan to tip Vicky off. At the other end of the bed, Vicky was moaning softly and her hips were grinding the bullet hard between them. Justine closed her eyes and arched her back.

"Not yet," Vicky said and shut the bullet off. Justine whimpered in frustration as she slumped back into the bed. Vicky laughed. "Do you need to cum, My Mistress?"

"You know I do."

"Ask nicely and I'll let you." She smiled sweetly at her. "But it has to be really nice!"

Oh, was she going to get it, Justine thought, but taking a deep breath whispered, "Please, Lady Felicia, please let me cum, please cum with me."

"I don't know." She shook her head.

"Oh please may I?" Justine pushed her lips into a pout, "Please, Felicia, I've been a good girl, please let your little girl cum!"

"Oh I like that!" Vicky clapped her hands delightedly.

Grabbing the remote, she turned it all the way up then, putting it down, moaned and shoved her pussy against hers. Justine gasped as the vibrator worked into her sore clit. But despite the discomfort, ground her hips into Vicky's as hard as she could. Vicky was moaning continuously and had begun playing with her nipples. Justine's nipples were so hard they were aching as were her shoulders from straining against the rope. She lifted her hips as she felt herself coming back to the edge yet again. She let out a whimper and then gasped as Vicky began to let out that series of short gasps that signaled she was about to cum. Justine bit her lip as she felt the orgasm just starting to take her over the edge. With a wicked smile Vicky held up the remote, her finger on the dial.

"No Vicky, please don't!" she cried out.

With a laugh Vicky dropped the remote, her laugh turned into a loud squeal as she began to cum. Her pussy thrashing wildly into hers sent Justine over the edge and she cried out as much in relief as pleasure as her exhausted body began to squirm and writhe as the orgasm sent waves of pleasure through her over stimulated clit. They sighed simultaneously as their bodies slumped. Justine was completely spent, even with her arms tied, she could fall asleep right where she was. With a groan, Vicky sat up and. crawling up to her, leaned over and slipped the ropes from her wrists. She gave Justine a soft kiss and. lying next to her, gave her a tired smile.

"I hope you forgive my game, Justine, I couldn't resist. A lot of fantasies were fulfilled for me tonight."

"You're lucky you have that once in a lifetime rule." Justine said quietly as she rolled over to face her. "Because favor or not, I should get a payback on this one."

Vicky smiled and. leaning over, gave her a kiss. Justine slipped her arms around her and the kiss went from a quick one to a long lingering one. Vicky sighed in her throat as their lips slid across each other's and their tongues explored. Justine breathed deeply, taking in the mixed scent and taste of their pussies. As sore as she was she knew the night wouldn't be over yet. A nap then....Vicky broke the kiss and laughed softly.

"What's so funny?"

Vicky placed her lips to her ear and whispered, "The once in a lifetime rule only applies to men. You, my dear Mistress are welcome in my bed anytime."

Part Five

Chapter One

Justine awoke with a sense of anticipation running through her. The meeting was only hours away. Justine always looked forward to the first Saturday of every month, but today she felt an extra sense of excitement. Tonight was Allison's first meeting. In addition to the thrill of having a new member, she couldn't wait to see the group's reaction, as well as Allison's when they played her initiation video. The original session had been cut down to the highlights and she could already see the looks of lust on the faces of her brothers and sisters.

There was another reason tonight would be special as well. In three days it would be Adonis's anniversary, the last he would celebrate as a member of the group, and Justine was going to make it memorable. Her plan would also, along with Mark's spectacular performance with Allison, create a buzz throughout the Circles. By the Monday after every meeting, e-mails would go around about what happened at the various meetings and this time it would be the East that would be getting some raised eyebrows. Mark had been right in the hotel three weeks ago; they had gotten a reputation as being one of the more prudish groups. Tonight that would change.

Every Master and Mistress knew their Circles were a reflection on them and lately Justine herself had been tiring of the endless games. Her Circle had slowly begun to reflect that, but again no more. Monday night with Victoria had left Justine both sex drunk and totally rejuvenated. Between Monday night and Tuesday morning, Justine had lost count of how many times she had come, as well has how many times she had brought Vicky to a screaming orgasm. The experience had left Justine so hot that on Wednesday she had gone out after work to a club and allowed herself to be picked up by an attractive brunette in her early thirties. She had spent the night with her, had an amazing time and planned on giving her a call soon.

She couldn't believe how much fun she'd had and planned on indulging in the fairer sex on a more regular basis. On Thursday Justine had still been wound up and going to a small bar, let a young cocky bartender take her to his little three room apartment. His cockiness quickly vanished and within a half hour she had him begging to jerk off on her feet.

The good thing about guys his age was they came around quickly and Justine fucked him three times making him go down on her in between each round. His cock had only made it into her mouth once and that was because it was the only way she could get him hard. By the last time he was exhausted and whimpering as she rode him so hard they had broken his cheap bed. When he'd tried to sound confident and ask when she would come by again, she told him he was proof of why she preferred men to boys.

After throwing a hundred dollar bill at him to fix his bed, she told him to stick with girls his age, they might think whimpering was cute.

She'd gotten home at two am and as soon as the alarm went off at seven was on the phone with Mark telling him she was going to meet him after work and they were going to drive up to New York together. They had taken his car and feeling as wanton as she could ever remember she blew him in the car. While she was sucking him, Mark had pulled alongside a tractor trailer and the driver had been blowing his horn as she blew him. After he'd cum in her mouth, Justine had given the driver an even better show, popping her tits out of her blouse, before putting put her feet up on the windshield as Mark fingered her.

Justine supposed she should be worried being recognized, but then again in all her years at Speak easy she might have appeared in the news once, and she doubted the middle aged truck driver had seen that particular bit. They hit Friday traffic and didn't arrive at the hotel until after eleven. They'd no sooner gotten the door closed when Justine dropped to her knees and pulling Mark's cock out, sucked him hard, hiked her skirt up, pulled her panties to the side and had him fuck her up against the wall. Justine was so hot she came with her legs wrapped around his waist and him driving his huge cock up inside of her while he sucked on her tit. When she knew he was ready, Justine had him drop her down and getting to her knees sucked his cock dry.

After another hard round of fucking during which they used every piece of furniture in the room, they had collapsed exhausted and fallen asleep. She had woken him at three am by sucking his cock, then hopped on and went for a long slow ride. They'd gone at it again when they woke up at nine and a couple of hours ago, after they had come back from lunch. Now she'd only been awake a few minutes and knew if she kept thinking about she would want more.

She would hold off for the moment. She was a little sore and knew they'd be tearing into each other after the meeting tonight. Justine smiled up at the ceiling. Forty eight, making plenty of money, and in the course of a week had sex with a super model, a kid twenty five years younger than her and was currently in bed with the hottest man she'd ever known. That man was lying on his side next to her, his muscular heavily tattooed arm draped across her stomach, and his slow steady breathing in her ear.

Justine decided to lay there for a little while so he could sleep longer. When she had met Mark at his office his eyes looked as bad as they had the week before and he said he'd slept okay a couple of nights, but the insomnia had quickly returned. It made her feel good to know he could sleep next to her, made her feel he did indeed trust her. Justine closed her eyes and tried not to keep thinking about the wildest week she'd had in years, it would just keep her revved up.

Looking over at the clock Justine was surprised to see it was after three. Because they weren't doing to dinner before the meeting, it was going to start at seven rather than nine and Mark would have to leave to get Allison before six. She was getting ready to turn over and wake Mark when she felt a gentle kiss on her neck.

"Getting up, Justine?" Mark asked.

"I think so," she turned and kissed him, relishing the scent of her pussy on his face. "I stay next to you, we'll be fucking again."

"You're in rare form this weekend." He said, sitting up against the head board.

"This weekend?" she laughed as she sat up as well. "Baby, it's only Saturday afternoon, the weekend hasn't even started yet!"

Justine licked her lips at the sight of the muscles rippling down his arms and across his chest. His stomach was smeared with her lipstick and she felt her nipples stiffening. She smiled as she saw his eyes lingering on her tits. "Like what you see?"

"Love what I see."

"Good you'll be seeing a lot more of them after the meeting. Because something tells me we're going to be damn hot by the end of it."

"I guess." He sighed.

"You're not excited?" she asked. "It's your video Mark. The group is going to love it! Best initiation in years."

"Yeah, but afterwards I know...."

Justine stopped him by placing her finger on his lips. "What happened afterwards?" she winked.

"Come one Justine, you...."

"No you stop right there. It's over Mark. You paid for your mistake and Allison will be allowed in, it's taken care of now we move on and enjoy."

"Speaking of prices, what did Vicky want?"

"Sorry, can't tell you." She replied, "But it was surprisingly easy to grant, so it really did all work out."

Swinging her long legs from the bed to the floor, Justine stood up and walked over to one of the two small chairs in front near the sliding doors that led out to the deck. Knowing he was watching, Justine put a little extra swing in her hips.

"Justine, don't take this the wrong way, but you look incredible for your age."

"No wrong way to take that," she replied as she turned and sat down, pointing at the other chair she asked, "Join me?"

Mark walked over and her eyes lingered on his cock dangling between his legs as he made his way over to her, even soft it was large.

"Mark can I ask you something?"

"Anything?"

"Do you enjoy seeing me?"

"Why would you even ask that?"

"Well it's been getting more often and I want you to know you don't have to, I'm not asking as your Mistress."

"It's my privilege to be with my mistress." He replied, "And a pleasure to be with Justine."

"You're smooth councilor," she laughed. Leaning back in the chair, it was her turn to stretch and watch Mark, watch her tits rise with the motion.

"Yeah, I suffer nobly."

She smiled, and then turning serious asked, "Will you still want to see me when I leave the group?"

"Why wouldn't I?" He asked spreading his arms. "You're stepping down, not vanishing."

"Yeah, but." She shrugged. "I've been thinking about it a lot because it's getting close. Feel like I'm being put out to pasture."

"Once a member always a member." He reminded her. "And once you step down it won't have to be a big secret if we spend time together."

"True." She nodded. "Mark, I've been thinking about the dating thing. I know I don't want a boyfriend, but I want fun and comfort and...." She hesitated, then looking away finished. "Mark I'd really like to see more of you, I hate waiting for the weekends, maybe you could drive up one night during the week? I enjoy you and I want to.... I don't know feel like I kind of have someone."

"I'd like that." He said without hesitation.

"Not like a couple though, "she said quickly. "You can still...."

"Justine, it's okay, you don't have to explain." Shrugging he smiled and said, "Just roll with it and enjoy. If it feels good do it."

"That's a new one for you."

"Allison said it's her motto."

Justine blinked at Allison's name and she tried to keep a neutral expression on her face. She noticed Mark was looking closely at her and could see he was fighting not to smirk, he was baiting her. Picking up the small pillow that was on the chair next to her she threw it at him.

"Asshole." She said, but couldn't help laughing.

"You're beautiful when you're jealous." He said, now flashing the smirk.

Not knowing how to answer that, Justine looked down at the table where there was a menu from the hotel's restaurant on the first floor. "Alex, Amado and Eros are going out together, wanted to know if I wanted to join them. Want to go or get room service?"

"Room service." Mark said. "I'm not up for the twenty questions game about Allison. You can go without me."

"Then they'll be asking where my car is, if I go in a cab." She pointed out. "The conference room is three floors beneath us, so they won't know that way."

"Unless Alex is checking for everyone's car down in the garage." He laughed. "He thinks Lexi and Loki are screwing around because they always ride up together. Shit they live six blocks from each other in Boston."

"'Alex thinks', is the key part of that sentence." She said, rolling her eyes. "But because he does, I don't want him having anything to think about with you and Allison."

Mark stared at her "So it's not over."

"I'm sorry," she told him, "But your mentioning Alex brought back to me something I meant to say earlier but," she pointed between his legs, "You're so damn distracting."

"Then say it and get it over with." He told her, not appearing to be flattered by her remark.

"I feel terrible I mocked you about Allison, especially after you told me that story. I didn't know you were ever in love and I'm sorry."

"It's okay Justine. A good Dom punishes through humiliation and the mocking of soft spots."

"A good dom would also know when to pull back and not hurt their sub, no matter what the transgression." She said quietly. "But back to Allison. I want some distance between you two for awhile okay? You have a function you want one of the ladies to attend with you; it's not to be her. When you're in New York you only go out with her if it's with another member understood?"

"Understood."

"And in a little while, when you go pick her up don't go into her apartment."

"She's not that bad Justine."

"I'm covering our asses Mark. Vicky will deliver the warning after the meeting and I don't want you being too close tonight."

"Whatever you wish My Mistress." Mark bowed his head to her.

Justine reached out and touched his cheek, when he looked up she smiled at him. "What I wish is this to be forgotten. What I wish for right now is for you and I to go take a nice long hot shower together. Then you're going to go get our new sister and have the honor of presenting her to the group."

"I thank you for that honor." Mark replied, taking her hand and kissing it.

"You can thank me properly later, because trust me Mark, it's going to be one wild night."

Chapter Two

The bar on the first floor of the hotel was exceptionally crowded even for a Saturday. Sitting there, drinking a martini, Justine had learned from the bartender there was a conference in town and the hotel was booked solid. Looking about the room, Justine could see that indeed many of the patrons were in town for business. The tables were full of professionally dressed men and women, exchanging business cards and talking shop. She wondered how long before some of the conversations would soon turn to other topics. There would be discussions about the lonely lives of the busy professional with no time to date or the horrible stories of boring marriages.

Justine saw a fortyish looking woman in a low cut black dress leaning over to speak to the man next to her. Her body language suggested she was saying something in a confidential manner, and she could all but hear her words, 'he just doesn't understand me'. Turning in her stool and surveying the large bar, Justine also spotted several pretty young women wandering the room dressed in short skirts and speaking only to the men. No doubt working girls, conferences were big business for them. Justine smiled as she wondered if any of the Ladies of The Circle who had been here earlier had been mistaken for prostitutes. The rules were the men dressed formally, always in suit and tie, but the women dressed as they chose, and usually to great effect.

Two months ago, on a whim, The Lady Lexi had attended the meeting dressed as a school girl, complete with her long auburn hair in pig tails. Her plaid skirt had barely covered her ass and the looks on the faces of the men as she wandered around the bar had been priceless. Victoria was always dressed to kill, but a bit more careful in her selections, in case she was recognized. Tonight, Justine herself, still in her sexed up, playful mood was wearing a simple one piece red dress that barely covered her ass and tight enough to show off every curve she had.

The dress was low cut enough to not only show most of the top half of her breasts, but the red lace of her bra. A pair of red stilettos making her taller than many of the men she had passed completed the ensemble As she continued people watching, she noticed many men as well as women looking her over and wondered how many pegged her as a high end call girl. Turning back around to face the bar, Justine smiled at her reflection in the mirror behind it. Thirty five tops is what she would give herself. Then again, she was biased. Glancing down at the red Rolex Amado had given her for her birthday last year, she saw it was six forty five. The meeting was due to start at seven and she would have to head upstairs to the conference room.

Mark had left to get Allison almost an hour ago and would probably arrive by seven fifteen. Finishing her drink, she signaled to the bartender, and holding up a twenty placed it on the bar. He called out a thank you and Justine slid off of the stool and began to head towards the door when she heard her name called. She turned to see Alex approaching her and smiled as she watched the head of every woman he passed turn to follow him. He was wearing a custom tailored black suit with an electric blue shirt that perfectly matched his eyes and a black silk tie. The suit showed off his broad shoulders and tapered down to accentuate his narrow waist. When he reached her, he leaned in and kissed her on the cheek. "Justine, you look incredible as always."

"Thank you, I would say you do as well, but you already know that don't you?" she asked, as she slid her arm around his neck and returned his kiss.

"Well yeah," he laughed. "But it's still nice to hear." He grinned. "Not like you don't know how good you look."

"True. Well in that case, you look damn good tonight," she told him. "I love that shirt."

"Victoria bought it for me in Europe; she got all of us one in some pretty wild colors. We're all supposed to wear them tonight."

"Should be a colorful meeting tonight then." She nodded. "So my sergeant at arms, have you made sure everyone is upstairs and no one is lingering to get a sneak peek at our new sister?"

"The few who haven't seen her you mean?" he laughed. "Between sending her the ghosts of Circle's present to entice her and Loki seeing the video, half of us already knows what she looks like." He shook his head. "Good thing everything went smooth, we took some chances here."

"Good thing." She agreed. Then extending her arm said "Shall we?"

Looping his arm through hers they walked slowly though the bar, both enjoying the looks they were getting from the crowd.

"Think they think you're paying me?" she asked softly.

"I thought they were wondering how much you were paying me."

"Yeah right."

"Hey, I am younger after all." He laughed, and then grunted as she elbowed him.

"Just remember," she said. "Women my age can't get enough, when men hit my age they need blue pills."

"Mr. Warner!" a voice called out to their left.

Alex stopped and they both watched a dark haired man in a cheap suit approaching them. "Josh McGinnly" Alex whispered, "Reporter for the times, society page."

"Oh press" Justine whispered back, "I'll play it up for you."

Feigning she wasn't aware of Josh coming up to them, Justine cupped Alex's chin, turned his face to hers and gave him a kiss. Alex kissed her back quickly and started to draw back, but still feeling playful, Justine slipped her hand behind his head, parted her lips and slipped her tongue into his mouth. Alex quickly responded in kind and Justine had to admit he was a hell of a kisser. Aware that Josh was now standing next to them, Alex slowly withdrew from the kiss and slipping his arm around her waist said, "Good evening Josh, you working or just having dinner?"

"Technically dinner, but always working," Josh replied as he extended his hand to Alex. "Never know who you're going to see." he smiled at Justine "And may I ask who your stunning companion is?"

"Justine Bates," she said allowing him to take her hand.

"Hmmm." Josh pursed his lips in thought as his hand held onto hers, "I know I've never met you, because you're too beautiful to forget, but that name sounds familiar."

"I'm the regional CEO for Speak Easy communications." She told him as she slipped her hand from his.

"Speakeasy?" his eyes widened. "So, hey seeing the two of you are together, does mean there's some type of technology merger coming up? Maybe Orion software in speakeasy's phones?"

"I can assure you the only merging between us won't be happening in the boardroom" Justine paused to let that remark hit home, "And sorry, but we do have to be going we're late for something far more pleasant than this."

"Oh, of course." Josh nodded. "Thank you for your time, nice meeting you."

"Good seeing you as well Josh." Alex said. As they started walking away, Alex turned back and said. "Oh, and Josh? If Justine's little comment gets quoted in the paper, the times will be hearing from my attorneys, again."

Josh gave Alex a half hearted wave and Justine laughed as they exited the room and caught the elevator. They exited onto the fourth floor which contained several conference rooms. Not too many people were using the rooms at night and the only people they passed were employees cleaning or cutting through the floor on their way somewhere else. When they reached the end of the hallway where their meeting was being held, Justine saw a large black man leaning against the wall. He was dressed in jeans and a short sleeve shirt that showed off a pair of enormous arms. As they approached he pushed himself away from the wall.

"Who's this?" Justine whispered.

"One of Mercedes people. I figured there's bound to be a lot of drunken idiots wandering around after the convention I wanted somebody at the end of the corridor so we won't be disturbed."

"We're with Mistress Mercedes." Alex said as they reached him.

The man bowed and waved towards a set of oak doors at the end of the hallway.

"There will be two more of us coming in about a half hour," Alex told him. "A man and a woman, after that, no one else is to be admitted."

"Understood." He bowed again and as Alex and Justine walked down the hallway she said,

"It makes me worry to have outsiders here."

"Please," Alex replied. "All he knows is his mistress is meeting with several of her friends and doesn't want to be disturbed. Besides, if he does as asked, Mercedes rewards him, if he should ever say anything he'll be punished severely. We have no worries."

"I suppose you're right, Mercedes dungeon has quite the reputation."

As they approached the doors, the one on the right opened and Larry McCaffrey exited and seeing them coming, immediately bowed, "Good evening my Mistress." He said softly.

"Good evening my dear brother Loki." She replied as they reached him.

Larry stood up and smiling took her hand and raised it to his lips. "Gorgeous as ever, and may I say that I love the playful look you have going tonight."

"As long as you start with gorgeous you can say anything you like!" she laughed. Looking closer at him, she nodded approvingly. "I see you shaved off that poor attempt at a beard."

"Yeah," Larry ruefully rubbed at his smooth jaw. "It wasn't coming in to well."

"It was barely more than fuzz." Alex laughed.

"Thanks." Larry rolled his eyes.

Justine reached out and ran her nails along his cheek, "It's okay to look young Loki, when you get to be Orion's age you will appreciate it, trust me."

He laughed, flashing Justine a huge smile that caused her to smile back. Larry was thirty three, but had a youthful appearance that still had him being carded at bars. In general he was the boy next door, blond hair, blue eyes and by far the best natured man she'd ever met. Quick with a joke and quicker to laugh, even if the joke was on him, which in the group, they usually were, he was a breath of fresh air amongst the rest of the men, who took themselves way to seriously.

"Everyone else in there?" Alex asked.

"Yes, and we have a situation."

"A situation?" Justine raised her eyebrows. "What's wrong?"

"Okay," he put his hands up and was trying not to laugh. "The Lady Felicia and The Lady Aurora have arrived wearing the same dress."

"Are you kidding?" Alex laughed, "Oh I have to see this!"

Moving past Justine, Alex walked through the door Larry had left partially open.

"Shall we My Mistress?" Larry asked, taking her arm as Alex had earlier.

"Lead the way my brother."

They entered the large conference room and Larry closed the door behind them. The room was dominated by a huge cherry wood table that had twelve leather office chairs around it. Against the wall directly opposite of her was huge flat screen television that had to be at least a sixty five inch. Along the wall to her right was a line of curtains that covered up sliding doors that led out to a terrace and to here right was a large fully stocked bar. At the bar was tonight's anniversary boy Daryl Winter.

Winter had played twelve years of professional football for The New York Giants before injuring his knee at the age of thirty four. Despite his forty nine years, Winter still carried an easy two hundred and forty pounds on his six three frame and not an ounce of it was fat. Coupled with his thick black hair, green eyes and still smooth perfect features, Winter well lived up to his Circle name of Adonis. At the moment he had several glasses and bottles lined up in front of him as he made everyone a drink. The rest of the group were sitting at the table, and all eyes were on Victoria and Sydney who were standing there facing each other, hands on hips in identical teal dresses.

"Really Aurora," Vicky was saying to her, "This is totally unacceptable."

"You say this like it's my fault," Sydney replied. "Am I to call all the ladies before the meeting and ask what they're wearing?"

"Aurora only got here a couple of minutes before you arrived so you haven't missed much." Larry said next to her.

The dress in question was a short strapless creation that tied behind the neck and featured a silver and black belt. Adding to the absurd image of the matching dresses was the fact Victoria and Sydney themselves shared quite a resemblance, down to the fact both had chosen to wear there long blonde hair down tonight.

"Well the how isn't the problem," Vicky stated, pointing at Aurora, "It's what to do about it, because this is ridiculous. Really this couldn't be more embarrassing."

"Sure it could." Amado spoke up from where he was sitting at the table. "Your sales people could have told you the dress was an original."

"This isn't funny Mephisto!" Victoria told him.

"No," Tonya Cooper, The Lady Mercedes said from the corner of the table where she sat filing her long red nails. "Pathetic is what it is, you two sound like you're at the high school prom."

As Tonya spoke, Sydney turned to look at her. Whereas Vicky and her shared quite a resemblance, Tonya couldn't be more opposite of Sydney. Tonya was black, short and petite. With long black hair that Justine knew she spent hours straightening during the week. Tonya as always was dressed quite simply, wearing a coral colored sundress that perfectly complemented her dark complexion and showed off her figure quite well.

"That's because unlike you, we are concerned with our appearance."

"No," Tonya said calmly, without looking up from her nails, "You care what others think; especially men, I don't care what others think," she smirked, "Especially men."

"And exactly what do you propose to do about this my lady?" Vicky asked.

Turning back to her, Sydney replied. "And why is it that I am supposed to do something about this?"

"Because I am the High Lady, I outrank you, therefore it is up to you to make this right."

"And how do you suggest I do that?"

"You have a room at the hotel correct?"

"Yes."

"Then go down there and change." Vicky said with a shrug.

"The meeting starts in a few minutes." Sydney said pointing at her watch. "I don't have time."

"I am sure our Mistress would delay the start for a few minutes while this problem is resolved."

"I doubt it."

"Ask her, she is right there."

Turning around, Sydney saw Justine and after giving her a slight bow, said. "Mistress, will you grant me the time to change my dress? The fashion nazi known as The Lady Felicia is quite upset someone else has the same taste as she does."

Trying not to laugh, Justine glanced at her watch and saw that it was almost seven. "Lovecraft will be here shortly and I'm not going to make our new sister wait in the hallway while you change. How would that look?"

"It would look better than the two of us dressed alike!" Victoria pointed out.

"Oh, it's not so bad!" A deep voice called out from behind her. Justine jumped and turned, she had not seen Eros leaning against the wall near the door.

He pushed himself away from the wall and walked up next to Justine as he continued speaking. "I think it's rather adorable, like little girls whose mom dresses them up. You should sit next to each other." He laughed. "If nothing else it gets me thinking about fantasies involving twins!"

"Laugh it up Eros." Vicky snapped. "I'm a member of your district and it is an election year."

"Now, now my sister," He replied, "Have a sense of humor."

"It was my sense of humor that was going to allow me to vote for you."

Justine bit back another laugh as she turned to see Eros rolling his eyes. Robert Moretti was a city councilman who had joined the group three years ago, with the Circles influence he was making a series push to become elected as the city treasurer this November and eventually wanted to take a run at Mayor. He was Justine's height with dark hair, beautiful hazel eyes and a tan that rivaled Vicky's.

"Well there you have it," Sydney shrugged. "We're at an impasse."

"Unacceptable!" Vicky snapped and crossing her arms, stamped her heeled foot like a child.

"Oh for Christ's sake, what would you like me to do, take the dress off?"

"That, my lady sounds like the perfect solution!" Amado laughed from the table.

"Stop causing trouble, my brother." Justine said as walking up behind him she put her hands on his shoulders. "Can't you see this is crisis of the utmost importance?"

"My forgiveness Mistress." He laughed, removing her hand from his shoulder and kissing it. "But it would a…."

"Fine!" Sydney snapped. "If that will make my high lady happy then so be it!"

Reaching up under her hair, Sydney untied the dress letting it fall and exposing a skimpy black bra. The cups were lace and her pink nipples were clearly visible through the material. Grabbing the belt she unhooked it and let it go sending the dress to the floor and showing off the matching black thong she was wearing.

'Oh, damn!" Larry said as he walked over to the table

"Is my lady happy now?" Sydney asked.

"I know I am!" Amado called out.

Sydney stepped out of the dress and turning, bent over to pick it up. The thong was nothing more than a string in the back and Justine stared at the firm round cheeks of her ass. She felt a tingling between her legs as she recalled riding Sydney's face as Mark fucked her. Picking up the dress, Sydney draped it over her seat at the table. "Problem solved." She declared.

"Aurora," Justine said. "Please put your dress back on, it's not a big deal."

"Yes it is!" Vicky spoke up and looking at Sydney, gave her a curtsey. "Thank you for your sacrifice my sister, it is appreciated."

"Damn straight it is!" Adonis said as he came over to the table. He was pushing a small cart and began putting drinks down where everyone would be sitting.

"Really my lady," Justine tried again. "Do you want to meet your new sister for the first time in your underwear?"

"It's better than The high lady and I meeting her as the Olsen Twins."

At that the entire room burst out laughing and Justine noticed even Tonya was smiling.

"Are you sure?" Alex asked as he walked over to the cart and picked up a glass of scotch. "I can call down to the desk we can get someone to go to your room and bring something up."

"We do not need your help oh, diplomat." Eros said as walking up to Justine, he leaned in and kissed her cheek, "Evening my Mistress, you look stunning as always."

"Thank you, my brother." She replied. "And no worries The Lady Felicia will vote for you." She shook her head. "As soon as she registers."

"Threaten to raise taxes on clothing she'll register." Alex remarked

Walking towards the head of the table, Justine was stopped by Adonis who handed her a martini. "My Mistress," he leaned down and kissed her, then whispered in her ear, "Allow me to thank you for my celebration after the meeting."

"Don't thank me yet, my brother, you have no clue what you're in for." She smiled up at him, and then sipping at the drink sighed. "Perfect as always."

"Aurora, you can put the dress on if you wish, you'll be cold."

"No," Sydney said sitting down, "I'm quite comfortable. I'm sure in this bra you'll be able to tell when I'm cold."

"Where's the thermostat?" Larry called out.

Walking up behind her, Alex removed his suit jacket and draped it over Sydney's chair. "Put this over you, if you get uncomfortable my lady."

"Killjoy!" Amado shook his head.

"Dogs," Tonya said. "Pathetic dogs, men of the circle and you show them a pair of tits, still in a bra and it's like they have never seen them before."

"I think the solution wasn't Sydney stripping," Eros said as he made his way to his seat next to Amado, "But a good old fashioned cat fight."

"With a lot of hair pulling." Alex added as he walked over to the head of the table and pulled Justine's chair out for her.

"One moment," Justine said and walking past him went over to Victoria who was getting ready to sit down.

"My Mistress," Vicky greeted her as she bowed her head.

Justine put her arm around Vicky and spoke softly in her ear.

"Thank you again my lady. And not just for your favor, but for an incredible evening. By the time it was over I felt the favor you desired was as much for me as it was you."

"I'm glad you enjoyed." Vicky whispered against her neck, "I've desired you for a long time my mistress and you were everything I knew you would be. Thank you for honoring my bold request and know that tonight I will take care of the matter at hand."

Placing a soft kiss on her neck that sent a shudder through her, Vicky stepped back. Still holding her shoulder, Justine gestured toward Sydney, "Really my lady?"

Vicky shrugged. "It's fun for the guys and I don't think she's really mad, it's all for show."

Justine rolled her eyes and turning, went back to her seat where Alex slid the chair in for her. As soon as she sat, Tonya stood and walking over to her, took her hand and kissing it said, "I did not get a chance to greet you properly my Mistress, you are as radiant as ever."

"Thank you Mercedes, and I love that dress it's, very playful?"

Tonya frowned. "Playful? Oh, that's not good."

"The men appreciate it I'm sure, this is much better than your usual leather ensembles."

"That's what I was afraid of." Tonya sighed disgustedly, muttered "Playful" and went back over to her seat between Adonis and Sydney.

"My Mistress."

Justine looked up to see the last member of the group, Alexis Winters, the Lady Lexi standing next to her.

"I didn't see you at the table," Justine said as she stood so that she could pet her arms around her. "I was distracted by all the drama!" she added with a laugh.

"I was just sitting there listening." Lexi replied as she kissed Justine on the cheek. "Besides, I was doing a little day dreaming while watching the anniversary boy make our drinks."

Justine looked Lexi up and down. Among the group Lexi was affectionately known as Little Scarlett. She had the same shade of red hair as Justine and it was just as long. Although much shorter than her mistress, Lexi had a similar build with some curves, but all in the right places. She was wearing a black blouse that was open over a red tank top that barely contained a pair of tits that were bigger than Justine's and a short black skirt with a pair of black stiletto heels. As she had done with Vicky, Justine drew her close and spoke softly, "And were you thinking about your little surprise?"

"I've been thinking about it all week." Lexi sighed in her ear, "And getting off to it. Damn this week went by slow."

"You're sure you want to?"

"Do you need to ask?" Lexi laughed "I will not disappoint you my mistress, tonight will be memorable. I have a fun idea for the end."

"Thank you Lexi, Adonis deserves this and I will see to it you are rewarded."

"Please," Lexi said. "Have you seen him? He *is* my reward!"

Justine laughed and as Lexi made her way to her went to sit back down. She heard her phone begin to beep and saw Mark had sent her a text,

"At the end of the hallway, text me when its time."

Typing the reply 'come in' Justine kept her finger on the send button and remaining standing, addressed the group. "Good evening my brothers and sisters, and welcome to the seventh meeting of the year. As always everyone here looks amazing...."

"Especially The Lady Aurora." Amado said softly.

"Do not interrupt me Mephisto or you'll spend the meeting in your underwear as well."

"Which would be a punishment for all present." Mercedes said.

Justine waited a moment for the snickers to die down before continuing. "As I know you have all heard, tonight is a special night. After our last meeting our diplomat Orion the Hunter came to me and again lived up to his name by presenting me with a woman he'd discovered who was perfect for us. Beautiful, talented and sexually dominant, a representation of everything we embody."

She paused to look around. No one was joking now. There were a couple of smiles playing on the lips of some of the group, but they were smiles of anticipation.

"Like many who've come here before, this woman wasn't where she should be in life and embraced the concept of The Circle to further her career, proving she truly is one of us. As we all know however, nothing in the Circle is free, especially entry. So two weeks ago, that special woman took a trip to Providence to be initiated by our enforcer Lovecraft."

"Lucky bitch." Lexi muttered.

"Our brother is not for the faint of heart, even by our standards. Alex's choice, again like all of us was proud. A woman who had total control in the bedroom since her college days, I'm sure she was under the impression she could handle him." Justine again looked around and allowed an evil smirk to appear on her lips.

"She learned differently. The initiation was one of the most brutal in quite some time and our candidate held out far longer than I would have expected, but in the end our enforcer proved the stronger and she broke, which means tonight brothers and sisters, our Circle will once again be complete."

Justine stopped as everyone clapped, and looking over to her right at Alex, spoke again, "Brothers and sisters, allow me to extend a special thank you to Orion. In his thirteen years in this group he this is the fourth member he has found for us, including the very initiator we will be watching tonight." Turning to Alex she bowed deeply, "Thank you Orion, for continuing to keep this Circle strong."

As everyone around the table stood and applauded, Alex stood as well and bowed to the group. "It's my privilege to be of service to my Mistress and my family." He said softly.

"Now if you'll all remain standing I...." Justine paused as looking down the table she saw Loki looking at Sydney rather than her. "Loki? Do I need to remove my shirt to have your attention?"

Again the table broke out in laughter and blushing, Loki bowed. "I'm sorry Mistress, but.... Damn she's distracting!"

"Thank you my brother." Sydney replied smiling at him. "Perhaps I'll show then to you later."

"Perhaps you will want to later." Justine replied. "Because allow me to tease and say the initiation video will not be the only surprise for this evening." She paused to let them think on that, then sent the text before continuing. "But now, with no further delay, it is time for you to meet our new sister."

A moment later the door opened and Mark stepped into the room.

"Good evening My Mistress and my family," he began. "Tonight I've been honored with the privilege to introduce to you to our new sister. Like my current sister's her beauty is beyond measure, she's driven, she's talented, and like all of us she has learned to take what she wants. Brothers and sisters please let me introduce to you the stunning, Allison Saunders, The Lady Pandora!"

Stepping to the side, Mark turned, and extending his hand through the doorway led Allison into the room. As the sound of applause filled the room, Justine took in her newest Lady. Allison was even more beautiful in person. Her long curly black hair was down and had been teased out, giving her a bit of a wild appearance and the short one piece black and red dress she was wearing showed off both her ample tits as well as the full length of her long shapely legs. She was wearing a pair of red sandals the heels of which had to be at least four inches, with straps that wound up her legs and tied behind her knees.

As the group applauded, Allison looked nervously around, nodding her head as if unsure what to do. Justine noticed with a frown Mark was still holding her hand, but told herself not to read anything into it. Justine waited for the applause to die down, and then gestured to Mark, who walked Allison over to the chair opposite her at the end of the table. Letting her hand go, he gave her a kiss on the cheek, then bowing to her turned and began making his way to his seat to Justine's left. He then stopped and did a comical double take as he saw Sydney standing there in her bra and panties. Seeing him looking, Sydney put her hands out and shrugged.

"Well hey less is more right?" Mark said, getting a few laughs.

Walking over to Justine, Mark dropped to one knee and kissing her hand said, "Thank you my mistress for bestowing the honor of our sister's initiation upon me, I hope I met your expectations."

"I will let the group decide that, Lovecraft." She replied as he stood. "But I don't think there should be any concern on your part." As Mark moved over in front of his seat Justine looked to her right. "Orion will you begin the introductions to our new sister?"

"It will be my pleasure, My Mistress. To the real world I'm Alex Warner the owner of Orion Software, but here and where it matters most, I'm Orion the Hunter. I have thirteen years of service to the Circle and currently serve as the diplomat. I am the liaison between our Circle and the others. Any favor you need from another member or group will go through me as will any favor a member asks of you." He bowed his head as he finished. "I greatly look forward to serving my beautiful new sister in any way I can."

When he finished he sat and Victoria spoke, "Victoria Redding, a very successful model who was recently compared to Elizabeth Taylor."

"Oh, for Christ's sake," Alex said slapping his head.

Ignoring him and the ensuing laughter Victoria went on, "Before that however, I was a struggling model getting nowhere near the attention I deserved. The Circle changed that for me and now I stand before you as The Lady Felicia. I am the High Lady, which means I am your big sister within this group. I will instruct you in the rules as well as be the one who will handle any requests for you involving granted time. If you have any issues within the group, I am the person you will take them to." Bowing she said. "I am eagerly looking forward to getting to know my new sister."

As she sat Adonis stood, "My name is Daryl Winter, A former linebacker for the New York Giants," he paused. "Perhaps you've heard of me?"

Allison didn't respond at first, then looking around awkwardly said, "I'm sorry, but no. I'm a Patriots fan."

Daryl waited good naturedly through the laughter and Justine smiled as she saw Allison beginning to smile. Many of the groups were serious to the point of being pretentious at their meetings; Justine however, enjoyed the humor at her table and could tell it was already putting Allison at ease.

"Despite the fact that you're the fan of a rival," Daryl continued, "I will welcome you to our group. Here I am referred to as Adonis. Sadly my time here is almost at an end, but I hope that in the short time we will serve together, I may have the honor of getting to know you and call you both sister and friend."

"Thank you my brother," Allison said softly. As he sat, Tonya turned to face her.

"My given name is Tonya Cooper, but that is a name I seldom go by. Years ago I became a professional dominatrix by the name of The Lady Mercedes, that is now my Circle name and who I truly am. I own The BDSM club, The Velvet Rope and freely provide my subs as entertainment to my brothers and sisters. They are trained to please and know if they don't they will answer to me. On that note my new sister, before you leave I will be providing you the name of a hotel nearby. Pick a night and I will book a room there and awaiting you will be a sub handpicked by me to please you."

"I...that's okay," Allison began "I don't have a problem finding...."

"It is my welcome gift to you and a tradition I hold dear," Tonya continued. "Please accept it. I can assure you, you will have an amazing evening."

Justine saw Allison's gaze shift to Mark and saw him nod out of the corner of her eye.

"Thank you Lady Mercedes," Allison said. "I look forward to your gift."

Mercedes bowed and as she sat Sydney turned to face Allison. "I am erotica author Sydney Stone, known here as The Lady Aurora."

"Notice she didn't ask if she read her books," Eros said.

"I have actually." Allison said. "I read Chained Reaction."

"But was it any good?" Amado asked.

"It um," she paused then smiled. "Did the trick so to speak."

"Thank you, my sister." Sydney nodded. "And allow me to apologize for my appearance; sadly my attire became the casualty of our resident fashionista. I myself have only been in the group for several months and greatly look forward to the two of us spending many years as sisters."

To Allison's left Larry stood up and turning to her said, "In a sense we have already met, my name is Larry McCaffrey, but within the group I am called Loki. You have seen a demonstration of what I can do. A private investigator by trade and a computer hacker by hobby, there is nothing I cannot find."

"Find a video of someone having sex with Mercedes willingly." Mark called out.

Over the laughter, Mercedes retorted. "Tougher yet, find a copy of that mongrel's birth certificate."

"Aside from those two impossible tasks," Larry said grinning, "I can get you anything you need to know about any of your clients or anyone else. I also handle the taping of our entertainment videos and will coming by one day to set up cameras in your room."

"I don't take them home with me." Allison shook her head.

"Then for your entertainment you will need to let me pick a place...." He paused, "But we will discuss that another time. But for now, let me say it will be my pleasure to be of service to you."

Smiling at her, Lexi curtsied to Allison, "I am Alexis Winters, simply called the Lady Lexi, a name which, very much like myself, is a bit short, but a lot of fun. I am a lawyer by trade, but try not to hold that against me," she laughed. "And like the others here, I am looking forward to getting to know my beautiful new sister."

Bowing deeply, Robert addressed Allison next, "Known within the group as Eros, my real name is Robert Moretti, I will not ask if you have heard of or voted for me to avoid any embarrassment."

"Good call." Allison said then blushed as the room immediately burst into laughter.

"Oh, I like her already." Mercedes said, "Good job Orion!"

"Set myself up for that one." Robert said, putting his hands up, "Be that as it may, I like The Lady Felicia was wallowing much lower in my career than I should have been and this group has elevated me to a solid position with the promise of more to come. Now my lady, I have a question for you, Next week there is a fundraiser for my cause and I am in need of some company, would you give me the honor of attending with me?"

"I...." Allison looked around for a moment then shrugged, "Will I get a chance to network?"

That got another round of laughs and Eros immediately spoke over it, "My lady you are truly perfect! In the Circle nothing is free so as you will be doing me the favor of providing me with a beautiful date and you will be gaining the opportunity to network with many wealthy people."

"I would love to go." Allison told him.

"And I will love to have you," he bowed. "Thank you my sister."

"Mephisto, at your service" Amado began, "Amado Rosario to the real world, originally from Spain I represent one of the wealthiest families on the west coast in all their business endeavors. I travel around the country constantly seeking more opportunities...."

"And dodging anything resembling work." Alex said quietly

"Opportunities," Amado continued as he casually flipped Alex off, "Not just for Rosario enterprises, but for my brothers and sisters. If I find someone who can make use of a member's talents I do my best to send them your way. It will be an honor for me to help see that you quickly achieve the type of success due to you."

He sat down and just before Mark began to speak, Justine reached under the table and gave his hand a squeeze. She knew he was nervous about speaking of the rules to Allison when he had broken them, and with that gesture hoped to convey to him that it was okay.

"To the world my name is Mark Phillips," he began. "But within this group my name is Lovecraft. I have nine years in the Circle and currently serve as its enforcer. To you I can be both a curse and a blessing. I enforce the rules which mean if any are broken I mete out the punishment. However, it is also my job to protect the members of this group. It is a job I take seriously and although that extends to my brothers, I take the job of looking out for my sisters even more seriously. If anyone should hurt you either professionally or physically I will make it right. That also extends within the Circle. If another member should ever make the mistake of harming you they answer to me. If a member of another group should ever think you should be punished and think they have the right to do it, they will have to pass through me first." He smiled coldly. "And I my lady am a road not easily traveled."

"Ain't that the truth." Allison nodded,

More laughter broke out and Mark paused to let it die down. "Now that was my introduction as to who I am. I will now, if My Mistress allows, tell you My Lady Pandora what we all are here including yourself."

"By all means Lovecraft." Justine said

Mark spread his arms out wide to indicate the room "Before me I see the best the world has to offer, I see beauty, success, power and all the privilege that comes with it. I see the elite, the cream that rises above the banality of the common man. Everyone in this room excels at what they do, and why is that? Because we my brothers and sisters quite simply put; are better than the rest."

Justine smiled, she'd heard all this before, but was thrilled Mark was back to himself and up for giving it.

"Arrogant?" Mark asked. "Narcissistic? Better than? Is that how I sound? Some would tell you that. Of course those who would use those words are the commoners, the lemmings, the people who because they are so far from perfect they have to try to justify their own meaningless existence by trying to say it's us that's wrong; that it's a sin to take pride in what we are."

Mark shook his head disgustedly before he continued; "Man's laws, Gods rules." He snorted. "Laws created to maintain a balance, to keep those of us who are superior lumped in with the herd. We are told to reign in what we are so those less than us will not feel they are less than. Well brothers and sisters we know differently don't we? Pride..."

He shook his head, "They say it's a deadly sin. No my friends, denial is a sin, and those who deny greatness are the true sinners. To keep this short and use a modern term these people are haters. They hate us because we're better and they are jealous. I am not supposed to take pride in my appearance because they don't look like me. I should hold back at work so my inferior co-workers look less inferior."

Mark sighed for dramatic effect and shook his head before continuing; "Beauty is skin deep?" He laughed. "Ugly people tell us that." Several people laughed at that one. "All men are created equal? Under achievers came up with that one."

"And guys with small cocks." Lexi called out."It's not whether you win or lose it's...." Mark trailed off and with a wave of his hand began to head for his finish. "Anyway enough of what they are. Now I will discuss what we are. What I am."

Mark once again put his arms out. "I am a true child of Levay. I am the best of the best. I am beautiful, powerful and successful, I ignore mans laws and practice my own. I live for indulgence over abstinence; I embrace each and every pleasure of the flesh and live each day as if it's my last because one day it will be. And when that day comes I will not be one of those who had wished he had lived to the fullest because I do that every day."

Mark flashed that killer smile and continued; "I am the true alpha, the wolf amongst sheep," He winked. "Every father's nightmare, every house wife's fantasy," Mark paused and looking around added the catch phrase he had been using for years;

"Every woman wants me every man wants to be me. And all of what I just said Lady Pandora now applies to you. No more will you watch opportunities pass you by, no longer will you watch those inferior to you succeed while they hold you back. No, my sister from this day forward you will do what I told you the night of your initiation, from now on you will live as we all do by one mantra."

In unison several members called out "We take what we want!"

"Damn straight we do." Mark declared, then bowing deeply to Allison added, "My sister it was a privilege for me to be the test you had to pass to gain entrance to the group and from this day forward it will be my honor to watch you grow in confidence and success. To become a true Lady of this Circle. Welcome Lady Pandora."

Everyone at the table stood and applauded and Mark bowed before sitting down. When the applause died down and the others had sat, Justine walked over to officially greet her new Lady.

Chapter Three

As the room exploded into applause, Allison awkwardly bowed as the others had to her. The entire night had a surreal feeling to it. Even earlier as she had dressed and applied her makeup she'd felt as if none of this were real. Waiting to be picked up to be brought to meet a secret sect of sexual deviants, it sounded like something out of an x-rated novel. What was real were the abrupt changes in her career. True to his word, Blake had called her into a meeting with him and in addition to giving her a ten thousand dollar raise in base salary, increased her commission percentage.

Allison had moved into Ben's office and upon request had brought Cindy with her and feeling confident in her new found pull had gotten her a raise as well. When Allison and Victoria had met with the Rapture, Blake had sat in and witnessed their enthusiastic response to "No Boy's allowed". Their only question about the campaign was how soon it could be launched. Blake told Allison to hand pick six people she would like to work with from the office. Once she had Blake told her from now on those people were her department, because she had just become A&S advertisings newest senior account executive.

In two weeks her career had gone from dead end to limitless potential and Allison hadn't even met the entire group yet, from everything indicated to her, this was just the beginning. Sitting there at her dressing table, Allison had looked down at her phone to see it was almost six thirty; Mark would be arriving any minute. In the two weeks since her initiation, Allison hadn't heard from him. Well not on his own, she had called him once on the red phone he had given her. He had answered "Lovecraft" and asked her if everything was okay. When she had answered everything was amazing and she had just called to say hi, he had paused and she felt like an idiot.

Mark had talked with her for a few minutes. He seemed genuinely thrilled to hear about her recent success, but otherwise she had the impression he was humoring her. He had then told her he was at work and needed to go. He added he was looking forward to seeing her for the meeting, but aside from that he seemed quite distant. That had made her feel even more foolish. No, not foolish, pathetic. Allison had felt like a high school girl with a crush. For all intensive purposes a crush was exactly what she felt like she had.

Although he had pissed her off that Sunday morning, she couldn't get him out of her head. For the last two weeks she had masturbated to him constantly. To her surprise a lot of what she kept recalling wasn't the time they had played, but how he had taken her. She'd lost track of how many times she had come to the image of being tied to the bed and him laying between her legs, teasing and tormenting her, making her beg and plead the way her subs did. She had also gotten off many times to the memory of that incredible mix of pleasure and pain as he tore into her ass, while she came harder than she ever had in her life.

Since her initiation Allison had been on a tear with her pets. Normally she would indulge two to three times a week, but last week had been every night. She currently had three she was juggling and had them all twice, one each night then back again. Even then there were times when they were on their knees between her legs she envisioned Mark.

She knew they weren't supposed do it again, because of the weird rules they had, but Allison had hopes that since he broke them with her once, he might again. If nothing else the thought he would be at her mercy next year was a hot one. But that was next year and Allison was never known for her patience. After all wasn't part of the reason they chose her because sexually she always got what she wanted? So although she knew Mark was probably being aloof because of what happened, she would keep a watch out for an opportunity between them. If nothing else she was truly hung up on finding out if he were more beauty than beast. Granted he had that brutal stuff down pat, but no one could be as sweet as he had been to her without wanting to have that in their lives.

Mark had arrived right at six thirty and Allison was again taken off guard by how damn perfect he was. Mark was wearing an expensive black suit with a bright fuchsia shirt and black and purple striped tie. She had never pegged him for dressing flashy, but he pulled it off well. He was clean shaved and his gorgeous eyes were as light as she had seen them. They were also red around the edges and she saw dark circles beneath them. When he arrived he went to kiss her cheek and Allison turned her head, trying to catch a quick peck on his lips. He had pulled away, then leaning in kissed just her cheek.

Feeling like an idiot, she let it go and was content in him taking her arm as they went down stairs to his car. They passed several of her neighbors and enjoyed the looks they received as they walked by. Mark was quiet on the ride to the meeting answering her questions with simple yes or no's. When they arrived and Mark had given the keys to the Firebird to the valet he again took her arm and the entered the hotel, making their way to the lobby and getting into the elevator. Allison mentioned she was nervous and that got a better reaction out of him. Taking her chin in his hand, he kissed her cheek and said softly, "No worries my sister, you're one of us. In fact you always have been it just took awhile for your family to find you."

She had nodded, and still holding her face gently in his powerful hand, he continued.

"Allison, everyone in that room started where you're starting now. A new member is a big event and the only thing they're thinking is how excited they are to meet you. Despite what we may come across to the real world, we're less judgmental than anyone you've ever met. What society deems as taboo we embrace. All we want is to have fun, make money and be good to each other. Just give them the chance that they're giving you. Go in there, be yourself and have fun. It's more casual than you think."

His words had made her feel better and as they walked past a huge black man who bowed and waved them down the hallway Mark spoke softly, "The only instructions I will give you, is one, you will be offered a gift by one of the Ladies, accept it. She will be hurt if you don't. Second, but more importantly, is when you greet the mistress you will kneel and kiss her feet."

"What?" she asked. "Her feet?"

"You don't have to lick and suck on them." Mark replied, and then grinned, "Not that anyone would complain if you did, but just a kiss, a sign of respect."

"You said she's the one that broke you?"

"Yes." Mark said.

"Then I guess that's a woman I should respect." She laughed nervously, "And fear."

By then they had reached the door and Mark had gone in ahead of her. She heard him call her name and reaching back he took her hand and had led her in. Allison's first reaction was she had never seen so many perfect people in one place. As she quickly scanned the faces looking at her, she saw every one of them man and woman alike were beautiful. It was like some type of ball. The men were all in black suits with various colored shirts, but the women all dressed differently and quite revealing, except for the shorter black woman who was wearing a plain sundress. Although she wasn't flaunting herself, Allison's gaze lingered on her face, her features were exquisite and she seemed to have a regal air about her as she stood looking back at her.

Breaking eye contact, Allison continued scanning the table, trying to ignore the ten sets of eyes that were taking her in. Directly opposite her was the woman who had to be the Mistress. A tall stunning red head, who's low cut dress, displayed a body that would send any of Allison's pets to their knees. Allison had a quick visual of this woman with Mark, tearing into him and somehow breaking him. Next to her was Alex, who gave her a wink. Victoria was standing to his right and looked as beautiful as ever. Amado was across from her wearing a yellow shirt and flashing his perfect smile.

As Allison looked over to her right, she paused and stared. She was looking at a tall gorgeous blond woman, who could pass for Vicky's sister. The reason for her staring wasn't her beauty; it was the fact that she was wearing only a black lace bra and a thong. Allison's eyes trailed up and down her amazing body, before coming to rest on her face. The woman had an amazing pair of bluish gray eyes, and as they met hers she winked at her. Her attention was drawn away, by Mark tugging on her hand, she let him lead her to the chair at the end of the table, across from the red head and then letting her hand go, he walked over to the edge f the table and dropped to one knee, kissing the hand of his Mistress.

As starting with Alex, they introduced themselves; Allison tried to remember all the names and careers. She felt like an idiot when she'd accidentally insulted Adonis. The rest seemed to find it funny and fortunately Adonis himself had laughed good naturedly at her. Then, although Mark had warned her ahead of time, she almost screwed up, initially trying to refuse Mercedes gift of a young man to please her. As she spoke to her softly in a slightly raspy voice, Allison felt that same air of power and confidence coming from Mercedes that the other she had met so far carried. Would people really feel that way about her some day, she wondered. She put her foot in her mouth again with Eros, who Allison distinctly remembered voting against.

Each time she had felt she had done something foolish, everyone had laughed and she felt that it wasn't at her, but more at the expense of who she had been talking to. The banter around the table had helped to relax her. Mark was right, they were nowhere near as stoic and serious as she had envisioned them being. Allison's nerves kicked back in however, as the tall redhead, her new Mistress, slowly approached her. Turning to her left, Allison took a step away from her chair and waited with her hands clasped in front of her. When the Mistress reached her, she gave her a surprisingly friendly smile and reaching out placed her hands on Allison's shoulders.

"Lady Pandora, you are even more beautiful in person," she said softly. "You have the most amazing eyes."

"Thank you my Mistress." Allison answered, hoping she didn't sound as nervous as she felt.

"My name is Justine bates, a CEO with speak easy communications. Here I am The Mistress Scarlett. I have eighteen years in the Circle and have served as its leader for the last six. It is my pleasure to welcome you to our group. I have no doubt you will flourish here as many before you have and you will greatly enjoy your time with us."

Allison looked up into Justine's deep blue eyes. Despite the heels, she was still several inches shorter than her mistress. It dawned on her that if all the members joined at thirty then Justine had to be closing in on fifty, yet even this close she would not have guessed her for more than a few years older than her. Allison dropped her gaze, taking in Justine's long curvy form and again could feel the confidence emanating from the woman before her. Allison caught a movement out of the corner of her eye and turning her head slightly saw Mark point to the floor.

"Thank you Mistress Scarlett, it is my privilege to be here amongst you." Sinking to her knees, Allison leaned over and placed a soft kiss atop each of Justine's feet. Wanting to make a good impression, she turned her head and briefly rested her cheek across Justine's foot. Sitting back up to her knees, Allison looked up and said softly, "I hope you will be pleased with me and consider me a worthy member of your special family."

"Very well said." Mercedes said from the table.

Justine extended her hand to her and helped her to her feet. Once she was standing, Justine put her arms around her shoulders and hugged her tightly. Whispering in her ear she said, "Welcome my dear Pandora, may your stay here be long, profitable and most of all satisfying in every way. Now," she was still whispering, "Let me properly welcome you."

Justine took her face in her hands and kissed her. Allison started to try to lean back, but Justine held her face tightly as her soft lips pressed into hers. She had never kissed a woman before and was taken off guard. Behind her she heard a couple of low whistles. Justine's tongue pressed against her lips, and not wanting to start off on the wrong foot, she parted her lips. Justine's tongue slipped into her mouth and caressed hers.

Allison heard someone else whistle and realizing the entire room was not only watching, but getting turned on, Allison darted her tongue into Justine's mouth and kissed her back. Justine's hands dropped from her face and Allison felt her arms slide around her waist. Unsure of what to do, Allison played along and put her hands on Justine's hips. Her tongue continued to play across Justine's and she heard herself sigh as she felt her hands slide up her back and through her hair.

Allison could feel her heart beating faster and could feel Justine's nipples pressing into the top of her tits. Justine kissed her harder and she felt her legs starting to tremble as to her surprise she began to feel her pussy beginning to respond. Justine's hands slid around and grabbing Allison's wrists pulled her hands up and placed them on her tits, Allison gasped, then let out a startled yelp as Justine's hands landed on her own tits and gave her nipples a light pinch. Justine stepped back and removed her hands from her tits and smiled, "I'm sorry my sister, but I can't remember the last time I saw such a perfect set of lips."

"I..." Allison paused to try to catch her breath, "I....." she exhaled. "Wow." She said simply.

There was laughter from the table and she could feel herself blushing. Laughing softly, Justine leaned into her and spoke in her ear. "Thank you for indulging me My Lady and for giving our brothers one of the cheap thrills they live for. And don't worry, you will never be asked to be with a woman," she laughed again, "Unless you would like to find out what it's like. I am available for private lessons."

She leaned back and Allison could feel her blush deepen and found that she had nothing to say to that. Giving her a wink, Justine turned and made her way back to the head of the table.

"You can sit now Pandora," Sydney whispered to her.

Allison sat and looked around to see everyone looking at her and either laughing or smiling. She felt something brush her right foot and looking down saw Sydney's foot against hers. She looked over and sliding her chair closer to her Sydney whispered, "Don't worry; they're not making fun of you, just having some fun with you. I'm pretty new myself and the mistress did that to me as well." She smiled. "Quite the kisser."

"Yeah." Allison nodded. "I...I'm not into women, but damn."

"The Ladies play from time to time just to get the guys going, but you never have to. And don't be surprised if your aversion to women doesn't turn to curiosity at some point."

"I doubt that." She said softly, "I have no desire to play with what I already have."

Sydney shrugged, causing her small perky tits to bounce. "You never know."

"Now that we have met our new sister," Justine spoke from the head of the table where she had sat down. "We can get to the entertainment we've all been waiting for."

There were several murmurs of agreement around the table and pointing at Allison Justine continued, "Just so you know Pandora, our meetings generally start with all of us meeting for drinks and dinner and...."

"Excuse me Mistress," Adonis spoke up, then turning to Allison said "I'm sorry my sister, I don't know where my manners are, what would you like a drink?"

Allison shrugged. "A Captain and Coke would be nice."

"As you wish." Adonis said and standing up, made his way over to the bar. "I'm sorry my Mistress," he said as he passed Justine.

"No worries my brother," she replied. "Tonight however, we skipped dinner because no one is to see you until your first meeting so next month things will be back to normal."

"Here you are my lady." Adonis said as he placed a glass in front of her, "Let me know if it is to your liking."

Allison took a sip and smiled, "Excellent, thank you."

Adonis nodded and as he went back to his seat, Justine continued, "Normally dinner is where we catch up on things and discuss any personal matters. Once in the meeting proper it is time for business. Usually that is strictly fun as it is tonight, but occasionally punishments are meted out. Depending on the offense that can be fun as well, but it can also be quite harsh and a warning to all, that although we are here for pleasure, the rules are here for a reason."

Justine was directly at Allison as she spoke of the punishments and she felt her stomach flutter nervously. Mark couldn't have said anything, if he had she would never have been allowed here, nonetheless she felt as if that were directed at her.

"Usually what we do is someone will be randomly called upon to provide us with an entertaining story. Tonight we had your introduction instead. After our little dirty tale we watch two videos. These videos consist of the members of the group performing with their pets, subs, or anyone for that matter. The only rule is that no matter what your personal style, the video has you in control."

"Can you say that again for Loki's benefit?" Amado asked.

"Hey," Loki spoke up from Allison's left. "The last one wasn't bad."

"Dear, you told the woman you were sorry at one point." Mercedes pointed out.

"Leave our brother alone." Justine said. "He is a work in progress, however as was decided when he was let in his talents and service to the group far outweigh what can eventually be learned."

"Thank you Mistress." Loki bowed his head to her.

"Teachers pet." Eros said.

"What was that Eros, you would like to be taught to be a pet?" Justine asked. "I'm sure Mercedes could arrange that."

"My apologies, my Mistress." Eros said softly.

"Next interruption will be rewarded with something humiliating that I will decide upon depending on the transgressor. So anyone else?" Justine looked around the room then nodded.

"Tonight we were due to see video's from Mercedes and…."

"Will she actually be having sex in this one?" Alex asked, "Or just more of her having the guy jerk off for her?"

"Mercedes, please stand up and hike your dress up,"

"Excuse me, my Mistress?"

"Do as I say my lady so that Orion can get down on his knees and kiss it for you."

"Oh, come on!" Alex exclaimed.

"Do as your told Orion, or I will arrange for a queens chair to be brought in next meeting and you can spend the night in it and amuse all the ladies."

Alex stared at Justine, then rolling his eyes stood up and walked over to Mercedes. Pushing her chair back, Mercedes stepped away from the table and turning around pulled her dress up to her waist, exposing her small firm ass, which was barely covered by a thong the color of her dress. When Alex reached her he paused and Mark called out, "In case you can't tell the difference her ass is lower than her face."

"Lovecraft!" Justine snapped as the rest of the table laughed.

"You wouldn't know what a woman's face looks like dog," Mercedes replied "They only let you have them from behind so they don't have to look at you while they earn what you're paying them to fuck you in the first place."

There was more laughter and leaning over to Loki, Allison whispered, "Why don't they like each other?"

"They get along fine." He answered, "It's just a game between them, that's why Scarlett lets it go, they come up with some good ones."

Alex had dropped down to one knee and placing his large hands on Mercedes hips leaned in to kiss her.

"I did not hear you ask Orion." Justine smiled at the head of the table.

With a sigh, Alex spoke, "My lady would you give me the privilege of kissing your beautiful ass?"

"You may, but be quick about it, I don't want you lingering and enjoying what you're not worthy of."

"My lady is to kind." Alex replied before placing a quick kiss on each of her ass cheeks.

"I think he should give her a rim job." Victoria said.

"What is your obsession with that?" Adonis asked.

"I don't know," Vicky shrugged. "I just like to watch tongues in asses."

"Then maybe you should attend Eros's fundraising dinner," Loki said, "There's sure to plenty of that there."

The room erupted in laughter, and Allison joined in as she watched Justine try to say something and burst out laughing herself.

"Touche my brother," Eros said bowing his head to him.

As they were laughing, Alex had stood up and after kissing Mercedes hand made his way back to his seat.

"He's going to have a cold sore tomorrow for sure." Mark said shaking his head.

"Enough." Justine said as she wiped at her eyes. "Excuse us Pandora, the mood here is very light tonight as we are all in high spirits having you with us."

"I'm enjoying it." Allison said.

"Because we're not mocking you yet." Sydney said with a wink

"As I was saying before I was interrupted again, Mercedes and Mephisto were due to have videos tonight, but that will be moved to next meeting. Now I see some people looking a little confused, well more so than usual in some cases" she added with a smirk, "And I know that's because they're thinking only one would be bumped in favor of Pandora's initiation video."

"Oh shit." Allison whispered.

"Please my lady, the reaction will be amazing you'll see." Sydney told her.

"So why is the first video moved as well?" Justine smiled. "Because we have a very special treat in store for us, my brothers and sisters. Tonight we will see something that hasn't been done here in quite some time."

She paused and took a sip of her drink, before going on. "But first I have to explain one of our traditions to Pandora. Although you learned our most important rule is no sex between members," Justine paused slightly, and Allison felt another stab go through her as she was looking straight at her again, her eyes moved over to Mark who she noticed was looking down at the table. "We do enjoy some fun from time to time." Justine continued. "One of those times is upon us. When a member has a certain amount of years in the Circle they receive a reward. Now in case Lovecraft conveniently left it out, your first years reward is a payback night with your initiator."

"He told me." Allison said then added, "I'm looking forward to it."

"As are we because they are taped." Justine said smiling, "You have a year to come up with something exquisite my dear, many here are looking forward to Lovecraft squirming."

"I'll promise not to disappoint." Allison said returning her smile.

"Aside from that, every fifth year of service is rewarded with a special treat. On the meeting of that anniversary that member is serviced orally by one of their brothers and sisters."

"Don't worry Pandora," Mercedes said turning to face her. "Not all the men here are as lousy at that as Lovecraft," she sighed disgustedly. "I have seen dogs lap out of the toilet with more skill than he licks pussy."

"Most men would prefer the taste of toilet water to that of your rancid snatch, whore." Mark replied.

Ignoring them, Justine continued, "The best part about this, the fun of it is we add some mystery to this event. All members know of these dates and leading up to them can volunteer to be the giver of that special gift."

"Damn I have to wait two more years." Loki said with a sigh.

"Only I know who has volunteered and if there is more than one I choose. After the meeting I go up to the member's room and as they sit in a chair I blind fold them. I then sit back and watch as the gift is given. The giver is not to speak nor is the person receiving the gift to touch in anyway. All members are not to wear any perfume or cologne that night. All men are to be clean shaven and the women to have their hair pulled back. There is no hint at all as to who is bestowing this special gift."

Justine spread her arms to indicate the table. "It adds a great sense of mystery to look around and wonder who over the years has taken care of whom and a special privilege of the Mistress to be the only one who knows." She smiled and touched her chest. "In case you're wondering I am also entitled to my gift and on my fifteenth anniversary Lovecraft was in charge of who bestowed that gift to me." Her smile widened, "And to whomever that was, a job very well done."

"Wonder who it was." Alex said rolling his eyes.

Justine frowned and shot him such a look that he immediately put his head down, and Allison noticed no one laughed. Justine stared hard at him for a moment and leaning towards Alex whispered something that caused him to drop his head even lower. Taking a deep breath, Justine turned back to the others. "This week for any not aware is our good brother Adonis' fifteenth anniversary."

Justine paused as everyone at the table applauded. "Sadly our beloved brother, although he certainly does not look it, is in his fiftieth year, which means this will be the last anniversary he celebrates. Pandora allow me to tell you that over the years few men have been as highly regarded as Adonis, a rare gentlemen amongst Masters and a man whose kindness to not only his sisters has rarely been matched. A man who in all his instances of granted time always deferred to the ladies, never once letting one submit to him, but rather to treat them as equals and enjoy the night that much more."

"And that has always been appreciated by us my dear brother." Vicky said softly.

"Because of that, the beautiful lady who has requested to take care of him has decided to make this a special night and treat the entire group by making it a public display. The first we've had between members in quite some time."

As several people clapped, Justine stood up and walking over to Adonis smiled down at him. "My brother, please remove your jacket then slide back from the table to provide some room and a better view for the others."

"My pleasure," he laughed as he stood and after sliding his jacket off put it on the back of the chair.

As he did Allison took in his huge shoulders that seemed ready to burst out of the teal shirt he was wearing. "He's a big boy." She said softly to Sydney.

"Wait until you see the shirt come off."

Adonis sat back down and rolled his chair back a few feet and coming up behind him, Justine reached around and began undoing his tie.

"Oh, so everyone gets to know but me?" He laughed as slipping the tie from his neck; Justine wrapped it around his eyes and began tying it behind his head.

"I'm sure you will suffer nobly." Justine told him finishing the knot. Reaching back around, she got some whistles as she began unbuttoning his shirt. When she reached the last button, she pulled his shirt open and rubbed her hands along his deeply muscled chest and carved stomach.

"Wow is he in shape for his age." Allison said.

"For any age," Sydney whispered, then leaning over to Allison added. "I volunteered, but lost out to someone else."

Allison's response was cut off, by Adonis crying out in surprise as Justine pinched his nipples. "Sorry, my brother, I couldn't resist," she laughed as she walked back over to her seat.

Justine waited until Vicky and Alex had rolled their chairs next to hers and Mercedes pushed back so Sydney would be able to see past her. Everyone around the table was now silent, a look of anticipation on their faces. With a start Allison realized she was about to see a live sex show.

"It should be obvious, but I will say it anyway, no one is to say a word."

There were several murmured yes's and Justine called out, "You may begin my Lady."

Allison sensed movement to her left and saw Lexi stand up from her seat and put her arms out to the table. Everyone applauded and Amado said softly, "Very lucky man, our brother."

Slipping her blouse off to expose a tight red tank top that looked as if it was straining to contain her tits Lexi walked around the table and stopping in front of Adonis put her hands on his chest kissed him. From where she was sitting, Allison could see his mouth open as Lexi kissed him deeply while running her hands up and down his chest. Sliding her lips from his, Lexi trailed them down to his chest and as she began to teasingly swirl around his left nipple, while sliding his shirt down past his shoulders. Adonis leaned forward enough for her to work the shirt off of him, showing off his well muscled arms.

As Lexi switched to his other nipple, her hand dropped between his legs and began to rub his cock through his slacks. Allison felt her heart beginning to beat faster as she watched Lexi's tongue leave his nipple and start to slide down his stomach. As her tongue worked its way down she sank to her knees and began undoing his belt. Allison took a moment to look around the table and saw Victoria's skirt was hiked up and her hand was slowly rubbing her pussy through the material of her thong. She watched Vicky's long blue nails drift up and down her crotch, then looked up to see her lips were parted, and she was breathing heavy.

Allison looked back to see Lexi had slipped Adonis's belt off and after tossing it aside, unsnapped his pants. By now her lips were just over the waistband of his slacks and she was sliding her tongue back and forth. His hands were resting on the arms of the chair and Allison could see him starting to breathe heavy as well. After unzipping his pants, Lexi grabbed the sides of them and tugged. Adonis obediently lifted his hips and with a sudden yank Lexi pulled them, as well his underwear down.

"Oh, look at that." Sydney whispered as Adonis's cock sprang free.

"Damn." Allison said quietly.

His cock was huge and hard, and standing at full attention. Grabbing the base of it, Lexi started slowly pumping it. The look on her face was one of pure lust as licking her lips; she bent her head and flicked her tongue around the swollen head. Pulling her head back, Allison saw a trail of his pre cum between his cock and her tongue and felt a warm sensation building between her legs. In front of her, Lexi had added her other hand and was now pumping his cock with both fists. The head of his cock was still visible and Allison said quietly, "He's huge."

Lexi had begun running her tongue from his balls up the length of his shaft. When she reached the top, she sucked the head into her mouth, causing Adonis to groan and twitch his hips, releasing his cock, Lexi teasingly ran her tongue back down where she started sucking on his balls. A soft moan escaped him, and Allison could feel herself getting wet. Next to her, she saw Sydney's hand reach up and start stroking her left nipple through the bra. Looking across at Victoria, Allison saw her face was flushed and glancing down her eyes widened as she saw that she had pulled her thong to the side and her finger was sliding in and out of her pussy.

Adonis moaned, bringing Allison's attention back to the show where Lexi had taken him into her mouth and was slowly bobbing her head, taking him about halfway down each time. She wrapped her hand around his cock, just below her lips so that she was jerking him off as she blew him. His hands begin to squeeze the arms of the chair and she knew he desperately wanted to reach out and touch her. She never let her pets touch her when she did that and seeing this older powerful man begin to squirm had her nipples stiffening. Shifting in her seat she felt her wet thong slide against her pussy. She let out a sigh and looked to see if anyone had noticed, but both Sydney and Loki were watching Lexi devour Adonis's huge cock.

Devouring was the word, Lexi was now taking his cock all the way down and her hand was resting at the bottom as her red lips slid up and down his long thick shaft. She started sucking faster and was now effortlessly taking him all the way down.

"Damn look at her go." Eros said quietly.

Lexi paused, then taking his cock all the way down held it there.

"Oh, goddamn!" Adonis gasped.

"She's licking his balls," Sydney said in a voice that was more a moan than a whisper, "Shit, she's good."

Allison looked towards her, and saw that Sydney had slipped her fingers into the bra and her other hand had dropped down between her legs. Looking up, she saw Vicky now had two fingers in her pussy and another sense of the surreal came over her, as she watched Victoria Redding, an elite supermodel, play with herself while watching a blow job.

"Hell yeah, look at that!" Loki called out.

Lexi had put her hands up over her head and was making a show of deepthroating Adonis and sucking him in and out faster than before. Again she took him down to his balls and was shaking her head back and forth. Lexi made a gagging sound and withdrawing his cock from her mouth left it open, allowing a thick trail of spit to run down his shaft. Quickly taking him deep again, she made a loud slurping sound as she sucked his cock clean.

"Look at that little pig go." Mark said softly, a wicked smile on his face.

Lexi repeated the maneuver, this time using just her tongue to lick the spit from his cock, before going to town on him again. As she sucked on him, Lexi reached up and grabbing his wrists tugged on them.

"Sorry my sister," he panted trying to speak as her mouth slid up and down his cock. "I...."

"Go ahead my brother." Justine called out. "I told you tonight would be special."

Lexi tugged again, and taking his hands, placed them in her hair. Still sucking she rubbed his hand back and forth and taking the hint he wrapped his hands in her long red hair. Slurping up to the head of his cock., Lexi stopped and waited.

"Go ahead," Justine whispered. "Fuck her mouth."

Adonis lifted his hips off of the chair, shoving his cock deep into Lexi's mouth. She moaned around his hard flesh as he pushed it all the way down her throat and holding her head started pumping his hips, driving himself in and out of her mouth. Lexi tapped his thigh and Justine called out, "Harder!"

Adonis gasped and this time rather than move his hips twisted his hands in Lexi's hair and began slamming her head up and down in his lap, plunging her mouth onto his cock.

"Oh shit." Sydney groaned.

Taking a quick look down, Allison saw that like Vicky, Sydney had slid her thong over and her fingers were buried inside of her. The sound of gurgling brought her back to Lexi, whose eyes were watering from Adonis fucking her mouth, but she was moaning as well. The gurgling sounds sent a thrill through Allison and she caught her own hand as she had unconsciously started caressing her aching nipple through her dress.

"Go ahead Adonis!" Justine called out. "Use your sister's mouth, fuck it like you fuck your pets, she's fucking loving it, the little whore."

Allison heard a moan from across the room and saw that Victoria had thrown one leg over the side of her chair and her fingers were now rubbing her clit. There was wet sucking sound and she looked to see that Lexi had pulled Adonis's cock from her mouth and was sitting back on her knees, her face was flushed and her huge chest heaving. There was a long trail of spit hanging down her chin, which leaning forward she wiped off on his thigh. Standing up she turned to look at Justine who with a smile said, "Go ahead my sister, give us a show."

Lexi grabbed the bottom of her tank top and after quickly stripping it off, reached back and unhooked her bra. Letting it slide off she held up her huge tits and leaning forward shoved one of her large rose colored nipples in to Adonis's mouth. He started to turn his head, but Justine spoke, "Refuse nothing my brother; this is my gift to you."

Lexi moaned as Adonis quickly sucked her nipple into his mouth. Grabbing his hand's she brought them up to her tits and letting her head go back, moaned again as he started teasing her other nipple with his fingertips. Lexi stepped back and grabbing the sides of her skirt shoved it down. As she did, she playfully shook her round ass at the table and several men called out their approval as there were no panties to be found. Turning back to Adonis she reached out and grabbing his legs, pushed them closer together. Putting her hands on his broad shoulders, she brought her legs up one at a time so that she was kneeling on his legs.

"Oh damn," Loki said softly, "she's going to..."

Adonis let out a loud moan as reaching back and grabbing his cock, Lexi guided it to her pussy and let her weight go. She cried out as she impaled herself on his huge cock and began grinding her hips into his lap. He moaned again and placing his large hands on her hips began to shove her back and forth, helping her to ride him. Sitting up, Lexi wrapped her arms around his neck and shoved her tit in his face. He began to eagerly suck on her nipple as she rode him.

Allison was breathing hard and squirmed in her seat as her pussy was beginning to make a puddle in her thong. Next to her, Sydney's eyes were half closed and she had now pulled the cup of the bra down and was rolling her tiny pink nipple between her fingers. Allison's hand dropped into her lap and she seriously thought of pulling her own dress up, no one would see her under the table, but still she felt....

Her attention snapped back as she heard Lexi cry out. She had sat up on her knees and holding her waist, Adonis was fucking the shit out of her. From her seat, Allison could clearly see his huge cock plunging into Lexi's glistening pussy and the sight sent a flood of wetness through her already dripping pussy. As she moaned Lexi looked over at Justine who nodded. Reaching around his head, Lexi untied the knot and tossed the tie to the side. As Adonis looked up into her smiling face, she moaned, "Happy anniversary my brother."

She kissed him deeply as he slowed down his thrusts and she started bouncing up and down, taking control of their fucking. His hand was on her ass and reaching back, she guided it to just above his cock. She broke the kiss and whispered something, then gasped as he shoved his finger into her ass. Lexi wrapped her arms around his shoulders and groaned as he started thrusting both his cock and his finger into her.

"Let me ask you Adonis," Justine began, "It's your anniversary and what's an anniversary if you can't enjoy a piece of cake." She laughed. "Wouldn't you like desert my brother?"

Lexi yelped in surprise as his answer was to wrap his arms around her waist and displaying his strength stand up easily while holding her up. Taking a couple of steps forward, Adonis lied Lexi back on the table, and dropping to his knees immediately plunged his face between her legs.

"Oh, fuck yeah!" Lexi screamed.

"Holy shit." Allison whispered as Lexi began bucking her hips wildly into his face.

Lexi grabbed Adonis's hair and started grinding her pussy even harder into his face. His answer was to bring his hand up between her legs and Allison could tell from the way his arm was moving he was pumping his fingers in and out of her pussy. Lexi was moaning and squirming on the table, her eyes closed and her mouth open as she moaned continuously. Allison saw Justine lean over and whisper something to Mark, who then leaned over to Amado. A moment later they both stood up and Justine said, "Gentlemen, help your sister come for her brother."

Leaning over the table, Mark and Amado each grabbed one of Lexi's tits, and bending their heads began tonguing her nipples.

'Oh yes!" she cried. Removing her hands from Adonis's hair she placed them on the back of their heads.

"This is crazy." Allison whispered.

"Are you kidding?" Loki asked. "She loves this, she's done gang bangs with four guys, wait until you see one of her videos."

Mark and Amado each hooked one of her legs behind the knee and were pulling back until her ankle's were close to being behind her ears. Allison now had a clear view between her legs where she could see Adonis sucking hard on her clit. Two fingers of his right hand were sliding in and out of her pussy, and bringing his left up he plunged two fingers into Lexi's ass.

Lexi screamed and started trying to pump her hips into his fingers which was impossible with her legs pinned back. She let out a long whimper of frustration and Allison saw Mark lift his face from her nipple and say something to Amado. When Mark went back to her nipple, he opened his mouth and bit down hard, she assumed Amado had done the same as emitting a sound that could only be described as a howl, Lexi began to cum. Even with her legs held up her body began to buck and writhe on the table as she wailed in pleasure. Between her legs, Adonis continued to drive his fingers roughly into her holes as his lips remained fastened to her clit.

Lexi released another long howl and then began to let out a series of short gasps; she stopped and seemed to pause then cried out. There was a wet sound and Adonis flinched back as her pussy convulsed and sprayed a thick stream of fluid in his face. Lexi yelped again and another spurt hit him as he was trying to wipe off the first one with the back of his hand. There was another loud cry, this one from Victoria. Looking that way, Allison saw her head was thrown back and her mouth open as her fingers blurred across her clit. Her hips were bucking in her chair and she released a long slow moan that might have been the sexiest thing Allison had ever heard. Her hand slid from her pussy and slumping further down in her chair she said softly, "Thank you my sister."

"Jesus what a mess." Eros laughed.

"Now you know how we feel," Lexi panted as she laid there on the table, her huge tits heaving.

Mark and Amado each gave her a kiss on the cheek before sitting back down and Justine said softly, "Well my brother are you going to let that wet pussy go to waste?"

Quickly standing, Adonis grabbed her ankles and after lifting her legs and spreading them as wide as he could, plunged his massive cock into her. "Yes!" Lexi called out as he began slamming his cock in and out of her.

Her pussy was so wet each thrust was accompanied by a squishing sound as well as another yelp as Lexi lied there with her arms by her sides letting him fuck the shit out of her. Allison heard a small gasp and looked over to see Sydney's hand moving faster between her legs. She looked away embarrassed and then whispered, "Oh, My God."

The sight in front of her was amazing. Adonis was covered in sweat, causing his muscles to show even more as he drove relentlessly into Lexi's sopping wet pussy. Lexi was lying there moaning continuously as he held her legs open and fucked her as hard if not harder than Mark had fucked her. Like Mark his control was amazing, no one Allison had ever been with could have held out that long. Lifting her head up from the table, Lexi gasped, "Step back."

Adonis let her legs go and did as she said. Lexi sat up and moving to the edge of the table slid off onto the floor. "You know how I like it, my brother." She told Adonis then turning around bent over the table.

Not needing to be told twice, he stepped forward, grabbed her hips and slammed his cock into her. Lexi gasped and folding her arms on the table rested her head on them as he began fucking her harder than he had been before. She yelped as Adonis began sliding his cock all the way out to the tip before using all the strength in his powerful hips he drove forward into her. He was fucking her so hard the table was rocking and next to Allison, Sydney began to let out a series of sharp yelps, as she came sitting less than two feet away from her. Allison's own pussy was begging for release and her clit was so swollen just the material of her thong was driving her crazy.

"That's it fuck me!" Lexi cried out, looking over her shoulder at Adonis. "Really fuck me! Show me how you take your whores Adonis, make me one of them!"

Adonis looked at Justine who nodded and swinging his arm up dealt a savage slap to Lexi's ass. "Harder!" she cried out.

Adonis hit her again and the slap sounded like a gunshot in the room. Lexi gasped and Adonis let out a soft moan and began fucking her even harder. His face was covered in sweat as well Lexi's pussy and he was breathing hard. Every muscle in his impressive body was bulging and Allison knew he wouldn't be able to hold out much longer.

"Is this how you want to take her?" Justine called, "Go ahead and give it to her where you know she loves it! Take your lady Adonis!"

Adonis pulled back, lifted his cock and slammed it into Lexi's ass. Her eyes bulged and she howled into the table as grabbing her hair he pulled back hard on it as he began fucking her ass. Lexi turned her head towards Allison and she felt something wet trickle down her thigh as she stared into Lexi's wide blue eyes. She was crying out with every thrust of that huge dick in her ass, but the look on her face was pure pleasure. Her hair was plastered to her face from sweat and as Allison watched her eyes appeared to glaze over as Adonis, placing one leg up on the table started fucking her even deeper. She opened her mouth and began letting out a series of squeals that had Allison's hand sliding up her leg again. Behind Lexi, Adonis moaned and his pumps seemed to have an air of desperation in them as he started fucking her even faster. Looking back at him, Lexi called out, "Sit down!"

Adonis gasped, and pulling his cock from her ass, all but fell back into the chair. Standing up, Lexi spun around and dropping to her knees immediately began sucking his cock.

"Damn she is a pig!" Amado said.

"Suck that cock!" Vicky called out, "Suck him off Lexi! Show him how good you are!"

"Oh fuck!" Adonis groaned as Lexi took his cock all the way down to his shaft then began sucking the entire length in and out of her mouth. He gasped and grabbing her hair began thrusting his hips into her mouth. His legs were shaking and closing his eyes he put his head back and started groaning.

"That's it!" Justine shouted, "Give it to her, cum in that little whores mouth! She earned every fucking drop!"

He started to try to answer then cried out as loud as Lexi had and started wildly thrusting his hips. Between his legs, Lexi started moaning and holding her mouth still she began to jerk his cock, helping him cum in her mouth. His hips started to slow down and with one last twitch, Adonis moaned and slumped back against his chair panting. Removing her mouth from his cock, Lexi turned on her knees to face the table and pointing at her mouth spread her arms as if asking a question.

"Swallow it!" Vicky called out.

'No, drool it onto your tits!" Amado shouted.

"Why not let Pandora decide?" Justine asked, pointing at her.

Allison stared as Lexi turned to look at her, pointing at her mouth. "I...." she shook her head "I... don't"

"Hurry my lady, Your sister has quite the mouthful," Victoria said, "Why not tell her to do what you would do?"

"Well," Allison forced her voice to remain steady "I like to swallow, spitting it out on my tits is for the man's benefit and I'd rather make me happy than him."

"Well said!" Eros said slapping the table. "You are perfect my lady."

On the floor, Lexi nodded her head then made a show of throwing her head back and swallowing. Still facing the table she opened her mouth wide to show she had taken every drop, then using her hand on Adonis's knee to help her stand, sat on his lap. Putting her arm around his shoulders she panted. "Happy anniversary, dear brother. Thank you for all you have done for us."

She gave him a sweet kiss and sliding his huge arm around her he pulled her close to him and kissed the top of her head. "Thank you my beautiful sister. You have made this an unforgettable evening."

"Brothers and sisters," Justine spoke up. "Some appreciation for the amazing Lady Lexi"

Everyone stood and applauded and Allison followed suit, part of her still trying to grasp the fact that not only had she just watched two people fuck the shit out of each other, but people were cheering as if it were a sporting event. Lexi bowed to the table and then stepping into her skirt, pulled it up to her hips. Adonis stood as well and pulling his pants up picked Lexi's shirt up off the floor and slid it down over her upraised arms. She kissed him again and as he sat down tiredly made her way around the table, pausing as Justine embraced her and stopping as both Mark and Amado, took her hand and kissed it. Loki stood up and pulled her seat out for her. After she sat she smiled tiredly over at Allison. "Hope I made your first meeting live up to expectations."

"Oh, I wasn't expecting this." Allison said then unable to help it asked "Didn't that hurt?"

"I'm used to it," she sighed. "God I love it in the ass."

"Better you than me," Allison shook her head.

"Something tells me, we're about to see otherwise." Lexi grinned. "I've seen Lovecraft's videos."

Before she could reply, she saw Mark coming over. "Speak of the devil." Lexi said smiling at him.

"No, just one of his servants," Mark replied as he handed her a bottle of water.

"Thank you." She nodded and taking the bottle, chugged half of it.

Next to her, Allison saw Loki open the lap top in front of him and begin to type. Picking up a remote he thumbed a button and across from her the huge tv on the wall came on to display a blank screen. Eros rose and walking over to the wall killed the lights. In front of her, everyone turned in their seats to face the tv.

"Now my brothers and sisters," Justine said, "As if that little treat wasn't enough to make this meeting memorable, we're now going to see what we've all been looking forward to"

The screen flickered and went black. A small flame appeared and began to spread in a pattern, a moment later the flames had taken the shape of the baphomet. The image burned on the screen for a moment then slowly faded to a black outline that as Allison watched became Mark's powerful back. The video panned back to show Mark standing there his back to it. He turned slowly and paused to stare at the camera, Allison could see his bed behind him and putting his hand out and caressing one of the carved ebony bed posts he began to speak.

"Good evening my brothers and sisters. It has come to my attention there have been rumors that the eastern circle has gotten soft. That we are no longer one of the elite groups and membership here is but a formality freely given." He shook his head slowly.

"Tonight that rumor will be proven to be exactly what it is, a lie. For you see The Mistress Scarlett upset at that rumor has granted me, Lovecraft, The Dark Prince of the Circle , permission to show the other Circles what it takes to gain entrance to our group. It is a mission I took very seriously as the reputation of my brothers and sisters were at stake. Tonight, you will see a woman who is a strong dominant in her own right come face to face with a true master of Women. One who could only be broken by the Mistress Scarlett herself, and is second in reputation to only Persephone."

Mark paused and the camera zoomed in close to his face, then to his eyes which were that beautiful shade of golden green. He continued to speak, "Tonight my brother's and sister's you will witness an initiation that other Circles only speak of as legend. So without further adieu, allow me to present to you," Mark's eyes suddenly darkened and he smiled, "The Breaking of Allison."

A cheer went up around the table and putting her head down, Allison muttered "Fuck me."

Chapter Four

The screen faded to black and Allison looked around to see all eyes were on the TV. At the head of the table Justine and Mark had slid their chairs over and were sitting next to each other. On the other side Alex had slid over to the right, but Victoria had stayed at the table, and had just her head turned towards the screen. The TV flickered and Allison saw herself sitting at the bar at Mitch's. She looked miserable and picking her cell phone up looked at it, and then shaking her head put it back and looked around disgustedly. A couple of people around the table laughed, as a moment later Mark walked right up behind her, and just stood there watching her.

His arms were crossed, displaying his massive tattoos and as he stared at her, reached out until his fingers were inches from her hair. She looked up and turned, but only to see that Mark had quickly turned and was walking away from her. Sitting there in the chair she frowned as there was another laugh; he had been stalking her the entire time she had sat there stewing. On the screen Mark came over and sat down next to her. She jumped as their voices came through the speakers behind her. She only half heard the initial exchange, then heard Mark set her up, "What do you think, you're better than me?"

"No hon," her screen persona replied, "Just out of your league."

"Famous last words," Eros commented.

The conversation went on and Mark's voice carried through the room, "Warner's a poser, he doesn't master his women, he buys them."

"Fuck you, Lovecraft." Alex said, getting a few snickers.

The scene shifted to Mark's living room and Allison watched as they entered his apartment. There were a few laughs as she spoke in her little girl voice, then some whistles as she put her arms up and slowly turned, flipping her skirt up and showing herself off to him. They moved to his bedroom door and she watched herself try to seduce him. As she trailed her hand along his arm and sweet talked him, there seemed to be an air of anticipation in the room. When Mark grabbed her chin and began insulting her again, she saw several heads bob, nodding in approval of what he was saying to her.

The screen winked and they were in his bedroom. Mark told her to strip and Allison felt her cheeks start to flush as eleven people were now staring at her completely naked.

"Well hello Lady Pandora!" Adonis exclaimed.

"Gorgeous tits." Amado said softly.

Allison flinched as she saw Mark's hand flash out and pinch her nipple. The sound of her yelp pierced the room and she heard Loki whisper, "Damn he's fast."

Mark slapped the collar and leash on her and yanked her down to the floor. The video zoomed in as Allison unzipped his pants. He slapped her hands away and when he whipped his cock out, the look on her face drew a few chuckles from the group. Those laughs quieted as she began to suck his cock. Allison felt like sliding down off the chair as a group of people she just met watched her give a blow job. Mark grabbed the back of her head and started fucking her mouth. To her left Lexi said softly, "Oh, you lucky bitch."

Mark put his leg up and began driving his cock deeper. Tears were flowing down her face and Sensing movement Allison looked to her right, to see Sydney once again playing with her nipple.

"Holy shit, Lovecraft." Eros gasped.

Allison looked back to see they were at the point where Mark had pinched her nose shut. Allison was looking up at him, her eyes bulging with fear as her already flushed face began to turn a darker shade of red.

"I thought there were rules these days?" Loki asked.

On the TV Allison was squealing around his cock, as he held her arms over his head. She cried out against his hard flesh and fell to her hands and knees as he pulled his cock from her mouth. As she knelt there gasping, he looked down at her,

'Were you trying to say something whore?"

On the screen Allison looked up at him, an expression of rage on her face. She began to say something then stopped. Her expression changed slightly and in a stronger voice than she had remembered using she said. "I was simply trying to thank you my master."

"The lady has a core of steel in her for sure." Mercedes said approvingly.

There were several murmured agreements and next to her Sydney said, "Well met, my lady."

The view on the television changed to Mark bending her over the bed.

"Nice tattoo." Loki told her.

Allison winced as Mark began spanking her, dealing blow after blow to her ass. Allison could see his hand prints on her and the sound of the slaps in the now silent room was deafening. She gasped as she realized she had been holding her breath while watching. In front of her, Mark backed up a step and then drove his enormous cock into her.

"Oh goddamn," Sydney whispered softly,

Something in her tone made Allison look over and she saw that Sydney, like Victoria had done earlier, had put her left leg over the arm of the chair and her hand was busy between her legs. That caused Allison to shift her gaze to Victoria. Her eyes widened as she saw that she had put both of her feet up against the edge of the table and had her hand buried in her pussy. She heard a sigh and turned to see Loki staring across the table where from his position he had a direct view of Victoria's pussy.

"Here we go." Lexi whispered. Back up on the screen Mark had released the manacles from his bed and Allison was lying on her back staring up at him with a look of naked fear on her face. As he went to grab her wrist she whimpered, "Please don't hurt me."

"So much for steel." Mercedes said shaking her head.

Allison bit back the urge to tell her to go fuck herself, but her attention was drawn back to the show in front of her. Mark had climbed up the bed and was fucking her mouth. Allison looked over at Loki and wondered how much work he had put in to editing this and exactly how many cameras were in Mark's room. The views was shifting from an angle that showed Mark's long cock driving into her helpless mouth and a view from above showing his powerful back and ass as he pumped his hips down into her. Mark slid back down on the bed and kneel between her legs. The camera was now pointing his over shoulder and directly between her wide open legs. Right on cue, Adonis said, "Beautiful pussy."

Her pussy was then covered as lunging forward on the bed, Mark slammed his cock into her and started fucking the shit out of her. This time the camera stayed still, focused on Mark's incredible body over hers as he assaulted her pussy. There were a few soft murmurs around the table that she couldn't make out, but didn't care anymore, right now her attention was on the glistening muscles in Mark's back and shoulders and the fact that she was getting worked up. She was beginning to sweat and there was a pleasant warm wet sensation building between her legs. She sat back and had to bite back a moan as the material of her bra rubbed across her nipples.

Looking over to the right she saw Sydney's eyes were half closed and that her hand was moving slowly, teasing her pussy as she waited for the climax of the video. Allison heard herself emitting a series of yelps as Mark began fucking her even harder. The camera had panned down and as he fucked her, his face was visible in the mirror in front of him. His black eyes were staring straight down into her face and his expression completely blank as he tore into her. Mark began speaking, telling her that he wished he could bring in her pets and let them gang bang her. She saw him begin to lift his hips higher and start slamming her harder. She was squealing loudly and to her surprise the sound sent a wave of heat through her pussy. She could hear Sydney breathing heavier next to her and to her left saw Lexi swing her foot up onto the table, and slide her hand down into her still moist pussy.

Loki was staring intently at the screen as was Eros and Adonis and Allison wondered if the guys ever masturbated at the table. Amado was now sitting straight up in his chair and was loosening his tie. Alex was also totally focused on the screen. He let out a low whistle as, Allison's cries took on an even more desperate pitch.

"Oh, that sounds so fucking hot!" Victoria purred in a tone that sent another surge through her.

"Go ahead, say it!" Mark snarled in her face on the screen.

Allison saw herself begin to speak, and then stop as Mark gasped and his breathing picked up. She stared as the expression on her face change again, and giving him a smile that she didn't recall at the time, she said softly, "Thank you, Master, for showing this unworthy whore what it's like to be taken by a real man."

To her delight the camera caught Mark's look of surprise, then obvious frustration as he was unable to hold back any longer.

Allison pouted and said sweetly, "Oh thank you Master!"

"What do you say to that Mercedes?" Lexi asked, and then turning towards Allison nodded. "A strong showing my lady."

Allison didn't reply as her eyes were drawn down to where, even as she had spoken, Lexi was still stroking herself. She watched Lexi's slender finger slide through the wet folds of her pussy. The same pussy that fifteen minute, ago had been stuffed with one of the biggest cocks Allison had ever seen. Speaking of huge cocks, several people whistled and commented as on the screen, Mark was spraying her face with cum. An hour ago she would have thought sitting at a table surrounded by people who were watching her get her face painted, would have made her hide her head. Instead she found she couldn't look away as she watched spurt after spurt of thick white cum splash against her face. Mark got off of her and the camera zoomed down into her sweat streaked and cum coated face. Sydney moaned softly and speaking for the first time, Justine said, "Oh what a beautiful sight."

Walking back to the foot of the bed Mark shoved the vibrator between her legs and after tying her legs together her, left the room. The next several minutes of the video was Allison lying there whimpering pathetically as the vibrator hummed, then shut off. Whenever it kicked back on, her eyes would widen and she would start moaning. Her hips were pumping as she strained to cum and she heard Victoria moan as on the screen she whimpered "Oh, no!" as again her orgasm was denied her. Allison slid down in her seat and this time a soft sigh did escape as she could feel her wet thong slide across her aching pussy. Again her hand dropped to her thigh and started sliding up towards her yearning flesh.

The screen flickered and Allison saw that her eyes were closed. She started to twitch then called out "No!" remembering that she had thought she had called out cease in her nightmare, Allison felt her stomach tighten. On the TV she shouted, "Please" but to her it sounded odd. Looking over at Loki, she whispered, "Did you fix that?"

"Fix what?" he winked then turned back to the screen where Mark appeared out of the shadows and approached her.

He cranked the vibrator again, and smiled sadistically as he stopped her from cumming, before untying her legs. Allison caught her breath as he crawled between her legs. This was the scene that she had been masturbating to for two weeks and she was about to watch it happen. Her lips parted to allow for her heavier breathing as she watched Mark spread her pussy open. The camera was showing the view from above and the sight of Mark's muscular, tanned body lying between her ivory thighs sent another shiver through her. His dark hands on her inner thighs and his tongue flickering out against her glistening pink pussy sent her hand up between her legs to brush against the soaked crotch of her thong.

The teasing went on and Mark began asking her if she did it to her pets. Allison's answers were barely more than whimpers as he had her right on the edge of cumming. Sydney's arms brushed hers and she heard her moan louder than she had before as she continued to stroke herself. Mark asked her if she always let her pets come and this time Victoria moaned as, with a look of utter hopelessness on her face, Allison began to beg him to let her come. Mark brought her close and when he backed off, she let out the most pitiful moan she'd ever heard. He immediately started licking her again and Lexi said, "Goddamn, he's good at that."

"I was enjoying my work." Mark said quietly.

There were a couple of soft laughs, but the room quickly went silent as Mark began teasing her more, asking her why she should be allowed to come. Allison bit her tongue to avoid moaning as she rubbed the edge of her hand along her pussy. She couldn't do this in front of people and tried to move her hand, but it didn't seem to want to listen. She jumped as her phone beeped on the chair next to her telling her she had a text, she quickly reached down to shut it off, and knocked it on the floor. Feeling stupid she bent down to pick it up and froze.

From her position she could see underneath the table all the way to the end and saw that Justine had her sandal off and was sliding her foot, up Mark's leg. Despite the sound of her moaning getting louder on the screen, Allison continued to stare and saw his hand was on Justine's inner thigh, his fingers were caressing her. Her hand was resting on his leg as well and their touching didn't seem urgent at all, rather it seemed comfortable and familiar. In an instant it struck Allison they were lovers. Apparently she who made the rules could break them and Allison wondered if that was why he had been so upset he had screwed up with her.

Realizing she was sitting there with her head under the table, Allison quickly sat back up just in time to see Mark starting in on her with that teasingly soft touch and get her close again, this time when he stopped Allison gave up all pretense of pride and began pathetically begging him. There was now heavy breathing from Lexi as well as Sydney and Allison again found her hand sliding against her soaked crotch. On the screen Mark sped his tongue up and Allison jumped as the speakers erupted with her long loud wail of pleasure. She squirmed and writhed on the bed as he licked her and she continued to squeal as came hard in his face.

Sydney let out a long loud moan that caused Amado and Alex to look back and stare as she came to Allison's orgasm. She turned to look next to her and saw that Sydney had thrown her other leg across the arm of the chair and was deliberately giving the men a show as she stroked herself through her orgasm. Lexi erupted into a long squeal to her left and unable to help it, Allison turned to watch her fingers stroke her swollen clit. Loki was looking straight down at her pussy and the look on his face was enough to make Allison rub herself harder and she released a moan that was covered up by her moaning over the speakers.

The screen flickered again and this time Allison saw herself being pulled off the bed by the leash. As she saw herself begin to crawl on all fours, she was again surprised that instead of humiliation all she felt was more heat between her legs. She couldn't remember being this hot without anyone actually touching her. The camera panned up behind her showing her ass and thighs framing her glistening pussy as Mark walked her like a dog. He took her into the shower And she watched herself being chained to the hook and scrubbed down, when Mark spun her up against the wall and started fucking her, she began rubbing herself faster and now with her fingers rather than the edge of her hand.

The scene shifted one more time and Allison took a deep breath as she saw Mark put her on her hands and knees and tie her hand behind her back. He got on his knees behind her and the camera focused on her face as he pushed his cock into her ass. He paused then Allison's mouth opened wide and her scream filled the room as he drove his huge cock into her ass.

"Jesus." Loki whispered as Mark began tearing into her and she howled in pain with each thrust.

Allison leaned back in the chair and started to bring her leg up. Her fingers began to slip into her thong and she groaned at how wet her pussy was. The sound of her screaming as Mark tore into her filled the room and Allison looked around to see everyone's eyes locked onto the screen. There were no more comments or jokes now; everyone was completely caught up in the show. Allison stared at herself on the huge TV, her mouth was open and her eyes squeezed shut in pain as Mark continued his relentless assault on her.

Her eyes shifted behind her and she gasped and pushed her finger into her pussy as she took in the sight of Mark. Every muscle in his chest and arms were bulging as he held her hips and fucked the shit out of her. His body was slicked with sweat and his dark eyes appeared to be glowing. He looked both dangerous as well as desirable and she could feel her heart pounding in her chest as she slipped her finger through her pussy. She gasped as she reached her throbbing clit and then heard a soft laugh next to her. Allison turned her head to see Sydney smiling at her.

"Enjoying the show?" she whispered

"I..."

Allison felt herself blush and started to pull her hand out from between her legs. She stopped as reaching down Sydney caught her wrist. "Go ahead, my sister." She said. "Don't hold back, this is your night after all." She smiled up at the screen "And such a show."

Allison jerked as she heard herself emit a long howl and looking up saw that Mark had pulled her back by her hair and was tearing into her even harder. There were tears on her cheeks and her hair was plastered to her face as she squealed again into the camera. She opened her mouth and started to say the word, then let out a surprised cry as Mark reached down and shoved the bullet into her pussy. Her squeals began to change in pitch as Mark began fucking her again and Allison saw the look on her face begin to change as well. Down the table Victoria, who had held herself off was moaning and her fingers busy on her clit. Turning to look at her, Victoria smiled, "And will you join me my sister?"

Victoria had been pointing down at her lap and Allison realized she still had one knee up against the table and her hand in her lap.

"Go ahead Pandora," Sydney whispered, "You know you need to."

On the screen Mark told her to read the banner and after she gasped out each word, she shrieked as Mark slammed into her even harder. At the front of the table Justine called out, "Oh yes! Make her sing my prince!"

Allison's screams were now mixed with moans as she watched her eyes began to glaze over into a look of lust that sent her fingers plunging into her pussy. As Mark tore into her ass and her screams turned into squeals, Allison's fingers found her clit and she cried out as she started rubbing it in hard fast circles.

"That's it Pandora," Lexi said, "Show us how much you love it!"

The room was pierced with a high pitched wail from the television, then Allison screaming, "Oh yes master, oh thank you!"

"There it is!" Amado called out.

Allison moaned as her fingers sped up, trying to come before the video ended; again her screams filled the room. "Thank you for showing me my place, Master! Thank you for fucking this unworthy whore, for treating me like the fucking pig I am! For showing me my place! Oh oh oh!"

Her scream turned into a wail as she began to come with Mark fucking her ass, down the table, Victoria threw her head back and released a wail of her own as her hips bucked off of the chair and into her fingers. Allison gasped as she felt her own orgasm building. Not caring if anyone was watching, she reached up and sliding her hand into her bra, caught hold of her nipple and started twisting it. She leaned her head back and as she saw Mark whip his cock out of her ass and shove it in her mouth, she released a series of sharp yelps and then as her pussy convulsed around her fingers screamed as loud as she had on the video.

She was aware of everyone, including Justine, turning in their seats to watch her, but she didn't stop. The orgasm was tearing through her and she was thrusting her hips into her fingers. Next to her, she saw Loki hit the remote and the TV paused as the entire table watched her come. Allison released a low moan, then with a sigh slumped gasping into her seat. Loki hit the button again and everyone turned as Allison whispered, "I see a once proud whore who now knows her place."

She moaned softly as she slid her fingers from her sopping wet pussy and watched, panting as she spoke again, "I have no will of my own," she whispered, looking up at him. Her lip was trembling and she whimpered, "My only desire's are my master's desire's"

She watched her heart pounding as Mark knelt down, and gave her that surprisingly gentle kiss.

"Welcome to The Circle my Lady."

The TV went off and immediately everyone in the room stood and turning to face her began applauding.

"An amazing initiation!" Justine called out, "This one will be spoken of throughout the Circles for a long time to come" pointing at Allison, she bowed deeply. "Welcome to the Circle Lady Pandora, you have earned it!"

"Yes!" Amado exclaimed and putting his hands up to call for silence, began speaking. "I want to take a moment to point out what an amazing lady our Pandora truly is! Lovecraft is one of the strongest doms in the Circle, and to gain passage through him will earn you instant respect amongst all the groups," he paused and bowing to her as Justine had done said, "You showed spirit my lady and held out quite well, We are all proud to call you sister."

Allison forced herself to stand and give a weak bow to the group. She had come so hard her legs felt like rubber and she again had that feeling as if none of this could be real. The applause stopped as Victoria raised her hands.

"And let me also point out my brothers and sisters, how privileged we are to have seen such an amazing initiation and how proud I am to say that the East has the best Enforcer of all the Circles. Let us pay our respects to a true master of women, my dark prince, Lovecraft!"

As they applauded Mark bowed, then putting his hand up for silence gestured to Allison,

"Again it was my privilege to introduce Pandora to this Circle. The initiation was hard fought and our new sister acquitted herself quite well. It truly was my pleasure to be with a woman of such beauty and talent." He paused and smirked, "And it will be with great trepidation that I put myself at your mercy next year."

"Payback's a bitch." She told him quietly, getting a round of laughter from the table.

"Pandora," Justine spoke haltingly though her laughter, "You are truly one of us!"

Chapter Five

Allison sat on the edge of the table sipping another Captain and Coke and relishing being the center of attention. Justine had ended the meeting right after her video and most of the group had gathered round to speak with their newest sister. Many of them commented on her video and how exciting it was. Allison had been a little embarrassed at first, but as she saw the same look of genuine respect on their faces, began to enjoy.

Lexi especially raved about it and leaning forward had whispered in her ear she was dying to get a chance to be with Mark. She admitted she preferred to be submissive and loved to be taken roughly and the only time she dommed was for her videos. As Allison listened to her, she remembered Loki telling her that Lexi liked to be gang banged and asked her about it. She got even more excited, telling Allison how incredible it was to just let go and be used like that. She told her she should try it sometime and laughing, Allison said she would pass.

Along with Lexi, Allison found herself very much enjoying talking to Sydney, who had finally put her dress back on despite some protests from Victoria. When Justine interceded by telling Victoria it would be her turn to walk around in her underwear, Victoria sighed and said she would not give the unworthy dogs around her the satisfaction. Allison liked the fact Sydney had only been in the group for a few months and was still getting used to things herself. She lived in Connecticut and told Allison she would love her to come up and spend a weekend with her.

Eros came over and told her he had to be leaving and presented her with his card, saying he would call her to discuss what time he would pick her up for the fundraiser. Allison had kissed his cheek and thanked him for asking her, he nodded then told her he couldn't wait to show her off. As he walked away she shook her head, dinner with a councilman. Even if it were just for show, it would put her in touch with a lot of potential big shots. Mercedes had then come over and handed her two cards, one was for her club and with a smile she told her,

"Present that at the door my lady. You will be brought to me immediately and I will see to it you have an excellent time and are well taken care of." As Allison looked at that card, Mercedes tapped the other one, "And I want you to set up a night at the hotel before our next meeting. That way you can report to me on the quality of my gift to you. Your chosen lover risks a severe punishment if he disappoints, but a sweet reward if you are happy. I trust you will have an amazing evening."

"Thank you, Mercedes," Allison smiled as she looked at the card, suddenly the idea of someone providing her with some fun didn't seem so bad.

"Thank you for a most entertaining video and for completing our Circle" Mercedes told her. "And do not take my comments to heart; you held out well, Lovecraft is not for the faint of heart."

"No he's not," she agreed, then asked, "You guys are friends right?"

Mercedes smiled. "I harbor no ill will for my brother, I just enjoy mocking him." Looking at her watch she frowned. "Well it's after eleven and I need to be at the club before midnight, I look forward to seeing you in Boston."

Allison looked at her watch and was shocked to see that it was almost eleven thirty. She looked up at a touch on her arm and saw Amado standing there. "Allison, tonight was amazing and please call me this week, I want to have lunch with you to discuss some business opportunities as well as spend some time with my new sister."

"I look forward to it," she told him. He kissed her hand and with a laugh she said, "That is not going to get old."

Adonis came by to say goodnight to her. After he did he went over to Lexi and gave her an affectionate hug as he thanked her for an incredible evening. Allison watched Lexi kiss him and holding him close tell him it was her pleasure. She still couldn't believe she had watched the two of them have sex in front of her and was amazed at how causal they were about it. Sydney's phone rang and stepping away from Allison she answered and walked over to the far corner of the room. Allison found herself alone and looking down towards Mark who was now talking to Loki, slid off the table and made to go over there.

"A Moment Pandora?"

She turned to see Victoria standing there and giving her a smile said, "Victoria this...."

"Felicia dear."

"Oh, sorry Lady Felicia," Allison laughed. "This is amazing!"

She smiled back at her, "Are you enjoying your first meeting?"

"That's an understatement!" she said.

"Good." Victoria replied and putting her arm around her, guided her away from the table, "Come with me my sister, I don't wish to be overheard."

Allison frowned as she walked towards the bar with her. "Is everything okay?"

"Let me ask you Pandora, is this group not everything Orion told you it would be? A place where you can relax and be yourself, where as you saw tonight, nothing is taboo? Your exploits will be thought of as amazing here, rather than disturbing as they would be anywhere else."

"It was something," Allison nodded. "I...I can't believe I sat there and got off in front of everyone."

"And as you can see your brothers and sisters are quite sincere are they not? We may appear aloof and better than to the world at large, but here you see we let our hair down and are quite fun."

"I see that. It's..."

"And most importantly," Victoria interrupted. "You see the opportunities for advancement. Not only have we already helped your career, but I know you're excited about the potential Eros's dinner has for you. I understand you have already received quite the promotion."

"I did, and it's...."

"Just the beginning no?"

"Absolutely!" Allison exclaimed. 'I can't wait for..."

"Well how would you like to lose it all?"

Allison turned her head to look at Victoria and found herself staring into her blue eyes which now seemed cold. "Why would I...."

"If you dare speak of the mistake you made, you will lose everything and far more quickly than you gained it."

Allison's stomach began to turn and trying to look confused she asked, "What are you talking about?"

"Lovecraft told me of what transpired after your initiation Pandora." Victoria answered softly.

Why the hell would he do that? Allison's mind began racing as she tried to hold Victoria's gaze. She tried to think of something to say, but could come up with nothing. With a nod, Victoria began speaking quietly. "Don't panic just yet. Lovecraft did not tell Scarlett, if he had you would have never been invited to this meeting. Instead, concerned you would not heed his warning he came to me. This now puts me in an awkward position, as it should now be me going to our Mistress about this offense."

"Vi...Felicia," she caught herself. "I know we screwed up and he told me what could happen. I promise I won't say anything."

"You promised him. You also seduced him, giving you the confidence to attempt it again at some point." Raising her eyebrows, she asked. "And you have thought about it haven't you Pandora? You're used to having your way and Lovecraft was like no man you had ever had, you have been planning on having him again at some point. I would be disappointed if you hadn't, after all that is our nature."

"I..." Allison let out a deep breath, "Maybe I have, but I...."

"Pandora, there is an expression we have; nothing in the Circle is free. When a member helps another it is because they want to, but there is always a price, sometimes sexual in nature if the Mistress allows it, but more often it is the calling in of a favor."

Victoria turned around and leaning against the bar reached down, and taking Allison's hand pulled her directly in front of her. Placing her hand on her shoulder she, she continued, "Several years ago I broke a rule and was to be punished. The rule I broke was minor, I was complaining I had been passed around to a couple of members and didn't want to be the club mascot. My punishment was to submit to yet another, the enforcer of the group. He did not like me or my attitude and whipped me. He got carried away and scarred me. In my career explaining whip marks would be interesting to say the least."

"Oh, my god." Allison whispered.

"To this day I wear cover up on my left shoulder so it is not seen. I was going to leave the group, but Scarlett, who set me up to be punished felt terrible and sent Lovecraft to see me. He has strong views against people who pick on those weaker than themselves and asked me to stay, promising that he would make it right."

Victoria paused and turned her head. Allison followed her gaze, and she saw Mark looking their way. He stared for a moment, then went back to talking to Alex.

"The next meeting he called out the enforcer as a coward and challenged him for his position. The next weekend we met at the private Gym that Alex works out in. The place was closed to all but us and in the ring Lovecraft and Tartarus faced off. For the next ten minutes, Lovecraft toyed with him, hitting him and dancing back, hurting him, but not finishing him. He would have won the fight easily, but something happened and he snapped. Before anyone could stop him, he broke several of Tartaru's ribs, and then kicked him in the knee snapping his leg back."

"Jesus." She whispered.

"To this day that man walks with a cane and my brother did it in my name. I am scarred for life and he is hurt for life an eye for an eye."

"And you're okay with that?" Allison asked.

"Was it extreme? Yes, but did that animal deserve it?" she smiled coldly, "I would rather it not been so harsh, but he brought it upon himself. After that I offered myself to Lovecraft as a reward. Knowing my issue was I did not enjoy being given away, he turned me down, said I was wanted for far more than my body and his reward was my staying."

"He..." Allison paused. "He seems like he's two people, crazy and sweet at the same time."

"Many demons drive my brother, it is not my place to know what they are, but he does have a sense of flawed nobility that tempers his capacity for revenge. However, he also knew that by doing that I was in his debt and now six years later, his favor has come due and he has asked that I speak with you and not involve Scarlett."

"I can assure you that nothing will happen." Allison told her. "I understand...."

"Nothing yet." Victoria cut her off. "First of all, your seduction of Lovecraft was a fluke. He suffers from insomnia and is prone to bouts of depression, why? Again not my place to know my brothers mind, but he was not prepared for that initiation. He then compounded his weakness by demonstrating his usual lack of control and indulging in far too much to drink. On your end you had been through a life changing experience, and was also drunk. Although not so drunk that you decided you wanted him on your terms. You caught him in a weak moment and took advantage to get what you wanted."

"I..."

"Trust me Pandora, nothing that you did warranted his giving in to you, it was a matter of timing. In reality there is nothing special about you to him."

"Thanks." She rolled her eyes.

"But you will think that and our concern is that you believe you would have this control over others. We fear that while enjoying your evening with our very attractive brother Eros that perhaps you would decide to indulge in him as well. Except he will turn you down, then go to Scarlett."

"I've been through this with M...Lovecraft." Allison said heatedly, she was getting tired of being lectured. "And I told him that...."

"You will speak when I'm finished." Victoria snapped at her. "I am above you in this group and you will know your place, understood?" Allison stared at her, before nodding.

"If Scarlett finds out, she will go to Lovecraft. If she does he will tell her of what transpired. He does not want to see you banned as he blames himself, but he will not lie to her. She is his mistress and he will confess. She will punish him, and it will be brutal. Scarlett is a survivor of the old guard and can be more vicious than you can possibly imagine. But whereas he will be punished you will be expelled from the group and be considered disgraced."

"Disgraced." Allison repeated.

"Yes for breaking the most important rule. See this is what you need to understand Pandora, if this was brought to Scarlett immediately you would have never made it to this meeting. But you have seen us now, all of us. The recruiter, Orion in your case, takes a risk when they speak of the group. I very much wanted to see you one of us and exposed myself as well. But now all of us will be at risk if you leave."

"I would never...."

She stopped as Victoria put her hand up. A moment later, Allison saw Lexi coming over and Victoria said, "My lady if you would excuse us for a moment?" Lexi nodded and turning walked over to Alex and Justine.

"We would make sure that you never did Pandora, trust me on that. Orion and Mephisto are millionaires and yes they have a playboy reputation, but being exposed as members of a sex group would be a bit much. I have a reputation in the industry of practicing discretion in my work and you have just witnessed me, stroking my pussy, in front of a live audience. Lexi is a successful corporate lawyer and you saw her take it in the ass from a man who works for ESPN. Eros is a public figure. There is a lot to lose here Pandora and we react accordingly."

"What does that..."

"For starters Orion and I will pull our work from you and if you say anything we will say it is because of incompetence. We will make sure word gets out that you are not reliable and ruin your name."

"But...."

"Speaking of ruining, you have seen what Loki can do. He has your initiation video in his possession, if we think for a second you have spoken of us, that video will be e-mailed to your employer and everyone you work with. They can all witness you crawling naked on a leash," she sighed. "As will your father."

Allison's eyes widened and she found herself speechless as Victoria went on. "Loki will take that video and upload it to every amateur porn site on the internet and there are hundreds of them. We will ruin you both personally as well as professionally and by the time we are done any allegations you make against any of us will look like the bitter accusations of sex crazed gold digger."

Victoria went silent and Allison could feel her heart pounding in her chest.

"All this over some sex?" she whispered.

"No, the sex will get you out of the group, any attempt at exposing us will lead to the rest. Although as I said your career will suffer as we will not be allowed to work with you."

Squeezing her shoulder, Victoria said softly, "Allison, we don't want that to happen. Mark was beside himself that he created this mess. It was expected you might make a pass at him, it happens frequently. He was the one who fell. That is why it is being handled this way."

"By threatening me?" she asked, "By threatening to humiliate me to my father?"

"I'm warning you Allison."

"What happened to Pandora?"

Standing away from the bar, Victoria put her arms around her neck, giving her a hug and whispered in her ear. "I like you Allison, I really do. You're beautiful, and driven and most of all fun. This was your fist meeting and you've already begun playing along with everyone. I look forward to spending time with you and I'm not talking about work. I look forward to lunches and shopping and teasing the boys." Turning her head, she kissed Allison's cheek. "I have two older sisters and always wanted a little sister. Most of the ladies here are not shall we say compatible with that, but I think we can have a lot of fun together and I don't want to see that lost to a mistake."

Leaning back, but still keeping her hand son her shoulders, Victoria continued, "I did not like issuing that warning, but that is all it is right now, it's up to you to leave it at just that." She sighed. "No one can know of this, anyone else would go to Scarlett and it would be ugly."

Allison nodded. "I promised Mark and I'll promise you..."

"But you have to mean it to me dear." Victoria smirked.

"I promise." She grinned back at her. "I already love it here vi... Lady Felicia, I won't jeopardize it."

"Good to hear." Victoria smiled.

"Besides," leaning closer to Victoria she whispered. "I would imagine Scarlett would be upset I was messing with her boy."

Victoria frowned and glancing over at Mark and Justine looked back at Allison. "So that's what you were doing under the table dear, spying?"

"Well..." she shrugged then laughed. "I guess the one who makes the rules can break them."

"Being the Master or Mistress has its perks Pandora." Victoria lowered her voice. "Including indulging in a member of their group, however I will ask that you don't make that statement to anyone else in this room. So I'm glad you said it to me."

"Why? If she can do what she…"

"Jealousy is an ugly emotion." Victoria interrupted. "And this group is full of it. Everyone here has always had what they have wanted and never been turned down by anyone they have wanted. The reason that granted time is both rare and kept secret is that jealousy. We do not need things going on like, "Lexi said okay to Adonis, but refused time with Eros" money and power doesn't necessarily equal maturity and this table does have its children."

"I can see that." She grinned. "Boys will be boys."

"Oh, the women can be as bad, but again never repeat what you said. Especially to Orion."

"Why?"

"He and Lovecraft are great friends, more like brothers, but are fierce rivals within this group and if he knew Scarlett enjoyed Lovecraft's company from time to time there would be a problem and it would be traced back to the person who brought it up." She shrugged. "Just consider it a dirty little secret, this group is full of them," she laughed. "But always feel free to tell your big sister, gossip is what I live for."

"So the mistress and master get free reign?"

"Not free reign, but they can have what they want. It is frowned upon to indulge in the table. It often creates favorites and jealousy and makes the position look like an excuse to be grabby. On the night a new Mistress or master is chosen they pick from the table someone to celebrate with, but it remains between them."

"Will we have a Master at some point?"

"Scarlett has to step down in two years, Orion is the heir apparent, so who knows Pandora, you could find yourself in his bed."

Allison looked over to see Alex had removed his jacket and tie. He had also rolled his sleeves up and was making a show of flexing his forearms to Mark who was rolling his eyes at him.

"Wouldn't be a bad thing." She smiled. "But it wouldn't be rough would it like the…"

"You'll never be treated like that again unless it was a punishment." Victoria laughed, "That little girl routine you tried on Lovecraft would be fine, that's what those nights are, yes your there to please but it is playful, we are equals here."

"No rough stuff," she nodded. "Good, I'm not…"

She stopped as Justine came over to them. "Getting acquainted with our high lady I see."

"We're going to have a lot of fun together," Victoria spoke up, "Isn't that right my sister?"

"Looking forward to it."

"Good," Justine said, then looking at Allison put her hand on her shoulder. "Pandora, a few of us are going to go out to a club, have a few drinks, dance and have some fun, we'd love it if you would come along."

Looking at her watch, Allison said, "It's midnight."

"The clubs close at two and Orion knows of one open until three, do you have a curfew my dear?"

"No," Allison said feeling stupid. "I would love to go dancing."

"Good, because I would love to share a dance with you," she winked.

"Oh." Allison said and could feel herself blushing.

Justine laughed, "All for fun my lady, I assure you I am quite harmless."

"That's good to know." Allison told her. "And I'm all about fun."

"That's good to hear," Justine told her, "Because trust me Pandora the night has just begun."

Chapter Six

"Hey ladies," a voice said from behind Allison, "These are from the gentlemen at the bar."

She turned as the young bartender placed drinks in front of her and Victoria. Picking up her drink, Victoria held it up in a toast and Allison looked over her shoulder to see two guys in their thirties wave and lift their beers. Allison toasted them as well. Turning to Victoria she laughed, "Think they'll come over?"

Victoria took a sip of her drink and shrugged. "Eventually, they're not punks. They're older, dressed decent, they're waiting on us, for now anyway." Waving her hand dismissively she said, "Who cares anyway? I have no interest in them"

"Too old?" Allison asked as she took a sip of her drink, then closed her eyes. The drink was strong and she'd already had several in the hour they had been at the club.

"No, I'm not into boys like you are. I don't enjoy teaching, but they're too boring looking for me."

"What do you like?"

"I like to toy with older men, the ones with money who think every pussy is for sale. Guys like Alex and Amado are my prey. I like to play along enough to get back to their place then flip the switch on them." She sighed. "It's hard though, if they don't recognize me that's fine, but the ones who do, I have to be different. Then again if they know who I am I generally won't be with them."

"That must be hard, finding people who don't know you."

"Not really." Victoria said. "Most men don't read the magazines I'm on, except for SI and one Maxim cover I'm more of a model for women's products and magazines. They know the name more than the face." She laughed. "I had one guy a few weeks ago tell me his friend had a modeling agency and I should try out."

"What did you say?"

"I told him the only time his tongue should be wagging is if it's on my pussy so be a good boy and go back to sucking my clit."

Allison laughed, "Great answer, except I would have made him go back to my feet and work his way back up."

"That's because you have a fetish for having your feet worshipped." Victoria shrugged. "Personally I like their tongue in my ass, I always make them eat me from behind so they can go back and forth."

"I've never really been into having my ass played with."

"When you go to the hotel have Mercedes gift do that for you," she sighed. "Nothing like a good rim job."

"I'll keep that in mind," she said laughing again.

Allison had spent a good part of the night laughing. In addition to Justine, Mark, Alex and Larry had come to the club with them and so far it had been a blast. In the beginning Allison had been a little hesitant; the club had a reputation as a trouble spot and was more suited to the early twenties crowd. She had mentioned it to Alex who had suggested the club, but he laughed and said wasn't that age group the one most of them hunted within? She shrugged and Justine told her not to worry about it, they were just going for a few drinks not to really mingle, and the guys were with them.

When they arrived, they went over to the huge bar in the middle of the club and Mark bought a round of shots, then Alex bought a round and within ten minutes, Allison could feel the beginnings of a buzz. Looking around she smiled as she saw every guy at the bar and those passing by staring at her, Victoria and Justine. The guys had all left their jackets and ties in the cars, but for the most part were still dressed better than most of the men there. Alex laughed when a man came up and after complimenting Mark on his shirt asked him if he wanted to dance. Mark told him he was barking up the wrong tree, but their friend Larry was into men so why not ask him?

They all watched as the man drifted down to where Larry was waiting for a drink and began to talk to him. Allison saw his eyes widen and he started shaking his head back and forth. They laughed, then taking her hand, Alex asked if she were ready to hit the floor. For the next forty five minutes they all danced, switching partners each time the songs changed and Allison couldn't remember the last time she'd had so much fun. All three men could flat out dance, especially Mark, who drifting away from the group had ended up sandwiched between two girls who didn't look as if they could really be twenty one.

The three of them drew an audience as they gyrated to the music and there was a series of loud catcalls, as Mark's hands slid up and began to fondle one of the girl's tits from behind as he ground his cock into her ass. The girl behind him had reached around and was unbuttoning the top of his shirt as they worked their way across the floor. Her attention was then drawn away as Victoria grabbed her hand and pulling her onto the floor said, "Let's give them a better show."

Before she could react, Victoria put her arms around her neck and slowly shimmied to the floor, before working her way back up, sliding her tits against Allison as she did. When she reached the top, she surprised Allison by giving her a quick kiss, then spinning around shoved her ass into her. There were several whistles from the men around them and playing along, Allison slipped her arms around Victoria's waist and stared sliding her hands up and down her sides. When she reached the sides of her tits, Victoria grabbed her wrists and put her hands over them.

As they spun around, Allison saw most of the people around them had stopped dancing and were now watching. In front of her, Victoria had kept her hands over hers and pushed them against her tits, before raising her arms over her head. Taking her cue, Allison kept her hands on Victoria's high firm tits and started making a show of squeezing them as, arms over her head; Victoria began swaying seductively against her. Reaching one arm back, she grabbed Allison's hair and leaning her head to the side, pulled Allison's face into her neck. Her eyes on several young guys staring at them, Allison made a show of kissing Victoria's neck. Their mouths dropped opened and then they laughed as she let out a surprised yelp as she felt a pair of hands slide around her and grab her own tits.

Turning her head, she saw Justine behind her and felt her begin to grind into her from behind. In front of her, Victoria spun around so she was now facing Allison and slid her arms around her waist. Justine's hands were around her chest holding her tits and the two of them began grinding her between them. She felt warm breath on her neck then gasped as Justine kissed her lightly between her neck and her shoulder. Justine's hands were still on her tits, and Victoria's hands had slid under her skirt and were on her thighs. Allison felt a shudder go through her and the guys in front whistled again as Justine ran her tongue along the length of her neck.

Victoria pressed her face next to Allison's and kissed Justine. A cheer went up as the two of them kissed with Allison in between them. Victoria leaned back and instantly pressed her lips to Allison's. She gasped as her tongue pressed into her mouth and now Justine's hands were sliding up and down her tits. Victoria pulled upwards and the guys let out another cheer as she lifted Allison's skirt above her hips, exposing her red thong. Behind her, Justine cupped her ass in her hands and gave it a hard squeeze. Allison felt her head turned and leaning over her shoulder Justine kissed the side of her mouth. Victoria backed off slightly and the three of them were kissing.

Allison's eyes popped open as she felt both of the women's tongue's sliding across her lips and as she did she saw Larry standing there with a small camera, taping them. That turned her on and opening her mouth she stuck her tongue out and played it across Justine's and Victoria's. Allison had never been into women and still had no desire to be, but her nipples were hard and her pussy wet as the three of them performed for the men around them. She jumped as she felt a hand on her shoulder and saw Alex in front of her. He also had his hand on Victoria.

"As much as I'm enjoying this, you need to be careful Victoria, you never know."

With a sigh, she nodded and stepped back. Allison started to tell Alex he was being a spoilsport when Justine slapped her bare ass hard enough to cause her to yelp. Several guys yelled do it again, and Justine obliged them, striking her even harder. Turning around, Allison shoved her skirt down. "That wasn't very nice." She made a show of pouting at Justine.

"Who said I was nice?" she laughed and then turning walked away.

Allison watched her saunter over to Mark who was now standing against a wall talking with the two young girls he had been dancing with. He had his arm around one of them, but when she approached, Justine simply put her hand out and taking it, Mark left the girls and allowed Justine to lead him out to the dance floor. That was when her and Victoria decided to sit and have a drink. Since then in between joking with Victoria, she had watched Mark and Justine dance. To her this was another sign they were more than occasional lovers. The way their bodies moved in perfect rhythm and the way Justine smiled at him a couple of times as he held her during a slower number demonstrated a familiarity that spoke of a lot of time spent together.

Across the room at another table, Alex and Larry were sitting. Larry was talking with an attractive brunette who was sitting to his left, and there was a young blond talking to Alex. Even as she was speaking to him, Allison saw Alex was watching Mark and Justine. Although he smiled at her when he caught her looking, Allison could see he was not happy watching the two of them. Victoria was right, he was jealous. That thought gave her a strange thrill. This group was going to be so much fun in so many ways it felt like it had to be a dream.

"She's amazing." Allison said pointing at Justine who had just kicked it into high gear as a techno number came on.

Victoria turned in her seat to watch Justine spinning around, her long red hair flying about.

"She has to be close to fifty if she's leaving soon no?" Allison continued.

"She's forty eight," Victoria answered, "But work hard play hard, and Justine knows how to do both."

"So would you lovely ladies care to dance?"

Allison looked up to see the two guys from the bar smiling down at them. She looked over at Victoria who shook her head, "Sorry, but we're together," with a wink to Allison she added, "No boys allowed."

"So not even a dance?" The second man asked.

He was tall with light brown hair and eyes. Attractive in a boy next door way. Allison smiled and asked, "So you would still want to dance even though you know you're not getting anything?"

"I'd be getting something," he smiled, "The chance to dance with a beautiful woman."

"Good answer!" she laughed, looking at Victoria she said, "Come on baby, let's be nice to the boys."

"Fine," Victoria sighed as she stood, "But I swear you just want to get me jealous."

"Now honey, you know I'm with you." Allison pouted at her.

"True, but I know you still like cock from time to time."

The looks on the faces of the men was priceless and without saying another word, Victoria took the hand of the one who had first spoken, "Come on and show me what you men think I'm missing."

Allison stood and as he took her hand, the guy said, "I'm Glen it's nice to meet you…." He trailed off.

"Allison." She told him as they walked out to the dance floor.

"You have beautiful eyes, Allison." He told her.

"That's what my girlfriend tells me all the time." She said trying not to laugh.

Glen was a pretty good dancer and they stayed out there after the first song. The second number had a grinding beat to it and Allison saw Victoria working her ass into her partner and putting on a show. Allison followed suit and decided to really give Glen a thrill by shimmying down to her knees in front of him before working her way back up and sliding her tits against him the entire way.

"So hey, so you really like guys sometimes?" he asked as she spun around and planted her ass against his very interested cock.

"Sometimes, but she gets mad." She pointed at Victoria, "And she's way too good to me, to piss off." She sighed. "She has an amazing tongue."

"I…well I guess I can't compete with that." He laughed behind her.

Allison saw Mark walk away from Justine and began to head back over to the bar. As he passed he glanced at her, "Need a drink?" he called out

She shook her head and then let out a surprised gasp as Glen's hand went across her tits. "Hey watch the hands," she told him.

"Sorry," he laughed. "I was just trying to get your girlfriend…."

He stopped and Allison saw Mark standing right next to them. "Got a problem with your hands?"

"Who the hell are you?" Glen asked stepping back from Allison.

"I'm the last person you'll see tonight if you don't watch yourself." Mark smiled coldly "And that's all you need to know."

"We're just messing with Victoria," Allison told him with a wink, "You know how jealous she gets."

She wasn't thrilled at the cheap grope, but had no desire for trouble. Allison had seen her brother in enough drunken rages, violence did nothing for her. Mark looked at her then back at Glen, shaking his head, he turned and headed for the bar.

"Who was that?" Glen asked.

"My big brother," she said, "But I think I'm done for the night," she gave him a kiss on the cheek, "Thank you for the drink and the dance."

"Thank you." He handed her a card, "Here's my number, you know in case you ever get a craving."

Allison laughed and shoved the card in her bra before turning around to see that Victoria had also sent the other guy away. Allison went to walk back to the table, but stopped when she saw Larry and

Alex coming over. Alex caught Victoria around the waist and gave her a spin as the music kicked back on again and coming up and taking her hands in his Larry asked, "One more dance my lady?"

Allison nodded and they moved over closer to Alex and Victoria and began dancing. At one point she spun around to find herself facing Victoria who leaned into her and kissed her as Alex held her from behind. Larry slipped his arms around her waist from behind and Allison continued to kiss Victoria as the Alex and Larry ground against them. Alex let Victoria go and moving quickly she grabbed Allison's hands and spun her around so that it was now Alex behind her and Victoria was with Larry. Again she noticed several people watching and grabbing Alex's hands put them on her tits.

"Why thank you my lady," Alex laughed in her ear, and then added. "I knew you were hot Allison, but that video, goddamn!"

Allison was going to reply, but stopped as she saw several people on the dance floor move out of the way and several heavily tattooed young black men wearing matching vests began walking across the floor towards the back of the club. They bumped into several people who all seemed to back off without saying anything. She saw one guy stop and say something to one of the waitresses who looked nervous, then nodded and handed him the drink that she was about to give to someone else. Allison saw the customer start to say something, then stop as the man pointed in his face.

"I think we should get off the floor," Larry said. "They look like ball busters."

"Yeah," she agreed, "I'm pretty damned tired anyway, and it's been a long night."

Holding her hand, Larry walked over to Alex and Victoria. "Alex let's go sit and have a drink," he said.

"Why?" he asked.

Larry indicated the group of men who were now circling the dance floor. "I think they may want to cut in, so let's go sit."

Alex rolled his eyes, "Really Larry? Why because they're in a gang?"

"Because they just came in at two am and everyone here is afraid of them so yeah Alex, let's take our designer shirts and white collar asses and go sit. Before there's a problem."

"Whatever." Alex muttered, but taking Victoria's hand began to head for the table at the edge of the dance floor where Justine was standing, waiting for them. They had just arrived at the table when a deep voice spoke from behind them,

"Hey, where you girls goin,' the parties just starting."

They all turned to see three of the guys standing in front of them. The one speaking was tall, well over six feet and Allison could see the muscles rippling in his arms as he crossed them over his chest.

"Oh jeez," Larry whispered next to her.

"Come on, don't you fine ladies wanna dance with some hot young guys?"

"Sorry sweetie," Victoria said, "We're getting ready to head out."

"Come on baby," One of the others said, smiling and showing off a gold tooth, "You got time for one more dance," his smiled turned nasty, "Then maybe we could go in the back and really party."

As he spoke the third man, who was as almost tall and muscular as the first one looked at Allison. "Yeah, let's go honey, there ain't nothing hotter than white skin like yours against a body like mine."

Shaking her head, Allison replied, "Not tonight, like she said we're leaving."

"Oh, I see." The first man nodded. "You bitches think you're too good for us don't you?"

"Hey watch your mouth kid." Alex said from Allison's left.

"Make me watch it pops." The guy said, smirking, "This ain't Wall Street, you just mind your business while we show these fine women a good time."

"Tell him Ricky," the one with the gold tooth said, "This is our house."

"We've had a good time already and we're done." Victoria said calmly.

"What about you red?" One of them asked Justine, "I bet fine ass cougar like you wouldn't mind some fun with a real man."

"I wouldn't." Justine replied, then made a show of looking around, "Where is he?"

One of the guys started to laugh then stopped as Ricky shot him a look.

"Think your funny bitch?" he asked. "Think your rich ass can come to our club and talk shit?"

"It was just a joke kid, calm down."

Alex stepped up between Justine and the guys. When he did, Justine looked over at Larry and made a gesture with her fingers. Allison jumped as she felt Larry take her arm. He had grabbed Victoria's as well and started slowly pulling them back away from Justine and Alex. Turning to look over his shoulder, he frowned, "Where the hell is Mark?"

Allison turned and scanned the long bar which was now mostly deserted. She didn't see Mark.

"I think you stuck up bitches need to watch your mouths." The guy said, and then laughed. "Or maybe we'll watch your mouths in the back."

"What's that supposed to mean?" Alex asked.

"We have a couple of rooms back there we party in and I think your snotty little white girls should come back there with us for awhile."

"Oh, please" Justine waved her hand. "This isn't the old west kid, you're not dragging anyone anywhere, the bouncers will…."

"The bouncers don't fuck with us, baby." Ricky said smirking. "Look around, you see one? We do what we want around here."

"Victoria, go find Mark." Larry said softly, "Now."

Victoria turned and started to walk away, then cried out in surprise as another one of the men had come up alongside of them and grabbed her arm.

"Where you going hot stuff?" he asked.

"Get your hand off of me," Victoria snapped, pulling away from him.

"Honey there's going to be a lot more than a hand on you if you don't learn to play nice."

Allison had begun to step back and he looked at her, "Oh no green eyes, you don't go anywhere, the three of you are going into the back with us."

"Fuck you they are!" Alex snapped now stepping in front of Allison "You punks need to back off before…"

"Before what pops? You gonna kick my ass?" he looked Alex up and down. "Gym muscle don't mean you can fight boy. Now tell you what. You two losers stay here and we'll bring your girls back in an hour or so," he laughed. "They might be a little stretched out, but they'll be okay."

"I'm done with this." Justine said, and turning started to walk away.

"I said you don't leave." The guy reached out to grab Justine then jumped back as Alex slapped his hand down.

"You keep your fucking hands to yourself." He told him.

"Oh Jesus." Larry said, "Here we go."

Allison looked around to see several people watching.

"Someone will call the cops." She said

"No they won't sweetie, trust me." The guy who had grabbed Victoria said. "They know better. Now let's you and me get to know each other a little better."

"Maybe we should make them strip for us first," Ricky said. "Damn they're fine."

"I want the redhead," The other one said, "Women her age know how to suck."

He reached out for Justine and again Alex got between them. "Last chance kid," He said quietly.

"Get your ass out of the way." The kid pushed Alex hard enough to get him to step back.

"Larry," Victoria whispered, "Tape this."

"What?"

"We're going to need them swinging first."

"Are you crazy?" Allison asked.

Larry pulled out the small camera he'd had earlier.

"Oh, no homes, that won't do." The guy next to Allison said, reaching across her to grab Larry. Larry stepped away from him and everyone turned as Alex said, "Go ahead kid, fucking try to get past me."

Smiling the kid went to push Alex then dropping his hand swung with his other. Alex whipped his head to the side, easily avoiding it then pushed him in the chest sending him backwards. "Try again."

"Mother fucker!" The kid snapped and swung again.

Again Alex ducked it easily, but this time snapped his left hand out, catching the kid in the face. His head rocked back and Alex, still using just his left, hit him twice more. As he staggered back, Alex brought his right arm around and hit him in the head hard enough to send him to the floor.

"Jesus Christ!" Allison exclaimed.

"Real cute old man," one of the others said and lashed out at Alex's face.

Alex jumped back and took a boxer's stance, his hands moving in slow circles as he bounced lightly on his feet. The guy next to Allison walked over to stand with the other two as Ricky approached Alex.

"Oh, shit look." Larry said pointing.

There were three more of them walking over and the one Alex had knocked down was slowly getting up. Next to her Victoria turned her back to the action and pulling her phone from her purse. Allison heard her say the name of the club and that her and her friends were being attacked. Allison looked back to Alex as she heard someone laughing. The tall kid was walking around Alex faking punches. At each one Alex swung back, his hands moving faster than Allison could follow, but the kid was easily slapping his hands away. "Come on old man that all you got?"

"What's the fucking problem here?" Mark's voice came from behind them.

"Thank God," Larry sighed as Mark walked past them towards where the others were all watching.

"Shit we have to get out of here," Allison said. "They're going to jump them we…"

"Don't worry Allison," Victoria said softly. "Our big brother's here, we'll be fine."

Walking up behind Alex, Mark grabbed his shoulders and pulled him back over to Justine.

"What the fuck Mark?" Alex demanded, "I…"

Mark turned away from him and slowly walked up to the others who were standing their smiling.

"Oh, look another pretty boy." Ricky said. "Nice shirt, your boyfriend buy that?"

"Listen guys," Mark said softly, his hands up palms out in a calming gesture. "Do we really need this?"

"Ask sugar Ray back there if we need this." One of them called out.

"Sugar Ray was pushed first." Mark said softly. "And we have it on tape as well as you threatening my sisters. So you see anything that happens from this point on is self defense and again, do you need this kind of trouble?"

Mark was speaking in a soft soothing voice and as he did Allison saw the men all looking at each other, maybe this would blow over before the cops arrived. Justine had moved over behind Alex and came around to stand between her and Victoria. Alex was standing between them and Mark and Larry had moved further off to the side where he was taping what was going on.

"This is crazy." Allison whispered, "We're not kids this is..."

"We don't want trouble pretty boy," Ricky spoke up. "What we want is some ass."

"Then go find some, I'm sure as charming as you are that's pretty easy." Mark said.

"Don't have to; there's three fine bitches right behind you."

"And they're with me."

"And they will be again, after were done." The guy laughed. "Not that they'd want your sorry little white dicks after we're done."

Another one laughed, "That's right man, once they've gone black...."

"Keep your stupid racist jokes to yourself and let's settle this." Mark interrupted.

"Yeah? How you gonna settle this?" Ricky asked, stepping forward until he was right in Mark's face.

"By buying all of you guys a drink and forgetting the whole thing."

He was still standing there with his hands up and Allison could see they were rock steady. Her stomach was in knots and she could feel everyone else around hers tension, yet Mark seemed dead calm.

"We're going to forget this over a drink?"

Mark sighed. "Kid, judging by the prison tats on your hands and neck I'm thinking you don't need any trouble here. So let me get you a round and then we'll be leaving."

"You can leave, but the girls stay."

"No, I think they should stay and watch." One of them laughed. "He said they were his sisters, maybe he'd like watching them get fucked."

"No one hurts my sisters." Mark said in a tone that stopped the one in front of him in mid laugh. "Now we're leaving. If you want the girls you'll need to go through me. So the choice is yours."

"Yeah, what choice is that?" The one with the gold tooth asked, grinning.

"Forget this and walk out, or keep it up and get carried out."

"Me? Carried out?" Ricky asked.

Mark spread his arms. "All of you."

"Crazy bastard." One of them whistled.

Ricky stared at Mark and no one moved. After a few seconds, Mark called over his shoulder.

"Larry, take the girls and go. We're done here."

"Let's go." Justine said grabbing Allison's shoulder.

"Going somewhere?" A voice asked from behind them.

Allison turned to see two more of them standing their grinning.

"We're done when I say we're done!" A voice called out from the front.

Allison spun around to see Ricky back up, but the one next to him throw a punch at Mark. There was a loud slapping sound and everyone froze as they stared at Mark who had caught his fist against his palm and was holding it there.

"Here we go." Larry whispered.

"Poor choice." Mark said, and then exploded into movement.

His right hand lashed out dealing a vicious backhand slap to the guy while still holding his hand. His head rocked back and continuing the motion, Mark swung his arm down into his stomach. When he doubled over, there was a sharp crack as he brought his knee up into his face. He fell over backwards, blood gushing from his nose. Mark's right, flashed out in another backhand swing, but this time catching the guy on his right in the throat with the edge of his hand. As he went to his knees gagging, Mark spun the rest of the way to his right, bringing his leg up and catching one of the men who had been rushing at him in the face, sending him to the floor.

Still spinning, Mark went down into a crouch, his leg sweeping out the legs of another of the charging gang members and dropping him to the floor.

"Fuck he's good!" Larry exclaimed as if he were watching this on television.

Mark came to his feet and ducked a punch, but then rocked back, as his attacker brought his other hand up, catching him with an uppercut. As Mark staggered backwards, the guy swung again catching him in the face. A second man came charging towards Mark and Alex leapt out from behind him and slapping his arm down dealt him a hard blow to the stomach, then another, Alex threw an uppercut and when his opponents head came back up, swung a right hook that sent him reeling into and over the table next to them.

Allison cried out as she was knocked to the floor by the two men that had been behind them charging past her to get into the fight. From her knees she saw Mark drop down to one knee to avoid a swing, then throw his fist directly into his assailants balls. As he doubled over, Mark rocked back onto his hip and kicked him in the face. As he staggered backwards, Mark came out of his crouch and slammed his arm across the man's chest. He had been in front of a table and Mark drove him down into it hard enough to cause it to shatter beneath him.

"My god!" she gasped.

"Where the hell are the cops?" Justine asked, looking around nervously, "And how many of these assholes are there?"

In front of them, Alex had blocked a bottle that was swung at his head, and holding onto the man's wrist slammed his elbow into the side of his head. As the man's knees buckled and he began to go down, Alex threw his head forward smashing his nose with the top of his head. Allison remained kneeling on the floor unable to believe she was watching Alex Warner in a bar room brawl. As he stood and narrowly avoid getting hit with a nasty roundhouse, she had the insane thought of her ad; *Orion knocks out the competition.*

Alex swung again, but missed and his opponent spun around behind him getting him into a head lock. Coming forward, Mark grabbed the man by the hair and started to pull him off. That was when one of the guys who had run past Allison grabbed him from behind, and started dragging him back. Mark was still holding the man's hair in front of him and as he was dragged back, pulled him off Alex. Letting himself be dragged, Mark delivered a brutal punch to the back of his head. As he went forward Alex met him with a left hook sending him spinning to the floor.

He started towards Mark where the man behind him had succeeded in pinning his arms down and had him in a bear hug. There was a loud cry and one of the men who had gotten back up, ran across the floor and threw himself into Alex sending them both down onto the floor where they began grappling. Another one jumped over them and swinging wildly struck Mark in the face. He hit him again and then a third time as the other man held him from behind.

"Help him!" Allison yelled to Larry.

"Don't bother." Victoria whispered.

"That all you fucking got?" Mark screamed.

The kid hit him again, and with a savage cry Mark yanked his feet up, drew his knees to his chest and kicked out, catching him in the chest and sending him to the floor. The move sent the guy holding him off balance and leaning his head forward, Mark threw it backwards, driving the back of his head into the man's face. There was a loud crack and he let Mark go. At least he tried to. Holding his left arm, Mark drove his right elbow back into his stomach several times before standing and with a wrench of his hips flipped the man over his shoulder slamming him to the floor. Stepping back Mark dealt him a savage kick to his side, then spun just in time to see a man dressed all in black try to grab him.

"Who the hell is he?" Justine asked.

"Bouncer." Larry said.

"Get the fuck out of my fight!" Mark snarled and swinging his arm around caught the bouncer in the side of the head, dropping him to his knees.

Mark kicked him in the face knocking him to the floor. Another bouncer came after him swinging wildly. Mark blocked the swing and coming forward, drove his knee into his stomach. When he went to his knees Mark slammed his elbow into the middle of his back. Then leaning over punched him in the mouth. Allison screamed as she saw a gout of blood spray from his mouth before he went face down to the floor.

"Mark they're the fucking bouncers!" Victoria yelled.

"They're with them!" Mark snarled

He went to turn back around to where Alex had gotten away from the one on the ground and was facing two others.

"What the hell is he waiting for?" Larry pointed at Ricky who was standing several feet away his arms crossed, watching the fight with a smirk on his face.

"For Mark." Justine said softly, "You see how fast that kid was? Alex couldn't touch him."

There was a loud scream of rage and they turned to see that two more bouncers had charged up behind Mark and jumping on him took him to the ground. A third one came diving in and they were all swinging wildly at Mark who was trapped underneath of them.

"Alex!" Justine cried out. "Mark needs you!"

Alex couldn't turn around, he was being stalked by two of them, but was standing his ground, weaving side to side his hands in constant motion. Allison could see blood dripping from his face, but as she watched he waved the kids in front of them on.

"Come on you little shits," he hissed. "Come see how a real man hits."

They both stepped in swinging, Alex faked to the right, then jumping to the left sent a straight punch into one of them, staggering him, then spinning around drove his fist into the side of the other. As the kid doubled over, Alex grabbed him and began delivering a series of short punches to his side. The other kid recovered and kicking out caught Alex in the back of the knee. As Alex dropped to one knee the kid stepped up and swung his elbow into the side of Alex's head driving him to the ground.

"Oh, no." Justine whispered.

Turning to see where she was looking, Allison saw that three of the bouncers were still on top of Mark, there was a windmill of arms and legs as they were all swinging. Allison saw Mark's legs kicking, trying to get them off of him, but they had him down by sheer weight.

"Alex!" Larry yelled.

They turned to see Alex on the ground curled into a ball as the man standing over him threw kicks at him.

"Larry!" Victoria snapped, "Go help!"

"Larry started to hand Allison the camera, when Justine pointed at him. "Stay with the girls."

Turning away Justine took three quick steps and yelled, "Hey!"

As soon as the guy began to turn around, Justine took another step and turning to the side lifted her leg up to her hip and kicked out. The guy cried out as the heel of her shoe drove into his stomach. As he staggered back, Justine pivoted smoothly and raising her other leg threw another kick, this one catching him in the chest. With no hesitation, she swung her right fist into his face, sending him to the floor.

"Holy shit!" Larry exclaimed as he followed everything with the camera, "They're going to be playing this at the conference for sure!"

Justine turned and started to kneel down to Alex when a voice called out.

"Oh, you're a tough bitch aren't you?"

Allison saw Ricky was finally walking over and heading for Justine who was now standing in front of Alex who was struggling to get to his feet.

"Where the fuck are the cops?" Allison demanded.

"It's only been three minutes." Victoria said looking at her phone.

"What?" Allison demanded, how could all this have happened so quickly.

There was a loud scream to the right and Allison turned to see one of the bouncers go rolling off of Mark clutching his bleeding ear. Another one flew off the pile with Mark's foot implanted into his chest. Mark rolled off the ground and into a crouch where he threw his leg out kicking the remaining bouncer that was trying to get up in the face. The man with the bleeding ear stood up and picking up a bottle off of the floor, swung it Mark who staggered back.

"Yeah let's go bitch!"

Allison turned back around to see that Justine had thrown a kick at Ricky. He stepped back and hiking her skirt up to her hips, Justine spun around and threw a kick at his face.

"Oh baby, you're good!" he laughed jumping back again.

Justine began throwing a series of kicks at him driving him back away from Alex. Ricky was laughing and slapping her foot down each time it came near him. Justine went to throw another kick with her right, then quickly dropping her foot, kicked out with the left. Her foot caught him in the thigh and he yelled as her heel dug into him. Stepping in Justine, swung with her right and Allison heard it connect solidly with his face.

"Justine, get away from him!" Alex yelled as he got to his feet.

"You fucking cunt!" The man snarled as Justine swung at him again, catching her wrist in his large hand, he backhanded her across the face. She spun around and landed hard on her stomach, her head hitting the floor.

"You mother fucker!" Alex shouted and charged at him.

Victoria ran past Allison and sliding down to her knees next to Justine grabbed her shoulders and rolled her over. Allison snapped herself into motion and ran over to join her. Getting down on the floor, she helped Victoria get Justine up into a sitting position. Allison picked a napkin up off the floor and reaching out dabbed at the blood flowing from Justine's mouth.

"Justine, are you alright?" Victoria asked.

"I..." Justine slowly shook her head. "My head hurts, I..."

"Too slow old man!"

They looked up to see Alex throwing punch after punch at Ricky. High and low, left and right, his hands were a blur, yet Ricky was blocking everything and egging him on.

"Shit man, boxing can't touch karate old man!"

Alex swung again, and this time Ricky stepped into it, there was the sound of several blows as he threw a series of rights and lefts at Alex's face. Alex staggered back and spinning around, Ricky caught him in the chest with a kick sending him to land on his back, a couple of feet from where they were all sitting. Allison saw Ricky start to come over and was aware of a couple of the others getting up. Alex somehow got to a sitting position, but his eyes were unfocused and he was gasping for breath. Nevertheless, he started to get to his feet.

"Stay the fuck down," Mark's voice came from the right.

Allison looked up to see him walking over and gasped. His shirt was torn and his face was covered with blood, but he was coming forward quickly. When he reached Alex he looked down at him. "I'll finish this bullshit, I...." Mark stopped and Allison saw that he was staring at Justine, who was holding the napkin to her bleeding mouth. "He..." Mark blinked. "Hit you."

Looking up, Justine removed the napkin, her eyes were wide and for the first time tonight she looked scared. "Mark," she started, "Don't..."

Mark snarled like an animal and spun around to face Ricky who was laughing at him.

"Come on pretty boy," he called out, "Let's see how good you are."

Stepping forward, Mark ripped what was left of his shirt off, tossing it to the floor.

"How pretty do I look now?" he screamed as his enormous tattoos were exposed.

The other two men started to come forward, but Ricky waved them back. "Stay out of this!"

"Let them go you piece of shit!" Mark snarled, "You're going to need them!"

"Don't think so, asshole" Ricky laughed as Mark came towards him. "I don't need help I'm....

"A chicken shit nigger who beats women!" Mark shouted at him. "Leave it to a ghetto spook like you to attack a woman!"

"Keep talking bitch!" Ricky snapped, "You're going to get beat down then watch me fuck your little red headed girlfriend."

Mark had come right up to him and raising his arms, Ricky began bouncing around as he had with Alex, "Come on boy let's see...."

His words were cut off as Mark threw a punch that went between his hands and struck him in the face. His head rocked back then again and again as Mark hit him twice more. He swung wildly and ducking, Mark punched him twice in the stomach, then jumping back kicked him in the face, knocking flat on his back.

"Get up you piece of shit, so I can knock you down again!"

"Goddamn." One of the other men exclaimed.

"Alex," Justine said, "Stop him, he's going to hurt that kid."

"Yeah so?" Alex panted as he wiped at his bloody face.

Ricky rolled over and jumping to his feet stepped forward and threw a vicious kick. Stepping forward, Mark let the kick catch him in the side but brought his arm down, pinning Ricky's leg to his side. Raising his elbow, Mark drove it into his thigh. As Ricky yelled in pain, Mark backhanded him across the face. Ricky couldn't fall, due to Mark's holding his leg and Allison winced as Mark dealt him several short jabs to his face, then letting his leg go went into a spin, kicking him in the chest and putting him down again.

"Get up!" Mark screamed.

One of the others came forward swinging, and turning Mark caught his fist and ducking down and spinning hurled him over his shoulder and onto a table. Standing back up he turned to see Ricky was back on his feet panting.

"Let's go!" Mark cried out.

Taking a deep breath, Ricky beat his chest with his right fist then letting out a loud cry began weaving his hands in front of his face. He was throwing short blows at the air showing off his speed then, then began to close in on Mark. Raising his hands over his head, Mark crossed them at the wrists then as he drew them down towards his sides, let out a bone chilling howl. Allison felt her blood freeze as the unearthly sound filled the club and looking around she saw the people who had been watching were all stepping back. In front of her Mark looked insane, as he pulled his arms down, every muscle in them bulged. His face was covered with blood, but his eyes were bright and wild.

When he finished the scream his own hands went into a wild flurry of punches, before he stopped and waved Ricky on. Stepping forward, Ricky launched a series of punches that were so fast, Allison couldn't tell where one started and the other ended. There was a series of sharp cracks as Mark's hands blurred out and blocked each one. The two of them stood face to face, Ricky throwing punch after punch and Mark slapping them all away. Ricky began to swing harder and seemed desperate as Mark stood his ground, blocking everything thrown at him.

"Goddamn." Larry whispered.

"Alex please stop him." Justine said, trying to get to her feet. She got halfway then went back down to her knees. "Dizzy," she whispered.

There was a loud cheer from the crowd as Ricky was now launching kick after kick. This time Mark was backing up, but still ducking and blocking every blow. Ricky spun low trying to take Mark's legs out, but he simply jumped over it. When Mark had backed up several feet, he slapped another kick away from him, then went into a series of kicks himself, driving Ricky back. Mark stopped and feigning a right, dropped to his knees and kicking out, caught Ricky in the stomach.

He doubled over, and snapping the same leg up, Mark caught him in the face, standing him up. From a crouching position Mark leapt into the air and spun. As he turned he drew his leg up to his hip. When he completed his spin and drove his leg out it caught Ricky high in the chest. He flew backwards, crashing over a table and rolling over several times before he stopped.

"Thank god it's over." Victoria sighed.

"It's not over." Larry said softly

Mark was striding over to Ricky who had somehow managed to get to his knees. Allison saw him cough and spit up blood. Seeing Mark coming, he stood and threw his arm forward, there was a click and a knife appeared in his hand.

"Mark, get out of there!" Alex yelled.

Mark kept going and Ricky slashed at him. Mark jumped back, and then whipped his head side to side as Ricky stabbed at his face. Mark feigned a punch then jumped back as Ricky slashed at him again. Ricky came forward thrusting the knife to the left and right. Mark kept moving backwards waving him on. Mark stopped and Ricky started to slash to the left, then spun to the right. Mark jumped back clutching his forearm, blood already flowing between his fingers.

Ricky spun again and this time drove the knife straight at Mark's stomach. Turning to the side, Mark let Ricky's arm sail under his, his hand flashed out and caught Ricky's wrist. Before he could pull back, Mark swung his other arm up hard. His forearm caught Ricky just under the elbow, there was a hideous crack and Ricky screamed as his arm snapped backwards.

"Oh my god!" Allison cried out.

Ricky was screaming, and swinging his elbow, Mark slammed it into the side of his head. "Shut the fuck up! You want to hurt my sister?"

Mark threw his head forward, smashing the top of it into Ricky's face. His knees buckled and he would have gone down, but Mark had grabbed his hair and drove his head down into his face again.

"Alex!" Justine screamed.

Jumping to his feet, Alex ran over to break it up.

"Think I'm pretty now?" Mark screamed and slammed his head down again.

Ricky had gone to his knees and Mark went down with him. He was holding his head back and sent another head but into him. Mark's face was covered in blood and much of it not his own at this point. "Like beating women?" He screamed. "Like hurting them?"

Mark drove his fist down into Ricky's face.

"He's killing him!" Allison shouted.

Mark went to swing again, but coming up behind him, Alex grabbed his wrist and yanked him up to his feet. Mark snarled and spun around, his left coming up in a wild round house. Alex ducked it and as Mark turned back to Ricky, grabbed Mark around the waist and lifting him off his feet began to carry him backwards.

"Mark, stop it's me!" He yelled.

Mark relaxed, then threw head back. The blow caught Alex in the side of the head and dropping Mark he staggered back. Mark screamed something at him and began to turn around again.

"Enough! Stop!" someone yelled.

Allison saw three of the bouncers heading their way. Seeing them, Mark let out another of those frightening howls and putting his hands up waved them on. "Now you want to fight?" he screamed. "After my sister's hurt now you give a fuck!" Come on then I'll give you a fucking fight! I'll...."

Mark stopped as running over and getting in front of him Justine shouted, "Mark cease!" Mark shouted something, Allison couldn't make out then stepped forward. "I said cease!" Justine yelled again.

Mark stopped and Justine put her hand on his heaving chest. "Please stop," she said to him. "We're all okay, your okay, just stop."

"Lady get away from him," One of the bouncers called, "He's fucking nuts."

"Damn straight he's nuts!" Justine shouted as she put her back to Mark to face them. "And I'm the only thing between you and him so shut up and get the hell away from us!"

"What the fuck is going on?"

A man in a suit had come up behind the bouncers. "You tore up my fucking club!'

"They tore up your club!" Justine snapped pointing at a couple of the gang members who had gotten to their feet. "They attacked us and your asshole employees let them!"

"Hey lady, you people were fighting and he's trying to kill people!" One of the bouncers pointed at Mark.

"We were defending ourselves because you wouldn't!" Alex shouted as he came up next to Justine. "They tried to hurt us, not these fucking thugs!"

"Yeah well we'll see what the police say asshole!" The owner yelled. "They're just getting here now!"

"Good, because we got all this bullshit on tape and take a good look around because you won't own this when I'm done suing!"

"Fuck you," The owner yelled. "I have lawyer and…"

"Go fuck yourself asshole," Mark screamed at him. "I am a fucking lawyer!"

Justine grabbed Mark's arm. "Come with me now."

Walking backwards, she dragged Mark over to where Allison, Victoria and Larry were sitting on the floor. Alex came over and looking around the floor, breathed a sigh of relief and picked up his red cell phone. He punched in a number and a minute later began speaking,

"Peter? It's Alex Warner. I know it's late, but I have trouble." He paused. "Me and some friends were attacked at club Benz." He stopped and nodded. "Yeah, some gang. They started with the women I was with and their bouncers just stood around so we got in a fight and…." He looked at Mark who was standing there glaring at the bouncers as Justine tried to wipe his face with a napkin. "One of my friends got a little carried away."

Allison heard shouting and saw several police officers striding over to the club owner who began yelling and pointing at them.

"Yeah," Alex continued. "Look we got it on tape all self defense." He sighed. "Peter I need your help man, can you…." He nodded again, "That's fine, what's his name? Okay, thanks, I owe you one."

He hung up and Victoria asked, "Who was that?"

"The chief of detectives, met him through Robert and pulled a couple of strings to get his kid into Harvard last year. He said a plain clothes detective named O'hara is going to show up in a few minutes and take over. We'll all go to the station with his people," he let out a breath. "We'll walk away from this no charges pressed and hopefully this stays out of the paper."

He then sat on the edge of the table and held his head in his hands. Allison went to go over to him then jumped back as Mark appeared in front of her. Looking at her through his bloody face, he asked. "Are you okay Allison?" As he spoke he reached out to her and stepping back she shook her head.

"Don't touch me!" She told him. "You're fucking crazy! You could have killed that kid!"

"I was…"

"You're a fucking animal!" she snapped at him.

Mark stared at her through his right eye as his left was swollen shut. He nodded then said softly, "Well I guess you know which one I really am now don't you?" Turning he added, "Told you I was the worst you could find."

He walked back over to Justine and Allison turned to see Victoria shaking her head at her. "He defended us Allison that was uncalled for."

"He wasn't defending us at the end, he was enjoying himself, he's nuts."

Victoria shrugged. "I prefer their beating to our being raped, you can disagree with that if you want."

Victoria turned and walked over to pick her purse up off the floor. Seeing Alex sitting on the table Allison went over to him. "Alex, are you okay?" She asked, putting her hand on his shoulder.

"I will be," he wiped at his bloody nose. "I'm getting old."

"You looked damn good out there Alex." Victoria said, coming over and giving him a kiss on the cheek. "And here we thought you were just a pretty face."

"Oh shit!" Larry said, "Allison we have a problem."

"What's the matter?" she asked.

"Well," Larry began as he looked at the display on the camera, "We have a problem with your campaign."

"What are you talking about?"

Larry turned the camera around so they could see the display. Allison saw it was a still of Alex lying on the floor. "I think the campaign has to be changed to 'Orion, knocked *out* by the competition.'"

"You…." Alex looked at him. "You little shit! At least I was fighting while your pansy ass was…." He stopped then looking at the screen again, shook his head, "You're a real shit Larry you know that?"

As Victoria started laughing, Allison saw two police officers talking to Justine and Mark. Looking back at the three of them she snapped. "How the hell do you people think this is funny? What's wrong with you?"

"Oh calm down Pandora." Victoria said, putting her arm around her. "Look at the bright side; no one will ever forget your first meeting."

"But this isn't…."

She stopped as kissing her affectionately on the cheek, Victoria laughed, "Welcome to the Circle, my lady!"

Chapter Seven

Justine sat at the table with an ice pack pressed to the side of her face, trying to focus through the throbbing in her head. She was sitting in one of the precincts interrogation rooms, along with Mark and Alex while they waited for Detective O'Hara to come back in. Forcing her head to the left, she saw Alex staring down at his folded hands. His right eye was swollen, his lip split and there was a large bruise on the side of his face. He also had an ice pack which he was currently resting on top of his right hand. His shirt had been torn open and Justine winced at the blood stains on the white t-shirt he'd been wearing underneath it.

Craning her neck, she looked past him at Mark, who, as he had been since they came into the room, was staring straight ahead. He was wearing just the tank top which was also covered with blood. She repressed a shudder as she wondered how much of it wasn't his. Facing front again she saw their reflection in the mirrored glass across from them. Mark's face was a mess. His left eye was shut, his lips swollen and there was a large bandage wrapped around his left forearm. The EMT that had arrived with the police had said he was lucky and it didn't need stitches.

They had arrived at the precinct just after three and were lead to the room, by O'Hara who had kept the police away from them as much as possible. O'Hara then told them what was going on. Victoria, Allison and Larry had all been allowed to go home from the club after giving statements and Larry had turned over his camcorder. Alex had whispered to her he was sure Larry downloaded it before he did and would have a copy in case they needed it. O'Hara went on to say very few people at the club wanted to say anything, but a couple did come forward and said the gang had started it. He explained it was looking like self defense, and all the gang members had been arrested. The problem remaining was the club owner wanted to press charges for damages to his club and assaulting his bouncers.

That was one of the few times Mark spoke, asking if the owner knew who Victoria and Alex were and was fishing for a pay off. He'd answered that the owner, Brian Wilcox, would have access to the police reports and would see the names. Whether he recognized who they were he wasn't sure. He then assured them his men had been told not to speak to the press. However if things became formal it would get out there one way or another. The key word was formal. The owner of the club would be the problem. He knew the gang bangers would have no money, but they were a different story. O'Hara had then left them alone again, to see what he could do. Justine put the ice pack down, and turning to Alex, put her hand on his arm.

"I don't think I thanked you Alex," she said softly. "I have to say you caught me by surprise in there."

"Yeah well," he shrugged. "You do what you have to." He sighed, "I'd be lying if I said I wasn't scared. Christ they just kept coming and that fucking kid was something."

"He's nothing now." Mark said quietly.

"He's still breathing anyway, no thanks to you." Alex snapped at him.

Mark didn't respond, just stared straight ahead as Alex glared at him. Turning back to Justine, he forced his bruised lips into a smile. "Speaking of something, you were pretty damn impressive yourself; you kicked that kid's ass."

"I had a good teacher." She leaned over to look at Mark and asked, "Mark, are you okay?"

"I'm sorry Justine, I should have gotten there sooner."

"You saved our asses Mark,"" she told him. "But you scared the shit out of...."

She trailed off as the door opened and O'Hara came in with Wilcox and another man in a suit. As the two sat across from them, O'Hara moved to the head of the table. He was carrying a folder and as he sat, placed it in front of him.

"Okay," he began, "What we have here is some good old fashioned stupidity which turned into some real ugliness. Now despite the ugly, only one person was seriously hurt, and that happened to be the one that pulled an illegal weapon. For all other parties we have shiners and some wounded pride, but no one's any worse for wear."

He paused and looked around the room. Justine saw the man next to Wilcox staring at Mark and following his gaze saw Mark staring back at him, a slight smile on his face.

"Now everyone at this table is fairly well off and I assume don't need this kind of hassle. All this can really amount to is a shitload of separate assault charges. We're looking at a mountain of paperwork, court appearances, and in the end, a bunch of anger management classes and wasted time."

"Why do I care about assault charges to a bunch of thugs?" Wilcox asked. "They can go to jail where they belong. But I got four bouncers who are hurt and several thousand dollars worth of damage to my club." He gave an exaggerated sigh, "And these guys got hurt on the job, which means my insurance goes up and...."

"So how much will make it right?" Alex asked softly. "That's where you're going with this right?"

"Well this wouldn't be the place to discuss that." O'Hara pointed out.

"Yes it is." Mark said. "If charges are dropped he has no recourse in a civil suit." He then sighed in the exact manner Wilcox had. "Unless of course some sort of back room deal was made and a check written here and now."

Wilcox looked over at Mark and frowned. He was a heavy set man and his jowls were red and sweating as he sat there in the small chair that barely contained his bulk.

"Before we go any further allow me to introduce my attorney, John Wescott."

"Who works for Powell and Cruise." Mark said. "Junior partner, works directly under Cruise who has ties to a reputed coke dealer that works the hell's kitchen area. One wonders if Mr. Cruise's lackey's involvement means coke flows in and out of the Benz like the watered down booze."

"Okay, we need to decide how far this is going to go." O'Hara tapped the folder. "In here are waivers releasing everyone here of responsibility and this goes in the clerks file no charges no court. If you don't sign then we start all the paperwork and there will be an arraignment." Turning to look at Alex he asked, "Mr. Warner do you wish to have an attorney..."

"He's right here." Alex put his hand on Mark's shoulder.

Mark smiled nastily at Westcott, "So how is Jack Powell these days? Still licking his wounds over the Johnson contract I got my client out of due to his shoddy paperwork?"

"Funny." Wescott nodded. "As funny as a person with two decades of martial arts experience beating up a bunch of kids barely out of their teens."

"You mean a bunch of gang bangers with records who were ready to commit rape?"

"Gentlemen." O'Hara began, "I think we all know I'm trying to work with everyone here."

"You're trying to work with them." Wilcox pointed out.

"Then let's get to it." Mark said. "State your charges."

"You and your friends tore up my club, the two of you assaulted my bouncers and...."

"Your bouncers who weren't doing their job?" Alex asked. "Those men were threatening to assault the women I was with and your security stood and watched. Then when they finally decided to get involved they defended the thugs."

"No doubt," Mark added, "Because they're paid to do so because they supply the nose candy sold at your club."

"Supposition." Wescott said.

"Easily proved." Mark replied. "Just like your bouncers sorry job performance, you see we have everything on tape. The thugs insulting and threatening the ladies and them pushing Mr. Warner. Then me trying to diffuse the situation and right there on video is them attacking me."

"I'm sure the audio may tell a different story."

"Sticks and stones." Mark said. "All physical contact was initiated by them. Now let's stop dicking around shall we? The person who taped that little scene is named Lawrence McCaffrey, Mr. Wescott may have heard of him. He is employed by my firm and is one of the finest PI"s in the business. He knows the game that's being played and is already bringing up dates people and places. Your club will be connected with drug trafficking as well as I'm thinking prostitution. Those boys were pimps and pushers, local muscle for Tobias Williams's small time Cartel." Sitting back in his seat, Mark pointed at Westcott, "Go ahead and dare me to prove it."

Westcott looked over at Wilcox and Mark continued. "Press charges against us and your quest for a quick payout will turn into more hell than you can possibly imagine. I am licensed to practice in the state of New York and I will make you my life's mission. We were defending ourselves against a gang of thugs. And doing so while your security guards watched." He smiled. "Add willful negligence to my list of charges."

Leaning forward he reached out and tapped the folder in front of O'Hara. "Or sign off and go back to being the sleaze ball you are."

"A moment?" Westcott asked O'Hara

"Of course."

Wescott and Wilcox stood and as they walked over to the corner O'Hara leaned over next to Mark "You need to watch what you say. You're scaring them, but I am a detective. If I keep hearing this and don't do anything they can come after me. My boss said to get you out of this, but you're pushing things."

Mark shook his head disgustedly and went back to staring at the wall. A few minutes later, Wilcox and Westcott returned to the table.

"We've decided we can just let this go for a small sum to cover damages to the club, and some compensation to the men who...."

"Fair enough," Alex began. "How's ten...."

"You get nothing." Mark cut in, putting his hand up in front of Alex's face. "Sign off or play your cards."

Wilcox slapped the table disgustedly, "Fucking rich assholes, get whatever the hell they want, do whatever they want."

"Oh, poor you." Mark retorted, "Shit or get off the pot."

"Give me the papers, but they sign too." Wilcox snapped.

O'Hara nodded and slid a paper over to Wilcox then coming around put a form down in front of Justine before moving down the table and giving one to Alex and Mark. Justine stared at the form, trying to focus long enough to read it. Her eyes blurred after the first few sentences and she whispered to Alex, "Is it okay to sign this?"

Alex put his finger up and after taking a couple of minute to read through nodded. "It releases the club of any responsibility I assume theirs says they assume responsibility for what happened meaning they can't come after us."

"That's correct." O'Hara said.

Grumbling Wilcox signed the form and rolled the pen over to Justine. Picking it up she signed and passed the pen to Alex who followed suit. He passed the pen to Mark, who tapped it on the paper several times then putting it down said. "No."

"What?" Alex asked.

"You two signed off, you're no longer part of this. I'm pressing charges."

"Whoa wait a minute." Wilcox said, "I thought we agreed to..."

"You agreed to do the right thing and not go after us because you know damn well you have no right to. You came here for money not justice. But I will not allow you to go unpunished."

"For what?"

"Those animals were going to fucking rape my friends!" Mark snarled and everyone jumped as his fist slammed down on the table. "They were going to drag them in the back and fuck them!"

"Hey," O'Hara said. "No one knows that for sure, they may have been trying to scare you and..."

"Look at her fucking face!" Mark shouted, pointing at Justine "Look at her! That mother fucker punched her in the mouth; you don't think he would have stuck his cock in there?"

"Mr. Phillips, please," O'Hara started

"Bullshit!" Mark snapped. "And your piece of shit bouncers just watched! Hell they probably would have went in the back and joined in!" Pointing at Wilcox he continued. "You think I'll let this go?"

"Mark stop it!" Justine turned to face him. "It's over, we're okay we're just going to let it go."

"And it's not like you didn't make that kid pay a price." O'Hara said. "I would say you're getting off easy Mr. Phillips that was...."

"I want them!" Mark pointed at Wilcox. "They work for you. Those animals were going to hurt my friends and would have if I wasn't there. This isn't over, it's just us now."

"Mark..." Justine began, and then stopped as Alex put his hand up.

"Mr. Wilcox, it's our turn. Would you and Mr. Westcott be kind enough to allow us some privacy?"

"Yeah, but you better talk some sense into your crazy friend while we're gone." Wilcox grunted as he got up.

The two of them got up and O'Hara walked them to the door where after knocking a uniformed officer opened it and let them out. Coming back over O'Hara pointed at Mark.

"Mr. Phillips, my boss is putting his name on the line to get you and your friends out of this. You know the law, everyone should be booked right now. They're playing along because you're right they were hoping for some money, you called their bluff and now everyone goes home. If you keep pushing I have to do my job and we're all going to regret that."

"Mark, let this go." Alex said. "You kicked the shit out of that kid, it's over its...."

"Do you see what he did to her?" Mark pointed at her again. "Do you know what they would have done? Fuck you this is over." He shook his head disgustedly. "Go home Alex, thanks for the help, but I'll take it from here, this fucker is going down."

Justine winced and put her hand to her head as she tried to come up with something to say, but her mind seemed sluggish. She was exhausted and her stomach was turning. Standing behind Mark, O'Hara made a cutting gesture across his throat. Nodding, Alex took a deep breath and spoke calmly.

"You push we all end up involved. It goes to court and they pull Vicky and Justine in. What was Vicky doing there the press will ask." Leaning close to Mark Justine heard him whisper. "How long before a video from the clubs camera's comes out of Vicky and Justine making out with Allison shows up. They were drunk and not thinking, but imagine what it would do to Vicky. Mark think of us, all of us, let it go."

Mark looked at Justine and whispered, "But they hurt her."

He had said it softly and Justine could hear the emotion in his voice. Something broke inside of her and she felt an overwhelming feeling of affection towards him. Her eyes began to fill and she quickly put her head down so he wouldn't think she was upset.

"And you hurt them Mark." Alex pointed out. "An eye for an eye, it's over."

Taking a deep breath, to get control, Justine reached across Alex and grabbed Mark's hand. "Let it go baby," she said softly. "Please."

As she stared at Mark, she was aware of Alex turning to look at her. Mark looked away and as she caught Alex's eye he mouthed the word "baby?" She gave him a dirty look then went back to staring at Mark. He had his head cocked slightly and his eyes were closed. He nodded then looked at O'Hara. "I'm sorry detective, I'm just upset about the whole thing. I realize you're putting it on the line for us and I'm in your debt." Picking up the pen he signed the paper. "It's been a long night; do you think we can get back to our cars now?"

"Absolutely." O'Hara nodded, taking the papers. "Just a few more minutes and I'll have an officer drive you back to Benz. We have someone there to make sure your cars were untouched."

"Thank God," Justine said, "I can't ever remember being this tired."

"You'll be able to sleep soon," Alex told her, and then, his split lips turning into a smirk, he whispered softly, "I'm sure your baby will tuck you in."

* * *

They rode back to the club in silence. After wincing every time her eyes were struck by the glare of oncoming headlights, Justine put her head down and stared at her hands in her lap. She noticed the nail of her middle finger had broken and idly wondered when she would be able to fix it. She could feel her face swelling and figured she wouldn't be going out in the next few days unless she absolutely had to. She was aware of Alex staring from where he was sitting next to her in the backseat, but deliberately avoided looking at him.

When they had gotten into the unmarked car, Justine had slid into the back seat, hoping Mark would get in next to her. Whether he wanted to or not, she wouldn't know because Alex, who had been right behind her, slipped in next to her. One look at his face told her he had done it on purpose and she wanted to smack him. It was amazing that despite the fact he'd been nothing short of heroic tonight, he could still piss her off. She had herself to blame for this one, she hadn't been thinking when she'd called Mark baby in front of him. Then again the look on Mark's face would have been enough to tip Alex off to… to what?

Justine tried to concentrate then grunted when the car hit a pot hole sending a stab of pain through her aching head. Something big had happened in that room. The level of emotion displayed by Mark towards her and her response couldn't be ignored. For months she'd wondered what exactly was going on between the two of them. Not just between them, but what was going on with her as well. Justine had been wearying of the games to the point she had been with just Mark. Then Victoria had sent her off on a tear and tonight's meeting had kept that mood going, Justine had let it get wild between Lexi and Adonis to feed her own fire, to prove to herself she wasn't getting old or softening.

But now Justine felt herself swing back the other way, and even further than before. It had been more than just concern in Mark's eyes and much more than affection in her hearts response to him. Looking up and staring at the back of Mark's head she now knew exactly where she stood. She was in love with him. She could no longer pretend it was otherwise. She had been close to admitting it when she'd been jealous of Allison, but convinced herself they were just close. Now there was no deluding herself. As the car turned the corner, Justine saw the club ahead and noticed both Mark's Firebird and Alex's Bentley were parked on the street. There was a patrol car in front of them and when they pulled alongside of it, the cop waved and pulled away. The detective pulled the car over and as they got out asked, "Do you folks need me to follow you anywhere, you all okay to drive?"

"We're fine officer," Alex said as he got out and extended his hand to Justine, "Thank you so much for your help."

Justine allowed Alex to help her from the car and as the detective pulled away, she walked over to Mark's car and leaned against it, waiting for him to come over and open the door for her. As she watched Mark and Alex standing there several feet in front of her, she felt her stomach begin to turn again, but this time it was not from the throbbing of her head, but nerves. As exhausted as she was, Justine was going to tell Mark how she felt, just get it over with and either he would feel the same way, or she would just add humiliation to the rest of what she had gone through tonight. Alex walked over to her removing his circle phone and putting it to his ear.

"Yeah Loki?" He spoke, "I just wanted to let you know we're okay, everything's settled. I'm heading home and Lovecraft and Scarlett are going to the hotel. I…" He stopped as Mark came over and put his hand out for the phone. "Hold on, Lovecraft wants to talk to you." Mark took the phone and stepping away from Alex began speaking,

"Loki, listen first thing when you get up, I want the name of every bouncer that was working tonight. I want their addresses and I want to know everything about them. I also want the names of every one of those cockroaches that attacked us and all the dirt on Wilcox."

"Oh what the fuck!" Alex snapped and came up behind Mark, who was now raising his voice.

"You heard me, I want their fucking addresses and where their little club house is, I'm…hey!"

Mark yelled in surprise as Alex snatched the phone from his hand. Mark tried to grab it back, but Alex backed away while speaking into it. "Ignore everything he just said, he's out of his fucking mind."

He paused then snapped. "I don't give a fuck who he is, call Scarlett and ask her and she'll tell you no. Go to bed and don't take his calls."

"Give me the fucking phone!"

Mark reached out to take it and spinning away from him, Alex screamed at him, "What the fuck is wrong with you?"

"I'm going to make this right! They..."

"Enough! You're fucking crazy do you know that? Fucking out of your goddamn mind!"

Alex was walking towards Mark and yelling. Oh, God, she thought as she forced herself away from the car to try to get between them, will this night ever end?

"Just give me the fucking phone," Mark snarled, "Just because you don't have the balls to...."

"You want the phone? Take it!"

Alex reared his arm back and threw the phone at Mark's head. They were only a few feet apart, but demonstrating his uncanny reflexes, Mark whipped his head to the side avoiding it. The phone sailed past his head and shattered against the trunk of Alex's car.

"What the fuck Alex?" he yelled.

"I am sick and fucking tired of your punk ass, that's what the fuck!" Alex shouted as he got directly in Mark's face. "How fucking dare you say I don't have any balls! I fought my ass off in that dump. Look at my face; do I look like I ran?"

"Stop it!" Justine called out to them as she stopped and leaned against the no parking sign a few feet from them. She had tried to run and her head was swimming. "Its five am and we're out here alone, let's just get some sleep and...."

"I didn't say you did, but it's time to finish this!" Mark pointed in his face.

"It is finished you fucking psychopath! If you had finished it anymore you'd be locked up for murder, and it wouldn't be the first time that's happened now is it?"

"Don't throw that in my face!' Mark shouted. "This is nothing like that! You heard what they were going to do! If you don't care than that's..."

"Fuck you I don't care." Alex shoved Mark, who caught off guard, staggered backwards. "You don't think I was fucking scared in there?"

Turning he pointed back at Justine, who couldn't get herself to move. For the first time she could remember, she was unsure of what to do. She couldn't think straight and had the sinking feeling she wouldn't be able to stop them if she tried.

"You don't think seeing her hurt pisses me off? But it could have been worse; Christ there was eight of them animals. When I went down all I could picture was them hurting my sisters!"

"Then let me...."

"But it's over, they didn't do anything, we protected the girls. Justine will be fine. Let it go Mark, for once in your life let something be."

"I always finish!"

"Then if you finish you'll be finished don't you get that?" Alex demanded. "You could have gone to jail tonight and you will if something happens to those bouncers. And speaking of finished? It's time we sat down and talked about you stepping down. You're an out of control animal and if I hadn't pulled you away, Victoria Redding would be in the papers for being good friends with a murderer!"

"It's my job to protect my sisters!" Mark shouted and coming forward pushed Alex backwards. "I always protect my sister!"

Move, Justine told herself, fucking move.

"And you did, but now you want blood, you and your Lex Talionis bullshit! I'm done with it Mark, you're not a kid anymore, you're a fucking lawyer not a vigilante!"

"I know what I am," Mark snapped, "And that's..."

"A fucking punk in a suit, that's what you are!" Alex snapped. "And an ungrateful one! I saved your ass years ago, saved you from yourself. Then I get you into the Circle and you know why? To give you something in your life besides your fucked up sister to care about to..."

"You don't talk about my sister!" Mark screamed. He swung at Alex who quickly jumped back out of the way. "My sister is not fucked up!"

"She was then!" Alex told him, "And go ahead and swing Mark, because I'm not afraid of you."

"Mark, stop it!" Justine cried out as she managed to push herself off of the pole and walk slowly towards them. He looked over at her and Justine felt her heart skip a beat, he looked as crazy as he had in the club. "Mark, please Alex is...."

"A fucking idiot, that's what I am!" Alex threw his hands in the air. "And know why Mark? Because I fought to get you into this group. They didn't want you, but I got you in and I did it for you, I did it to give you a chance to live up to your potential and to have a family to make you a part of something. I thought it would change you!"

He shook his head disgustedly and pointed at Mark's shirt. "Yeah, you've changed all right, still the same crazy fucked up animal you always were. You're proof you can never take the street out of the kid. What did they call you back then? Mad dog? Take a good look at yourself, because that's exactly what you are, a fucking mad dog!"

"Fuck you Alex!" Mark lashed out and Justine cried out as there was a crack and Alex's head snapped back. He staggered and stepping forward, Mark began to raise his hand again, but went reeling backwards as Alex's fist came around and caught him in the side of the head.

"You're proving my point asshole." Alex said, putting his hands up in front of him, fists clenched "All we've been through and you swing at me." Alex stopped and lowering his hands also lowered his voice. "We had each other's backs in there Mark, like we've had each other's backs for years, and that's how it should be, because we're more than friends we're brothers. Or at least I thought we were.

"But you don't know how to treat the people who are good to you do you? This isn't the first time you've shit on me or the group. Only person you never shit on was Megan who spent most of her life shitting on you, good old easy bake."

"Don't ever call her that!" Mark screamed and coming forward through a wild punch that had Alex not ducked would have taken his head off.

Alex jumped backwards and almost knocked Justine over as she reached them. Stepping in front of Mark she put her hands up. "Mark enough! Alex is right; you're out of control! You need to stop now!"

Mark took a deep breath and again she saw him close his eyes and cock his head slightly. When he opened his eyes, he appeared calmer. "I'm the enforcer of the group," he said softly. "It is my job to avenge any wrongs done to my sisters, not his. It's my call and...."

"And I am your Mistress, Lovecraft." She told him, trying to sound calm. "And I'm telling you he's right. It's over and you're not right," she shook her head. "I told you before if you can't get a grip on yourself than..."

She trailed off as the look of anger left his face and was replaced by that strangely childlike look of hurt that he had sometimes after his nightmares.

"Oh, I get it." He said quietly. "In there it was baby, because you needed me to play along, now it's Lovecraft."

Justine swallowed against the lump rising in her throat at his words. Five minutes ago she had been planning on telling him she loved him, now she had just broken his heart. "Mark, it's not like that." She said her voice tight with emotion. "You just need to calm down."

"She's right." Alex said behind her. "For tonight, but I'm calling for a meeting, we're going to sit down and talk next week about this. I think it's time you walk away. You have some kind of crazy crash and burn attitude, fine, but crash alone, you're not taking any of us with you."

Mark stared over her shoulder at Alex then shifted his gaze to her. "Do you agree my Mistress?" he asked.

"I..." she nodded. "I think we should all talk, but that doesn't mean that...."

"Okay." Mark nodded. "I understand, my mistress is not pleased with me and I shall report to her next week."

"Mark please," she whispered, "I...we need to talk. I want to...."

She trailed off as leaning forward; Mark whispered in her ear, "Shall I bring the gag?"

Justine felt her heart sink, and struggled to say something. It didn't matter, he had turned and walking past her and Alex headed for his car. Turning to face Alex, she whispered, "Please stop him."

"Let him go Justine." He told her, putting his hands on her shoulders. "We'll give him a couple of days and one of us will call him."

"No," she shook her head. "I...need to talk to him now, I...." She stopped as she felt the lump in her throat rise and could feel tears beginning to run down her cheeks.

"Justine, are you alright?" Alex asked his good eye wide with concern.

Behind him she heard the roar of the Firebird.

"I..." her words were cut off by a choked sob and she tried to push past Alex to get in front of the car. It was too late as with a squeal of tires, the firebird tore away from the curb and sped down the street.

"No, no, no!" she cried as she took a couple of steps towards the corner as if she were going to catch him.

"Justine, he'll be fine!" Alex said, coming up behind her.

She turned around quickly, planning on asking Alex to try to follow him. She stopped as the street spun in front of her and she felt herself begin to fall.

"Justine!" Alex yelled as he caught her by her around the waist and held her up.

She tried to tell him she was okay, but all that came out was a pathetic sounding sob. Her trembling legs gave out and she felt herself beginning to slide down his body. Her head was pounding and there were spots of color floating in front of her tear filled eyes. As if from a distance, Justine heard Alex call her name, then everything went dark.

Chapter Eight

Justine sat in front of Mark, her hands clasped nervously in her lap. He was looking at her expectantly and when she didn't speak asked, "What is it Justine, you said you wanted to tell me something."

She nodded and taking a deep breath began, "Mark, you know how we've been spending a lot more time together lately?"

"What about it?"

"I've been telling myself that we're just friends with benefits and we're comfortable together. I've been telling myself I enjoy your company because you know just what I like, I can play the game and you love it or we can just have fun."

"We've had this conversation before." Mark pointed out.

"When you told me about Allison and I got jealous, I thought it meant something, but wasn't sure." She paused and prepared herself to take the plunge. "The other night at the police station, the way you looked at me, Mark, it was more than concern and I could feel myself wanting to just get up and have you hold me, Mark I…." Here we go, she thought. "Mark I love you."

Mark nodded, "Of course you do."

"I…what does that mean?"

"You love me because you need me." He shrugged. "Now anyway, before I was just fun, but hell Justine you're pushing fifty and the Circle is putting you out to pasture. Your clocks ticking and you want to lock me up while you're still hot enough to hold my interest."

"Mark…" she swallowed as she felt those damn tears building again, "That's not true…"

"Sure it is." He shrugged, "I don't blame you, I'd be worried too, Christ Justine in ten years you'll be sixty years old, your tits will be sagging, you'll be getting wrinkles. If you don't make a move now, you'll be paying guys to have sex with you like the old men do." He laughed, "Either that or you'll be the hottest babe at bingo night!"

"So…so you don't love me?" she asked, feeling the tears flowing down her cheeks

"If you tell me to I will."

"I…I don't understand."

"You're my Mistress and I always do as you tell me. That's why I spend time with you in the first place. You ask me to be with you and I obey. But, don't worry; it's a privilege to be with you."

She tried to speak, but couldn't around the lump in her throat. Looking at her, Mark laughed, "Oh, come on Justine, you're not going to tell me you thought I had feelings for you are you?" When her answer was a sob, he frowned and said, "I'm sorry Justine," a look of panic spread across his face. "I'm sorry my Mistress, please don't hurt me again, I'll tell you I love you, I promise I'll....."

Justine's eyes flew open and she found herself staring at a red ceiling. No, it wasn't a ceiling; it was the silk top of a canopy bed. Turning her head to the side, she saw the matching curtains had been drawn completely around the bed. In between the curtains, Justine saw huge mahogany columns and realized she had no idea whose bed she was in. She sat up quickly and immediately pressed her hand to her head as it began to pound. Ignoring it as best she could, Justine looked down to see she was wearing a black t-shirt with the Orion software logo on it. She let herself relax; she was in Alex's bed

She leaned against the headboard and rubbing at her temple, tried to focus back to last night. At first she couldn't remember much after the argument between Mark and Alex, but then she recalled waking up in Alex's car. She had been sitting in the passenger seat, and he must have been calling her name, because as she opened her eyes, he had sighed with relief and asked her if she wanted to go to the emergency room. She remembered asking him to call Mark, but he refused. Her next memory was of them walking through the foyer of his building. She was leaning heavily on him, and someone made a crack about Alex's face and saying something about her being a drunken hooker.

She couldn't remember Alex getting her into bed and it dawned on her the last time she had looked it had been five am. Wondering what time it was, she reached up to the ornate rope dangling from the column next to her head and drew the curtain back. There was an intricately carved end table next to the bed and seeing her purse on it, Justine leaned over and pulled it onto the bed with her. Her eyes widened when she saw that it was two pm. She saw she missed a call from Victoria and smiled in relief as she saw one from Allison as well, Justine had been afraid last night might have scared her off.

Her smile caused pain in the right side of her face and as she experimentally opened her mouth, that entire side felt tight. She gingerly touched her cheek and winced. Dialing her voice mail she listened to Allison asking her if she were okay and to call her. Victoria's was the same, except she added she was leaving for Colorado at one to visit her niece for her birthday. Justine put the phone down in disappointment. She'd wanted to talk to Victoria today, to ask if she would call Mark and find out how he was doing. Odds are he would ignore her and Alex for a few days, but he and Vicky were close, he would answer her.

Not as close as the two of them were she thought, and then felt a pang of sadness as she recalled the dream that had woken her. Justine's concerns about Mark had mainly been along the line of the depth of his feelings for her, or how much feeling he was really capable of. The dream had put another thought in her head, did he really only spend time with her because of who she was? She doubted it was that she was his mistress, but the fact she had broken him, and had many times early on called the shots in their games, had made the relationship unequal.

Justine, however, hadn't been his mistress in the bedroom in months. That was until last week when she'd punished him. Sitting there, it occurred to her that was really the night her feelings came to the surface. She hadn't been jealous of Allison sexually, she'd been upset he had shared things with her, and then made love to her. Two things he'd never done with her. Her tear of last week had been denial, Mistress Scarlett trying to convince Justine she still only wanted sex games and no attachments. There could be no denial after last night. True, she had been exhausted and maybe not in her right mind from the blow to her head, but her emotional breakdown after Mark had thrown that gag comment at her left her no room for doubt.

Not that Justine had ever experienced love, but as her sister, who constantly bugged her about being alone, had told her many times, when the time came she would just know. Justine grunted disgustedly as she wondered if this were some kind of record, forty eight years to find an interest, then fucking it up in minutes. She shouldn't have mentioned them talking about the group, she should have just gotten him away from Alex then back to the hotel.

"Shit!" The hotel, it was after checkout time.

She called and once she gave her name started to apologize and offer to pay for another night. The clerk interrupted her and told her the room was already covered until tomorrow and not to worry. Hanging up, Justine tossed the sheet from her and swinging her legs off the bed, stood up. She waited a moment to see if she were still dizzy and breathed a sigh of relief as the room stayed still in front of her. The t-shirt barely went past the cheeks of her ass, but after looking around the room, she didn't see her dress. Oh well, it wasn't as if Alex hadn't seen her body.

Justine had never been in Alex's room before, but he'd spoken recently of remodeling the bathroom off of it. Looking around she saw a door that she figured led to it and began to walk over. She stopped as she passed the bed and saw a leather arm chair pulled up to it. There was a pillow on it and she smiled at the thought Alex had spent the morning next to her, making sure she was okay. It was amazing how he could be so endearing and yet so infuriating.

After using the bathroom, Justine took a deep breath and turning towards the sink looked at her face. She frowned as she saw it looked as bad as it felt. Her cheek was swollen and there was a large purple bruise in the middle of it. There was also a good size lump on her forehead just under her hair. The lump she could pull her hair over, but her face was another story. The location of the bruise made it obvious she'd been hit and, as she'd thought last night, she would have to work from home for a few days. Justine turned the faucet on and after rinsing her face, turned to go find Alex.

He was in his living room, sitting in a huge recliner facing a mammoth flat screen TV that took up most of that wall. Justine saw he was watching The Wall street report on CNN and heard him speaking into his cell. "Bill, are you watching this? Is there a reason I pay you to invest for me other than I must be a masochist?" he paused and added. "I'm not fucking kidding you, if that shit doesn't pull up by week's end, I'm pulling my portfolio."

He flipped the phone onto the table next to him, then seeing Justine, shook his head, "How is it that in all of the years I've been in this group, not one Circle has come up with a stock broker?"

"I guess it's a boring profession." She said, trying not to wince at the sight of his closed eye and battered face. Reaching his chair she leaned over and kissed his cheek. "Thank you Alex."

"For what?"

"For taking care of me last night. I...I was a mess to say the least."

"No problem Justine," he shrugged. "That's what friends are for."

"And thank you for letting me sleep in your bed that was nice of you. You do have a spare bedroom after all."

"My Mistress in the guest room?" his left eye widened. "Never!" he sighed, "Although admittedly that's not the way I envisioned you in my bed." As she stood up, he grinned and pointed at her. "You do look good in that t-shirt though. Damn you have some long legs."

"Thank you." Raising her eyebrows she said, "I don't remember changing."

"I..." he looked away, "I may have helped you out of your dress and into the shirt. You know, just being chivalrous."

"I have no doubt you were." she nodded. "I notice my bra and thong are still on."

"Give me some credit."

"I give you a lot of credit," she began as she sat down on the matching recliner across from him. "You were unbelievable last night. I knew you used to box, but goddamn you put on a show."

"Fear will do that to you." He said quietly.

"The great Orion the Hunter was afraid?" she laughed then stopped as she saw he was serious.

"Justine, those kids weren't playing. I meant what I said when I was yelling at Mark, I was scared, if those kids got past us…" he trailed off then said softly, "Thank God he was there."

Justine nodded. "I saw what he could do against Tartarus, but that was years ago and one guy." She shook her head. "He was like something out of a movie."

"Back when he was around twenty, he was considered a prodigy." Alex said as he stood up and walking past her went around the counter that separated the room from the kitchen. "He was invited to join The Thunderbolts, an elite group of Martial Artists. He was supposed to tour Japan to compete against some of the best in the world."

He paused as he filled up a kettle with water and put it on the stove.

"I sense that didn't happen for some reason." She prodded.

"Attempted murder was the reason." He said as he removed a mug from the cupboard above him. "When they acquitted Mark they still put him on parole because of the level of violence he demonstrated. Part of the conditions was that he avoid any situation that would lead to fighting. He had to quit his job as a bouncer and was banned from competing in tournaments."

"They might have done him a favor." She said as she leaned back into the comfortable chair and pushing a button on the arm raised her feet up. "He could have snapped if anyone got a couple of good shots in."

"You're right there," Alex said while leaning against the counter. "Mark was," he paused. "Mark *is* a time bomb."

Justine didn't respond. She knew Alex was right, and it was another piece to add to the puzzle. Mark, who had always had moments of being erratic, was slowly becoming nothing short of unstable. Could she handle that? Then again, perhaps she could help him if he let her inside. Maybe if he knew how deeply she felt towards him, it would calm him down. The teapot began to whistle and she watched Alex drop a tea bag into the mug then pour the hot water into it. Carrying the mug over to her, Alex carefully handed it to her, before returning to his seat.

"Thank you." She said as she sipped at the tea. "And while I keep thanking you, let me add one for the hotel. I assume that was you that took care of that."

"I was going to have Larry swing by here and get your key, then go get your stuff." Looking down he continued. "But then it occurred to me that since you came up together, you and Mark might be sharing a room and he didn't need to know that."

He had raised his gaze and as his open blue eye stared into hers, she could see the question he wanted to ask. Not ready to go down that path just yet, she nodded. "Good call. You took care of everything Alex, especially with the police." After taking another sip of the strong tea she told him. "If your friend ever needs anything that's within The Circle's power you tell me, and we'll see that he gets it."

"Oh, I'm sure he won't let me forget this one."

"I'm getting tired of saying thank you."

"You could always show me instead." He winked.

"Ah, there's the Alex I know and love!" Justine laughed.

"I know, I know, in a couple of years we'll have our night."

He was giving her that same look, as if waiting for her to react. Hoping her face didn't give anything away, her mind did react to that thought. If she got a chance to make things right with Mark, and he was open to exploring a relationship with her they would be....exclusive. On the heels of that was another even more disturbing thought, she would have to leave the group. They both would. They wouldn't be able to entertain and.... She took another sip of tea and forced her mind to stop racing. One thing at a time was all she could handle.

"So how are you feeling?" Alex asked, mercifully changing the subject.

"My face hurts, but I'm not dizzy." She shrugged. "Always a plus I guess. You?"

"Like I took a beating." He laughed. "But not too bad, mostly just sore. And by the way, thank you Justine."

"For?"

"For kicking that kids ass and getting him off of me." He gave her a low whistle. "Talk about impressive, those were some damn good kicks." He laughed. "I like when you hiked the skirt up to get more height on them, gave the club a pretty good show!"

"I didn't think of that," she rolled her eyes. "So you're lying on the floor half conscious and you're looking at my ass?"

"Well I...."

"Alex you kill me," she said, "But don't worry Larry has it all on tape so you'll see it again."

He nodded smiling, and she paused to drink her tea. Alex watched her as she did, and she knew it was coming. However when he spoke he said, "I called Mark, he didn't answer, but I left him a message and told him if he didn't want to call me to call Larry or someone else so they can let us know he didn't kill himself driving back to Providence last night."

"He drove five hours after that?"

"Did you doubt he would? I told him we were all out of control last night and need to talk."

"Think he'll call?" she asked.

"Eventually," he sighed. "Mark and I have gone at it worse than that. It's just he wouldn't stop and when he gets like that all he reacts to is more of the same."

"No, he listens to me, I...I was dizzy and couldn't think straight. I made it worse by looking like I was taking your side."

"You should have been on my side." he pointed out.

"Do you really want him out Alex?"

"No," he answered immediately and Justine felt relief flood through her. "He needs the group. I meant what I said; I got him into it to give him something to be a part of."

"The family he didn't have."

"No, he has a family, his foster parents were very good to him, but he has a me against the world attitude so he doesn't acknowledge that. They were Megan's parents not his, is how he sees it. Speaking of her, I shouldn't have brought her up; I know what it does to him. I was just so damn mad at him."

"You called her easy bake." Justine said. "What the hell is that?"

"When she was baked which was often, she was easy. She had a reputation for fucking guys for drugs and Mark knew it." He shook his head. "I can't imagine what it would be like to know things like that. I was out of line."

"That's tough." Justine agreed. "Alex, I don't want him out either, but I already warned him. I won't leave you with that problem; we need to get him to get some help. Maybe we have Victoria talk with us, they're close."

"Speaking of close…." He trailed off.

Justine met his gaze and knew there was no avoiding it. She took a moment to tell herself to be calm; Alex had saved her ass at the club and been damned good to her last night. As she had told him last month they were more than just members of the group they had been friends for years. Alex was also very close to Mark, he deserved to know. Know what? She asked, as he waited expectantly, what was there to know?

"Go ahead Alex," she said softly, "You've earned it."

"You were extremely upset last night Justine."

"I had been threatened to be gang raped, watched two of my friends get jumped and got punched in the face. My head hurt and I…."

"Even so, you didn't get really upset until Mark made that crack about you playing him."

"I know, I…"

"And the way you two looked at each other in that room?" Alex shook his head. "I think I have the answer, I would just like to hear your side of it."

Justine looked away from him. She'd just told herself to be straight with him, but was now hedging. She was the Mistress of the group. It was one thing to have a pet, but to admit more would be suicide. "I think that maybe, we shouldn't take this any further." She said. "I know I just said you earned it but…."

"Justine," Alex slid off the chair and sitting on the table between them, took her hand. "I want you to listen to me. I know how I come across. I like to play games and stir up shit. I instigate and push buttons. It's just how I am. But when it counts I have never nor will I ever betray a confidence. Right now I'm interested in what's going on between one of my best friends and a man I consider my brother."

Looking down at his hand, she turned hers over and holding his, squeezed it. "You mean that Alex? Because I want to believe it. But the Circle and the rules and…"

"Speaking of the rules, Justine." Alex said. "I heard that remark Mark made about the gag. There's a lot going on and it's obviously all tied together. Just tell me, I gave you my word, I won't say anything, even to Mark when he decides to talk to me again."

"Okay." She said quietly. "I…I'll tell you what's been going on, but when I'm done, just know how many of us will be screwed if you get stupid with any of this."

"And there's the Scarlett I know and love." Alex replied with a smirk.

"I think it really started back at Mark's initiation." Justine began. "You and Lazarus were the only two that ever knew how it really ended."

"And note I have never said a word."

"True." She agreed. "I was upset with myself, I almost sent him into a break down. I…there was a point when I couldn't get him to calm down that I saw myself going to jail," she sighed. "And I would have deserved it."

"You didn't know Justine, you had no idea what that would do to him and why."

"No, but I was beyond control. I couldn't break him and was getting as cruel as the old masters. Alex I rubbed salt into the cuts on his back, for Christ's sake."

"Persephone still does that."

"She's also a sick individual, and feels the need to instill fear. But afterwards I felt terrible. I went to see him a few days later and made it a point to always spend some time with him at the meetings." She shrugged. "I just wanted things to be okay between us."

"Seems like it worked." He grinned.

"Are you going to make me regret telling you this?"

"No, but I can't help a little teasing." He told her. "I can only be so good you know."

"As time went on I started to worry about my payback night. Mark's first entertainment video was brutal and I'd learned firsthand what he was capable of. Lazarus told me he would deny the payback, due to the extreme nature of the initiation, but fair was fair and after what I'd done he deserved to do whatever he wanted to me. I went into that night more nervous than I had been since my own initiation."

"You mean your gang rape?" Alex asked disgustedly.

"I don't speak of those things, let it go." She told him. "When I arrived at Mark's apartment I was prepared for the worst." She sat back and smiled at the memory. "Instead he went in another direction and decided to just go with being playful but embarrassing me a bit nonetheless."

Alex laughed and clapped his hands. "Shit, I forgot about that, he had you dress in a blue baby doll, put your hair in pigtails and act like a nervous little girl. It was classic," he laughed again. "Who knew you could be demure?"

Justine rolled her eyes. "Glad you enjoyed. Point was he refrained from taking his well deserved revenge. He learned a hell of a lot of respect from Lazarus and many others at the table. By deferring Mark proved that he wasn't the animal they thought he was. He also won a lot of points with the ladies. I was high lady at the time and he chose not to take the opportunity to treat me like a whore."

"I'm sure he was rewarded in granted time requests." Alex said. "Mark knows how to manipulate."

"No, Mark was showing me it was going to be fine between us, that he forgave what I did to him. I rewarded him myself two years later when on the night I ascended to Mistress I chose him for my celebration. After that things were normal between us. He became enforcer two years after that and I again rewarded him with my bed, because he not only rid us of the pariah that was our enforcer, but convinced Victoria to stay, had she left it would have been on my head."

"You also caught your first glimpse of how out of control he could be. Even with Adonis helping we could barely pull him off."

Sighing she shook her head. "From there I kept my distance sexually. He had already been with me several times and as much as I enjoyed him I didn't want to make it a habit. Then about a year ago, I was having a difficult time. I was in a funk. I was forty seven and getting tired of the games. I was fighting for my job when ownership changed hands and my sister was sick and at the time it was touch and go. I had a lot going on and Mark approached me after a meeting and asked to speak with me. He said he could see something was wrong and wanted to know if I wanted to talk."

She stopped as Alex stood and sliding the cup from her hand put it on the table then returned to his chair.

"We went out for coffee and I ended up telling him everything. Mark doesn't say a lot, but he's a good listener. He was very comforting and I..." she shrugged. "I needed someone so we went back to his place and played. Up until then I was always in control. This time I just relaxed and enjoyed. It was the best time I'd had in a long time. No expectations, no reputation to uphold. For the first time in years Justine, not Mistress Scarlett was enjoying being in bed with someone."

"Justine?" Alex frowned. "I don't understand what you mean."

"I had been Mistress for several years and had to uphold that mystique. Masters can make their table a buffet and its fine. But Mistress's cannot do so. Many nights my enjoyment was provided by men Mercedes arranged for me. I was getting tired of it. Mark came along at the right time and I started seeing him after each meeting."

"Just the meetings?" he raised his eyebrows.

"After a few months I needed to entertain. So I gave the group what I know they enjoy, I went out and found some punk ass kid who thought he was something, took him to a hotel room and made him beg to suck his own cum from my toes. He was a good looking kid and didn't do a bad job of fucking me. He turned obedient quickly and it should have been exciting."

She sighed and put her hands out. "Instead, I couldn't really get into it. I felt like a robot just going through the motions. Hell I faked an orgasm when I was riding his face."

"It was pretty convincing."

"Just goes to show men never really know now do you?"

"Ouch."

"That was the last time I slept with someone other than Mark. For the last six months I'd only been with him and the last couple of months it's been at least once a week."

"You two have been exclusive?" he asked shocked.

"I was with him, but you know damn well Mark has Stephanie, and he initiated Allison. I figure he assumed I was with others. But I was content to be with him. No games and I got what I wanted. But I did start to wonder what was going on."

"Maybe it's a phase?" he asked as she went silent.

"I thought so, in fact a week ago I ended up having a chance encounter that sent me off and running. I had the wildest week I'd had in a long time. A guy, a girl, Mark." She shrugged.

"Damn, now that's more like the old Justine."

"Even last night's meeting. I was so sex drunk over the week I called our resident exhibitionist Lexi and asked if she would be up for a live performance. I wanted to show the group their Mistress was as wild as ever. I was also trying to move myself past Mark. Telling myself it wasn't right and not just because of the group. Truth was I was starting to play a game I had no idea what the rules were."

"Are you talking about love?"

"I...I'm not ready to use that word" she told him, at least not aloud, she added to herself. "But I was flirting with the idea of more and tried to get past it. I mean look at the other half of it. Mark, The Dark Prince, settling for one woman? But that look he gave me last night Alex...."

"He was upset you were hurt Justine. He would have been if it was Victoria or Lexi or any of the girls."

"No Alex, he would have been angry as hell, what I saw in his eyes and heard was more than that. He..." she exhaled loudly. "You saw it, you just remarked on it. There's something between us."

"And you're thinking of pursuing this?" he asked, as he leaned back and resting his arm on the chair, put his chin in his hand.

"I was thinking of speaking to him last night when we got back. As exhausted as we were I didn't want to wait, then you two got into it and I fucked it up."

"What was he talking about with the gag?"

Justine looked down and again questioned how wise this was. She couldn't tell Alex she punished Mark without saying why. But as she sat there Alex swung the door wide open.

"Something went wrong after the initiation didn't it?"

"Why do you…"

"Give me a break Justine. I had my suspicions and last night confirmed them. You came to me about who Allison reminded Mark of. At my office you mentioned his little welcome aboard kiss. So when the time came at the end of the video I watched closely and I saw what you meant, but only because you brought it up."

"Well…." She began.

"Then Mark brings up a gag. I doubt he was talking about ten years ago. You punished him very recently and I hope to hell you didn't actually use that on him."

Justine put her head in her hands and fought to keep control. Just the thought of what she had done had her eyes burning. After having never remembered crying as an adult, that night with Mark had apparently broken the seal.

"Do you need some aspirin Justine?"

"No," she put her head up. "You're right Alex, the initiation went bad. Well not the actual breaking part, you saw that unedited. He was perfect, maybe a little too rough, but he pulled it off."

"So he did something to her after the fact?"

"Yes, he slept with her that night."

Alex started to speak, but she put her hand up.

"This is the second time I'm telling this and I'm already tired of it. He was in the middle of an insomnia bout, he was exhausted, and not in a great place mentally. Allison was also exhausted as well as overwhelmed from the experience. He decided to let her stay at his place. They went out got drunk, bared their souls to each other and upon returning back to his place proceeded to have quite the night, which ended with her spending the night in his bed."

"Holy shit." Alex said softly. "So I get it, he's in a funk, drunk and Allison happens to look like his sister. He's fucked in his head and sees her as a bit of a surrogate for his misplaced affection and fucks her."

Justine nodded and waited for him to continue, but he was finished. Breathing a sigh of relief that he wasn't going to go on and on, she continued, "I was away during this and he called me and sounded terrible and said we had to talk. I figured he was just in a funk and told him to come see me Friday. In the meantime I'd seen the video and I couldn't wait to get my hands on him. I planned on him spending the weekend and having fun and celebrating our new sister and… then he tells me what he did."

"Yet Allison is still here."

"I'll get to that. I was livid Alex, absolutely lived. And because you know there is something between us I'll admit it wasn't just the rule he broke that had me angry. I was pissed off that after all the time we had shared he would never tell me a damn thing about himself."

"Welcome to the club." Alex grunted.

"Then he tells me he and Allison are sharing stories about their past. Then he caves to her. This is a man who declined a night with Victoria Redding. He's also a man who has been with some of the most amazing women of the group, hell he has his Mistress hung up on him. Yet he gives in to this nobody, this whore off the street, because she pouts at him and…."

"Easy Justine, Allison is a member of the group now; she is far from some slut. Besides she had the advantage of his condition and resembling a woman he longed for when he was younger. A woman he could never be with. There was a point Mark used to seek out women who looked like her. I can see how..."

"I'm surprised you're defending him."

"I was afraid this might happen." He said softly.

"What?" she asked surprised.

"Back at the hotel I wasn't trying to get you to bypass Mark for the initiation because I was afraid he would scare Allison off. The second I saw her I knew who she looked like and thought something could happen if he got into one of his weird moods."

"Why didn't you...?"

"What Justine?" he laughed humorlessly, "Excuse me Justine, but don't let Mark near Allison, she looks like his sister." He looked at her and put his hands out as if saying "See?"

"I guess you're right." She nodded, she paused for a moment then continued where she left off, "I was pissed off Alex, angrier than I had been in years. But it was more than that. I was jealous and to make it worse, he asked me if I was. That was the last straw. It was hard enough to realize I was jealous of Allison, but for him to throw it at me?"

"So you punished him."

"Damn straight I did, but you know him. He came looking for that. He knew he let the group down, knew he jeopardized Allison being in the group, he wanted to be punished. Had I been rational I would have sent him away. Thought about it, made him wait then done something."

She shook her head disgustedly. "But I was too far gone. I laid into him in a way that would have put the old masters to shame. Whipped him so hard I hurt my shoulder and he just took it, not a sound out of him."

"Pissed you off even more."

"I strung him up from my ceiling then put a cock ring on him so he couldn't go soft on me. I left him there then when I came back, made him fuck me, then go down on me. The entire time I made him call me Allison."

"Nice touch." Alex said as if he were admiring what she did.

"I made him beg 'Allison' to lick her pussy, to fuck her. The entire time I was getting more and more angry. He was just taking all of it and I wanted him to be hurt the way I was hurt."

"You mean because you were upset?"

"I mean the things I and Morrigan and many others had to endure. Being that rough on him brought back some nasty memories of what they had done to me, including my initiation. I...I wasn't thinking straight and I decided to do the only thing I could do get him to react."

"The gag." Alex said quietly.

"I tied him to a chair, slipped the gag into his mouth, and as he screamed and cried, I hopped onto his cock and rode him."

"Holy shit Justine!"

"I told him the only thing he was good for was sex so show me how good he was. I told him that gag would stay in his mouth until he came for me. So I rode him and held his face still while he begged behind the gag and whimpered like a baby even with the ring his cock was getting soft and I told him he would be there all night." She stopped and felt another wave of tears trying to get past her eyes as she saw Alex looking at her, disgusted.

"Then he changed." She said softly."His eyes got dark and his cock got hard. He even started fucking me, slamming his hips into me and I got nervous. I thought he was going to get violent when it was over. But as soon as he came he started to whine again. I let him go and as he laid there on the floor sobbing and saying he was sorry. I told him to get the fuck out of my house and to plan on how he was going to announce to the group that Allison couldn't join and why."

She stopped and pointing at her Alex said. "Justine that is the most brutal thing I've heard even in this group!" he threw his hands in the air. "Do you know what you could have done to him? Over what, a rule? Kick her out, kick him out, you don't fuck with someone like that!"

"I...I know." She said and could now feel the tears trickling down her cheeks. "I told him to shower before he left." She shook her head. "The Circle has done amazing things for me, but over the years I've lost track of who I was. Mistress Scarlett needed to punish him, but what the fuck was wrong with Justine to literally gamble on his sanity?"

She started crying harder and standing; Alex picked a box of tissues up from an end table and handed them to her. After she took one, he sat back down on the table and rested his hand on her leg.

"He trusted me, even after how we started. He fucked up and came to tell me. He deserved to be punished, but who the fuck was I to do that to him? What the hell was wrong with me? All this over a fucking group of perverts?"

"So what happened, you two were obviously all right until last night."

"I went into the shower with him and held him and said I was sorry. We went into my bed and just lied there. He said he was sorry to me and I started crying. He held me and I'm thinking how pathetic I am. I hurt him and he's consoling me. He should have never wanted to see me again. I told him I would let Allison stay. I had hurt him enough I wouldn't make him responsible for that."

"So Allison knows you know?"

"No, if she did she would have to leave, you know that."

"So you're crossing your fingers that Mark telling her not to say anything will work? Why would she listen to a guy she seduced?"

"You're right, which is why I went to Victoria. We spoke and you know she feels she owes Mark. She went to Allison after the meeting and told her she knew. Gave her the warning of how she would not only be tossed, but now that she knew us totally ruined. That was why I let her attend to see what she would lose out on and put more fear in her. I don't think we will need to worry. At least not about her saying anything."

"What do you mean?" he asked.

"I warned him to stay away from Allison, no taking her to work functions or dinner if he's in town. I think he learned his lesson, but he broke her and she may still want more of him at some point and think she can..."

"Last night took care of that."

"How do you figure?"

"I guess you missed their little exchange last night. After the fight he went to ask if she were okay and she told him to get away from her, called him an animal. He seemed strangely un-offended, now I know why. It just fixed a possible problem."

"Speaking of problems Alex, you see why you can never repeat this story. Now that you know each of the four high positions were involved in this. Persephone would have a field day."

"I have no desire to see anyone punished and have our reputation tarnished." Looking up at her he grinned. "But I have to ask. Whether she owed Mark or not Victoria would not have done this for free."

"She didn't."

"Was it a high price?" he asked.

"Yes, but so was the favor and I won't speak of it" She said while dabbing at her eyes.

"So now that I know the sordid details, where does this leave things with you and Mark?"

"I'm not sure. I have feelings, I know that now. The mishap with Allison brought them up and last night clinched it. I think he feels the same way, but doubt he'll bring it up."

"You know," Alex said quietly. "We're talking about this as friends, but you realize you might have to leave the Circle. If you two went exclusive, what about entertaining? Plus if that ever got out, it would make the Allison thing look like a minor infraction."

"I don't know." She shrugged. "I don't have a lot of time left. That would be more his decision." She tapped Alex's hand. "Just think Alex if something comes out of the two of us, you get to be master sooner."

"Yeah, and needing to replace you and find an enforcer." Sitting back, he again rested his head in his chin, a thoughtful expression on his face.

"So you would really consider for lack of a better term, dating Mark?"

"Wow," she laughed. "I haven't dated since sophomore year in college."

"Seriously," he told her. "You're open to a relationship?"

"Yes." She said nodding. "At least to give it a try anyway. Why?"

"Justine before I make my point I want you to know something."

"What's that?"

"Although last night may have shown otherwise, Mark and I are close. I've known him since he was seventeen. Mark was a great success story. He survived a brutal childhood and became a straight a student, who was a gifted athlete, martial artist and even had the cute little girl next store girlfriend. He tested at the genius level and he excelled at everything he tried. The all American boy."

He paused and shook his head. 'That was on the surface. Underneath there was something wrong. His past never left him, just got buried. He started getting carried away in the tournaments, hurting the kids he was fighting. He was trying to get rough with his girlfriend and she eventually left him when he broke a guys jaw for insulting his sister. He was also already heavily into the occult. He had mastered Latin by seventeen and was reading books that had been banned for good reason. He was also in love with a woman he could never have which made him more bitter. When he ran into Max I feel what happened had been inevitable all along. Sooner or later he would lose it and in a way fate was kind to him and he lost it on the one person who really deserved it."

"Thank you for the history lesson," Justine began, "But…"

"I used to spend time with his foster parents. Doug, Megan's father, used to fight with Mark quite a bit, he always thought he was up to something. When the trial was going on, Doug told me there was something wrong with him and he had known it for years. He told me there were times you could look in his eyes and see something moving, something ugly. Behind the good looks, talent and intelligence, there was something dark that was just waiting to get out. Years later I still see that in him sometimes."

"If you're warning me Alex, I appreciate it, but you saw me stop him last night. I can…."

"Control him? Is that what you want? To be with someone so unstable you have to get in his face and yell a safe word to get him to stop?"

"He can sleep when I'm next to him" she said softly. "He trusts me, if we were together he would be calmer, go back to the way he was before his sister left."

"You want to be a babysitter? Justine, everyone has their problems. Look at the group, on the surface everyone would want to be any of us, but we all have our heart aches and problems just like they do, we're far from perfect. Justine, you're a beautiful, successful woman with a lot going for you. If you choose to offer your heart to someone then that someone is a very lucky man. Do you want to give that to someone with more baggage than you can fathom?"

"I can...." She paused as he rolled his eyes.

"What? Change him? I know Mark better than anyone other than his sister. I can tell you he is broken in ways you can't understand. There was a time I wanted to know so I could help him. Then I had the lie detector incident. When Mark attacked me, I found myself looking into the eyes of a maniac. I had never seen so much hate. It's still there Justine; we saw a flash last night. I'm telling you this as your friend."

"I know you are" she said softly as she again took his hand. "But sometimes all that's needed is the right person. He thought the only one who he could be with was the one person he wasn't allowed to be with. I can be that person now."

"Justine, the idea of a good woman fixing the perennial bad boy is something that Harlequin Romances made popular. In reality those women end up hurt. Usually just emotionally, but sometimes worse. You can't fix Mark because he doesn't want to be fixed. All you can do is contain the damage when he snaps."

"Alex," she began as she squeezed his hand. "I appreciate not only what you're saying, but the reason you're saying it. It makes me feel bad I think poorly of you sometimes. You're a good man underneath all of your games, and I think Mark is too, he does do a lot of things for people."

"I'm not saying he's a bad person. He couldn't be where he is without having some control, but any time he goes through a phase like this it could be the time he throws it all away. Again last night, you don't get it, he would have killed that kid."

"Extreme situation." She said trying to convince herself as much as him. "Like I said Alex, thank you, but as you just said, no one is perfect; everyone has a skeleton or two in their closet."

"It's your call Justine, and you're right, a lot of people have skeletons." Looking her in the eye he said quietly, "But trust me, Mark doesn't have a skeleton, he has a graveyard"

Chapter Nine

Justine sat in her Porsche staring across the street at the building that housed Mark's firm. She'd been sitting there for the last ten minutes, checking her e-mails, fixing her make-up and trying to convince herself to get her ass out of the car. Tapping her fingers on the steering wheel she could no longer deny the reason she was stalling, she was nervous. Justine was never nervous, concerned at times yes, but never nervous. She sure as hell couldn't remember being this nervous over a conversation with a man. Let alone a man she'd dominated at times for years. That was part of the problem, Justine was here to speak to Mark as an equal and more importantly do something she had never done before, offer her heart.

Picking up her phone she saw it was eleven fifty and decided to give it until noon. She'd called his office earlier and asked if he had court today and was told he would be in the office all day. Mark rarely took lunch and odds are he wouldn't be tied up in a meeting. Justine could have made sure he would have been available by calling first, but she wanted to surprise him. No, the reason was she didn't want him wondering why she was coming down in the middle of the week. She had planned on waiting until Friday as when she had finally gotten him to call her back yesterday morning; he had said he would still like her to come down. As she sat there waiting for noon she replayed the brief conversation back in her mind. Although it hadn't started out well, it had ended better than she had thought.

She had called and left three messages on Monday and he hadn't called back. On Tuesday, feeling upset she had tried again, vowing she wouldn't leave him another message. However when his voice mail came on she couldn't hang up. Instead, her voice, choked with emotion, said, "Mark, please call me back, please?"

When she'd hung up she had been upset at herself. She sounded like a pathetic teenager. Shame of it was it worked. Ten minutes later he sent her a text saying he was in court, but he was fine and asked how she was. She sent him a reply she was okay, but they needed to talk. He didn't reply to that one and she had given up. A half hour later he called her and after she answered said, "I only have a couple of minutes Justine, are you okay?"

"I'm better now that I know you are." She told him, and then a thought occurred to her. "So you're in court with a black eye?"

"What choice do I have? And trust me I've been hearing about it."

"Mark we need to talk."

"I know, we established that Sunday Morning. My Mistress was...."

"Fuck the Circle Mark." She snapped into the phone. "That's not why I want to talk to you. I was supposed to come down this weekend. I would still like to, or would you rather not see me?"

Mark was quiet and she felt her stomach sink, but a moment later he said softly, "I always want to see you Justine. I figured you wouldn't want to or you'd come down with Alex to talk about what happened."

Justine laughed in relief. "That's funny I figured you wouldn't want to see me. Alex won't be involved in this. I'm coming down for us to talk Mark."

"Okay, how's Blue Grotto sound? I'll make eight o clock reservations."

"Sounds good, I'll see you then?"

"I look forward to it."

Justine had felt better after that conversation. The fact he wanted her to come down told her things could still be open for them. The only issue then was waiting until Friday to see him. From there either she would have an amazing weekend, or things would be awkward and she might end up coming home before Sunday. Justine had tried to lean towards the great weekend. She thought of being in that magnificent bed, watching in the mirrors as they fucked. More than that, she found herself just as excited about waking up in his arms, holding her close. They had done that before, but this time she would know there was emotion behind it as well as physical comfort.

Unfortunately that was when work reared its ugly head. There was a last minute conference taking place in Houston this weekend to discuss the new launch and finalize all the details and she would have to leave on Friday morning. Justine had been furious, but there was no way out of it. She also wanted to attend to make sure the people at tech didn't grandstand about how they miraculously fixed the audio bug. The conference would run until Monday and seeing as she'd be out that way, Justine decided to stay out there and from the conference travel to Dallas to visit her sister Debra for a couple of days. She hadn't seen her or her nieces since Christmas and it would be nice to take it easy for a couple of days.

This completely screwed her weekend with Mark and knowing there was no way she would wait until next weekend to speak with him she decided to drive down to Providence today. It was Wednesday and if things went well she could stay with him until Friday morning. Because her face was still bruised, she'd been working from home and could do that from Mark's place while he was at work. This also gave her a little bit of an element of surprise. She didn't want Mark to have time to plan how their conversation would go on Friday. This way she could get his unguarded reaction to her proposal.

The only way she was going to get any reaction was to get her ass in gear and go get this over with. Looking in the mirror one more time she shrugged, her face was still discolored, but it was yellowish rather than the purple it had been the first couple of days. The swelling had also gone down quite a bit. She gathered her long hair which was a mess from having the top down on the way from Boston. After putting her hair up, she got out of the car and took a moment to smooth out her dress.

Justine's recent nervousness, and teenage like behavior, had even extended to her spending a half hour sitting on her bed wondering how to dress. She quickly decided against provocative. She needed to have him pay attention to what she was saying, not what she looked like. Professional would be too far the other way. Remembering the dress Mercedes had been wearing at the meeting, Justine had opted for something simple. She had chosen a plain white sundress that was short enough to show off her legs, but not inappropriately short. In similar fashion the dress was low cut enough to show some of her breasts, but that was due as much to their size as the style of the dress.

Justine had only lightly applied her makeup and mostly cover-up over the bruise. Despite the extremely attractive women Mark spent time with, she knew he had a thing for girl next door cute and she figured this was about as close as she could come. Hitting the alarm on her car, Justine took a deep breath, told herself to stop acting like a sissy and most of all, "Take what I want." She whispered.

* * *

Justine could feel the butterflies in her stomach as she made her way through the suite of offices that made up Howard Bloch & Price. Mark had a corner office and as she followed the intern from the front desk to the back where he was located, she kept telling herself to calm down. They reached his receptionist Melanie who asked who she was and told her to hold on, that Mark was in one of the conference rooms. She picked up the phone and after listening for a minute hung up. "Mr. Phillips is in with a client, but he'll be finished shortly. He said for me to have you wait in his office, so right this way."

As Justine followed her, she couldn't help but smile. Melanie was in her early twenties and really couldn't handle much more than typing and answering the phone. What she could handle, and according to him quiet well, was Mark's cock. He told Justine he had met her at a goth club a couple of years ago and last year she had called him because she needed a job. Although she dressed conservatively and didn't give the impression of being an office slut, Melanie was submissive and Mark had amused himself with her many times at the office.

This in between a twenty year old blond pet, Justine, and any other chance encounter he might land himself in. Justine's smile faded, she was going to ask Mark to give all this up for her. For most men Justine would be more than worth being exclusive with, but someone like Mark was a different story. She had seen him pick up women ranging from eighteen year old students to married women in their forties and he never failed to land who he wanted. She stopped that train of thought; she would have her answer soon enough.

Instead her mind focused on Melanie's grey skirt, which although it was knee length, was quite tight and showed off her ass. Justine looked at her round firm ass, then let her gaze work it's way down the backs of her well shaped legs. When Melanie reached the door she opened it, stepping aside gestured for Justine to enter. As she passed, she checked out the front view as well. Melanie had long blond hair, blue eyes and a sweet smile. Below that smile, she was wearing a black blouse unbuttoned enough to show the top of a lacy red bra. She had fair skin and the swelling of her breasts looked damn good against the red.

Okay, would she be able to stay exclusive? She laughed to herself. Maybe her and Mark could compromise and share a woman once in awhile. They weren't even there yet and this already seemed complicated.

"Have a seat Miss Bates, he'll be right in."

"Thank you."

"There's a bar against the wall, feel free to help yourself."

"I'll wait for Mr. Phillips to make one for me, thank you." She winked at her.

Melanie winked back and smiled. No jealousy whatsoever. Then again one of Mark's little tricks usually involved making his pets watch him fuck someone else so they knew they were nothing to him. Games, everything was a game to them. Melanie closed the door behind her and just before she turned away something caught her eye and she laughed out loud. On the back of the door someone had hung a poster of Sylvester Stallone as Rocky, complete with black eye and bloody face.

Still smiling she turned away from the door and looked around the office. It was huge and completely full. All along one wall was a row of bookcases. Most filled with legal reference books, but the last two were Mark's personal collection. Mostly philosophy and religious texts along with quite a few occult works that she believed he put there to throw people. Then again, the two enormous oil paintings behind his desk were enough to do that. The one on the left was Hieronymus Bosch's The Garden of Earthly delights where a plethora of scantily clad demons and humans were cavorting and carrying on lewd acts.

The second painting was one of Mark's sisters. It showed an endless line of people standing before two thrones. In one sat an angelic figure with a crown and long flowing robes. Behind his throne was a pair of golden gates with light emanating from inside of them. To the left was the hideous looking Goat thing Mark had tattooed on his back. It was sitting cross legged on thrown made of skulls and behind it was huge pit where demons were using pitchforks to cast people into it. Each figure had an arm out stretched and between them they were holding the Scales of justice. At the bottom of the painting, the title was written in blood red gothic lettering "The Final court of Appeal."

Justine shook her head at the detail in the picture. She could almost feel the serenity coming from the figure on the right as well as the malevolence in the eyes of the beast. Mark had told her that since she had become sober his sister had finally started selling some work and was getting as much as Ten thousand a painting. Both paintings were disturbing to say the least and the firm had requested several times Mark take them down. At that point he would reach into his desk and wave the stack of envelopes that contained standing offers from several firms around the country. Jim Howard, the head of the firm, would always cave, which was why Mark stayed where he was; he pretty much did whatever the hell he wanted.

Turning to her right, Justine walked over to the other wall which in addition to the small bar consisted of a series of glass cases that contained all of Mark's trophies. There were dozens from karate tournaments and all first place finishes. There were also several from when Mark played baseball in high school and college. The last case was full of plaques and scholastic awards. All of this spoke of how tremendously gifted he was, yet he could barely get through a night without waking up screaming and at times, recently for example, seemed as if he were ready for a breakdown.

Justine smiled at a framed picture on one of the shelves. It was a newspaper clipping that featured Mark as a teenager. Standing next to him, shaking his hand and smiling, was Alex Warner. The headline proclaimed. 'Classical Student Mark Phillips wins coveted Orion Best of The Best Scholarship'. Best of the Best was how the Circle was frequently described and Mark fit it to a tee. An alpha even amongst alpha's, but broken nonetheless. After walking away from the cases, Justine made her way over to his desk

The huge cherry wood desk was as always annoyingly neat. His lap top, piles of folders, note pads, pens, pictures, everything perfectly lined up and organized. Mark had OCD and smiling mischievously, Justine picked up a stack of files that were in alphabetical order and shuffled them. Putting them down she looked at the three different colored pens he had lined up over a yellow legal pad and switched them around. As she did she looked at the pad and saw that all of his notes were written in Latin. Mark had two sets for every case. The ones he would share with the firm and his personal ones in Latin, which always contained one or two points not in the shared versions.

She looked around to see if there was anything else she could switch up on him and stopped as she looked at a couple of five by seven pictures he had lined up on the desk. One was of Mark and Victoria at an awards ceremony where she had won cover girl of the year. Justine knew Mark kept this one quite visible to add to his player reputation. It, along with all of his trophies, played well with the boys club.

There was another picture with him and Alex. In this one they in black suits and toasting the camera with wine glasses. Mark was holding up a rolled up diploma and Justine assumed it was from his Suffolk graduation. Again she was amazed at how far back they went, yet they could turn on each other in a heartbeat.

Justine felt her heart skip a beat at the last picture in the row. It was of the two of them from when Mark had taken her to Newport two months ago. They had been sitting at a table outside of a beachfront restaurant and Mark had the waiter take the picture. Justine was wearing a red bikini and her wet hair was down across her shoulders and chest. Mark was shirtless, and sliding behind her had wrapped his arms around her waist and put his head on her shoulder. Just before the waiter snapped the picture, Mark had slipped his finger under the cup of her skimpy top, brushing it against her nipple and getting her to laugh. He was smiling and it wasn't the fake pretty one he used on his prey, it was genuine, and even in the picture she could see how green his eyes were.

The pictures he had with Victoria and Alex were formal, two friends out together somewhere. This picture was different. Justine could see how happy they both were and admired how good they looked together. The thought hit her they looked like a couple. This was the type of picture a guy kept on his desk of his girlfriend or wife, not an acquaintance. She winced at a sharp pain in her face and realized she was smiling so hard her cheek hurt. Resisting the urge to pick the picture up to look at it closer, she went to walk back around the desk to sit in one of the leather chairs in front of it and wait for him.

Justine stopped and her eyes widened as she caught sight of the only picture on the left hand corner of the desk. It was two pictures in one large frame and they were both of Mark and Megan. The pictures looked like a past and present. The first one was quite sweet. It was just of their faces and the two of them appeared to be in their teens. They were cheek to cheek and smiling. Megan's smile was huge and Justine noted a little crooked which gave her and endearing appearance. Mark's smile was... after a moment Justine had to settle on the word sweet, he looked a little nervous, and she could picture his sister saying something to get him to smile.

The second picture appeared to be fairly recent and Justine could tell from the wall of paintings they were in front of it been taken in Abigail Lefay's club, The Black Flame in Chicago. Mark was wearing a black suit with a blood red shirt and had his arm around Megan who was wearing a long black and blue dress that was slit up the left all the way to her hip. The dress was sleeveless and Justine noticed a huge tattoo of Medusa that covered her arm from shoulder to elbow. Next to them was a gruesome painting of some type of ghoul in a cemetery that Justine assumed Megan was unveiling at the club.

What really caught Justine about the pictures was Megan's resemblance to Allison. This time she did pick up the picture to get a closer look. Megan had the same ivory skin, long black hair and large full lips as Allison; again the only real difference was the eyes. That and Megan had higher cheekbones, but all in all the two of them could be sisters. Justine frowned as this left no doubt the woman Mark was once in love with had been his sister.

In the back of her mind Justine heard Alex saying Mark had more baggage than she could fathom. That was followed by the graveyard crack. Still holding the picture she tried to convince herself not to worry about it. Mark had been a screwed up kid. Megan was the first one who was good to him. Even while telling his story and not admitting it was his sister, Mark had said nothing happened, that she turned him away. Alex had backed that up with his asshole stunt during Mark's trial. It was in the past. On the other hand, it seemed more than coincidence Mark had gone downhill when his sister went to Chicago. Then again, the fact that she did proved nothing odd was going on there.

Her mind stopped spinning as hearing the sound of the door behind her; Justine quickly put the picture down and turned to face the door. Mark came in wearing a pair of black slacks and a white dress shirt that looked damn good against his tan. He wasn't wearing a tie and had his sleeves rolled up exposing his muscular forearms and she could already feel herself wanting him. Her eyes then found his face and she winced. Mark's left eye was barely open and as he approached her she could see where his lower lip had been split. There was also the same yellowish coloration on his right cheek as she had on hers.

"Sorry to keep you waiting." He said as he veered off toward the bar. "Martini?"

"Sounds good." She said as she took the last couple of steps past the desk and sat down in one of the chairs. He was looking at her as he walked to the bar and she hoped to hell he hadn't seen her with the picture. Wanting to keep the mood as light as possible she said, "Nice poster."

"Oh, please." Mark said as he stood at the bar and pulled two glasses from the rack over it. "Fucking Jim."

"Well you said you were hearing about it."

"Think that's bad? Someone passed out little bells to all the partners and they hit them when I walk by."

Justine laughed. "Well you're better than all of them so this probably makes them feel good to be able to make fun of you."

"I suppose."

"But in the end, they're still jealous, how many of them could have defended their women like that?"

"You mean how many of them would almost kill someone?"

"Mark, we wouldn't have made it out of that without you. Regardless of you getting carried away, you saved our asses. Literally, those kids weren't playing; Alex said that Sunday, you did what you had to."

"I suppose." Mark said as he walked over to her carrying two drinks.

Placing one on the desk he reached down and handed Justine hers. "Thank you," she said as she took it, then raising her eyebrows added, "Do I get a hello?"

Mark leaned down and gave her a quick kiss. He started to pull back, but reaching up and grabbing his head, Justine pulled him back to her and kissed him softly. She felt him hesitate, but only for a second. His lips lost their stiffness and she sighed as he kissed her back. Parting her lips, she slipped her tongue against his lips and felt her nipples stiffen as he opened his mouth to accept it. Their tongues played across each other, and she felt his hands on her shoulders. As the kiss deepened, his left hand slid around her shoulder and began caressing the bare skin of her back. Justine broke the kiss and for an instant had the urge to tell him she loved him. She resisted that urge, the sex and attraction had always been there, she needed to discuss the rest before she would go that far.

"You look cute," Mark told her as he straightened up. "I like the dress."

"Cute?" she asked, trying not to smile. "Is that bad thing?"

"No, I like it. You pull it off pretty well considering I know you're really a bad ass Mistress."

"Not today I'm not."

"No?" he asked as he sat down. "What are you today?"

"Today I'm just a woman who came down to spend some time with a good looking guy."

"Speaking of time, what happened to Friday? Is everything okay?"

"No, well not as far as the weekend goes." With a sigh she told him. "I have to go to Houston for work, I'll be gone a few days, I won't be able to stay with you."

"Oh." He said. "Well you have to do what you need to. You didn't have to come down here to tell me that."

"No, but I told you yesterday we need to talk and I'm not waiting. Do you have time now or should I come back?"

"I'm clear until two."

"Good, first off, are you okay Mark? You took a pretty good beating that night."

"I'm fine." He said. "Trust me this is nothing compared to what I've taken."

"Are you sleeping yet?"

"Not much, no." He told her then pointed at her. "Are you okay? You're head okay?"

"I'm fine now, Sunday was a rough day. Fortunately I didn't have to drive home."

"Shit Justine," he said shaking his head, "I'm sorry I left you like that. I'm such an asshole."

"It's okay, I think it might have been better that you did. Alex was as angry as you were and I was in no condition to break the two of you up."

"I still shouldn't have left you, but I...." he trailed off. "I'd lost it and Alex was right, I was out of control, he should want me to leave."

"But he doesn't and you know I don't. I do want to try to help you Mark and so does he. Please, at least take some damn sleeping pills."

"They don't work, it's hard to explain. But if you did want me to step down, I..."

"Mark, will you do something for me?" she asked.

"Of course."

"Stop talking about the fucking Circle. I am sick of it, I really am. I came here to talk to you about something else. All I will say is that will be the day an enforcer is tossed for defending his sisters. Aside from that, I'm here for another reason."

"Sounds good." Mark nodded. "How did you get home?"

"Alex called Lexi and asked if she minded knocking around New York for awhile and I rode home with her. He also covered the hotel Sunday morning, because I didn't go back and he figured you wouldn't so I have your things and..."

"You didn't go back to the hotel?" he asked. "Where did you go?"

"I spent the night at Alex's and...."

"You spent the night with Alex." Mark said softly.

Justine started to respond that it wasn't like that, but was struck by the tone in his voice. He had looked away from her and was staring down at his desk. Was he...? Hating herself for it, but needing to know, she took it further. "Yes, we went back to his place. Why, does that bother you?" She'd deliberately said the last part with a tone to see if she could get more of a reaction out of him.

"I..." Mark hesitated, "Well you can do whatever you want, you're the mistress and if you..."

He paused again and she asked, "I know I can do what I want, but I asked if it bothered you?"

Looking up at her he responded immediately "Yes it does, but I guess I deserve it for leaving you, I... I hope you had...."

"Jealousy is an ugly emotion Mark," she cut him off, "Isn't that what you always say?"

"What can I say, I'm an ugly person." He said softly.

He was jealous! As childish as it was, Justine felt her heart leap at the thought. It wasn't one sided between them. "It wasn't like that Mark," she said quickly.

"You don't need to explain."

"Yes I do." She told him. "After you left I was…I was very upset and my head hurt and I ended up fainting. Alex took me back to his place so he could keep an eye on me."

"You passed out?" his eyes widened. "Now I really feel like…"

"No Mark you were…." She paused and tried to think of what to say next. Mark frowned and picking up the pencils, switched them back to their original places. "Mark, were you really hurt the other night?"

"I told you I'm fine, just some bruises."

"No, I mean when I called you Lovecraft and you got upset."

Mark's eyes narrowed and he pursed his lips in thought. Justine sat back in the chair and finally took a sip of her drink. Hopefully he wasn't going to turn this into a game. When he remained silent she went back to what they had been talking about.

"Anyway, Alex was a gentleman, I slept in his bed, he stayed in a chair. He's worried about you, so please call him."

"I'll think about it." Mark said. "He said things he had no right saying."

"He knows, he admitted he was as out of control as you were. No one was thinking Mark, and that included me."

"I was hurt."

"Excuse me?"

"What you asked earlier. I was hurt; you looked at me in that precinct and called me baby. You know I like that and you said it so sweet." He sighed. "Then you turned into Mistress Scarlett and I over reacted. I can handle rage, but I can't handle things like that so I…I left."

"I'm sorry I hurt you." She said softly. "And you were very sweet to me as well. In fact that's why I'm here."

"What do you mean?" he asked as frowning again, he picked up the stack of folders and rolling his eyes started putting them back in order. "Did you do this?"

"Yeah, sorry." She grinned, glad for the distraction, she needed to think.

"Really Justine? Are we in high school?" he shook his head as finishing the files he put them back, then made a show of looking around his desk.

"I can't resist you're so goddamn neat. And I…."

She stopped as Mark reached out and turned the picture of he and his sister towards him, she had put it down quickly and it had been facing away from him. Still holding it in his hand, he looked at it, then back at her. Picking it up, he turned it to face her. Taking a couple of long swallows of her Martini, Justine felt her heart begin to race. She'd fucked up again. Lowering the drink she looked at him where he was waiting in silence and said, "I'd never actually seen a picture of your sister. She's beautiful."

"She is." He agreed. "Our real parents were losers, but I guess they were pretty ones."

"You look sweet in that picture." Justine said, "It's something to see you so young, how old were you?"

"I was sixteen she was eighteen, it was at Christmas I had just come to live with them."

"Sixteen?" she smiled. "You both look so innocent."

"We were never innocent." He said softly, "Our innocence was taken from us by monsters."

"I'm sorry." She said quickly.

"That's okay. The animal that raped Megan when she was a little girl died of pancreatic cancer in prison he died slowly and in pain. He had also been raped twice while in there. So he's dead and Max

Thompson is wishing he was after I was done with him." His eyes darkened and he gave her an evil smile. "Lex Talionis. Justine, life has a way of making things right."

Justine nodded and again tried to force Alex's warning from her mind. Mark was silent and as he picked up his drink, chugged half of it while looking at the picture. Putting his glass down he said, "Justine, it's not what you think."

"What isn't?" she asked

"Come on Justine, you don't miss a trick. I told you my unrequited love story and that Allison looked just like her and you were staring at this picture when I came in. You know."

"I..." she paused, she couldn't tell him she talked to Alex about it, "It was a long time ago Mark, you don't have to tell me anything."

"Have to? Usually no, but in this case I do."

"You don't." she shook her head.

"Maybe I want to." He said quietly. "You say you would like me to open up with you. So here's your chance to hear something about me."

"If you trust me." She said.

"Completely."

"That's more than I deserve," she said. "After what I did to you I don't..."

"It's called the Westermarck theory."

"What is?" she asked, confused.

"It's about Siblings. The first part states how while as early as in the womb we are conditioned to not be attracted to our blood. The back half of the theory speaks of how, if Siblings are separated at a young age and are reunited later in life that it is highly likely they will be strongly attracted to each other."

"Okay." She nodded. "I understand Mark, I'm not judging."

"Megan and I were taken to the pound by our sorry excuse for a mother when we were four and six. I wouldn't see Megan again until she was eighteen." He turned the picture back to himself and looked at it. "She was the most beautiful girl I had ever seen. She thought that about me as well. She used to call me her beautiful little brother."

"That's cute."

"Megan was taken in by Doug and Denise when she was eleven. They adopted her a year later and were damn good to her. They found out about me years later and helped me get placed in her custody since she was eighteen. I had a lot of issues, mostly besides my temper I wouldn't speak. I would speak to her, but even with her not much more than a few sentences. Nothing to anyone else."

He paused and finished his drink. "Megan wouldn't give up though. Night after night she would come into my room and just talk to me. Most of the time at me, I would just sit and listen. She would talk about everything from books to music to how the cute guy at school asked out her friend instead of her. She didn't quit on me and eventually I started talking to her, then her parents then other people."

"Wow, all my sister and I used to do was fight over boyfriends and clothes." She said trying to keep the mood light.

"Our bedrooms had an adjoining bathroom and every night I would have nightmares and she would hear me wake up screaming. Megan knew what I was going through; she had some pretty bad ones herself. One night she comes into my room, gets in my bed and holds me. She used to do that when we were little and our mother had company as she called it and we would be scared because they were drunk and yelling. Megan would hold me and tell me she would never let anything happen to me."

His voice was so soft she could barely hear him and she could see he was struggling not to get emotional. Leaning forward, she reached across the desk and put her hand out. Mark looked at it for a moment, then put his hand in hers and squeezed it. Justine felt her own emotions begin to build as she realized how big this was. It sure as hell wasn't a pleasant story, but she had the feeling Mark had very few of those, but it was an important one and he was sharing it with her.

"So we began sleeping together. Always dressed of course and in the meantime I had a girlfriend named Krissy, Megan's best friend's younger sister. We went out of a year and a half and I loved her, or thought I did. In the meantime I was thinking more and more of my sister. We would lie there and talk for hours, we would hold each other when we were upset and we never had nightmares when we slept together. I felt myself falling in love with her. I couldn't fight it."

He stopped shook his head. "I started changing in other ways too, getting more violent, darker. I got carried away with Krissy a couple of times in bed and she dumped me. Then she took me back, but left after I beat the shit out of Megan's ex boyfriend. I didn't care though, by then I knew who I wanted. I started to feel her wanting me as well."

Justine looked down as she wondered if she really should be hearing this. The words be careful of what you wish for came into her head. No, she would have to learn to take the bad with the good.

"I remember one Saturday morning we woke up and we're lying there listening to the rain. I made a joke and she laughed and next thing we're staring into each other's eyes and I can feel it, better yet I could see she did too. I leaned into her and kissed her." He paused and shook his head. "I know how bad this sounds, but nothing had ever felt so right at the time. She kissed me back and we kept kissing. I pushed her back and,"

He stopped as he must have noticed the look of unease on her face. "Anyway her father scared the shit out of us, banging on my door and asking when I was going to help him move some shit in the basement. So he stopped us from making a big mistake. At least I see that now anyway. Back then though I was thrilled, I knew she wanted me. Then like I told you I took her out for dinner and dancing and back to my place. I tried to love her and she brushed me off. Years later she would tell me how hard it was, how she had cried all that night, but it was for the best."

He stopped and still holding his hand, Justine asked. "Did it take you long to get past it? It must have been hard; you saw each other all the time and...."

"My sister's addiction took care of that. Once she started using coke she went downhill quickly. You start to see someone in that shape and see what they do, it changes things. She became what she was, my sister and one I tried to look out for. It wasn't easy."

"I can imagine."

"You heard Alex call her easy bake?"

"I did and you don't have to say anything I can put that one together myself."

"I was bouncing at a club called baby Head and one night I'm leaning against the bar and I hear these two guys talking behind me. They're talking about some girl they're calling easy bake. One of them is saying how he had some coke and she gave him a blow job for a couple of lines right in the back alley."

"Mark, please don't do this to yourself." She said.

"The club had been in some trouble and they didn't need dealing and prostitution, so I wander to the back and walk out into the back alley and there's my sister, on her knees in front of some guy."

"Mark, I'm sorry." She said putting her other hand over his. "That must have been...."

"It was heart breaking." He put his head down. "I…I didn't even do anything, I turned around and walked away. They called her that for years and it got worse. She started stripping and working in clubs where the dancers fucked in the back rooms, she was arrested for prostitution. It went on for years. At one point she ran to New York and no one heard from her in months, we thought she was dead. I had ads in New York newspapers. Alex was trying to find her, no one could find anything."

"Well obviously she turned up."

"One day her ex fiancée that she had screwed over royally called me and said she called him from Hell's kitchen in New York looking for money. She said it wasn't for her, but a guy who helped her he was going to get thrown out. Her fiancée was an ex addict and didn't buy it, but she claimed she was dying and only wanted to help someone before she went. He didn't know what to do and told her he would call back. He calls me and I tell him send the money and tell me where. I went up there and got her. It wasn't easy I literally had to fight my way through some people to get to her."

"But you got her."

"I did." He nodded and Justine could see there were tears in his eyes. "She was so far gone Justine, she was skin and bones, covered in sores and she….she pissed herself on the ride home and didn't even know it, She kept begging me to let her die. I told her she saved me years ago and I wouldn't stop until she was saved. I got her home had a doctor come see her and after a week took her to her parents. She checked into a clinic right after that and next month makes five years for her."

"That's a tough story." She said, fighting back her own emotions. "But an amazing one. Mark you realize how few people are strong enough to deal with that?"

"You do what you have to. But it was Lex talionis again. She saved my life I saved hers. It's not always a negative thing. It's about what comes around goes around."

He sighed and after wiping at his eyes said quietly, "But as you can see there's nothing there now, but a healthy brother sister relationship." He laughed. "Right down to her calling me and yelling at me that I don't visit my foster parents enough."

"Oh, I know the feeling," She laughed. "I left Texas out of high school and my sister still claims I stuck her with our parents."

"But, that night with Allison," he began.

"Mark, I want to forget about that."

"And I want to tell you," he countered, "So you know it won't happen again."

"Okay." She nodded.

"She had told me a story about her brother, who was an alcoholic, he was drunk one day and hit her. His father beat his ass and disowned him. He still blames her and she has a niece she isn't allowed to see."

"We can change that." Justine said, already thinking of the group in Florida, one of them would have some pull with the courts down there.

"I offered and she declined for now. But she got pretty emotional, the story, the booze, the initiation, it all got to her and she was in tears. I comforted her then she put me on the spot about my past and I shared a couple of things. I got closer to her than I should have, I should have stayed more aloof, but I couldn't help it."

He paused and looking down at their hands, began lightly caressing the back of hers with his thumb. It was a small sweet gesture and Justine found herself more willing to let him keep talking.

"When we got to my place and she came on to me, I did try to back off. But over dinner I had explained to her how even though her real brother was an asshole that I and Alex and the others were her new bothers and we would take care of our sister. So she started giving me that pout and asking me to please take care of my sister and I...."

He hesitated and Justine kept looked down at their hands as well. She knew where this was headed and had to admit, the thought was more than a little disturbing.

"I was so tired, and so drunk and just so.... fucked up." He continued softly. "When she looked at me and asked me to be good to my sister, I lost track of reality and even though I still knew who she was, I had flashed back to that night and knew who I wanted her to be. So you know, I didn't really see her as my sister, but it was the emotional aspect that caught up with me.

"I understand," she began then stopped. "No, actually I don't, but I do if that makes sense."

"More sense than I'm making." He sighed, "But I know you were worried it could happen again, but it won't. In fact after the meeting I'm not sure she would even want to be alone in a room with me."

"I know, Alex mentioned it to me, he overheard it."

"It's for the better, for now anyway." He shook his head. "Well now you know. I think maybe now you can see why I just like to leave the past where it belongs, the past."

"Thank you for sharing that with me Mark," she said giving his hand another squeeze. "It means a lot to me."

"You mean a lot to me." He said softly.

His words sent a thrill though her and not wanting to let it wait she whispered, "Mark, can I ask you something?"

"What is it?"

"I think the two of us have been kind of confused about things lately, or maybe just I am and that's why I'm here today."

"Confused about what?"

"I think you know. But I understand why you haven't said anything, because I'm in the same boat." She paused as he looked down at where they were still holding hands. He was going to make her come out and say it. "Mark, have you ever considered just being with one woman? I mean recently, not back then."

"I hadn't really thought of it, but...." He stopped and seemed to be trying to pick his words. "When I see someone happy, like Cerce for example, I don't mock them like others do. I have nothing to prove in the bedroom. I think if I had the chance I would take it."

"You..." she began, but he shrugged and added.

"But she would have to be an amazing woman."

"Well obviously." She said, "Look at this office, you're an amazing man."

"And listen to the story I just told you, I'm an amazing mess."

"No, you've just had a difficult past that you can't change." She smiled nervously at him. "But you never know, you might find someone to make the future a lot happier"

"Yeah?" he nodded. "You know someone who likes fucked up sleazy lawyers?"

"I know someone who likes bad boys that are sweeter than they let on."

"Is she amazing?" Mark asked, giving her a sweet smile that made her heart flutter.

"I heard she's good in bed and can hold her own in a fight." She said.

"I don't know." He sighed. "I'm a little preoccupied these days."

"What do you mean?"

"There's this beautiful redhead, I've been carrying on with and she's the jealous type."

"She should be, I heard she can be a real bitch." She said.

"True, and a little self centered, but there is one thing about her that I could never deny."

"What's that?"

Bringing her hand to his lips, he kissed it and whispered, "She's absolutely amazing."

"Do you…." She put her head down as she felt her eyes filling. "Do you mean that?"

"I always say what I mean." He sighed. "For better or worse" He kissed her hand again, and then asked, "Justine, are you sure about this? You said the word confused a couple of minutes ago."

"Yes." She nodded. "I think I knew the night I was jealous of Allison, but tried to tell myself I was just angry."

"And when you were jealous and after you," he thought for a minute then shrugged. "After you did what you had to, when you were upset I thought it meant there was something between us. Then next time I see you you're back in the saddle telling me how hot your week was.

"I…" she shrugged. "I think I was still confused. "The last couple of months I've tried to tell myself I was leaning towards more because of age and leaving the group. Then when I was jealous I thought I was denying it I think Scarlett keeps trying to tell Justine it's all about games, but Justine is tired of them." Looking at him she asked, "Mark do you think you could do it? I mean just us."

"I… don't see where I'm losing out." He laughed.

"We're wired different from other people. The last few months both of us have known we've been getting closer, but you've had a pet, you've assumed I've had others, but it never bothered us, we see sex differently."

"What's the point?"

"The point is, if we agree to try this, I'd expect you to break it off with Stephanie. I…if you don't want us to be more than things can stay the way they are. I'll still enjoy being with you, but as a friend with benefits. But if you want more, then I want it just us."

"So you're talking about…." He shrugged. "Dating?"

"I guess." She sighed. "I'm not saying a fairy tale wedding in a year, but all I know is I was sobbing like a baby when I hurt you that night. When I wake up in your arms I feel so peaceful, so happy. I'm not going to fight that because I'm supposed to be a Mistress."

"I hate to bring it up, but what about the group?"

"I don't know. I don't have to entertain for four months and you have six. We have time to figure that out. "

Removing her hand from his, she wiped at her eyes then looking at him, bit the bullet and gave him an out. "I understand this is easier for me. I'm older and I don't have a lot of time left in the group. You have a lot of time left in the Circle and you're still playing the games. The ones I'm getting tired of. You're losing more than I am out of this."

"If you're sick of playing games Justine, why are you making this one? I sat here and told you I've been feeling the same way and said I would like to be with you, why are you hedging?"

"I….I've been hedging for months."

"I told you I would drop the group in a heartbeat if it meant being with someone I enjoy. I'm not worried about your age and as far as games go?" he laughed. "I highly doubt you and I are done with the game, well just be the only players. We'll be each other's pets." Taking her hand again, he looked into her eyes as he continued, "Justine you're beautiful, have a great career and oh, let's see you're running a sex club, yeah I'm losing out here."

"You really mean it Mark? You're willing to give us a try?"

"I think I've said that several times." He sighed. "Maybe that age thing might matter if you're already losing your hearing."

"Mind your tone L...."

She stopped as he put his finger to her lips. "Sorry Justine, you can't talk to me like that anymore." He grinned. "Well maybe in the bedroom, but that's it."

"Fair enough."

"So when do you leave for Texas?"

"Friday morning."

"So when do you need to go back to Boston?"

"I don't," she smiled at him. "I'm flying out of Green and I have my luggage with me. I'm in Rhode Island until Friday."

"Really? You have a place to stay?"

"I suppose I could find a hotel." She shrugged.

"I don't know. Pretty thing like you could get picked up in a place like that."

"If I was lucky."

"I don't think you should take that chance. I heard you're boyfriends the jealous type."

"My boyfriend?" she laughed, "Oh my God, how funny is that?"

"Thanks." Mark rolled his eyes at her. "Okay I heard your lover is jealous."

"He is and word on the street is he's nuts." She added.

"Well he'd be nuts to let you out of his sight here for two days."

She started to say something when he pulled away and leaning over picked up his phone. "Melanie? Do me a favor, cancel my afternoon appointments." He paused then rolled his eyes "I don't care what you tell them, but I'm going to spend the afternoon with," he winked at her. "My girlfriend."

Chapter Ten

Although Mark only lived a few blocks from where he worked, it was lunchtime and they were mired in traffic. At first Justine had been upset; she couldn't wait to get to his condo and swore when they caught the same red light for the second time. She felt like an anxious young girl who couldn't wait to get laid, rather than the confident woman who had spent her life always in control. By the second red light, Justine was looking out the window of Mark's Lexus, stewing and tapping her foot. They had left her Porsche at his firm's garage in order to ride over together and planned on picking it up later. When they drove two more blocks and came to another stop, she rolled her eyes, "Christ I didn't think this many people lived in this little city!"

Looking over at her, Mark patted the seat next to him. "Why so far away?" he asked. "The traffic wouldn't be so bad, if you were closer."

She hesitated, refusing to act like a girl on a first date, but when he flashed her that killer smile, she laughed and slid across the seat until their hips were touching. Mark put his arm around her and Justine relaxed and put her head on his shoulder. This time they moved forward an entire block before catching yet another light. Before she could say anything, Mark made it so she had no complaints with this one. As soon as they stopped he turned in his seat and taking her chin gently in his hand, kissed her. She kissed him back eagerly as his hand slipped under her dress and began caressing her inner thigh.

Her hand found his lap and felt his cock straining against his pants. She gave it a squeeze, then gasped, as his hand moved higher and began stroking her pussy through her thong. Mark's other hand was lightly caressing her cheek as they kissed and that sweet gesture had her as worked up as his hand between her legs. She let her head fall back onto the seat and shifting his position, Mark began kissing her harder. She opened her mouth and sighed as his tongue accepted her invitation. She began stroking his cock through his pants as he worked a finger into her thong, rubbing it along her wet flesh. The sound of a horn blared behind them, and she looked up to see the light had changed.

'What the fuck, man! The driver behind them yelled, "Get a damn room!"

"Oh, sure now we move." Mark muttered, as he gunned the motor and sent the car through the intersection.

Justine laughed then put her head back on his shoulder. Looking into the rear view mirror at their reflection, she had to say, Mark's bruised face notwithstanding, they looked damn good together. He had slid his arm back around her shoulders and nuzzling into his neck, she let herself relax. They would be spending a lot more time together and there was no need to rush. When they arrived, Mark got out of the car and as he always did, opened the door for her. Taking her hand, he helped her out and as soon as she stood, greeted her with a kiss, before leading her across the garage to the elevator.

They held hands on the ride up, and during the walk down the corridor to his condo. As they past them, she saw a few people smirk at Mark. He was pretty poorly thought of amongst the high society of the Promenade and they were getting a kick out of him looking like he'd taken a beating. For his part, Mark seemed oblivious, just walking along and occasionally looking over at her. Each time he did, he would give her a little smile and squeeze her hand. It dawned on her he was relaxed, the most relaxed he'd seemed in weeks. Had their relationship been weighing on him as well?

When they entered his place, Mark led her through the living room and down the hallway to the closed door of his bedroom. Looking at the runes carved there she asked, "I hope at least this time around all I'll find behind this door is pleasure."

Taking her face in his hands, Mark kissed her softly and whispered, "I hope you find more than pleasure in my bed, Justine."

Before she could respond, he opened the door and his hand at the small of her back, gently ushered her into the room. Once he entered and closed the door, he hit the switch on the wall that caused the electrically wired candelabra's to light up. As the room filled with their flickering glow, Justine walked over and stood at the foot of the bed, admiring the intricately carved ebony columns and the black velvet enclosure that hung along the sides. Looking up, she smiled at her reflection and could feel the heat growing between her legs as she envisioned what she would be watching in that mirror. Lowering her gaze, she looked across to the head of the bed and in addition to her front, could also see her back in the mirror behind her.

In the mirror she saw Mark sliding his shirt from his shoulders and she felt her nipples harden in anticipation as she took in his well muscled chest and chiseled stomach. Coming up behind her, Mark slipped his arms around her waist and softly kissed the side of her neck. The sensation of his lips sent a shiver through her, and she let herself go, leaning back against him. Letting her head fall to the side, she sighed appreciatively as he took advantage of it, sliding his lips along her soft flesh. As good as their reflection looked; Justine closed her eyes as his lips trailed up and down, placing soft kisses from just below her ear to the top of her bare shoulder.

His arms tightened around her and bringing her hands up she placed them over his forearms, caressing them lightly with her fingernails. Mark had worked his way to the back of her neck, and Justine turned her head the other way, allowing him to able to pleasure that side. As he began sucking on the soft flesh between her neck and shoulder, Justine started slowly working her hips side to side, pushing her ass into his hard cock. Mark's hands left her waist and a chill went through her as they slid up her arms. Grabbing the straps to her dress, he slid them off of her shoulders and started kissing her upper arm. He pushed the straps down further and started working his lips across the top of her bare back.

As he unhurriedly slid his lips to the top of her right shoulder, he pushed the straps down to her elbows. Taking her cue, Justine slid her arms from the straps and raised them over her head. She watched in the mirror as he pushed the dress down past her hips and let it fall to the floor, exposing the white lace bra and matching thong she was wearing. Once again sucking on the inside of her neck, Mark began rubbing his hands across her back, then with practiced ease unsnapped her bra, and as his tongue trailed down the middle of her back, slipped the bra from her shoulders.

Justine pulled the bra off and tossed it to the side. Mark's arms slid back around her waist and after teasing her stomach lightly with his finger tips, reached up and cupped her full tits in his hands. Justine smiled as she saw him watching over her shoulder as he kissed her neck while presenting her tits in the mirror. Mark began to nibble playfully on her ear, and she moaned as, still holding her tits, his thumbs found her nipples and started tracing slow circles around them. She began rocking harder into him, loving the feeling of his hard cock grinding into her through his pants. Part of her couldn't wait to taste it, but more of her wanted to stay right where she was.

Mark's lips were on the back of her neck again, and she marveled at how slow he was going and how she had no problem whatsoever with it. He began working his lips lower, leaving a trail of soft sweet kisses down her back. She saw him get to his knees behind her and she began working her thighs back and forth, teasing her pussy with the material of her thong as his lips reached the small of her back. His thumbs were still on her swollen nipples and she put her hands over his, squeezing them and encouraging him to fondle her tits. Mark's tongue traced a line across the string of her thong, then sliding his hands from hers, placed them on her back and gave her a gentle push.

Justine placed her hands on the bed so that she was bent over in his face and groaned as she felt him begin kissing the cheeks of her ass. Like he had with her neck and back, Mark took his time, working up and down both sides of her ass and getting her to emit an uncharacteristic giggle when he started sucking on the bottom of her right ass cheek. Her giggle turned into a moan, as sliding her thong to the side, he ran his tongue through the crack of her ass. She bent over further and started pumping her hips, urging him to find her aching pussy.

She gasped when his tongue press into her asshole, and then moaned loudly as it slid down and into her warm wet flesh. She resisted the desire to start pumping her hips and instead remained still while his tongue worked its way through the folds of her pussy. Her hips did twitch and she let out a soft whimper as he found her clit and began lightly flicking his tongue across it. His hands slid underneath of her and caught her nipples as they hung over the bed and started rubbing them between his fingers, as he slid his tongue back and pushed it into her pussy. Unable to help it, she started to rock slowly back and forth, pushing his rigid tongue in and out of her dripping flesh.

Looking up, she saw that her lips were parted and her eyes were beginning to get that glazed over look she knew so well. She groaned as Mark slid his tongue from her pussy, but started to flow even more as he stood up behind her. It was going to be her turn and how she wanted to taste him! Grabbing her shoulders, Mark pulled her back to her feet and turned her around to face him. She wrapped her arms around his neck and pulled him into a long deep kiss. Justine moaned as he pushed his tongue into her mouth and she started sucking on it, enjoying tasting herself from him. As they kissed she started rocking side to side, sliding her nipples across the hard flesh of his chest.

Mark sighed into her mouth and putting his arms around her waist pulled her tightly to him. Justine fumbled with her hair and after loosening it, leaned her head back and gave it a shake, letting her long red hair cascade down across her back. As soon as she leaned back, Mark's lips fastened to the creamy skin of her throat and began sucking gently. She smiled up into the mirror as she was presented with the view of being held in his arms, while his face was buried in her neck. She could see his powerful back and reaching around him, began running her hands across it, enjoying the way his hard muscles felt beneath his tanned skin.

Mark's head dipped lower and she gasped and grabbed his hair as he sucked her right nipple into his mouth. Justine lifted her leg and began rubbing it along his as he switched to her other nipple. Again Mark crushed her to him and she could feel his cock shoving into her soft stomach. Bringing her head back forward; she pushed against his shoulders to get him to step back. Sinking to her knees, she began kissing and sucking on his stomach, while unzipping his pants. As he had done, she teased her tongue across the waistband of his underwear. Mark began running his fingers through her hair while she pulled his pants and underwear down.

His cock sprang free and hit her in the face, leaving a wet spot on her cheek. Grabbing it in her hand stare she gave it a hard squeeze that sent more pre cum dripping from it. She gave the tip of his cock a playful kiss and looking up at him whispered, "All for me?"

"From now on its only for you." He told her.

Oh, how good did that sound? Giving his cock another slow pump, she swirled her tongue around the head, savoring the taste of him and the feeling of his sticky fluid on her lips. Turning her head, she rubbed him against her cheek as she kissed the top of his balls, she turned again, rubbing his hard flesh along her other cheek, before taking the tip into her mouth. She began sucking gently, moaning as his precum trickled down her throat. Mark sighed as she began to slowly bob her head, taking a little more of him each time. When she had him halfway, she reached up and started massaging his balls.

Justine opened her mouth wider and slowly took him all the way down. When her lips were at the base of his shaft she shook her head side to side, then just as slowly eased him back out. Pushing herself up, Justine wrapped her tits around his cock and began, sliding it between them. Bending her head, she opened her mouth and each time the head of his cock poked out between her tits swirled her tongue across it. Mark moaned and his fingers found her nipples as she continued to work her tits along the length of his cock.

Sinking back to the floor Justine took his cock back between her lips and began moving her head in a slow steady rhythm. She had both hands on his balls, kneading them gently as she worked his hard flesh between her soft lips. She had her tongue pressed tightly against his shaft and his hips started pumping in rhythm to her sucking. Normally Justine devoured his cock, but right now she was taking her time as he had with her, just playing with and savoring every inch of his beautiful flesh. She moaned in pleasure as she took him all the way and stayed there loving the sensation of her mouth full of him.

Mark's hands left her nipples and moving to her shoulders gave her a tug. Justine sucked him deep into her mouth one more time, and then allowed him to help her to her feet. Mark put his arm around her shoulders and kissed her. She yelped in surprise when he swept his other arm down behind her knees and effortlessly lifted her into his arms. Justine laughed and smiled at their reflection as he carried her around the foot of the bed towards the pillows. Stopping at the side of the bed, he bent his head to hers and they shared another long tongue filled kiss. Still kissing her, Mark lowered Justine to the bed and sliding his arms out from beneath her stood and looked down at her.

"Damn you're beautiful Justine."

"You make me feel that way." She told him softly.

Mark walked around to the foot of the bed and as Justine watched, heart pounding, he climbed up onto the bed and crawled up between her legs. When he was directly over her, he leaned down and after giving her a soft kiss, nuzzled his face into her neck and started working his lips across her neck and down her chest. Justine sighed contentedly as his lips worked their way lower and fastened onto her nipple. She looked up into the mirror and felt herself getting even wetter at the sight of his muscular body over hers. That body was sliding down lower as his lips were now kissing her stomach and heading for her aching pussy. Kneeling between her legs, Mark slipped the thong over her hips.

Justine raised her legs so he could slide it off and after he tossed it to the side, he started to lower his head to go down on her. She hooked her leg around his waist and when he looked up beckoned to him with her finger. "Come up here baby," she whispered, "We'll play later right now I just need you inside me."

Mark gave her that heart melting sweet little smile of his and once again crawled up between her legs. Justine wrapped her arms around her shoulders and as she pulled him down into a kiss, he slowly entered her. She moaned into him as he slid deep inside her willing flesh. He stayed there motionless as they kissed, then began to slowly move within her. Justine sighed softly and looking up in the mirror smiled at how good he looked between her legs, how good they looked together.

Wrapping her long legs around his waist she moaned as that pushed him even deeper into her and she closed her eyes as Mark began sliding further out before sinking back in. Her nipples were pressing into his chest and rather than teasing, the long slow strokes he was using felt incredible. As impatient as she normally was Justine had no desire to get him to move any faster. Mark nuzzled his face into her neck and as she turned her head, he began kissing the side of her neck.

"Oh, baby, that feels so good." She moaned in his ear.

His reply was to turn his head and begin planting soft kisses on the top of her shoulder. He was still using those slow steady strokes, but had moved up higher, changing the angle as he did. Justine moaned as his long hard shaft was now stroking her clit on its way down into her pussy and she felt a shiver go through her each time it did. She squeezed her legs tighter around his waist and gasped as that brought him even deeper inside. Justine began running her finger nails lightly across his back and through his hair, causing him to make a soft whimpering sound in his throat that she'd never heard before. She again slid her fingers down the length of his back, and smiled as she was rewarded with another of those oddly cute noises.

Justine then made a whimpering sound of her own, as pushing himself up, Mark bent his head to her right nipple and sucked it into his mouth. She sighed and closed her eyes as he switched to the left, before bringing his lips up to meet hers. He began to thrust harder into her, not faster, but hard enough to start to really stroking her clit.

She moaned into his mouth and wrapped her arms around his neck, pulling his mouth harder into hers. She started running her fingers through his hair again and received a soft moan from him. Mark had not slowed or paused once, but just continued that deliciously slow rhythm. Justine began to move her own hips, slowly and in time with his. Her hands drifted from his neck and began rubbing up and down his arms, loving the feel the muscles rippling beneath his skin.

Justine could feel an orgasm beginning to build, but rather than speeding up, she continued to let Mark go slow and easy, letting it take its time. Besides she was in no hurry for this to end, lying here with him taking his time like this was better than anything she could remember. She placed her hands on either side of his face and pushing him up from her neck, parted her lips for him, inviting another kiss. Mark lowered his mouth and began sliding his lips softly across hers. Justine had never kissed like this, so slowly and sweetly. For that matter she had certainly never had sex like this slow and easy it was...Justine's eyes opened as she realized this wasn't sex. Mark was making love to her.

That thought caused more than just her body to respond to him. Justine could feel how much she cared for him, how much she wanted him. Not just his body, but all of him. Better yet, she could feel it in him as well. She could feel it in those soft teasing kisses and those slow gentle strokes. They weren't fucking, they were using their bodies to show each other how much they cared how much they...

Her mind stopped racing as her body took control. The orgasm she had been teetering on the edge of for such a delightfully long time was about to reach its conclusion. Normally when Justine was at this point the orgasm would just take her, yet even now, knowing it was right there, her body stayed on the edge awhile longer. Her thighs started to shake and breaking the kiss, she started moaning each time his cock stroked her clit, her hips twitching harder into his. Mark sped up as well. He was still going nowhere near as hard as usual, but was going faster than before and using short strokes that were rubbing her clit harder and faster.

"Ohh," she gasped looking up into those beautiful golden green eyes. She squeezed her fingers into his arms and gasped again. The orgasm was starting, but was flowing slowly through her. Instead of a rush it was more of a slow steady stream of pleasure.

"Oh Mark," she moaned, "Oh God, that…."

Justine let out a series of long moans that got louder as Mark sped up more. He was breathing heavier as he closed in on his own climax. The orgasm reached its peak and exploded through her. Wrapping her arms and legs tightly around him, she bucked her hips into his. Justine let out a long drawn out groan as the orgasm lingered, sending a continuous wave of intense pleasure through her. She squeezed her legs around his sides and arched her back into him as her body convulsed beneath him. Mark moaned in her ear as his body tensed up and he began pumping her harder and faster. Justine groaned as the orgasm continued.

"That's it baby," she moaned. "That's it Mark, cum with me. Let me feel it."

Mark came hard, exploding deep inside of her as he continued to thrust in and out. He moaned in her ear, as he continued to cum. Justine gasped at the sensation of his cock twitching inside of her, filling her with his cum while her lingering orgasm still flowed through her pussy. Mark let out a soft whimper as her pussy contracted around his spurting cock, milking him as he continued to thrust into her.

"Oh ," she moaned in his ear, "Oh baby, I…." she paused then let herself go completely. "I love you!" she gasped out.

Mark groaned as his cock twitched one more time and let his weight go so that he was resting on his forearms. His chest was pressed against hers and she could feel his heart beating against her. He was looking at her and she couldn't read his expression. She hoped she hadn't pushed things, but she didn't regret saying it she…Leaning down and resting his head on her shoulder, Mark whispered in her ear, "I love you too Justine."

He kissed her gently and smiling at him she said, "My God that was amazing."

"So are you."

They lied there in silence, and Justine held him close to her, enjoying the feeling of his cock softening inside of her. She looked up again at their reflection and this time as she smiled she felt a surge of emotion go through her as she saw her holding him close to her. With a sigh, Mark rolled over onto his side and smiled tiredly at her. "Well that's not one for the group now is it?"

"No." she laughed. "They make fun of that stuff."

"They don't know what they're missing."

"I used to make fun of it too." reaching out and touching his cheek she said, "I'm not saying I'm ready to give up the game, but baby feel free to treat me like that anytime."

"Yes Mistress." He grinned.

"Hmmm, make love to me you worthless dog!" she shook her head. "Nah, it doesn't have a good ring to it."

Mark laughed softly, then yawned. Looking at the large circles under his eyes she said, "I know it's only the afternoon, but it's been a long week. You tired?"

"I've been tired for weeks."

Rolling onto her side to face him, Justine put her arms out to him. "Come here baby,"

Moving over to her, Mark put his arms out to pull her into him, but putting her hand on his chest she said, "Slide down a little bit." He hesitated and she added, "Let me hold you Mark."

Mark slid down and wrapping her arm around his waist Justine drew her into him. Putting her other arm behind him, she put her hand on the back of his head and lowered it to her chest. She sighed as Mark's arms slipped around her waist and pulled her to him. Justine began running her finger nails across his back. Mark sighed into her chest and placing her lips close to his ear, she whispered, "I love you baby."

"And I love you," he said softly.

Justine felt her eyes fill up again, but didn't fight it, these weren't bad tears, but good ones. She continued to rub his back as she stared at the flickering candelabra and wondered what this meant for the Circle. Justine only had to entertain twice more. She had a video from last year she had never used and if she had to she could even entertain with Mark, make up a reason even if she said it was a parting gift to herself. That could be fun, she thought. The Circle watching the two of them fucking the shit out of each other and never suspecting they were so much more. But that was her, what about Mark? He would have to....

She stopped and listened. Mark's breathing had become slow and deep and his body was completely relaxed. Turning her head to look up into the mirror she could see his eyes were closed and he looked peaceful.

Justine smiled and closed her eyes. Screw the Circle for now; she didn't have to worry about it tonight or next week, not for a few months. All she needed to think about right now was how good it felt to be here. Her sister had told her she would know it when she felt it and there was no doubt in her mind. As she listed to Mark's slow steady breathing, she recalled Alex's warning to her. Yes Mark had issues and a lot of baggage, but he had finally opened up to her and was now lying asleep in her arms.

Justine let her head rest on the pillow and reveled in how good she felt. Unlike Mark, she had always had a good life. She had a caring family, a good education and a great career. In addition to that, through the Circle she had made some amazing friends who had become a second family to her, albeit a dysfunctional one. In fact as her tired mind dwelt on that thought the only truly bad times she'd had were her early days in the Circle when she'd been treated harshly at those monthly meetings. Even then, that had been her choice, essentially letting her body be used to get to where she was today. Yet although she had never been truly unhappy, she had never been at peace. There was always another goal in her career, man to dominate, woman to enjoy, or a new game to play. As much as she had, she never seemed satisfied, as if there was a hole she couldn't quite fill.

Now, lying there, in Mark's bed holding him as he held her, Justine felt a wave of peace come over her. This was what Hollywood glorified and she and the others in the Circle had mocked for years, this was love. Closing her eyes, Justine smiled and as she felt herself beginning to succumb to sleep's warm embrace, one last thought entered her mind. Alex had been wrong; there was nothing about Mark she couldn't handle. He was in love with her and from now on she would be all that he needed.

Part Six

Chapter One

Mark awoke with a pounding in his head, the taste of Jack Daniels in his mouth and the smell of pussy on his face. A morning pretty much like any other. The only questions were whose pussy was it, and where the hell was he? Unlike most people, whose first reaction upon waking is to open their eyes, Mark had learned to keep his shut until he was sure it was okay to open them. After all, a sleeping child is a quiet child and quiet children don't get beaten.

His eyes snapped open in an effort to force himself completely awake and send images like that back into the room in the attic they had escaped from. As quickly as his eyes opened, he shut them as a searing pain went through his head. How much did he drink last night? Mark took a deep breath, once again inhaling the sweet scent of sex. The smell wasn't just under his nose; it was in the air. It was the unmistakable mixed scents of sex and sweat, the kind of smell that could only be generated by a long night of hardcore fucking.

Slowly releasing the breath, Mark felt his senses coming back to him as his mind began to shake off the cobwebs of sleep. He was lying on his back with his face turned to the left and the feeling of the cool silk pillow as well as the flickering light he could make out through his eyelids told him he was in his bed. He became aware of the pleasant feeling of a warm body pressed against his. Now deliberately keeping his eyes closed, he savored each individual sensation. His arm was around his companion and he could feel her soft skin beneath his heavily calloused hand. He could feel her hair across his arm and shoulder, as well as her hand resting on his stomach.

He could feel the slow steady rhythm her breathing and concentrating harder could pick up the scent of Coco Chanel beneath the animal smell of lust. Letting his mind wander down his body Mark could feel her breast pressing into his side and beneath the sheets her warm leg was draped over his. He could also feel the heat of her sex against his thigh. His mind now clear, Mark knew who he was holding.

"Your girlfriend Justine!"

Mark squeezed his eyes shut against the pain the Voice's shouting had caused and the mocking laughter that followed it. Once the fresh wave of pounding subsided, he tried to remember if he had taken the Risperdal yesterday. He thought he had because he recalled counting the pills yesterday to make sure he had taken one every day since refilling the script on Monday. Today was Friday, four days and the goddamn Voice was still there. Normally two days had it fading away and by day three he was clear. This was the first time it had spoken since Wednesday morning, he had thought it was gone.

"Nope," it whispered in its dry raspy tone, *"I've just been hiding out, all that sweet bullshit you've been slinging with your lady love was making me sick."*

Then go back in your room where you belong, Mark responded in his mind.

"My room?" again its laughter caused him to wince. *"You know damn well I come and go as I please."*

The Risperdal will....

"No, it won't because you need me."

No, I don't.

"Oh, but you do, ever since Meg went to Chicago you've needed me more and more. You keep playing games with the pills so I'll be around" it laughed again, *"So you'd have someone who would talk to your fucked up ass."*

Go to hell, I don't need you anymore. Besides, I'm not sleeping any better and still have the dreams so what good do you do anyway?

"Got time for a list? If I recall I was the one who got your damn cock up, when little red riding hood was torturing us. You were too busy crying so I gave her what she needed."

Mark forced himself to not replay that image and began trying to 'go away', let his mind drift so the Voice would have nothing to respond to.

"Got no answer for that do you? Oh, and what about the club there bad boy? I was the one who got the damn dog you let out back in its room."

You were also the one that got me to fuck Allison, Mark came back to reply, got us in trouble to begin.

The Voice laughed, but softly this time. *"Sorry Mark, but you wanted Allison and you know why you did. All I did was encourage you to enjoy her."* It made a disgusted sound. *"You should be fucking all the whores at that table, since when do we follow rules?"*

Since breaking all of them don't seem to work anymore. I'm taking the pills; you'll be going soon.

"That's what you think, all week and I'm still here. You've played too many games with your meds Mad Dog, you're not going to get rid of me."

I will because I don't need you anymore and you know it.

"Oh, and why is that?"

Before Mark could form a reply, he heard the sound of fingers snapping in his mind.

"That's right, I forgot! You're in love!"

I...

"In love with a woman who gagged and beat the shit out of you! In love with a woman who thinks you're no more than a pet!"

Knock it off.

"You're not in love with Justine, Mark. You know who our love is."

I know who we'll never have. Justine loves me and...

He stopped as the Voice sighed. When it spoke again, it had lost its mocking tone. *"Mark, we will have our love, I've told you that. It's our destiny, but in fates time, not yours."*

She doesn't want us in that way.

"She will. Justine's hot and a great lay, you want to fuck around with her fine, but she's not for us and you know it. Besides she's using you."

No she's not.

"Yes she is. Christ Mark, she's almost fifty! Sure she looks good now, but in a few years that little ruby in her stomach will be between her sagging tits and she'll be dying her hair and collecting social security! You're her insurance policy to not be alone when the looks fade. You're nothing more than a pet to her always have been always will be."

I said stop it.

"You're pathetic Mark, all it took was for her to say she cared and you think you're in love."

I'm not pathetic.

"Yes you are. You have everything, you can have any woman you want, but you fall to her because she says she loves you. Because you still believe Max."

Don't say that name.

"Max told you no one wanted you and you believe it! That's why you're happy to be with her, she said the magic words!"

Shut up!

"Oh, Mark!" It was now speaking in Justine's voice, *"Oh, how I love you! Oh, make love to me my baby!"*

"Shut the fuck up!" he hissed.

"Mark?" Justine's voice spoke in his ear. "Are you okay?"

"You're talking out loud asshole!"

Opening his eyes, Mark turned his head to see Justine propped up on one elbow looking at him.

"Bad dream, baby?"

"Awww, baby!"

"I..." his voice came out as choked whisper and he paused to swallow. "I guess, I don't know."

Lifting her head, Justine peered over his shoulder to look at the clock on the nightstand. "It's only four am, I don't have to get up until five thirty and you can stay in bed while I shower and get ready." Her hand trailed up his stomach and then touched his cheek. "Go back to sleep okay?"

"I'll try."

"Damn Mark," she whispered as she continued to caress his cheek with the back of her hand. "We got shit faced last night, didn't get back until midnight and fucked for two hours, how the hell can't you sleep?"

"I just can't." he answered then thought someone won't let me.

Justine's hand left his cheek and she began trailing her long fingernails down his chest and across his stomach, just above where the sheet covered them. Mark could feel his cock beginning to stiffen at her touch, and could feel her nipple hardening against his side. Looking more closely at her, he found it hard to believe she was that much older than him. Even with her hair tousled, her blue eyes bleary from sleep and no makeup, she looked damn good. Never mind her body.

"Check her out in ten years; you'll have to get on your knees to suck her nipples."

Justine looked down and he could tell there was something on her mind.

"What's the matter?" he asked as he began running his hand along the smooth skin of her back. He stopped at the curve of her ass as she shrugged, "I don't know, I...I feel bad you can't sleep."

"I've been this way my whole life."

"When I came here Wednesday you slept great in the afternoon and again at night. But the last couple of nights you've been tossing and having nightmares and..."

"Like I said, I've..."

"I guess I thought you felt good enough with me that you could sleep."

"Don't flatter yourself bitch!"

"It's not you." He told her. "No one can help when I'm like this."

"Liar!"

"Sorry, I was hoping I was special."

"You are." He replied softly and kissed her. "You're very special to me.

As he dropped his head back to the pillow, Justine rolled over so that her tits were pressing into his chest and kissed him. Mark's hand slid past the small of her back and squeezed her ass. Sliding her lips from his, Justine kissed his neck just under his ear, and her hand sliding under the covers whispered, "Well let's see if I can get you to sleep."

Her hand closed around his cock and began stroking it as her lips moved from his neck, down his chest. He moaned softly as leaving his cock, her hand slipped between his legs and started massaging his balls. Drawing her leg up, Justine kicked the silk sheet from them and rolling over between his legs, crawled up so that her tis were hanging in his face. Mark cupped them in his hands and eagerly, one at a time, began tonguing her hard pink nipples. Justine sighed and swinging her leg over his, started sliding her damp pussy along his thigh. Pulling her tit from his mouth, Justine leaned down and kissed him softly, before beginning to slide her way down his body.

"Showtime!"

Mark looked up into the mirror and smiled at the sight of Justine's long curvy body working its way down his muscular form. She was now kissing his stomach and her long red hair was fanned across his chest and thighs. Justine was on her knees and reaching down between them pressed her tits around his cock, as her tongue now played across the line of his pubic hair. Her tongue dipped lower and Mark sighed as he felt her soft wet flesh swirling around the head of his cock. He began rubbing her back and running his fingers through her hair as he felt the tip of his cock engulfed in her warm mouth.

Justine started rocking back and forth, sliding his cock between her huge tits while sucking on just the tip. Mark watched her firm round ass in the mirror and felt his cock stiffen even more as he could make out several small bruises on her hips from where he had been holding her as he fucked the shit out of her last night. As he watched, she stretched her long legs out and sank to her stomach. He moaned softly as she started bobbing her head, slowly taking his cock further into her mouth. She had slid her hands up and one was stroking his cock, while the other teased his balls with her fingers.

Mark gathered her hair in his hand so he could watch Justine work his cock and was rewarded by her looking up at him, and winking as she quickly took him all the way down. He groaned in appreciation as while her lips were wrapped around the base of his shaft, her tongue slid out along his balls.

"Well she does have her good points."

Justine moaned around his cock, the vibration causing him to moan as well, and slowly worked her way back up his cock. Her tongue was pressed to his shaft and the feeling of her soft full lips against his hard flesh caused his hips to twitch. When she reached the tip of his cock, she paused, her blue eyes looking at him expectantly. Taking his cue, he started lifting his hips, slowly fucking her mouth. Justine closed her eyes and moaned again as he pumped his long thick cock into her mouth. Using her hair he began pushing and pulling, guiding her head up and down his cock in time with his thrusts.

She let go of his cock and resting her hands on his thighs sighed against his flesh as she lied there letting him use her mouth. Mark's gaze again went to the mirror, where he watched her bend her knees, and begin slowly kicking her feet back and forth. As he let his eyes linger on the soft smooth soles of her feet and red toe nails, he thought to himself not bad for a street rat. He'd come from a broken home and survived a hellish childhood. Now here he was a senior partner in a prestigious firm, lying on silk sheets in a twenty thousand dollar bed, while a gorgeous CEO let him fuck her mouth.

His attention was snapped back to the present as Justine began sucking him hard and fast, taking his cock all the way down before coming back up and releasing it with a loud slurping sound, before taking it back down again. Mark gasped and started thrusting his cock into her attacking mouth and then winced as her fingernails dug hard into his thighs. Justine let his cock pop out of her mouth one more time, before she got back up onto her knees and crawled back up along his body. Her large tits were dangling just low enough that her hard nipples were sliding along his skin and her eyes were again locked into his.

Justine crawled up further and swinging her legs one at a time over his, straddled his hips. Her hands were braced on his chest and she began rocking, sliding her wet pussy along the length of his throbbing cock. Justine placed her right tit in his mouth and sighed as he began sucking on it. Wrapping his arms around her waist, he began thrusting his hips, causing his cock to slide through the wet folds of her pussy. Justine hissed when the head of his cock stroked her clit and he stayed still so she could grind herself against him.

She rose up, sliding the head of his cock back until the tip was pressing into her soft lips. Lowering herself, they both moaned as his cock sank into her warm welcoming flesh. Justine began sliding her hips back and forth, slowly riding him, as she leaned over, again letting him enjoy her tits in his face. His hands found her hips and began helping her slide across his cock. Justine sat up straight, and then cried out as raising herself up on her knees she drove down hard, impaling herself on his cock.

Bracing her hands on his thighs, she began bouncing, driving him deep inside of her. Mark grabbed her tits and as she continued slamming herself onto him, caught her nipples and began rolling them between his fingertips. Justine stopped riding him and leaning all the way back, grabbed his ankles and started sliding herself into him. Mark moaned as his cock was bent straight between them and her movements were teasing him. Mark saw her head was back and she was looking up as well. She smiled at him in the mirror and began pushing herself harder into him. Watching his cock disappearing into her beautiful red haired pussy, Mark dropped his left hand from her tit and reaching between her legs, found her swollen clit with his thumb.

"Oh yes!" she groaned as he started rubbing it in slow hard circles, "Oh, right there baby!"

Mark sped his thumb up, causing her to release a long moan as she started pushing harder into his cock. He gasped and started moving his hips, trying to plunge himself deeper into her. Justine started rocking faster and now balancing on her right arm; she brought her hand up to replace his on her nipple. Mark started squeezing the nipple he was playing with while his thumb moved in ever faster circles. She emitted a high pitched whimper and feeling her thighs trembling against his, Mark gave her nipple a hard pinch.

Justine cried out and began grinding her hips into his as her pussy contracted around his cock. Mark looked back up to see the look on her face as she squirmed and writhed on top of him. Justine's eyes were closed and her full lips parted as she let out a loud squeal of pleasure. Mark moaned as her movements were more of a tease than ever, but smiled as her beautiful features were etched in an expression of pleasure as her orgasm continued to flow through her. He moaned as he felt her pussy begin to convulse against his hard flesh and with a long drawn out squeal, he felt her pussy spasm and felt a warm gush of fluid around his cock.

Justine pushed herself up until she was leaning forward again; her hands on his chest and looked down at him, as she gasped for breath. Grabbing her hips, Mark started fucking her, his cock making wet sucking sounds as he drove it into her soaking pussy. Justine slipped her arms under his and, her tits pressing against his chest, gave him a long lingering kiss. Mark slowed his thrusting as her soft tongue slid into his mouth and she hugged him tighter to her. He had slowed his thrusts down and her hips were moving with his. Justine looked into his eyes and whispered, "I love you Mark."

"Oh, for Christ's sake!" The Voice groaned. A moment later, Mark winced as he heard the sound of a door slamming somewhere in his mind.

Looking into her eyes, he whispered, "I love you too."

Bringing his hand up behind her head, he brought her lips back to his and wrapping his arm around her waist pulled her as close to him as he could. He slowed his thrusts even more, wanting to enjoy her for as long as he could. Justine's lips left his and letting her head go, she buried her face in his neck as her hips moved with his. Mark looked into the mirror again and felt an unfamiliar lump in his throat as he took in the sight of her wrapped in his arms. As amazing as their bodies looked together, he was caught up more in the way her head was resting on his shoulder and how he was holding her close.

Each time, her hips descended, pushing him deeper inside of her, Justine sighed in his ear and the sound sent a thrill through him. They were not the sounds of lust or the brutal fucking he had become accustomed to, these were sounds of affection. The comforting sounds of a longtime lover, a sound made by someone who was exactly where they wanted to be. Holding her even tighter, Mark gasped as he could feel himself getting close.

"There you go," Justine whispered, "Let it go baby."

He moaned as forcing himself to continue to go slow he could feel his legs trembling as he strained to cum. Justine began kissing his neck, just under his ear and as her soft lips and tongue pressed into his flesh, he lost the battle and she yelped in his ear as he gave her several hard fast thrusts. Mark let out a cry of his own as his cock twitched and began spurting inside of her. "Oh, yes," Justine purred in his ear, "That feels so good!"

Mark continued to pump his hips, each thrust ending in another squirt of cum entering her already sopping pussy. With a low moan, he stopped moving and Justine took over, grinding her hips down into his and managing to get another weak spurt from his cock. She stopped moving and he relaxed, then let out a pathetic sounding whimper, as contracting her pussy, Justine milked a couple of more drops from his spent cock.

"I like that little noise," she laughed.

"Glad I make you happy." He replied with a sigh.

"Mark, you make me very happy."

They lied there in silence, and he could feel his cock softening inside of her. Justine's head was resting on his shoulder and he could feel his eyes beginning to close. They opened as, after kissing his cheek, Justine rolled over onto her side. "Why don't you roll over and I'll rub your back?" she asked.

He wasn't going to argue and rolling over onto his stomach, Mark let out a contented sigh as Justine began training her nails across his back. A moment later he felt her kiss his back softly and rest her head on the back of his arm as she began to trace the outline of his Baphomet tattoo. Closing his eyes, he let his mind drift; focusing only on how good it was to have her with him, to hear her say she loved him. The Voice was wrong, he could be happy.

* * *

"It's time to go Mark."

Mark looked up from the spider man comic book he'd been looking at to see a tall older woman with blonde hair looking down at him. When she saw him looking she smiled and put her hand out. He looked around the room trying to find Megan. The room was big with some chairs along the wall like the one he was sitting in and a really big desk in the middle with a big fat guy sitting behind it. He had no idea what the room was for and where it was, Mom hadn't said much in the car on the way over.

Mark thought it must be a nice place because mom had helped him get dressed in his best pants and that white shirt with the buttons he hated. Megan was dressed up too, in the pretty red dress that had been in a bag of clothes someone had given mom. Mark had sat in the back seat with Megan who seemed nervous so he held her hand. She looked over and gave him a big smile. He laughed at her because one of her front teeth was missing and she told him he wasn't being very nice, but still held his hand.

Mom parked and they got out and went into a huge building and took an elevator way up and after they got out came to the room where Mom told him to sit. Then for some reason took Megan with her and had her sit across from him. There were a couple of women in the office besides the fat guy and one of them gave him the comic book. The women and the guy all talked to mom, he wasn't sure what they were saying, but heard his name and Megan's. He also heard her say;

"And you promise there's no way for their father to find them?"

After a while Mom stood up and after hugging and kissing Megan, came over and leaning over, hugged him tight. "Mommy has to go Mark; you're going to stay with some nice people for a little while okay?"

"Ummm okay," He said. "Meg too right?"

Mom didn't answer. Instead she kissed his cheek "Mommy loves you Mark."

She stood up and it looked like she was getting ready to cry, walking away she left the room, closing the door behind her.

"Mark?"

The woman reached down and taking his hand, gave a little tug. He got up from the chair and let her lead him over to Megan, who was standing with another woman. "Give Megan a kiss good bye Mark."

He looked at her wanting to ask why, but he didn't know her and didn't want to talk. The woman knew what he was going to say though because she told him; "You're going to stay with some nice people, but they don't have a lot of room, so your sister is going with some other nice people for now, but you'll see her real soon okay?"

Megan came over and hugged him tight. When the woman tried to pull him away he held on and so did Megan. The woman behind him succeeded in pulling them apart and as she led him away he heard his sister call his name and start crying. He turned to see her being led away and started crying too. The woman opened the door and started to pull him through. He saw Megan still looking at him getting scared yelled out to her; "Megan!"

The woman was closing the door on him and he couldn't see sister anymore.

"Meg!" Mark cried out, as he sat up in the bed his heart pounding. He immediately clapped his hands over his mouth, he had just yelled, what if Max had heard him? Looking around the room wildly, he felt a wave of panic go through him as he saw the bedroom door was open partway. That means Max would have heard him! He had to hide, kicking the sheet of the bed, Mark swung his legs off the bed, he would drop to the floor and slide under the bed, Max would....

"Mark!" The Voice called out. *"Snap out of it! It's just a dream!"*

Mark took a deep breath and releasing it slowly; put his head in his hands and fought against the tears that were welling up in his eyes. He couldn't shake the image of Megan as a scared six year old girl calling out to him. They were supposed to protect each other, but he had been taken from her. Megan had gone to a home where she had been raped repeatedly and he couldn't help her because he thought she was dead and was being beaten and...

"Easy Mark," the Voice spoke softly.

"I... thirty years," he whispered, "Thirty years I still can see it. Is it ever going to stop?"

He sounded pathetic and knew it, but instead of mocking him the Voice spoke in a soothing tone, *"Yes Mark, when all is as it should be, for now you have to get through it."*

Mark nodded and tried to clear his head of the visual of he and Megan being separated.

"Here."

Mark heard the sound of footsteps in his mind and a moment later the sound of a door swinging open. He jumped as it slammed shut, but the vision he had carried with him from the dream was gone. As his mind stopped spinning, he realized he was alone in the bed and looking behind him saw that it was six fifteen, he had to get Justine to the airport for seven thirty. Closing his eyes, he could faintly here the shower running. Good, she wouldn't have heard him cry out. Sensing the Voice's presence he said quietly. "Thank you."

"My pleasure." The Voice replied with no hint of sarcasm. *"It's what I'm here for."*

* * *

There wasn't much traffic and Mark had the pedal down in the Firebird, taking the Thurbers avenue S-curve at ninety five, one handed while his other hand rested on Justine's soft thigh. She didn't seem to mind his driving as she leaned back against the head rest watching the cars fly by them. She also didn't seem to mind his hand caressing her thigh as she had her leg bent up so he could rub higher. If the shorts she were wearing weren't so tight, he would have tried to work his fingers into her pussy to give her a little goodbye treat, but the things were all but painted on.

"They say timing is everything," she said, cutting into his thoughts about her attire. "I can't believe this had to be this week," she sighed. "Damn, I wish I could stay a couple of more days."

"When you come back next Friday you can stay the weekend." He pointed out as he looked over at her.

She shrugged and he admired the way her huge tits strained against her tight white tank top. "What about Stephanie? She's bound to come looking for you."

"Nope." Mark said smiling at her. "I told her, I was done."

"Giving up a well trained twenty year old for me," she laughed, "Most people would think you're nuts."

"Oh, you don't know the half of it!"

"Besides," he said. "I remember what happened the last time my girlfriend got jealous!"

"I'm sorry!" she said, "You don't know how bad I feel about that."

"Not bad enough skank!"

"Don't worry." as he spoke he took the airport exit and as he came to a stop at the light looked at her. "Justine everything happens for a reason and that night was what made you realize how you felt so we wouldn't be happy now."

"Are you happy baby?"

"For now," he said with a smirk, "We'll see if you can keep up with a younger man."

"I won't be the one that has a problem!" She said. "I know just how to put young guys like you in their place."

"Looking the way you do, I can see how."

Justine laughed again. "I'm wearing shorts and a tank top. You've seen me in lingerie and dressed to kill, what's so sexy about this?"

"That the shorts are up your ass and the shirt looks a size to small." Putting his hand back on her thigh, he continued. "You look damn fine Justine and you know you wore that to fuck with the losers you're flying to Texas with."

"I don't know what you're talking about."

"Oh please," he waved at her as he entered the airport. "I bet you're going to sit between them and watch them fight to keep their eyes in their heads."

"Maybe." She said as she looked around evasively.

As they pulled along the curb for departures Mark frowned. "Speaking of losers, I guess they're waiting for you."

Justine saw Bill Reynolds and Paul Wilson standing near the entrance in front of a baggage cart. "All I know is I'll have much hotter waiting for me when I get back."

"That wouldn't be hard," He shook his head disgustedly as he looked at Bill who, even from a distance Mark could see was sweating like a pig, his gut over hanging his belt. "How the hell do people let themselves go like that?"

"I don't know."

"I'll circle and help you get your luggage on a cart and you can walk over and meet them."

"Why?"

"You really want them to see me drop you off?" He asked.

"Mark, pull over right here." She pointed at the curb, not a dozen feet from where Bill was standing.

He did as she asked and saw Bill look over at the sound of the car. He said something to Paul and pointed.

"Mark, its one thing to keep this quiet in the Circle, but I'm not going to hide us from everyone."

"But we work..." he began, but she cut him off.

"You work for Speakeasy's legal department, not me personally. And their dating policy amongst management is that it's allowed as long as you work in different departments."

"Okay," he said. "I just don't want you hearing anything."

"Like what?" she rolled her eyes. "Like how I'm dating a hot successful lawyer who's a decade younger than me," she clapped her hands to her cheeks. "How embarrassing!"

"Okay, okay." He laughed.

"Besides," she smiled and leaning over kissed his cheek. "It's a game, just look at the looks they're giving us already."

Before he could reply, she got out of the car and following suit, he made his way around to the trunk to get her bags. He heard Bill call her name and peered around to see them walking over. Mark had to hold back a laugh as, pretending she didn't hear them, Justine bent over to adjust the strap on her sandal. He watched both men's jaws drop as they took in the impressive sight of her ass. Straightening, Justine turned to face him, but still ignoring them, made a show of putting her hair up. The tank top rose up, exposing her stomach and pushed her impressive tits out even more. Finally turning towards them, she exclaimed, "Bill, Paul, how nice of you to wait for me!"

"Umm yeah," Bill began, "We...we got you a cart."

"Thank you!" Justine gave him a huge smile Mark could tell immediately made him nervous.

"You seem happy today." Paul said.

"Why shouldn't be?" She asked. "It's a glorious morning!" She sighed for effect and added, "It couldn't have started any better that's for sure!" Mark had come around the car with her bags and she put her hand on his shoulder, "Isn't that right baby?"

"You are a morning a person," he said, nodding to Bill and Paul while effortlessly tossing her bags onto the cart, making it a point to lift them high enough so they could see the muscles bulge in his arms. Looking at Bill, he dropped his voice to a confidential whisper, "Woman doesn't get enough."

"I..." he looked over at Justine who was smiling provocatively at Paul, "Really?"

"Had me begging for mercy." Mark told him with a wink. Turning away from him, Mark walked over to Justine who this time with a genuine smile, threw her arms around his neck.

"Bye baby," she said softly, "I'm going to miss you."

Mark's reply was cut off by her leaning in and giving him a long hard kiss. As her tongue plunged into his mouth, Mark opened his eyes partway to see Bill and Paul gawking like idiots. Sliding his hands down her back, Mark cupped her ass in his hands and gave it a squeeze as she continued to devour his lips with her own. Closing his eyes, Mark forgot about the game and sliding his hands back up hugged her tightly to him and slowed the kiss down. Her hand reached up and he sighed as her fingers ran through his hair. Justine stepped back and with a disappointed look on her face took his hand and said softly, "I really am going to miss you Mark."

"That's okay," he told her, "You've wanted to see your sister."

"Yeah, I miss the girls." She nodded, still holding his hand. "Debra is going to be thrilled when I tell her I'm seeing someone. She's going to want you to come home with me at Thanksgiving."

"Whoo-hoo! We're going to meet the family!"

Looking over at Bill and Paul, she sighed, "I have to go," leaning up, she gave him a quick kiss and winked, "I'm going to go through a lot of batteries thinking about you."

"And we're going to be jerking off like a teenage loser!"

Mark watched her walk away with Paul as Bill struggled to push the luggage cart behind them. He stared at her amazing ass and long legs until she had entered the lobby. He was starting to turn away, when he saw her turn and blow him a kiss. Returning it, he continued to stand there as she left his line of sight.

"Hey, you know what?"

What is it?

"She really could be our love."

How do you figure, he asked it, curious despite himself.

"Well she just hopped on a plane and left us. Isn't that what the women we love do?"

Chapter Two

Mark got into the firebird and smiled at the roar of the 455 engine he had put in six months ago. Unfortunately the sudden sound wiped the smile off his face as the noise crashed through his throbbing head. Easing up on the accelerator, he tried to think when the last time he had this much trouble trying to put the Voice away. For that matter when the last time he had a headache this bad. The headache was probably because of…

"That's not me. That's called a hangover." The Voice said indignantly

The voice. It was the only thing he'd ever called it. Years ago when he'd first heard it Mark had asked it if it had a name and it said its name was Mark, so "the voice" it was. What it really should be called is the curse. His father Matthew had been a paranoid schizophrenic who snapped and murdered someone in a bar fight, and died in an institution in New York before his forty fifth birthday. His grandfather William had also had it, the way the story goes, he was pretty much the town loon walking around all day talking to himself.

"I'm not a curse, I'm a gift and you know it!"

Mark turned the radio up, exchanging the noise of the music for the one in his head. If he didn't respond to the remark's it would usually stay quiet, if he spoke to it, the voice would go on and on.

"You used to like to talk to me when you were a kid."

That's because I needed you.

"You still do."

"Shit!" Mark said out loud. It was impossible not to speak in your own head.

A loud laugh rang through his mind as the voice mocked his efforts to ignore it.*"Gotcha!"*

"Shut up."

Mark shook his head, he was arguing with himself. The Voice disturbed him now more than ever, because after days of Risperdal it should be gone. Unless he was getting used to the dosage, or, he thought nervously, the Voice was getting stronger.

"Why are you out of your room?" He asked out loud.

"You tell me. I only come out when you want me to."

"Well get your ass back in there then, I'm doing just fine."

"Oh come on Mark! Don't be an asshole, it's not like I bother you. Hell you're better when I'm around and you know it."

Arguing was useless, if the voice was out then it was going to be around until he did something about it. That meant a trip to Florida where, as Jason Streets, he would have to see his doctor. The Voice had a point however; when it was in his head he did feel different. He felt faster and stronger and seemed to pick up on things faster as well. In work if he couldn't recall a precedent, the Voice would "show" it to him; an image of the correct page of the reference book flashing into his mind's eye. Over the years there were many times Mark had the disturbing feeling The Voice was more experienced than he was, as if it were older than him.

Unfortunately what the voice really represented were his baser instincts. It was him stripped down to the core; concerned with only two things; survival and violence. The Voice fueled his already destructive temper. When it wasn't around Mark had ways to maintain control, when it was here things tended to get real nasty real quick. It was the voice that, several years ago had caused him to break Tartarus's leg. Mark had him beat, but the Voice had been screaming about Lex Talionis and how no one would ever hurt his sisters.

Except for Megan, and even then not until they were in their twenties, Mark had told no one of his curse. When he was in the group home it would have gotten him locked up. If Megan's parents had found out they would have sent him away. As it was there were times people noticed he wasn't always there all the time. The doctors said it was from being traumatized; that it was part of all those years he was forbidden to talk. They believed Mark talked to himself in his head and it sometimes led to "spells" or as Megan had always called it "Going Away." The doctors were right, he was conversing in his head they just didn't know it was a two-way conversation

He arrived at the All-Star gym and, after grabbing his bag out of the trunk, went inside. At eight o'clock on a hot Friday morning the gym was pretty much deserted. There were two young couples over near the boxing ring, the guys staggering around with gloves on, and the girls egging them on. He walked past them and two other guys who were working out on universal machines. One of the guys called his name. Mark thought he recognized him from the courthouse, maybe one of the bailiffs, but ignored him. He repeated his name and he kept walking, a minute later Mark heard him call him an asshole.

"Are you going to take that?"

No I'm going to go kick his ass and get arrested over an insult from some lemming I don't care about. See why I lock you up? Mark went into the locker room and changed into a pair of loose fitting karate pants and a black tank top. Seeing there was no one else in there with him, he sat cross legged on the floor in front of one of the mirrors. Closing his eyes, he softly chanted the Ave Satanna. He normally did this first thing in the morning, but his routine had been screwed up. The voice chanted along with him. Mark had started in Latin as did the voice, in the middle he switched to English, the voice however, stayed in Latin.

Finishing, he closed his eyes and began taking slow deep breaths, letting go of everything including the voice. No worries, no fear, no pain just peace. As his breathing slowed down and he relaxed, Mark drifted to a place somewhere between conscious and subconscious. He felt as if he were floating and after a few minutes he opened his eyes to find himself standing in the attic he had created in his mind.

When he was sixteen and had been in karate for a few months, Mark had lost his temper and unloaded on a couple of kids who had tried to hurt him. Technically it was self-defense, but he had broken the right arm of one kid and the jaw of the other. The voice had told him to hurt them so badly they would never even think of hurting him again. It had taken three people to pull him off of them.

The social workers were pretty close to writing him off, but his Karate instructor, a man named Joe Cabral, who gave free classes once a week at the home, stepped in and said he could help. Cabral had sat and talked to Mark, or more accurately at him, as he really didn't really talk to anybody. After all, you never knew when you might make too much noise. At that thought Mark felt a ripple of unease go through his peaceful state. A growl came from down the other end of the attic. Mark took a deeper breath and refocused.

Unfazed by his unresponsiveness Cabral continued to give him private lessons working out with him three times a week, much to the distress of the social workers who thought Mark was already too dangerous. After every lesson Cabral would talk to him about discipline and control and how he could have them if he wanted them. After a while Mark started to trust him enough to speak with him and told him he had no control over his temper. All he saw was red and it was all over. This wasn't completely true, what he saw was Max Thompson's screaming face and massive fists. Mark was careful not to mention he had a voice in his head telling him to hurt before he was hurt.

Cabral told him he'd had the same problem and for the same reason. Cabral had also been abused as a child and as he got older began to have serious problems with fighting. His mother had sent him to a therapist who had taught him a mental exercise to control that rage. The trick was to picture your rage as some type of animal and then create a cage for it in your mind. Then meditate every day with that image, until you had it firmly envisioned in your head. Once it was complete, you put the animal in the cage and locked it. The idea sounded ridiculous, but Mark had a good imagination and gave it a try.

Mark envisioned his rage as a dog; a big black hound with red eyes and fangs that were so long they came out over its lower lip. Rather than a cage he created an attic, an old musty one that no one would ever go in. Mark put the dog in the room at the end of the corridor and after closing the door put a wooden brace across it so it couldn't break through. This worked surprisingly well.

Mark found he was able to control himself much better. If someone touched him the dog would get out and all hell would break loose, but eventually, as he got better at karate that improved as well. As Mark learned how to defend himself by being faster, and more proficient than his opponents, he didn't need to lose his temper to protect himself. Even now when trouble started, he could usually remain calm and talk his way out of it. If he had to act, Mark was able to do so in a controlled manner, doing just enough to end the fight quickly with minimal damage to his opponent. Sunday morning at the club had been an exception. When Mark saw Justine hurt he had thrown the door to the dog's room open and allowed it to run rampant. Only the Voice had been able to contain it.

The room for his rage worked so well Mark created several rooms for the attic, each one containing specific things so that when he needed them he could find them. In one were his work studies, whenever he couldn't remember something right away, if he concentrated hard enough he could go into the room and the answer would be there. Mark had one for his occult studies as well and one for the women he had slept with, which was always a fun one to go into.

Mark had also created one for pain and emotions in general. Anything he didn't want to deal with went up there. He quickly turned from that room and found himself staring at the room that housed the Voice which was wide open. Another growl sounded and he turned to face the door that contained the dog. Mark walked up to it and putting his hand on the wood could feel the vibration of the dog's growl. The dog was the embodiment of years of hate and pain, and every year more was added to it. Each time he let it out increased the chance of never getting it back in there.

Mark opened his eyes and found himself staring at his reflection. He might be broken on the inside, but nature had more than compensated on the outside. Megan always referred to him as her beautiful little brother, and although beautiful wouldn't ordinarily be the word used to describe a man, Mark had to say, it fit him to a T. Staring into his stunning multi colored eyes, the ones that darkened whenever the Voice began to get control of him, he playfully flexed his arms. "Am I not beautiful?" He asked, smiling, his even white teeth flashing through the dark scruff of the five o'clock shadow he was sporting.

"Oh mirror, mirror on the wall!"

As Mark grabbed the bag from the floor he had to admit that was a good one. He went over to the corner of the gym he always worked out in where there were a couple of mats on the floor and a hundred pound punching bag hanging from a chain. Tossing the bag down, he took a few minutes to stretch, wincing at how sore he still was from the fight. Not just the fight, three straight nights with Justine was like a fight in itself.

Mark sat down on the bench and removed two bricks from the bag. After placing them on the floor and wrapping his hands tightly with ace bandages, Mark got down and began to do pushups on his knuckles on the bricks. After the first ten he felt the stiffness in his muscles begin to loosen and by twenty five he was feeling pretty good. Mark would do fifty of these and as part of his mind continued to count he drifted off and thought about the voice.

He'd first heard it when he was eleven years old. He had just taken a vicious beating from Max that had ended with him hitting Mark in the face several times. When Max turned to start screaming at his wife Julie, who was yelling at him for hurting him like that; after all how were they going to explain it to the school? Mark turned and running downstairs to the basement, hid behind the washing machine. He sat there bleeding from his nose and mouth, and holding his right eye that was already swelling. Mark started crying, knowing that on top of the pain this meant no school for a while, which meant more time with Max.

He started sobbing louder. He wanted Megan, he hadn't seen her in a long time, but the woman, who was there when he was taken from her, had said that someday they'd be back together. Mark put his head down and cried harder. Whenever he would cry when he was little Megan would give him a hug and tell him she loved him. Now no one loved him, he was alone, even in school he didn't have any friends. All the kids made fun of him for not talking, they were the stupid ones; didn't they know they would get hit for that?

"You're not alone Mark." A dry raspy voice said in his head. *"You have me to talk to."*

"Who are you?" he asked.

"SHHH" the voice said. *"Talk in here, that way Max doesn't hear you."*

Who are you?

"I'm you, but a better, stronger, smarter you. I'm your friend Mark."

He began to slow down at fifty, when in a mocking tone the voice spoke; *"Fifty? Do seventy five you pussy."*

Fuck you, he replied, but continued up to seventy five. On the last push up Mark kept his hands on the bricks and bringing his legs up did a handstand. Grunting with the effort, he lowered his head until it touched the floor then pushed himself up until his elbows locked and stayed there. His arms were trembling with the effort as he waited for the voice to count to sixty. Letting his legs drop, Mark rolled onto his back and started doing stomach crunches. As the Voice started counting to a hundred, he continued to let his mind wander into the past. From that day on the voice talked to him constantly. If he read a book they would discuss it. The voice was funny and always got him to laugh, making comments like; *"Do you think Nancy Drew ever fooled around with the Hardy Boys?"*

In school if he didn't know the answer, it did. Sometimes the voice protected him; warning him when Max was around, making sure he stayed quiet and out of his way. Other times it was of no use and

Mark would get beat anyway. Max would hit him hard, until he cried, then when he was crying, yell; "Are you still making noise?"

He would then hit him again, and again. One time Mark started screaming and Max shoved a sock in his mouth, threw him into a dark closet and left him there all night. He was so scared he had an accident and oh did he get beat for that one. Finishing the last crunch Mark drew his knees up to his chest and kicking out, threw himself to his feet. Mark quickly spun and delivered a vicious kick to the bag. The bag came back, and picturing Max's fat face in his mind, he launched a right left combo hitting the bag hard enough to feel the vibration up to his shoulders. Mark turned to the wall and jumping, caught the pull up bar and hoisting himself up, counted the first of the twenty five he would do.

He had spent years with Max, twice during that time he had been pulled away for an investigation and both times was brought back. The second time he had come back he was thirteen and on one of the few occasions Max actually talked to him, he told Mark he kept coming back because no one else wanted him; that he was fucked up even for a state rat. Mark told him that wasn't true, he had a sister and someday he'd be back with her. Max had shaken his head sadly and said; "Christ Mark, didn't they tell you? Your sister died two years ago, she got sick and died."

Dropping down from the pull up bar Mark rolled backwards and springing up, went into a stance and started throwing a series of combinations, his hands blurring through the air. Mark's breathing was picking up and his heart pounding. He could feel its beat in his still throbbing temples, but refused to slow down. Throwing himself to the floor he rolled, and coming to his feet went into a series of spin kicks that took him from one end of the mat to the other.

He had believed Max and now he was all alone and always would be. Mark gave up and didn't even try to talk. He still did his schoolwork, because it gave him something to think about, but at home all he did was read in his room, and try to stay away from Max. This went on for another year. Julie had the school convinced there was a physical reason he couldn't talk and they taught him sign language. Mark would use that in school because he wouldn't have to make noise, so he thought that was great. Apparently he enjoyed it too much because once, when he was doing it at home, Max broke two fingers on each of his hands by stomping on them.

Mark finished the last kick, which had landed him within a few feet of the bag. Turning to it he started circling, bouncing lightly on the balls of his feet as if it was an opponent and he was waiting for an opening. Mark shook the sweat from his eyes and could feel himself ready to explode. It was the same every day.

"You know who you want it to be!"

He threw a couple of quick kicks at the bag and, unable to help it, completed the cycle and went back to the last day with Max. He'd come home from school and went into the parlor. Max was sitting there hunched over the coffee table. Mark had to walk past him and tried to do so as quickly as he could. Max was leaning over a silver platter with white powder on it. Max had a straw in his nose and was sniffing the powder. Mark had never seen anything like that before and kept staring as he walked by, which was when he tripped over one of Max's boots that he had left on the floor.

He lost his balance and fell into the table. At the last minute he reached out to try to catch myself on the edge of the table and ended up hitting the edge of the platter. The platter flipped over sending the powder everywhere. Max stood up and started screaming at him. Mark tried to get up to run, but he grabbed him and hit him, screaming that was all he could get for the week. Mark tried to pull away, but couldn't. Still screaming, Max picked up the silver platter and swung it at his head.

Stepping into the bag, Mark threw a savage right hook, then a left. The bag rocked back and when it came back he drove another left, right into it. He threw a jump kick that sent the bag flying and when it returned went into a series of lefts and rights, nothing fancy just hitting the bag as hard as he could. As he hammered away, all he could see was Max and that platter heading for him, Max stomping on his hands, telling him his sister was dead.

"Harder!!" The Voice called out.

Striking the bag, Mark could feel his shoulders burning and his heart was beating so hard he thought it was going to come through his chest. Mark kept swinging anyway, hitting the bag again and again.

"But we showed that motherfucker didn't we?"

"Yes." Mark hissed as he continued to hit the bag. In his mind, Mark saw Max in his apartment the day he had lured him there. Max's fat face was covered with blood and he was screaming. He was lying on the floor, his leg snapped backwards and his right arm hanging useless by his side. Mark was standing over him, screaming and driving his fist repeatedly into what was left of Max's face. The dog was out and it and the Voice were howling in his head. As Mark beat him he punctuated each blow by screaming Max's favorite expression.

"Are... you... still... making.... noise!?!?!"

Mark snarled like an animal and slammed his left fist into the bag so hard it flew several feet away from him. When it came back he wrapped his right arm around it then started delivering a series of short brutal left hooks. He was swinging with everything he had and found he couldn't stop. Mark kept swinging, envisioning myself crying and helpless, his shoulders hurt and he was gasping in-between punches.

"Mark Stop!" Mark hit the bag one more time then leaned his face against it, panting for breath. *"Easy Mark."* The voice was using that soothing tone it had used when he was younger. *"We got him, he's not dead, but I bet there's still days he wished he was."*

Mark stepped back from the bag and almost lost his balance. He had nothing left, to the point where he could barely lift his arms to pick the bricks up and toss them into the bag. Sitting down he pulled a bottle of water out and after drinking half, poured the rest over his head. Mark put his head in his hands and, staying there for a few minutes, let the story play out to the day he finally caught a break.

Mark had bounced back and forth between various group homes never being allowed to stay long. No one wanted a sixteen year old kid who wouldn't talk and had rage issues. One day, he was brought into a social workers office to meet Doug and Denise. Denise was very nice to him, telling him the reason they had come to see me was that his sister, Megan, lived with them and how would he feel about seeing her again after all these years? Looking at Denise, Mark uttered a sentence for the first time in over a month; "My sister died a long time ago."

The next day he was brought back into the office where a tall beautiful girl with long dark hair and crystal blue eyes was waiting for him. Even after ten years Mark knew who she was, it really was his sister! Max had lied to him to cause him even more pain. As he stood there stunned, Megan came over and hugged him. He hugged her back and put his head on her shoulder just like he did when he was little.

"I missed you Megan." Was all he could think to say.

He could feel her tears on his neck but her voice was steady when she said; "Come on Mark, let your big sister take you home."

Tossing the empty water bottle in the bag, Mark forced himself to his feet and slinging the bag over his sweat slicked shoulder, walked across the gym towards the locker room. Mark was aware of the other people in the gym watching him. As he passed the kids that were messing around in the ring and their girlfriends, his Voice enhanced hearing picked up their whispers.

"Fucking crazy."

"He's a lawyer?"

"The guy that owns the place told me he's a Devil Worshipper."

"Goddamn, he's fine!"

"Shit, I wish I had those moves."

Mark entered the locker room and after showering, dressed and decided to go into the small bathroom where he knew they kept aspirin and some first aid supplies. The mirror to the cabinet was already open and after poking around the crammed shelves he found some packets of advil. Opening two of them, Mark dry swallowed the pills and reaching out closed, the cabinet. He frowned as he saw the mirror was broken and he staring at his face with a jagged crack down the center of it.

"How symbolic." The Voice giggled.

* * *

Mark awoke to the sound of the door opening and footsteps running across the room. He sat up trying to get out of bed, but he was too late. Before he could react they were on top of him; two of them pinning his arms and a third boy jumping on top of the bed and straddling his chest. Mark tried to yell, but before he could get anything out, the boy on top of him punched him in the mouth.

"Yeah, not so bad now are you Mark?"

He tried to throw him off but couldn't. Mark recognized the boy who had hit him, his name was Royce and he had made fun of him at lunch. That didn't bother him, but when he tried to take his lunch Mark had pushed him and when he swung at him, had grabbed him and smashed his face into the cafeteria table.

"What got nothing to say freak?" Royce asked, hitting again this time in the eye.

"He's never got anything to say." One of the other boys said.

"Yeah, he doesn't even make noise when you hit him!" The third said and proved his point by slamming his fist into the side of Mark's face.

"That's cause he's fucking crazy aren't you Mark?" Royce asked, slapping him in the face. "Fuck it, he don't make noise, no one knows were in here!"

Royce swung and hit him, then again and again, the next punch hit Mark in the nose and he felt it break. "Let's see how pretty you are tomorrow you little freak!" Royce laughed.

Mark jerked awake and panicked as he felt himself beginning to fall; he flailed out with his left hand and just caught the edge of the desk, saving himself from toppling out of his chair. Sitting up, he let out a deep breath and swallowed hard, he must have dozed off while looking though some revisions he had been making in a contract. He jumped again as his cell phone rang. He looked at the number and seeing it was Justine, answered, "Hey Red,"

"Hey baby," she answered, "You okay?"

"Yeah, I was just working."

"Oh, you sounded funny. I just wanted to let you know I just got settled in and had a great surprise!"

"What was that?" he asked as his watch began beeping telling him it was five o'clock.

"My sister met me at the airport with the girls, she's going to stay in Houston for the weekend, then drive me to my parents on Monday."

"That's great." Opening his drawer, Mark removed the bottle of Risperdal and shook one out into his hand.

"Really, you asshole?"

"It is!" Justine said happily. "And I told her I was finally serious with someone and showed the picture you printed for me of us at the beach."

"You sound excited," He told her as he popped the pill into his mouth and swallowed it as the Voice cursed at him. "Like a teenager," he finished.

"I kind of feel like one," she laughed. "It's nice to say I have someone." She paused. "Do you think so? Or am I just acting stupid?"

"No, it's great I..." he winced as The Voice continued its swearing. "I'm just tired."

"Well it's five out there, go home Mark, get some rest."

"Yeah, I think I will."

"Well your silly girlfriend won't keep you. I just wanted to let you know I landed and I'll call you tomorrow okay?"

"Okay," he paused then said softly. "I love you, Justine and I'll miss you tonight."

"Mark, you just made my night!" she laughed.

"Mark, you just made me sick!"

"I love you too," she continued. "Now go get some sleep."

As he hung up, Mark's mind was filled with the sound of a cracking whip.

"Yes Mistress!"

* * *

Mark walked listlessly down the corridor to his condo. He'd stayed another hour at the office, trying to finish the contract, but his eyes were stinging and kept feeling as if they were ready to shut. That was just a tease. Mark knew damn well as exhausted as he was the second he lied on the couch or went to bed he would be wide awake. Insomnia, as he had learned over the years, had quite the sense of humor. Unlocking the door, Mark entered and as he stepped into the living room and tossed his jacket and tie onto the chair froze. Narrowing his eyes and taking a deep breath, he caught the unmistakable scent of strawberry.

"Megan!"

"Hey little brother!"

Mark spun around to see his sister sitting on the couch wearing his black silk robe, her long dark hair pulled into a pony tail.

"Meg!" He cried out happily, all but running over to the couch.

Standing up, she flashed him one of her trademark big crooked smiles and throwing her arms out shouted, "Surprise!"

Catching her around her slim waist, Mark lifted her off her feet and crushed her to him. "Damn I missed you!"

"I missed you too," she laughed as she wrapped her arms around his shoulders and hugged him just as tight. "I'm sorry it's been so long."

She kissed his cheek and putting her down, Mark stepped back, keeping his hands on her shoulders and looking into her amazing crystal blue eyes. "When did you get in?"

"I landed around eleven and got here about noon."

"The folks know you're here?"

"Nope," she shook her head, "You know I always come see my little brother first. We'll go see them tomorrow, it'll be nice, the four of us can do lunch."

"I thought you couldn't come up for another month?" He asked.

"I changed my schedule," she replied as she put her arms back around his neck. "I figured I'd surprise you."

"You look great," he reached out, playfully tugging on her pony tail.

"Thank you," she then frowned, "But you, my beautiful little brother, aren't looking so good." Shaking her head she asked, "You're not sleeping are you?"

"No," he said softly as he trailed his fingers through her hair, before touching her cheek. "You?"

"Very well actually," she told him.

"So you're doing okay? You still..."

He stopped as she rolled her eyes. "I'm doing fine, I go to an NA meeting every Sunday and AA on Thursdays." She smiled. "It'll make five years in a couple of months," taking his hand between hers, she squeezed it, "I promised you Mark, I'm never going back."

"Good."

"But, enough about me," she let his hand go and placed hers against his cheek, "You look so tired Mark, that's why I came up, I could hear it in your voice the other night, you're having one of your spells aren't' you?"

"Yes." He whispered as he pressed his cheek into her hand.

"Well no worries, you're big sister's here to take care of you." Her blue eyes looked into his and he could already feel himself relaxing, he would sleep tonight. He tried to put his arm around her, but she skipped back away from him. "So who is she?"

"Who?"

"You're lady friend you were with last night."

As he looked at her confused, Megan laughed. "After I showered, I took a nap in that wonderful bed of yours and all I could smell was Coco Chanel, that isn't the kind of perfume one of your little tarts would wear."

Shrugging, Mark reached down to take her hand, but laughing, she stepped away again.

"Who is it Mark?"

"Justine, I've mentioned her before."

"The Redhead," she nodded. "The leader of your weird little sex club."

"The one you don't know about."

"Know about what?" she smiled and as always he couldn't resist smiling back at her. "You two have been spending a lot of time together lately."

"Yes," he answered. "A lot of time."

"Ohhhh," she cooed. "Are you getting serious? Is Justine special to you?"

"I... we're seeing where it goes."

"Don't lie to your big sister," she waved her finger at him showing off her black nail polish. "Is she special?"

"She is." He said softly as his eyes wandered down to her bare feet to see her toe nails matched.

He approached her again, his gaze working their way up her long slender legs. Mark took a moment to admire how good her ivory complexion looked against the black silk, before he looked back up at her face. Since she had become sober, Megan looked better than ever, as beautiful as when they were younger and the demons of their past hadn't caught up with them yet. This time she didn't step away and as he slid his arms around her waist she smiled at him.

"So Justine's your special girl?" He nodded as she slid her hands around his neck and stared up at him. "But she's not your favorite girl is she Mark?" she asked softly.

"Of course not." He answered and felt his heart begin to beat faster as she ran her fingers through his hair.

"And who is your favorite girl little brother?"

"You are."

"Me?" she asked, leaning her face close to his. "Your sister is your favorite girl?"

"Of course she is," Mark whispered

"Yeah, she's still your favorite?" she pushed her full lips out into a pout. "Even with all those hot girls you fuck?"

"You'll always be my favorite girl." He told her placing a soft kiss on her cheek.

"We promised we would always be each other's favorite didn't we?"

"We did."

"That's right, your Megan is your favorite isn't she?" she gave him a sweet smile and moving her hands to his chest began unbuttoning his shirt. "After all I was your first girl wasn't I?"

"My best girl."

"I like that," she whispered in his ear, "Did you miss me, baby?"

"You know I did."

"Well then what are you waiting for Mark?" Stepping back, Megan undid the robe and letting it fall to the floor raised her arms over her head, presenting her naked body to him. "Come over here and show your sister how much you missed her."

Mark took her into his arms and as he felt her breasts pressing into his bare chest, lowered his head, allowing her soft lips to press into his. As Megan wrapped her arms around his neck, drawing him deeper into her forbidden embrace, Mark's head echoed with the sound of the Voice's laughter.

To be continued.

Afterword

Thank you for reading my first installment in the Circle series! There is much more to come, including several shorter works as well as the full length follow up already in the works. I would like to take a moment to touch upon the ending of this book. From here Mark's story takes two paths, the future Circle works, and the previously published series Broken that details his dark past and features the Circle in book 8. More details on that series and much more on the Circle including future projects and a complete bio of all twelve members can be found by visiting me at llcraftpublications.wordpress.com Once again thank you for supporting my work, LL Craft.

www.ingramcontent.com/pod-product-compliance
Lightning Source LLC
Chambersburg PA
CBHW080742250626
47162CB00010B/2989